WARRIOR FAE

AURORA ACADEMY

WARRIOR FAE

CAROLINE PECKHAM & SUSANNE VALENTI

Warrior Fae
Ruthless Boys of the Zodiac #5
Copyright © 2019 Caroline Peckham & Susanne Valenti

Interior Formatting & Design by Wild Elegance Formatting

All rights reserved.
No part of this publication may be reproduced or transmitted by any means, electronic, mechanical, photocopying or otherwise, without the prior permission of the copyright owner.

Warrior Fae/Caroline Peckham & Susanne Valenti – 1st ed.
ISBN-13 - 978-1-914425-19-6

This book is dedicated to all the hard working Mindys who toiled tirelessly behind the scenes of this story to keep the Pride's clothes washed and ironed, working into the late hours to remove countless suspicious stains from Elise's undergarments, her sheets, a tiny hat and an unfortunate Tiberian Rat's fur who happened to be in the splash zone of an outdoor orgy extravaganza.

Sadly, several Mindys were harmed in the making of this series, one lost their fingers to a magical sewing machine, another broke her leg when diving out of Altair Halls to be the first to answer their king's call, whilst another unfortunate Mindy fell to her doom while scaling the Vega Dorms to ensure Leon's toast was delivered to him before it went cold. Sources say her only regret was that the toast in fact did go cold as she tumbled to the earth, but in the true spirit of all Mindys, they all agreed that not one casualty was in vain.

Well done Mindys, we couldn't have done it without you.

Long live your king.

WELCOME TO AURORA ACADEMY
HERE IS YOUR CAMPUS MAP TO HELP YOU FIND FRESHMEN TO TORTURE AND WHIP INTO REAL FAE.

Please take note of where The Lunar Brotherhood and Oscura Clan have claimed turf to ensure you don't cross into their territory unintentionally. Faculty will not be held responsible for gang maiming or disembowelment. Enjoy your final days basking on Devil's Hill and hanging out in the Iron Wood. This land has seen you grow into a true Fae and it'll miss you as much as you will miss it

Lake Tempest

The Iron Wood

Lunar

The Capella Observatory

The Dead Shed

The Weeping Well

Rig

The Cafaeteria

Kipling Emporium

Os

The Acrux Coutyard

L

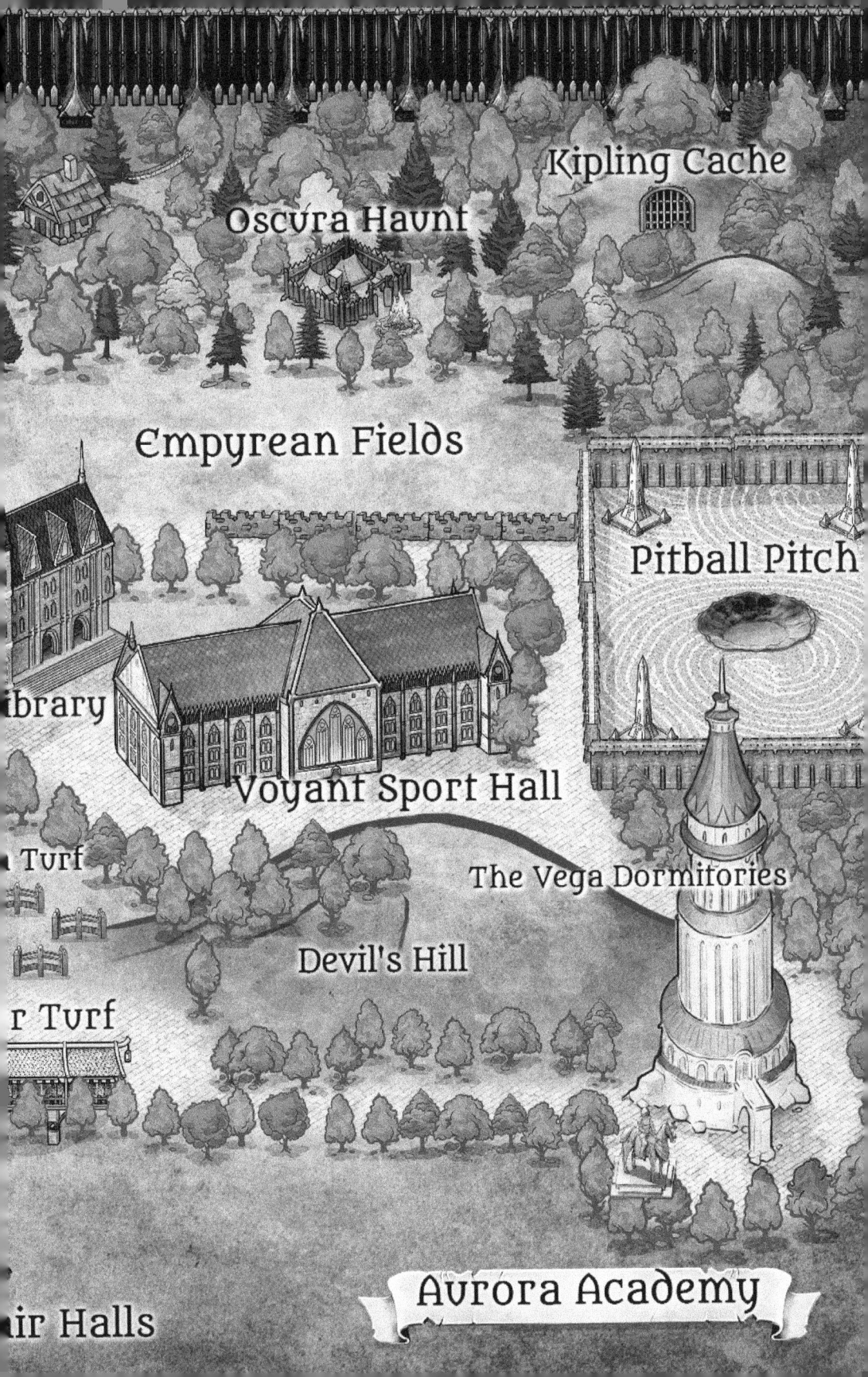

Aurora Academy

- Kipling Cache
- Oscura Haunt
- Empyrean Fields
- Pitball Pitch
- brary
- Voyant Sport Hall
- Turf
- The Vega Dormitories
- Devil's Hill
- r Turf
- ir Halls

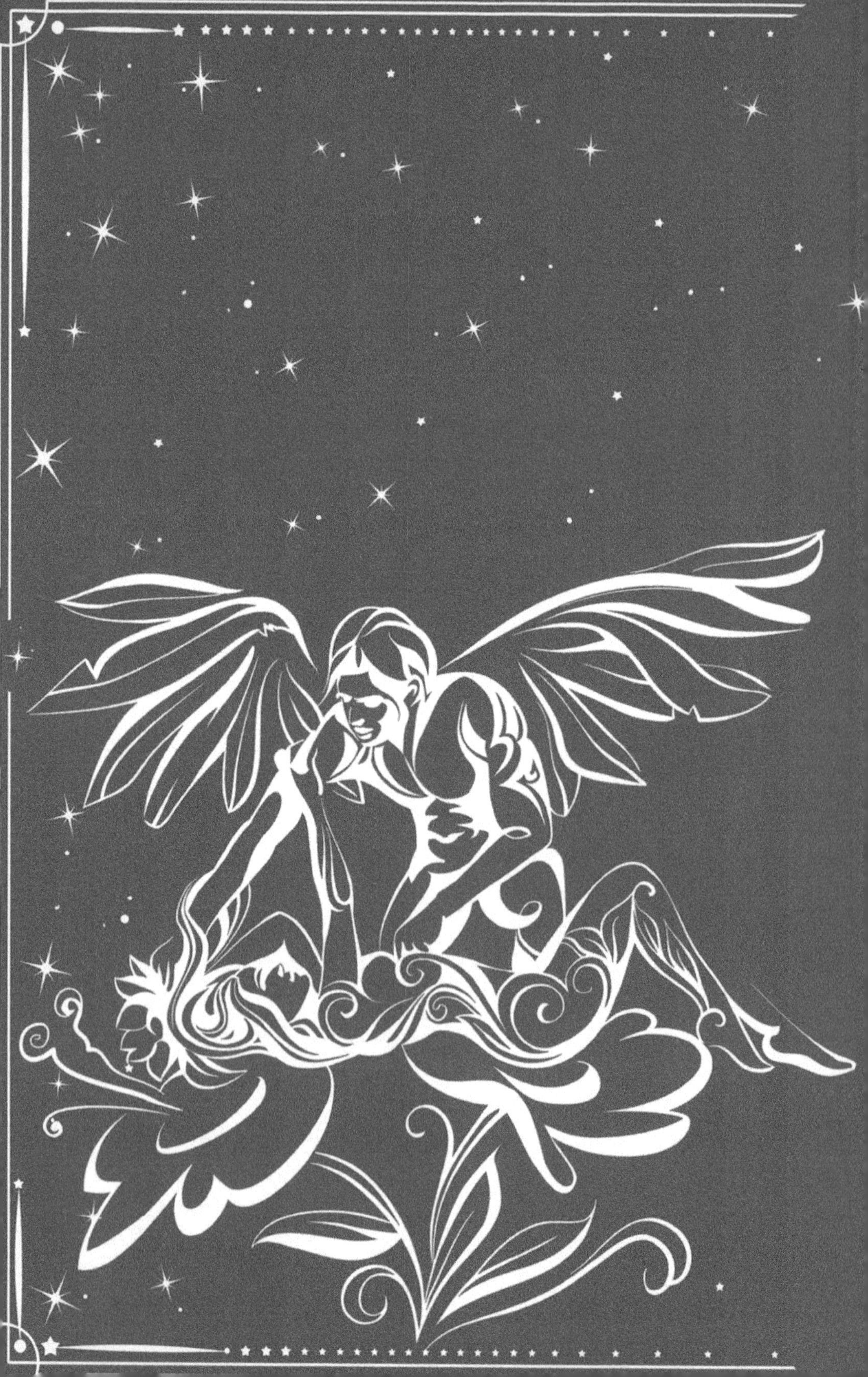

GABRIEL

CHAPTER ONE

I pushed into the power of The Sight over and over, seeking out my dark angel with everything I possessed. But if King had her, he was using some power to hide her from me and nothing I did could break through it.

Seeking her out was like wading through an endless tunnel of black, my hands roaming blindly in the dark. But she was there somewhere at the far end of it, her presence calling to me in a way that made me fucking ache. It was the most excruciating kind of torture.

"Gabriel," Ryder growled, his hand clamping down hard on my shoulder as I blinked out of my trance. "Anything?"

"No. Nothing," I sighed, hating myself for this failure. I was letting her down. I was letting everyone down.

We were in one of the empty classrooms in Altair Halls, the sound of chaos still reigning around campus. The war was over and the professors were hurrying to restore order after the fight.

Leon had run off to search the tunnels beneath the Weeping Well, but my gut told me he wouldn't find Elise there. She was gone and now she was somewhere so far away I just couldn't grasp her. The agony that caused me was unbearable. And I knew if I didn't find a trace of her soon, I was going to lose my fucking mind.

The small comfort I could take was that sense of her on the edges of my gifts told me she was still alive. And I prayed to every star in the heavens that that would remain the case. Because if King tried to steal her from this world, there was no force in Solaria which would save that motherfucker from my wrath.

My Atlas buzzed and I snatched it out of my pocket, finding a message in the group chat Leon had made for us so that we could keep in touch if we found her.

Dante:

Any news?

He'd had to head home with his family and ensure his cousin Rosalie was tended to by a professional healer who worked for the Oscuras. I'd seen him breaking, torn in two directions when she'd told us about Elise. But we'd all forced him to leave with Rosalie. He'd be back soon enough and he'd already sent half his family to search the city for our girl.

Between the Oscuras, my visions, her Elysian Mate desperately hunting for her, and the most fearsome Basilisk to roam the land willing to kill anyone for her location, surely we could find her. The four of us alone would rip apart the whole world to get her back, I knew that. I just didn't know where to make the first tear.

As new and unsteady as this relationship was between Dante, Leon, Ryder and I, there was one thing I did trust them on these days. And that was doing anything and everything within their power to save Elise. I'd witnessed how far they'd gone for her in the past, and the darkness in their eyes told me they were willing to go far further than that too. In fact, I didn't think there was anything the four of us wouldn't do to get her back in our arms.

I replied to the group chat saying I had no news and Leon sent a response too.

Leon:

She's not in the tunnels. I'm heading to the Iron Wood.

I sighed, not having the heart to tell him to stop searching campus. Because I knew she wasn't here. It wasn't a tangible thing I could *see*; it was just a feeling. But the kind that was intrinsically linked with my gifts.

"Where do I go?" Ryder demanded of me, his shoulders tensing up. "Give me a direction, point me toward the fucker who took her, Gabriel."

"I can't." I gripped his arm. "I can't fucking *see* them."

Desperation pooled in his deep green eyes and his jaw ticked with the need for violence. I'd deliver it to him in a heartbeat if I could and I'd be right there at his side making King pay when he caught up to the fucker. But this wasn't going to work.

"I need to go to the Black Card," I decided. "It's the only way I can think of to get closer to King. I'm still in their ranks, they don't know I'm their enemy. Maybe I'll be summoned soon."

Ryder nodded firmly, his brows pulling sharply together.

The door banged open suddenly, making us turn towards it and Bryce strode in with a couple of sneering Lunars at his back. He pushed a hand over his black hair, taking in Ryder and me with suspicion in his gaze.

Ryder wheeled toward him with his hands fisting and his shoulders stiffening as he disbanded the silencing bubble around us.

"What the fuck do you want?" he snapped.

Bryce's eyes moved from me to Ryder then he wet his lips. "Our people need their king," he said curtly.

"So you sniffed me out like a rat did you, Bruce?" Ryder hissed, a deadly rattle echoing through his chest.

"Everyone's looking for you," Bryce defended himself. "It's not just me. And my name is Bry-"

"I'll come to you when I'm good and ready!" Ryder barked and the assholes flinched but didn't run.

Something in their eyes made my skin prickle uneasily and my upper lip peeled back as The Sight flickered at the edges of my mind, offering me a vision. I let myself fall into it as Ryder laid into them and I found myself watching an army of Lunars dragging Ryder to the heart of them, tearing the shirt from his back while a fire Elemental burned the Lunar crest of a moon with a serrated edge from just below his collar bone.

My throat tightened as the mob closed in with murder in their eyes, though I couldn't recognise any of them, their faces shadowy and indistinct. The vision spat me back out and I found Bryce and his friends gone and Ryder looking to me with hope in his gaze.

"Did you *see* her?" he demanded, but I shook my head, unsure if I should tell him what I had *seen* or not. But it was only one of many possibly futures ahead of us and right now we had something more pressing to focus on.

"Fuck," he spat. "I have to talk to the Brotherhood. I'll get them searching our territory in the city."

"Ryder." I caught his arm before he could leave, my heart beating furiously as I lowered my voice. "I'm not sure you can trust your people anymore."

His eyes darkened to pitch. "I never trusted my people, Big Bird. I just rule them. They will fall back into line by the end of the night."

I nodded and one look at The Sight said that future was a possibility. He was in no immediate danger, but I was left with a knot in my gut as he walked out the door. The Lunars were a ticking time bomb waiting to explode and I would do whatever I could to make sure Ryder wasn't a casualty when it inevitably detonated. But there was nothing I could do this second.

I cast a new silencing bubble around me and called Bill as I exited the room, heading down the corridor at a fierce pace.

"Hey kid," Bill answered. "Everything okay?"

"No," I growled, hurriedly explaining what had happened. "There was a huge fight at the academy tonight. Felix Oscura came to try and kill Dante and shit got pretty intense."

"By the stars, are you safe? Why didn't you fuckin' call me?" I heard him light up a cigarette and my heart yanked at the worry in his voice.

"I was busy shielding a Storm Dragon," I sighed and he sucked in a breath.

"You're working with Dante Oscura now? Did he win then?"

"Something like that. And yeah, Dante won, Felix is dead. But I can't go into all of that right now," I muttered, hurrying on. "Look, I need your help. Elise is missing. The Black Card have her and I can't *see* where they've taken her. Is there anyone you know who might have some information?"

Bill had the dirtiest of contacts from his P.I. work. He'd squeezed the throats of nearly every low-level scumbag in the city to get information for various jobs. He used his Cyclops gifts to tug memories out of their heads, made them forget all about the invasion, then left them thinking he was their best friend. Fucking genius if you asked me.

"Yeah...there's a few pricks I can ask. You sure you wanna do this though, kid? She's got an Elysian Mate to save her ass now, it's not your responsibility."

I gritted my jaw at the mention of the star bond, a fierce longing in my heart making me burn for her. "She's got me too, Bill. Nothing's gonna change that ever again."

"Alright," he sighed like he didn't want to agree, but he'd never let me down and he knew once I made my mind up on something there was no going back.

Except Elise. I'd changed my mind on her. I'd tried to force her away, treated her like shit and blackened my soul just a little further as I painted myself out as a heathen. And maybe I was, but now I was *her* heathen. Always would be. I was destined to love her whether the stars said so or not, and even if I had an Elysian Mate waiting for me out there in the world somewhere, nothing could tempt me away from Elise. She was my little angel. And I may not have been her perfect match or her other half or even her other quarter, but she still owned me. All that there was to give, even if it didn't fit her entirely right.

"Call me if you hear anything." I hung up and tucked my Atlas away, running out the front exit of Altair Halls and letting my wings burst free from my back.

I took off towards the Vega Dorms, gazing down at the devastation of the campus, huge holes blasted in the ground, areas of the forest still burning.

Students were being lined up outside the dorms and counted by the faculty, so I cast a quick illusion spell to hide myself, making my body blend with the dark clouds above. I hunted for any of the Black Card among the crowd, but I couldn't see them and as I came down to perch on top of the roof of the Vega Dorms, I sat on the edge and waited to be summoned. Because King would surely gather his followers soon enough. And until then, I would wield The Sight with all my power to try and find the girl I was so perilously in love with, that I knew with absolute certainty losing her would be the death of me.

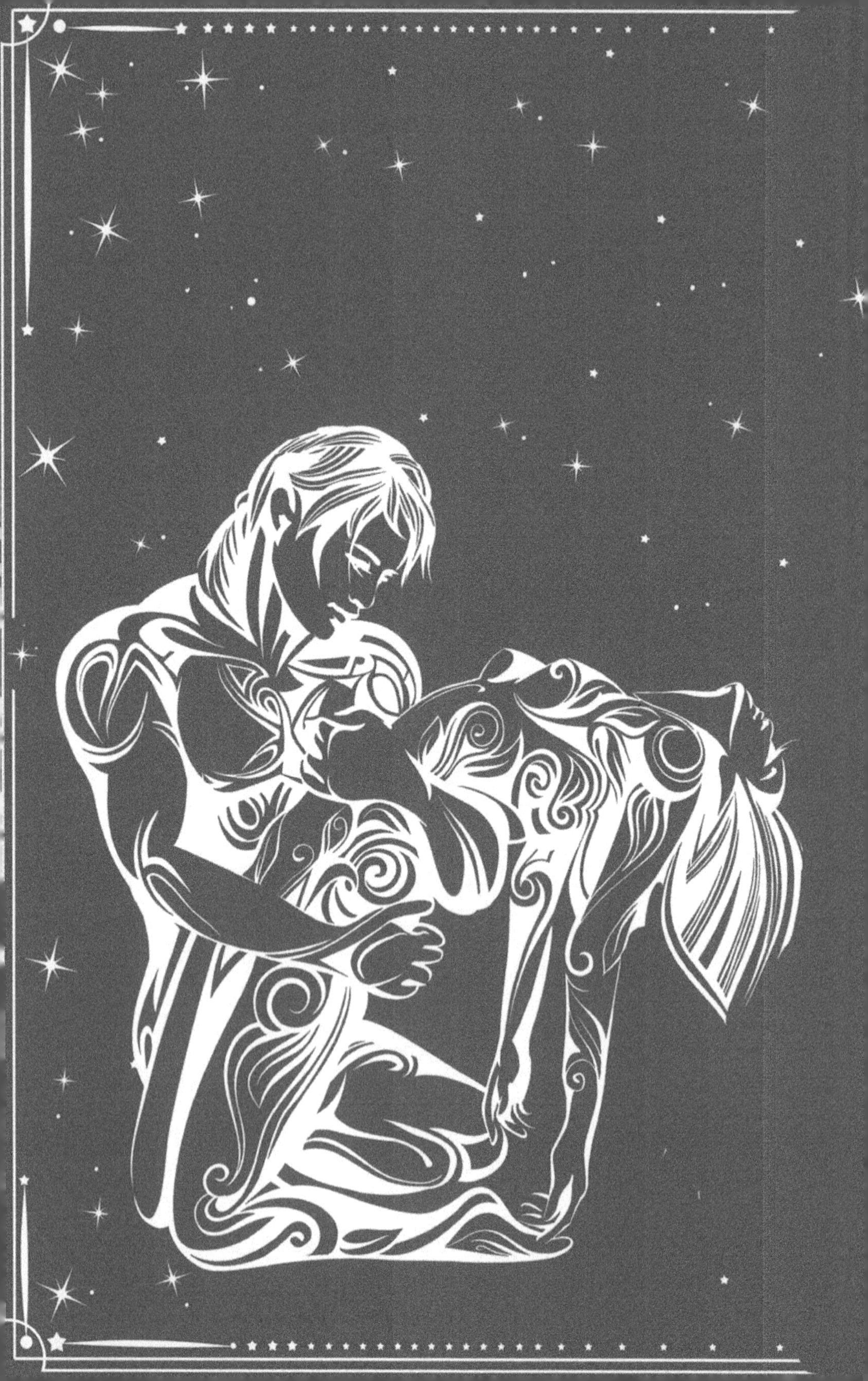

RYDER

CHAPTER TWO

I stood down in the basement with my gang after the head count was done and the teachers had started work on fixing up campus. Professor Mars had taken charge as Greyshine was apparently still hiding in his office and because he was the only teacher with a backbone on campus, he'd restored some semblance of order.

Now, I stood in front of my gang feeling weighed, judged, and measured. And I planned to eradicate all the suspicion I saw flaring in the eyes of my people for good.

Ethan Shadowbrook was at my side in nothing but a pair of sweatpants, his inked muscles tense as he sensed the danger in the room. There was only one way I was going to crush the doubts I saw gazing back at me from the Lunars and that was by spilling blood. But that was just fine by me. I had so much fucking rage in me over Elise that I was hungry to get started. But not yet. I'd test them first, let the rats show their faces.

"Elise Callisto was kidnapped from campus during the battle," I said loudly. "Did anyone see anything that might help us find her?"

"*Us?*" Bryce spat. "Why would we care about some random girl? She's not even a Lunar."

The snake in me curled through my flesh, readying to strike, but I held myself in check as I waited for more people to chime in.

"What were you doing out there helping the Oscuras?" a girl at the back called and a murmur of ascension rippled through the crowd.

"Why should we do anything you say? You're a traitor!" Bryce snapped and a large Minotaur, Russel Newmoon, behind him nodded his agreement. The guy was always backing up Bryce in class whenever he bullied Eugene Dipper and I didn't like his cocky little face.

I looked to Ethan beside me, needing to assess my second's response to this and he raised his chin higher as more of my people started hollering angrily about my actions tonight.

I didn't give a fuck what they thought of me, but I found I did care what Ethan thought. I wanted his allegiance; he was a man of his word and an Alpha I could see eye to eye with. But if he had turned on me too, he would be the first to bleed.

"Speak, Shadowbrook," I commanded, and the crowd quietened to let him talk.

Ethan's blue eyes swirled with darkness as he turned to me. There was still blood on his flesh from the fight and a smirk danced around his lips like he was in his element right now. He'd fought without question, fiercely and with his pack behind him, tearing through Felix's ranks like cannon fire. He hadn't questioned my orders for a second, but perhaps he was questioning them now.

"Ryder is our king," he barked out powerfully. "Anyone who says he isn't should pay the price of those words." His pack howled their agreement and plenty of my people called out their support for me too.

Interesting.

I nodded, turning my head slowly to look directly at Bryce and the Fae still clustering around him, clearly defining themselves from the others. "Do you dare to still stand against me, Bruce?"

He glowered at the name I used to belittle him, taking a foolish step towards me. "We deserve an explanation for the betrayal we witnessed tonight."

"I owe you nothing!" I bellowed, making the crowd wince back and Bryce nearly leapt out of his skin. "I am your king. So if you wish to rise up against me, then go ahead." I opened my arms wide, striding towards him at a slow pace, giving him the opportunity to attack. I'd relish the fight, crush him thoroughly and tear his head from his neck to punctuate my point. But he didn't attack me. He shrank like the coward he was, glancing left and right for back up that was now fast abandoning him.

I walked forward until I was nose to nose with him, gazing down from my superior height and baring my teeth.

"Kneel," I commanded and his eyes flared with defiance. A defiance I would cut out like rot.

If I was going to get my people hunting the city for my girl tonight, this had to be dealt with fast. I wouldn't have treacherous words being handed back to Scarlett who I already suspected had betrayed me. No, this was a delicate matter and death might not be the answer right away. That might only cause more rebellion tonight. Fear was the tool I needed.

Bryce hesitated before lowering down to his knees and I gazed at him as the crowd fell back to give me more space. I could feel the power shifting in the room, their respect for me forcing them into line. But respect wasn't enough today. They needed a reminder of why I was the most feared Fae in Alestria.

I pointed to the Minotaur who'd backed up Bryce, beckoning him forward. "Name?" I demanded of him even though I knew it. But I wasn't going to let him think even a single brain cell in my mind was reserved for him.

"Russel," he said, swallowing hard as he looked me in the eyes, a flicker of anger there that awoke the demon in me.

I cast a wooden blade in my hand as sharp as a knife and tossed it to him. He fumbled the catch, a murmur of terror escaping him as he held it like it was a cursed object.

"You will cut one of your own ears off before I finish beating Bryce, or you will regret it, Russel," I told him simply.

He gasped in horror and Bryce winced as I threw my fist into his face, the word pain on my knuckles smashing into his jaw. He hit the ground and I leapt on him, pounding my fists into his body as he took it all like a good little scumbag, not even trying to fight me as I spilled his blood, drinking in his pain.

"I don't hear any cutting!" I roared at Russel and he wailed, starting to beg. Fuck, I hated when they begged. It disgusted me.

I beat Bryce bloody, my breaths coming heavier as I thought of Elise, of that fucking robed asshole stealing her away from me. My punches became deadly as I crushed bones and made him scream so loud, it shook the walls. But nothing was going to get beyond my silencing bubble, and even if it did, I doubted there was anyone in this school with enough of a backbone to come save him from me.

Bryce started fighting back as he realised I might just kill him, using his Vampire strength to slam furious punches into my sides. I relished his suffering, growling as my magic reserves swelled and the blinding pain juddering through me gave me some relief from the aching loss of Elise.

When Bryce tried to run, I caught him by the throat and pinned him beneath me, squeezing as tight as I could. He was a rat, maybe I should just end him. But then I'd have to hide the body and I didn't have time to fuck about. Besides, I didn't kill my own unless I had entirely valid reasons and as much as he was questioning me, he hadn't outwardly taken a stand against me. This should be enough to squash any more fancy ideas of rebellion he might have. And to teach the rest of my gang a lesson.

When his head was about to pop and I had ice coating my arms from his water magic, I released him and Ethan stepped forward, pressing a hand to my back and immediately healing me without a word.

I nodded to him, getting up as sweat ran down the back of my neck and I took heaving breaths as I turned to Russel. Two ears. No blood. Not even a cut.

"Oh Russel," I tutted, shaking my head. "How bitterly disappointing you are."

I strode toward him as he whimpered, trembling from head to toe as I snatched the blade from his hand. "Both ears it is then."

I shoved him down at my feet and he screamed, casting a dome of ice over himself in protection. I slammed my boot through it and grabbed hold of his shirt, ripping him out of it and binding him in vines before holding him up against the nearest wall. I fingered the blade as I moved toward him, letting him squirm and scream and beg while I just sneered at the pitiful display before me.

I took the first ear slowly, letting him wail and hurt, but the second I cut off in one furious slice that would be a bitch to heal. The pain was enough to fill the last of my magic reserves but it did nothing to heal the aching hole in me over the loss of my girl. I spat venom onto my hand and rubbed it over his wounds, making him scream even louder. Now these wounds would scar horribly and there'd be no chance of him growing them back with a potion.

I turned to Ethan with bloodied hands and he nodded to me.

"What's the plan, boss?" he asked brightly, clearly not remotely affected by the violence. He was my kind of Fae.

"Send word to the entire Brotherhood to hunt our half of the city for Elise Callisto," I ordered him.

"Aye, aye captain," he said with a smirk then turned and led my people out of the basement.

A couple of guys dragged Russel and Bryce out, but they didn't have the gall to start healing them in plain sight of me. And nothing would fix

Russel fully.

Things were back in order for now. But this was a Band-Aid on an open wound, and it would keep bleeding until death was near again. I couldn't escape the path I was on. It was already too late. My men would follow me now, but for how much longer?

I wasn't afraid of death, but I was afraid of losing the glint of life Elise had offered me. If I couldn't stem the betrayal running through my gang like poison quickly, then my time as the king of the Lunar Brotherhood was going to come to a bloody end. Our enemies wound up in ten pieces, but our traitors wound up obliterated. If they turned on me, my death was inevitable. So I had to rescue Elise and find a way to keep her safe for good. Because I wasn't the only one they'd punish now they knew she was my weakness.

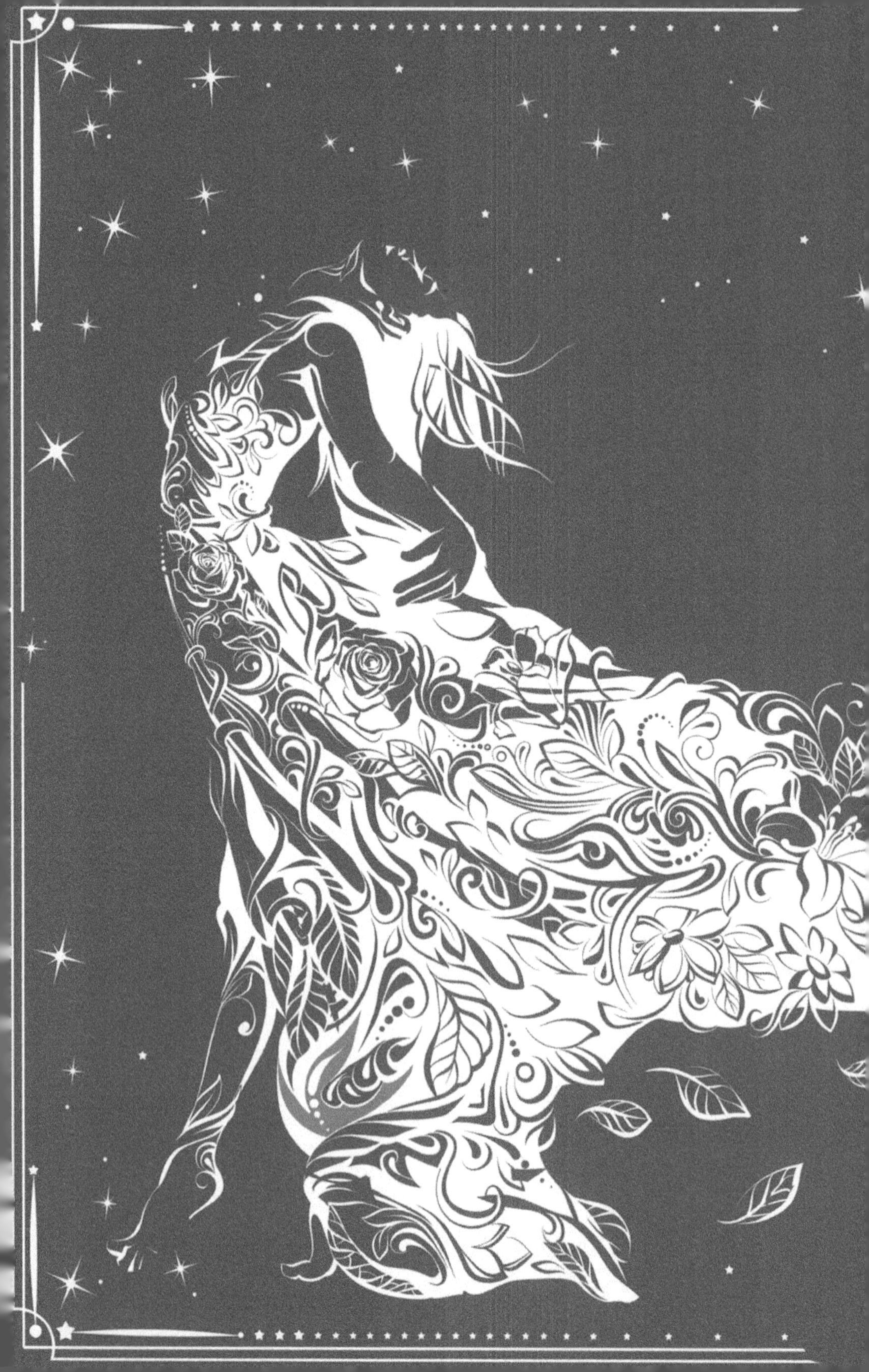

ELISE

CHAPTER THREE

My *fucking head.*

By the stars what the fuck had happened to me and where the hell was I?

I groaned as I pushed myself up into a sitting position, squinting at the dark, stone chamber I found myself in and brushing bits of grit and gravel from my side that had stuck to me while I was out of it.

I reached for the well of magic which should have been living inside me and my heart lurched as I found it severely lacking. My tongue swept over my fangs as they snapped out and the bloodlust hit me hard and fast.

Shit.

A snarl slipped from my throat as I looked around in the dark urgently, hunting out some form of prey to sate this thirst in me. How long had I been out to be this desperate for it? I felt dizzy and achy, and my throat fucking hurt with how much I needed blood.

I hadn't been tapped out like this in a long damn time. Not since my kings had become my Sources. I was a damn addict for the taste of all four of them and I made sure to take my fix daily. They were a habit I had no intention of quitting and I'd been spoiled by how regularly I'd been partaking. But this feeling...*fuck* I swear it actually hurt.

I took a deep breath and fought the bloodlust back as best I could, trying to focus on where I was and what was going on.

"Hello?" my voice rasped out and I licked my dry lips as I looked around at the dank space I found myself in.

I got to my feet, my legs more than a little wobbly and pain ricocheting through the left side of my skull, causing me to press my fingers to it. Sticky, half-dried blood clung to my fingertips where it was matted in my hair, but there wasn't any wound, so I had to guess someone had healed me. Though not well enough to banish the ringing in my skull or the dull thump of a headache that was pressing in on me.

No one answered my shaky call and I took a deep breath as I focused on my senses, listening with my gifts as I tried to hear anything or anyone nearby. It was almost entirely silent beyond this space and I cursed as I realised I was within a damn silencing bubble. And with no magic in my blood, there was nothing I could do to remove it.

Just as I was about to return my hearing to normal, I noticed a faint sound like the lapping of water coming from above me and I stilled as I tried to concentrate on it and figure out what it meant.

I tilted my head back, using my gifted sight to pierce the darkness that surrounded me and noticing the faintest sheen on the ceiling overhead. It was hard to make out much, but I was almost certain there was a small amount of silvery light up there somewhere, way above my head, just about reaching me in the gloom.

"Hello?" I tried again, walking towards the edge of the room and stopping when my outstretched hand met with cold stone.

There were patterns carved into the rocks that surrounded me but even with my Vampire gifts, I couldn't see well enough in the gloom to pick them out.

I started walking, keeping my fingers pressed to the cold rock and feeling my way around the circular chamber. The walls were only broken once by a single solid, wooden door which must have been the only way out of here.

I felt all around it before realising there was no handle on the inside then steeled myself as I gathered my gifts and built up the strength in my limbs.

I backed up several steps before shooting towards the door, slamming into it with my shoulder and making it rattle. But it didn't give.

I threw myself at it again and again, ignoring the pain that burst through my arm as I just kept going.

I had to get out of here. There was no alternative.

"Let me out!" I roared, wondering if the silencing bubble went both ways or if whoever was out there could hear me.

As I backed up to run at the door again, air magic slammed into my body and I was hoisted off of my feet, cursing loudly as I was suspended in the centre of the room. I kicked and thrashed but it achieved nothing, and I fell still as a faint sound reached me from beyond the door.

The door burst open and I squinted as the flickering orange light of a burning torch assaulted my eyes, lighting the space outside and a little of my prison too.

The carvings on the walls were thrown into sharp focus and I glanced at the countless images of every kind of shifter intermingled with constellations and words written in a language I couldn't read. Above my head, I realised the roof was glass and I sucked in a breath. I was in an amplifying chamber, somewhere deep beneath the ground with water overhead. This was a place designed to boost The Sight, but I had no such gifts so why was I here?

A figure stepped through the doorway, shadows seeming to cling to their very being and a cloak pulled around them to conceal their features. I stopped trying to fight the magic that was holding me and just hung there, fixing all of my attention on them as I waited to see what would happen next.

This was him. Or her. *King*. The one I'd been hunting for so fucking long. The reason I'd enrolled at Aurora Academy. The reason my brother had died.

"Hello, Elise," King purred in a tone that was at once familiar and alien, male and female. "I suppose it's time we got to work."

I opened my mouth to scream or curse or just call this asshole out on being a psychotic motherfucker with Daddy issues, but before I could do any of those things the cloaked figure lifted a hand filled with glittering purple powder and blew it into my face.

I inhaled it before I could stop myself and my limbs fell instantly slack. If their magic hadn't been holding me suspended off of the stone floor I would have fallen flat on my back in the blink of an eye.

My consciousness began to slip away from me as I felt myself floating out of the chamber at their command, my eyelids fluttering closed while my heart raced in fear.

I battled to stay awake with the last few ounces of my strength, and my mind filled with pain and panic as I thought of the four men who had captured my heart and wondered where they were now.

When I'd first started out on this mission to avenge my brother's death, I'd foolishly believed one of them had been my target. Who would have thought that I'd be relying on them so heavily now? Because I knew in my soul that I couldn't get myself out of this. I had no idea where I was or what was going to happen to me, no magic at my disposal and no way to fight back.

The only thing I had was hope and love. I needed to believe that my kings would find me somehow. I needed to place my faith in them unlike I ever had before. Because without them I was certain that I would find out Gareth's fate clearly enough by succumbing to the same darkness myself. I was going to die here.

A single tear slipped from the corner of my eye as the darkness pulled me under and the last thing I thought of as I was drawn into the shadows was that I didn't want to die. I'd been willing to sacrifice everything I had and everything I was in the pursuit of justice for my brother. But that was before. When I didn't have them. And now that I did, I knew with an unending certainty that I couldn't give them up. I needed them more than I'd ever needed anything in my life, and I was almost convinced that they felt the same way about me.

The darkness pressed closer and a tremor ran down my spine as it drew me away.

Please don't give up on me, boys. I need you.

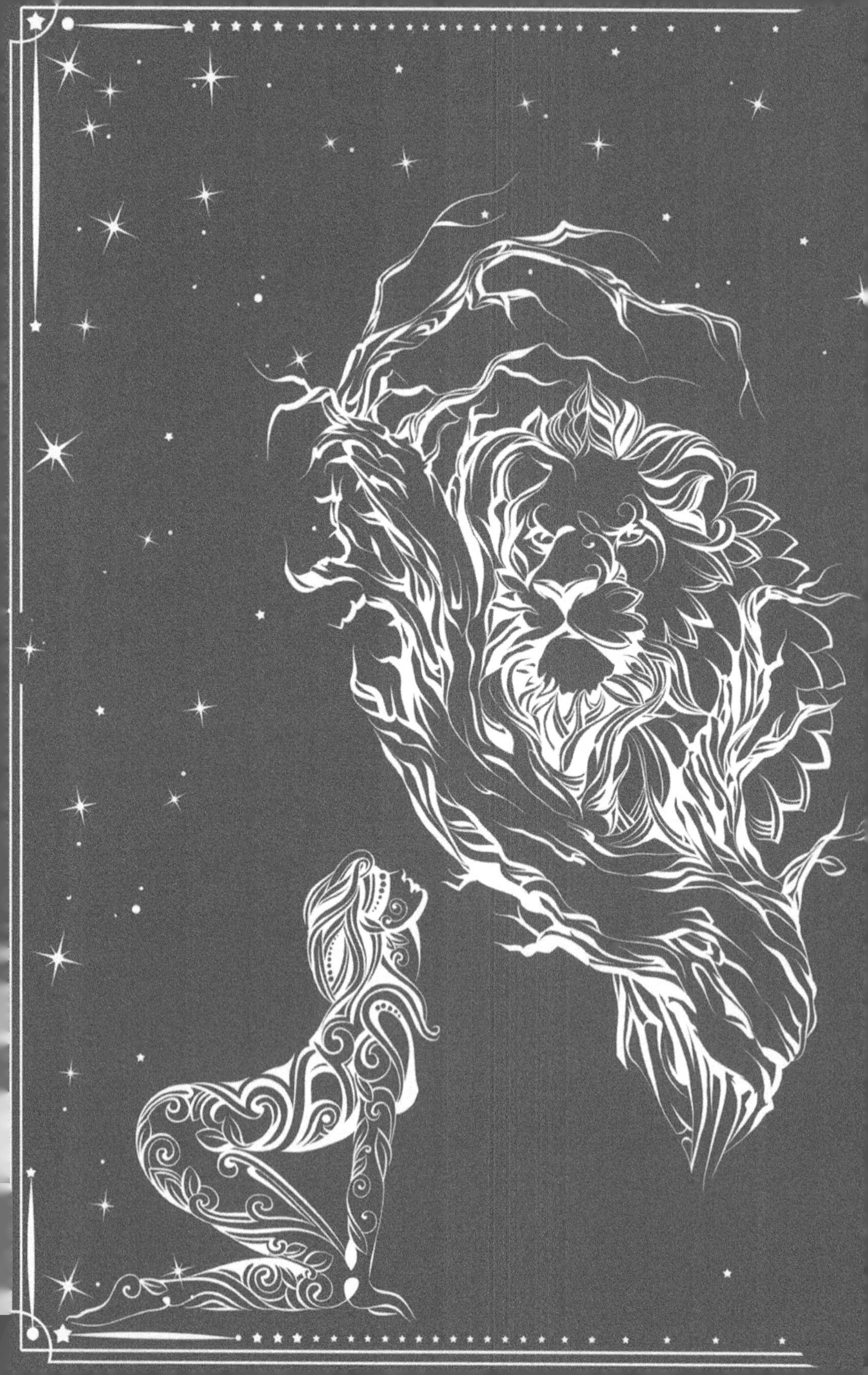

LEON

CHAPTER FOUR

Two weeks and there hadn't been a single sign of my little monster. The stars made me burn for her in an eternal fire, the strength of the Elysian Mate bond between us fiercer than ever. Losing her had been the most unthinkable possibility to ever cross my mind. So much so that it never really had. And now the worst had happened. And I was fucking useless to her.

I hunted day and night, barely sleeping and keeping myself perky on energy booster spells. It was taking its toll, man, I knew that. But I'd straight up die if I didn't find her, and I wasn't sure that was even an exaggeration.

Gabriel landed beside me in a dingey alley on the rougher side of Alestria. It was weird it even had a rougher side considering it was ninety nine percent rough wherever you went. But this here was deathsville for any weak and stupid Fae who wandered into this particularly nasty corner of hell.

Gabriel's black, velvety wings folded behind his back and he nodded to me, his jaw tight and his eyes as hollow as my chest felt. I moved into him, hugging him firmly and nuzzling into his neck. He wrapped one arm around me and released a noise that spoke of how much he needed this too. My bro wasn't much of a hugger, but I didn't really take no for an answer, so he was coming 'round to the idea.

Footsteps sounded behind me and I broke apart from Gabriel, finding Dante striding out of a glimmer of stardust, his shoulders rigid as he approached us. He clapped me on the back and I shared a look of desperation with him before we turned to Gabriel.

"He's going to be on the corner of Firefly Street in five minutes," he said and a growl rumbled through my chest, my Lion pushing against the inside of my flesh.

"Let's go," I insisted and Gabriel nodded, leading the way out onto the road, casting an illusion over us to keep our identities concealed.

He was one powerful fucker and I could feel the weight of the magic as it trickled over me. I didn't really care if my enemies saw my face tonight personally - they wouldn't survive 'til dawn to remember it. But keeping Gabriel's involvement in this a secret was important considering he was our only connection to the Black Card, and if they figured out he was helping to hunt out important members of their twisted little cult, King might take an interest in killing him deader than dead.

Of course, King hadn't shown his face since he'd taken our girl, but he had been as busy as a little bastard of a bee. Killblaze was spreading through the city like free cake and junkies were popping up all over the place like freaking jack-in-the-boxes. But Gabriel hadn't been summoned to a single Black Card meeting since Elise had been taken and it was making me anxious as a shit on a Tuesday.

I knew she was still alive though. The star bond roared as loud as a claxon in my head, begging me to find her. And I was sure I would have felt it if she was dead. Gabriel said he felt it too through The Sight and though Dante and Ryder hadn't said anything of that affect, I could see it in their eyes. They felt her because we were all meant for her. The four of us were cast from stardust in the exact image of the soulmates she needed. And I may have had silver rings in my eyes, but that didn't make my love any fiercer than my brothers' love for her. It was clear in the way they hunted for her, their desperation equalling mine in every way. I hadn't had a whiff of a doubt about any of them before, but if they'd had doubts themselves, I hoped they could see now how much we all deserved her now.

We headed along the street where a Harpy with one beaten up black wing was begging for money and a half shifted Lexian Goat woman was frying up some kind of bugs in a rusty old pan over a magical flame. I mighta had one for a laugh once and said Hakuna Matata before I ate it. Not anymore though. I hadn't smiled since Elise had been taken. And the only food I ate was the meals Gabriel made for us at his apartment. I'd only been home once, unable to bear the look of sadness in my parents' eyes after I'd told them what had happened.

They were already broken over the loss of Roary, now they were broken over Elise too. And not just that, I'd seen the way my dad had looked at me. Like I'd done this. Like I should have been there to protect her. And I felt the same way. I'd let her down. The one person I'd vowed to love and cherish for the rest of time, the one the stars had chosen as my perfect match, who I'd claimed as my Lioness queen. I hadn't protected her when she needed me most. What kind of Lion did that make me?

Gabriel led the way down a dark street as the moon shifted behind the clouds above. There was a betting shop across the road where punters were placing bets on the Pegasus sky racing that was playing on the screens inside.

We leaned against a wall side by side, waiting for our mark to emerge. I had the urge to shift, tear in there and grab the bastard between my teeth. I'd rip limbs off until he told me where my little monster was, and I'd make his death the most painful I could if he had the answer. But that wasn't the plan. I couldn't go off half-cocked. I had to be fully cocked. We handled every target the same way; we captured them discreetly and Ryder came to collect them.

"How's Rosa?" I murmured to Dante and he sighed.

"Better," he replied with a heaviness to his voice. "But she won't talk about Felix. I've tried to get her to open up, my mamma has too. She just refuses to talk about what he did to her. And I'm afraid she won't ever open up now."

I shook my head at that, hurting for Dante's kid cousin. The scars left on her body by Felix would never heal, they'd been left there by a Sun Steel blade. There was no undoing that shit. And it broke my heart to think of what she'd faced at the hands of her own father.

"It's time," Gabriel murmured and we all stood upright as the asshole in question stepped out of the betting shop.

He was a grisly fucker with a weathered face and slicked back grey hair. He pulled up the hood of his coat then started walking up the road and a low growl rolled through my throat.

As one, the three of us crossed over the quiet street and followed him while Dante worked to draw the shadows closer around us for cover. We were three predators on a hunt and the beast housed in my body hungered for death keener than it ever had. This danger in me wasn't new, but it was at its peak. There was nothing more deadly than a star bound Fae parted from their mate by force. They'd tear the heavens apart for one another. And if King thought they could hide her from me, they were going to be proven seriously wrong when I got my hands on them. I'd bleed every drop of blood from their veins, spill their magic into the earth and let it rot there. Elise Callisto belonged to four powerful creatures who would happily see every star in the sky fall if it would return her to us. And I would be the first to rip one down.

Our mark turned onto the next street and we closed the distance between us and him as he slipped through a gate into a dark park that had murder-me-in-the-shadows written all over it.

"Like before?" Gabriel murmured and me and Dante nodded.

My Harpy bro flexed his wings and took off silently into the sky, the darkness swallowing him up instantly. Dante's fingers sparked with electricity and I cracked my knuckles as we stepped through the gate, using a silencing bubble to hide the squeak of hinges.

I raised my palms as Dante and I closed the distance between us and our target a little more until we were within five feet of him on the shadowy path, the dull orange light of a lamppost flickering up ahead.

I threw out my hands, sending a blast of fire ahead of me and casting it in a huge circle around the asshole. He gasped in alarm as Gabriel dropped down like a bullet from above, landing on top of him and forcing him to the ground. I flicked my fingers, opening up a gap in the fire which Dante and I strode through. Dante jogged ahead of me, dropping to his knees beside Gabriel and slammed his hand down on the back of the guy's head. One good shock of electricity cut off his screams and made him pass out. That wouldn't be the last of his screams tonight though. This guy was a Killblaze dealer and was no doubt responsible for countless drug related deaths across the city. And if that wasn't reason enough to torture his pasty ass, we had a reason beyond all others. He might know where our girl was.

Gabriel's eyes glazed for a moment then he sucked in a breath. "Shit, Ryder's not coming. He's stuck in a gang meeting at The Rusty Nail."

My jaw locked at that. We didn't have time to wait. This piece of shit could know where Elise was. He could be the key we'd been waiting for. And I'd already waited long enough.

I marched forward as Gabriel got off of the guy, lifting him into my arms and throwing him over my shoulder.

"What are you doing?" Dante balked.

Gabriel's eyes glazed then he looked to me, his mouth parting to try and make me stop what I was about to do, but I was already throwing the stardust into the air and leaving them behind. Dante had given us all supplies of the rare substance in the name of finding Elise, even though using it was like burning a thousand auras every time. But he had a large stash and he hadn't exactly paid for it. At least not with money. And there was no better reason for using it than finding our girl.

I was dragged away from my friends, tearing across Alestria and landing outside The Rusty Nail, a bar that looked like a crime scene waiting to happen and which was the headquarters of the Lunar Brotherhood.

I strode right up to the door with nothing but flames in my heart and a furious determination to find our girl. I'd do anything it took. And I wasn't going to waste another second debating how to act when this motherfucker could lead us to her. What if she was being hurt? What if she needed me right this second and I wasn't there? What if time was running out for her?

I'm coming, little monster, just hold on.

Panic warred in my chest as I shoved through the door, feeling the resistance of a strong silencing bubble as I made it inside and couldn't hear beyond it. The bar was packed with angry, muscly people with tattoos on their faces and leather jackets galore.

Ryder was standing up on the bar and whatever he was saying within the silencing bubble fell dead on his lips as every eye in The Rusty Nail turned on me.

"Ryder!" I barked. "I need your help. Now."

His jaw ticked angrily and he started shouting, though I couldn't hear him beyond the barrier of magic. It suddenly washed away in a huge wave and the sound of his voice exploded over me.

"-do you think you're doing walking in on a Brotherhood meeting?!" he bellowed and his gang members shared looks, sniggering and smirking like they expected Ryder to forge an axe in his hand and cut my head off with it.

Scarlett Tide was sitting on the bar beside him, her eyes narrowing on me with suspicion before she looked up at Ryder, awaiting his orders. She had a Scorpio tattoo on her cheek and her long, brown hair was pulled up into a ponytail, giving her resting bitch face more ammo.

"I brought a Lunar traitor," I called, figuring it was best not to end up dead tonight as I gestured to the asshole over my shoulder.

A murmur of interest ran through the crowd, but eyes were dragging over me too, some filling with recognition.

"Isn't that one of the Night boys?" someone muttered.

"He's friends with the Oscuras," another hissed and I realised my hot head had just caused Ryder a serious issue. But I couldn't wait. Not when our girl was in trouble.

This bond between us clouded everything else. I'd lost all sense the day she was taken. I couldn't function right. I was in dire need of another energy booster spell and my brain fucking hurt. I'd have tortured the guy myself if I hadn't needed Ryder's gifts to get inside his head. Black Card members were bound by all kinds of spells, but Ryder's hypnotism could work its way beneath all that, seek out the truth by sifting through their pain and cutting to the heart of it. I needed him. And I needed him right now.

Ryder's throat worked, then he crouched down and murmured something in Scarlett's ear. She nodded slowly, glancing at me once more with a sneer before rising to her feet. "We're going to take a break. Who wants a drink?"

A cheer went up from a few of the gangbangers but most of them were still glaring at me with suspicion. Especially as Ryder strode down the bar and jumped off the end of it to land in front me, then steered me away through a door to my left.

His grip on my arm was iron tight as he dragged me along a corridor then down a dark stairway to a heavy metal door. He unlocked it with the press of his palm, a magical lock reading his signature before we headed inside and I dumped the Black Card member on the concrete. The room was just a stone chamber with a drain in the centre of the floor and a wooden chair behind it. It was clear what this place was for and I couldn't wait to get started.

Ryder shoved the door shut and a silencing bubble wrapped around us before he caught me by the throat and threw me against the wall. I didn't fight. I knew in the back of my head I'd screwed up, but I was so desperate I couldn't find it in me to care.

"What the fuck do you think you're playing at, Mufasa?" Ryder spat, his fingers icy cold against my skin as he tightened them.

"That asshole could know where she is," I growled.

He shook his head at me, his upper lip peeled back. "Do you have any idea of the pressure I'm under right now? My gang already suspect I'm disloyal, you coming here is like adding a fucking log to their bonfire."

The weight of what I'd done fell on my heart and a Lionish mewl left me in apology. "I'm sorry, I'm not thinking straight."

He slammed me against the wall again so my head snapped back and hit it. "Get it together," he barked. "If you fall apart, you're no use to her. And if you get my gang to fucking kill me, I'll be no use to her either."

I swallowed guiltily, nodding and he released me, stepping back with a curse.

He turned to the unconscious guy on the floor and took a slow breath as he started rolling up his sleeves, revealing the ink decorating his forearms. The atmosphere around him was ripe with violence and I drank it in, feeding on it as I let the darkness envelop me.

"Let me help," I growled and he glanced back at me with a vaguely bemused expression.

"You're no help here. Go back to your little friends." He sneered.

"Don't pull that shit. They're your friends too," I muttered as I stepped closer. "And I'm not going anywhere."

"You've not got the stomach for what I'm gonna do to him. First in his head, then right here in this room," he said, his face cast in shadow as he leaned down to bind the man's hands behind his back with vines.

"I can stomach anything for her," I said seriously and he looked back at me over his shoulder as he assessed me.

"Come here then, Mufasa."

"I'm feeling more Scar today," I commented as I moved to help him carry the guy to the chair and Ryder finished tying him up with his earth magic.

"You can't be Scar," he muttered.

"Why not?" I sniped. I had a little Scar in me. I could be the big, bad Lion when I wanted to be. And right now, that was all I wanted to be until I got Elise back.

"Because *I'm* Scar," he said then he strode forward and grabbed the guy's face to wake him up. I got there first though, setting a flash fire at his feet and relishing the wail of pain that left the asshole as he woke.

Where's my little monster, you piece of shit?

Ryder's hypnosis exploded over me in a wave and I found myself in a room just like the one we'd been in before, only the floor was wet with blood and the sounds of screams and torture echoed beyond the walls.

Our faces were disguised as twisted lion heads and I smirked at the jagged scar running across one of Ryder's eyes. This would have been the best moment of my life on any other day of the year. As it was, I wouldn't be having any good days again until my mate was returned to me.

Ryder forced his will over the guy in the vision with us and he jerked awake with a gasp, fear filling his eyes as a whimper of alarm escaped him.

"W-what is this?" he stammered.

"This is hell," Ryder answered in a gravelly voice that wasn't his.

I smiled twistedly to unnerve him. "And we're your unending suffering."

Nothing. The guy hadn't given us a single hint to where Elise was. And I was left feeling more hopeless than ever. I'd really thought he'd be the one. That he held the secret we'd been desperate for all this time. But he'd died spilling all he knew, and it was no good to us at all because it had nothing to do with Elise.

I shoved out the door as I wiped blood from my face with the back of my hand. Ryder followed me out, slamming the door shut and locking it with a flash of magic. He caught my arm before I could storm off, because all I wanted to do right then was shift and run as far away as possible then roar my pain into the night.

"Look at me," he demanded and I did, wondering if he had some words of comfort to offer me or maybe a warm hug. But I was yanked into his hypnosis instead and I blinked in surprise as he spoke to me within it.

"Some asshole in my gang is watching us. He's using a concealment spell by the wall up there. Follow my lead." He released me from the hypnosis and jerked his head in a command for me to follow him.

I headed up the steps and my gaze slipped to the shadowy corner by the wall and the very subtle tingle of magic emanating from it.

"If you wanna join the Lunars, you're gonna have to prove yourself more than that," Ryder said. "You've got ties with the fucking Oscuras and the information you've given me on them isn't enough for you to win my trust. You'll only manage that when you hand me something that can get me close to Inferno so I can destroy him."

Holy shit.

I twisted my expression into a dark smile and shrugged. "Dante trusts me, it'll be easily done. I just need more time."

"I expect some more tip offs soon or I won't grant you anything but a knife in your gut, Lion," he snarled.

We headed out a side door onto the street and Ryder kicked the door shut behind us, casting a few spells around it before turning to me again and creating a silencing bubble.

"You'd better go," he muttered, glancing at The Rusty Nail with a grimace like going back in there was unappealing.

"Come with me," I urged. It was the weekend and I didn't want Ryder to be stuck here alone. He was Elise's snakelet. I needed him close.

"Is Inferno staying there?" he asked, meaning Gabriel's apartment and I shook my head in what may or may not have been a lie. I mean yeah, Dante could have been staying there tonight, or my bro could have gone home. Impossible to know for sure really. But Ryder only ever went there when Dante wasn't around or if he had no choice but to speak to all of us about our plans to find Elise.

"Your nos are often yeses," he pointed out with narrowed eyes.

I huffed a breath, clawing a hand through my long hair. "Alright, whatever dude. I'm gonna go." I was too tired and too fucking disappointed to beg him. I just wanted to destroy something then pass out for a few hours before I started my hunt again.

I walked off down the street, figuring Gabriel's place was only a couple of blocks away from here anyway. No point wasting the stardust. And I might find a wall or two to take my rage out on along the way. Or an unfortunate dipshit who looked at me funny.

"You're covered in blood, Mufasa," Ryder called after me like I gave a damn right now.

I waved a hand in a vague goodbye and picked up my pace, my vision darkening around the edges. When was the last time I ate, or slept, or felt anything but stress?

I rubbed at my eyes and stumbled a step as exhaustion ripped down the centre of my chest. Sleeping felt like a betrayal to my mate, but I had to give in to it occasionally. My mind was a haze of death and destruction, loss and pining that I wanted to escape but I felt guilty escaping it too. She was out there all alone and I wasn't even a single bit closer to finding her.

"I'm sorry little monster, I'm so fucking sorry," I murmured, hating myself for letting her down. I looked up at the moon and wondered if wherever she was, she could see it too. Or if she was buried away somewhere that no light could find her. My beautiful, lilac-haired Vampire hidden away in the dark.

The roar of an engine sounded behind me then Ryder pulled up beside me on his forest green motorcycle.

"Get on," he ordered, not even looking at me, just staring straight ahead down the road like if he didn't acknowledge his own kindness it wasn't happening.

"It's fine, bro," I tried but he finally looked at me with a sadistic glint in his eyes.

"Get on or I'll hogtie you to the bitch seat," he warned and I was too tired to argue, moving up to him and swinging my leg over the back of the bike.

I clutched his leather jacket as he took off down the road at a fierce speed, a concealment spell washing over us as he tore along the streets in the direction of Gabriel's place. My head lolled forward, pressing to his back and he smelled like leather and oatmeal. It was sucha homely smell and sucha comfy back, I found myself drifting off to sleep.

"Sucha nice snakelet…" I murmured, snuggling closer as a purr ran through me, the first shred of peace I'd found in a long time.

An elbow drove into my gut and I jerked awake with a curse, squinting as I found myself in the underground parking lot of Gabriel's apartment block. I slid off the seat with a yawn and Ryder got off too, looking to me with his brows pulled sharply together.

"Come on, asshole," he muttered.

I followed him to the elevator, and we were soon sailing upstairs towards the penthouse. I leaned back against the wall, my eyes fluttering closed again as I thought of Elise and pictured her wrapped around me, her ear to my chest, my arms locking her to me and never letting go.

"I fucked up," I groaned. "I'm the worst Elysian Mate there ever was, Ryder."

"There's probably someone worse," he commented and I almost, almost smiled. "Not many. But maybe one. Probably not though," he backtracked, but it was too late. The compliment had left him and I loved him for it.

"Thanks, Rydikins," I mumbled, sleep gripping me again and I was half aware of a loud snore leaving me as I passed out.

Consciousness half slid back to me as Ryder gripped my arm and yanked me out of the elevator and I tried to crack my eyes open to see where I was going, but I couldn't manage it.

"By the stars," Gabriel cursed. "Here, let me get the blood off of you two." The kiss of his water magic ran over me and I murmured a thanks, reaching vaguely in the direction his voice had come from before Ryder yanked on my arm again and towed me through the apartment.

"Well? Did you find anything, serpente?" Dante growled. *Whoops, looks like he was totally here after all. My bad.*

"No," Ryder grunted then shoved me and I fell face down onto a soft bed.

"Mmm," I sighed, stretching out across the cool sheets.

"I can help him," Dante's voice drew closer. "You can leave now."

"He should stay," Gabriel called.

"I don't want to fucking stay," Ryder growled.

"Well you have to because if you go back to The Rusty Nail tonight, you'll be questioned and I don't see that ending well for you," Gabriel said and I reached for Ryder blindly.

"Stay, Scar," I begged. "Cuddle me."

"I'd rather cuddle a bag of butcher knives," he growled.

"Someone cuddle me," I pleaded as two sets of strong hands started pulling my clothes off.

"I can do it, Inferno," Ryder hissed in warning.

"He doesn't need you, I'm his best friend," Dante clipped.

"Are you hungry Leon?" Gabriel called. "I can make something?"

"Nah, I'm okay," I slurred as someone flipped me over and I cracked my eyes, finding Ryder and Dante fighting to unbuckle my jeans.

My Charisma was slipping out of me like water from a shattered dam and I was too tired to even try to stop it. It looked like my pride were happy to accommodate my needs though, so I wouldn't deny them the satisfaction. It would have been enjoyable if my queen had been here. But she was gone, lost, stolen. *Oh little monster, come back to me.*

Dante got my belt undone and Ryder yanked my jeans off, tossing them into the laundry basket. Dante gripped my shirt, tearing it over my head and smirking victoriously as he tossed that in the basket too.

"I got you some hot milk." Gabriel walked into the room with my favourite mug. It was shaped like Simba's head and had a little leafy crown along the top. I'd moved quite a lot of stuff in here actually, but Gabriel didn't mind. Well, he'd only shouted for a couple of minutes, but he'd gotten over it.

"Thanks, Mindy," I sighed.

"What?" Gabriel asked sharply.

"I said thanks, Gabe." I smiled as I took it, shifting back in the bed as Ryder tugged the comforter down and Dante dove to the other side of the bed to grab the other corner of it.

Gabriel looked like he wanted to reprimand me for calling him Gabe, but he held his tongue as Dante and Ryder tucked me into bed. I was as snug as a bug in a rug as I nestled back against the pillows and sipped my honey sweetened milk. I drank it down in a few long gulps then Dante hooked the mug out of my grip and placed it on the nightstand before stripping out of his clothes and climbing into bed with me in his boxers.

"I'll stay with him," he told the others, moving under the covers and Ryder hissed under his breath, stripping out of his own clothes and getting into the bed on my other side.

Gabriel moved to the window, gazing outside then moving to perch on the low chest of drawers beneath it. "I'll keep watch," he said.

"Wake us if you have a vision about her, falco," Dante urged and Gabriel nodded, the promise in his eyes helping me relax.

I slipped lower under the sheets, the presence of the two bodies either side of me giving me more comfort than I'd had since I'd lost her. I could practically taste the pain in each of my Lionesses and I reckoned Ryder was having a feast on all of it as it surrounded him too.

A low purr started up in my throat as I drifted into the dark and hoped the nightmares wouldn't come for me this time. All I ever saw in my dreams was Elise bloody and screaming, begging me to help her. But with my pride surrounding me, I felt like I might just be lucky enough to slip into pure darkness instead. Then tomorrow, the hunt would begin all over again.

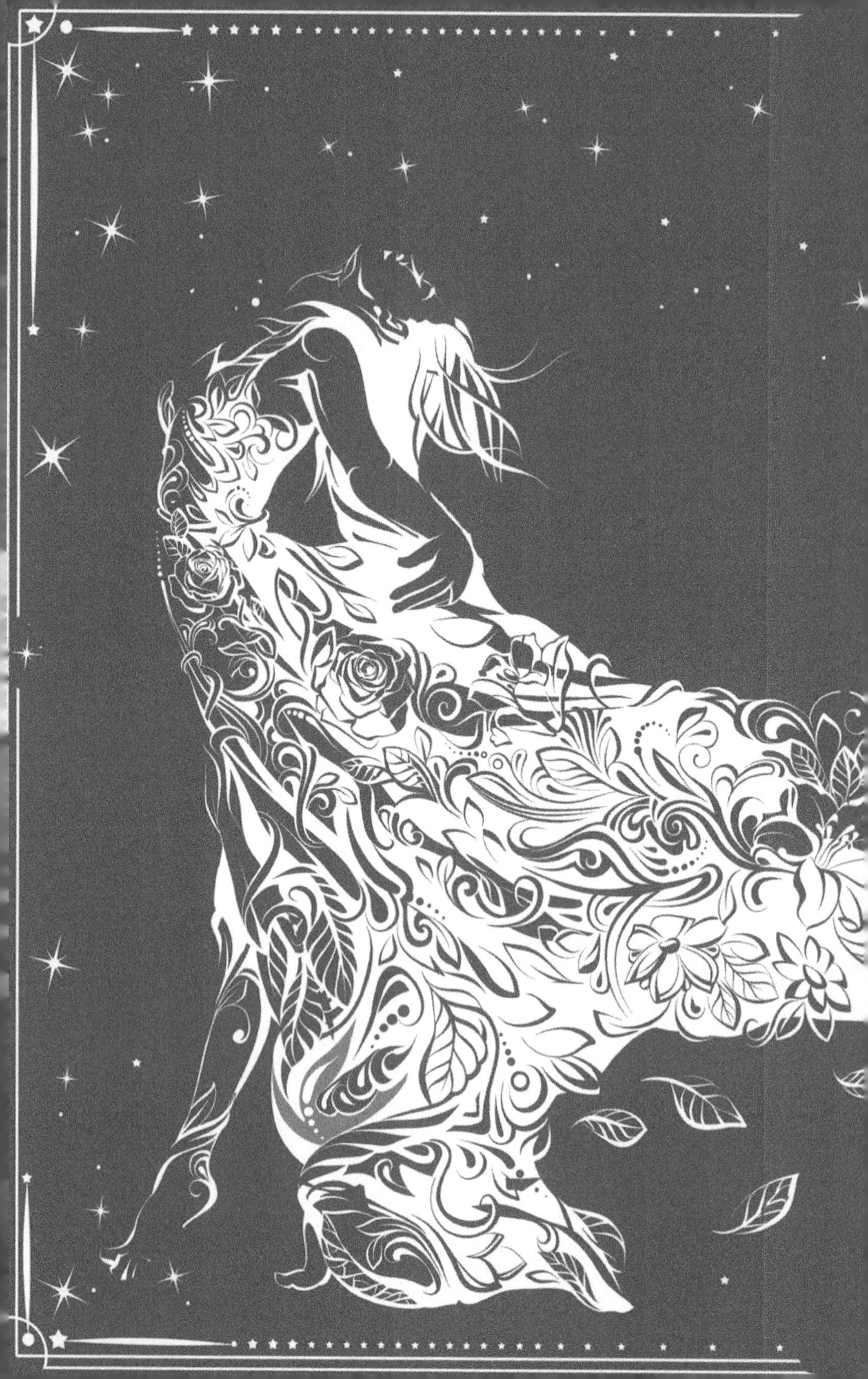

ELISE

CHAPTER FIVE

I woke in the same stone chamber, though this time I found myself on a thick bed of blankets with an everflame burning to the side of the space warming me through.

I groaned groggily, feeling weaker than ever, the thirst near unbearable as I tried to climb back up out of my dreams. Dreams of my kings and my fangs in their veins, their hard muscles pressed against my soft curves and all the best bad things happening at once.

The ache in my throat was unbearable and a snarl ripped from me as I shot to my feet, racing toward the heavy wooden door and throwing myself against it with my full strength. Over and over again, I launched myself at it, not stopping until I was panting and sweaty, my shoulder and arm aching with pain I couldn't heal away.

"Let me out of here!" I screamed, my fangs snapping out as I thought of what I'd do when I escaped this place. I'd pounce on the first unlucky fucker to cross my path and drink them dry. It was the least they deserved for locking me up like this. I wouldn't feel at all guilty over it.

Silence. The void of nothingness beyond that door pressed in on me more firmly than the bars of Darkmore Penitentiary. I was trapped down here. Alone.

I bit down on my tongue, groaning at the taste of blood that spilled through my mouth and aching even more at the lack of magic residing in it.

I stumbled back a few steps, hunger, thirst and exhaustion sapping my energy now that I'd worn myself out attacking the door.

My feet tangled in the nest of blankets and I sank down onto them, half falling, half just giving in to the inevitable.

A sob caught in my throat as I looked up at the glass dome that made up the roof of this chamber. With the light from the large everflame flickering and reflecting against the glass, I could make out more details and this time I was certain that water sat above me.

Why the hell was I down in this place?

I licked my lips, coating them with blood from my tongue and using the pain of that injury to try and focus my thoughts. If this went on much longer, I was going to be lost to the thirst. I knew more than enough about that curse which held all Vampires in its grip. And worst of all, I wasn't used to this anymore. With my kings available to sate my thirst whenever I'd been in need of blood recently, I'd grown complacent. I hadn't had much practice of going without and now when I needed my thoughts clear and rational, they were clouded by the desire for blood and death and carnage.

I flopped back onto the makeshift bed, breathing in deeply as I tried to calm myself and staring up at the water beyond the glass.

Come on, brain. Why am I down here? What's the point of placing me somewhere that is intended for Seers when I don't have The Sight?

I tried to remember the things I'd learned in Arcane Arts, the methods of divination I'd learned, and the methods Gabriel had tried to take control of his Sight.

Focus.

I needed to focus if I wanted to *see* anything, but what was I supposed to focus on?

I breathed in and out slowly, trying to let my mind fall into that place of calm deep within me even though my hunger for blood kept creeping up on the corners of my mind, drawing my attention. I exhaled slowly, thinking about the most important things to me in this world.

The faces of my kings swum before my eyes and I moaned softly as I could have sworn I almost felt their touch on my skin, their voices in my ears.

They were together, all four of them in Gabriel's apartment in the city, none of them looking happy but none of their anger pointed towards each other.

"What's wrong?" I breathed, my eyes falling closed until I actually *saw* them and they really were all together just like I'd pictured.

Everything looked grainy somehow, like I wasn't able to grasp the finer details of the room and I had no sense of time to judge whether this was happening now or if it belonged to the future. Gabriel sat on the end of his bed with Dante and Leon's hands on his shoulders. Ryder stood before him and offered a hand, his jaw gritted with determination and a pain I was certain only I could see. He was hurting. They were all hurting. And it was because of me.

I stared at the four of them, united in pain and fear as Gabriel tried to force a vision, his brow furrowing and his grip on Ryder's hand looking strong enough to crush bones.

"It's no use," Gabriel snarled. *"I don't know where that motherfucker has taken her, they're clearly doing something to mask her location from me."*

I sucked in a sharp breath as realisation hit me. That was why I was down here. This place was designed to focus the energy of the stars, make it easier for us to *see* them and the visions they offered. But it worked both ways. The focus was all outward which meant that while I was down here, I was effectively hidden by this room and the water above me. The stars had lost track of my fate and without them being able to *see* me and the paths I might take, Gabriel couldn't *see* me either.

The flurry of thoughts that burst through my mind were more than enough to break my meagre hold on the vision and my eyes snapped open just as a tear slipped loose and cast a burning track along the side of my cheek before sinking into my hair.

My chest shook as I fought to bring it back, to bring *them* back, to feel close to them once more even though I knew they weren't truly here.

"Wait," I murmured, my heart racing as pain took my chest in a vice and squeezed.

The sound of the door unlocking had me gasping and sitting up with a flash of speed, my fangs snapping out once more as I prepared to dive on whoever was coming in here.

Nothing else mattered beyond the solid thump of their pulse as they drew closer and the moment the door swung open, I shot forward with my lips peeled back, fangs bared and the need to drink filling every part of my brain.

But a moment before I could pounce on the cloaked figure who had arrived, I slammed into a wall of magic and it wrapped around my entire body like a fist.

I bucked and snarled as I was hoisted off of my feet, snapping my teeth together and straining my neck as I tried to reach them.

Just a drop. I only needed a drop to sustain me. Just a little...and then a lot. Then I'd keep drinking and drinking and drinking until the pathetic excuse for a Fae before me was nothing but an empty shell and their magic and blood pounded through my veins, injecting me with life once more.

"I come bearing gifts," King said in that ever-changing voice of theirs as the robed figure stepped further into the room.

Another dude scuttled in behind them, pushing a little cart with several metal domes on top of it like the ones fancy hotels placed on top of food. He backed away again the moment he'd delivered it then closed the door, leaving me alone with King in the small chamber.

"I'm going to fucking destroy you," I snarled, still thrashing against their magic and cursing the fact that I didn't have a drop of my own power to fight back with.

"Now, now, Elise, I know you're thirsty, but there's no need for violent outbursts," King said, sounding entirely unconcerned about my promises. But that was a mistake. I hoped the motherfucker really was underestimating me though, because it would only make it all the sweeter when I finished their miserable life.

"Why the fuck am I here?" I demanded, still thrashing.

"I would like to have a civilised conversation with you," King said, eyeing me from within the dark confines of their hood. "And I am aware that Fae of your particular Order have trouble being civilised when they are in need of blood. So…"

I watched as King strode over to the little cart and removed the first of the metal covers, showing me the pint of thick, red blood waiting there for me with a little pink straw jammed into it like it was a milkshake.

I snarled as I scented it on the air, my throat burning with need as the beast in me rose to the surface of my skin and forced control over my body, making me thrash harder.

King just waited, watching me while I couldn't see their face in return. There was nothing inside the hood today, no changing faces or identities. Nothing but a mass of shadows too deep for even my gifted eyes to penetrate.

When I calmed down a little, the next cover was lifted, and King raised a pair of matching metal cuffs to show me.

"These were very hard to get hold of," King said, taking a step closer to me. "They're the cuffs the FIB use to restrain the magic of Solaria's worst criminals. They're the same as the ones used inside Darkmore Penitentiary to stop the inmates from using their magic while they're locked away down there."

"So what?" I snapped.

"So, I'd like you to wear them. If you agree, I will allow you to drink blood regularly to save you from the agony of the thirst."

"Why?" I demanded, but I was practically ready to beg for a taste of that blood, my gaze glued to the glass and my heart pounding as I was overwhelmed by my need for it.

"Because I don't want you to end up like the Vampire you released from the tunnels beneath the academy. I'm attempting to be civilised about this. I need you for my work, yes, but that doesn't mean you should have to suffer unnecessarily. If you need more time to think about it-" King turned towards the door like they intended to leave me here and my heart lurched with panic.

"Wait," I gasped, saliva pooling in my mouth as I stared at the glass of blood. I knew I shouldn't be giving in to this so easily, but what difference did it make? Without drinking blood, I had no magic anyway. At least with the cuffs I would be free of the thirst. I'd have the magic inside me and this all-consuming need for blood would let me think in peace. And I really needed to maintain my sanity if I wanted any chance of getting out of this place. Especially now I knew my kings wouldn't be coming for me.

"Do you accept?" King asked, seeming surprised. But I wasn't a fool. I knew I'd end up agreeing to this deal one way or another. The thirst was only going to get worse, and I'd cave in the end. So why prolong the inevitable? At least this way I could drink my fill of blood and regain my own mind.

"Yes," I growled.

The magic restraining me shifted until my arms were forced out in front of me and King moved closer to snap the cuffs around my wrists.

I bared my teeth and hissed at the feeling of the cool metal against my skin as they used a small key to lock them up tight before pocketing it.

The moment it was done, King released their hold on the magic restraining me and I fell to the floor, landing on my feet.

I lunged at King, my gaze set on the shadows within that hood as the desire to tear their fucking head clean off and bathe myself in their blood consumed me, but I slammed straight into a solid air shield and stumbled back.

I didn't waste any more time on trying to fight my way through it and turned for the cart instead, practically pouncing on the glass of blood and raising it to my mouth with a snarl.

I ignored the straw, letting it jab me in the cheek as I tipped the glass up into my mouth.

Blood ran over my chin and down my face as my desperation made me sloppy and I groaned as I drank deeply, my throat bobbing with every single swallow as the empty pit inside me slowly began to fill.

The blood was bland, stale, the kind of warm that suggested it had been sitting out for a while in that fucking glass and my fangs tingled with the need to bite, drink, feed properly from a Fae worth drinking from.

I finished the glass and cursed as I pushed my fingers into it, swiping them around the inside and coating them in red before sucking them clean.

It helped but it wasn't enough. Not nearly enough.

"Who did you get that blood from?" I growled as I spun back to face King, still sucking my fingers clean and no doubt looking like something from a horror show with blood coating my chin and dripping down onto my clothes. "The weakest fucking Fae you could find?"

King chuckled, the voice stranger than ever as the sound was at once like a young girl, old man and everything in between.

"I'll make certain the next delivery is sourced from a more powerful Fae if you'll do something for me."

"What?" I had no intention of doing anything for this motherfucker, but I was all ears for whatever information they were willing to give up.

King moved to the cart again, removing the last couple of covers from it and revealing a large plate of food alongside a neatly folded stack of fresh clothes and a pile of newspaper cuttings.

"I want you to try and understand what I'm doing here," King said, moving away from the cart to the far side of the chamber where I watched as they began to build something using earth magic. "I require your assistance in my work, though in all honesty the only thing I truly need from you is your blood."

My skin prickled at that suggestion and I scrunched my nose up as I took a step back, instinctively reaching for the magic inside me. But as I tried to wield it, the power ran down my arms towards my hands then slammed to an abrupt halt as it reached the fancy new cuffs I was wearing. My fingers didn't so much as tingle. Nothing. Not a damn thing. *Fuck*.

"While I'm gone you should relax, eat, and read those articles. Each and every one of them. Then you might begin to understand exactly why I think we need change in this city. Alestria is drowning in gangs and violence. We need to rise up from the ashes of this carnage like a Phoenix being reborn and to do so, we need a new leader to guide the people into the light."

"And let me guess," I said scathingly. "That leader is you?"

King spread their arms innocently as they finished building the stone tub. "Someone must bear the burden of leadership if we want to see a brighter dawn rise and for the gangs to fall." They finished constructing the tub and my skin itched with the desire to bathe. I wasn't certain how long I'd been down here, but it was long enough to know I needed it.

"What does reading that shit have to do with it?" I asked, pointing at the pile of cuttings.

"I want you to face the reality of the gangs. Of their atrocities. Of the innocents who have been caught in their crossfires. I want to remind you that Dante Oscura and Ryder Draconis are men capable of terrible things. I want you to remember that they are Fae with two faces and they only allow you to see the ones the light shines on. I want you to see how they've fooled you."

I wanted to snap and bite and defend my men, but I wasn't a fool. King didn't want to hear that. And if I was going to get myself out of here then I needed to play along with these games.

"Fine. I'll read them," I agreed with a shrug. "Then what?"

"Then we'll talk again." King waved a hand over the tub and I watched as heated water poured into it, steam rising to coil up towards the glass roof above us.

I remained still as King turned and walked away from me, my gaze glued to their back and my mind whirling.

The second the door locked behind them and I was left alone again, I moved over to the cart and grabbed some fries from the huge stack of food that had been left for me, munching on them as I picked up the first article.

Family of four killed in crossfire as The Lunar Brotherhood and The Oscura Clan collided today in downtown Alestria.

It wasn't exactly a new story. I'd heard hundreds of them growing up here. I knew full well how dangerous the gangs were and that it was never wise to get close to them when a turf war kicked off. They didn't aim at unallied Fae as far as I was aware, but there were plenty of accidents like this when magic started flying and Fae began shifting on the streets.

My gaze roamed over the picture of the little kids and their parents who had been killed and something twisted in my gut. Of course I didn't support this. But I knew for a fact that Dante and Ryder wouldn't either. Though I guessed as the leaders of their people, they did own some responsibility for it. The thought of that made me uncomfortable and I sighed as I scanned the details of the article. It looked like their car had been hit by a rogue fireball and had collided with an oncoming truck. I guessed they died instantly, or someone would have been able to heal them.

My gaze lingered on the little brother and sister and for a moment I almost envied them because at least they were together wherever they'd gone now. But even as that thought crossed my mind and the ache I was always going to feel over the loss of Gareth rose up sharply inside me, I realised I didn't truly feel like that. Not anymore. There was a time when all I'd wanted or cared about in this life was gaining vengeance on his behalf and I'd been more than willing to trade my life in the pursuit of that. In fact, I was pretty sure I'd been hoping that it *would* cost me my life because I definitely hadn't had any thoughts of an after.

But that wasn't true anymore. I thought of an after now. I thought of my men and the love I felt for them. I had the beginnings of some dreams outside of this unrelenting pain. I was beginning to want...*more*.

I grabbed the stack of articles and the plate of food then moved across the chamber to the steaming bathtub before placing them down on the edge of it. There didn't seem to be much point in me refusing to read them and I had nothing else to do in here anyway.

I quickly stripped out of my dirty clothes and climbed into the tub, almost sighing at how good the hot water felt against my tense muscles.

I sank into it, closing my eyes as I dipped below the surface and wishing I had use of my air magic so that I could stay there. I used to love doing that. I'd just hide out beneath the water, using my magic to let me breathe and I'd allow my troubles to stay above the surface.

Lilac hair floated around me and I released a stream of bubbles from my lips as my tears slipped away unseen.

I miss you, Gare Bear. And I don't know what to do. Can you help a girl to figure it out?

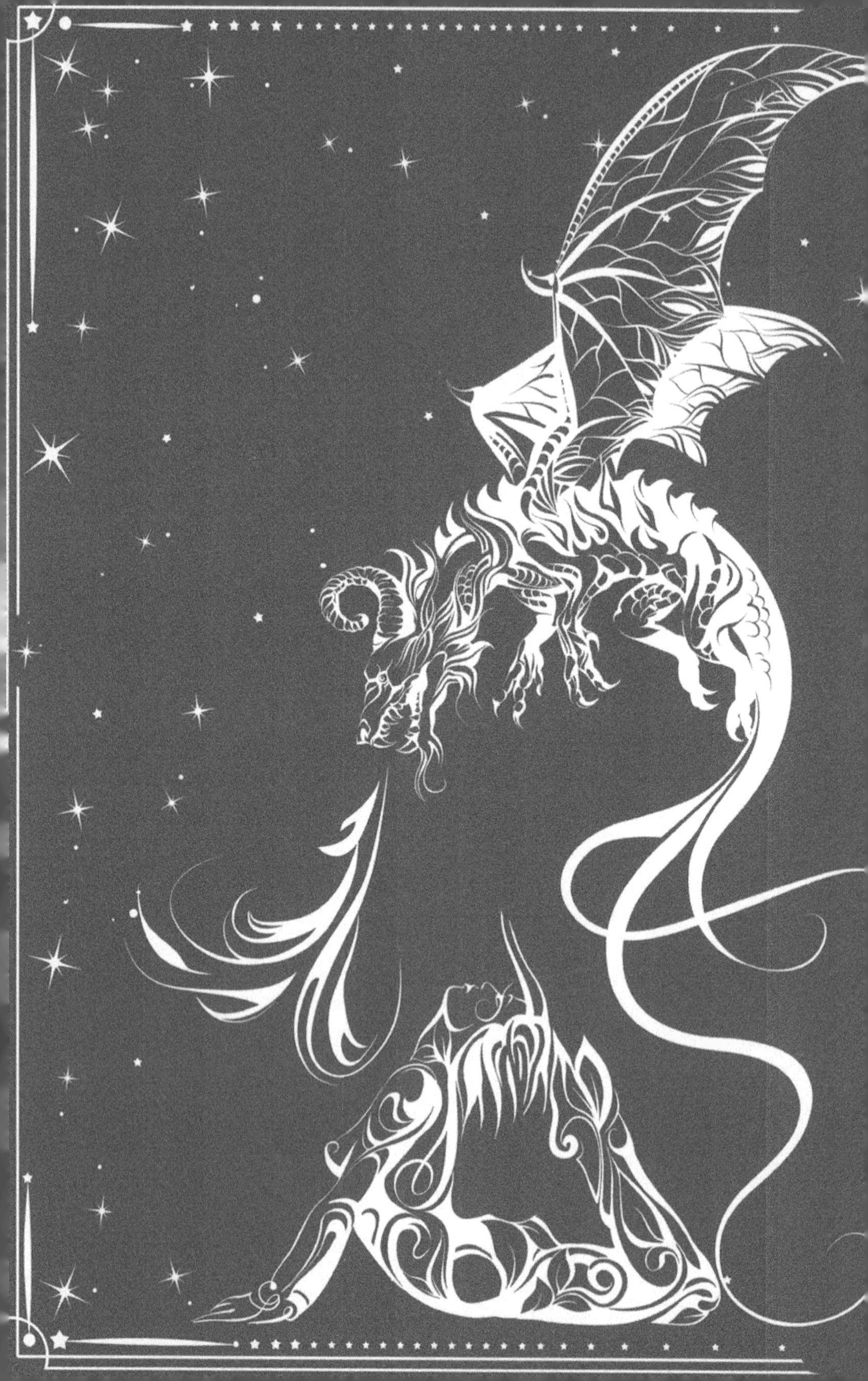

DANTE

CHAPTER SIX

I ate dinner at home, forking mouthfuls of bolognese between my lips as I barely tasted it at all. My full attention was given to my family as they reported any and all news they'd gathered from around Alestria on the whereabouts of Elise. Again and again, they gave me nothing of use and my mind was starting to buzz loudly, panic threatening to come for me again. But I held it in check as my papa had taught me a long time ago. Sii sempre la calma in ogni tempesta, figlio mio. – always be the calm in every storm, my son.

The one good thing my people had reported was that all of Felix's followers had now been accounted for and executed. I'd shown no mercy for what they'd done. Countless atrocities had been committed at their hands and I had ensured not a single traitor was left alive, a choice which now ensured the safety of my true famiglia.

I took a long breath and my eyes flicked to my cousin Rosa as she stood from her seat, her eyes full of something that looked important. But Nico kept harping on about a suspicious acting Heptian Toad in the eastern quarter who was high on Killblaze.

"All Blazers act like that, Nico," I said, my tone a little sharp and making him bow his head as he lowered back into his chair with a doggish whine. But dalle stelle, that was the fifth Blazer he'd pointed me to this week. "What is it, Rosa?"

Rosa had thrown everything she had into the challenge of helping find Elise. She wasn't even Awakened, but I couldn't have stopped her from helping if I'd locked her up and thrown away the key. When Rosa wanted to do something, hell or high water couldn't hold her back.

She was wearing a baggy sweatshirt and jeans, the only difference she let show since what Felix had done to her. She might be pretending she was fine, but the way she hid her scars spoke volumes and I knew I was going to have to confront her about it soon if she didn't come to me herself. But right now, my priority had to be Elise.

"Well, it might be nothing, but…"

"Tell me," I pressed, my stomach twisting as I looked into her dark eyes. There was something broken there now which I couldn't heal. And it hurt me every day.

She still refused to speak to me about Felix, acting as if it had never happened. But the scars peeking out around the left side of her neck and disappearing beneath her shirt told me all I needed to know. Those marks ran deeper than her flesh, and more than anything I wished I could heal them away forever.

"I think I might have found a Killblaze lab," she announced and a couple of excited howls went up around the table.

"Pfft, no chance," Nico said dismissively and I growled loudly, banging my fist on the table, making the whole pack fall silent.

I felt Mamma's eyes on me from the head of the table, her chin lifting with pride.

"Speak Rosa," I urged. "I'm listening."

"So, I've been monitoring the old crystal roads that lead out of the city.

No one really uses them much except the crystal farmers since the highway was built. And there's a lot of abandoned mines out that way since the Cursus Crystal reserves all dried up." She bit her lip. "Anyway, I made a chart of anyone who comes and goes that way, licenses, car makes, any details of the faces I saw. And every day at nine pm, a large black van drives that way then returns back down the road at one am. I've watched it all week and thought it was just one of the crystal transport vehicles at first. It's the exact same make as those. But I decided to get closer to the road last night to take some photos of the drivers coming back and forth that way and when that van showed up, I felt it."

"What?" I asked, hooked on every word that fell from her lips as I prayed they could lead me to amore mio.

"Nothing," she replied, shaking her head. "No feel of any magic at all. And I thought…that's odd. The crystal transport vans have all kinds of protective spells on them, but it was more than that. Normally, the crystals radiate power too and even the Fae driving would give off something. But this vehicle felt like a ghost. Like if I closed my eyes, I wouldn't know it was there at all."

I realised what she was saying and my heart thrashed wildly with excitement. "That's how they're getting so much Killblaze into the city." I carved my fingers through my hair. "Fuck, you're a genius Rosa."

"Language, Dolce Drago," Mamma hissed, but I was lost to my thoughts, barely hearing her.

When the Blazer problem had started to get out of control in Alestria a couple of months ago, the FIB had put up magical checkpoints throughout the city and at its boundaries. Every vehicle had to pass through them daily and their contents were assessed by the spells so they could try and find the dealers moving the Killblaze. A couple of shipments had been found that way at first, but not a single shipment was discovered after that. They went completely off the grid. And *this* was how they were doing it. King must have been using some dark magic to hide the vehicles, let them slip through magical barriers like they were nothing but smoke.

I rose from my seat, nearly knocking it to the floor as Rosa smiled hopefully.

"I can show you where it is?" she offered and I checked the time. It was eight thirty. We needed to get there fast.

"We'd better hurry." I nodded.

"You need a pack," Uncle Filipe urged. "I can lead one."

"No, Uncle," I said firmly. "This needs to be covert." *And I have friends who will be joining me.* I didn't share that with my famiglia though, they'd only take offence. "I'll call you if I need you."

A few mournful howls went up as I nodded to Mamma and strode from the room with Rosa racing after me.

I made it to the hall, pulling on my leather jacket as Mamma jogged after us. "A word Dolce Drago," she asked, her eyes full of concern.

"I need to go Mamma," I said anxiously, leaning in to kiss her on the cheek, but she caught my arm, giving me a firm look that told me she wasn't going to let me go anywhere until she'd said what it was she needed to say. "What is it?"

Mamma threw Rosa a look as she kicked on her sneakers.

"I'll wait outside," my cousin said, getting the hint and slipping out the front door.

Mamma cast a silencing bubble around us, and I gazed at her silver ringed eyes with a squeeze of my heart.

"I have held my tongue until now, but I must say this." She pressed her shoulders back and though she was small, she still always carried a weight of power about her. "I like Elise, mio figlio, I do. But the entire Oscura Clan is hunting for this girl as if she is your mate."

I shook my head, lies on the tip of my tongue to explain my way out of this, but Mamma didn't let me speak them as she went on. "I know you love her. I see it in your eyes, in the way you search for her, the way you don't rest, don't sleep, the way you run off every night with your amico Leon Night. But *he* is her star-chosen mate, Dolce Drago, I cannot see your heart break over a girl who isn't yours to keep."

My throat thickened, full of lead as I stared at the sincere love in her eyes, her need to protect my heart blazing in her expression. She reached out to cup my cheek. "But I also sense there is more to this because I have seen the three of you together in this house. A son cannot hide the truth from his mamma, and a girl's eyes reveal her soul. So answer me this, Dolce Drago, why does a girl who has found her Elysian Mate stare at my son like he stands right at the centre of her world with her Leone?"

I couldn't breathe for a long moment, staring at my mamma and knowing she didn't deserve a lie. She would stand by me no matter what I said in this moment, no matter how controversial. It wasn't like Werewolves were strangers to polyamorous relationships. But Dragons certainly were. Though I was no ordinary Dragon.

"It is as you see it, Mamma," I admitted on a breath, pulling her hand from my cheek and squeezing it in my fingers. "I love her. She's my una vera stella and both she and Leon know this. We have…an arrangement."

She nodded slowly and tears filled her eyes, making me fear that she couldn't accept this. And I realised those fears had lived in me for a long time now. Mamma had always spoken of me finding my Idol - my Dragon mate - or perhaps an Elysian Mate of my own. She had pictured me with one girl and no one else, someone who would fulfil the possessive need in me to claim a single Fae as my own. But I'd been around plenty of Wolves who lived in packs with their lovers, I'd just never imagined I'd end up in a relationship with a girl who loved three other men.

"This is unheard of with Elysian Mates," she breathed. "Your father and I could never have imagined wanting anyone else."

"I know it's strange, but it works," I said firmly. Even though I knew in my heart Elise may never want me as deeply as she wanted Leon, that was okay. Because she could have whatever pieces of me she desired, and I would be there for her in any way I could. "I'm happy with them, Mamma," I promised, wanting to eradicate the fears in her eyes. "Truly."

"Oh Dante," she breathed, her face splitting into a wide smile. "Then I am so happy for you. Leon is already like a son to me and when you are all married, he will be a part of this family alongside Elise and then-"

"Enough," I stopped her, shaking my head. "Let's not get ahead of ourselves. I need to find her first." *And tell you about Gabriel and the fucking snake.* Dalle stelle, she was hardly going to welcome Ryder Draconis into the family. And fuck if I would either.

"Then go, Dolce Drago." She pushed me toward the door and dissolved the silencing bubble around us. "Bring her home."

My heart squeezed at those words, the idea of Elise having a home here, truly being a part of my family made me ache for that life. I would give anything for it. *Anything.*

I strode out the door, taking a deep breath of the night air as Rosa gave me a hopeful look, jumping up from the porch steps.

"Ready?" she asked.

"Yeah, you wanna fly tonight, piccola alfa?"

Her eyes brightened and she nodded excitedly. "Hell yes."

I pulled my clothes off, tossing them to her and jogging down from the porch. I dove forward, letting the huge beast within me tear free of my flesh and landing on the dusty ground with a roar.

Electricity crackled down my spine and I let myself bathe in it for a moment before taming it so it wouldn't hurt Rosa. I lowered my wing so she could climb on and she tucked herself in behind my shoulder blades as I flexed my wings and took off toward the sky. The hope of finding Elise made me fly faster than I ever had before as I moved into the cover of the clouds and soared toward the old crystal roads beyond the city. The clouds hugged my body, begging for a storm, but I wouldn't be bringing one tonight. Nothing to give away my approach.

When I was half a mile away from the roads, I landed in one of the fields and shifted back into my Fae form, pulling on my clothes as Rosa passed them to me.

"It's this way, come on," Rosa called and I ran after her, casting concealment and silencing spells around us to give us cover.

We soon headed into a thick cluster of trees that bordered the road and Rosa started climbing up into a large oak with all the agility of a monkey. I followed her at a slower pace, my huge body making it more difficult to squeeze between the branches.

"Come on, grande Drago, tuck those shoulders," Rosa laughed as I pulled myself up onto the wide branch she was perched on.

I dropped onto it behind her and she tucked herself up against me so I could see down to the road. My heart hit a powerful beat as I thought of my girl. This could be the night I got her back in my arms, the night we found King and destroyed the bastardo for good. I'd call on the others just as soon as I was sure. There was no need to draw them from their hunts around the city if this was another dead end. But a feeling in my gut told me it might not be.

We waited in the dark as the time ticked by, just a few minutes left to go until nine pm. Rosa was as still as a statue, poised like a predator ready to pounce.

Lights flared further down the road and I held my breath as the van approached, trundling along the narrow lane as it made its way towards us. Rosa crept further along the branch and I followed her to where it overhung the road. Then we kept very still as I drew the shadows tighter around us.

The vehicle got closer and I felt no magical signature coming from it at all. The man driving had a hood up and I couldn't see much of his face beneath it. As the van passed beneath us, I made a snap decision, grabbing hold of Rosa and throwing us out of the tree. I used my air magic to lower us silently onto the top of the van and flattened us to it, holding Rosa down beside me. Her eyes sparkled as she gazed at me and I let a small smirk pull at my lips in response.

I'm coming for you, amore mio.

The van wound down the roads before eventually turning onto a track that led up to one of the old mines. I lifted my head as we closed in on a gaping tunnel that disappeared underground and my gaze fell on the Fae standing outside it in black robes, illuminated by a floodlight.

A glint of magic around the tunnel entrance made my heart clench up into a fist and I pulled Rosa against me then lifted us off of the roof with a hard gust of air, carrying us down behind a hulking boulder a hundred yards away from the tunnel entrance.

I cast a silencing bubble around us and Rosa frowned at me.

"Why'd you do that?" she hissed as I let go of her.

"Because that tunnel has protection spells on it and I can't tell specifically what they are from here. It could have killed us for all I know. Besides, the floodlight would have revealed us even with my concealment spells."

She sighed, sitting down in the dirt as she hugged her knees to her chest. "What do we do then?"

"We need backup." I slipped my Atlas out of my pocket and hit dial on Leon's number, holding it to my ear.

It rang on for several seconds then Gabriel answered, panting heavily.

"What's up Dante? Oh shit, you found something?" he asked before I even told him. The Sight was strange sometimes.

A wail of pain rang out in the background then the sound of Leon bellowing questions reached me. "Where is she, you motherfucker? I'm gonna shove this Killblaze up your ass along with every other item you've got in your pockets."

"Get him on his front, Simba," Ryder growled.

"I've got a lead," I said quickly. "Rosa found something. It might be a

Killblaze lab. It's the perfect place to hide someone too. She could be here."

"Shit…I can't *see* it," Gabriel cursed. "But I can *see* you and then… okay I know what to do. Help's on the way."

"When will you be here, falco?" I demanded.

"Just hang in there." He hung up and I pursed my lips at the screen. *Real fucking helpful, stronzo.*

"Is he coming?" Rosa asked.

"I guess," I muttered, leaning back against the boulder.

Rosa moved to my side, resting her head on my shoulder. Silence rippled between us and I hated that. There'd never been any silences to fill before Felix had died. It was like a weight rested on her soul that I couldn't remove. And I didn't know what to do about it or how to be there for her in the way she needed.

"Rosa, are things…better since Felix died?" I asked carefully, tiptoeing around what I really wanted to ask. *Are you okay?*

"Yes," she said firmly. "It's like I can breathe again."

"That's good," I said with a knot easing in my chest. "I know you don't want to talk about what happened, but I just need to know if…if…" I didn't know how to finish that sentence without making her recoil from it. She was so strong that she acted like the world didn't affect her. But it did. Pain wasn't weakness. She was a survivor. And the hardness in her eyes, the toughening of her soul, all of that was a mark of what she'd made it through. But I didn't want to see the weight of those things break her. Or us.

"It's okay," she whispered. "I didn't want to answer you before, but I can now. Ask me, Alpha."

"Are you going to be okay?" I let out in a rush of air.

"Yes," she said slowly. "Someday, I think. But I hate my scars, Dante. They show everyone in the pack how weak I am."

"You should celebrate them," I growled fiercely. "They aren't your weakness, Rosa. They're your strength."

"Mmm," she said dismissively like she didn't believe that.

A glimmer of stardust in the air made me stiffen, magic crackling at my fingertips as Ryder appeared out of it and immediately crouched down in front of us.

"Holy fuck!" Rosa kicked dirt in his face, shoving me in the side to try and make me move. "Attack – attack!"

"It's alright, cugina," I said, gripping her arm to hold her against me as I bared my teeth at Ryder. But how the hell was I gonna explain this to her? "What the fuck are you doing here, serpente?"

"You tell me, Inferno," Ryder hissed. "One minute I'm beating the life out of some scumbag on the ground and the next Big Bird is throwing stardust in my fucking face."

Rosa glanced from me to Ryder in confusion. "What's going on?" she demanded.

I reckoned the fact that she'd seen Ryder help kill Felix was the only reason she wasn't completely panicking right now. But a lifetime of being enemies with this bastardo wasn't going to be easily forgotten. I didn't plan on forgetting it myself. But we were kind of out of options for help right now.

"Ryder is helping search for Elise," I told Rosa. "We've come to a sort of…truce." The word tasted bitter in my mouth as I glared at him.

"I would call it a temporary ceasefire," he corrected. "And when Elise is back in my arms, I will gladly cut your head from your shoulders as slowly as I can manage."

"You and him…and Elise?" Rosa asked, her eyes wide. "What about Leon?"

"Long story short, the Lion isn't going anywhere so we have to suck that up," Ryder said bluntly. "Big Bird too."

"Big Bird?" Rosa's brow creased in confusion.

"Stop telling her shit, it's not your responsibility," I snarled then turned to Rosa with an intent look. "You can't tell anyone this, cugina." I didn't want to use a memory potion on her later but if she couldn't keep this secret, the consequences were too dire to risk it. My entire family could lose faith in me if they knew I was working with Ryder Draconis. But I trusted Rosa, I didn't want to take that route if I didn't have to.

She looked to Ryder again then shoved her hand out at him. "Make a star vow with me that you won't hurt Dante tonight."

"You're not even Awakened," Ryder scoffed, but Rosa kept her hand outstretched, her jaw locked tight.

I glared at the serpente, expecting him to just stardust away again and not put up with this shit, but then he grabbed Rosa's hand.

"I won't hurt Dante tonight and I won't hurt you either, Wolf girl." Magic flashed in his palm, but it didn't really mean anything without her magic to latch onto. Still, it made me feel some kind of way about him. Not respect. Definitely not that. But something.

"Okay, now what do we do?" Rosa asked me without taking her eyes off of Ryder like she expected him to attack at any moment. But he wouldn't do that while the possibility of returning Elise to us hung in the balance.

"There's a tunnel up there," I told Ryder. "It's got magical protection spells on it and a couple of guards outside. Can you get close enough to detect what we're dealing with?"

Ryder shrugged and pulled his shirt off, revealing the myriad of scars covering his body between his tattoos. Rosa stilled beside me, staring at him closely as her gaze moved over the marks, her hand drifting to the scars on her neck as some desperate question filled her eyes. She didn't let it out though, biting down on her lip as Ryder stripped out of the last of his clothes, tossing them in my direction, his shoe bouncing off my head.

"Pezzo di merda," I growled, shooting a zap of electricity at his chest but he only growled like he enjoyed the pain. *Psicopatico.*

He shifted into a small black snake which I could have crushed under my heel, but I resisted the urge to do that as he slithered away beyond the boulder, keeping to the shadows as he made his way over to the tunnel.

Rosa turned to me with wide eyes. "Mamma is gonna kill you if she ever finds out."

"That's why she won't find out," I said with the hint of a warning in my tone, but she gave me a stern look.

"I'm not stupida, Dante. You guys are Astral Adversaries, bound to despise each other by the stars until your feuding ends in death. Fae can't just put aside that shit for anything. You love Elise. And he does too. Don't tell me otherwise, the moon always knows."

I locked my lips tight. Her and her damn moon abilities. It wasn't even worth lying to her, her gifts were something I knew to respect and there was no point denying what she had already sensed from both me and Ryder. The serpente loved Elise - as unlikely as it was to know he had a heart at all – and there wasn't anything I could do about it. I'd seen how he was with her, I wasn't blind. His heart existed and he'd given it to her. And she had given hers to him too as readily as she'd given it to me. That was a crux I had to bear as part of loving her. She would always love him too. How that was going to work out long term was a fucking mystery to me, but so far we were managing by avoiding the subject entirely and tolerating one another whenever we had to. I imagined once we had her back in our arms, things would continue in a similar manner.

I'd been plagued by thoughts of the discussion we'd had about his father back at the Christmas cabin though. He hadn't known about Vesper's sacrifice or the peace deal I'd tried to establish with him. Someone had betrayed him. And that someone was potentially responsible for countless deaths and this endless hatred that burned between me and the Lunar King. That knowledge was a plague because it meant our reasons to remain at war became a little thinner. And as hopeful as I was that that might mean a peace deal could be struck at last, it also meant I would have to let go of the animosity between Ryder and I. And not just for the city. But for Elise.

"I'm afraid for you, Dante," Rosa breathed. "You know how it works with Astral Adversaries – your fate is to clash again and again until one of you is dead. That means that fate has decided that either Ryder will kill you or you'll kill the man Elise loves. Do you think she'd still be able to love you after that?"

I frowned at her, my heart knotting at the thought of either fate. I had no intention of dying, but she had a point. How could Elise still look at me the same if I killed him?

Ryder returned, shifting back into his Fae form and tugging on his clothes. "It's detection spells, nothing else. I can break them."

"We should call the pack," Rosa whispered.

"Not yet," I growled, giving her an intent look. "You need to go home, Rosa. Ready the Wolves for a fight and be prepared to come if I call you." She looked about to argue, but I took a pouch of stardust from my pocket and gave her an Alpha stare. "That's an order, cugina."

She released a harsh breath then nodded. I tossed the stardust over her, sending her home and the knot of wire around my heart loosened a little at knowing she was safe. But now I was just left with Ryder and the death glare he was shooting at my head.

"We'll do this covert, sneak in, see if we can locate her," I growled, getting to my feet, but staying low behind the boulder.

"That definitely wasn't you giving me an order, Inferno," he gritted out, the word *pain* aimed at me from his knuckles as he crunched them into a fist.

Electricity crackled along my flesh and I wondered why the fuck Gabriel had thought it was a good idea to send the serpente along. I had to guess he'd *seen* something that made Ryder suitable for the job, but I wasn't going to acknowledge that right now.

He cast a sharp wooden blade in his hand and I cast a subtle air shield against my flesh in case he planned on driving it into me the second he got a chance.

"You take out the floodlight with your fancy little storm powers and I'll kill the guards," he said and I bristled.

"Now who's giving orders?" I hissed, squaring my shoulders and the two of us descended into a stare off where neither of us blinked.

The amount of Alpha testosterone in the air was making my temple thump with a furious pulse. But I didn't have the desire to force him beneath me like I did with most Fae. It was the same way I felt about Leon or Gabriel. He was on my level power wise and in any other scenario I would force myself to respect that. So I guessed I was going to have to try. Because amore mio needed us and the longer we lingered here, the more likely it was that something could happen to her.

I took in a breath, composing myself as the Oscura King I was and taking a step toward him. My father had taught me to be the bigger man. And I would do him proud today. For a moment, I felt like I was standing in front of Vesper Draconis again, the similarities to him in Ryder stark. He'd been a man willing to die for his people and I realised that Ryder was that too. Only his people was just one person. A girl who had offered him the love he'd lacked his entire life. And as much as I didn't want to feel anything for him, I found myself wanting to return Elise to him. Not as much as I wanted her returned to me, but Ryder truly had no one. He had held no concern for his own life at all until her. He would have died in countless battles; no fear had ever entered his eyes in a single fight I'd faced him in. But since Elise, I'd seen things change. He didn't fight to die anymore, he fought to live.

I reached out to him and he eyed my hand like it was a bomb about to go off. Then I released a trickle of air from my hands, wrapping it around him in a tight shield. His eyes widened in surprise, but he said nothing, clearly preferring not to acknowledge it. And that suited me just fine.

"We'll take one each," I said then snapped my fingers and electricity burst away from me underground, tearing along toward the floodlight, shooting up the pole and hitting the bulb.

Sparks showered down as the glass exploded and the guards cursed in surprise. I ran out from behind the boulder at Ryder's side, the two of us drawing the shadows closer to keep us hidden for as long as possible.

We split apart and I charged toward the Fae on the left of the tunnel as Ryder went for the right.

"-the hell happened to the-" My target cast a Faelight in his palm, but it stuttered out as my hand slammed to his forehead and electricity burst from my body into his, frying his brain in seconds. He hit the ground and I turned, finding Ryder lowering his target to the ground, his knife buried in the guy's neck.

I gathered a storm of air in my hands, carrying the bodies towards a hill of dirt to the side of the mine. Ryder opened up the earth before I dropped them into it and he closed it up again, all evidence of their deaths gone.

I nodded to him as we moved in front of the tunnel and we both raised our palms. I felt out the detection spells and the two of us worked to disable them, our combined power slicing through them in record time.

We ran side by side into the dark and my heartbeat quickened as I thought of finding Elise down here somewhere. I'd never let her go. I'd bring her home, make her part of my family and never hide my love for her again.

Ryder's shoulder bumped against mine as he sprinted along, starting to outpace me and I pushed myself harder so we were running flat out down the winding tunnel, the descent becoming steeper and steeper beneath our feet.

We didn't dare cast a Faelight, but the faint crackle of electricity over my skin gave us just enough light to see by.

A rumbling noise reached me from somewhere deeper in the tunnel and a glowing blue light up ahead made us slow. We approached a corner where the passageway swung to the left and I tightened the air shields protecting us as I threw a glance into the cavern beyond. A huge glass tank stood at the heart of the rocky space full of glowing blue liquid, the whole thing twisting like a massive whirlpool and thousands of tiny blue Killblaze crystals glittered within it.

"Dalle stelle," I breathed as Ryder glanced out too.

This place had taken Killblaze production to a whole other level. Beyond the strange water chamber was a long conveyer belt where the crystals were being poured onto it from a large pipe connected to the tank. The belt juddered, shaking the crystals out across it and the water poured down into a waste tank below it. The crystals disappeared off into another tunnel, still glowing and lighting a trail away into the dark.

Ryder stepped out and I headed after him as we crept through the cavern then started following the conveyer belt deeper into the tunnels.

The sound of voices echoed up ahead and Ryder grabbed me by the collar and hauled me into a dark alcove in the cave wall, covering us with concealment spells while I cast a silencing bubble.

I was pressed right up against him, the cool skin of his arm flush against mine as we breathed the same air.

"Grazie," I muttered.

"That better be fuck you in your fancy language, Inferno," he growled in a low tone.

"Vaffanculo," I added a fuck you because why the hell was I thanking the stronzo?

The voices drew closer and we fell utterly silent as we listened.

"-wants us doubling shipments by the end of the month. Between this place and Site R, I think we can serve half of Alestria," a guy said excitedly.

"Nuvis City and Lanica District have taken to it well. The Black Card are spreading far and wide. It's going to be a new world," a girl cooed.

"The Card Master will rule," the first guy said assuredly. "And the whole of Solaria will bow."

As they stepped past us, Ryder's arm moved like a whip and both Fae were snared in vines by their throats. He snapped the guy's neck in a flash then ran forward and grabbed hold of the girl, raising her above him on his vine so her feet started kicking in the air.

"Where is Elise Callisto?" he snarled as she opened her palms, about to fight with fire, but Ryder smothered the flames with dirt and bound her hands behind her. She was too weak of a Fae to fight his power and I gazed on darkly as I watched her thrash and panic.

"She needs to be able to speak to give us an answer, serpente," I muttered and he dropped her in a flash, her knees hitting the floor hard.

She screamed for help, the sound echoing within the silencing bubble and going absolutely nowhere.

"Tell us or you'll die," I growled, stepping forward and gazing down at her with electricity snapping through my veins.

"I don't know who that is!" she wailed.

"Lilac hair, Vampire, fucking perfect," I spat and her eyes widened as she continued to shake her head.

"I don't know, I swear I don't know."

Ryder grabbed her by the throat, staring directly into her eyes and she fell still as he snared her with his hypnosis. They stayed like that for a long moment and I folded my arms as I waited. *Couldn't have brought me with you, bastardo?*

He snapped her neck and tossed her to the floor before looking to me with a scowl. "Elise isn't here, but this bitch showed me someone who might know. He's the boss here."

My gut dropped with bitter disappointment, but I latched onto the hope of finding someone who did know. It was a lead. Something at long last.

"Alright, where?" I demanded as I threw the two bodies into the alcove and concealed them there with shadow.

When I turned back, Ryder was already stalking off down the tunnel without me and I growled under my breath as I followed.

The tunnels split apart and he turned left away from the conveyer belt of Killblaze and back into the dark. It wasn't long before we arrived at a wooden door, clearly cast by earth magic to fit into the tunnel perfectly.

"Tear it down," I murmured.

"That sounded like another order," he hissed, glaring at me.

"You ever heard of a suggestion, stronzo?" I growled.

"A suggestion would sound like 'ciao serpente, maybe you could tear that bastardo door down'," he mimicked me in a stupid fucking accent, and it was so ridiculous coming from him that a breath of laughter escaped me.

A smirk tugged at his mouth which he quickly flattened then turned to the door again.

I brought air to my fingertips, ready to blast a hole through it instead, but he touched his palm to the wood and it exploded like a cannon ball had just torn through the centre of it.

A scream came from within the room beyond and we strode inside, finding a middle-aged bald man who started blasting shards of ice at us. I threw out my hand, blocking them with a wall of air and they smashed against it, shattering and hitting the floor. I choked off the Fae's air supply and he clutched his throat with a look of terror.

Ryder rebuilt the door behind us with a wave of his hand, inspecting the room around us. It was full of CCTV cameras showing the entire Killblaze lab throughout the mines. It made my heart riot in my chest to see the enormity of this place. Those assholes had been right, this place could hook thousands of Fae on fucking Killblaze. And if they were already serving other cities, how long would it be before King was powerful enough to make a bid for the throne? I may have hated Lionel Acrux and his posh little friends who ruled the land, but they weren't destroying the kingdom. They at least had some semblance of decency. King would ruin Solaria if they got into power.

A flashing red light under this stronzo's desk drew my attention and I cursed in Faetalian, striding over to it and finding a panic button beside it. "We're on borrowed time, serpente."

"Then let's take this party home," Ryder said darkly and though it was just some offhand comment, I wondered if he actually thought of Gabriel's apartment as some semblance of that. Which was kind of fucking sad really.

My gaze moved to the wires running across the ceiling over this place then to the same ones stretching across the walls throughout the entire lab. I smirked, raising myself up on a gust of air and touching my fingers to one of the wires.

"Get ready to stardust us away," I told Ryder and he didn't question me on that order this time.

Electricity built and built in my body and I brought all of it to my fingertips, calling on every scrap I possessed. Somewhere, far, far above us, thunder roared and I drowned in the heady feeling of all that power charging my veins. I was going to pour everything I had into this place, leave my mark and hope that King got the message that a Storm Dragon was hunting them. And I would not rest until they lay dead at my feet.

"By the stars, watch it, Inferno," Ryder barked and I looked down, finding our mark thrashing as he continued to struggle for air. Ryder's hair was short but it stood on end from the static in the air and I offered him a mocking grin. I could kill him right now if I wanted to and there was nothing he could do about it. But I found I didn't want that. I supposed I needed him for the interrogation after all.

Ryder knocked out the bastardo we'd caught just before I released my power in a roaring tidal wave of lightning. It shot into the wires and blasted away around the entire lab. The following boom, boom, boom told me chaos was descending and I smirked as I saw the explosions on the screens, the panicking Fae as they ran for their lives. Then Ryder tossed stardust into the air and we were yanked away into the grip of the stars, spinning through a haze of endless light.

We landed in Gabriel's apartment with our unconscious target at our feet between us and Leon was suddenly diving at me, nuzzling against my neck.

"Gabe said you found a Killblaze lab," he said in desperation. "Who's this guy? Did you find Elise? Does he know where she is?" He dove on Ryder next who shoved him onto his ass with a growl, though I swear a hint of mirth entered his eyes.

"Don't call me Gabe," Gabriel clipped as he walked up to us, gazing down at the guy on the floor who was now bound and gagged by Ryder's vines.

"Calm down Gabby," I said and his eyes narrowed on me with murder in them.

"Watch it, or I'll start calling you Dragonella," he warned then grabbed hold of the guy on the floor and hauled him through the open plan space then into the bathroom.

We followed him and as I stepped inside, I found the normally plain white room had been transformed with earth magic into a killing chamber with nothing but stone walls and a toilet in one corner.

"Guess you *saw* what we'd be bringing back, huh?" Ryder muttered, sharing a hint of a smirk with Gabriel.

"Yeah. I can't *see* what he's gonna tell us though, but I get the feeling you can find out," Gabriel said and Ryder stepped toward him.

"Give me ten minutes with him alone," Ryder growled.

"Not happening." I folded my arms.

"Just bring us into the vision with you, Ryder," Leon demanded and Ryder sighed before shrugging. "Take us inside. Take us deep with you."

"Fine, but don't get in my way. I need him scared so he doesn't feel me breaking down the barriers in his head that King put there," Ryder gritted out.

I flicked my fingers, sending a shock of electricity at our mark and he woke with a loud gasp.

Ryder snared him in his hypnosis then spun his head to look at the rest of us. I forced my barriers down as his eyes locked with mine - no matter how unnatural that felt with him. His hypnosis dragged me away and I found myself on the bank of a river, the guy strung up above it while crocodiles leapt up and snapped at his heels, making him scream like crazy. The magic was kind of impressive, not that I'd be telling the stronzo that.

All of our faces were disguised in twisted masks which were freaking Lion King characters. Leon was Simba, Ryder Scar and Gabriel Zazu. One snort from Leon told me mine was a fucking joke and he mouthed the word *Pumba* to me. I didn't give a shit anyway, I was here for Elise. And I wasn't in the mood to play games.

I felt the power of the hypnosis around me and as I focused, I could tug at the edges of it and wield it. It felt like pushing through tar at first, but it came easier the more I relaxed my mind. If Ryder needed this bastardo frightened, then I would happily deliver on that request.

"What do you want?" the guy screamed as a crocodile ripped his shoe off.

"We're looking for Elise Callisto," Leon called. "She's my Elysian Mate and if you think anyone can keep her from me, you're going to pay for that stupidity."

I shifted closer to Leon in solidarity, raising my chin to glare at the guy. Ryder was quiet as he worked to break through the walls of the bastardo's mind, so it was our job to keep him afraid.

I pushed my will into the water beneath him and it changed to a roaring fire, flaring up and burning his feet.

"Ah! Please, I don't know anything," he yelled so I burned him more, letting the flames climb higher and higher. The power of this vision was immense, and I realised that Ryder wasn't even trying to keep control of it, he was allowing us full rein to do as we pleased.

A hungry fire beast lurched out from within the flames with red eyes and huge teeth and I realised Leon was wielding it as he focused on the fire.

"Where has King taken her?!" Gabriel boomed and the heavens opened up above the stronzo as more fire poured down on him and singed the skin of his shoulders.

He wailed and I urged heat into the flames with my mind, my jaw locking as I wielded the hypnosis. I made him hurt, made him pay. He might not have had a hand in taking our girl, but he was responsible for the Killblaze running through my city. He was happy destroying countless lives and I was more than happy to destroy his in return.

"Where is King?" Gabriel roared.

"The Card Master is....is..." he grunted, unable to say any more than that because of King's dark control and a growl of frustration ripped from my throat.

I let the flames burn the skin from his bones, wanting him at absolute breaking point. I'd remain here making him suffer until every barrier in his head snapped and shattered. And I knew in my heart that every one of these men would do the same. For her. The girl who had captivated all of us deeper than any magic which lived in this world.

"Where is she?!" Leon bellowed and he willed the fire beast under his control again, making it tear one of the man's legs off. The illusion didn't just look real, it felt real thanks to Ryder. And a small part of me had to stand in awe of this power he could wield.

The man screamed a new scream, one that spoke of utter fear, the terror that his death was coming, and it would hurt more than he could even comprehend.

"In the sea, in the sea. The King lies in the sea!" he wailed.

"Keep going," Gabriel urged Ryder and I looked to him, his eyes glazing slightly as he latched on to some vision.

Leon willed the beast to rip the man's arm off next and Ryder gritted his teeth as he worked to crack his mind. I wielded my own electric power, adding it to the flames and letting it burn beneath the stronzo's flesh as well as outside it. The pain in his eyes was like a blazing beacon and I could almost feel the weight of that power as it wrapped around Ryder and he drank it all in.

"Yes," Gabriel gasped. "I've *seen* where he means. That's enough Ryder, he doesn't know any more."

Ryder's hypnosis came crashing down like falling rain and he stumbled into me as we returned to the bathroom. I steadied him instinctively then yanked my hand back as he blinked through the power swimming in his eyes. He looked almost drunk on how much pain had just been fed to him and he took a long breath as the magic settled within his blood.

"Fuck that's good," he muttered like a psycho.

The man lay twitching on the floor as Ryder kept him locked in some vision and I turned to Gabriel anxiously.

"What did you *see*? Where is she?" I demanded.

"King is hiding somewhere near the Rustian Sea. I *saw* the Black Card being summoned there and I was among them. I didn't *see* her, but I felt her. She's there." A hopeful glint entered his eyes.

Ryder stepped toward the guy on the floor, cracking his knuckles. "So we don't need this piece of shit anymore?"

"No," Gabriel agreed darkly, and Ryder used a vine to snap his neck in a flash.

I strode over to Gabriel, grabbing his shirt in my fist. "When can we go?"

His chest heaved as his eyes gripped mine and I felt Leon pressing up beside me, his need for that answer ringing in the air as loudly as my own.

"Two days," Gabriel said as though it was an eternity. And in a way it was. Because every day we were parted from Elise was another day spent suffering in hell.

But now we finally had something to go on. A direction to aim our rage. And when we unleashed it, every star in the sky had better be watching. Because we were going to make them fear ever painting a fate which took her from us again.

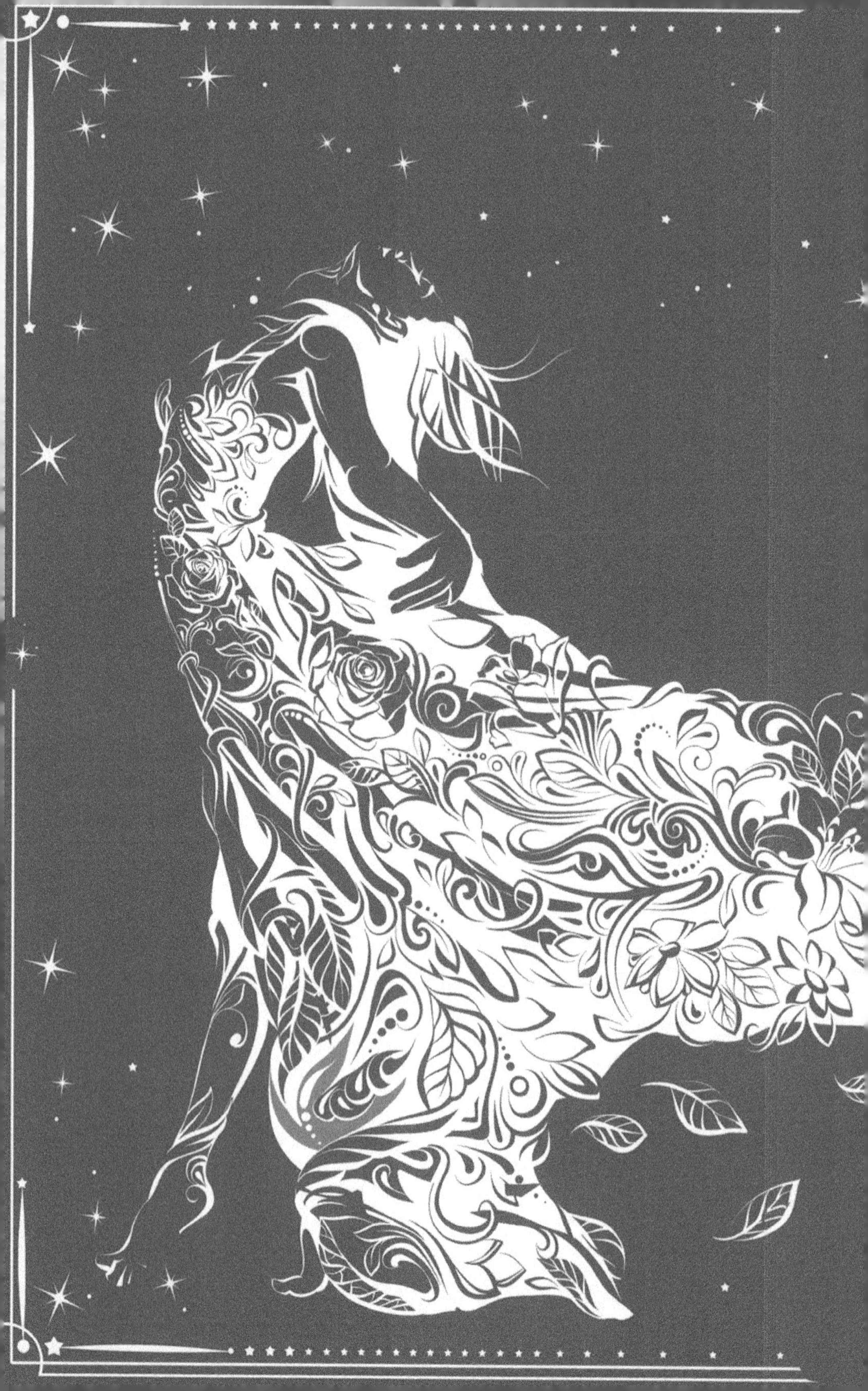

Elise

CHAPTER SEVEN

I wasn't sure how much time had passed between King's last visit and now. Days had come and gone, and I'd been brought meals alongside the occasional glass of blood. Though some of the donations had been from more powerful Fae, there was no escaping that stale, old taste that came with each mouthful. I wasn't certain how long it had been since the blood had been taken from the vein, but I was desperate for a taste from the source. And not just any source. I wanted my kings.

I also wasn't being given nearly enough of it. Even with my access to my magic blocked off by the damn cuffs, my body burned through a small amount of it every day naturally. It wasn't natural for Fae to be cut off from their power like this. And though it wasn't as bad as when I'd been entirely tapped out all the time, I felt the lack of it coursing through my veins like a missing limb.

Fae had gone insane for being unable to use their magic. The power trapped inside them festered with its need to be set free into the world and it turned into rot. How long did it take for that to happen? I knew that the Fae locked up in Darkmore Penitentiary had to wear cuffs like these most of the time so I guessed you could withstand it for a while, but I was already itching to rip them off of me. Fuck knew how the prisoners coped with wearing them for years.

As I thought of that hell of a prison where the worst and most deadly Fae in Solaria were locked up for their crimes, my mind turned to Roary and my heart twisted with pain. Leon had asked him to help us get that spyglass in the hunt for answers about my brother's death and in doing so, he'd lost his own brother.

The guilt I felt over that gnawed at me, whispering to me in the night and making me replay the events that had led to his capture over and over again. He'd been a hero, saving Rosa from the FIB, but he'd lost his freedom in payment for it.

The more I thought about Roary being locked up in that underground tomb, the more I found myself thinking about Gareth too. Those newspaper cuttings that King had brought for me had been filled with stories of deaths just like his - of family members left grieving a loved one who had been entirely innocent, caught in the crossfire. I knew that there had been a lot more to Gareth's death than that. He'd been tangled up in something dark and more dangerous than I was sure he ever would have wanted to get himself caught in, but he had been innocent. At least in my eyes. I would never believe him capable of any act of real evil. Anything he'd done, every sacrifice he'd made had been in aid of me. Which meant his death was on me too.

Grief crippled me in here. I spent hours just lying in the nest of blankets I'd been given for a bed or in the tub of heated water which never seemed to cool. I had nothing to do anyway. My only companions were my grief over Gareth and my pain at being separated from my kings.

I'd tried to use the power of this place to steal more glimpses of the future from the stars, but they hadn't given me much. I'd caught sight of my men a few times, though the image was always blurred and distorted. Once I'd seen Leon and Ryder painted red with blood and the fear that had left me with still hadn't shifted from my soul.

They were out there somewhere, hunting for me. That much I knew. But beyond that, I couldn't be sure of anything. And all the time that King was using this place to hide me from Gabriel's visions, I knew they'd never find me.

My mind whirled with possibilities as I tried to figure out who the fuck King was. They had to be connected to the academy, and they clearly knew me. They knew me well enough to know that Gabriel would be hunting for me. But I just couldn't figure out who it was. I felt like I had all the pieces of a puzzle and yet I just couldn't make them fit together.

Memories of hanging out on the rooftop of The Sparkling Uranus with my brother pressed in on me so hard that I could have sworn I was back there when I closed my eyes. I could feel the warmth of Gareth's arm pressed up against mine and see the stars sparkling overhead as we gazed up at them, talking shit and smiling about nothing. Had the stars known then what his fate would become? Had there been a point at which I could have changed it?

The sound of the door unlocking had me jerking upright, using my speed to swipe the tears from my cheeks and take a deep breath before King appeared in the doorway.

I kept my face impassive as the hooded figure strode into the chamber with me, pushing my hands into the pockets of the pink sweats I'd been given to wear.

"Sorry to have kept you waiting, Elise, but there has been a lot of work for me to do in the city. The world is changing after all."

I stayed silent, not knowing what they meant by that and waiting to see what they wanted from me now.

"It is the full moon tonight," King said, staying by the door and blocking my escape. "Which means I need some of your blood, I'm afraid."

I wet my lips, glancing past King to the stone corridor I only ever caught glimpses of and wondering if I should just make a run for it. With my speed I could make it, but I got the feeling there would be magic there waiting to stop me too, and with my own power locked down I wouldn't be able to break through it.

"Why?" I asked, though I already knew why. King wanted the blood of a Vampire for the spell they used to steal the magic of the Fae they were pressuring into suicide. It was sick, twisted, and I didn't want my blood to be any part of it, but I was pretty sure that saying that would only mean I was forced to submit so my blood could be stolen by force.

King regarded me for several long moments then turned and walked out of the door.

"Walk with me, Elise," their ever-changing voice called back to me and I arched my brows in surprise.

But I wasn't quite as dumb as I looked and I absolutely wasn't going to waste the chance to get out of this chamber, so I shot after them and caught up halfway along the stone corridor outside.

It felt damp out here in a way the chamber didn't, and the roughly hewn stone passages spoke of hurried earth magic unlike the beautiful amplifying chamber.

"Did you read the articles I gave you?" King asked conversationally as I fell into step at their side. The brush of magic against my arm told me they had a strong shield in place around themselves though, so I knew they didn't really trust me at all. Probably a good shout because I would have been more than happy to tear their throat out with my teeth given half a chance.

"Yeah. I get it. The gangs, Alestria in general - it's a shit show. But I'm not sure why-"

"Because that's precisely why I'm doing this. The people of this city - and of Solaria as a whole - deserve to live in a peaceful place where they don't have to fear for their lives every time they leave their homes. I want to create a shift in the balance of power, disband the gangs and create a new, safer place for my people."

Oh they were King's people now, were they? Such altruistic words for a dude who so clearly hungered for power. Was that how they justified everything they did? By pretending it was all for the greater good and that sacrifices had to be made?

"Sounds great," I said, my voice holding little inflection, so it was unclear whether I was being sarcastic or not. I mean, it did sound great if you took away the part where we'd all be ruled over by this crazy, identity shrouding megalomaniac.

"I know that you have experienced loss, Elise. I know that you would want to protect others from feeling the grief you have suffered through."

"If I'm getting wishes granted I'd probably be asking to raise the dead, not change the world," I muttered.

King sighed and for a moment I could have sworn they actually understood where I was coming from with that.

We walked on in silence for a few more moments before turning a corner and stepping out into a huge open cavern filled with cloaked people.

My lips popped open as we stepped into a silencing bubble and I stared at the robed figures as the sounds of their chanting carried to me. My gaze lifted to the roof and my eyes widened a little as I realised this was another amplifying chamber, bigger than I'd ever seen before.

A prickle danced along my skin at the taste of dark magic on the air and I suppressed a shiver as I looked out across the crowd. There were tunnels and doorways leading off of this chamber in multiple directions, any of them could be the way out of here, but I needed to pick right.

"What is this?" I asked, straining my ears, eyes, everything in my gifts to try and get some clue as to where the exit was.

"I have been busy recruiting more like-minded Fae to my great task," King said proudly. "Each and every man and woman here wishes to see a world without the violence of gangs and criminals. They want something better. They have been helping me scour Alestria for recruits and sacrifices alike, and tonight I am hopeful to take on enough magic to ascend to a position of true power and lead this city into greatness."

"Sacrifices?" I asked uncomfortably, noticing an alcove on the far side of the room where a group of Fae lay on couches and sat in chairs, their eyes glazed and skin sweaty. Robed figures moved between them, offering out tubes of Killblaze and I had to swallow a lump in my throat as I tore my gaze away from them.

"Only Fae who are beyond salvation will choose to take their lives and offer me their power," King said. "Only those who it is already too late to save. And what better way to repay their sacrifice than by using their power to bring about a better world where no more Fae will suffer the way they have?"

"Mmm." I needed to get the fuck out of here. Now. Ten minutes ago. Like yestergone.

"Do you understand what I'm trying to achieve?" King pressed.

"Oh yeah. Sounds great." I beamed at him or her or whatever the fuck and they nodded.

"Good. Because I don't like to cage you. I would like you to help me achieve my goals willingly, as my old friend once did. All I need is a little of your blood for the spell and I would prefer for you to give it willingly."

I tore my gaze away and looked out over the crowd of chanting Fae once more, noting the vacant expressions on the faces shrouded beneath the hoods and knowing full well that they weren't even really aware of what they were doing here. For supposedly loyal followers, King sure did like to keep them in the dark. Were they worried about their secrets getting out or were they worried that these followers might be disillusioned when they realised their great Card Master took power in the form of Fae sacrifices and preyed on the weakest people to do so? Whatever it was, they definitely wouldn't assist me in any way. No, I was going to have to get myself out of here.

I noticed that more figures kept trickling into the chamber to join the chanting, all of them arriving from one of the tunnels on my right and I was willing to bet that was the way out of here.

"Okay," I agreed, making a snap decision and looking back to King. "How much do you need?"

"I just need you to fill this chalice." They took a silver cup shaped like a small wine glass from within their robes and held it out to me.

I accepted it reluctantly before raising my wrist to my mouth and ripping into the vein. I watched as my blood spilled from the wound, running into the chalice and filling it for them. I didn't like giving King this, but it was my best shot at an escape. I only needed a couple of seconds for a distraction and I'd be out of here before they even noticed I'd run. That was all that mattered. I needed to get away from this place. Escape. Get back to my kings.

The moment the chalice was full, King reached out and pressed two cold fingers to the wound on my wrist, healing it for me. The press of their stolen magic against my skin made me shudder at the slimy sensation it left me with but I held still, accepting that it would be better not to bleed out while I ran seeing as I couldn't heal myself.

I pulled my hand back once it was done and as King reached for the chalice of my blood, I shoved it towards them, tipping it up and spilling it everywhere.

King lurched back with a surprised gasp, trying to save the blood with water magic but I was gone before I could see if they managed it.

I shot away in a blur, my feet moving faster than I ever thought they had before as I raced for the exit with every bit of power my Order form could allow, using my gifts to their maximum potential.

I sped into the chamber I'd seen, passing more robed Black Card members who were heading inside as I raced on down the narrow passageway which was lit by blazing green everflames.

It couldn't have been more than a few seconds, the whole world was practically a blur around me and only my gifts saved me from crashing into something or someone as I sped for the exit.

The taste of fresh air washed over my tongue and for the briefest of moments I could have sworn I saw a glimpse of rippling light up ahead. But then I was ripped off of my feet in a whirlwind of air magic that flipped me upside down and yanked me back into the main chamber even faster than I'd been running.

I fought and screamed, swearing and cursing as I tried to break free of King's power and the world tossed and turned around me until I was suddenly deposited in the heap of blankets back in the amplifying chamber that had become my prison.

I scrambled onto my hands and knees, my gaze locking on King just as they threw the door shut in my face and locked me inside again, their words hanging in the air as my failure sank down on me like a descending cloud.

"How disappointing."

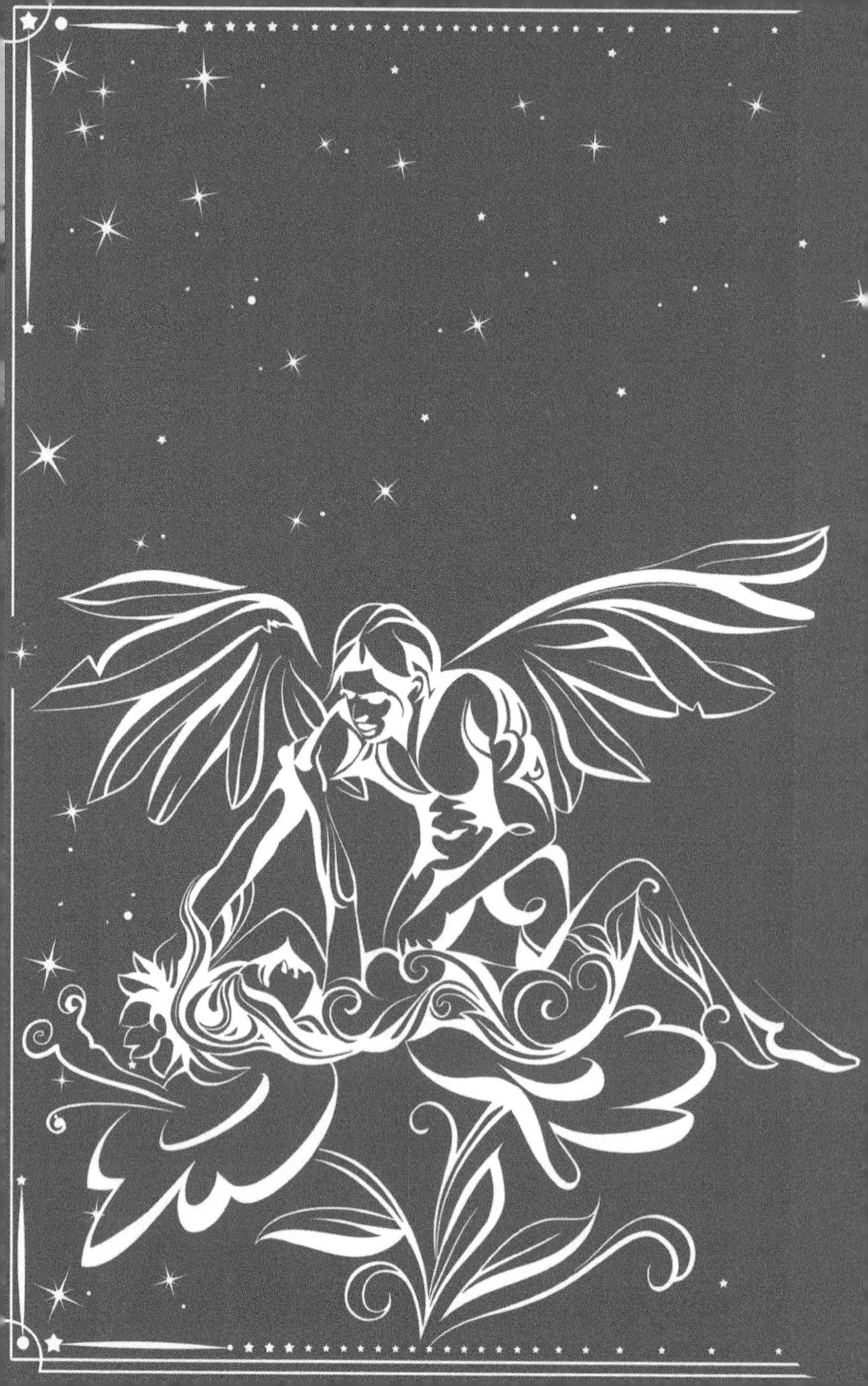

GABRIEL

CHAPTER EIGHT

I stood staring out at the Rustian Sea with my heart as heavy as a lump of iron in my chest. This place was fifty miles from Alestria, just an old town perched on a weathered cliff. The beach was an endless stretch of sharp rocks and the sea was a dark grey beast frothing at the mouth.

Elise was out there somewhere, perhaps hidden within the smugglers caves that ran beneath the cliffs from the times when the Hermetic Pirates ruled the oceans. There were only a few pockets of their kind left, but this place was long since abandoned by them. I'd been brought here on a field trip once in my freshman year at Aurora Academy to learn about this historical place, so I had some grounding on where Elise might be hidden. But I couldn't be hasty, I had to stick to the plan. The stars weren't offering me any more insight on her whereabouts, but my gut told me she was here, I was sure of it. And that meant I was drawing closer to her with every second that passed as I waited to be summoned by the Black Card.

Leon stepped outside to join me on the balcony of the little cliffside beach house we'd rented. None of us had wanted to wait any longer to come here, hoping that I might get another vision which led us to Elise earlier than expected. But so far, there was no sign of that happening.

Leon pressed a hand to my shoulder and I looked at him with a taut smile of acknowledgement. His golden eyes glinted with the silver rings of his star bond and I found myself studying them for far too long, reminded of Elise, stealing a tiny moment with her in his eyes. Then I yanked my gaze away and stared back across the churning sea, the waves exploding in a wave of foam against a jagged rock out in the water.

"I hate all this waiting," Leon muttered, resting his forearms on the balcony railing as he followed my line of sight to that rock. My heart felt like those waves, torn to pieces on a jagged stone.

"Yeah," I sighed. "Me too. But it'll be today, I can feel it." *It has to be. I can't bear another day without her.*

"Is it weird knowing everything, dude?" he asked curiously. "Do you *see* all kinds of possible fates in your mind like cars whizzing by on a highway?"

"It's not like that." My brows pulled together as I thought on it. "I have to focus to *see* anything at all unless the stars choose to show me something. Otherwise, it feels more like intuition, except its stronger than that, more tangible. I know the best paths for myself by that alone. But for others, it's more complicated. And things change so often. Like you for example."

"What about me?" he asked, looking to me with a hopeful buzz of energy about him. He truly was placing his faith in me completely today, and I really wanted to deliver what he was expecting of me.

"Your fate bounces from one thing to the next, sometimes within milliseconds. Especially when you're excited."

He released a low snort. "Is that a bad thing?"

"No, you just live in the moment I guess. You see something shiny and you go for it. I think if I'd lived my life like that more often, I'd probably be a happier person."

Leon nudged his shoulder against mine. "There's still time, bro. Once we get Elise back, the world's your juicy oyster."

I pulled a face. "Eating sea food should be a crime."

He barked a laugh. "Now *that* I agree with. Who was the first person to ever look at an oyster and think ooh that looks like a tasty treat, then cracked it open and sucked out the snotty goo inside?" He mimed retching. "They had to be starving, man, there's no other explanation."

"Agreed," I said on a breath of amusement then my mood descended again, my mind hooking on my little angel and the fear of what could be happening to her.

I couldn't stand this much longer. I had to see her, and I had to see King bleed for daring to take her.

Leon's aura was so heavy I knew this was taking its toll on him too. I'd never seen him the way he'd been during the last few weeks, like a man possessed as he hunted for his mate. It hurt me to watch. And not just because of Elise. This search for her had brought us all closer in ways I hadn't ever imagined would happen. Now she was gone, the time to argue and bicker over her seemed so fucking pointless. I'd give anything to have her back in any capacity. If she wanted the four of us in her harem plus a whole division of bright pink fucking pixies in it too, I'd be star damned happy with that fate. Actually fuck no. I'd have to kill off the pixies. But I'd put up with them for a while.

It wasn't that I didn't still want her to myself, I guessed I just saw how much the other guys needed her too. They loved her as fiercely as I loved her. As much as I might have wanted to deny that once, it was plain to see now. And The Sight changed things too. I could *see* a life unfolding for us, one where this worked out. It was just glimmers. But the possibility was there. And any time I leaned into it, it felt fucking amazing. The hardest thing was adjusting the possessive streak in me to this situation, my need to protect my loved ones at any cost. Up until recently that had included a sum total of Bill and Elise. Now that circle was widening, and I didn't exactly hate it. But was it really going to include a Lion, a Basilisk and a Storm Dragon?

"What does Elise's fate feel like?" Leon asked and I felt his eyes on me. "Does she know what she wants? Is she always going to be happy?"

The question was so candid and hopeful, I had to like the Lion a little more for it. "I can't *see* 'always,'" I replied. "Fates changes constantly, but Elise wants what I always refused to accept she wanted."

"What's that?" he breathed, leaning right against me, the heat of his body pressed flush to mine. He literally had no boundaries, but I didn't push him off. I wasn't really sure why, but if I was being totally honest with myself, it was because it felt kind of nice.

"Freedom. To never be bound or ruled by others, including the stars. It makes her fate feel like an ever blowing wind, trying to snare her in it but never catching her unless she chooses it. It's why I don't fit her the way you and the others do. She chose to be caught by each of you. I'm here because I couldn't let go of what was never meant to be mine. And I still don't intend to, regardless of me knowing that. But so long as she wants me too, I'll be here." My heart clenched at those words, my darkest truth spilling from my lips. Something about Leon was just plain trustworthy and despite wanting to hate him for his star bond to Elise, he made it so fucking hard.

"Gabriel," Leon growled, grabbing my face and forcing me to look at him. "She chose you. You deserve to be here as much as anyone. You're her protector. You can literally *see* any harm coming her way. I'll never be able to do that for her. I'd make the stars mate you to her if I could." I stared at those silver rings in his eyes, practically hearing the stars laughing at me. What a fucking joke I must have been to them. After all the insanity I put Elise through over assuming she was my mate, they'd been toying with me all along.

I pushed his hand off as he unwittingly exposed my greatest failure. "But I didn't protect her, did I?" I snarled. "She's been taken by the only motherfucker in Solaria I can't *see* and he's buried her from me. So what use am I?"

I glanced away toward the glass balcony doors and spotted Dante and

Ryder on the floor inside doing push-ups opposite each other. They'd been working out for hours, both of them refusing to stop until the other one did. The sweat coating their skin and the grunts and curses leaving their lips all indicated how exhausted they were getting. It was fucking ridiculous.

Leon nuzzled against me, but I pushed him away. "The only reason we have a chance at getting her back is because of you. We wouldn't even have a lead if you hadn't *seen* this place."

My throat was tight, full of insecurities that I held back. I didn't need a pep talk. I knew my place in this arrangement. And I had accepted that. Dante and Ryder weren't mated to Elise either. We were always going to be the puzzle pieces that didn't fit her quite right, but what did it matter so long as we loved her with all of our hearts?

A fierce tugging sensation in my chest made me curse as my magical bond to King took hold of me, but hope crashed through me at the same time.

"King's summoning me," I gasped, looking to Leon with utter hope tearing through my veins.

"Yes!" he cried, whooping loud enough to scare a seagull off of the balcony with a furious squawk.

Ryder and Dante burst outside, panting and shoving each other to get in front. I climbed up onto the balcony railing, pulling my sweater off and tying it around my waist.

"He's been summoned," Leon informed them and I slid the smooth black rocks from my pocket which disguised the Magicae Mortuorum book and spyglass, tossing them to Leon.

"I'll come back as soon as the meeting is over," I told them, letting my dark wings burst free of my shoulder blades.

"Find her, Big Bird," Ryder growled in an order and I nodded before letting myself fall from the balcony, my wings flexing and catching the updraft as I sailed out over the cliff, following the line of the rocky beach below.

The summoning spell drawing me to King blazed beneath my skin, demanding I answer it but I felt the kiss of power from the ring I'd found in those faraway caves burning hotter inside me. It kept the dark pull of King's spells from possessing me and offered to burn right through the summoning spell too, but I didn't let it, needing this connection so it could bring me right to my girl.

I followed the beach for almost two miles, soaring lower as the sky darkened and the sunlight filtered away beyond the horizon.

I felt the brush of magic over my wingtips and it accepted me into it like an embrace, but I had the feeling that wouldn't have been the case if I wasn't a member of the Black Card. As I passed through the veil of magic, Card members were revealed below me walking straight out into the sea, the rough waves crashing against them, making me frown in confusion. As they made it fifty feet into the water, a huge wave swallowed them up and they disappeared beneath it. More of the hooded members walked confidently towards it and the waves dragged them under, all signs of them vanishing as they went into its depths. *What the fuck?*

I circled down and landed where piles of black robes had been left on the rocks, picking one up and pulling it on as I banished my wings. The rest of the members seemed to be in a trance, silently walking straight out into the water with blank expressions and empty eyes. I felt King's power swirling around me, trying to drag me into that same glassy hollowness, but the fiery gift from the ring burned it away again.

I let my features fall flat as I filed after them into the water and waded straight towards the huge waves heading this way. I had the Element of water in my blood, but it was still slightly unnerving to walk into the embrace of a stormy sea like this. I felt its power tugging me in and I fought to keep my face neutral as I made it up to my waist in the water. A huge wave towered above me, curling over and casting me in its shadow like a hulking giant. It crashed over me, dragging me under, but suddenly my feet hit solid ground and I stumbled a step forward, somehow entirely dry.

I was in a long tunnel with sconces on the walls with flickering green everflames within them. Fucking ominous if you asked me, but that wasn't exactly surprising. I was in a maniac's lair after all.

I glanced back and found a swirling bulge of water that seemed to rotate as Black Card members stepped through it and marched off down the tunnel. The magic was some of the most powerful I'd ever seen, and my fingers itched as I brought my Elements to the surface of my skin, wanting to be prepared in case this went to hell.

I followed the other members as the tunnel wound deeper under the sea and we arrived in an enormous chamber with a domed glass roof that looked up into the ocean. It took everything I had not to fucking gasp at this place, realisation thumping through my head. This was why I couldn't find Elise. This was an amplifying chamber, designed to magnify the celestial signals from the stars. It would block The Sight. It would easily keep me or anyone else from finding Elise or King or anyone spying on his plans. *Holy shit, this asshole is one clever piece of shit.*

Tunnels leading off of this main room gave glimpses into further amplifying chambers and my heartbeat quickened at the thought of Elise being so close. She was here, her soul was practically calling to me, but despite how fierce the urge was to try and find her, I couldn't do that. Not while so many Black Card members were here. I wouldn't get two steps out of this cavern without being caught, killed. Then what good would I be to her?

No, I needed to follow the plan. Take in every detail of this entire place and report back to the monsters waiting for me to return. Then I could unleash them here when it was time to save our girl.

The chamber I was in was full of chanting assholes in robes. There were so many of them that I had to guess this had been going on a while already. King must have been summoning his followers all day and I was kind of glad I was clearly among the last to arrive so I hadn't had to wait around with these creeps longer than necessary.

The last of the members filed in behind me and the shadowy figure of King stepped up onto a stage at the far end of the chamber, raising their hands in the air. Everything about them changed from male to female, old to young within flashes of a moment. I tried to see beyond the fog of concealment they were hiding behind, but it was impossible.

One day soon, I'll expose you and cut your heart out for taking my girl.

My hands curled into fists as the tug of magic along my skin told me to kneel, and as the rest of the Black Card dropped down around me, I followed suit, thankful I wasn't really under King's control like they were.

The chanting fell quiet and my gaze moved to the twenty people kneeling at King's feet, none of them in robes, the sound of them muttering nonsense reaching me. The Blazers looked to King as they produced a silver blade from within their robes and their currently young, male face looked out over the crowd.

"Tonight marks the beginning of the new future," King called. "The blood of those who no longer wish to live will pave the path for a better, safer world. It is time to take our movement to new heights. We must draw as many of those who wish to die to us as possible to ensure I can protect you from the gangs which have spilled the blood of your family, your friends, and the rulers who have crushed the weaker Fae beneath them to rise to power and take everything they can from you and your kind. We will take back what we are owed. I shall offer you the kingdom, dear friends, if you offer me the power to seize it!"

He handed the blade to the Blazer at the far end of the line and sickness filled my gut as I kept myself still, the urge to destroy this asshole taking over nearly every piece of me. But in here, The Sight shone clearer than ever, and I could see my death from every angle. The only chance for me to save Elise was to remain quiet and return to the others. And as the first Blazer drove the blade into his own gut, a coldness fell over me and I knew I'd allow a river of blood to flow in this room so long as not a single drop of it was hers.

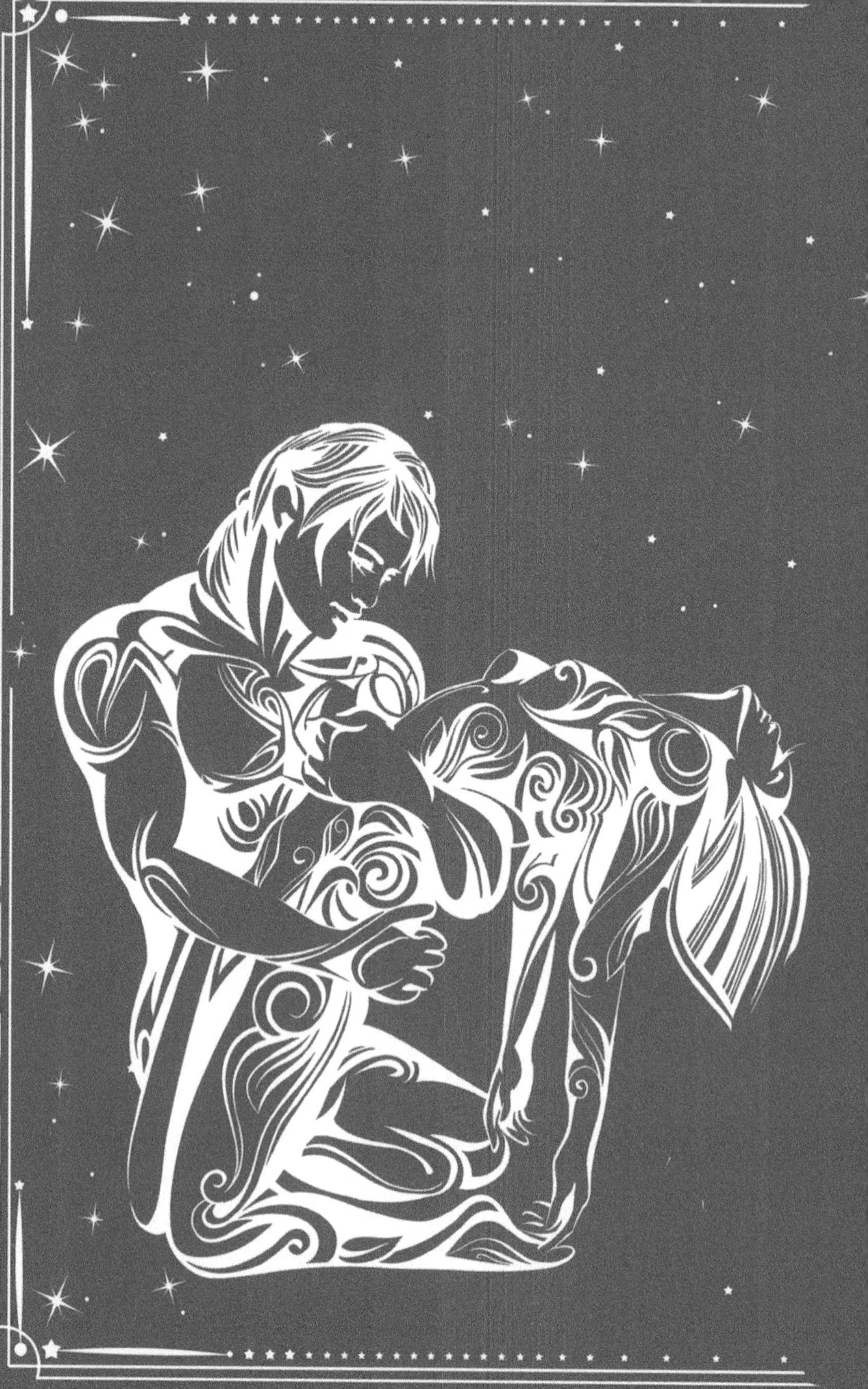

Ryder

CHAPTER NINE

"Now?" Leon asked.

"No," Gabriel growled.

"Now?"

"No."

"Nooow?"

"I'll tell you when it's time, Leon," Gabriel barked and thank fuck for that because I'd been one second away from wringing Mufasa's neck.

Leon huffed, throwing himself onto the couch and I watched from my position against the wall, my arms folded as I waited. Big Bird had been back for hours and though I wanted to charge right into that fucking sea palace to claim my girl back, I also had years of experience in executing plans like this. Timing was crucial. And the stoic silence that Dante had fallen into as he sat in the armchair with his feet up on the coffee table told me he knew that too. He was preparing himself just like I was, descending into the darkest, most calm place in his mind ready to do everything and anything it took to succeed tonight.

Of course, Inferno's state of mind didn't have an inch on mine. I could switch off everything inside me, become nothing but an emotionless creature with one goal in mind. For Elise, I would do anything. But Dante always had others to consider. A doting little mamma who would miss him, brothers and sisters who'd cry at his funeral if he wound up dead tonight. I ignored the strange pang in my chest over that thought. If I died, no one would mourn me except maybe my girl. A small part of me hoped she would anyway. That I meant something to someone on this earth. Though I wasn't sure why I cared. I never had before.

Gabriel was studying the Magicae Mortuorum, leaning over the coffee table as he read one particular spell using the spyglass Leon had stolen from Lionel Acrux. I'd had a rare smile over that. The Dragon Lord who ruled the kingdom with his friends was some entitled prick who'd been 'born for greatness' or some bullshit. It was all very well being born for greatness when you've got golden candlesticks coming outa your asshole and servants taking care of every worry you have in life so you could focus on that 'greatness.' People born in cities like Alestria didn't stand a chance of being great. They couldn't afford to be fucking *great*. Not that I gave a fuck, but I still thought the rulers were dipshits.

Leon kicked his feet like a toddler, bashing his head back against the couch. "I need to kill someone," he groaned. "Come on Gabriel, let me go get her. I'm gonna *die* if I don't go now."

"You're not gonna die, Leone," Dante said sharply. "Leave him be, we're not going anywhere unless he gets that spell right."

Gabriel nodded, continuing to read the book and Leon gripped the back of the couch, hauling himself onto it dramatically and flopping over the top of it out of sight, a thump sounding him hitting the floor.

I shook my head and Inferno caught my eye for a second before I wrenched my gaze away from his. *Fucking Oscura filth.*

I didn't feel that insult down to the depths of my soul like I usually did though and I sure as fuck wasn't going to examine the reason why.

Leon started pushing himself along the floor like some sort of demented seal, his arms dragging at his sides and his knees bending and pushing him along as his cheek grazed the floorboards. He peeked up at Gabriel as he made it to the coffee table and Dante kicked him as he stuck his ass in the air.

"Leon!" he snapped and I strode across the room, grabbing Leon by the back of his shirt and dragging him out of the room, throwing him into one of the bedrooms.

I followed him inside, slammed the door shut and folded my arms as I pressed my back to it to block his way out.

Leon got to his feet with a loud huff. "It's taking forever, Ryder," he complained. "I need to go and get her. She's all alone. She needs me."

The rings in his eyes seemed to shine with that need too and I could see this was more than just the suffering the rest of us were going through.

I jerked my chin at his eyes. "That bond causing you trouble?" I asked blandly, unsure if I wanted to know or if I even gave a fuck.

"Yes," he gasped, lunging forward and knotting his fingers in my shirt as pain crossed his features. "It's like someone's stabbing my heart with a fucking pickaxe then shoving a grenade in it and pulling the pin. I can feel how close she is, but I can't go to her. It's agony, Ryder, fucking *agony*." He slumped against me and I vaguely patted his shoulder as he took a hug I definitely hadn't consented to. But the guy was such a mess, I just let him fall apart on me, taking what his Order needed and trying not to think into it too much. But when he nuzzled into my neck with a mewl, he'd gone too far.

"Mufasa," I warned.

"I can see why she likes your hugs," he purred, actually shitting *purred*.

"Get off me, asshole." I shoved him back and his ass hit the bed before he hung his head like a sad animal.

"I'm gonna kill anyone who stands in my way tonight. I'll rip apart any and all Fae who tries to keep her from me another second."

"That's more like it," I clipped. "Don't be sad, be angry. You're gonna need all the rage you can muster tonight."

"Can't I be both? You're both," he said, his eyes round and wide. "Remember that Siren who gave us the keys to this place while you were concealing yourself as my friend Barry?"

I didn't answer, my lips pressed tightly together as I gave him a death glare to warn him off of rehashing this story. Again.

"She said she could feel how sad you were and wondered if you needed a tissue, remember?"

"That's not what she said," I gritted out.

"Pretty sure she did, that's why I added those tears to your concealment spell to keep your cover."

"I remember that part," I growled, as my fists clenched.

"And then Gabriel reminded you that you could have just shifted into a tiny snake and hidden in his pocket instead of embarrassing yourself as sad boy Barry."

"Yes," I hissed. "I remember, Leon. You don't have to keep-"

"And then I showed you that website where you can buy tiny hats for tiny snakes and bought a whole range for you to cheer you up, and I almost smiled about it, but then I remembered Elise was gone and-"

"I was fucking there," I barked. "And if you put a tiny hat near me in any of my snake forms, I will shift into my biggest form and eat you whole. That isn't a threat, that is a promise."

"Aww, look at us making pinkie promises, Elise would be so proud," he said with a twitch of a smile.

"I don't *pinkie* promise things," I snarled.

"Sure you do." He stood up, striding toward me and holding out his pinkie, trying to hook it around mine as I kept my hands in tight, impenetrable fists.

"I will snap your little finger off if you don't stop this second," I hissed, a rattle sounding in my body in a dangerous warning.

"Come on, just give me your pinkie." He gripped my fist with the word *lust* on it, trying to unfurl my little finger from it. "Promise you'll eat me, Rydikins. It'll cheer me up."

I clenched my jaw, wondering if Elise would forgive me if I snapped her mate's neck. But I guessed she wouldn't.

"Stop," I growled, my hackles rising.

He was damn strong and was actually getting close to hooking my little finger out of my fist.

"Mufasa," I snapped. *Don't kill the Lion. Don't kill the Lion. Don't kill the Lion.*

The door opened and I turned, hope rushing through me as I found Gabriel there.

"It's time," he announced just as Leon yanked my little finger out and locked his around mine.

"Yes!" Leon whooped, squeezing it tight for a second and I shoved him off with a snarl before he went bounding past me and tried to kiss Gabriel on the cheek, but Big Bird swerved it like a bullet. "Let's get our girl back!" He ran to the front door and we all chased after him as he made it outside.

Gabriel cursed, racing out in front to stop him and turning to face us all.

"I'm leading the way," he said firmly. "I can get us in and out but if any of you make rash decisions, it could mean one of you or Elise dies. If you wanna go off on a suicide mission, fine, but I'm not risking Elise for anything. So you follow my orders or I will leave you behind."

The Alpha in me reared its head, desperate to take charge and go barrelling into war. But Gabriel had The Sight and he had the best chance of getting me to my girl and getting us the fuck out again in one piece.

"Fine," I agreed.

"Lead the way, falco," Dante urged and Leon nodded keenly.

Gabriel turned and we followed him down the steps onto the path and he led us around the house toward the edge of the cliff. The night was thick, and darkness was our friend tonight as we made it to the steep drop off.

"Dante, can you lower the others to the ground? It could draw attention if Ryder and I use earth magic, someone could see," Gabriel said as he shed his shirt and let his wings burst free from his back.

"Sure," Dante said. He cast air beneath Leon's feet and carried him over the edge of the cliff before lowering him down to the rocky beach far below.

I glanced at Dante with a sneer. "I'll make my own way down."

"You can't use your magic," Gabriel said. "I've *seen* that we'll be spotted."

"He can just stay here then," Dante said with a shrug.

"He won't let you die," Gabriel told me, placing a hand on Dante's shoulder to stop him heading over the cliff. "And we don't get Elise back without all of us, so do as I say."

Dante sighed, looking to me and it took every piece of love I had in my heart for Elise to step forward and let the Dragon asshole cast air beneath my feet.

The magical wind carried me out over the cliff and I gazed down at my doom as my life hung in Dante's hands. If this wasn't proof that I'd do anything for Elise, I didn't know what was.

Dante started lowering me down to the beach, then the air beneath me suddenly vanished and I cursed as I shot toward the sharp rocks below. Dante caught me at the last second and his laughter rang out from above, making a deep hiss seep through my teeth.

I stepped onto the sharp rocks and the Lion stood there with wide eyes.

"Dante just saved your life," he gasped.

"That's not what happened," I growled.

"Pretty sure it was, dude." He clapped me on the shoulder as Gabriel flew to the ground and Dante floated down to land beside him like a fucking butterfly.

"You think you're real funny, don't you Inferno?" I spat and he smirked tauntingly.

"I said I'd get you down and I did. Didn't realise you had a fear of heights, serpente," he remarked casually and I lunged at him, casting hard metal knuckle dusters over my fist as I swung it at him. It smashed against his air shield as he laughed a little louder and Gabriel shoved his way between us.

"If you don't work together, Elise isn't coming home tonight," he snarled, his steel grey eyes flaring. "This needs all of us to work. But Leon and I will find another way if you two can't cooperate."

"Just suck it up," Leon barked. "Don't do this right now. We can have marital spats later when Elise is home."

"Marital spats?" Dante balked.

"Yeah, I mean we're not married yet, but we all will be to Elise one day, right? So Ryder will be your husband-in-law."

"Stop talking." I shoved my way past Leon. "I'll work with Inferno tonight."

"And always," Leon whispered like he thought I wouldn't hear.

"Stop. Talking," I reiterated and he thankfully listened as Gabriel took the lead again and we all followed him along the beach, drawing the shadows closer around us. We picked up the pace and I strode forward to walk at Gabriel's side.

"Aim me wherever you need tonight," I said in a low voice. "It's not gonna haunt me no matter how many lives I take to get her back."

Gabriel glanced at me with an arched brow. "Who are you worried about it haunting?"

"No one," I growled. "I'm just saying, there are no lengths I won't go to for her. I won't hesitate. I won't suddenly grow a conscience. So if a dirty job needs doing, assign me to it."

"Fine," he agreed.

"Don't go thinking that makes you the boss though, asshole," I added.

He tsked. "You think I want to lead a group of men who hunger for the girl I love?"

Venom slid over my tongue as I glanced back at Dante and Leon behind us, their eyes dark and full of determination. Then I looked back at Gabriel with curiosity rising in me. "You could see us all dead tonight if you didn't want us getting in your way. You'd just have to point us towards the deaths you *see* for us in your head."

"True." A smirk pulled at the corner of his mouth. "Unfortunately, I need all of you to get her out. Doesn't mean I won't bump you all off in the future though."

I released a breath of amusement. "You take the Lion, I'll take the Dragon."

He shook his head. "Thing is, Ryder, if I actually did that, you'd kill me for it according to The Sight. Should I look into your alliances a bit more?"

A hiss escaped my lips in irritation. "I don't care if those two don't make it out tonight. It would make my life a whole lot easier."

His arm brushed mine, his eyes glazing for a moment as he *saw* some vision and a dark chuckle escaped him.

"What?" I grunted.

"Nothing."

"Don't do that, Big Bird, what did you *see*?"

"You'll just deny it," he commented like a prime prick.

"I'll rip your eyes out and look through them myself it you don't-" I walked straight into a forcefield of magic and stumbled backwards, my foot slipping on a wet rock.

I threw out my hand to soften the ground with my earth magic before I dashed my head in on the rocks, but strong hands caught my shoulders and yanked me upright.

I twisted around with a growl as the temperature of my blood rose by one degree, finding Inferno holding onto me. I yanked my shirt out of his grip and he gazed at his own hands in confusion like they'd just betrayed him. Leon grinned at us with his fucking golden eyes sparkling and I turned to

Gabriel with a snarl on my lips.

"You *saw* that coming, why didn't you fucking stop me?" I accused.

"I didn't *see* anything, I was too busy looking for Elise," he said lightly, but I could tell from his fucking face that wasn't true. "I thought we were-" I cut off those words, strangling them until they choked and spluttered until they died. I was not friends with Gabriel Nox. Or anyone. And he'd just proved that.

"You saved him, bro," Leon breathed to Dante in awe and my teeth ground to dust in my mouth.

"I didn't," Inferno denied, his eyes meeting mine for a moment. I tried to figure out his motive, but maybe it had just been a kneejerk reaction. I sure as shit didn't care enough to think into it.

Gabriel raised his hands to the forcefield, pressing his palms against it and a flicker of blue light shimmered beneath his palms. He closed his eyes and started murmuring some weird ass words which I guessed he'd memorised from the Magicae Mortuorum, then he created a blade of wood in his palm and slit his thumb open. His pain flickered through me for a second as he smeared the blood over the forcefield, painting a symbol there made up of the four interconnecting Elemental triangles, circling around in a jagged ring. His blood shone blue then Gabriel pressed his palm to the symbol, pushing hard and a glowing triangular door opened for him in the forcefield.

"It's a door-to-anywhere spell," Gabriel announced with a triumphant smirk as he looked back at us, gesturing for us to follow. "It'll close as soon as we're through. Come on."

I stepped after him, eyeing him closely. "Was that dark magic?"

Gabriel shrugged one shoulder, giving me my answer.

"Teach me that spell and I'll forget about your little mind slip back there, Big Bird," I said in a low tone and he grinned.

"No, it's dangerous and I won't be using it again after tonight. Blood magic can steal away pieces of your soul. And by the way, if I'd warned you about walking into that forcefield, Leon wouldn't have stopped walking and would have fallen and cracked his head open on a rock. Straight up dead. Funny how fate works, isn't it?"

"Oh my stars, dude," Leon jumped at Gabriel, nuzzling his fucking face. "You love me."

"I do not *love* you," Gabriel said through tight lips. "As I keep saying, I need you all to save Elise. I'm not going to be your twenty-four-hour lifeguards after tonight." Gabriel didn't push Leon off for a second though and I saw the glimmer of some emotion in his eyes.

I didn't say anything in response to Gabriel's words, but the weight in my chest over his disregard for me suddenly eased. *Ergh, who the fuck am I becoming?*

"Which way do we go, falco?" Dante asked and Gabriel jerked his head to beckon us.

Leon dropped back to hurry along beside me as we followed Big Bird and he leaned closer to whisper in my ear. "How cool is it that we're all on a rescue mission together? One for the scrapbook, right dude?"

"Please tell me you don't actually have a scrapbook," I muttered.

"I've been stuck in that house waiting to get news of my mate for two days, what else was I supposed to do with all the photos I took these past few weeks?" he hissed.

"Not make a scrapbook," I deadpanned. *And what fucking photos?*

"Then how would I show Elise all the stuff we've been doing, Scar?" He tutted like *I* was the insane one.

Gabriel raised a hand to halt us, going all still and shit as his eyes glazed and he stared off toward the crashing waves for a long moment. Then he started moving again, striding straight towards the sea at a fierce pace.

"Keep behind me!" he barked and we all hurried forward to follow.

The cold water washed over my feet as I marched straight into the sea with my breaths coming heavier. I could sense her out here somewhere, so close I could almost taste her. And hell, I'd make sure to taste every inch of her the moment I had her back. I wanted her heart, her soul, her pain, all of it was mine. And I didn't care how far I had to dive into the ocean tonight to save her, because when I returned to the surface she'd be back at my side and there wasn't a journey I wouldn't have made for that.

I followed Gabriel into the dark water as the waves crashed furiously against us and my heart thumped slightly harder than its usual slow pace. I didn't feel the cold and Leon's skin practically blazed with his fire magic as he kept himself warm, his hand going to Dante's arm to offer him the same relief without a word.

The waves rolled up higher and higher and as we made it up to our waists in the water, an enormous one swallowed us in its shadow. It curled down from its immense height, frothing and foaming before washing over us. I expected to be cast away in its power, but instead found my feet hitting a hard stone floor and I stepped out into a tunnel lit by flaming green torches on the walls.

Gabriel cast a silencing bubble around us as Leon and Dante stepped out from the swirling wall of water behind us, looking around in surprise.

Leon released a low whistle. "I want one of those in our house."

"What house?" Dante whispered as we headed along the tunnel.

"The one we're gonna buy together after we marry Elise," he whispered back and I released a growl. As if I'd ever share a living space with Inferno, or any of them for that matter.

Gabriel paused as he reached a turn in the tunnel, beckoning me forward. "Feeling bloodthirsty, Ryder?" he asked.

"Always," I replied, stepping to his side and he nodded to encourage me further on.

"One on your left," he said.

I cast a steel blade in my hands with a wooden handle and strode forward, Gabriel's silencing bubble extending ahead to remain around me. I turned into the adjacent tunnel and found a Black Card member standing to the left of it in long robes, gazing into a large chamber ahead of him.

I crept right up behind him before slamming my palm over his mouth, casting a silencing bubble right into his mouth to steal away his screams before ramming my knife up between his shoulder blades. His death was quick and easy, but I drank in the sharp pain of it before he went, then heaved him backwards by the shoulders towards the others.

"There's nowhere to hide him down here," I hissed. "Use a concealment spell."

"Nah." Leon opened his palm as I dropped the guy on the floor and fire burst along his body at such a fierce temperature that it dissolved him into dust in seconds. Dante waved a hand and the dust went flying away in the direction we'd come from before splashing into the wall of water and vanishing for good.

"Fuck," I breathed, hating being impressed, but what a way to dispose of a body.

"You're up next, Dante. There's five tunnels out of the chamber up ahead and each are guarded by a Black Card member," Gabriel told him.

"He gets *five* kills?" I growled in frustration.

"Storm powers, serpente." Inferno smirked as he stepped past me. "It's why I'm the most feared Fae in Alestria."

"Bullshit," I hissed dangerously, stepping forward but Gabriel pressed a hand to my shoulder, giving me an intent look.

"You'll get the most kills today regardless," he said in a low tone and satisfaction filled me.

"Lo vedremo," Inferno muttered as he walked off down the tunnel and we headed after him.

We reached the edge of the passage, shrouded in concealment spells as Leon and Gabriel worked together to hide us. Electricity crackled along Inferno's body and he raised his hands as he gazed out at the robed figures standing in the tunnel exits around the huge amplifying chamber. I gazed up at the glass domed roof above and a school of fish rushing overhead with a sneer. *You think you can get away with hiding my girl under the ocean like a fucking polyp in Ursula's garden in The Little Mermaid? I'm gonna squeeze every drop of pain I can out of you, King. It'll be a star damned feast.*

Dante released an explosion of electricity, five shots tearing toward his prey and slamming into their chests. They all crumpled in unison and Gabriel ran out ahead of us, beckoning us after him as static licked across my body.

"Leon, Dante deal with the bodies. We've got two minutes until someone heads out this way. Ryder, you're with me," Gabriel commanded and I chased after him as he turned down one of the tunnels and leapt over the body in the middle of it.

I glanced back at Leon, finding his eyes burning into mine.

"You find her and you bring her back, Ryder," he snapped at me and I nodded, too caught up in how close I felt to Elise to be pissed over all the orders I was receiving left, right and fucking centre.

I ran on behind Gabriel, winding into another dark passage before he drew to a halt and appeared to be counting under his breath.

When he was done, he looked to me. "Four Black Card members, the guy on the right is the one you wanna watch out for," he told me. "I'll take the three about to come up behind us." He turned back past me, striding away and I ran forward without hesitation, casting a vine whip in my hand and readying my other palm, charging it with magic. Energy crackled along my veins in anticipation of the coming kills, my emotions entirely disengaged, my heart a cold, black thing that only beat for one Fae in this world. She was the reason it worked at all, the reason it wanted to keep pounding. Elise Callisto was the life I'd been lacking since I was a boy, and I was here to claim her back along with every dream of the future she'd given me. I didn't want to just exist anymore. With her, I could experience every flavour the world had to offer.

I rounded into a long passage that ended in a black door and water magic blasted at me from the guy on the right. I threw up a huge wall of rock to block it, using the whip to yank the two assholes to the left off of their feet before casting sharp wooden spears at them. They died with yelps and their pain sizzling through my veins as I rounded the rock wall.

The huge water Elemental cast a tumult of ice shards at me and I blocked them with another wall of earth, my adrenaline rising as one whistled past my ear. I released a grunt of anger, diving out from my cover and slamming my fist into his ugly face. His head snapped back and hit the wall, my surprise attack leaving him dazed long enough for me to drive a wooden blade into his chest. He died with a moan and I shoved him to the floor, leaving my blade in his heart as I wiped a speckled of blood from my cheek.

"Now where's number four?" I growled as I headed down the tunnel, finding him scratching at the door and calling out for someone to open it from the other side. Didn't look like anyone was coming to his rescue though.

I cast his head in a silencing bubble, stifling his screams and he turned to fight me, a magical wind whipping around me as he desperately tried to wrangle his air Element. I grew a sharp stalactite out of the ceiling above him and it slammed into his head, killing him in an instant, taking my rage out on this piece of shit who dared keep my girl from me.

Gabriel came running back to my side, his hands bloody and his eyes dark as he stepped up to the door. "She's in here," he murmured and my heart rate picked up. I fought to open the door with my earth magic, but some dark power halted me from using it.

"Open it," I urged and Gabriel started casting his door-to-anywhere spell across the black door, extending his silencing bubble out further ahead of him to keep his work quiet. A curse left him as he worked and I could see him struggling against the dark magic he was using, making me less inclined to wanna learn that spell.

When it was done, he pushed through the triangular door carved into the metal and I followed him through it, seeking her out in desperation as we arrived in another amplifying chamber. The door sealed up behind us in an instant and Gabriel took a breath as he recovered from the dark magic. His hand suddenly shot forward and a robed girl with black hair was caught in the grip of his vines, his silencing bubble stretching out to include her.

She looked vaguely familiar and as Gabriel sneered at her, her eyes widened with recognition. "Gab-riel?" she rasped.

"This is partly for the frogs, Karla, but mostly for my girl." He whipped his hand sideways and snapped her neck, his gaze merciless as she crumpled to the floor.

I shoved past him, hunting for Elise and my gaze locked on a lock of lilac hair peeking out from a pile of blankets she was curled up in on the floor. I ran to her, lowering to my knees and dragging the blankets back as I evaporated the silencing bubble around me.

She lolled in my arms and panic set in to my bones. "Gabriel, what's wrong with her?" I demanded, the heat of her against my icy flesh the only comfort that she was still alive.

His brows pulled together in concern. "She's drugged with Nellaweed to keep her subdued," he growled and my teeth lengthened to sharp points in my mouth as I prepared to give her my antivenom.

"Wait," he hissed. "Not a large dose. King has been draining her and she's starved of blood. If she wakes fully, she'll lose herself to the bloodlust and kill you before she realises what she's done. We can feed her once we get out of here."

Rage burned through my chest at those words, what that fucking piece of shit King had done to my girl. I'd make every nerve ending in his body scream when I got my hands on him. I'd feast on his pain, drawing out every drop of it he could give.

I brushed a lock of lilac hair away from her neck then bit down, letting a little antivenom flow from me into her veins. I pulled back, fighting the urge to give her all she needed and running my thumb over the teeth marks to heal them away. She blinked sleepily and those bright green and silver eyes of hers found mine. Fuck me, she was so beautiful.

"Hey, baby." I smirked, my heart beating harder than it ever had, practically fighting its way out of my chest. "Did you really think I wouldn't come for you?"

"Ryder," she gasped, reaching for me and I crushed her to my chest, a fierce growl of protectiveness leaving me.

Her lips clashed with mine and I took the kiss I'd been thirsting for for weeks. My whole world was right here in my arms. This girl was the beginning and the end of my life and everything in between.

Gabriel was suddenly there, hauling us to our feet and Elise broke away from me with a moan of need, stumbling toward him and wrapping her arms around his neck as she kissed him too.

"How did you find me?" she begged against his lips and I found I didn't even want to cut his head off for touching her like that. His need for her was as keen as my own, and if he'd punish, torture and kill for this girl like I would then I guessed I had to deem him worthy.

Gabriel didn't manage to answer that question as Dante and Leon started hammering their fists on the door and shouting out to let them in. A deafening boom followed and static electricity made the hairs on my arms stand on end.

I tore across the room to the dead bitch on the floor, rifling through her pockets but finding no key. "How the fuck do I open it, Big Bird?"

"She's got a mark, use her palm," Gabriel said urgently and I dragged the girl to the door by her arm, slapping her hand against it.

The door opened and Dante and Leon spilled inside before I slammed it shut on a guy's arm. I kept slamming it until he withdrew it with a wail and the door fixed into place.

Dante and Leon were bloody and panting, but as their eyes fell on Elise, all the darkness in them lifted like a veil. Gabriel and I cast vines across the door to stop it from opening again, but from the sounds of it, there were a hell of a lot of Fae out there trying to get in. And it wasn't going to hold forever.

"Little monster!" Leon ran to Elise, tearing her from Gabriel's arms and spinning her around as he kissed her like a maniac.

"Leo," she croaked, clinging to him as best she could in her weakened state before gripping on to Dante too as he kissed her.

"Let's just keep the reunions for when we've actually fucking escaped," I snarled as Leon clutched her ass and looked one second from having a mid-shitstorm fuck.

But then she drooped in his arms and her eyes slid closed for a moment, making all of us share a look of worry. Leon nuzzled the side of her head with a growl of concern and I felt that same feeling down to the core of my bones. We needed to get her out of here. Fast.

A loud bang sounded from the other side of the door and it trembled ominously.

"She needs to feed," I growled as I looked to Gabriel anxiously, my jaw clenching.

"No, it's too dangerous right now," Gabriel said firmly. "We'll feed her as soon as we're out of here."

"Then tell me you've got a plan, future boy," I demanded.

Gabriel's eyes glazed and Elise lifted her head, watching him with an ache in her eyes, her expression drawn. I'd feed her every last drop of blood in my veins just as soon as I got her to safety.

Gabriel snapped out of his vision as the door shuddered and nearly gave. I added more magic to the vines, but another thundering attack made more of them snap.

"Got it," Gabriel said in a tight voice that spoke of imminent doom. "No one panic."

He raised his hands, gazing up at the glass ceiling above and his fingers curled as he wielded the water beyond it. A spiderweb of cracks splintered across the glass and my breaths came a little quicker.

"*That's* your fucking plan?" I hissed, but he didn't answer, his decision clear in his eyes.

I ran to Elise, taking her from Leon's arms and holding her tight to my chest as the others clustered around me.

"You sure about this, Gabe?" Leon asked.

"No," Gabriel ground out as he focused.

"If you kill us, I will come back from beyond the veil to murder your ass so fucking hard, falco," Dante warned.

"Seconded," Elise said breathlessly, then her eyes fluttered closed again and my heart thrashed.

"Get close to me, all of you," Gabriel demanded and we grouped around him. Leon snuggled in next to me, a deep purr resounding in his chest as he leaned close to lick Elise's hair.

"Leo." Elise swatted him weakly. "We're about to die, dude."

"Nah, Gabe will save us," he said lightly.

"Don't call me Gabe," Gabriel hissed and I dragged him into the middle of our group with me and Elise. He was the only water Elemental here so that meant he was the only asshole who could save Elise from this. And the rest of us. The stars really were testing my faith in these dipshits today.

The door crashed open and a wave of robed Black Card members poured in like a tide. I threw out my palm, spearing three of them on huge spikes of wood before Dante cast a powerful air shield around us. Magic exploded against it, making him curse under his breath in Faetalian as he fought to hold it up.

Elise's fingers curled around my arm and I met her green and silver gaze, making a silent promise to her. I'd get her to the surface no matter what happened. The ocean would have to tear her from my arms if it wanted her.

A huge hole burst into the glass ceiling above us and water came crashing through in a torrent just before the entire dome gave way under the weight of the sea. I took a breath, but the water never touched me, tumbling down around Dante's sphere of air. The lights were knocked out just as the Black Card members were washed away and we were completely submerged.

Gabriel used his magic to propel us towards the surface and I lost sight of everything as the dark ocean consumed us, the feel of Elise's breath on my neck the only reassurance that she was still here in my arms. Leon's breath on my ear was another kind of reassurance I didn't fucking need, but maybe I was one percent relieved the Lion had made it out alive.

Gabriel used his water Element to push us towards the surface and I cast a Faelight above us so he could see.

Elise sagged against me and I took in the magic blocking cuffs on her wrists with a growl. She looked hungry and desperate and thinner than before. It made anger curl through my veins like flames and the most fearsome need for death filled me. I would kill King for this. I would peel the skin from his bones and make him scream in penance. He was going to know the full force of my wrath, learn the reason why I was the Lunar King. And no one would ever dare touch a hair on Elise's head again when it was known what happened to her enemies.

We breached the surface and Dante kept his air shield tight around us as we bobbed on top of the dark waves. He cast a wind behind us, driving us towards the shore.

We'd done it. We'd saved our girl and no force in this world would ever steal her from us again. But there would be a price to pay for this. King would retaliate. And I knew in my bones, that we would soon be going to war.

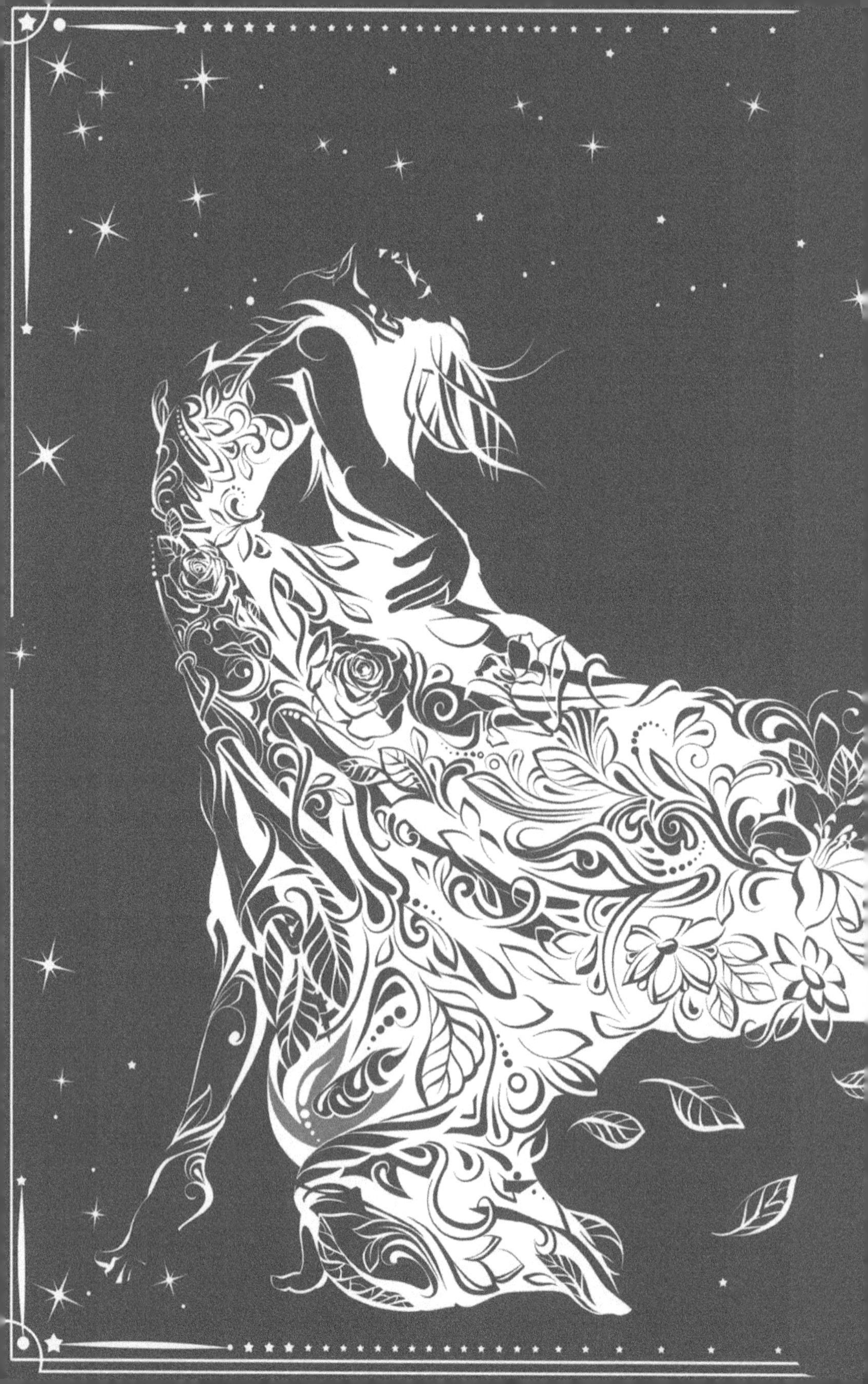

ELISE

CHAPTER TEN

My skin tingled as Ryder's antivenom coursed through my body, seeking out whatever the fuck King had given me back in that chamber to keep me subdued while they stole as much of my blood as they wanted. I'd been dreaming of my kings the whole time I was zombied out on that stuff and I hadn't quite believed that I was really in their arms until this moment.

As my strength returned to me, I blinked around at the little beach house they'd brought me to, pushing out of Ryder's arms so that I could stand on my own two feet between the four Fae who were crowding close around me.

My throat was raw and burning with the need for blood and I inhaled deeply as I fought against my baser instincts with all I had, taking a moment to absorb the fact that I really was free before I allowed myself to indulge in the taste of their blood.

I stood, looking between my four kings as they surrounded me with my heart pounding and desire coursing through me as I realised they'd come for me. All of them. They'd put aside all of their shit with each other because they'd cared about me that much.

I knew how they felt about me in theory, I'd heard the words they'd spoken and felt it when I was with them, but having them do this for me, seeing the way they'd worked together and proven themselves was more than I could take.

"I don't deserve all of you," I breathed. I was just a broken girl with a vendetta. I'd only wanted one thing when I'd started at Aurora Academy and now they'd given me more than I ever could have dreamed of.

Leon growled low in his throat, stepping closer behind me as electricity sparked against my skin from Dante. Gabriel caught my jaw, forcing me to look at him on my right as he gazed down into my eyes.

"You're all I want, little angel. You're all any of us wants. And we were never going to let you go."

Tears pricked the backs of my eyes and I swallowed thickly, not knowing how to live up to this person they thought I was. I didn't deserve so much from them. I wasn't worthy of it.

"We're just so relieved to have you back, carina," Dante said, taking my left hand and making me suck in a breath as the static lining his skin crackled along mine.

"We love you, little monster," Leon said, closing in on me from behind, his arms slipping around my waist and his rough fingers moving across my skin as he pushed my cami up an inch.

The little beach house they'd brought me back to was unfamiliar, but with the four of them surrounding me it felt like home.

"You should all be angry with me," I breathed. "For getting myself caught and falling into King's grasp-"

"I am angry," Ryder snarled, gripping a fistful of my hair and yanking on it to tug my face from Gabriel's grip as he made me look at him standing in front of me. "I'm angry at that motherfucker for taking you from me. I'm angry at the time we missed out on while you were gone. I'm angry that your lips aren't already pressed to mine and that we're still all standing here talking."

A breath of laughter escaped me but as Dante's electricity flared and struck against my skin, it turned into a gasp of pleasure, the bite of almost-pain stinging my nipples beneath my shirt.

"Are you angry too, Elise?" Ryder pressed.

"Yes," I admitted, letting that feeling soak through my limbs as Leon's fingers curled around the top of my sweatpants and he tugged the drawstring open. "I'm really fucking angry at King for taking me, for trying to make me turn on you. For keeping me from you and blocking off my magic and stealing my blood-"

"What?" Gabriel hissed, tugging on my arm to make me look at him again.

Ryder didn't release his hold on my hair though so as I turned my head, prickles of pain flared across my scalp. It was overwhelming being at the centre of them like this, but it was exhilarating in all the best ways too.

"Did that bastard hurt you?" Gabriel demanded.

"Not as much as I wanted to hurt him," I replied.

"What else did he do, bella?" Dante asked, reaching for the strap of my cami and tugging it down over my shoulder.

"He kept me thirsty," I said, my fangs snapping out at the mere mention of that. The meagre hold I was maintaining over the thirst started to crumble as I flicked my gaze between Gabriel and Ryder, not knowing which of my kings I wanted to bite first. "And the blood he did give me was weak, old, bland and from a fucking glass."

Ryder's lip curled back in anger on my behalf and my gaze locked on the throbbing pulse at his neck as I lost control of the beast in me and lunged.

But before I could get close to Ryder, Leon wrapped an arm around me from behind, pressing his wrist to my mouth and my fangs sank into his flesh without me even making the decision to do it. It was an act of the beast within me and my nature took over as I dug my fangs in deep. I felt Gabriel's hands hold onto me like he was afraid of how far I might go and I felt my bloodlust rise so keenly it blinded me.

I growled as I bit Leon too hard, the thirst and my anger pushing into my instincts and making me reckless.

Leon growled too, the Lion in him all too clear as the taste of sunshine washed over my tongue and his blood ran hot and fast into my mouth and down my chin. He pushed forwards behind me, his solid cock driving against my ass and telling me just how much he liked my bite.

Dante gripped my sweatpants and yanked them down my legs as I moaned, drinking deep and closing my eyes as I lost myself in the heat and taste of my Lion. This whole reunion was headed one way fast and there wasn't a single piece of me that wanted to change that.

But before I could get lost in the taste of Leon, Ryder used his grip on my hair to tear me away. He shoved me at Dante who had already removed his shirt, baring his huge, muscular frame for me.

The bloodlust had me lunging at him in a furious, desperate pounce and he chuckled as he muttered something in Faetalian which sounded dirty and made my muscles clench with need. He was so tall that I didn't even reach his neck, my fangs sinking into his pec and making him hiss in a mixture of pleasure and pain as I tore into his skin.

Fuck I'd needed this. My kings surrounding me, the taste of them coating my tongue. All of it. All of them. And I needed a whole lot more than this too.

I kicked my sweatpants the rest of the way off as three more pairs of hands started tugging at my cami, tearing it off of me with a violent ripping sound as they fought to be the one to do it.

My hands found Dante's belt and I fumbled with it in my haste to rip it open before Leon's hands encircled my waist and took over for me.

Dante slapped Leon's hands aside with a grunt of irritation in Faetalian and shoved his jeans off just as Gabriel yanked me into his arms, pulling my fangs out of Dante as he spun me around and lifted me by gripping my ass in his big hands.

My arms and legs went around him as he kissed me, the thick length of his cock driving against my panties as I realised he'd already ditched all of his clothes.

He kissed me hard and desperately, like he needed to feel that I was really there in his arms and in his haste, his lip was torn open on my fangs.

I moaned as I swiped my tongue over the cut before sucking his lip into my mouth and biting down again to get access to more of his raw power and drawing it into me.

With the fucking cuffs still blocking the use of my magic, I couldn't do anything with the power I was taking from all of them, but I could feel it building inside of me with every swallow I took, and it was making my entire body hum with energy.

The cold press of Ryder's mouth against the side of my neck drew my attention to him behind me a beat before he bit down, and a mixture of pain and ecstasy exploded through my flesh.

I broke my kiss with Gabriel, moaning loudly as I threw my head back and bathed in the feeling of Ryder's fangs in my skin.

"Fuck, little monster, how do you make blood look so hot?" Leon purred, his eyes alight with fire as I met his gaze and found him in his boxers, his golden skin seeming to glow with the heat of his Element.

"Because it is hot," I purred right back, licking my bloodstained lips and earning growls from all of my kings.

Leon's eyes lit with an idea and he grabbed hold of me, tugging me away from Gabriel and Ryder before practically tossing me into Dante's arms.

I looked up at Dante as he placed me on my feet again and my gaze instantly fell to the bleeding wound on his chest. I leaned forward to lick the blood that had run down to his boxers from his skin, and he groaned before catching my chin and lifting it until I was looking into his honey brown eyes.

"Sei il mio mondo, amore mio."

"I love you, Dante," I breathed in reply, feeling the heat of those words washing over my skin.

"Bene. Then don't leave me again. I can't be without you a second time, bella."

Before I could reply, Leon whistled sharply, drawing my attention to him and my eyes widened as I found him smearing blood from his wrist down the centre of Gabriel's chest before shoving him so that he fell back onto the bed in the centre of the room.

Gabriel began to curse him out, but I shot forward and pounced on him before more than half a word could escape his lips. I leaned forward and began to lap the blood from his chest, moaning as it coated my tongue before driving my fangs into his abs so that I could taste both Leon's and his blood at once.

Gabriel knotted his fingers in my hair, pulling me closer as I drank from him and Ryder peeled my panties off of me from behind as Leon and Dante moved onto the bed either side of us.

I moaned loudly as Ryder ran his fingers around my pussy, feeling my wetness and groaning as he teased me.

I pushed my ass up as I continued to drink form Gabriel, wanting more from my Basilisk.

Leon and Dante's hands slid over my back and removed my bra between them so that I was fully naked in the heart of my men, feeling all of them so close to me that my head spun.

Ryder placed a kiss in the centre of my spine before moving his mouth lower and lower, the icy pad of his tongue raising goosebumps all over my flesh as his fingers kept stroking through my wetness without actually giving me what I wanted.

As his mouth made it to my ass cheek, Ryder bit down and I cried out, pulling my teeth from Gabriel's skin and arching my back just as Ryder pushed two fingers inside me.

"Fuck," I gasped as my whole body buzzed and throbbed, reminding me of exactly how long I'd gone without an orgasm in King's fucking dungeon.

Gabriel leaned up to suck one of my nipples into his mouth and my moans got louder as Ryder continued to fuck me with his hand.

Leon leaned closer, nuzzling against my neck and purring as he reached behind me then pushed two of his fingers into me too, making my breath catch at the combination of his and Ryder's fingers inside me at once. I was so full, the two of them stretching my pussy and making it throb as they worked some kind of magic with their hands, the combination of Ryder's ice cold skin and Leon's flaming hot flesh making me dizzy.

Dante started kissing my neck as I rocked my hips back into them and Gabriel sucked harder on my nipple, tugging on the other one with his fingers.

The moment Dante's statically charged fingertips brushed against my clit, I came for them, throwing my head back and screaming my ecstasy to the moon as Ryder and Leon kept pumping my pussy through it.

When they finally pulled their fingers back out of me, Leon slapped his hand down on my ass right over the bite Ryder had given me. The jolt of pain had pleasure pulsing through my pussy once more, prolonging my orgasm even further as I cried out again.

A hand wrapped around my throat and Ryder pressed his other wrist to my lips as he dragged my back against his chest, the hard press of his cock driving between my ass cheeks and making me whimper with the desire for more.

"Drink, baby," he commanded and I bit down hard, knowing he liked me to be rough with him and giving him what he wanted.

But I'd barely even gotten a mouthful of his sinful blood before he tore his wrist out of my mouth, my fangs slicing through skin and veins as he used his grip on my throat to control me.

Blood poured from the wound and I gasped at the sight of it, but Ryder just chuckled in my ear before holding his wrist so that his blood spilled down over my tits, painting me red for him.

"You're fucking crazy, stronzo," Dante muttered as Ryder released me and let the blood spill down his body too, relaxing his grip on me so that I could watch it run down over the curves of his muscles, painting his tattoos red and staining his scars.

It might have been the hottest thing I'd ever seen.

The moment the blood spilled over the hard length of his cock, I pounced, knocking him onto his back beside Dante on the mattress and sinking my teeth into his neck as I straddled him.

His dick slid between my thighs, the mixture of my arousal and his blood making it slick and causing me to moan as I shifted my hips, trying to line us up so that I could feel him inside me.

But before I could manage that, Leon snarled and snatched my hips, pulling my ass up higher and slamming his cock into me without warning, making me cry out.

Ryder cursed him and Leon growled right back, the dominant side of him showing itself as he fisted my hair and tugged until he pulled my fangs from Ryder's flesh.

I hissed my irritation at him for that, but he silenced my protests by slamming his thick cock into me even harder, making his balls slap against my clit and curses spill from my lips.

"I wanna watch you suck his dick, little monster," Leon growled, pushing my head down again as Ryder's pissed off gaze lessened a little.

My eyes fell to Ryder's cock, smeared with blood and beaded with precum and I found I had absolutely no objections to that as Ryder shifted up the mattress to give me the space I needed to follow through on that command.

Leon slowed his pace a little as I ran my tongue up Ryder's shaft, feeling Dante and Gabriel's eyes on me as I slid my lips over the head and tasted the blood coating him. It was sinful and fucked up and pretty much the culmination of my dirtiest and best fantasies brought to life.

The moment Ryder's cock was in my mouth, Leon stopped holding back, a snarl tearing from his throat as his fingers tightened around my hips and he began to drive himself into me like a man possessed.

I moaned and screamed around Ryder's cock, sucking and licking him and loving the taste of his blood coating my tongue alongside the taste of him.

Dante and Gabriel's hands moved over my body, sliding in the blood which painted my front and smearing it all over me.

I dug my fingernails into Ryder's chest as his cock thickened in my mouth and just as I felt them break the skin, he thrust in deep and came hard, his cum spilling down my throat as he growled my name.

I swallowed greedily before releasing him and my moans filled the air as Leon used his grip on me to pull me upright again before laying back on the bed so that I could ride him reverse cowgirl style.

My eyes fell on the lust filled looks my other kings were giving me as I rode Leon's cock and tasted the blood that was still staining my lips.

I slid my hands over the blood that wet my body and moaned as I smeared it across my flesh, looking between the three god-like creatures before me while Leon held my ass and drove his cock up into me so hard that I could barely catch my breath.

One of my hands found my clit and I moaned louder as my pussy pulsed around Leon's shaft and I touched myself provocatively, wanting to goad the others into joining in.

But all three of them stayed exactly where they were, watching me with hungry eyes and hard cocks. Even Ryder looked ready to go again already and the sight of him so turned on so soon had me gasping as I came for them. Pleasure rushed through my body and I arched my spine as my eyes fell closed and I bathed in that eternal feeling.

My pussy clenched around Leon's cock and I called his name as he thrust into me harder and harder until he was coming too, growling like the beast he was and burying himself deep inside me as the two of us rode out our pleasure together.

But of course the others weren't going to let me waste time catching my breath.

I gasped as a pair of vines snaked their way around my wrists, yanking my hands above my head and dragging me up and off of Leon until I was on my feet.

Gabriel smirked as he cast vines around my ankles next and I was suddenly flipped upside down, the vines coiling around my thighs and shins, tying my legs in a bent position so it was as if I was kneeling upside down, my lilac hair brushing the bloody bedsheets beneath me.

"What are you-" I began but I was cut off as my wrists were bound to my ankles and my knees tugged apart, baring me to all of them.

"Dalle stelle," Dante murmured as he moved to stand before me, running his electrically charged fingertips down the insides of my thighs and making me shiver.

"Do you want us both, little angel?" Gabriel asked as he stood behind me, running his fingertips over my sensitive pussy and making me moan at the kiss of cool water magic he had slicking his skin.

"Yes," I begged as blood ran to my head and made me dizzy. Of course I wanted both of them. I wanted all of them. Always.

Gabriel's fingers pushed into my ass as Dante rubbed the head of his cock over my clit, sliding it back and forth and making my whole body ache for him as the electricity that accompanied his touch set me alight.

Gabriel pumped his fingers as he used his water magic to lubricate my ass and I moaned, wanting him to get on with it so that I could feel them both inside me now.

"Ready?" Gabriel asked me, his other hand squeezing my ass cheek and making the bite Ryder had given me throb.

"Yes," I panted, feeling Leon and Ryder moving in on either side of me again as Gabriel chuckled darkly.

He slid his hard cock between my cheeks then slowly began to push it into my ass.

My breath caught at the feeling of fullness and he groaned as he worked his way deeper, letting me adjust to the strange sensation of being upside down while he began to fuck me.

I tugged on the restraints holding my wrists against my ankles and cursed as I found myself unable to break them even with my gifts. And with my weight suspended from the vines, I had absolutely no control over the movements of my body at all.

Dante groaned as he watched Gabriel thrusting in and out of me, still running his cock over my clit, making my pussy clench and tighten with need.

Leon's fingers dipped inside me as Gabriel began to up his pace, and I moaned as he stroked my inners walls, pressing on that thin divide between my pussy and my ass so that I could feel Gabriel's movements even more intensely.

"Please, Dante," I panted, wanting him inside me. But he only chuckled as he kept rubbing it over my clit.

"I'll fuck you once you come for me, Bella," he said. "I want to push into your sweet pussy while its pulsing and throbbing and you're begging me for it even more forcefully than you are now."

I wanted to demand he do it now but as Gabriel drove his cock in harder, my words caught in my throat and suddenly Ryder's lips found mine as he lay down on the bed beneath us.

I kissed him hard and hungrily, tasting more blood on his mouth and guessing he'd smeared it there just for me. He pushed his tongue between my lips as Dante rocked the head of his cock against my clit even harder, finding the perfect pace with Gabriel as my head spun from the dizziness of being suspended like this.

My orgasm hit me like a freight train and my pussy clamped down on Leon's fingers as I cried out into Ryder's mouth and Gabriel fucked my ass even harder.

True to his word, I felt Dante grasping my thighs, forcing them further apart as he worked with this strange angle and finally drove his cock inside me.

Leon kept his fingers there too and I came again almost instantly as the three of them drove into me in perfect synchronisation.

Ryder found my nipple then tugged hard on it and as I opened my eyes I found him pumping his cock in his fist, the sight so fucking hot that I swear it made my orgasm go on and on even longer.

I was completely at the mercy of my kings as Dante and Gabriel fucked me furiously and before long, Gabriel growled deep and low as he came too.

The moment he drew out, Dante gripped my ass cheeks in a brutal grip and drove his cock into me harder and harder, electricity sparking all over all of us until I was screaming and coming with him for the final time, my body wrung out and heart racing.

Leon's cum spilled over my tits as he finished himself off and one look at Ryder told me he'd finished again too.

Gabriel released me from the vines as Dante pulled out of me, lowering me onto the bed where we all collapsed into a heap of bloody, sweaty limbs, panting and tingling with pleasure, each of us grinning over what we'd just done.

Even Ryder had the hint of a smile playing around his lips.

"You and me are gonna have a lot more fun with blood play, baby," he promised me and my fangs tingled at the mere thought of it even though I was absolutely brimming with power from all I'd drank.

"Stay with me," I said, my words for all of them and meaning forever, not just tonight.

"Always," Leon agreed, reaching out to tuck a lock of bloody, lilac hair behind my ear.

"Sono tuo," Dante murmured, his arm curling tight around me.

"You're the only future I want, Elise," Gabriel promised, his words followed by the kiss of water magic as he washed all of us clean of our sins. But the stains of what we'd all just done would stay branded to my flesh forever, no matter whether the blood and sweat was cleaned away. Which was exactly how I wanted it.

"I'm yours, baby," Ryder muttered, his words low like he only wanted me to hear them and I leaned towards him so that I could press a soft kiss to his lips.

"Good," I said as I lay back in the heart of the four muscular bodies of my kings. "We'll just have to figure out a way to make that happen then."

No one bothered to mention the fact that with the gangs' involvement that was going to be damn near impossible and as I closed my eyes and began to drift off, I hoped that was because they all wanted to find a way just as much as I did.

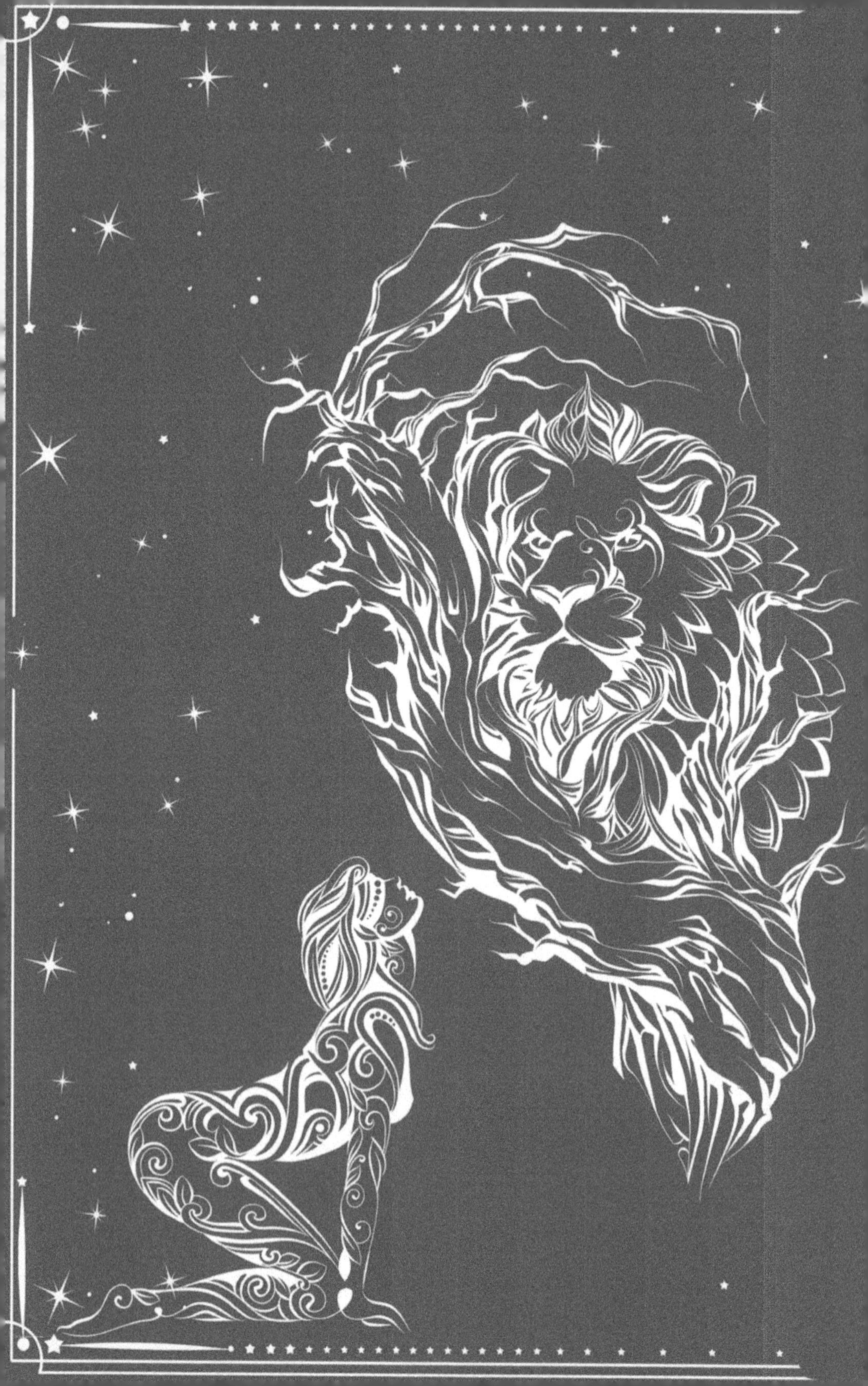

LEON

CHAPTER ELEVEN

*B*est.
Day.
Ever!

I used a waking spell to get me up at dawn and crawled out of the bed full of sleeping bodies. I adjusted my boxers and snatched up my Atlas, snapping a photo of them all where they were curled up with Elise at the middle of the mattress. Gabriel lay behind Ryder with his arm hanging over his hip, his fingers grazing Elise's waist and his crotch pressed to Ryder's ass. *One for the scrapbook.*

I grabbed my Pitball bag from under the bed which had my clothes in it for the trip, unzipping it and pulling out the scrapbook from within the folds of a shirt.

I slipped out of the room and headed to the coffee table in the lounge, sitting on the sofa and flipping the book open before aiming my Atlas at the next blank page. I used my Snapaflap app and a flash went off before the image appeared printed in the book. *Purrrfect.*

"What are you doing Leo? It's not like you to be up so early," Elise's sultry voice fell over me and a hungry growl rumbled through my chest.

She leaned over the back of the couch, laying a kiss beneath my ear. I caught her arm, dragging her onto my lap and nuzzling against her face before claiming a filthy kiss. My tongue moved in time with my mate's and I groaned against her full lips, tasting all of her and fighting the urge to devour her whole. I could totally do that. Just shift into a Lion and eat her up. She'd taste like cherries and starjuice, my fucking favourite flavour in the world.

Our lips broke apart, leaving us breathless as I crushed her against my chest and when she pulled away, I reluctantly let her go. She slid onto the floor between my thighs, folding her legs beneath her and tipping her head right back to look at me.

"Can I see the book?" she asked cutely and I nodded, reaching forward and flipping it open to the first page.

There was a photo of Ryder and Gabriel sitting side by side on the roof at Gabe's apartment, the sun dipping below the horizon in the distance. They hadn't realised I was taking photos. Not at first anyway. I'd taken them for Elise in the times where I had to wait for another mark, another kill. It had kept me semi-sane knowing that the next time I saw her I could show her how her boyfriends had all come together, united for her.

The next page showed Ryder running at me with a snarl on his lips, his hand outstretched for my Atlas. Gabriel was standing up behind him, his wings spread wide and a half smirk on his lips.

"That was just before Ryder punched me in the face," I said wistfully then turned the page to show a photo of Dante and Ryder sitting at opposite ends of Gabriel's dining table in a glare off. The next picture was of me spread out on the table between them, knocking their food flying as I posed for the photo which was set up on a timer on my Atlas. Gabriel was stepping out of the bathroom with a towel around his waist and that same little smirk on his lips as he looked directly at the camera. And something clicked in me as I looked at him, then quickly flipped the page. *Hang the fuck on, Patrice.*

A photo of Ryder standing over a map on Gabriel's kitchen island was next, his finger pointed at some place in the city while Dante shouted at him and electricity daggered toward Ryder. The next photo showed Ryder blasted back against the wall while I did the peace sign at the camera as I smooshed my face up against Dante's. Gabriel was stepping into the kitchen with that very same smirk.

"Oh my stars," I gasped as Elise chuckled.

"What is it?" she asked, turning the page eagerly. "These are hilarious."

"Look at Gabriel," I commanded, pointing to the next photo and the next and the next. Gabriel stood in the back of them all fucking smirking. Which could mean only one thing. "He knows!"

"Knows what?" Elise turned to look back at me with a frown on her brow.

I smoothed it out with my thumb then cupped her chin and grinned cattishly at her. "He knew I was gonna take these photos, but he didn't stop me, little monster. And look at that face." I jammed my finger down on the last smirk of his. "He wants it. He wants us to be boyfriends-in-law or else he'd stop me. But he never has. Not once." I beamed at her and her eyes sparkled, the silver rings in them glittering. Shit, it was so good to see her right here in front of me. It made my heart beat like a drum and my soul flash like a fire in a pan.

I hurriedly flipped over to the last photo I'd taken just a couple of minutes ago of them all in bed and leaned in close to look at Gabriel's face. A ghost of a smirk lay on his lips and I roared a laugh, pointing it out to Elise as I beamed at her. "He. Knoooows."

She grinned at me, climbing back into my lap and nipping at my ear. "Don't tell him, Leo. He'll only deny it."

I winked at her conspiratorially. "Okay. I can keep a secret."

She arched a brow like she didn't believe that and I spanked her ass.

"I can," I impressed and she curled up against my chest again like a little cub, making my heartbeat settle as I felt the weight of her against me. Here. No longer lost. My sweet, deadly little monster.

I rested my cheek against her head as I held her, a deep purr resounding through me as I just soaked in the feel of my Elysian Mate back in my arms. There was no feeling in any kingdom, in any world, in any universe that topped this one. So long as she was here with me, I would never want for anything else.

"No one's ever going to take you from me again," I swore to her, holding her tighter. "I missed you so much, it was like you took my heart with you."

Her palm slid up to rest against the thrumming organ within me which loved her to its core. Her fingers circled over my skin and drew my magic to the edges of my flesh. All of me wanted her, down to the dust of the stars which made up my soul.

"I missed you too," she said, her voice tight with emotion. "It's worse than going without my magic."

I traced my thumbs over the cuff on her right wrist holding down a vital piece of my girl. I swallowed back a growl as I worked out a plan in my mind to free her from these. It was crazy, wild and reckless. Which meant it was definitely going to work.

We stardusted back to Gabriel's apartment before noon and I worked over the plan in my head as Gabriel and Dante started making lunch. Ryder sat with Elise on his lap at the breakfast bar, his mouth running up her neck as he spoke to her in a low tone.

I moved over to join them, perching my ass on the island, serving me a side glare from Ryder.

"We have a thing to do," I announced, taking out my Atlas and bringing up the spell I'd found a few days ago. The fear of losing Elise had made me protective as hell and I wasn't going to be in that situation ever again. "I found a tracking spell that binds Fae to one another. We can do it and I'll never lose you again." I leaned forward to tuck a lock of lilac hair behind her ear and she narrowed her gaze.

"I'm not gonna be kept on a leash at all times, Leo."

"It's not like that. I'll be able to feel where you are, but only when I tap into the magic, little monster. And you'll be able to feel where I am too."

I brushed my fingers down to her neck and she leaned into my touch with a little sigh of content. It made my heart do all kinds of aerobatics and I grinned at her as Ryder's hands tightened on her waist.

"Well, that doesn't sound so bad," she mused, her eyelashes beating like the wings of a butterfly. I wanted to catch those little butterflies and eat them raw, but I resisted the urge.

"I'm doing it too," Ryder announced and Elise turned her head to look back at him.

"We're all doing it," I said with a grin. "Aren't we, little monster?"

She looked at me again, then over my shoulder to Dante and Gabriel and I felt them drawing closer. "Yeah," she agreed. "We can keep each other safe."

"Great," I said excitedly, scooting closer to her. "Everyone get over here and touch Elise skin on skin. Use your hands or lips or dicks, whatever works."

Ryder's hand immediately slid under her pink cami as I threaded my fingers between hers. Dante and Gabriel came to stand on either side of her, placing their hands on her shoulders. I pushed my magic out towards her and shut my eyes as I focused on the spell. "Everyone let your magic flow toward mine. You can feel it in Elise, really deep in her. Can you feel me inside her?"

"Dalle stelle, do you have to say it like that?" Dante breathed as Ryder grunted.

"What's wrong with how I'm saying it?" I asked tauntingly. "I'm just making it clear that you can feel my power really deep and now I'm reaching it out to you all. Can you feel it burying itself in you? Can you feel the tip of it pushing in?"

"For the love of the moon, Leon," Gabriel snapped. "We can all feel it."

I chuckled mockingly then concentrated on the spell again, loving feeling this close to all of my Lionesses. We made such a good pride.

The magic blazed between us and I felt my soul connecting to each of theirs, making us all gasp as it ran through our veins like magma. It slowly faded away as the spell settled in and a growl of relief left me as the magic faded. None of my Lionesses would ever be lost again.

"What the fuck, Mufasa?" Ryder blurted. "I don't just feel Elise, I can feel you standing right there as well as the rest of you assholes."

"Leone," Dante growled in warning and my eyes flicked to Gabriel who was suspiciously quiet. *Yes.* He knew this would happen. He was my secret best friend.

Elise stifled a laugh as I jumped off the table and hooked her out of Ryder's lap.

"Whoops," I said dramatically, tugging a pouch of stardust free of my back pocket. "Oh well, guess we're all soul brothers now – bye!" I tossed the stardust over me and Elise, a raging Storm Dragon and Basilisk diving at me as we disappeared into the stars.

Elise's laughter rang in my ears and I felt her essence twisting around me as we were carried through a wheel of galaxies. My feet hit the ground and my boot caught on something, making me stumble forward. Elise grabbed the back of my shirt, hauling me upright and I looked down at the root sticking up from the ground with narrowed eyes.

"Thanks, sugar puff." I turned to her, pulling her against me for a kiss, but her head was turned away as she took in where we were.

"Why are we here?" she asked in surprise as my lips met her cheek and I made out with it anyway. "Leo," she laughed, shoving me off and I smirked.

I linked my fingers between hers as I turned, squinting against the bright sun as it soaked into my soul and made my magic reserves swell. The huge fence ringing Darkmore Penitentiary cast us in criss-crossing shadows and my heart started to sink as I thought of my brother locked up in its depths. I hadn't given up working on getting him out, but there wasn't much hope. Lionel Acrux had the best lawyers at his disposal and apart from that, he was a fucking Celestial Councillor, he made the damn laws. If he wanted Roary stuck in Darkmore for the rest of his life, he could figure out a way to ensure it. Roary had said it was probably a damn blessing he'd only gotten twenty five years, but screw that. He didn't deserve to spend a single day in this hell, let alone a huge chunk of his youth.

Rosa had asked about him constantly, messaging me with links to lawyers she thought might be able to help and begging me to find a way to bring her here to see him. But Darkmore didn't let anyone underage visit the inmates, and even if I could have found a way to sneak her in, Roary had said himself he didn't want her to see him behind bars as a failure – his words, not mine. According to him and my dad, he'd brought shame on the family and now he was no longer a part of the pride. But I was never gonna cut out my brother, even if that was the 'Lion way' as Dad put it. I'd already spent too many years resenting and envying Roary, I wasn't gonna waste any more time being an asshole to him. He needed me now more than ever and I'd be here fighting for his freedom no matter what.

I gave Elise my leather jacket and tugged down the sleeves as she put it on, making sure the magic blocking cuffs were concealed fully then she inhaled a sharp breath.

"You can't get a key for them from here," she hissed in realisation of my plan. "If you steal from a guard in this place you'll be caught on camera and-"

"I won't steal it." I smirked at her, pushing a hand into my golden mane. "I'm the most charming Fae in Solaria, little monster. Just let your mate provide for you."

She arched a questioning brow, but I just turned away and towed her along behind me toward the main gate. I explained to the guards that we were here for visitation and we were soon driven up into the compound, passing through a second fence ringing the entranceway to the prison. It was all underground except for a huge dome which towered up above us. Inside was a large expanse of magical habitats from tundra, to forest, to baking hot desert, everything each Order needed. At least for the short amount of time the inmates were allowed access to it anyway. My gut clenched at the thought of Roary only getting a few short hours every couple of days to shift into his Lion form in there. It must have been excruciating going without it for so long, being restricted with the Order Suppressant they pumped into the lower levels of the prison must have been hell. I'd seen the darkness creeping into his eyes just a few days after he'd been incarcerated. If he spent the next twenty-five years in there, surely it was going to destroy him. And I couldn't bear the thought of it.

We headed into a stone outbuilding and passed through a high-tech security barrier before we were allowed into the elevator to descend into the complex. My heart beat harder as we sailed down within the large metal cube with its dark grey walls and air of doom. I hated this place. I hated it for Roary. And with each passing day, I feared that he really wasn't going to get out of here.

Elise ran her thumb up and down along the back of my hand as a growl rumbled through my chest.

"I already despise this place and I haven't even stepped out of this elevator," Elise said in a low tone. I glanced at her, finding her chewing on her lower lip. She looked tired and desperate and I knew it was because she couldn't reach her magic. My little monster was in pain and I wouldn't be leaving here until she was relieved of it.

The doors slid smoothly open and we stepped out into a waiting room where a guard with thick red hair sat with his arms folded behind a desk. There were a few other Fae sat around with glum expressions, but I didn't lead Elise over to join them, I guided her straight up to the guard.

"Hey there, I'm booked in to see Roary Night today," I told him and he nodded, checking a list on his Atlas.

"Yep, I've got you down," he said with a warm smile. "Take a seat, I'll call you when it's time."

"Sure, sure...can I have a word though first?" I asked with my most charming grin, loosening my grip on my Charisma and letting it come out to play.

His eyes lifted to meet mine and the second I had him in my gaze, I could see his allure to me growing. I couldn't go gung-ho on the Charisma in here, but if I was subtle about it, he probably wouldn't even notice my influence.

"What's the problem?" he asked as my eyes dipped down to his badge to read his name.

"Officer Lyle," I purred and he smiled, a blush rising in his cheeks. Bingo. "Can I put a silencing bubble up?"

"Oh, no sorry I can't allow that for security reasons," he replied and I nodded, feeling Elise's curious, pretty eyes on me.

"Well, it's just I'm in a bit of a situation," I began, leaning in closer but not really bothering to lower my voice. He'd had a chance for a silencing bubble and now he'd made his bed. I lifted Elise's hand which was locked with mine and yanked her sleeve up to show Lyle the cuff on her wrist.

"Leo," she gasped, trying to pull her hand free but I held on tight as Lyle's eyes widened to two perfect circles.

"Goodness, what on earth are you doing wearing those, ma'am?" he spluttered.

"Well um-" she started, but I cut over her, my story already constructed and ready to go.

"I paid way too much money for these from a buddy. I know, I know, I'm not supposed to be able to buy these things, but he promised they'd spice up our sex lives and I'm a man who follows his cock, if you know what I mean?" I asked, mutters breaking out behind me in the waiting room as Lyle turned beet red.

"Oh, I see," he gasped. "Well, er, why are you showing them to me, sir?"

"Well the thing is, I got a little too excited when I put them on her and tied her to my bed last night. My girl was just lying there, naked, with no magic, completely at my mercy, legs spread wiiiiide." I wiggled my eyebrows and the guy flushed somehow even redder.

"We're experimental like that," Elise chipped in in a husky voice that made my cock twitch with the fantasy. Fuck, why hadn't I actually taken advantage of these cuffs while I had the chance? "Leon likes to see how far he can push me, but he doesn't realise I don't have any limits."

"She really doesn't," I laughed, reaching out to clap Lyle on the shoulder and he blinked hard, his gaze flitting to Elise then back to me. "Anyway, she fought like a wild thing when I was trying to get them on her – she really commits when we roleplay – and once I got them in place, I thought it would be a great idea to swallow the key so she couldn't escape."

"Oh no," Lyle breathed.

"Yeah, that's what I said after he'd fucked me every colour of the rainbow," Elise said with a light laugh, slapping my arm. "Didn't I, baby?"

"Yeah, and then you asked why my ten inch cock wasn't in your mouth and we did that thing with the Basilisk vibrator until you almost choked out."

"Well you know what I always say," she said lightly, beaming at Lyle. "You can't use a safe word with a cock that far down your throat."

"She does always say that – not while my cock's down her throat though, obviously," I chuckled while Lyle seemed to shrink from a grape into a raisin in his chair. "Anyways, I thought I could just do a little digestion spell or two to speed up the process of dumpsday, but I got distracted when the moment finally came-"

"He loves watching cartoons on his Atlas while he's on the pooper, don't you baby?"

"Yeah," I said guiltily, shrugging one shoulder. "I forgot all about the damn key and flushed it right away!"

"Oh dear," Lyle breathed as horrified silence started to reign behind me, the muttering gone cold.

"He's quite forgetful, but I love him anyway," Elise said with a grin. "But obviously this time it's caused us quite an issue."

"It has indeed. So we'd love to be discreet about this and just grab a little key from you and pop off those bad boys, if you don't mind?" I asked.

"Discreet…yes," he mumbled, glancing past me to the waiting room full of people who'd just heard every colourful word of that story. "It's not really protocol though, I should really call the Warden."

"Sure go ahead, I'll tell her the story myself," I said and he scrambled for words for a moment as he took the radio from his hip then promptly put it back.

"Actually, I'd better not bother her. Here, I'll take them off for you, ma'am. I just need to do a quick security check first in case you're an escaped inmate." He laughed at his joke and I guessed it was kind of funny. No one got out of Darkmore. Ever. You couldn't escape this fortress, it was designed with magic and monsters and all kinds of crazy shit to keep dangerous psychos housed in its belly. I knew that well enough considering I'd already looked into breaking in and rescuing my brother. By the looks of it, I'd be dead before I even dug one foot into the earth up on the surface. Even that fancy door-to-anywhere spell of Gabriel's wouldn't work here. There were special measures in place to block dark magic just like everything else. It was fucking hopeless.

Lyle reached into his pocket, taking out a scanner and holding it up to Elise's face, lines of magical light running over her skin for a moment before it beeped.

"Good," he said then produced a triangular cuff key and I fought the urge to grin like a madman as Elise offered him her wrists and he unlocked them. She moaned her relief, a storm of air immediately whipping around her as she wielded her Element and I bathed in the power of my girl as I nuzzled her hair.

"I'll have to keep these, they're valuable property," Lyle said and I nodded, waving a hand for him to take them and he slid the cuffs into a drawer in his desk.

I turned to look at the shocked faces in the waiting room, while one beast of a man gazed lustfully at Elise and I gave him a death glare which made him promptly look down at his hairy knuckles.

We didn't have to wait long before Lyle told us to head through another security door with some flashy spells that hummed over our flesh. Then we headed along the corridor to see Roary and Elise continually made little tornados in her hands as we walked, her eyes alight with happiness. That look was what I wanted her to have every day of her existence. My little monster never deserved to frown, especially after all the shit she'd been through over Gareth's death and her butt plug of a mother.

We were directed to the third door along the hallway and I pushed it open, finding it empty as we moved inside. We barely got two steps before the door on the opposite side of the room opened and Roary entered wearing an orange jumpsuit with a Lion symbol on his breast beside the water Elemental symbol. I ran at him, crushing him in my arms and he squeezed me back with a breath of relief.

"Hey, little Leonidas," he growled as I released him, stepping back to take him in. His hair was a fucking mess and his stubble was getting to the point of a beard.

"Holy shit, Roary, our moms would kill you if they saw you looking like this. And what would Dad think of your mane?"

Roary ground his jaw. "Doesn't matter, I'm not a part of the pride anymore according to him."

Pain flashed through me at those words and I shook my head in refusal of them. "We'll get you out of here and he'll get over his bullshit. We stole from Lionel Acrux, it was the best heist of our lives. How can Dad stay mad at that forever?"

"The best heist of *your* life," he corrected, bowing his head a little in shame. "Nights don't get caught, Leon."

"It wasn't your fault," Elise said sadly as she stepped closer and wrapped her arms around Roary in a firm hug. He held onto her almost as long as he'd held onto me and I got the feeling he was starved of company in this place.

"It was entirely my fault," Roary sighed.

"You saved Rosa," I bit out. "She told me exactly what you did for her and she feels guilty as hell."

Roary's brows pulled together at that. "She has nothing to feel guilty for."

"I know, but she doesn't see it that way. She's killing herself over what happened. And after what Felix did to her…"

Roary growled deeply, his eyes burning holes in my head. I'd told him all I knew on the matter and I could see the pain it caused him having saved her from one fate only to find out she'd faced a far worse one. Sometimes I reckoned he blamed himself for that too, like if he'd been out there, he could have protected her. But shit happened, and he wasn't her Ward. I just hoped he didn't beat himself up over it forever, because being in this place was enough punishment without him torturing himself too.

We took seats opposite him at the small table in the centre of the room and I started telling him all about our rescue mission for Elise as if it was a book I was writing. We'd come up with the plan so I could fill him in on all the illegal shit I got up to on the regular without me incriminating myself or having to hide anything from him, all of our names changed in the story but I gave enough hints so he knew who I was talking about. His features lightened as I put on a show and embellished the story wherever I could to give him the best distraction as possible. But when it was time for us to leave, he headed back through the door into Darkmore with his head hanging low and my heart hurt at having to part from him.

"Don't worry, Leo," Elise said gently as we headed back out of the room and pain splintered through my chest. "We'll find a way to get him out."

I nodded, but it seemed so hopeless right then that it felt like a dark cloud was descending on my brother's fate. And nothing I did could save him.

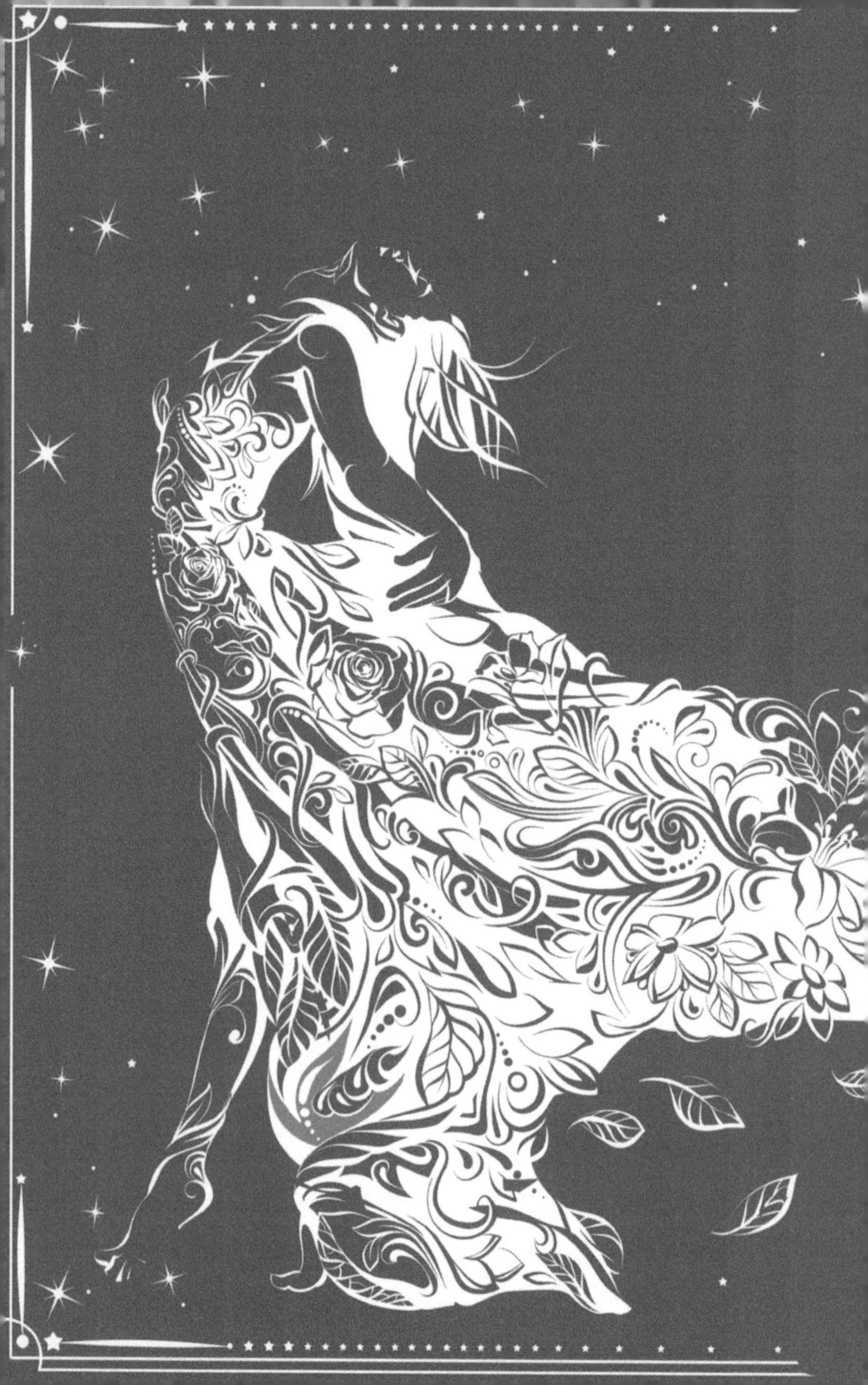

ELISE

CHAPTER TWELVE

Walking back through the gates of Aurora Academy with Leon and Dante flanking me felt kinda like walking towards my own execution. I knew we couldn't just hide out in Gabriel's apartment forever and I knew that if I chose to hide like that it would only seem like we were afraid of King, but my skin still prickled as I stepped onto the grounds.

I couldn't help but glance up, my gifted eyesight allowing me to see Gabriel high above me as he swooped across the sun, little more than a speck of darkness to anyone else. Ryder was with him, shifted into a tiny snake which was riding in his pocket so that they could both keep watch. It was the cutest freaking thing – not that I could say that to Ryder of course.

I hated that we couldn't all be together while we were here. I hated that I had to pretend I was only with Leon while the others stayed in the shadows, hiding what we were to each other. Though now that Gabriel's cover in the Black Card had been blown, I was planning on outing him at least. Not that he'd agreed to that because he was still worried about his mystery enemies, but I was done playing pretend.

He'd used the ring he'd found in the caves to burn the last remaining bonds between him and King away now though. There was no point in him staying linked to them and none of us wanted him to still have a connection to that monster.

"It'll be fine, bella," Dante murmured, the electric touch of his power caressing my skin as he walked beside me.

Leon gave my shoulders a squeeze as he tugged me closer to him, the solid weight of his arm around me making me feel protected, cherished.

We'd left it as late as possible to return, turning up just as breakfast was about to end so that we could head straight for class first thing and avoid too many awkward questions. As far as the academy was aware, me and Leon had gone on a slightly belated mating-moon vacation following the fight that took place here almost a month ago.

The academy had been closed for a week while the FIB carried out their investigations into what had gone on anyway and I knew that Dante had had to give them an interview. Luckily, it wasn't exactly like the FIB could blame the students at the school for fighting back when Felix and his pack of psychotic mutts had attacked, so none of the students had been charged. And as Felix and everyone he'd brought with him had been killed, the investigation had been closed, funerals had been held and now it was back to class as usual. Just another bloody day of carnage to add to the history books for Alestria.

Leon's dad had smoothed over the issue of mine and Leon's absence with this vacation crap, and I'd been given a fancy brochure and some random facts about an island retreat off the coast of Larulia where we'd supposedly been. Leon always had a tan anyway and I was never going to achieve his sun kissed glow regardless, so I was going to hope no one questioned me too much on the fact that I wasn't showing many signs of having been abroad.

Gabriel had faked some emergency as an excuse for his absence and Dante had blackmailed Greyshine into telling everyone that he'd given the gang leaders some extra time out of school to let the dust settle after the fight.

All in all, we were covered. The only thing I had to worry about was the mystery madman or woman who had their eye on me and wanted to lock me up again to be their own personal blood supplier. Hence my bodyguards.

I was no longer allowed to go anywhere without one of my kings and I'd promised to keep an air shield permanently in place over my skin to make sure I was protected from surprise attacks. That coupled with Gabriel keeping a close eye on my future and the fact that the guys hadn't even come close to managing to convince me to stay away was what had led me back here.

I chewed on my cherry gum as I remembered taking this exact route on my first day and the lazy, sexy Nemean Lion Shifter who had turned up to show me around, left out half of the important facts and had tried to make me his Mindy.

I leaned into Leon then grasped his nipple through his shirt and twisted.

"Ow!" he yelled, slapping my hand away. "Why?"

"That's for trying to make me a Mindy when we first met," I said, flashing him a grin as he frowned. He was so damn tense over us coming back here and I wanted to break through his moody mask and find my laughing Lion beneath it again.

Leon cracked a smile and drew me closer so that he could press a kiss to the top of my head.

"You can't blame me for wanting to have you under my thrall, little monster," he said. "I knew the wolves would descend and try to claim you the moment they laid eyes on you."

"And now look," Dante teased. "You ended up being the one to enthral all of us instead. If anyone got themselves a pack of Mindys, it was you, bella."

"I'm good with that," I assured him.

Dante stepped forward to pull open the door to Altair Halls, holding it wide for me and Leon to step through and Leon smirked at me.

"What's that look for?" I asked him, narrowing my eyes as I got the feeling he was up to something.

"I was just thinking what a great Lioness Dante makes," he teased, looking back over his shoulder with a taunting smirk for the Storm Dragon who promptly zapped him in the ass with a bolt of electricity.

Leon yowled like a cat and leapt half a foot into the air and I laughed as Dante dove on him, skipping aside as they began to wrestle. It was pretty fucking hot when they got into it like that. I wondered if they'd consider doing it for me on command. Shirtless. And oiled up.

I filed that little idea away for later with a grin.

The door swung open behind the two of them as Dante managed to straddle Leon and Gabriel strode in, shirtless with his wings in the process of fading away.

I blatantly checked him out as he glanced around before smirking at me, reminding me of the way he looked when he was about to do something wickedly sinful, and I found myself wishing he would.

"Hi, Gabriel," I said all innocently, like we were casual friends and he hadn't pinned me to the wall of the shower this morning and made me scream so loud that my throat still felt hoarse from it. I could have healed that shit of course, but what could I say? I liked the reminder.

He looked around to make sure there wasn't anyone else nearby even though I'd already used my gifts to check, then smiled in return as he pulled his shirt on.

"Nice to see you, Elise." Neither of us said anything about the two idiots who were still wrestling on the ground and he moved a little closer as he began to button his shirt.

I flicked my fingers to cast a silencing bubble around us and he cocked his head, clearly worried I was going to say something important.

"Is that a snake in your pocket?" I began, biting back a laugh as an angry little snake head poked out of Gabriel's pants pocket and hissed his hatred at this joke which I would never get tired of. "Or are you just pleased to-"

The mini snake lunged out of Gabriel's pocket and sank its little fangs into my finger, making me curse and laugh at the same time before it fell from my hand and slithered towards the door to the men's room on our left. He hadn't used his venom though, so I guessed he wasn't *that* pissed.

Gabriel laughed too, following Ryder and opening the door for him before tossing a bag into the bathroom behind him which I guessed was filled with the Basilisk's clothes.

"Catch you later, Elise," Gabriel said, striding away and leaving me to disband the silencing bubble as he headed to class ahead of us.

I could still hear plenty of students milling about the corridors further into the building so we weren't late yet, but it was quiet where we stood by the external doors.

"See you in class boys," I called, walking away from Dante and Leon as the sound of ripping material filled the air and I glanced back to see Leon's pants half hanging from one leg, leaving his thick thigh and boxers on show.

"Dammit, Dante!" he barked though he was laughing too. "Now what am I supposed to do?"

"You'll have to go get a fresh pair of pants from our dorm," I said, grinning widely.

"Ughhh, *no*," Leon groaned. "That's way too far. I'll get a Mindy to do it."

"You can't come to class like that," I pointed out as Dante boomed a laugh. "Just go. You're my mate now, everyone will associate me with your ass hanging out if you turn up looking like that."

Leon's eyes flashed with mischief at that comment and I shrieked as he lunged at me. I tried to shoot away from him with my speed but a flash of fire burst into existence in front of me and I skidded to a halt a moment before I could set myself alight.

Leon's strong arms latched around me and he threw me over his shoulder, making me squeal.

"Come on, little monster, I'm going to show you exactly what it's like to be embarrassed by me. If you thought me walking around with my ass hanging out was bad, then wait until I carry you into every class like you're a sack of sexy potatoes."

I called out for Dante to help me, but he only teased me in Faetalian as he followed along behind us, dusting off his uniform as he walked and healing away a bruise that had started to form along his jaw.

I kicked and wriggled as Leon carried me to our Potions Class, half trying to fight my way free and half dying of laughter every time I caught sight of his ass hanging out the back of his pants.

The corridors were near empty as we went and by the time Leon shoved the door to the Potions lab open most of the students were already seated.

Leon flipped me the right way up and set me on my feet by the door as plenty of people sniggered at us. I pouted at him as he tossed me a wink and strode towards his desk.

A series of chairs were flung back as I felt a tide of Leon's Charisma washing over me and a cat fight ensued as every Mindy in the room tried to fight their way to the door first.

"I will get you the best pants you ever wore, Leon!"

"I'll cut all of my hair off and braid it into a pair of pants for you!"

"I'll kill every bitch in my way and then skin them for their pelts to make your pants!" Erica shrieked, punching another Mindy hard enough to knock her out cold before vaulting a desk and diving out the door.

The rest of the Mindys tore after her, screaming insults mixed with promises to find Leon the best pants ever seen in all of Solaria and the class fell into shocked silence as the sound of their fighting faded away.

Leon took an exaggerated bow as Eugene Dipper began to clap and I laughed along with the others as he took his seat, not giving a single shit about his shredded pants as he spread his legs wide and leaned back in his chair.

I however had no intention of letting any other bitch in this room get an eyeful of my man's junk, so I cast a concealment spell at him from my position across the room, covering his lower half in shadow.

Leon smirked knowingly at me and I shrugged innocently in reply.

"Elise?" Professor Titan breathed, drawing my attention and I turned to find him standing behind his desk, staring at me like he'd seen a ghost.

Before I was entirely sure what was happening, he strode towards me and pulled me into a hug. I kinda froze where I was for a few seconds before awkwardly patting him on the arm and he released me again suddenly.

"Sorry," he muttered. "I just heard a rumour that you were missing. That something might have happened to you in the battle and I've been so worried-"

"She's just been off sunbathing with her Leone," Dante called from his seat, laughing off Titan's fears and I nodded my agreement as I scrambled to remember the details of our cover story.

"Yeah, um, Leon's moms and dad felt it would be best for us to take a few weeks out following the chaos here to celebrate our mating," I explained, rattling off our rehearsed bullshit. "So I'm totally fine. Not sure where you heard that rumour, but maybe someone was confused or-"

"I'm just so relieved to find it isn't true," Titan said, reaching out to squeeze my arm, his eyes brimming with emotion and I remembered him saying something to me before about losing a daughter.

Had he really been that concerned for me? I doubted my own mother had even realised I'd been missing, let alone cared. And if I was totally honest, I hadn't really thought many people would besides my kings. But here he was, giving me a look that said he actually had been worried about me and I was getting all the warm fuzzies in my chest.

"Thanks," I said a little awkwardly, giving him a genuine smile before turning and heading to my desk.

Ryder strode into the room just as I sat down, his gaze locking on me as he stalked closer.

I could feel Bryce watching us, knowing he'd have a sneer on his face without even having to look his way.

"Hey Elise!" Eugene squeaked as he plopped down into Ryder's chair, throwing his arms around me and giving me my second unexpected hug of the day.

"Hey, man," I said as I untangled myself from him, noticing the way he tipped his head to the side and exposed his neck to me like he thought he might tempt me in. "How have you-"

"Move," Ryder snarled as he reached us, his imposing figure casting a shadow over Eugene and making him straighten in his chair.

"Actually, I thought that I should pair with Elise for a while," Eugene said, raising his chin and looking up at Ryder. I was fairly certain his gaze had only made it to somewhere in the region of the Basilisk's jaw, but I was still pretty impressed that he'd managed that much. "She's missed quite a few classes and I can help her catch up on what-"

A vine shot out of nowhere and wrapped itself around Eugene's chest, heaving him out of the seat beside me and into the air.

Eugene squeaked in surprise then threw his arms out, magic making the floor rattle as he tried to fight back.

"Ryder," I warned, seeing the violence flashing in his eyes and making it clear I would be pissed if he hurt my friend.

Ryder rolled his eyes then flicked his fingers, wrapping Eugene in so many vines that he looked like a caterpillar inside a cocoon. With his arms trapped like that there was no way he could fight back, and Ryder promptly deposited him across the room in his usual seat before dropping down to sit beside me.

Bryce began laughing loudly before flicking his fingers at the cocoon that held Eugene and surrounding it with a bubble of water magic.

I gasped as Eugene began to thrash violently within the cocoon, clearly in danger of drowning in there. But before Titan could put a stop to the insanity or I could even think about shooting across the room to help him, Bryce let out a scream of agony and the water magic splashed to the ground in a wave that swept between seats and took out school bags.

"Did I ask you to get involved in my fight?" Ryder demanded in a deadly quiet voice as the vines fell away from Eugene too and I spotted a wooden dagger which had impaled Bryce's hand, fixing it to the desk in front of him.

"It was just meant to be a laugh," Bryce hissed, his face pale from the pain as Eugene coughed and glanced around in fright.

But as I looked closer at my friend, I realised there was more than that to the look in his eyes. He was pissed. And as he took in the scene, I saw the moment when he realised who had just tried to drown him.

"Are you two fighting?" Eugene demanded loudly, pointing between Bryce and Ryder and Ryder scoffed dismissively.

"Not worth my time," he muttered, making Bryce blanch.

Eugene didn't need any further encouragement though because he leapt out of his seat with a roar and before Bryce could do anything to shield himself, a heap of dirt poured down on his head. The soil forced its way into his mouth and choked him as the rest of the class squealed and leapt out of the way.

The pile of dirt kept growing and growing and Bryce didn't appear from within it, the only sign he was still in there a patch of water that started to leak through the side of the mound.

The seconds ticked by and when it was clear Bryce wasn't about to leap out of there, Eugene roared his victory to the ceiling, ripped his shirt open, sending buttons flying everywhere and ran out of the class whooping and cheering. I was guessing he was off to do a victory lap and a stunned silence fell over the class as the door slowly swung closed behind him.

"Err, Mr Nox, would you be able to assist us in removing the soil and water from the room?" Titan asked eventually and suddenly the class burst into conversation all at once, some laughing, some gasping, I even heard a girl saying how hot Eugene was and I couldn't help but grin as Gabriel removed the mound of soil from a near-dead looking Bryce Corvus.

His friend Russel leaned forward to heal him as Gabriel pulled the dirt up out of his lungs and Professor Titan sent him to go see the nurse to make sure there weren't any stones lingering in his stomach.

Bryce shot a poisonous look back over his shoulder at Ryder as he stumbled from the room and the King of the Lunar Brotherhood just gazed back impassively.

I subtly cast a silencing bubble around us and glanced at Ryder. "Should we be worried about him?" I breathed.

"Bruce? *Please*. He's nothing more than a pain in my ass. But if he keeps pushing me, I might end up putting a blade in his heart just to shut him up."

My lips parted on some follow up to that conversation, but Ryder's fingers landed on my thigh beneath the desk and slipped beneath the hem of my skirt.

"If you make a joke about me being Big Bird's trouser snake one more time, I'm going to have to punish you, Elise," he murmured.

"That's hardly a discouragement," I replied, tipping my thigh towards him and letting him skate his fingers higher.

He pinched me and I gasped as I snapped my legs closed, locking his hand between them and hissing at him like a cat.

"Are you sure Bryce isn't a problem?" I pressed because despite his insistence, I wasn't convinced.

When I'd first come to this school there was no way Bryce would have looked at Ryder the way he just had, and I didn't like the edge of venom in his gaze. No, he wasn't a match for the Lunar King, but dissent amongst his followers couldn't be a good thing.

"You let me worry about the Brotherhood, baby," Ryder said. "All rabid dogs need a firm hand to keep them in line. That's all."

There was a glint of something in his eyes that said that wasn't all, but this really wasn't the place to push him on it.

My Atlas flashed, drawing my attention to it on the desk and Ryder took his hand off of my leg as I picked it up to read the message.

Principal Greyshine:
Good-mornaroo, Miss Callisto. I would like to offer you the chance to have a chin wag about the classes you missed during your vay-cay and to make sure you're all good in the hood to keep up. Please come to my office alone, NOW. Principal G.

I arched a brow as I read the message over and let Ryder take a look too.

"You're not going anywhere alone," he said in a stern voice.

"I got the memo," I assured him. Though a rebellious little part of me was already itching to run from my watch dogs and laugh while they chased me around campus.

My Atlas was suddenly plucked from my hands and I looked up to find Gabriel standing over me, looking all gorgeous and shit. I really was one lucky bitch.

"Dante can deal with this," he said in that I-know-everything voice he liked to use when he'd *seen* something.

"So I don't have to go?" I confirmed in surprise and he just smiled all mysteriously before walking away and handing my Atlas to Dante.

Dante read the message over then tossed me a wink just as Greyshine's announcement started up over the tannoy. I watched my Storm Dragon as he casually leaned back in his chair with his Atlas pressed to his ear without so much as a glance at Titan behind his desk.

"Good day fine Fae and cool kids!" Greyshine's voice boomed out. "Just a few quick announceroos this morning. There have been several complaints about the new mural of a rather large Dragon fornicating with a surprised looking Pegasus that appeared on the side of Altair halls last week. I am pleased to say that we have now managed to remove most of it and have grown a patch of ivy over the Dragon's dongle which proved to have been spelled to stick longer than all other parts of its anatomy. In other news, there are even more Pop Tarts now available in the Cafaeteria at breakfast times and this week marks an entire month since someone died on campus grounds. Let's keep up the good work! I'm also proud to announce that-"

The sound of an Atlas ringing in the background wherever Greyshine was interrupted him and he paused for a long moment before continuing.

"There - er - have been some. Umm... I ah, should get that actually, kids. So, catch you on the flop." Greyshine cut the announcement off abruptly and whispers broke out amongst the students.

A sharp whistle caught my attention and I turned in my seat to look at Dante, finding him smirking at me as he beckoned me closer. I shot out of my seat and hopped up to perch on the desk in front of him in less than a second, slipping inside a silencing bubble he'd created around himself and pointedly ignoring Cindy Poo as she scowled at me from her seat. No doubt she'd been hoping I wasn't coming back. But boohoo for her, there was no getting rid of me.

Dante pointed to the Atlas which was still pressed to his ear and I trained my heightened sense of hearing on the sound of ringing coming from it just before the call connected.

"Er, um, hello?" Greyshine's voice came down the line.

"Elise Callisto isn't coming to your little meeting, Randal," Dante said in a casual as fuck tone, his accent sliding over the words the same way his eyes slid over me.

"Oh, erm. Well, I just wanted a quick word with her about-"

"Are you deaf, Randal? Or did I fail to make myself clear?" the slightest hint of a Dragon growl coated Dante's words that time and a shiver ran down my spine.

"N-no. Nope. Okey dokey. No worries, I'll just-"

Dante cut the call and handed me my Atlas. "You owe me a favour now, carina," he said in a low tone.

"I can think of worse positions to be in," I replied, tossing him a salute before shooting back to my chair with my Atlas in hand.

Ryder let out an irritated breath but that was about as far as his frustration over my relationship with Dante seemed to be going at the moment, so I was taking it as a win.

"So," Titan called over the mutters of the students. "Who's ready to brew a balm of everburn?"

I felt so out of sorts with my education that I had absolutely no idea what that was, but the moment we started working on it and Ryder took control of teaching me, I fell into the rhythm of the work. It might have felt strange to be back at the academy after what I'd been through at the hands of King, but I was still certain that this was the best place I could be if I wanted to get the answers I craved over Gareth's death.

So I settled into my work while in the back of my mind I was thinking about my brother and trying to spot some more clues which I may have left behind. Because now that King was growing in power, I knew we were running out of time to stop them and to unravel this mystery, but I was determined to get to the bottom of it soon.

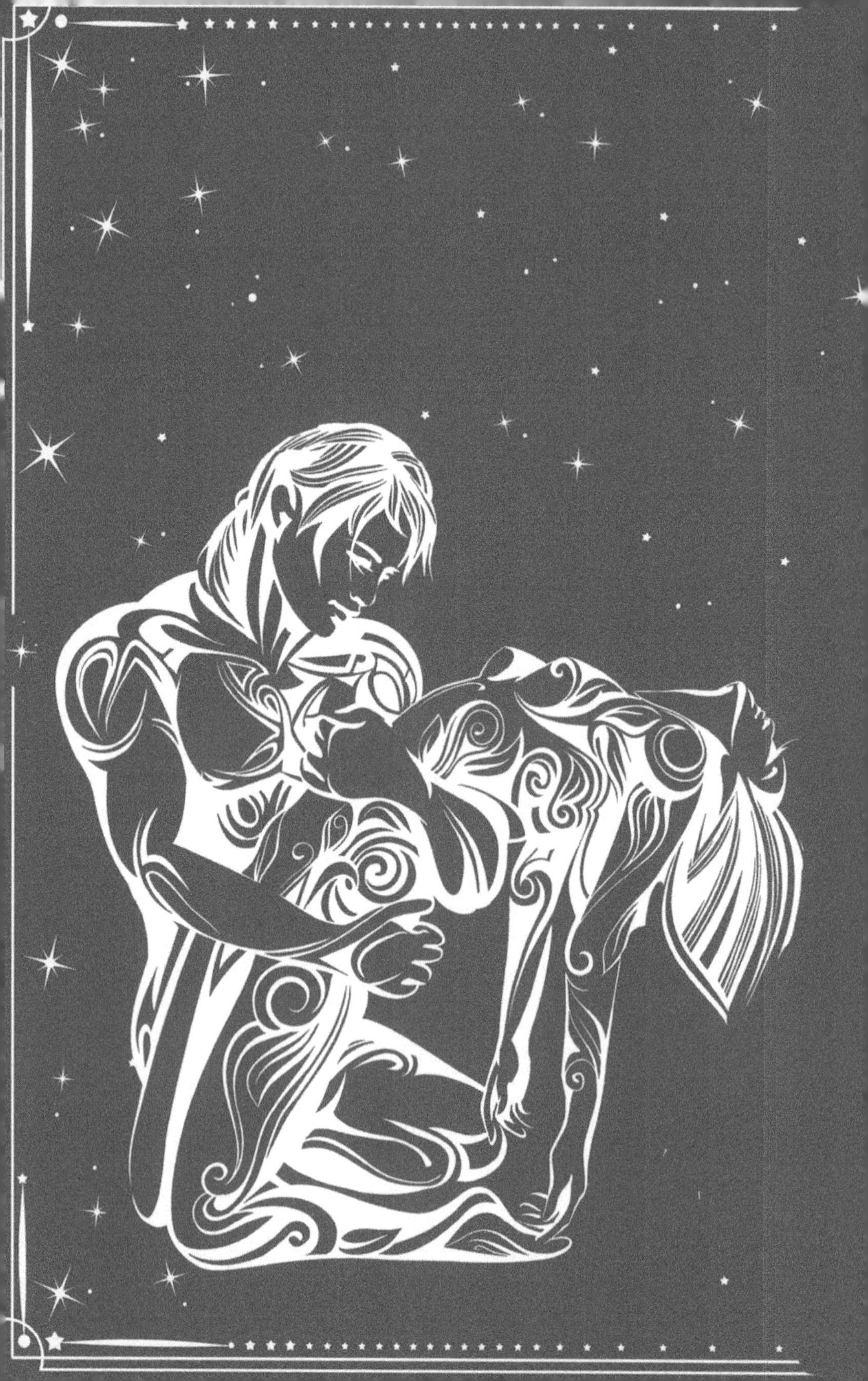

Ryder

CHAPTER THIRTEEN

I dreamed of Elise, her silky soft hands on my flesh, tracing my scars and panting my name in my ear. It was so real, I swore I could feel her fingers brushing along my throat and onto my naked chest as I moved toward consciousness. My eyes cracked open and the hand on my chest remained there.

"Snuck out of the Lion's bed for some real fun, did you baby?" I reached for the shadowy figure beside my bed, my hand curling around her arm, but I jerked violently upright as my fingers tightened over bulging muscle.

I cast a Faelight, about to attack, when my eyes locked with Gabriel's as he gave me a guilty look and cleared his throat.

"Why the fuck were you touching me like that?" I balked, wondering if I should have given him access to my room if this was what he planned to do with that liberty.

"Because I had to wake you up and The Sight showed you trying to kill me if I woke you any other way. And it was around fifty-fifty odds of me dying in that attack, so here we are." He shrugged and a low laugh escaped me.

"I would have killed you so good," I agreed, pushing out of bed and knocking the comforter onto the floor. "What's going on?" I looked at the clock on the wall, it was nearly four am, so my alarm would be going off soon to wake me for my workout. I took out my Atlas and switched it off.

"I had a vision," Gabriel said, his brow dipping in concern. "King has sent an assassin to kill me now that they've realised I was a traitor in their ranks, but I can't *see* many of the details. I have a location and the urge to talk to Eugene Dipper, but that's it right now."

"Shit," I breathed. "What's the rat got to do with it?"

"I think he might have some information, it's hard to say…" His eyes glazed for a moment then he snapped out of it and straightened his spine. "Get dressed. We've gotta go."

"What did you *see*?" I pressed as I cracked my neck. "Was it the rat? Do we need to kill him? I'll bring some rat poison." I took a step toward my supplies, but Big Bird caught my arm.

"No, just get dressed," he demanded and I grabbed some sweatpants instead, pulling them on with a shirt before kicking on my sneakers.

My slow heartbeat quickened with the lust for the kill, and I silently followed Gabriel out the window before we started climbing the fire escape to the top floor. He opened the window to his dorm, creeping inside and as I followed, he flicked up a silencing bubble around me like he knew I couldn't be as stealthy as him. *Asshole.*

He approached the bed where Eugene was curled up in a nest of chewed pieces of socks, underwear, and a Zodiass Weekly magazine. Gabriel extended the silencing bubble around the little white-haired rat boy then flicked him in the ear.

Eugene squeaked in alarm as he woke up then threw his hands out, blasting a wall of dirt at us that Gabriel sent flying out the window with a simple movement of his fingers. Eugene shifted into a rat and started running for freedom.

I lunged forward to catch the little bastard, missing several times as he swerved left and right on his nest. He dove off the end of the bed, his tiny front legs outstretched in a desperate bid for freedom and I lurched forward and caught him, locking my tattooed fingers around his belly. His teeth sank into my hand and I growled as the pain washed through me, but it would take a grenade going off in my palm to make me even think about letting go.

"Good catch," Gabriel commented with a smirk, grabbing a pair of sweatpants and shoes from Eugene's things and gesturing for me to head back out the window. Eugene squeaked, wriggled and bit, but I just ignored him as I climbed outside and waited for Gabriel in the pile of dirt on the fire escape.

"Give him here." He held out a hand and I passed Eugene over.

Gabriel froze his body within a block of ice with his water magic, everything but his little rat head falling still before putting him in his pocket. He tugged his shirt off, tossing it back through the window then looked to me and patted his other pocket.

I grunted irritably. "I can stardust wherever we're going."

"It will take you too long to make it to the boundary at the edge of campus. And there isn't time for you to do that. So shift and let me carry you, or stay here."

My lips twitched in anger, but I gave in, the desire to get my hands bloody tonight outweighing my frustration at being carried around like a twig in a bird's beak.

I stripped out of my clothes, tossing them to Gabriel a little aggressively before shifting into my smallest snake form. Gabriel scooped me up, slipping me into his pocket and I wriggled around to get more comfortable.

He started laughing, patting me lightly. "Stop it, that tickles."

I hissed angrily, managing to poke my head out and glaring up at him which only made him laugh harder.

"You're so fucking cute like that, Ryder," he snorted then his wings burst from his back and he took off into the sky.

I bit his leg through his sweatpants to show him what I thought of that comment, but he only laughed louder as he raced for the stars. Maybe I'd use venom next time. I knew I wouldn't though. Gabriel might have pissed me off from time to time, but he was also under my skin now in a way I couldn't ignore. The word friend did not generally make an appearance in my vocabulary, but if I had to use it on someone, I supposed it would be him.

He flew toward the city and the wind brushed over my scales as I stared down at the dark streets below, the scent of bad deeds crawling within its depths. This place was the only home I'd ever known, but it was somewhere death thrived and danger lurked. We were the ugly scar on the face of the kingdom that the rest of Solaria tried to ignore. But that was what I liked about it. The feeling of lawlessness on these streets and the sense of power which could only be achieved when you emerged from the muddy dregs of this hellish society.

If you could survive living here, then you were a stronger Fae than most. And it wasn't just the wars I was talking about, it was the people. Elise was the epitome of a queen to me because she had faced the demons presented to her in her life, from a useless mother, no-show father and growing up in poverty to losing the only person in the world she could rely on. Then she'd walked into Aurora Academy as a warrior and had been prepared to die in the name of finding and destroying her brother's killer. So I would be her weapon in that endeavour, willing to destroy whoever she directed me towards.

Gabriel circled lower as we arrived on the north side of Alestria and my sharp teeth snapped together as I spotted Inferno and Mufasa standing on the rooftop beside my girl. Gabriel landed smoothly beside them, taking me from his pocket and I shifted fast, snatching my clothes from his hands and tugging them on.

"You didn't mention the tagalongs," I clipped at him and Gabriel shrugged innocently.

Elise leapt forward, her lips crashing against mine and the taste of cherries ran over my tongue as I sank it into her mouth and branded her in front of them all. *Mine*.

My hand pressed firmly to the small of her back as I kept her against me, my other hand locked over the base of her neck.

By the time she pulled away, my anger had melted marginally and she slipped easily into Gabriel's arms, kissing him too while I fixed Inferno in my glare. He glared right back and I refused to blink first, my jaw ticking as lightning glittered on his skin.

"Problem, serpente?" he spat as my eyes burned and he continued not to blink.

"You are my problem, Inferno," I said darkly. "But not forever."

"Chill out dudes," Leon insisted, smacking Dante around the back of the head and making him blink.

I smirked over my victory and Dante scowled at Leon.

"Stavo per vincere, stronzo," Inferno snipped at him.

"No comprende, dudeo," Leon said like he didn't understand, but something in his eyes said he did.

"What have we got to do, Gabriel?" Elise asked him as she held his hand, concern etched into her features. And that was enough to focus my attention entirely. Elise was worried and my...friend was in trouble. I would bring death to King's assassin tonight in the most painful way I could and leave that hooded asshole a message that ensured he did not send anyone ever again.

Gabriel reached into his pocket, taking out the little frozen rat boy and melting the ice around him, leaving Eugene shivering violently in his hand.

"Oh no, poor little dude is all chilled to the bone," Leon cooed, stepping closer and running his fingers down Eugene's white fur, a glimmer of heat washing from his hand. Eugene relaxed, squeaking softly in gratitude.

I cracked my knuckles as I moved closer. "Make him shift," I muttered to Gabriel. "If he knows something, I'll get it out of him."

"That's not necessary," Gabriel told me then looked to Eugene. "You're going to cooperate, aren't you? We just need some help with something."

Eugene's tiny nose twitched before he looked to Elise and she reached out to take him into her hands.

"It's okay Eugene, I won't let anyone hurt you," she promised and he snuggled against her tits like a fucking tit nester.

My eyes narrowed, but I held myself in check, knowing we needed this information. And if I wasted time beating up Eugene for touching my girl's tits, it could cost Gabriel his life. So I *supposed* I had to bite my tongue.

"Shift back, okay?" Elise urged and Eugene nodded, jumping from her hands and shifting into his Fae form.

Gabriel tossed him the sweatpants and shoes he'd brought for him and Eugene got dressed then stood there with his pale chest reflecting the moonlight almost as brightly as his white hair.

"What's going on?" he asked nervously, glancing between us all. "Is this about your panties, Elise? I only borrowed a few for my nest, they're just so silky and-"

"You took what?" I snarled at the same time as Inferno lunged at him.

Gabriel threw out a wing to stop us attacking him and I got a mouthful of feathers as he swatted us back and closed his wings again.

"Not cool, Eugene," Elise said, folding her arms. "But no, it's not about that. It's about-"

"We need your help with a special mission," Gabriel cut in and I frowned at him.

"You...need me? For a mission?" Eugene asked in surprise and hope and Gabriel nodded. "No one's ever needed me for anything before."

"Well, we do," Elise said brightly, catching on and nudging Leon so he nodded keenly too.

"Yup, I need you like I need good blowjobs," Leon said and Eugene's eyes widened in alarm.

"Is that why I'm here?" he gasped in horror.

"No, stronzo," Dante stepped in. "We need your help with something."

Eugene turned to me, quivering like a dandelion before a hungry cow as I gave him a blank stare. Gabriel gave me a prompting look, but I said nothing. Ergh, did I really have to encourage the little shit?

"Ryder? We need him, right?" Elise pressed, giving me a pleading look over Eugene's shoulder and the rat stared at me hopefully.

I released a long sigh then nodded once stiffly. "Evidently."

"Oh wow, I mean oh goodness me. The sun and the stars and the moon, this is exciting! Eugenie is going on an adventure," the rat boy said, talking a mile a minute. Great, now I'd made him peppy and give himself a nickname.

"Do you need me to thread a fuse through a drainpipe into someone's home, then boom you guys explode the whole building while I run from the flames like *this* and like *that*." He weaved back and forth, darting around me and I gave Gabriel a deadly stare.

"Go ahead. Tell him, Gabriel," I said flatly, my irritation with the little rodent rising as he pointed his fingers at me and squeaked, "Pew, pew, pew."

"We're trying to catch a bad guy," Gabriel said simply. "We need to split up into pairs and corral him into that alley." He moved to the edge of the building and pointed down to the dark alley below. "Dante, you'll come with me to Grandcloud Street where we'll push him north. Leon and Elise, you guys will go to the end of Starstruck Street and chase him east, and Ryder and Eugene, you guys will push him into the alley from right down there." He pointed.

"No," I blurted. "Simba, you're with the rat," I commanded, directing Leon towards Eugene but the Lion just side-stepped over to Elise and tugged her against his waist.

"No can do, Scar," he said lightly. "We're going to Starstruck Street. Gabe's orders."

"Don't call me Gabe," Big Bird muttered then nodded to Dante and they jumped over the edge of the building, Dante following him down to the

175

road below on a gust of air magic.

"Elise," I growled, striding toward her. "You'll stay with me. Eugene, go with Leon."

Eugene squeaked, looking between all of us in confusion as Elise gave me a stern look.

"Don't be a dick, Ryder," she replied. "Gabriel knows what's best, I'm not gonna risk his life because you can't follow a simple order."

"I'm not working with the rat," I snapped.

"Woah dude, you sound totally Orderist right now. I think you need to check yourself," Leon said, folding his arms.

"I don't care that he's a rat, I care that he couldn't crack a walnut in half with his earth magic," I hissed.

"I could too," Eugene squeaked defensively, but I ignored him.

"This will be good for you," Elise said with a smirk, then waved goodbye, threw Leon over her shoulder and leapt off of the building while Leon cried *weeeee*.

My hands balled into fists as I was left there alone with Eugene Dipper. Why the fuck had Gabriel even brought him along? Didn't he say he had information? Why hadn't he gotten it out of him if that was the case?

"Um, Mr Draconis?" Eugene said and I snapped around, making him flinch.

"Don't call me that, I'm not your fucking accountant."

"Okay, um, Mr Ryder…" He paused, waiting to see if I had any objections to him using my name. I could have come up with a few just to make him piss his pants, but then I thought of Gabriel's life being in danger and knew I had to go along with this bullshit. I couldn't risk him being murdered for the sake of snapping this weak ass Fae's neck. Tempting though.

"Stay close, and don't talk unless I say so," I commanded, heading to the edge of the roof and casting a long vine over the side of it that ran all the way down to the ground.

Eugene's eyes widened as he stared down at the huge drop and for a second I thought he was going to start panicking, but then he cast his own vine beside mine, grabbed hold of it and walked backwards over the edge. Interesting. Maybe he did have half a backbone after all.

I gripped my own vine, walking backwards and letting it slide through my hands as I lowered myself to the ground and Eugene made it down even quicker than I did. We banished the magic and I turned to lead the way out of the alley, but Eugene caught my arm.

I snapped around, about to break every single finger laying on my flesh, but his nose was twitching like crazy and the guy looked on the verge of having a fit. Maybe his weak little heart was giving up on life just like that and my problem was about to be solved.

"Wait," he whispered. "Someone's coming this way."

I frowned. "Your nose told you that?"

"I can sense magical signatures. And sometimes I can sense…danger." He fell still, his nose twitching up a storm and I was about to turn and leave him there in the alley when he threw out a palm, casting a shield of wood in his grip half a second before a blade of ice slammed into it on the other side right in line with my head.

"Fuck," I gasped, throwing out a wall of dirt as more ice blades came tearing towards us from a hooded figure at the end of the alley.

The shitbag turned and fled and I cursed, chasing after him but as Eugene followed me, he tripped over his own feet and fell on his ass. I hauled him up by one arm and dragged him along.

"Find him with that nose of yours, Ratatouille," I ordered and he nodded as his nose went into hyperdrive.

I wasn't going to mention the fact he'd just saved my life, but I planned on saving his before the night was done so it cancelled it out and we never had to speak of it again.

"That way," he squeaked as we turned onto the street and he pointed towards a shadowy doorway up ahead.

I released his arm, casting a spear of wood out of the ground beneath the fucker's feet in the doorway and a bloodcurdling scream said I'd hit my target. I dispelled the spike he was impaled on and he tumbled out of the doorway onto the pavement in a pool of blood.

"Well, that was easy." I smirked, taking out my Atlas to call Gabriel. "I knew he didn't need a whole team of assholes for this job."

Eugene suddenly gasped and the ground swallowed us up, my stomach lurching as I dropped into a large pit underground before the street sealed over above us, leaving us in the dark. I pressed my earth magic out around me to shift the mud and give my shoulders more room.

"Shh," Eugene hissed.

I could just make him out as a crack in the street above let in a slit of light.

"Where'd they go?" a deep voice growled and footsteps pounded on the concrete somewhere up on the road.

"I dunno. Was one of them the Harpy?" a girl hissed in reply.

"Nah, Luke had eyes on him two streets over," the first guy replied. "I definitely saw a tattooed man and a girl down here though, so maybe she was the Vampire. I bet The Card Master would bless anyone who brought her back."

Eugene pouted indignantly as they drew closer and I raised my hands as rage coiled inside me like a hungry beast. I waited for my new friends Dead and Deader to walk over where we were hidden then blasted the street apart with the full force of my magic, a hiss of fury leaving me.

Their screams echoed through my skull and their pain fuelled my soul as I rose out of the ground on a pillar of dirt like a demon from hell with Eugene at my side, letting them look me in the eyes as my vines wrapped around their throats.

Fire and ice blasted toward Eugene and he shielded us while I focused on ripping them to pieces on the ground. Their screams cut off and Eugene squeaked, cringing from the gore and nearly falling off the pillar of earth we were balanced on.

I caught him by the throat, steadying him and lowering us to the ground before releasing him. I started typing out a message to Gabriel, but he replied to it before I could even hit send.

Gabriel:

Yeah, we've killed a few too. The Sight says I only have one to be worried about and I'm pretty sure we have eyes on him. We're all pushing him your way from the east so be ready in four minutes thirty three seconds.

Ryder:

Got it

I tucked my Atlas away and picked up my pace down the street, seeking out the perfect spot to lay in wait for our mark.

"If you can sense danger, how have you spent so much of your damn life in trouble?" I shot at Eugene as he jogged at my side to keep up with my fierce pace.

"I've only just started to get control of my Order senses," he said a little shamefully and I glanced at him with a frown.

"Some of them take years to master." I shrugged, not saying it to comfort him or some shit, it was just the truth.

"Are there gifts *you* haven't mastered?" he breathed in surprise.

I didn't reply to that for a moment, guiding him off the street and onto the wooden porch of an old boarded up library. We had a good view of the alley from there and the end of the street where our mark would be coming from.

"Are there?" Eugene pushed as we crouched in the shadows and I cast a couple of concealment spells around us along with a silencing bubble.

"It's a pointless one anyway, I don't need it," I said dismissively.

"What is it?" he pressed and I grunted in irritation.

"I'm supposed to be able to change colour and camouflage and shit. My Basilisk form is black anyway, what do I need that for? I'm not a fucking chameleon."

"Oooh, that would be cool though, wouldn't it?" he cooed and I punched him in the ribs to shut him up. "But like, imagine if you could do it when you weren't in shifted form too? Then you wouldn't even need concealment spells, you'd be totally invisible whenever you wanted to be and no one would even be able to detect the magic because it would be coming from your gifts. Seems like it would be handy in your line of work."

Dammit, that did sound pretty fucking handy. Gah.

I watched the street in silence and felt Eugene shuffling closer as I tried to ignore him. I checked my watch for the time and didn't understand how we still had three whole minutes longer to wait.

A board suddenly snapped beneath Eugene's foot and he squeaked in pain, giving me a hit of power as his boot went through and he cut his leg on the sharp wood.

"Mother trucker," he hissed, pulling his foot out and healing the cut as I watched him impassively.

I noticed a long number written on his thumb in what looked like enchanted ink as it glimmered a little even in the dark.

"What's that?" I muttered, unsure why I was bothering to ask.

"Oh, that's um…" He cleared his throat. "Well it's um, a thing."

I remained silent, figuring he didn't want to tell me and not really caring, but then he went on anyway.

"In my first year at Aurora, me and Bryce Corvus were sort of um, friends for a bit."

My eyebrows arched at that. "Oh yeah?"

"Yeah...and we made a star vow to hang out every Friday evening while we were at the academy. I didn't really know the weight of a star vow back then, but we said we'd just release each other from it if we ever couldn't make it. It was just so we both knew we'd have someone to rely on during our time at Aurora."

"I see," I murmured, unable to help but take an interest.

Eugene carried on in a splurge of words. "Anyway, after a while he got deeply involved with your gang and then you promoted him to your second and...his friends didn't like me. I was struggling to make other friends of my own and stuff. We kept meeting every Friday, but he said we had to go to secret places and he told me not to tell anyone we were friends. Then one day his buddy, Russel, showed up while we were together in the Iron Wood and Bryce got defensive when he accused him of hanging out with a..." He cleared his throat as pain flooded from him into me. "A weak Fae with no future." He gazed down at his knees as I felt the sting of those words in him. "Bryce got all flustered and angry, saying we weren't friends and that he'd just been there to beat me up. And to prove that was true, he did it. He beat me until he broke bones and then he left me there and no one found me for nearly two hours." He squeaked sadly and my brows drew tighter together. *Fucking Bruce.*

"I didn't show up the following Friday to meet him. I was stupid. I didn't think about the consequences of breaking the star vow, but when I did it, that was it. I was cursed with seven years bad luck and there was nothing I could do about it. Bryce came to me the following day and forced me to release him from the vow and I did because I was afraid of what he might do. But he didn't release me in return." He bowed his head and pointed at the number on his hand. "This number is a countdown of how long I have left, it runs down every day. I usually cover it with a concealment spell but you kinda took me by surprise when you woke me up so..."

Silence fell and anger slid through my veins like poison. "Bryce is a piece of shit."

He lifted his eyes to mine. "You think so?"

"Yeah, and from what I've seen of your magic tonight, you're more powerful than you let on."

"You really believe that?" He batted his eyelashes at me like I'd just told him his dick was a girl magnet.

"I'm just stating facts, don't take it as a compliment."

His shiny little eyes said he did though, and I shook my head as I turned away from him to watch the street.

One impossibly long minute to go.

"The problem is, even when I do better, the stars always trip me up. I'm not gonna be free of this bad luck until long after my education is over. I won't make it that far in life with this curse hanging over me. Especially not in a city like Alestria."

"Fuck the stars," I muttered. "They don't make your decisions. And if you don't have confidence in yourself then no one else will. You think anyone's been there cheering me on while I fought my way to the top of the Lunar Brotherhood? Ninety nine percent of people in life wanna see you fall. But you can thrive alone, Eugene. The strongest Fae do."

He lifted his chin like my words affected him or some shit and I looked away again. Didn't know why I was giving advice to the little bastard anyway, maybe just to spite Bryce. That motherfucker was pissing me off to no end lately.

"Thank you," Eugene whispered.

"No," I hissed in rejection of those words. "I'm not being nice, I'm being frank."

"Okay, Ryder," he said like he knew better and I growled, about to put him in his place when his nose started twitching wildly again.

I gazed down the street, my fingers tingling with magic.

"Ryder," Eugene whispered urgently, tugging my sleeve and pointing up at the roof of the porch above us.

I ran my tongue over my teeth and slowly got up, my hands raised as I listened for any sound of movement above. A car alarm went off down the street and a wind brushed my cheek, swirling around me. A trashcan rolled out of the alleyway opposite us on a breeze and I smirked. An air Elemental was here and if he thought he could distract me with those childish tricks, he was a fucking fool.

A low buzz sounded then a gravelly voice answered a call somewhere above us. "Yeah? I know, I got the photo he sent me. Looks like they killed some of our guys. But from that picture, it looks like the girl is definitely down here with the Lunar King, she's a small little thing with a nice ass and a tiny waist, easy to round up."

I snorted a laugh. They obviously thought Eugene was Elise. Fucking idiots. Eugene's ass had nothing on my girl's.

"For frick's sake," Eugene muttered as I climbed out onto the side of the porch and cast vines to lift me silently up to peer over the edge of the roof.

The hooded man was still talking on his Atlas and the way he was leaning on an invisible barrier told me an air shield was around him.

"Yeah, okay head this way. Oh shit, Lily, are you okay? What's that screaming? Ah fuck…" A storm of air blew around him and whipped his hood back, revealing his blonde hair and pig ugly face which was twisted in rage.

I cast a blade in one hand and coated my right fist in metal, silently creeping onto the roof and keeping the shadows hugging my body to hide myself. One good punch and I might be able to break through his shield if he wasn't too strong.

I crept closer and closer, my breaths slow and measured as I prepared to kill this motherfucker and bathe in his blood.

When I was near enough, I lunged forward, driving my knuckles into the back of his shield with a furious thwack. I felt his magic splinter, but it didn't give and the guy wheeled around, throwing out his hands and sending me flying away from him on a huge blast of air. I sailed across the street with my gut lurching, and I cast thick moss on the wall behind me before I slammed into it and hit the ground.

I was back running across the street the moment I was up again and I cast walls of dirt to block the violent wind rushing toward me.

A whip of air caught me from behind, throwing me backwards once more and slamming me onto the concrete which I just managed to soften in time before he broke every bone in my body.

A battle cry sounded from Eugene and I lifted my head, finding our enemy rounding on the rat as he launched himself off of a pillar of dirt with two wooden blades in his grip. He slammed them into the guy's air shield, and it looked like he almost broke through it before he was thrown back on a blast of air that sent him spinning away down the street in a tornado.

I shoved to my feet, my chance to engage him again opening up. We wouldn't team up like some unFae fuckers, but there was no rule against taking it in turns to attack the asshole.

My opponent leapt from the roof, running toward me through the air like a fucking pixie and I threw out my hands, throwing a torrent of razor sharp wooden spikes at him. They slammed into his air shield and it shuddered from the power I'd used.

Eugene squealed as he was whipped around and around us in the tornado, unable to get free of its grip and I snarled. I'd kill this asshole for thinking he could try and take my girl and murder my friend.

I rode a tide of earth towards him as he tried to blast me back, but I was the Lunar King and if he thought he could take me on, he was going to soon find himself in his rightful place beneath my feet.

I collided with his air shield and started pounding my fists into it. Fear flared in his eyes and a whip of air snared my waist just as his shield came crashing down. My hand locked around his wrist as he sent me flying away from him and I dragged him with me, my grip unyielding. We landed in the alley, tumbling across the ground and I punched him with the totality of my strength, feeding on his pain and relishing every cut on my body.

He hit the ground on his back and I cracked his head down on the ground before his gaze met mine and that was his final mistake. My hypnosis took hold of him and I sent him into an eternal fire where he would burn until I was ready to finish him. I stood up, leaving him unconscious on the ground within my power, finding Eugene stumbling down the alley behind me, clapping loudly.

"That was incredible!" he cried just as my girl shot into sight behind him.

She raced up to me, diving into my arms and hugging me with her whole body. I squeezed her ass and kissed her, smirking against her mouth as she clung onto me like I was the centre of her world. And I liked that a whole fucking lot.

"You're so hot when you go psycho like that," she said with a grin.

"You saw?" I asked with a sinister smile and she nodded, biting her lip.

She dropped out of my arms as Leon, Dante and Gabriel appeared, walking into the alley as a unit. I belatedly realised I shouldn't have kissed my girl in front of Eugene, but I knew plenty of ways to make sure he never told a soul.

"Well that went perfectly," Gabriel announced and I shot him a glare.

"How? And what was the point of Eugene being here at all?"

"One, he saved your life, and two if he hadn't been here, King's men wouldn't have thought he was Elise and focused their efforts here. Without him, Elise would have been recaptured and I would have been murdered," Gabriel said with a shrug and my heart pounded furiously at that.

Big Bird never did share his plans fully in case us knowing changed the path we were on, but I supposed it had worked out for the best. I just didn't like the idea of how bad our fate could have turned out tonight. *Thank fuck he can see the future. He'll never let any of us die.*

We all looked at Eugene who turned the colour of a plum and he shrugged like he'd done nothing. But dammit, he had.

"So am I...part of the harem now?" he asked, stepping towards Elise hopefully and licking his lips like he might win a kiss from her.

I yanked her back to my side by her hand. "Who said anything about a harem?" I barked, figuring it was probably time to take Eugene back to my room and force feed him a memory eraser potion.

"Oh, um," Eugene squeaked. "It's my senses…"

"Bullshit," Leon growled, gripping him by the back of the neck and twisting him around to face him. "You've been spying on us again, haven't you?"

"Not s-spying," Eugene stammered. "J-just watching."

"That's spying if you're watching what you shouldn't be, stronzo," Inferno warned, squaring up to the rat.

"I won't tell anyone," Eugene said in alarm, finding himself boxed in between three muscled killers who could all snap his neck with one hand.

"He won't," Gabriel backed him and we all looked to him as he folded his arms. "Eugene's known about us for a while and the stars say we can trust him."

"Why didn't you tell us?" Elise asked, her lips parted in shock.

"I can't tell you too much of what I *see* or it will change things," Gabriel said with a guilty frown. "But I wish I could tell you some of the stuff I've *seen*, little angel, because you'd know how fucking happy we're all going to make you."

Elise's expression softened and she smiled at him seductively like he'd just won himself a prime blowjob tonight.

"We really will," Eugene said, creeping toward her with an outstretched hand and Leon cast him in a circle of flames to stop him getting any closer to his mate.

"You won't be doing shit, Eugene," Leon warned. "You're not a part of the harem."

"You don't have to have sex with me, Elise, I'll just be like your sidekick. You can drink from me anytime you like, and I'll give you massages and clean your room and-"

"No," me and the rest of Elise's men snapped at once.

"That's sweet, Eugene, but let's just stay friends, okay?" she said with a sideways smile, moving forward to pat him on the head.

"Okay," he sighed in disappointment.

"Now that that's clear, let's do some killing," Leon said excitedly, rushing forward and dousing the flames around Eugene.

"I might head back to school…" Eugene said, looking a bit pale and Elise took some stardust from her pocket.

"I'll take you back, Eugene. I'm gonna have a bath and some girl time at Gabriel's while they're all here doing dirty deeds anyway."

"Mm, a bath, bella?" Dante purred. "Penserai a me mentre sei nuda e bagnata?"

"I don't know what that means but I know it's dirty." She grinned at him, walking over and brushing her fingers across his cheek. "None of you are allowed to come and spoil my peaceful bath time when you get back though."

"Okay, we promise," Eugene said and Gabriel slapped him around the back of the head.

"You're not a part of that 'we', dude," Leon warned, his teeth bared and it was weird to see him so protective. Why the fuck did he seem so happy that me, Dante and Gabriel shared his girl when he looked ready to kill at the idea of Eugene joining in? What made us any different?

"Bye guys." Elise grabbed Eugene's arm and he winked at us before she threw the stardust over them and they disappeared in a flash. Leon lunged into the space Ratatouille had vacated and swiped a palm of flames through the air.

"He's dead if he tries it on with her," he growled.

"You really think Elise isn't capable of handling his advances?" Gabriel scoffed.

"True," Leon conceded. "It just gets my back up. It's us five and no one else. I'll kill anyone who touches her except you guys."

"Because that makes sense," I deadpanned.

"Exactly," he agreed.

"Why does it?" I pushed because as much as I was all in with this, it did seem like a weird line to draw. He'd been close with Dante before all of this but not me and Gabriel, so why work so hard to include us if the idea of Eugene sent him batshit?

"Because," Leon said with a sigh like I was tiring him. "You guys are prime Lioness material. And the prime number of Lionesses is three. You're top shelf specimens so we already have a full line up. Elise is ours and that's it."

"Wait a fucking minute, I'm not your Lioness and if three is such a great number then how come you want it to be the four of us?" I demanded.

"Gah! Elise isn't a Lioness, she's a Lion. So she needs three Lionesses." He pointed at me, Dante and Gabriel in turn then gave me a look to say *see*.

"What about you?" I snapped.

"I don't count. I'm not a Lioness." Leon chuckled and shook his head, slapping me on the shoulder like I was just so amusing to him before turning to look at the guy I'd left writhing in agony on the ground.

I looked to Gabriel and even Dante for back up, but they just shrugged and focused on the guy we were here to kill too. Fine. But it was still fucking weird.

I released the fucker on the ground from my hypnosis and he groaned as he came to. I threw out a palm, casting a vine which wrapped around his throat, feeding on his pain, a dark expression pulling at my face as I watched him choke.

"Sky blue…cobalt…sapphire… ooh cerulean," Leon cooed as he watched him changing colour, standing close behind me. He leaned in near to my ear, his breath on my neck. "Make him indigo for me, Scar."

"Fuck off," I grunted, my power reserves swelling from the guy's trauma. I was going to make him suffer before this was over. I didn't kill easy. Especially not when I was killing in the name of my girl.

"Scar would make him scream," Leon purred. "Make him scream, Rydikins."

"Get away from me," I growled, throwing an elbow back which he somehow evaded.

Gabriel gazed at me with his arms folded, shaking his head. "I don't *see* this ending well."

Dante suddenly shoved me and electricity snapped through my veins, making me hiss angrily as my magic fell away and the piece of shit on the ground gasped down a lungful of air. "What the fuck do you think you're doing, Inferno?"

He squared up to me with a snarl, his eyes turning to dark, reptilian slits. "How come *you* get to kill him, stronzo?"

"Because that's my fucking forte," I snarled, getting up in his face.

"Don't bother, Ryder," Gabriel said. "You're not gonna kill him. I've already *seen* it."

"Shut up, Big Bird. No one decides my fucking fate," I snapped, not turning my gaze from Dante as the cocky little Storm Dragon raised his hands to fight me. "I'll put you on the ground right beside this motherfucker and bleed you dry."

"Sono il drago dei lupi, il mostro del cielo-"

"At least insult me in a language everyone can understand, *stupida*," I mocked him.

"It's stupid*o*," Dante scoffed like I knew nothing about anything.

"Guys," Leon called, but we ignored him.

I shoved Dante's chest. "It's *stupid* to the rest of the world, fuckwit. Take a language class."

"Um, guys?" Leon pressed.

"Says the stronzo who can only speak one. I'm going to send you to the stars in ten pieces just like your father did to mine," Dante spat.

"Guys!" Leon snapped and me and Dante swung around in fury.

"What?" we demanded at the same time and I growled a curse as I found him standing there holding the guy's severed head by the hair, swinging it back and forth like a fucking incense lantern. I hadn't even been focusing enough to feel the asshole's pain. Now I'd missed my chance to watch the light go out of his eyes.

"For fuck's sake, Mufasa," I snarled.

"Told you so," Gabriel said with a shrug, casually flexing his wings. "We've got two minutes before the FIB show up. Let's go." He patted his sweatpants' pocket and a ripple of frustration ran through me.

"I'm not flying in your damn pocket again," I huffed. "It's fucking emasculating."

"Well it's either that or you can fly on Dante's back with Leon because Elise took the stardust with her," Gabriel reasoned as Leon tossed the head into a dumpster and started doing a victory lap around us as if he'd just scored a Pit.

"He's not riding me," Dante refused.

"Like I'd ever ride you," I muttered with my upper lip curling back and I walked over to Gabriel. "I'd ride your mamma though."

"What did you say about my mamma?!" Dante roared and I smirked, stripping out of my clothes and handing them to Gabriel to carry.

I shifted into a small snake and Gabriel scooped me up in his hands while I hissed furiously at the oncoming Dragon asshole.

Gabriel gripped my jaws and snapped them closed with his finger and thumb. "Stop it, we need to leave." He was lucky I mildly enjoyed his company, or he'd be dead for that. I was certainly tempted to break a few bones for it. "Back down Dante."

Inferno snarled, turning around and dropping his sweats, tossing them to Leon. Gabriel carefully placed me in his pocket and I poked my head out, tasting the air with my tongue as he released me. Blood and electricity was thick in the atmosphere and I had to just be thankful that at least Inferno hadn't gotten the kill.

Gabriel took off into the sky and the city dropped away beneath us, the wind rushing over my face. He soared into the clouds and cast an illusion to hide us all as an enormous navy Dragon flew after us with Leon on his back, singing Fly Me to the Moon by Frank Sinatra.

Sometimes that Lion really needed a good punch in the face.

Gabriel's apartment was as quiet as the grave. Before we'd lost Elise, I usually spent the weekends at The Rusty Nail, heading out fighting Oscuras with the Brotherhood. But this was the first weekend where I could return to that old life now Elise was safe, and I found I didn't want to go back to it.

I lingered in the kitchen with a pang of some uncomfortable emotion coiling through my chest like barbed wire. Gabriel and Leon had taken Elise where I couldn't follow. Hanging out with a Night was damage to my reputation enough, visiting his family home like some kind of relative was out of the question. Besides, I had work to do. I'd spent too much time apart from the Lunars as it was, I needed to pull rank, eradicate any scrap of doubt in their minds that I was their king. But I was still standing in the kitchen doing something I never did. Procrastinating.

Well, I suppose I have to eat.

I tugged open the cupboard where the cereal was kept, automatically reaching for the oatmeal before pausing. My gaze hooked on an all-too-happy Minotaur holding a bowl of chocolatey rocks. I read the name beneath it, my mouth watering and not with venom. *Mino Pops.*

My hand shot toward them before I was aware I'd made any kind of decision and I yanked the bright yellow box from the shelf, grabbing a bowl and pouring in enough to almost spill out of it.

I fetched the milk and filled the bowl up to the brim before stuffing a large spoon into the Pops and bringing it up to my mouth. I shoved the whole lot between my lips and sugar exploded over my tongue like a fucking firework. A groan left me and I fell apart, shovelling mouthful after mouthful between my lips and crunching through the lot. When I finished the bowl, I started pouring another lot into it then the sound of someone clearing their throat made me stiffen. I whipped around with a snarl, finding Dante watching me with his arms folded and an eyebrow raised.

"That was quite the entertainment, serpente." He smirked and I bristled.

"What are you doing here?" I spat. He was supposed to be at home with his doting little family, not here at Big Bird's place spying on me like a fucking Squirrel Shifter in a tree.

"Watching you spill milk all down your shirt apparently," he taunted and I looked down, finding a wet mark splashed over my white t-shirt.

I growled under my breath, lurching forward a step ready to rip him a new asshole in his face, but I collided with a wall of air.

"Coward," I hissed, venom dripping onto my tongue and washing away the lasting chocolate taste in my mouth.

"I didn't come here for a fight, Ryder," he said, his eyes levelling on me. "The exact opposite actually. And if you don't hear me out, I might just send your gang the video I just took of you scoffing Mino Pops like a ten-year-old left home alone."

My upper lip peeled back. "I'll tear you to pieces, use your severed finger to unlock your Atlas then destroy that video."

He snorted and electricity flashed in his eyes. "I'm kidding, stronzo. There's no video. This place is neutral ground, right? For Elise."

My jaw clenched as I glared at him then nodded stiffly.

"For what it's worth, I think it's kind of sad that you can't eat cereal without feeling like your whole gang is going to turn against you, serpente." His brows dipped like he actually gave a shit, but I wasn't fooled. I couldn't quite figure out what his angle was though. It was probably just another way to taunt me.

"Well we aren't all in a gang with our Mommy who gets you to suckle on her teats every time you win a battle," I mocked and his expression contorted.

"Talk about my mamma like that again and I'll turn you to dust," he snarled then carved his fingers through his hair, turning away and heading for the door. "This was obviously a waste of my time."

I bit my tongue for several seconds, but my curiosity won out as he made it to the door. "What was?"

He glanced back, eyeing me closely as if assessing how this conversation might progress from here. He took a breath as a decision solidified in his eyes, then he slid a hand into his pocket and took out a worn looking envelope.

"What's that?" I grunted, jerking my chin at it.

He slowly walked back towards me, opening the envelope and taking out a piece of paper. "This…is a letter my father left for me after he died."

I nodded minutely, my interest slightly heightened. "And?"

"This didn't come into my possession until a while after his death. Mamma found it in his writing desk and merda…I regret not finding it sooner."

"Why?" I muttered.

"Because I did terrible things in the name of revenge for my father's death. Felix Oscura took me under his wing. I wasn't Awakened, but he gave me ways to harm my enemies. Your people. And I did." His voice cracked in a way that made my eyes narrow. He was either an exceptional actor or this was the truth. And before I could question him on it, he extended a hand to me.

"I swear every word I tell you on this subject is the truth as I know it." His throat bobbed and I felt the air shield falling down in front of me.

I hesitated, assessing whether it was worth risking my life to place my hand in his right then. No one was around to stop him blasting a thousand bolts of electricity through my body, but he'd had plenty of opportunities to do that before now.

I slapped my palm into his and we gripped each other's hands tightly as the magic clapped between us. Before my hand could fall back to my side, he placed his father's letter in it, his jaw pulsing with the weight of what he was offering me. This most precious thing he put into the hand of his enemy and could be so easily crushed in my fist.

"Read it," he urged and I growled at the command, but my eyes still fell to the words on the page.

Dante,

My dear Alpha, if you're reading this, I have gone beyond the veil and our Clan needs a new leader. There are many in our family who are worthy of the position as Alpha, but none who were born for it like you. I knew the moment I held you in my arms as my tiny pup that you were destined to rule. Your strength shone so bright even then, and over the years I have watched it grow into a light blinding enough to rival the sun.

Our pack needs you, Dante, whether you are ready or not. But as I think upon my death now, I also think upon the future I hope for you and my other children to have. Your mamma and I never wished for a life of bloodshed for you. We hoped to build a world full of peace, of safety. Nothing quite brought that home to me until I had pups of my own. For many years, I have fought to try and conquer the Lunars, to bring peace by winning a long, hard war. But as I grow older, I have come to understand something I wish to impart to you. Hatred is no way to build a foundation for peace. Bloodshed only reaps more bloodshed, and because of that, this war is eternal. My body now lies in the ground among countless members of our family, and I cannot say we were any closer to peace than when my father first handed the Clan to me.

In the end, family is all we have, and we must protect them at all costs. How will you protect them Dante? Think on this. Because if war is not the answer, then what is?

Your loving, adoring, ever-proud father.
A morte e ritorno. May we meet again.
Micah Oscura.

My throat was tight as I stared at those words, rereading them, the familiarity of them burning a hole in my black heart. From what I knew now, they could have been the words of my own father. He had talked of peace too, but only as if it was an idle dream never to come to pass. Had he truly gone to the Oscuras and offered himself as the price of that peace? Why hadn't he told me?

Emotion blazed so thickly in my veins that my muscles locked up as I struggled to process this alien feeling. I never thought of my parents. I buried that kind of pain in me, but I let it out now, inch by inch, allowing it to feed the desires of my Order. The pain was so potent, it filled me to the brim. All pain to Basilisks was strength, and emotional pain bit deeper than physical.

I handed Dante back the letter and forced my eyes up to meet his. A powerful connection between us hummed in the air and I swear the stars were whispering something in my ear, something I couldn't quite hear, but drew me toward him.

Inferno and I were two sides of the same coin. But whereas he fought for family, I fought for nothing. I was the king of a raging army who held no purpose except to make the world bleed. It was what I stood for. Pain and blood and suffering. I killed because I was so filled with hate that it was all I could see. And I hated so fiercely because of Mariella. She'd moulded me into the monster she'd wanted me to be to keep this war going. And I'd done just as she'd hoped.

"I came here to fulfil our fathers' wishes, Ryder," Inferno said in a low tone. "I want the war to end. What do you want?"

I could count on one hand how many times I'd been asked that question in my lifetime. Elise had been the first in years, now Inferno stood before me asking that very same thing. As if it mattered.

I searched the darkest places inside me for the boy I'd been before Mariella had twisted him into a vengeful man. I searched for his wants, for the things he'd dreamed of long before he'd become a bloodthirsty king. And I found him still there like he'd been waiting for me to look for him all this time. Elise had seen him when I couldn't, but now I could see him too, and it felt like taking a gulp of air after being trapped beneath a dark sea on the brink of death.

He had wanted – no, *I* had wanted to be a warrior like my dad. I'd wanted to protect my people like he did. I'd wanted my mom to give me brothers and sisters who I could charge into battle for. But then she'd gotten sick with a rare magical virus and nothing Dad did could save her. He would have paid every dime he had plus the whole weight of his soul for her life, but there'd been no cure. She'd faded away from us like she was turning into a ghost before our very eyes. And I remembered how impossibly painful it had been to say goodbye.

"I want peace," I admitted as that old memory tore my heart to pieces and made me miss my mother so deeply it burned. Somehow, I knew she'd wanted this, I could almost feel her standing at my back with my father now, urging me on and it was the first time I'd sensed them close to me like that in a very long time. I'd probably been lost to them almost as much as they'd been lost to me. But thanks to Elise, I'd realised that the boy they knew was still here, still living inside me, desperate to come out.

Dante's eyes brightened with hope. "You do?" he asked, taking a step closer.

"Yes," I said firmly. "We'll divide the city in two."

He nodded hard, getting closer still and for some reason I didn't back away. Electricity was skipping along his skin like little fish jumping out of the water and I fought the urge to smirk at him.

"We'll draw up rules – no, *laws*. And we'll punish anyone who doesn't obey them."

"I like the sound of that," I said darkly, a grin twitching at the corner of my lips.

He clapped me on the shoulder, his hand gripping my arm tightly and I felt something shift in my chest. "Of course you do, you fucking tyrant." He barked a wild laugh. "Let's make this binding now then. You and me."

"You want to swear it now? Break the cycle of war and hatred between our people for good?" I asked and Dante stood up taller raising his chin as he looked me in the eye and held a hand out to me.

I drew in a deep breath as I moved to stand before him, eyeing his hand and feeling the stars watching us as the future of our people hung in the balance.

As my hand hit his, my heart thumped to a deep, purposeful rhythm and I met his gaze as he spoke, wanting to lock this moment into my memory as I finally fulfilled the promise which had been made between my father and this man.

"I swear to make peace between our people. To end the war between The Oscura Clan and The Lunar Brotherhood for good and to find a way to rule in peace over our territories," Dante said firmly, his words imbued with power.

"I swear it too," I agreed firmly and a clap of magic rang between our joined palms which was so powerful that I was certain the only way the two of us managed to stay standing was because of our holds on each other.

That was it. We had just changed the course of fate for countless Fae and the future of Alestria would be forever altered by this decision.

"We'll tell our people then meet tonight to discuss the details of our alliance. This will work Ryder, I know it will."

I nodded, my heart rising in my chest as I thought of truly making this happen. "Bring everyone," I growled. "The entire gangs will witness this shift in and there will be no chance for insurgence."

"We'll stand together at the top of Moonview Hill tonight and show all of them that we are united in this as we end the war for good. But it is already done now. They can't fight it. We have finally made peace, fratello," he said, his eyes widening the second he realised what he'd called me. *Brother.* He turned sharply away and headed for the door. "Oh, and fuck you, serpente."

"Fuck you, Inferno," I tossed back, smirking as he slipped out the door, throwing me a sideways grin before he disappeared into the hallway.

A rare laugh escaped me and I turned back to my bowl of Mino Pops, knowing I was going to gorge myself on sugar. And fuck anyone who thought less of me for it.

I had the Lunar Brotherhood gather at The Rusty Nail but didn't head there until I was certain they'd had time to arrive and would be waiting for me.

I drove my motorcycle down the road and the low growl of it was enough to have the people on the streets diving for cover. That had given me the kick of power I needed once, but I found my chest hollow and quiet in the face of it today. A part of me felt like a stranger as I approached the bar I'd spent countless hours in, the place my father had once stood at the centre of. An army I had risen to the challenge of ruling and left my mark on.

But I didn't want to be the callous king who had nothing but blood trails in his wake, I wanted to be something...more. Something my own father might have been proud of. Inferno had that. And I was far more envious of it than I could have anticipated. Reading that letter had shone a light on a void in me which I'd resolutely ignored for too many years. And maybe it was time to fill it with something good.

I parked up in the alley alongside the bar and an animal whine caught my ear, making my head jerk around. At first I thought the stumbling idiot of a Fae in the alley with me had cast a little ring of fire around a small dog. But then I saw the creature's light blue coat, its three swirling tails and the flare of magic in its gaze. It was the size and stature of a fox, but its ears were larger and pointier, its eyes like two moons. *Holy fuck*, that was a ghost hound. They were rare as shit and usually lived out in the forest, what the hell was one doing down here?

"Hey little pupper, wanna have a cuppa – tea with me? While you flick your curly tails in the sea with me?" the guy started rapping – fucking terribly might I add – and my hands tightened into fists. *Fucking Blazer.*

The hound yelped and I growled in response. "Hey!" I barked at the asshole and he twisted around, nearly falling backwards into his own fire.

The ghost hound was trembling, shrinking away from the flames, which was about one of the only things that could kill it if you could even catch one at all. The fact that this guy had done it while off his fucking head on Killblaze was a damn miracle. I'd chased them around the Iron Wood for hours when I was a kid while my mom had laughed and told me not to bother. But I'd been one determined little asshole, though I never had caught one.

I was pretty sure they'd liked running circles around me for a laugh, especially the time one had led me into a river and I almost drowned before my mom found me and yanked me out. They were tricksy, intelligent little bastards and I'd never much liked them since then. But something in me wasn't gonna let me stand here and watch some druggy asshole kill one. Maybe it was the reminder of my mother, or maybe I was just a fucking sap today. Either way, looked like this Blazer was dead.

"I caught a cat!" the Blazer announced excitedly. "Come and see its ears. I bet it can hear smells with those ears. I bet roses sound like donkeys. Ee-orrrrre." He beckoned me over, but flames burst out of his fingertips and set his hair alight.

He stood there like a damn lemon for three full seconds as he raised his eyes to his burning hair then screamed like a man possessed and ran face first into a wall. A crack sounded and he hit the ground, knocked out for good and saving me a job. The fire sizzled out in his hair, but the one around the ghost hound kept rising and I walked toward it, holding out a hand.

Dirt sprayed from my palm as I smothered the flames and the hound looked up at me, sitting within the circle of earth.

I wafted a hand to try to make it move, but instead of running away, it carefully stepped over the dirt like it didn't want to get its toes muddy and approached me. Its three fluffy tails lifted behind it, moving ethereally, becoming near transparent as it used its weird ass gifts to make its body like a ghost's. It could move through walls this thing, hence its name. They often hung around graveyards too, feeding on the crypt slugs that lived in the soft soil. Of course, that meant there were all kinds of myths about them, like they were the spirits of the dead, but if they were then my guess was that they were the spirits of dipshits who liked to play pranks on Fae. Leon would definitely come back as one of these.

"Go. Be free. Or whatever," I muttered, wafting a hand again but it kept coming closer, its eyes round and pupils wide. "What do you want?" I growled. "I don't have food. Go away before the prick wakes up, I won't save you a second time."

The creature cocked its head, its long ears dropping back as it leaned up and sniffed me.

Maybe there was something wrong with it, but that wasn't really my problem. In fact, I wasn't sure why I was even still standing here.

I turned to leave, but suddenly the thing was in front of me, barring my way forward. It moved like a star damned lightning bolt.

"What do you want, beast?" I snarled, squaring my shoulders at it, but it didn't seem to get the message about me being the wrong Fae to piss off.

It started sniffing me again, its wet nose pressing to my right fist, snuffling at the word *pain*. Then it opened its jaws and just as I was about to stop it from biting me, its tongue flicked out and licked me.

I stared at it, stumped, figuring the thing must have had a brain injury and was most likely a dead beast walking. Then it turned and shot through the wall to my right which led into The Rusty Nail, disappearing in a flash.

"Bad choice. Now you really are dead," I muttered, heading to the side door and wrenching it open.

I walked into the main bar, finding the place heaving with my people, the smell of booze and smoke in the air. There was no sign of the ghost hound and I wished it good luck on its suicide mission today.

Silence fell as the crowd noticed me and I climbed up onto the bar, striding down it towards the middle where Ethan was sitting with a whiskey in hand and a few of his pack members around him. He nodded to me and I inclined my head a little in acknowledgement. Scarlett climbed over from behind the bar, smiling at me in greeting before dropping down to sit staring out at the crowd.

"Good evening, boss," she said. "Any news?"

"Plenty," I said and she frowned before I turned to face the crowd.

I ran my tongue over my teeth as I measured my words. Each one was crucial. There would be opposition to this news, but there would be support too. It was my job to ensure I gave no room for negotiation. The city would be at peace and if I had to weed out those who sought to rebel against that peace, then I was more than happy to deal out the price of an insurgence.

My gaze hooked on Bryce near the back of the room with the earless Minotaur Russel and a couple more of his skeevy little friends. They watched me with diligence, and I hoped that meant I'd squashed all doubts they had about me. But if it hadn't, there would be no mercy the next time they spoke out against me. I had been fair, one more infraction and I would be their darkest nightmare.

"How many people have been taken from us this year alone by our war with the Oscuras?" I called to the room and sad glances were exchanged. "Twenty? Thirty? And how many have died over the years since this war began?"

I felt Scarlett's eyes on me but mine never wavered from the crowd as I assessed each face, sought out my enemies and my allies among this army I ruled. "And how many lives have we taken in return?" I continued. "If all the spilled blood from our people and the Oscuras could be seen today, there would be a river running through the heart of Alestria."

Some people cheered at that and my jaw tightened.

"I don't say this to celebrate it," I spat and their cheers died in their throats. "I say it to condemn it."

Silence rang out and hope filled the eyes of some of my people, husbands and wives looked to each other like I might offer them the answer they'd been praying for. And my heart twisted in a way it never had before. Because I had never looked at them in all these years and thought of them or their children in this war. I'd been so focused on death and vengeance, it had blinded me to the pain I'd caused, the wound I was ripping open in this city. I was responsible. And the weight of that responsibility fell on me then like a ton of bricks. It was time to do my father proud.

"There will be no more war!" I cried, my voice filling every corner of the quiet, finding every ear in the bar so I could not be misheard. "Today, I have struck a peace deal with Dante Oscura and from this day forth, the death will come to an end."

Gasps of relief and anger tangled together and suddenly a din of shouts rang out, people praising me, others cursing me, and I took stock of them all. I looked down at Scarlett, her knuckles turning white as she held onto the edge of the bar. She gazed up at me, her eyes wide, but she said nothing, her silence leaving me uncertain on her stance.

"Hell fucking yes!" Ethan hooted and my gaze whipped to him, finding him in the middle of a group hug with his pack, relief hanging over them all.

My heart beat harder and I let the chaos descend for a minute longer before shouting out to regain control of it. "The peace deal will be upheld, or I will personally take the price from you in flesh and blood," I warned. "Half the city will be ours. Our people will be safe, the Fae of Alestria will no longer have to fear the night. Our future is peace!"

I climbed down off the bar and Ethan leapt at me, wrapping me in a hug before I could stop him. "Watch it," I growled in his ear and he stepped back with a smirk, sweeping his fingers over his styled blonde hair.

"Wolf moment, boss. Sorry." He grinned and I shoved his shoulder as more of his pack crowded around me. But I wasn't going to be involved in any kind of group hug. Fuck that.

I turned to Scarlett, stepping in front of her and eyeing her closely, seeing a hint of her conniving Griffin Order in her eyes. "Have you got anything to say?"

She hesitated then cleared her throat. "No, boss. If these are your wishes, then they'll be done." She bowed her head obediently and I scrubbed a hand over the stubble on my jaw as I started giving orders to prepare for tonight.

I needed the entire Brotherhood at the meeting. They would watch as I placed my hand in Dante's and struck the deal that would save our city from being run into the ground forever. By the time I had everything taken care of, I was already hankering to go so I left Ethan and Scarlett to deal with the questions from the rest of the Lunars and slipped away.

A path parted for me in the crowd, people darting out of my way like I was a reaper of death and if they touched me they'd fall dead at my feet. A glimmer of blue in my periphery made me look up and I found the ghost hound watching me from one of the wooden beams that ran beneath the ceiling.

Strange animal.

I headed outside through the front exit and a knot eased in my chest. I probably shouldn't have dipped out so soon, but I wanted to go back to Gabriel's place, and yeah okay, maybe I wanted to eat more Mino Pops. Was that a crime now? There was nothing more I could say to the Brotherhood anyway. This was happening. They needed to accept it and back my decision. Ethan and Scarlett would report to me with anyone who was going to be a problem, and no doubt tomorrow I'd be busy correcting those problems.

I rounded into the alley where I'd parked my motorcycle and immediately felt a cold wind at my back. I turned sharply, hitting a wall of air and finding Russel standing beyond it beside a girl with short blonde hair, her hands raised as she cast the barrier between us. I was pretty sure her name was Viola and from her expression I was also pretty sure she was a cunt.

Cindy Lou was lingering behind them with her long, black hair pulled into a ponytail. She was wearing a bright pink dress, looking totally out of fucking place in Lunar Territory and just as nervous about standing there too. But both Russel and Cindy had their hands on Viola's shoulders, offering her power to fuel the power of her air magic.

"You got something to say?" I barked, casting vines in my palms as I readied to batter my way through her shield and teach them all a fucking lesson.

Viola flicked a finger and stole the air from my lungs and I started fighting her shield with every drop of magic I could conjure. They all winced in concentration as they fought to hold the shield up and Viola's eyes flicked over my head, giving me one second to tell me to wheel around.

I twisted aside, but the force of a truck hit me from behind all the same and sharp fangs suddenly drove into my neck. Bryce clung onto me like a fucking animal and I threw myself back against the air shield, crushing him to it as he fed from me like a starved monster, my magic locked down by his venom. He groaned his satisfaction and I half expected his boner to dig into my back as I rammed him against the air shield again and again. When he didn't let go, I gripped Bryce's hair and yanked furiously, throwing him over my shoulder.

UnFae piece of shit!

He hit the ground, his mouth wet with my blood and suddenly the ghost hound was there driving its fangs into his shoulder and shaking him violently. Bryce screamed and I fell on him, my head beginning to pound with blood as the seconds dragged on without air and I fought with everything I had to stay conscious. I threw my fists into him with all my strength, trying to coat them in hardened metal to break his bones, but he'd already taken so much of my magic and his pain wasn't filling up my reserves fast enough to cast the complex spell.

Bryce thrashed, using his Vampire strength to force me away and trying to punch the ghost hound instead. It moved like the wind, evading him as it snapped its sharp teeth down on Bryce's shoulder once more. Bryce snarled, shooting to his feet with his speed and chasing after the animal as it tried to escape. It ran for a wall, disappearing through it like a wraith and Bryce slammed into it full force with a curse.

My vision darkened as I tried to get up, my lungs burning. As Bryce came at me again and sank his teeth into my wrist, I felt the last of my magic ebbing away and my mind being pulled down into darkness. Bryce's victorious laughter followed me into oblivion and rage took root in my gut.

My mind hooked on Elise and I held tight to that vison, taking her with me into the abyss. My love for her was eternal and it gave me comfort that if I was going beyond the veil, at least nothing could steal that from me.

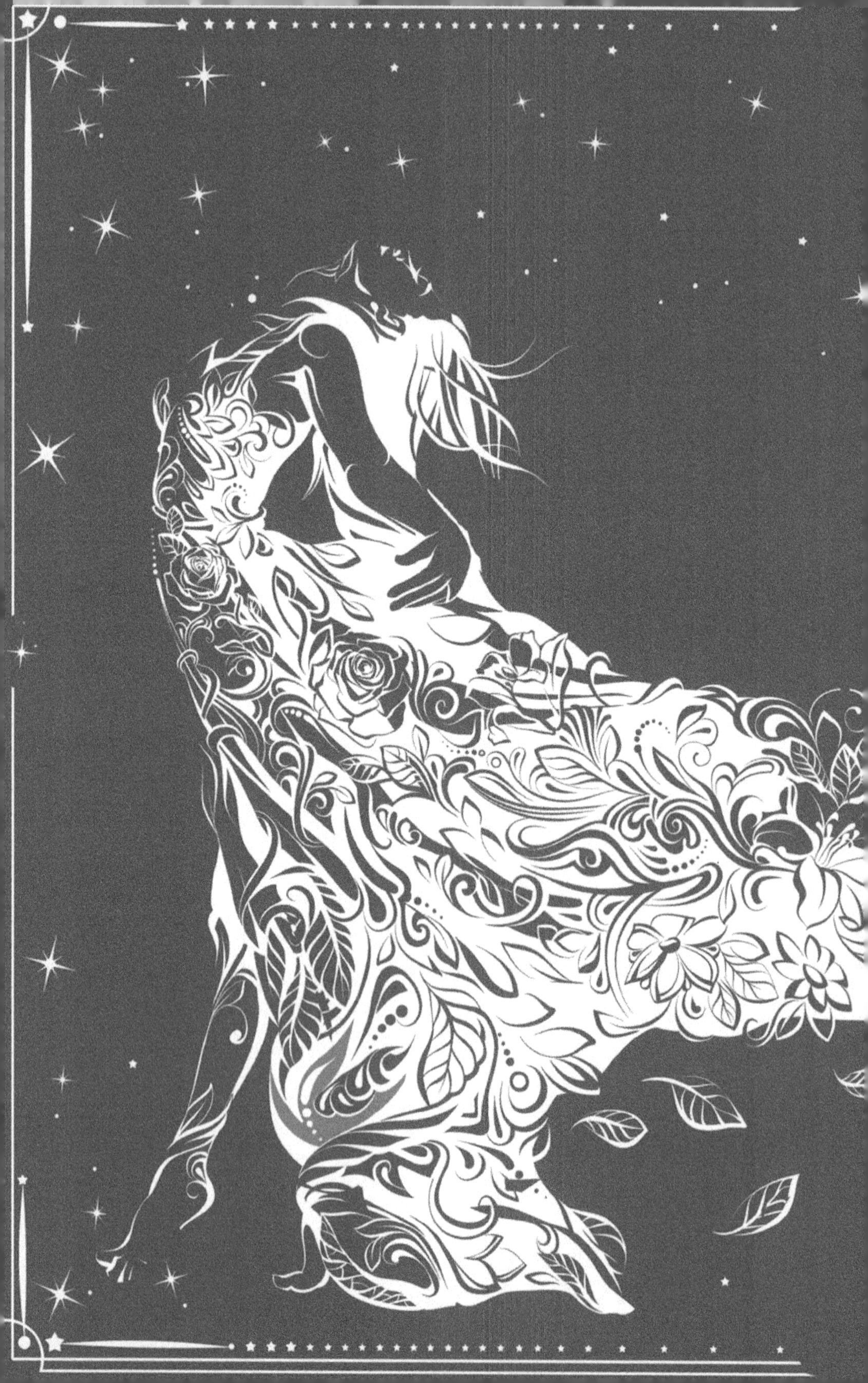

Elise

CHAPTER FOURTEEN

"This is weird," Gabriel said as we drove up to the imposing house where the Night family lived, and Leon parked the flashy Faerarri he'd stolen in front of the steps.

"It's not weird, man," Leon interjected. "It's weird that my moms and dad haven't met my boyfriend-in-law."

"I'm still not okay with you calling me—"

"Well, I can't call you my Lioness, and I can't call you Gabe, you won't let Ryder call you Big Bird and now you're being weird about meeting your in-laws. Honestly, Gabe, you need to get over your lonely loner thing and just accept that you've got a family now." Leon shook his head in exasperation and got out of the car, tossing the door closed behind him and jogging up the front steps, leaving me to deal with Gabriel alone.

"It'll be fine, I promise," I said gently, reaching between the seats from my spot in the back so I could take Gabriel's hand in mine.

He looked around at me, his brow furrowing. "It's not just this meet-the-parents thing Leon is forcing on me," he muttered.

"Then what is it?" I asked.

Gabriel frowned, his eyes beginning to glaze the way they did when a vision was pressing in on him and I leaned forward, closing the distance between us and stealing a kiss from him.

Gabriel's hand slid into my hair as he drew me closer and I complied, hopping between the front seats with a spurt of my speed and landing in his lap.

Our kiss deepened, his tongue driving into my mouth as his hands moved to grasp my waist.

"Maybe we can just stay out here," he murmured against my mouth and I breathed a laugh.

"No." I swatted his chest, leaning back and forcing some distance between our lips as I looked down at him. "I know this is kinda weird for you and believe me, the first time Leon brought me here it was pretty fucking weird for me too, but his family are great. And..."

I trailed off, the thought that had just come to my lips, surprising me as I turned it over in my mind.

"And what?" Gabriel pushed.

I met his steely grey eyes and blew out a breath before just saying it anyway because it was true.

"*And*, Leon's family are my family now too. I love them. His moms message and call me all the time and his dad is a bit intense but he's pretty cool when you get to know him, and they welcomed me into their pride without hesitation. I've never felt so easily accepted as I do within this house."

"Not even by me?" Gabriel teased.

"The man who literally tried to avoid me like I had Fae fanny rot for months because you couldn't bear the idea of being mated to me?" I teased right back and his frown deepened.

A growl escaped him and for a moment I swear I could feel his power humming around us, making the air vibrate with its intensity. My tattooed Harpy was one seriously powerful Fae.

"You know I only did that because I was trying to protect you. And I might have given in to my feelings for you now, but I still worry every day that the people who want to harm me will find me and then they'll find you, and Leon, and the others and now Leon's family too and I-"

I kissed him again, silencing those thoughts and cupping his jaw in my hands, feeling the rough bite of stubble against my palms as a shiver ran down my spine and I ached to feel it on more of my flesh.

Gabriel's cock grew thick between us, driving against me as I rocked my hips over his, the fabric of our jeans rough against each other and rubbing over my clit too. I was seriously tempted to ditch the pants and ride him hard and fast until I was coming all over his dick. With the use of my speed, we could probably make it the quickest quickie ever known to Fae and barely even be late...

"If you don't stop that, little angel, I'm going to fuck you right here in this car and we won't even make it inside in time for dessert."

I breathed a laugh, loving that we were considering the same thing and forced myself to lean back again. "I don't want you to worry about the people who forced you into hiding," I said to him firmly. "Maybe they're still hunting for you. Maybe they're not. But either way, they don't get to stop you from living your life. They don't get to stop you from having a family." I placed my hand over his black t-shirt, right above his heart. "I'm your family now. So is Leon and Dante and Ryder too. Fuck knows how we'll figure out their shit long term, but that's what I feel in my soul. And that means Leon's family are yours now as well. You've been without people to love and care for you for so long because of the fear hanging over you from the mysteries of your past, but it's time you started living for your future. The small boy who was forced to go into hiding is a powerful man now. I've never met a Fae as strong as you before, no one could hurt you even if they tried."

"You've met Lionel Acrux," Gabriel pointed out. "He's one of the four strongest Fae in the entire kingdom, so you absolutely have met a Fae who is stronger than me and-"

I placed my palm over his mouth to silence him and gave him a stern frown. "I seriously doubt one of the Celestial Councillors is behind the hunt for you. Chances are your family just got caught up in some gang bullshit or something and no one would even remember to look for you now. It's not like *you* can even remember why you're supposed to be running. So why don't we focus on the stuff that counts?"

"Like getting out of this car and not making Leon's family wait any longer?" he teased.

"Yeah, that. But they're Lions so being late is kinda expected."

Gabriel laughed, blowing out a breath and frowning once more.

"What is it?" I asked.

"I...I'm not sure. Probably nothing. The Sight is niggling at me, but my mind is too full up with all of this shit to let the vision in."

"Are you sure it's not important?" I asked.

Gabriel tried to concentrate for a moment then blew out a breath and shook his head. "Between borderline freaking out over meeting my supposed in-laws and having you straddling my cock, my brain is too busy to *see* whatever it is. But you're right here in my arms and if there was a threat heading straight at us then I'd definitely *see* that, so it can't be anything important."

"You sure?" I asked.

Gabriel shifted forward to place a peck against my lips and I leaned into it. "Come on. We don't need them hating me in advance for making them wait to eat."

I scoffed a laugh as I opened the car door and hopped out. "No chance of that. If we're late to the table, it's more likely that they'll have finished their own meals and will be starting on ours."

We headed up the steps to the house hand in hand. Leon had left the door open for us and I sent a silent thank you to my mate for giving us a few minutes alone. Leon was always so in tune with the rest of us emotionally that somehow he knew what we needed before we even did half the time.

I strained my ears to listen out for the occupants of the enormous house as we stepped through the door and the sound of male voices caught my attention from the conservatory at the rear of the property.

I kept hold of Gabriel's hand as I led him through the immaculate corridors and he drank in the sight of the artwork hanging from the walls and displayed on little pedestals in fancy alcoves. The Lions were definitely very proud of their accomplishments and the things they owned/had stolen, and I remembered feeling like this place reminded me of a museum when I'd first come here. But I didn't see it like that so much now. Despite the apparent coldness to the decor, I now knew countless stories behind the pieces which were on display and understood their importance to the family.

The tension in the room was palpable as we stepped into the conservatory and I looked to Leon where he stood by the windows beside his father, holding a leatherbound book in his hand and frowning down at it.

Reginald looked around at the sound of our arrival and a wide smile broke across his face as his eyes fell on me. He was impeccably dressed as always, his long, golden mane brushed to perfection and shining in the light.

"Ah, Elise! We were so worried about you, my dear!" He crossed the room towards me and before I knew what was happening, I found myself enveloped in his arms, the rich scent of his cologne - or maybe it was Lion musk - wrapping around me as my face was buried in his chest.

A trio of excited mewing and a shriek of excitement announced the arrival of Leon's moms and I lost my grip on Gabriel's hand as I found myself in the centre of the pride. I was crushed, nuzzled and my hair was ruffled so much I was pretty sure it would be standing on end by the time they released me while the sound of raucous purring surrounded me.

Safira tugged me out of the Lion pile at last and she grabbed my face between her hands tutting and fussing as she ran her fingers into my hair and stroked my face. I couldn't help but grin at the affection no matter how strange it may have seemed.

"Poor little cub," she murmured. "Did they forget to feed you where you were being held?"

"And what happened to your poor hair?" Latisha added sadly, her fingers combing through my lilac locks from behind. I was pretty sure that aside from them scruffing it up, my hair was just fine, but the Lion's had higher standards about that kind of thing than I did.

"Umm, no I ate okay," I tried, but they weren't listening, already talking between each other and suggesting manicures, pedicures, hair conditioning treatments and a bunch of other shit I wasn't even certain I understood.

"Ohhh and is this the latest addition?" Marie cooed, suddenly noticing Gabriel as he tried to hide against the wall.

Within less than a heartbeat, all three of the Lionesses had pounced on him, stroking his black hair and complimenting his physique.

"Oh, he's ever so strong," Latisha purred, squeezing his bicep.

"And impressively tall," Safira added, whipping a measuring tape out of somewhere and gasping as she checked his height. "Six foot six!"

A chorus of 'six foot six' rattled between the three of them and Leon purred his damn head off as he watched.

"Ohhh, you have a lot of tattoos, don't you?" Safira commented, tugging on the bottom of Gabriel's shirt and lifting it up to get a look.

Gabriel looked more than a little flustered, his eyes wide and on me as he mouthed 'help' and I snorted a laugh.

"How thick would you say his thighs are, Marie?" Latisha asked, brandishing the tape measure again but before Gabriel was forced to endure any more measuring, Reginald snapped his fingers.

"Weren't you saying something about manicures, my loves?" he asked, arching a brow at his wives.

The three Lionesses released Gabriel suddenly, giggling as they compared notes on Gabriel and what a fine addition he would be to Leon's pride before running from the room with excitement pouring between them, and I bit down on my lip as I tried not to laugh. Okay, so being a Lioness might have been as far from my nature as I could imagine getting, but I had to admit that I kinda loved being a part of this family. Leon's moms fussed over me in a way I wasn't certain my mom ever had, and his dad was pretty damn cool most of the time too. I kinda felt like Gabriel was meeting my family coming here as well as Leon's - I certainly had no intention of dragging any more of my kings out to meet my sorry excuse for a mother anyway. And Gareth...

I blew out a breath as a pang of sadness slipped through me for a moment. My sweet, overprotective, weirdly innocent brother would have lost his damn mind if he could see me now in the centre of this pack of heathens. Polyamorous relationships were common enough among Fae that I knew he would have accepted that side of it even if he may have been surprised to find out I'd chosen that. But the guys themselves were all pretty full on and intimidating and I was fairly certain this situation would have featured in his nightmares.

"Dad, this is Gabriel Nox, my boyfriend-in-law," Leon announced, drawing my thoughts away from my lack of blood relatives and I swung around to face them again as Gabriel offered his hand, still looking pretty damn flustered and more than a little uncomfortable.

"Nice to meet you, son," Reginald said with a purr, his smile widening. "When Leonidas told us his pride was growing, I can't tell you how excited we all were."

"I'd call it Elise's pride if we're being totally honest," Gabriel said, cutting me a warm look which had Reginald beaming at me.

"Yes, of course. And I'm not in the least bit surprised. That one is a rare treasure and we were more than thrilled when she claimed our little Leonidas as her mate. Have the two of you officially-"

"I dunno how Harpies do that, Dad, but that's between them really, don't you think?" Leon cut in, saving Gabriel from having to reply.

"I'm just wondering whether the three of you have made the bond official yet or not? And of course, whenever that young whippersnapper Dante can find time to come and visit with-"

"*Dad,*" Leon hissed. "Remember how I told you you're not supposed to know about Dante yet?"

I snorted a laugh as Reginald rolled his eyes. "All I'm asking is whether or not young Gabriel and Elise have officially mated yet or not. Because you can't exactly take part in a pride bond until each of her men have made that promise to her first." He looked back to Gabriel expectantly and I swear my big, strong, Seer of a boyfriend had actually been caught off guard for once.

"Err," Gabriel shot me another 'help me' look but I just shrugged, not really sure how I could do that. "I mean, clearly Leon is the best matched to her. They have their Elysian Mate bond in place, so I don't see how I could-"

"Leon!" Reginald scolded, disappointment flashing over his features as my Lion growled at Gabriel. "I would have thought that you knew how to run a pride better than to allow thoughts of *ranking* to be present within your circle."

"Gah, I know, Dad. It's not like I haven't told him *a lot* of times that it doesn't work like that, but Gabe won't listen, will you, Gabe?"

"Don't call me Gabe," Gabriel muttered but no one was listening to him.

"Chapter eighteen, son." Reginald banged his finger down on the top of the book which Leon still held and I looked at it curiously, trying to read the title between Leon's fingers.

"Don't worry, I'm on it, Dad," Leon said firmly. "No one in my pride will feel inferior by the time I'm done with them."

Gabriel looked like he wanted to protest against the fact that Leon had just claimed him for his pride, and I had to bury my amusement again. He just looked so damn out of his depth and I couldn't help but smirk a little, remembering how I'd felt when I'd been thrown to the Lions for the first time.

"Well, anyway," Reginald continued, turning his attention back to Gabriel with a warm smile. "It's a pleasure to welcome you to the family, son. Elise really is quite the Lioness- I mean, quite the, erm Vampiress?" He flicked a questioning look at me and I shrugged.

"She's the Lion, Dad. We're her Lionesses," Leon said with a wide smile that said he was in love with the idea of that.

Reginald laughed loudly and nodded. "I can certainly see that. She has quite the Charisma of her own. Even Roary was taken in by-" He cut himself off abruptly and the smile fell from his face as he realised he'd just mentioned his oldest son. My heart twisted at the pained look which crossed his features then he cleared his throat. "Where is the food?" he asked abruptly, looking around like he'd expected the table to be laid out with it already.

"Dad-" Leon began, but Reginald cut over him.

"They've gotten so excited that they're going to forget to feed us," Reginald muttered with a shake of his head, turning suddenly and striding towards the door. "I'll just go and check on how your mothers are getting on."

He walked out without another word and silence fell between us as he left.

Leon tried to keep his composure, but I could practically feel his pain over Roary's incarceration and I shot towards him, throwing my arms around his waist and squeezing tight, crushing the book between us.

Leon nuzzled the top of my head, winding an arm around me and holding me for a moment as Gabriel stepped closer and placed a hand on his shoulder too.

Of course, that wasn't enough for Leon who instantly threw his arms around Gabriel as well, dropping the book and crushing me between them which honestly wasn't a terrible place to find myself.

"I love you guys," Leon said, his voice heavy with pain over his brother and I tiptoed up to press a kiss to his rough jaw.

We broke apart again and I spotted the book Leon had been holding on the floor, stooping to pick it up.

"What's this?" I asked, reading the title *A Pride To Be Proud Of* and flicking it open.

"It's a book that Dad had copies made of for me and Roary from the one his dad gave to him when he was a cub. He gave my brother his one on his sixteenth birthday but when it was *my* sixteenth he said I was 'too immature' and 'the time wasn't right for me to have mine yet.'" He pouted before going on. "It was like this ultimate sign of our Dad's favour and he never seemed to think I was good enough for it. There was a time when I would have given my right arm to get my hands on it, but now..."

He shrugged, taking a seat on the couch and Gabriel moved to sit down beside him.

I flicked the book to chapter eighteen, wondering why Reginald had told Leon to read it and laughed as I read the title. *'How to ensure your Lionesses all feel equally cherished - a guide to avoiding inferiority complex within the pride.'*

"What is it?" Gabriel asked and my amusement slipped away as I looked at him over the top of the book.

I shot forward, landing in his lap and dropping the book into Leon's hands as I met Gabriel's steely grey eyes and held his gaze.

"You don't really feel like you mean any less to me, do you?" I breathed, willing him to see how much I cared for him in my eyes, to feel it in my touch, to know it in his soul.

"I..." He frowned as his hands slid up onto my thighs and he let out a long breath. "I feel *this*," he said eventually. "The strength of what there is between you and me. I feel all of it. But he's the one with silver rings in his eyes so that has to mean he's the one who's best suited to-"

Leon smacked Gabriel around the back of the head with the book so hard that he almost head butted me and only my speed saved me from a busted nose.

"*Hey*," Gabriel snarled while Leon burst into laughter.

"Dude, you're the one who told me you could *see* shit like that coming. You can't blame me for The Sight letting you down like that," Leon sniggered.

"Yeah, well, Elise was distracting me," Gabriel muttered, rubbing the back of his head and giving me a look that said he really did blame me. "With all of this shit going on today, I can hardly *see* a damn thing."

"Hey, I can't help it if you think with your dick around me," I protested and Gabriel gave me a shrug.

"How *do* Harpies mate anyway?" Leon asked thoughtfully. "Maybe you and Elise need to do that to help you feel better about the whole silver eyes issue."

"I don't really want to talk about this here," Gabriel said in a low voice.

"Lions have to dominate their mates," Leon said, ignoring him. "So when me and Elise came back here after the Divine Moment thing I overpowered her, pinned her to my bed naked, forced her beneath me and-"

"Yeah. I *saw*," Gabriel said, rolling his eyes.

"Oh yeah, I forgot you were peeping on our sex life with The Sight. Did you used to jerk off over it? Can you jerk off while inside a vision?" Leon asked excitedly.

"Lunch is here!" Marie called cheerily as she strode into the room with a huge tray laden with food.

I slipped off of Gabriel's lap and into the space between my two kings as the three Lionesses made quick work of laying the table with a huge spread of food.

Reginald returned, no sign of his earlier distress on his face as he took his seat and his wives hurriedly dished up plates of sandwiches and salads then handed them out to us. They fed the boys first, so I made sure to steal a sandwich from Leon's hand, biting into it like a savage as he growled and tried to wrestle it back from me.

We all fell into conversation as we ate and the moment I finished my food, the Lionesses descended on me, stealing me away for a pamper session like they had the first time I'd come here as Leon's mate.

They cooed and fussed, dyed my hair freshly and did all kinds of girly shit to me while we caught up on all the things they'd been up to while I'd been gone. The only weird thing was the way none of them even mentioned Roary. It was like he didn't even exist and when I tried to prompt them into speaking about him by bringing up my visit to Darkmore to get my cuffs removed, they started dumping water over my head to wash my hair.

I gave up on that fast enough when I realised my attempts were upsetting them, but it made me so sad to think of them pretending he didn't even exist just because he'd damaged their sense of pride by getting himself locked up.

When they finally finished with my pamper session and I'd officially had more than my fair share of girl time (which included way too many questions about my sex life with multiple men considering one of those men was their son) I headed away from them to find my boys.

I was wearing a lilac crop top and yoga pants combo that Marie had bought me - she loved matching my clothes to my hair and I wasn't really complaining.

I used my enhanced hearing to listen for them and the sound of laughter drew my attention to the far side of the house so I shot that way, heading for the room me and Leon had been given after our mating.

I sped inside, throwing the door closed behind me and finding that the sliding door to the balcony was open, the sounds of Gabriel and Leon's laughter coming from beyond the white curtains which billowed in the breeze.

I skidded to a halt between the two of them and Leon startled a little.

"Hey," I said casually. "What are you laughing about?"

"Gabe was just telling me about what Harpies do to seal a mate bond."

"Oh?" I asked with interest, looking up at Gabriel and trying not to let it show just how much I wanted to hear about that. I mean, it wasn't like I needed to be mated to him beyond what we had now, but after mating myself to Leon the Lion way, I couldn't say it hadn't crossed my mind to bond with my other kings in the way of their Orders.

"It's kinda dumb," Gabriel said dismissively but I nudged him to urge him to spill. "I just...have to present you with a branch."

"A branch?"

"Yeah...like the perfect branch to start building a nest. Because for Harpies our nests are kinda like the basis of our home and our territory and offering your mate a place in that is meant to be, like, important or some shit... Like I said, it's dumb."

"I don't think it's dumb," I said, a smile tugging at the corners of my lips. "If you...ever wanted to find me the world's prettiest stick then I'd be honoured to use it for our nest."

Leon snorted a laugh and I elbowed him in the ribs.

"What?" he asked. "I'm just saying, getting a stick isn't quite so exciting as what I gave you when we mated the Lion way. I mean, I guess it was kinda like a stick, but bigger and thicker and a lot more-"

I elbowed him harder and Gabriel rolled his eyes.

"Yeah well, like I said, it's dumb."

"Does it have to be that way around?" I asked. "Or could I get you a branch instead?"

Gabriel looked down at me and his eyes flashed with the power of his Order form for a moment, letting me see how much the beast in him liked that idea.

"Okay, I'm gonna do it," I announced, looking out into the trees beyond the balcony.

"It's supposed to be the male," Gabriel began but Leon cut him off.

"Little monster doesn't conform to gender stereotypes, Gabe. Don't be so close minded."

"He's right, I don't. So why don't we play a game? I'm gonna go and find the perfect branch and you have to try and catch me before I do."

"What do I get when I catch you?" Gabriel asked.

"Well if I've found the perfect branch, you're gonna be my mate."

He swallowed thickly, glancing past me to Leon who was grinning his fucking head off.

"And if you haven't found it?"

"Then you can see if you can overpower me, and we can mate the Lion way."

"What way do Vampires mate?" Leon asked curiously and I shrugged.

"I dunno, never really had any Vampires to ask. But I'm good with doing things your ways."

"You really want to be my mate?" Gabriel asked, a flash of vulnerability in his gaze as he looked at Leon again.

"I told you," I growled. "It's all of you, Gabriel. I want you all the same so unless you're going to say no..."

"No chance of that," he replied fiercely. "But I think I wanna be the one finding a branch for you."

"Then you'd better catch me and go all Lion on me, Harpy boy because if you don't, I'm going to find the best fucking branch you ever saw, and you'll swoon so hard you'll fall right out of the sky at my feet."

I hopped up onto the railing surrounding the balcony, preparing to race into the trees as Leon stripped his shirt off in anticipation of a shift, but Gabriel caught my wrist to halt me, his eyes glazing as a vision pushed in on him.

"What is it?" I asked as his brow furrowed with concern.

"I..." He paused for several seconds, concentration lining his features before he shook his head and relaxed his hold on me again. "I dunno. I lost it. For a moment I felt like there was somewhere else I had to be...but then I got a vision of me claiming you the Lion way and it faded away." He smirked at me, letting me know just how much he'd enjoyed that vision and I bit my lip in anticipation.

"Sounds like you're exactly where you need to be then, Gabe," Leon joked, dropping his pants and grinning at me before leaping over the balcony and shifting in mid-air.

He hit the ground on four enormous golden paws, shaking out his mane and roaring so loudly that I swear the windows rattled.

"Catch me if you can," I taunted, leaping after Leon and using my air magic to slow my descent before Gabriel could ditch his shirt and shift too.

In his Harpy form he was as fast as me, but I had the advantage of the trees and a head start.

That mating branch was gonna be mine and I'd be claiming Gabriel all for myself before this game was up.

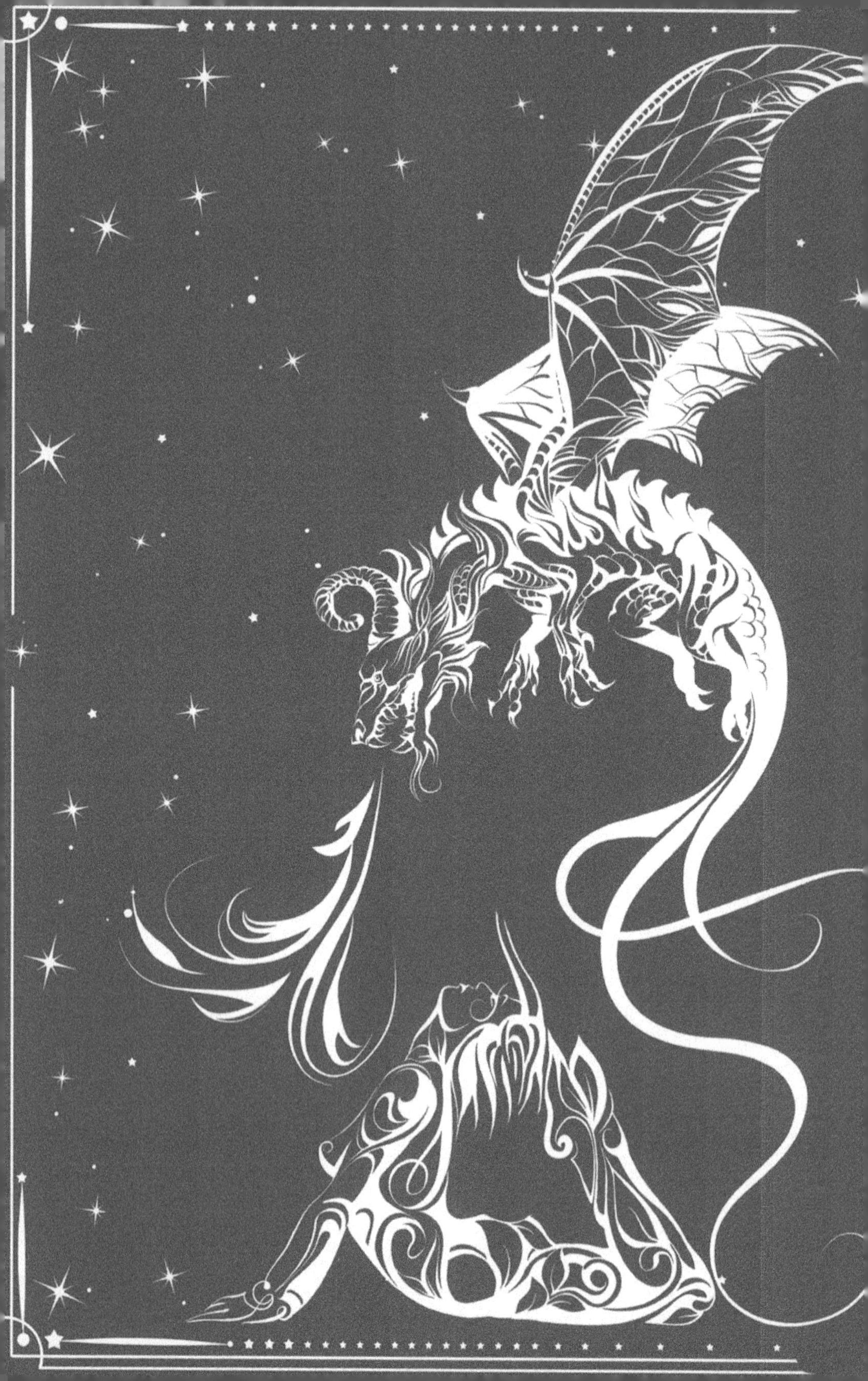

DANTE

CHAPTER FIFTEEN

My family were partying like it was their last day on Earth and I accepted my third glass of wine into my chalice as I danced with my baby cousins.

Rosa was on the table with Aunt Lasita's dingy stick in her hand, waving it in the air while Lasita clapped from her chair. Mamma was being swung around the room by her brother Claudio, a bottle of wine in her hand as she went. I couldn't stop smiling as I watched my family celebrate the news that we had struck a peace deal with the Lunars. It hadn't even sunk in yet; I couldn't believe Ryder had actually fucking agreed.

I desperately wanted to call Elise and Leon - fuck it, Gabriel too - and get them all here to party. But I didn't want to interrupt their time together at Leon's house. His bond with his family needed nurturing now more than ever since Roary had been sent to prison, so I wouldn't interrupt that. I'd see them back at Gabriel's place later this afternoon anyway, and I really wanted to see amore mio's face when I told her the news.

I took a long sip of my wine and just let myself enjoy this day. They'd know soon enough, and I had no doubt Leon would have us celebrating long into the night.

"Ragazzo Drago, dance with your old aunt," Lasita called to me and I moved to help her out of her seat, nearly gaining myself a whack from the dingy stick Rosa was swinging around.

"Watch it," I laughed and she beamed at me.

"If you wanna use that stick properly, cucciola, give your Uncle Luigi a smack about the head," Lasita called to her. "He's riddled with the mindworts." She pointed at him where he was passed out in a chair across the room, a bunch of pups in his lap drawing on his face with everlasting pens. *Well, merda, that was gonna be a bitch to get off.*

"I think he's just drunk," I said as I guided her onto the dance floor.

"That's what the mindworts want you to think." Lasita tapped her temple knowingly. "Careful, ragazzo Drago, they'll infest your brain too if they sense any weakness. I'll have to get you a dingy stick of your own."

"No," I growled, remembering how she'd gotten the first one. "There'll be no more dingy sticks."

"A flapper japper then," she decided, taking out a charm on a necklace beneath the collar of her bright yellow dress. It looked like a bottle cap with the words *flapper japper* etched onto it, which was probably because that was exactly what it was. "It only cost me a naked tea party with a leprechaun – and let me tell you, that leprechaun wanted to do a lot more than just have tea."

"Dalle stelle," I cursed under my breath. "Don't go getting naked for anyone else, Lasita, I forbid it. Leprechauns don't exist."

"Ha! Tell that to the leprechaun. He was the tallest leprechaun in Solaria, did you know? Over six foot and as hairy as a Yeti foot. Speaking of Yeti feet, last year I had to suck a Yeti's toe to earn myself this fertility bone." She pulled out another charm on her many necklaces, showing me what looked like a chicken bone. "He wanted me to suck a lot more than that too, I can tell you-"

"Yetis don't exist," I gritted out, trying not to let Lasita's stories sully my mood. I'd already stationed a couple of Omegas near her house to make sure she didn't go back to the damn 'spright' bridge, but I was going to have to get eyes on her twenty-four-seven at this rate.

"Well what else do you call an eight foot man covered in hair with horns and bull's face?" She scoffed.

"A Minotaur," I growled, narrowing my eyes and she laughed like I was being ridiculous. "And you're way too old to have more children. You already have eighteen anyway."

"Thanks to my bone," she said, wiggling her eyebrows.

"You only got it last year!" I scolded but she just rolled her eyes.

My Atlas started buzzing in my pocket and I hooked it out, finding my cousin Felipe calling. I guided Lasita into the arms of my mamma as Uncle Claudio took a break, dipping out of the room as I answered the call.

"Ciao."

"Ciao Dante, there's a girl looking for you at the front gate," he said. "She says she has some news for you."

I frowned. "Who is it?"

"She says her name's Cindy Lou Galaxa. Pretty girl, crazy eyes though."

"Hey, I heard that," Cindy snapped in the background.

My hackles rose. "Tell her I'm busy." And how the fuck did she find my home?

"I tried that, but she's persistent," Felipe muttered. "She says she has some important information."

"What information?" I growled, anxiety jacking up in my chest for some unknown reason. But my instincts were burning, telling me something was wrong.

"She won't say," he answered.

"Fanculo," I cursed. "Okay, I'm coming down."

I hung up and stuffed my Atlas in my pocket just as Rosa bounded into view.

"Everything okay, Drago?" She cocked her head to one side and I shook my head minutely.

"Something's up." I strode for the door and she fell into step with me. I didn't tell her to stay behind because from the look of her, her Alpha instincts were roaring and I wasn't going to suppress them.

We headed onto the front porch and I quickened my pace to a jog down the track between the vineyards while Rosa kept up with me, the dingy stick in her hand held like a sword.

We made it to the gates and Felipe nodded to me, opening them and I stepped through a magical barrier to the road where Cindy was waiting. She wore a tight-fitting pink dress and her eyes were pinned on me with hunger in them as she ran forward as if to greet me, but she smashed into my air shield instead. Rosa sniggered and I folded my arms, glaring at this psycho who had made a star damned shrine about me.

"Speak," I commanded and her eyes darted left and right nervously as she composed herself.

"I've got you a gift," she said, batting her lashes. "To make up for everything." She bit her lip. "I know what I did was wrong, I just want things to go back to the way they were, Dante. Me and you…"

"There was never a me and you, Cindy," I growled. "How did you find my house?"

"Oh, well…I may have followed you home once. Or twice." She batted her lashes innocently and electricity sparked over my skin as Rosa growled. "I didn't mean any harm. I was just curious, that's all."

Rosa suddenly whacked her around the head with the dingy stick and Cindy shrieked, leaping back in surprise.

"What the hell?" Cindy planted her hands on her hips.

"Oops, thought I saw a mindwort, but it must have been one of your brain cells jumping ship. My bad," Rosa said innocently and I breathed a laugh.

"Get out of here," I told Cindy. "And don't come back. If I see you within a mile of my home again, you'll regret it." I turned to leave, but Cindy Lou called out to stop me.

"Your Astral Adversary is going to die because of me, Dante. I helped catch him. It's probably already happened. You don't have to worry about the Lunars anymore. He's gone."

I stopped dead in my tracks, my pulse pounding, worry gnawing at every nerve in my body.

"What?" I gritted out, spinning around to face her once more.

"I did it to make it up to you," she said with hope in her tone, taking a step closer to me like I might drag her into my arms and hug her for this. "He's never going to be a problem again. All because of me. Isn't that great?"

My teeth nearly ground to sawdust in my mouth, but I forced myself to control my expression, sensing Felipe listening in.

"Where is he?" I demanded in a measured tone.

"Um, I'm not sure exactly. Bryce took him away to finish the job," she said with a grin.

I'd never hit a woman, but dalle stelle if there had to be one…

I tried to compose myself, but I lost control on my rage, the full brunt of it pouring out of me in a wave. "Tell me what you know!" I roared, storming toward her as electricity tumbled from my body and she winced away in fright.

"I don't know anything!" she screamed in alarm. "Bryce took him from outside The Rusty Nail. That's all I saw." She fell down to her knees, pressing her hands together in a prayer. "I thought you'd be happy."

"Get out of my sight before I kill you," I spat and she scrambled to her feet, tripping over something and face planting the road with a wail. I realised it was the dingy stick as Rosa picked it back up and twirled it between her fingers casually as Cindy got to her feet then sprinted off down the road crying loudly.

Rosa touched my arm and I whipped my head around with a snarl, her eyes lifting to mine as she read my expression. She could probably see exactly how worried I was, but whatever she thought of that, she didn't voice it.

"Go back to the house," I commanded. "I need you to cover for me."

"Okay," she said, squeezing my arm. "Will you explain this to me later?"

I gazed at my little cousin, my heart squeezing in a vice. "Yes," I promised. Because I would. I trusted her to the moon and back and she deserved the truth on this.

I strode away from her, pulling my clothes off and diving forward to shift into my huge Dragon form. Then I took my pants between my teeth and focused on that place inside me which was now bonded to Ryder thanks to Leon. I sought out his location with all of my senses and the magic of the tracking spell tingled along my body. Then I felt a pull like an anchor attached to my heart guiding me toward him and a knot of tension in my chest eased a little.

He was still alive. And I didn't focus too much on why I felt so relieved about that knowledge as I flexed my wings and took off into the sky. All I knew was that I was going to rain down hell on the Fae who'd taken Ryder Draconis, and I would do everything within my power to save his star damned life.

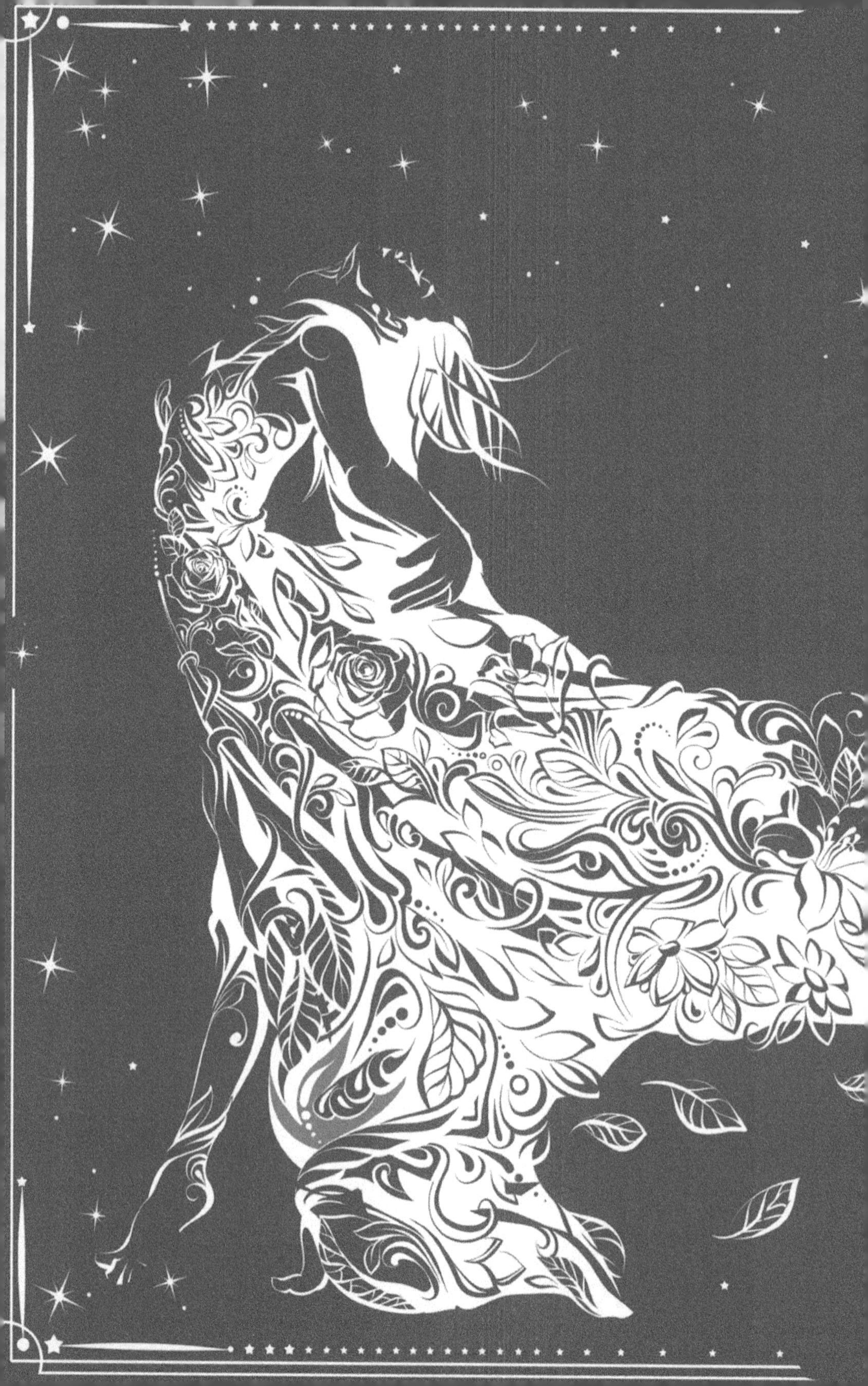

ELISE

CHAPTER SIXTEEN

I shot between the trees, using the cover of the leafy branches overhead to hide from any eyes in the sky, my hearing trained on the forest surrounding me as I ran. The sounds of Leon battering a path through the forest in his gigantic Lion form followed me and I had to guess he was sniffing me out or something because no matter which way I turned, he continued to pursue me. Or maybe he was just cheating and using the tracking bond to chase me down, that would definitely be his style.

Gabriel was harder to keep track of and I knew it was pointless wasting too much energy on trying to lose him anyway. He'd only use the The Sight to find me again and I had a branch to find before he managed it.

I grabbed sticks from the floor, inspecting them and tossing them aside one after another as I hunted for the perfect one. I didn't know why it was so damn difficult. I'd been planning on grabbing the first one I could find, stripping naked then waiting for Gabriel to find me in a clearing. But the second I'd started grabbing branches from the forest floor, I'd gotten a gut instinct about them, knowing they weren't the one. I didn't know if I was losing my mind, getting feelings from sticks, or if the stars were nudging me away from the inferior scraps of wood I kept finding, but I had the strongest feeling it was the latter. This wasn't supposed to be some random stick. It was important. Too important to pick on a whim while shooting through the forest. But I kept grabbing more and more of them all the same.

It wasn't like I had any objections to Gabriel finding me and claiming me the Lion way - he could try his luck at dominating me into submission just as much as he liked. But I knew that it wouldn't bond us the way it had for me and Leon. Even after us gaining our Elysian Mate bond, I'd felt the power of Lion bond taking hold of me when Leon had pinned me beneath him and claimed me like that. It had held more power than a normal fuck fest between the two of us and I knew in my heart that this perfect branch thing would be the same for me and Gabriel. If only I could find one that met the standard.

I glanced up between the trees and flinched as a huge, winged shadow passed across the sun, Gabriel's figure perfectly outlined as he hunted for me.

I turned back the way I'd come and shot away again, racing between thick boughs and taking a chance on darting through a clearing just as the earth began to tremble beneath my feet.

I skidded to a halt, trying to change direction once more but a shadow shot from the sky, aiming straight for me and I threw my hands up instead, blasting a gust of air at Gabriel as he sped towards me with his wings tucked tight to his back.

But before my attack could even knock him off course, the ground opened up beneath my feet and I screamed as I fell into a huge pit that opened up below me.

I caught myself on a blast of air magic and leapt back up out of the hole, speeding skywards in an attempt to get above Gabriel's dive. But of course he *saw* that coming and his wings snapped open just as I passed him. My magic caught him on the updraft I'd created and within less than a heartbeat, his arms had locked tight around my waist and we were plummeting towards the ground again.

"All mine, little angel," he growled triumphantly and I laughed as I lunged at him, aiming to sink my teeth into his neck to disable him.

Vines snaked around my throat and tugged me back at the last second, making me gasp before they cut off my air for a moment.

The next thing I knew, I was on my feet again, the vines falling away as Gabriel's mouth collided with mine and he shoved me back against the thick trunk of a tree.

I tried to bite his bottom lip and he growled as he lurched back, giving me just enough space to slam my palms against his chest and knock him away with a blast of air once more.

"Elise!" Gabriel snapped, his tone rough and commanding and doing all kinds of things to ruin my panties as I laughed, shooting away again.

"You didn't think I was going to make it easy for you, did you?" I taunted as I ran, choosing a route between the closely packed trees so that he couldn't fly after me.

A low growl drew my attention to my left as I sped past a huge boulder and I shrieked in alarm as a massive Lion leapt from it, a roar bursting from his lips as he pounced.

I tried to speed by but he'd been lying in wait, clearly figuring out that I was coming, and as I attempted to dart into the woods to escape, I found a wall of fire blocking my way.

Leon's paws collided with my chest, knocking me off of my feet and I cursed as I fell to my back beneath him, marvelling at the enormous size of him in his shifted form as he showed me every one of his razor sharp teeth.

I pushed my fingers into his shaggy, golden mane and a purr echoed through his powerful body a moment before he shifted into a very naked, utterly gorgeous man.

Leon's mouth captured mine as his body crushed me into the dirt and my heart pounded as he caught one of my wrists and slammed it down above my head, pinning me beneath him as he ground his solid cock against my aching pussy through my leggings.

"Admit it, little monster," he said in a low growl. "You like being submissive."

I bared my teeth at him and bucked hard, using my strength and the element of surprise to send him rolling off of me.

"Wrong," I replied, leaping to my feet again and grabbing a branch from the ground in the process. "I don't like submitting - I like being dominated."

"Same difference," Leon teased, getting to his feet too and circling to his right like he was preparing to pounce again. My eyes dragged over his perfectly defined physique before catching on his huge cock, standing hard and proud, ready for me when I was willing to give in.

"It's not," I disagreed. "Because I could submit to any Fae if that was what got me off. The way I like to be dominated means I want to know I'm beat. I want to be shown who owns me. I don't want to give it. I want you to take it."

Leon grinned, his gaze darting over my shoulder for a split second, giving away Gabriel's advance behind me.

I threw a hand up in the air, blasting magic out from my body with the full force of my power before shooting up into the air on a gust of wind.

I glanced down, seeing the two of them flat on their backs from my attack, but my advantage barely lasted a second before a vine snaked around my ankle and I was yanked down out of the sky again even faster than I'd shot up.

More and more vines coiled around my body, quicker than I could sever them with the whips of air magic I was creating and I cursed as I fell to my knees between the two of them, trussed up like a feast ready to be devoured.

My heart was racing and my pussy throbbing as I looked between their bare chests and Leon casually fisted his cock in his hand.

"I found a branch," I gasped, aiming to wrestle back some control as the two of them looked down at me.

"Really?" Gabriel asked, his eyes flaring with a heated desire that made my blood prickle as he dismissed the vines controlling me.

I got to my feet, holding out the branch I'd snagged and smirking at him as he reached for it. But as his fingers brushed the other end of it, I jerked it back suddenly, frowning down at the lump of wood in my hand and shaking my head.

"Wait," I said, glancing between the stick and him. "This might sound crazy but...I don't think this is actually the one."

Leon snorted a laugh and Gabriel's lips twitched with amusement as I tossed the stick aside.

"I know what you mean," he said. "I might have spent a bit of time thinking about this before now, but whenever I picked a branch it just wasn't right."

"I guess that means we'll just have to mate you Lion style, little monster," Leon said, grinning in a way that made my toes curl.

"I like the sound of-" Gabriel cut off midway through his sentence and his eyes glazed as I tried to decide on the best way to escape them - not that I really wanted to, but I was willing to play along with the game and make them work for it.

"What is it?" Leon asked him curiously, reaching out to ruffle the feathers of Gabriel's wings.

Gabriel snapped back out of the vision with an angry snarl, whirling on Leon as his wings spread wide at his back.

"Hands off the feathers," he warned. "And you fucked up my vision too."

"What did you *see*?" I asked him. "Was it something big?"

"Like my Lion dick?" Leon added, instantly drawing my gaze back to his cock and making me ache for it.

"What? No," Gabriel snapped. "It wasn't your cock, asshole. It was something...I dunno, it felt important and there was some heavy breathing."

"Sounds like you *saw* us fucking to me," Leon insisted. "Which means you might as well just give in now, little monster."

"Oh yeah?" I teased, wetting my lips and looking between the two of them. "I think you're still gonna have to overpower me though."

I turned and sprinted away, but a flash fire bloomed into existence right in front of me and I yelled as I leapt back.

Strong arms wrapped around my waist a moment later and Gabriel chuckled darkly as I fought and bucked against him, whirling me around and yanking on the front of my crop top so hard that it tore down the centre.

I smacked his arms as I tried to break free, but his hand fisted in my hair and he used his height to tug my neck back, making my spine arch and my tits thrust forward as he pushed his hand down the front of my leggings.

I sucked in a gasp as Leon appeared in front of me, his teeth closing around my nipple through my bra just as Gabriel found my bare pussy within my pants.

"No panties?" he asked in surprise, his teeth grazing my ear.

"At least I can still take you by surprise sometimes," I teased before moaning again as Leon bit down harder.

Gabriel chuckled, pushing two thick fingers into my aching core without warning and making a loud cry spill from my lips.

"Beg us to fuck you, Elise," he growled.

"Fuck off," I hissed through my teeth as he drove his fingers in harder and my traitorous pussy clamped tight around his fingers.

"Looks like she hasn't learned her place in this interaction yet," Leon teased, drawing back and grinning at me as he used his fingers to snap my bra strap against my skin.

"Maybe it's time she did then." Gabriel used his grip on my hair to bend me over at the waist, the bulge of his hard cock driving into my ass through his jeans and making me moan.

I tried to struggle back upright, opening my mouth to tell him that I was gonna shove him down in the leaves and ride his cock like a cowgirl, but before I could even begin on the threat, Gabriel pushed my mouth down around Leon's dick.

I moaned in surprise as Gabriel's grip in my hair tightened and he forced my head down harder, making me take Leon's cock right down into my throat. I wanted to push back, snarl and show them exactly who they were messing with but another part of me fucking loved this. I loved the feeling of them using me, my body giving them exactly what they needed while I was nothing but a vessel for their pleasure and my own.

I moaned around Leon's cock as he thrust it between my lips with a Lion's growl, his fingers tangling with Gabriel's in my hair as he fucked my mouth and I took it like a good girl.

Gabriel released his hold on my hair as Leon took over and the sound of his zipper rolling down had me moaning even louder.

My pants were tugged down next, baring my soaked pussy to the world as I pushed my ass back, needing to feel him inside me even more than I needed air in my lungs.

Gabriel's cock slid between my thighs, brushing against my clit and making me moan his name around Leon's shaft as I pushed my ass back at him needily.

He rubbed his length over my pussy then kept going, my own arousal mixing with his water magic as the head of his cock pushed against my ass instead.

"Do you want my dick in your sweet pussy, angel?" Gabriel taunted, his hips flexing so that the tip of his cock pushed into my ass.

Leon jerked me off of him suddenly, yanking my head back so that I could look up into his golden eyes which were hot with desire.

"What's it to be, little monster?" he asked.

"I'm not begging," I said defiantly.

I had meant to say more on the subject, but Gabriel took that as the perfect opportunity to thrust his cock into my ass with a savage move that had my breath catching and my nails biting into Leon's thighs to stop me from falling.

"You will," Gabriel promised, pulling back and thrusting in again.

I groaned at the feeling of his hard cock in my tight hole, feeling so full and so empty at once as my pussy clenched with the need for some attention.

Leon watched his friend fuck me in the ass for several long minutes while I just gasped and moaned and bit my tongue against begging on behalf of my pussy before driving his dick into my mouth again.

I almost chocked on Leon's cock as he thrust in hard, but I loved that, I loved the feeling of him using me for his pleasure, I just wished my pussy could get in on some of the action too.

The two of them growled my name as their fingers bit into my flesh and I fought to keep my legs planted between the onslaught of what these two monsters were doing to my body.

Gabriel jerked sharply, and for a moment I thought he was coming before I realised he'd fallen completely still.

"What is it?" Leon growled, still fucking my mouth, his cock thick and hard and the taste of him driving me wild with lust.

Gabriel remained entirely still and I pulled back slightly. Leon took the cue to withdraw his dick from my lips and I looked up at him, panting hard as the immobile hardness of Gabriel's cock deep inside my ass make me quake.

"Please," I gasped, not even realising I was giving in before I'd already done it, but my pussy was throbbing and I couldn't take much more neglect on its behalf.

"What?" Gabriel muttered, seeming to come back to us.

"I need more," I said louder. "Please, I'm begging you."

Leon purred as he pushed me upright in Gabriel's arms and I leaned back so that my spine pressed against his chest. A moan escaped me as the change of angle made Gabriel's cock fill me in a whole new way and my two kings groaned in response.

Gabriel began to thrust in and out of me again slowly as Leon dropped to his knees and dragged my shoes and yoga pants the rest of the way off of my body.

"There are visions dancing around my mind," Gabriel breathed in my ear, his hand finding my nipple and tugging on it.

"What about?" I gasped as Leon knocked my thighs apart and leaned forward to suck my clit into his mouth.

"Ryder, I think," he muttered. "But there's so much lust too, I can't concentrate to *see* it properly. You're too damn distracting."

"Maybe the stars are telling you to be rough with me like he is," I teased.

"Oh, am I not being rough enough?" Gabriel growled, his fingers moving around my throat to hold me in place as he began to fuck my ass harder, his thrusts fierce and stealing my breath away.

With Leon's tongue working on my clit, I fell apart in no time, my pussy clenching and ass squeezing tight around Gabriel's thick shaft as my cries of pleasure coloured the air.

Before I could even begin to recover, Leon got to his feet again, a cruel smile on his lips which were wet with my desire as he hooked my legs around his waist and positioned his cock to finally give my pussy what it was aching for.

"I think I want to hear some more of that begging," Leon growled. "And Gabe, you need to tell the stars to fuck off while you're balls deep in our girl. I want you on your A-game, not lost in your fucking head."

"Shut up, asshole," Gabriel snarled but he thrust in even harder like he was determined to prove he wasn't slacking on anything.

And as Leon drove his cock deep into my core too, I forgot all about visions and stars and every other bullshit thing in our lives as I lost myself to the feeling of being destroyed by the two of them while my tits bounced and they fucked me breathless. There couldn't be anything as important as this going on right now anyway.

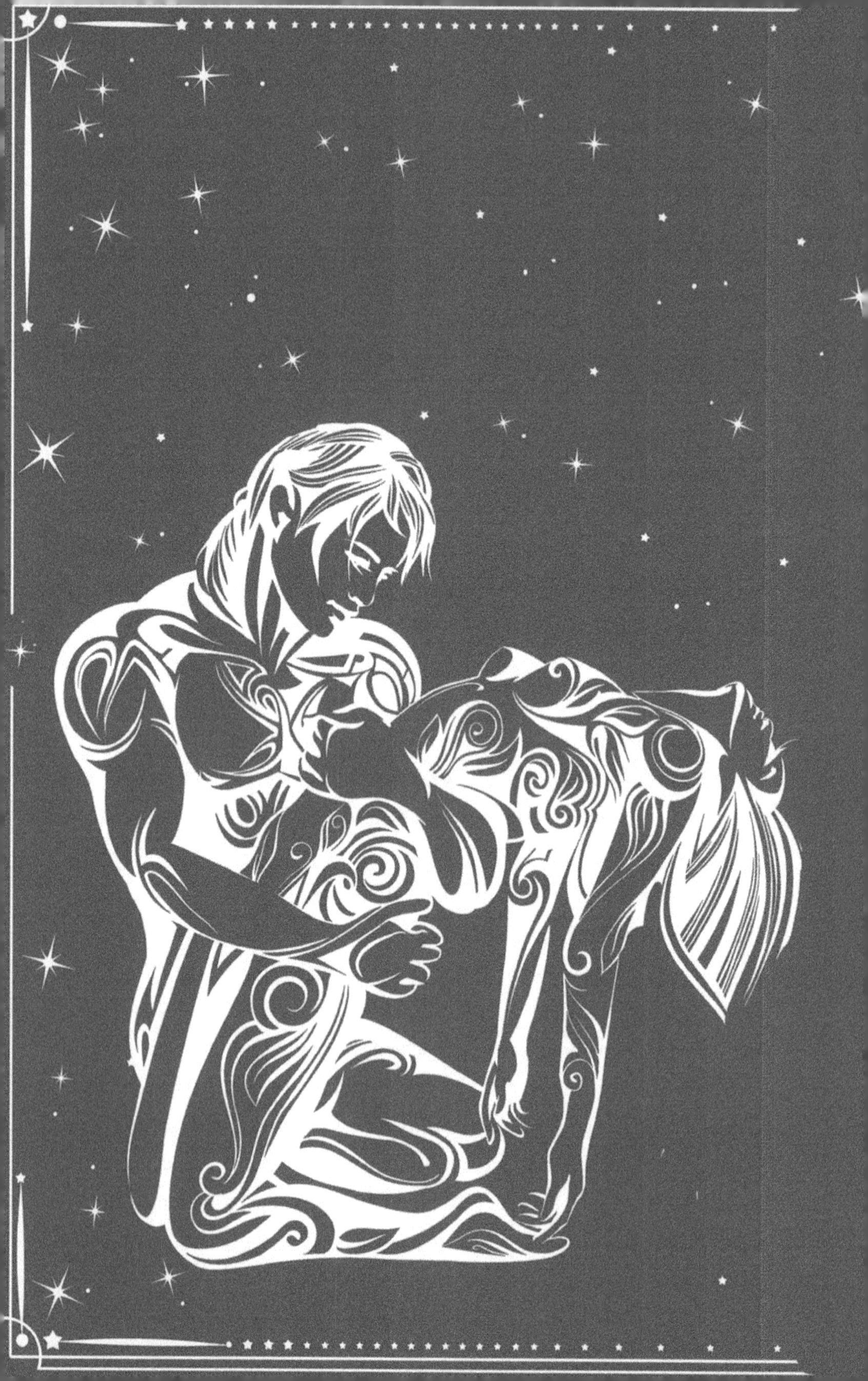

RYDER

CHAPTER SEVENTEEN

"I think you killed him, Viola," Russel hissed. "It's been ages."

"He's not dead," she snapped.

"His skin's cold," Russel muttered, his fingers pressing to my neck as my senses slowly sharpened.

"He's a Basilisk, idiot, his skin's always cold," Bryce said to my right and I felt pain ebbing from him. It was a deep, throbbing agony that drove deep and I recognised it instinctively. Venom.

A hand smacked across my cheek with the force of a truck and my head wheeled around as I tasted blood in my mouth and pain caressed my chest. *Bad fucking move.*

My magic reserves started to feed on the pain, but my hands were locked together behind me in a hard ball of ice so I couldn't use what little I had at my disposal to free myself.

I opened my eyes, finding Bryce there shaking out his hand from the blow, a smug as shit grin on his face as he looked at the others for approval.

"You just bitch slapped the Lunar King," Viola whooped and Russel laughed nervously, but as his eyes fell on me, he shrieked and leapt back a meter.

"He's awake," he stage whispered like I wouldn't hear him.

I guessed the holes where his ears had once been allowed him to still hear just fine, but I wondered how well he'd be able to hear when his head was cut off and buried fifty feet underground.

I took in my surroundings, finding myself in some dusty old stone building with nothing but the wooden chair I was sitting on for furniture. A layer of sand covered the floor and the square hole in one wall where a window had been let the afternoon sunlight pour into the space and tint everything in gold. But this whole place would be red by the time I was finished with it.

I yanked against my restraints and Russel raised his hand to keep the ice in place while I gave him a death glare and he trembled like a leaf. Viola pressed a hand to his arm, offering him more magic for the job and the ice grew colder and firmer against my hands, keeping me contained. I couldn't shift with my arms held like that, I'd rip them clean fucking off.

Fuck.

Bryce smiled when I didn't break free, stepping closer to me and my eyes flicked to the blackish blue stain over his right shoulder where the ghost hound had bitten him. A smirk tugged at my lips as I realised the mutt had poisoned him. And apparently it wasn't the type of wound he could easily heal.

"This is the end of your reign, Ryder," Bryce announced, raising his chin like he was some almighty asshole. He looked kinda sweaty and his eyes were a little bloodshot. Whatever was in the ghost hound's venom, it wasn't pretty, but it also wasn't acting fast enough for my liking.

"We'll see about that," I said darkly as Bryce forged a blade of ice in his hand. He took his time approaching me like he was a big, bad man and I just waited with a bored expression as he tried to frighten me. Pain was my weapon, but it looked like he'd forgotten that as he held the sharp tip of the blade to my throat and pressed down until he drew blood.

He wet his lips at the sight, his fangs lengthening and his eyes twisting with some vicious desire.

"You're a traitor, Ryder," he growled. "You've befriended Dante Oscura. Struck a fucking peace deal without even asking the rest of us what we thought of that." He spat on the floor at his name, and I continued to glare at him without reaction. "Don't you have anything to say in your defence?"

"I think that the only thing this little power trip is achieving for you, Bruce, is convincing your friends that you have a tiny cock," I said calmly and he slammed the blade of ice into my shoulder.

I laughed through the pain as it ran deep into my body and gave me strength.

Viola sniggered and Bryce shot her a glare over his shoulder.

"Shut up," he snapped. "That's not true."

"Why do you always shower back in the dorms after Elemental Combat lessons then?" I mused and he stabbed the ice blade into my gut, making me cough heavily as blood poured into some vital space inside me.

He stabbed again, hitting a lung and blood rose in my mouth, the taste of death surrounding me. Was this really how the Lunar King died? At the hands of some rat and his mouse friends? I'd surely earned a better death than that from the stars.

I thought of Elise with the kind of pain in my chest that made my magic reserves swell. Never seeing her again was a far worse agony then being stabbed by this motherfucker. If I had to die, couldn't I at least have looked at her while I did so? Gazed into the depths of my sweet saviour's eyes as I was cast into damnation for the hellish life I'd led?

"I don't have a small dick you piece of shit." Bryce started stabbing over and over, simply proving that he did. And I coughed out laughs that sounded more and more choked as he hit organ after organ.

"Stop or he's gonna die before we've had any fun!" Viola complained.

Bryce stepped back and I blinked through the haze of darkness around my eyes, my magic reserves almost full. I fought to get free, the ice cracking as I forced my earth magic to battle against the frozen block restraining my hands.

Blood dripped from my mouth onto my chest and their voices reached me through the fog in my head.

"-need to finish him now before he gets away. I can't hold him forever," Russel hissed.

"You can, use our power and keep him in place," Bryce commanded.

"I wanna play with him next," Viola insisted and I felt her warm fingers brush against my cheek.

Healing magic swept through my body and my wounds started to heal over, though not fully as she stepped away again. She gripped my chin, tugging my head up to make me look at her. She was clearly on a power trip, her blue eyes buzzing with excitement as she held me at her mercy.

She brushed her fingertips down to my throat and blocked off my air supply with her power, a smile pulling at her lips as she kept her eyes on mine. I stared blandly back at her, showing none of my discomfort as my lungs tightened with the need for air.

The ice started cracking around my fingers, but the fucking earless wonder worked with Bryce to seal it over once more, their water magic combining to form a powerful seal.

"Give me a knife, Russel," Viola demanded. "I want to cut out his tongue when it turns blue."

"You're a psycho," Bryce laughed as Russel stepped forward and handed her a blade of ice. She grinned at me, pressing the tip of it to the corner of my mouth. "Smile, sweetie pie." She cut a line up my cheek on one side then did the other to match, a clown's smile pissing blood down my face. I'd survived far worse than this pathetic excuse for torture though. I'd spent months at the hands of Mariella using a Sun Steel blade to mark my body permanently. This was child's play, a handful of weak Fae on a power trip who didn't know the intricacies of inflicting real pain.

When my lungs were about to pop, she gave me back my air and I gasped down the oxygen I desperately needed.

"D minus for the torture," I spat. "Poor effort."

Her eyes flared with rage and she drove her fingers into my mouth to try and get hold of my tongue. Fucking idiot. I bit down hard, my teeth sharpening at the point of contact and I unleashed a wave of venom into her veins. She screamed, trying to rip her fingers free of my grip, but I bit harder and she started stabbing me to try and make me let go. But I bit through flesh and bone until I tore them free from her hand and spat them back at her. She reared away with a wail as she hurried to heal the wounds and Russel leapt forward to help her. You couldn't grow back fingers though. They were one of the three Hs. Head, heart and hands were impossible to regrow as they were the source of our magic. How unfortunate.

I laughed threw the blood in my mouth and the pain wreaking havoc in my body.

"Pathetic," I mocked her.

"I'm gonna die, oh my stars, I'm gonna die!" she wailed.

"Calm down. I think him cutting your fingers off stopped the venom from getting into your system," Russel said placatingly.

"Oh great!" she shrieked. "But what about my fucking fingers, Russel?!"

"Maybe we can reattach them," Bryce offered weakly and Viola started screaming abuse at him about how she'd never be able to wield magic with them again.

I battled with my restraints, feeling the ice cracking again and while they were all distracted, I had a real chance at getting free. A splintering noise sounded as the crack deepened and Bryce's head snapped around to look at me.

My heart rate picked up as I raced to get free before he could act. But it was already too late. Bryce shot forward with a snarl, his fangs bared as he drove them into my neck and drank from me. I cursed as he drained my magic, taking mouthful after mouthful of it, ripping away what power I'd accrued. He healed me of the damage Viola had done while I tried to feast on the pain coming from the bites on his shoulder, but it wasn't enough.

My hope started to fade as he stole away my only chance of freedom before stepping back and smirking triumphantly at me, a line of blood spilling from the corner of his lips. He wiped it away with his finger and sucked it off, groaning lustfully. "Now I know why that whore of yours is so obsessed with you," he said with a sigh. "It never made sense to me on account of you having no personality, *boss*. But you taste like a rainbow."

"Your insults are as effective as your tiny cock, Bruce," I said lightly.

"I do not have a tiny cock and my name is not Bruce!" he roared, his ears turning red. He rubbed at the oozing patch on his shoulder where the ghost hound had bitten him, green healing light flashing under his palm. "Fucking monster. How do you heal the venom from those things?" he demanded of me and I frowned thoughtfully, faking knowledge of it. I could just give him my antivenom and save his ass, but I'd die before I gave it to this scum.

"You can't," I said with a smirk. "It'll rot through your shoulder then your arm will fall off eventually." Could have been bullshit, could have been the truth. The blood draining from his face was worth it either way.

"There has to be a way to heal it," he insisted, a note of fear in his voice.

"Nope," I said simply.

"He's lying, Bryce," Viola said as she moved to his side, her fingers now healed over to stumps and a look of utter, violent rage in her eyes.

"Am I?" I questioned dryly.

"Shut up. I'm sick of your attitude," Viola growled then looked to Bryce. "Let's finish him, he only enjoys the torture anyway."

Bryce considered that then nodded, stepping forward. "Traitors get cut into ten pieces, isn't that right boss?" He smiled.

"I'm gonna start with the fingers," Viola said bitterly.

"Then I'll take his cock." Bryce smirked.

"Go ahead, but be warned, it'll only remind you of your own cock failings," I said dryly.

"Shut up!" Bryce shrieked.

"Or is that what this is really about, Bryce? The way you've always hungered for my cock like a power hungry whore looking to fuck your way to the top?"

Bryce flushed beetroot but he couldn't deny it fast enough. I was guessing he had assumed I hadn't known about his little crush on me, but the way he panted like a bitch in heat around me had clued me in a long time ago. It was a shame for him that I'd never been attracted to little bitches with a fetish for hero worshiping then, wasn't it?

"Shut up," Bryce hissed.

"Is that what really happened between you and Dipper?" I added curiously. "The two of you started hooking up but then he caught sight of your micropenis and told you he just wanted to be friends?"

"You told me you just liked biting the femoral artery," Russel said, narrowing his eyes on Bryce in suspicion. "I knew you'd been going for Dipper's Dipper!"

"No I wasn't!" Bryce shrieked. "I can't help it if the best blood flow is in the groin. I had no interest in his fucking Dipper."

I started laughing and Bryce looked ready to cut my throat for it, his eyes flaring with rage.

A shadow blotted out the light streaming through the window for half a second and my three worthless kidnappers turned to look out of it.

"What was that?" Russel hissed and I had to admit I was damn curious myself.

"Nothing," Bryce muttered. "Just a cloud covering the sun. Come on."

"Gimme another blade, Russel," Viola demanded but Russel moved to the window, staring out and shifting from foot to foot.

"Something's out there," he murmured and a clap of thunder rang in the heavens far above as if to punctuate those words.

The sunlight dissolved like night was descending and rain started pounding down on the tin roof, a sound like bullets pinging off metal surrounding me. My mind went to one person capable of such things, but if he was here, what did that even mean? That he'd come to pull up a chair and watch my demise?

Static made the hairs rise along my arms and a murmur of fear left Russel's lips. He started backing away from the window, shaking his head in refusal of whatever he'd seen out there.

"We gotta go. Kill him and run," Russel demanded, racing for the door.

Bryce and Viola shared a look but the door was blasted off its hinges by an explosion of electricity, sending Russel flying across the room before they could figure out their next move. He smashed into the wall beside me, his bones breaking on impact and he hit the floor in a crumpled heap. My magic reserves swelled as he groaned in utter agony and I drank it all in before he released a rattling breath and died.

Fuck yes.

His magic weakened in an instant and I blasted away the ice holding my hands, two huge vine whips smashing through it. Bryce ran with the speed of his Vampire Order, evading my first whip while the second snared Viola around the throat. I stood from my seat with a growl, lifting her above my head on the vine and watching as her feet started kicking, drinking in her pain to fuel my magic even more.

She raised her hands, cutting off my oxygen, and holding a hand to her chest to fill her lungs with air and keep herself alive. I laughed manically, whipping the vine sideways and tearing her head from her shoulders, her horrified expression etched into her features forever as blood rained down on me.

A tremendous Dragon's roar made the walls shake and I took a moment to heal myself fully as I headed to the doorway where Bryce had escaped.

I stepped outside, the rain beating down on me as I found myself at the base of a huge, sandy quarry. Dante's navy blue belly soared over my head, his tail whipping out behind him and painting a line of electricity through the sky. He flew after a blur in the distance that was tearing along the huge valley of sand in an attempt to escape. *Bruce.*

Lightning blasted out of the sky, turning the sand to crystalised pillars of glass as it hit the ground, and as he shot a huge semi-circle of electricity ahead of Bryce, I realised he was capturing the asshole. And whether he was my enemy or not, I wasn't gonna miss out on the chance to make Bryce pay for what he'd done.

I used my earth magic to wield the ground beneath me, rising up on a wall of dirt and moving it like a wave heading for shore as I rode towards my prey. Bryce was captured within the glass, throwing himself against it as I blocked the only exit with the earth beneath my feet, then glared down at him in our trap. He stared up at me in fright, his fists bloody from punching the glass and true terror filled his eyes.

Dante landed beside me with a thump that shook the ground beneath my feet and he roared down at Bryce with the full force of his lungs. I looked to Inferno beside me as the wind tore around us and rain beat over my bloodied flesh, my heart pounding with some strange, powerful connection to him.

I stepped out onto a pillar of earth that appeared at my will, lowering myself down into the pit and walking toward Bryce at a calm and measured pace, cracking my neck. He shrank back against the wall of glittering glass, terror flaring in his eyes. Then he fell to his knees before me, bowing his head and sobbing like a child.

"Please don't kill me!" he wailed as I cast vines out from the ground. They latched around his legs, his arms, his neck then pulled tight so he was forced to lay on his back on the sand, spread out like a meal for the vultures.

"Please!" he screamed as I forced the vines to tighten, yanking and yanking as I fed on his pain and pulled his limbs out in opposing directions. I tasted the rain on my lips and the death in the air. Vengeance was always sweet, but today it was sweeter than all the candy in the world.

"I am the Lunar King!" I bellowed at him and he screamed to the stars for help, but no force in this world could save him from me.

I made it slow, let it hurt so bad that my magic reserves swelled to the brim once more. And when I was finally tired of his screams burrowing into my skull, I forced the vines to rip him into ten pieces, his blood soaking into the sand, his treacherous tongue eternally silenced.

My heart beat a fierce tune that seemed to drum into the very core of my body. I turned to find Inferno gone and wondered if he'd even admit he'd ever been here.

My gratitude to him outweighed so much of the hatred I'd felt toward him. He'd saved my star damned life. He'd been there for me. More than most people had ever been there for me.

I climbed back out of the pit, the rain beginning to ease and the clouds parting above me. But it wasn't the sun that appeared, it was the stars.

I frowned at the heavens, the edges of day meeting the darkest of nights right at the centre of the sky. I tried to blink away the illusion as shock rang through me, but it remained there and two constellations shone bright and burning at the centre of it all. Serpens and Draco. The snake and the dragon. The ones linked to my Order and Inferno's.

I looked for Dante as the beating of my heart in my chest seemed to sound from outside me too. The world became a blur at the edges of the night, the sunlight turning to a milky haze beyond the circle of darkness I was cast in.

"What the hell is happening?" I breathed as a figure walked toward me through the glowing fog.

Dante appeared in a pair of sweatpants, his lips parted in awe as he turned his head to the sky to take in the beautiful and frankly strange as shit view of the night sky above.

The beating in my ears became louder and louder, then turned to ethereal whispers. The stars winked and sparkled and I knew in some deep, instinctual place inside me that it was them I could hear.

"Adversaries born and raised," they spoke. *"Your challenge has been heard. Your bond of blood and death hangs in the balance."*

A deep tug in my chest drew me to Dante and I found myself walking towards him, needing to be closer. *Wanting* to be.

He stood before me like a mirror image, a prince of darkness born to rule the opposing side of the same war. As his eyes locked with mine, a piercing ringing tore through my skull and I fell to my knees, clasping my hands to my ears as the power of it ripped through my head.

"Countless souls have been cast into the sky because of the hate that lives between you both," the stars cursed us, their rage over this fact making everywhere in my body hurt. And it was the kind of pain that offered me no magic. It was torture in its purest, most refined form.

I was being punished by a power that ruled every cell in my body. It could strip me down to dust or build me up into a god. I could feel the source of all my magic in that power, could sense the gift of life it had offered me, the fate it had painted for me. It gazed upon my bared soul, judged and weighed it, separated the good from the bad and counted every piece like they were coins that amounted to my total worth.

"Many chances have been given to end the suffering in this land. But you and your fathers ignored it in favour of your blinding hate." The stars hissed and spat like a raging fire beneath my flesh. *"The bond has tested you and you were both found wanting. But now you stand as allies upon this hill, and we cannot ignore the question you ask of us."*

"What question?" Dante gritted out and I managed to raise my eyes again, finding him just in front of me, on his knees, his back bowed as he faced the same wrath as I did.

"You ask for the bond to be changed," the stars answered, their anger seeming to simmer a little as the pain in my body eased.

I knew what they said was true, but I wasn't really sure how. I'd never asked for things to change, never thought I wanted it. But now I knelt before the man who'd saved me, who loved the woman I loved, who reflected me in so many ways it was suddenly impossible to ignore.

"So what's your answer to that question?" I forced out, feeling Dante's gaze on me as I looked to the sky.

The stars were silent and the pain ran out of my body like water from a shattered dam. My head tilted down to look at Inferno and I almost stopped breathing as I found two glimmering lights floating between us, like tiny stars had dropped from above. They pulsed and flickered, one deepest blue and the other a fiery red.

"Blue is hate, red is love. Choose. But if you do not choose the same, the answer will be hate," the stars whispered, then their power released me from their grip.

I suddenly couldn't see Dante, a wall of light parting us and I gazed at the choice before me. Red or blue. Love or hate. Life as it had been, or life as it could be.

My throat was tight, my heart thrashing more powerfully than it ever normally did. Hate was the path I'd always walked. It was a comfort, the only thing I knew. It was what had always felt right with Inferno. To hate him until he found his death at my hands. But now...

Things had changed. Elise was the reason for that in part, but not just her. I'd seen pieces of Inferno, I had come to like and respect him in ways, though I'd never admit that to anyone. But how could I stand here and choose to *love* him? Just yesterday the idea of that would have seemed abhorrent. But this morning we had placed our hands in each other's and sworn peace. Peace for our people, for the city, for Elise. So how could I refuse this offering from the stars when it could save the whole of Alestria?

And maybe it was more than that. Maybe I wanted the hate to end, to start a life where every day wasn't driven by my desire to hunt and kill. Elise had shown me there was more to the world than that. Dante knew the taste of it. And maybe this was my chance to take a bite out of it too.

I raised my hand, starlight surrounding me, drawing close like it was watching me. Then I reached out to the red star and pressed my fingers into its depths, heat running up my arm in a flood. The wall of light separating me from Dante melted away and my hand met his within the red star.

Our palms locked together and heat burst up into my flesh, rolling through my body on a magnificent wave that made me suck in a breath. It unlocked something in my heart, releasing me from a powerful bond I'd been under the weight of my entire life. Then the light started to lift away, the stars dissolving before us, the clouds beginning to close over and hide the unnatural night once more.

The sunlight broke through, spilling over us and we stood up, standing with our hands in each other's, shocked to the fucking core.

I stared at a man I no longer hated, no burning need to destroy him tearing through my being any longer. He was bonded to me in some new way that felt entirely alien and yet fiercely good.

"Dalle stelle," Dante said heavily, our hands breaking apart.

Then he lunged at me, wrapping me in his arms and I grunted in surprise before winding my arms around him too and holding him tight. I noticed a mark on my hand like half of a figure of eight as it locked around Inferno's shoulder. As he stepped back, I pointed out one on his too, nestled between the crook of his forefinger and thumb just as mine was.

"What is that?" I murmured.

"A mark from the stars." He admired it in the light and it glimmered with some deep, unknown magic. I stared at him as he looked up at me once more and a grin split across his face which I immediately returned. He held his hand out to me to clasp and where I hands joined, the marks created an infinity symbol connecting us to one another. "Holy shit, fratello. I think the stars just made us best friends."

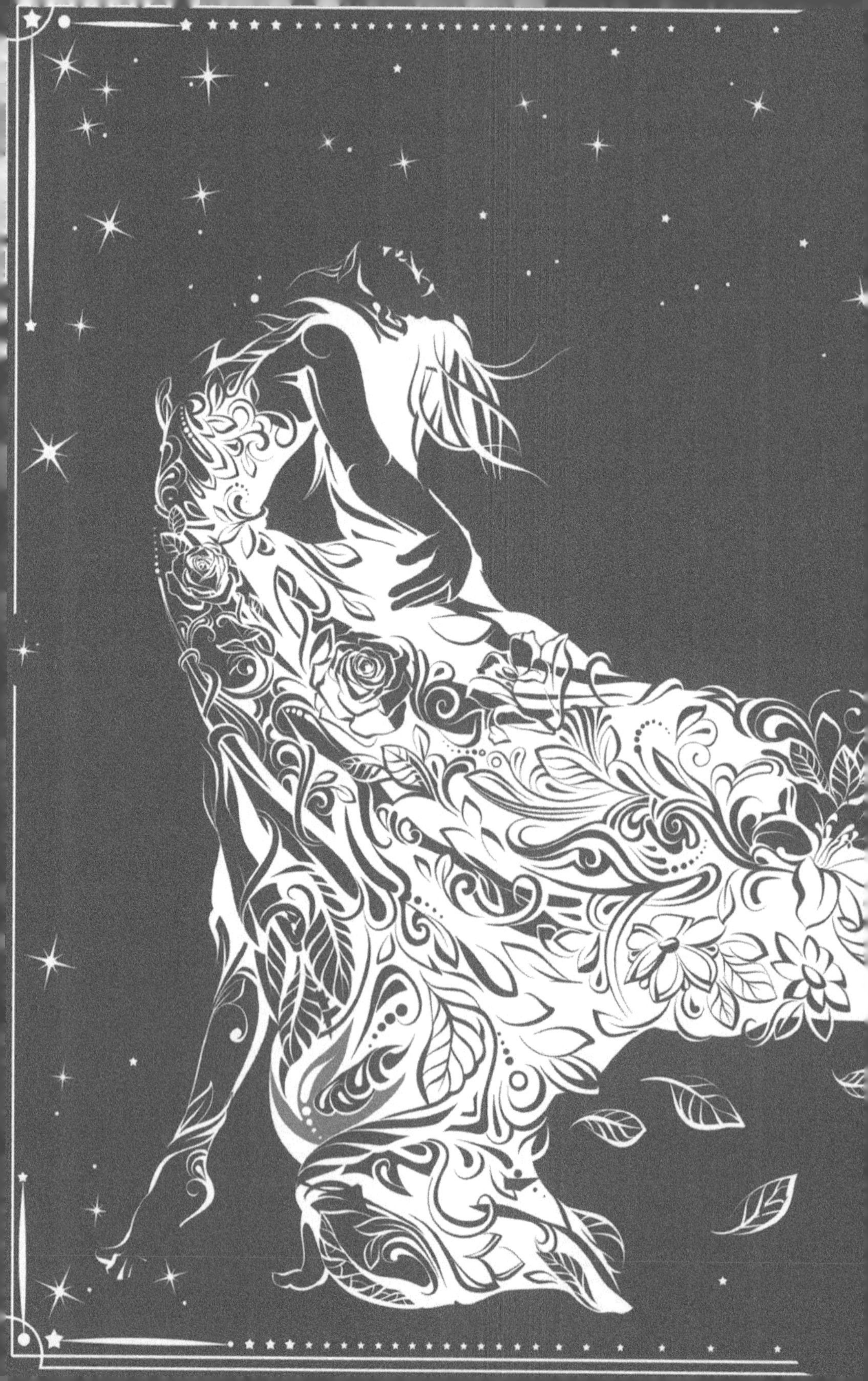

ELISE

CHAPTER EIGHTEEN

"By the moon, you're so fucking tight," Gabriel growled in my ear, his cock thrusting deep into my ass as I leaned back against his chest, panting and moaning through the sensation of him and Leon destroying my body.

"Use me," I moaned, loving the way their fingers were digging into my thighs as they held me up between them.

"You want more, little monster?" Leon asked, thrusting in harder and making me see stars as he slammed his thick cock against my g-spot.

My response was a pleasure filled moan as his thumb found my clit and Gabriel bit down on my neck from behind me.

They changed up their pace, Leon slamming into me as Gabriel drew back then vice versa, making sure there was never a moment where I didn't have one of them fully sheathed within me.

"I'm gonna come," I panted, unsure if I could really take any more as Leon rubbed my clit and Gabriel lifted a hand to tug on my hardened nipple.

"Then come for us, beautiful," Gabriel commanded in a rough and possessive voice.

Ecstasy exploded through my body and my muscles clamped tight around their cocks as I cried out, every inch of my flesh overwhelmed with pleasure.

"Fuck," Leon gasped, his hand on my ass tightening painfully as he held off his own release and Gabriel groaned as he fought against his too.

My muscles throbbed around them, my fangs snapping out as I hungered for more, wanting to bring them to ruin too. But the look in Leon's eyes as I met his golden gaze said that he had no intention of being done with me yet.

"Look at you," he growled. "So fucking perfect. So fucking beautiful. So fucking insatiable."

"One man never would have been enough for you, would it, angel?" Gabriel added. "You breathe sex like the rest of us breathe air."

"She's our filthy girl," Leon purred, rolling his hips and making me gasp. "I say we see how much she can take of us."

Gabriel's dark chuckle was a clear agreement and he drew back too, adjusting his hold on me as Leon looked at him over my shoulder and I tried to prepare myself for what they had planned. I knew they meant what they'd said, but I had no complaints about that. I wanted them to push me, punish me, use me and fuck me until I couldn't take any more of it and my body was fully sated.

But just as the two of them began to move inside me again, a tug of need pulled in my chest and I gasped as I tilted my head back to look up at the sky.

A curse drew my gaze back down and I blinked in surprise as I found myself crouching on the ground, Leon flat on his back ten feet away from me and Gabriel shoving himself upright from the same distance away behind me.

"What the hell, Elise?" Leon asked, a confused frown pinching his brow, but I couldn't form the words to explain why I'd just thrown the two of them off of me using my magic. In fact, I couldn't even really remember doing it.

The tug in my chest was growing more demanding and I turned and shot away from them before another word passed between us.

I sped through the trees, but lost track of time for several seconds before blinking and finding myself back in the room Leon and I shared in his family's house.

I'd pulled on one of Leon's white dress shirts which I guessed I'd grabbed from the closet though I had no recollection of fetching it, let alone putting it on. Half of the buttons were fastened over my otherwise naked body and I looked down at my hand in confusion, finding a pouch of stardust in my grasp.

I shot out of the room again, aiming for the gates at the far end of the Nights' drive without any understanding of why I was heading there.

I blinked and found myself in the grip of the stars with no idea of where I was heading or even any memory of me tossing the stardust in the first place.

My bare feet landed in the dirt and I frowned around at the sandy quarry I found myself in, wondering where the fuck I was as my skin prickled with a strange kind of energy.

My feet started moving of their own accord, drawing me towards a little stone building but before I could reach it, I fell still, the air around me seeming to fall still too, like I was cocooned in a bubble of silence.

My skin prickled as the hairs along the back of my neck stood on end and I sucked in a surprised breath as two figures suddenly stepped around the building before me.

Ryder was covered in blood and the two of them looked like they'd been through hell and back, but something about the way the two of them stood so close to each other, their arms brushing and the hint of a smile on their lips made my pulse quicken.

I opened my mouth to ask them what had happened to them just as they noticed me standing there and the question got caught in my throat.

They strode towards me side by side and I found myself unable to move as the sky seemed to twist and swirl above us, clouds parting and the sand kicking up in a vortex that surrounded us and yet somehow stayed outside of the space we stood in.

I gasped as I realised the sense of déjà vu I had pressing in on me was because of the way the heavens were converging overhead. I'd stood in a sphere of magic like this before, had answered the call of the heavens like this too, and my lips parted in a gasp as the stars realigned themselves in the sky above us. How could this be happening?

My star sign appeared right overhead, the Libra constellation shining bright and clear right between Dante's Gemini constellation and Ryder's Capricorn.

"Dalle stelle," Dante murmured in awe as he stared up at the heavens too, taking in the enormity of what was happening to us.

This shouldn't have been possible. There had never been a case of this in the history of our world, and yet here I stood with two more men, answering the call of fate and feeling a pull to them just as deeply as the one I had felt to Leon all those moons ago.

"I always knew you were meant for me, baby," Ryder breathed, drawing my attention back down to him and Dante.

They still stood side by side, their arms touching and bare chests painted in blood. I had so many questions about what they'd been doing here, why they looked like that and what those strange new marks were on their hands. But the only thing that really mattered right now was the question being asked of us.

"This is why we didn't have this choice before," Dante said, drawing his eyes from me to Ryder. "While fate held us pitted against one another we couldn't have been this to her."

"But now we're free to choose," Ryder replied, though his gaze never wavered from my face.

"What does that mean?" I breathed.

"We broke our bond, bella," Dante purred. "We're not Astral Adversaries anymore."

Shock rattled through me at that news and tears of joy brimmed in my eyes.

"Which means, we can be yours," Ryder added.

"Together?" I asked, because I knew this couldn't just be about them choosing me. They would be picking each other too by making this choice. If we really were being offered the chance to become Elysian Mates, then we would never be able to unravel the bonds between us. We would be family.

I stepped towards them as they exchanged a loaded look and when they both turned back to face me again, I could see the decision clear in their eyes. They wanted this. Wanted me. More than any hatred or rivalry or any of that bullshit, they just wanted us.

The three of us moved together as one, their arms winding behind me as I reached for both of them, my chin tilting up as they leaned in. Our mouths met in the middle, all three of us at once, lips parting, tongues caressing and a bond wrapping around our souls as the stars made good on their offer and mated us to one another.

I moaned softly as I felt the power of that bond taking root in me, gasping as their hands tugged at my shirt and teased my body.

I was already hot and needy, my flesh aching for more after my hook up with Leon and Gabriel had been cut short and I moaned as the bond urged us even closer.

I wanted more of them. No - I needed them. I needed to feel the power of their bodies surrounding me and taste the flavour of this bond on their flesh as I claimed them in every way I could think of.

The magic echoed through my bones as the bond between us was solidified and my flesh shivered with the pure joy of what we'd just become.

A sound drew our attention from each other for a moment and I gasped as a little blue ghost hound barked at us.

"We shouldn't linger here," Ryder growled, seeming to remember the reason for the two of them being covered in blood as I realised the heavens had settled once more and the magic was fading from the world around us.

Dante grabbed a pouch of stardust from his pocket, tossing it over us and whipping us away through the stars without another word and I clung to them as we were dragged across time and space.

We landed in Gabriel's apartment in the city, and the ghost hound shot off towards the kitchen with a happy yip.

I barely had time to take in my surroundings before Ryder tugged my chin forward so my mouth met his again, pulling me with him as he fell down onto the bed.

A surprised laugh escaped me as I steadied myself on his chest, looking down into his green eyes which were now ringed in silver, my heart racing with the heady thought of knowing I'd claimed him even more thoroughly than before.

"A morte e ritorno," Dante growled in my ear as he crawled onto the bed behind us, and I turned my head to find a silver ring in his honey brown eyes too.

"To death and back," I breathed in reply.

"Your eyes are almost entirely silver now, bella," he purred, excitement filling his gaze as he stared into them. "Only the smallest line of green left surrounding your pupils."

I bit my lip as I took that in, wondering how the hell I could have ended up so blessed as to claim so many ferocious creatures as my own, but before I could say anymore on the subject, Dante leaned forward to kiss me hungrily.

I moaned into his mouth as Ryder unbuttoned the shirt I was wearing and sucked my hardened nipple between his lips, biting down hard enough to make me gasp.

Dante pulled back with a dirty laugh and tugged the shirt the rest of the way off of me, leaving me naked between them before standing to remove his own pants.

I reached out to unbuckle Ryder's belt as he continued to suck and bite my nipple, tugging on the other between his calloused fingers and sending a mixture of pleasure and pain spiking through me.

I used a spurt of my speed to yank Ryder's jeans the rest of the way off of him and moaned in excitement as his hard cock was freed, his piercing catching the light and making my pussy clench with need.

Ryder gripped my ass and tugged me into position over his throbbing dick, rocking me back and forth so that my arousal coated his shaft and his piercing rubbed against my clit, making me beg for more.

Dante's hands ran down my spine as he moved onto the bed behind me, his mouth finding my neck as he traced kisses over the sensitive skin, sending goosebumps blossoming across my flesh.

"Ti amo, mate of mine," he growled hungrily, his hot dick driving against my ass as his muscular chest pressed against my bare back.

"Ti amo, Dante," I panted while Ryder continued to rub his cock back and forth against my opening and over my clit. "I love you, Ryder."

"I love you too, baby," Ryder swore and the intensity of the look in his newly silver ringed eyes, coupled with the feeling of that piercing rubbing over my clit once more had me coming so hard I saw stars.

Dante growled something which I just knew was filthy in Faetalian and Ryder groaned headily at the sound I made before driving the full, solid length of himself into me with one hard thrust, making my orgasm sharpen and heighten as I fell prey to the two of them.

Dante pushed me forward so that I was leaning right down over Ryder and I found my Basilisk's mouth, kissing him with a desperate kind of passion which showed him exactly how much he meant to me.

Ryder fucked me from below, his thrusts long and slow, driving the breath from my lungs with every strike of his cock deep inside me.

Dante trailed kisses down my spine as he moved even closer behind me and I moaned in encouragement, wanting to feel the thickness of him in my ass so much that I was only moments away from begging for it.

Before I could break my kiss with Ryder to do that, Dante shifted his cock between my thighs just like I'd been wanting. But instead of claiming my ass like I'd expected him to, I felt the head of his dick pushing against the wet heat of my pussy right alongside Ryder's.

I gasped as I broke away from Ryder's kiss, glancing over my shoulder at Dante as my pulse flickered with surprise and a little fear, but more than a little anticipation too.

"Do you want this, bella?" Dante asked, his eyes lighting with excitement as electricity danced across his skin and sparked along mine as well.

I moaned loudly as Ryder continued to guide my movements on his cock with his hands on my ass, glancing back down at him to see what he wanted.

"You can handle us, baby," he purred with a sinful smile gracing his lips and melting any lingering hesitance.

"I want it," I said, my voice catching as Ryder drove his cock in deep once more.

Electricity crackled across the room as Dante took in those words and I sucked in a breath as he waited for Ryder to draw back out of me until only the head of his cock was inside me before driving his dick into my core as well.

The moan that escaped me was all animal as the two of them pushed inside my pussy at once, moving slowly to allow me to get used to the way their thick cocks stretched and filled me. It was so much. I could hardly even breathe. I felt so full that it made my head spin. And yet my whole body was humming with so much pleasure that I knew there was no way in hell I was going to be asking them to stop.

Dante chuckled darkly as he began to move, his weight driving me down onto Ryder even harder as the two of them sandwiched me between them and began fucking me together.

Every thrust was the most intense form of ecstasy and the noises that were escaping me were pure animal as I came again almost instantly, my pussy clenching around their cocks as I gasped and panted, blinded by the sensation of the two of them owning me as one and never wanting it to stop.

And it didn't stop, they weren't even close to done with me, their bodies finding a rhythm together as they pinned me between them, these two men who had once been mortal enemies now bound by something so much more powerful than hate. They were bound together by me.

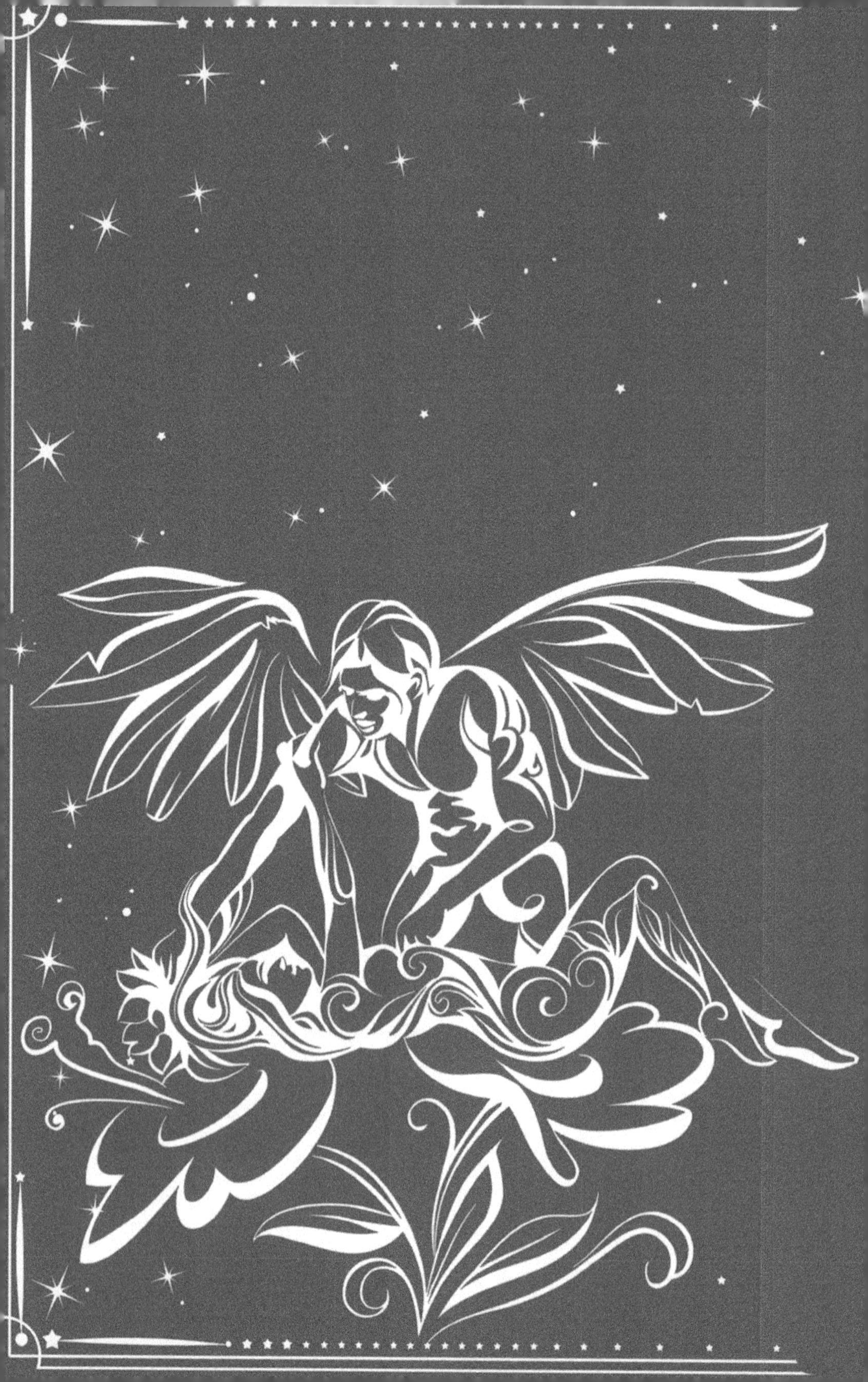

GABRIEL

CHAPTER NINETEEN

"Holy shit!" I cried as Leon took a corner at speed in his fancy silver sports car and I braced myself on the window as he pumped the gas. We flew up the road and I whooped in time with him as my heart rose in my chest and my stomach did backflips.

I'd been pissed as hell after Elise had run off on us, and especially when we'd felt out exactly who she'd run to through the tracking spell that now bound us all. Apparently, she wanted to be in the arms of Dante and Ryder right now, and one flash of The Sight had shown me all I needed to know about how much they were fucking at this very second. I'd been on the verge of a full blown tantrum when Leon had dragged me to his car with promises to cheer me up. And hell, I had to admit it had worked.

We'd driven up into the mountains north of his family home and he sped along the winding roads almost fast enough to outrun The Sight. Or at least it was distracting enough to keep me from focusing on visions of Elise moaning and coming on someone else's cock. Instead, I used it to *see* around every corner ahead of us which meant Leon could drive as fast as he wanted without worrying about a crash.

"Guide me, Gabe!" he yelled, slamming a hand over his eyes and I roared a laugh as I saw us plummeting over the nearest cliff.

"Right!" I called and he spun the wheel. I yanked on the other side of it as we took the bend hard, levelling us out and Leon cursed excitedly as he dropped his hand so he could see again. "Faster!" I demanded.

He slammed his foot on the accelerator and we tore into a dark tunnel carved through the mountain. He blasted the horn and flashed his lights as we zoomed a hundred miles an hour toward the circle of light at the far end.

As we broke back out of the tunnel, he took a sharp left and a vision of a truck colliding with us made my heart bunch up into my throat.

"Get up on that verge!" I shouted, pointing to the mossy patch off of the road and Leon immediately obeyed, the car bumping onto it as a truck came tearing towards us out of another tunnel as he slammed on the brakes.

The driver blared his horn as he sailed by and we both fell apart laughing, trying to catch our breath as Leon pulled the parking brake.

"I love almost dying with you, Gabe," Leon panted, throwing a hand out to slap down on my shoulder.

"Fuck yes." I grinned at him. "And don't call me Gabe."

"Yeah, yeah." He waved a hand, snatching his Atlas out of the cupholder, his eyes falling to the screen with a pout. "She hasn't called. Is she alright?" He looked to me and I let myself fall into the nagging visions of my girl being DPed. Was that actually necessary, stars? How was that an important vision I needed to *see*? I swear they just liked to mess with me sometimes.

"Yeah, she's fucking swell," I said with a look that told him exactly what she was still up to.

Leon ran his tongue over his teeth then unclipped his belt and lunged out of his seat, climbing on top of me and shoving my shoulders down under his weight.

"What the fuck are you doing?" I balked, pushing him back as he started nuzzling my head.

"Shhh, shhh," he purred, trying to shove me down harder and I fought with two hundred pounds of Lion muscle as he boxed me into my seat and kept pressing his weight on me.

"Dude!" I barked, not wanting to hurt him, but I sure as shit would. I called on The Sight for help, but only got a vision of Dante's cock in Elise's mouth, so that was just great.

"Leon!" I snapped, punching him in the kidney and he blinked hard, seeming to snap out of some stupor.

"Oops, sorry dude. Went all Lion instincts there." He tried to pat down my hair which he'd nuzzled up into a fuck nest and I slapped his hands away. Sometimes I wasn't convinced these so-called episodes of *Lion instincts* were as hard for him to avoid as he made out.

He slid back into his seat, taking a long sip of the rainbow coloured slurpee he'd bought on our way here.

"You need to lock that shit down. What's it even about?" I asked, trying not to Order shame him, but by the stars, I would never understand the social Orders and their weird ass tactile ways.

"It's a dominance thing. I'm an Alpha Lion, I get urges to dominate my Lionesses from time to time," he said casually and my eyes narrowed.

"I think we need to have a discussion about our group being called a 'pride'. I'm not a Lioness, and I'm sure as shit not submissive."

He finished his slurpee, sucking loudly on the straw as he tried to get the last of the juice out. The noise went on and on until it annoyed me so much, I smacked the cup out of his grip and he was left with the straw sticking out of his lips and no slurpee to slurp on.

He plucked the straw out of his mouth and tossed it into the backseat. "Well, that wasn't very nice, Gabe."

"Don't avoid the subject. And don't call me Gabe," I said firmly.

He reached over, gripping my thigh and squeezing as he stared at me. "Look Gabe-"

I pushed his hand off my thigh with a growl and narrowed my eyes. "Don't. Call. Me. *Gabe*," I warned.

He sighed dramatically. "Fine. Look *Gabe*-riel, I'm a Lion. And you can call a duck a horse, but it still quacks and has a beak."

"I don't know what that's supposed to mean," I said in confusion.

"It *means* we're a pride, dude. There's no changing that. Our pride is our family. And my instincts get all over excited sometimes because my nature is to be the head of the pride. So just don't worry about it. The next time I dom you, just go with it. Let me grind you down beneath me, let me put you in your place."

"My place is not beneath you," I said.

"Sure it isn't," he said lightly like he didn't actually mean that. "It'll just keep my inner Lion happy, that's all. Nothing to worry about. I won't tell anyone I topped you."

"You didn't top me, Leon. And I'd prefer if you used some different phrasing."

He rolled his eyes. "By the stars, you're so touchy. Fine. I pushed you down beneath me and bent you to my will. Happy?"

"No."

"Good." He started driving off down the road. "Shall we go see our little monster?"

"Alright," I agreed. "But I'm pissed at her."

"Even better. We can have make-up sex and show her who does threesomes better."

"I still can't believe she just abandoned us for them. Was my game off today?" I didn't exactly want his opinion on that, but I was also feeling one percent self-conscious about it now I'd gone and said it. The Sight had been distracting me a lot and I'd ended up in a fuzzy headspace which hadn't been good for visions *or* fucking. But if there was one person I could talk to about that, I guessed it was the no boundaries Lion with one hundred and fifty percent confidence. He'd been pissed she'd left, but hadn't taken it personally at all. How did he even manage that? Maybe being her Elysian Mate quieted any worries or jealousies. I already felt like the lesser party in this group, so I didn't need much convincing to spiral into doubts.

"You were hot on your game, bro," Leon said reassuringly. "You were all thrusty and dirty and then you said that thing that was all like, 'you breathe sex like the rest of us breathe air'," he said in a husky impression of my voice and I cringed.

"That doesn't sound sexy now you're saying it back to me," I commented.

"Nah, it totally was." He reached over blindly, vaguely rubbing my face and I leaned away from his weird stroking. "You made her come so hard. Maybe she just had to leave because she was too turned on."

"I don't think so," I muttered.

"It's a total possibility. One time, before me and Elise had hooked up, I had a boner over her for three days. Three *days*, Gabe. I had to get Mindys to hold strategic objects over the bulge in my pants. Cups, bagels, a potted plant. It was a long few days, but I got away with it."

"Actually, I remember that," I replied with a snort of a laughter. "And *everyone* noticed. It was in the school newspaper. Principal Greyshine did that announcement asking some of the girls following you around to report to him if they were in any kind of trouble."

"Nah," he said dismissively like I was just plain wrong and I shook my head at him, a smirk pulling at my mouth. He was a complete headcase, but it was kind of impossible not to like him most of the time.

We descended from the mountains and made our way back to my apartment on the west side of Alestria. Leon parked in the underground lot and we took the elevator up to the top floor where Elise wasn't even trying to conceal her screams of pleasure within a silencing bubble. Leon grinned darkly as he opened the door and we stepped inside, finding Elise spread out naked on the breakfast bar with Ryder and Dante's faces buried between her thighs, their heads bobbing in time with one another's. *For the love of the stars.*

"You're in trouble, Elise," Leon called, marching straight toward her as she came with a shudder and a moan, her hands fisting in both of the guys' hair between her legs.

She propped herself up on her elbows, panting furiously as Dante and Ryder stepped back. They were in matching grey sweatpants, the outline of their hard cocks standing out through them. At least they'd made some attempt at getting dressed since the last fucking vision, but it had clearly been heading in the same direction anyway.

"We need to talk," Elise panted, her gaze fixing on me as I drew closer and I frowned as I took in her eyes. The silver in them seemed thicker somehow...

"Oh my stars!" Leon roared, diving on Ryder and Dante and dragging them into a group hug as he bounced up and down. "How did this happen? It's not possible, but by the moon it has happened. It has. Tell me it has!"

"It has, Leone," Dante said with a wide grin.

Elise slipped off of the breakfast bar, pulling on a white silk dressing gown which had been abandoned on the floor. "Gabriel." She caught my hand, but my gaze fixed on Dante and Ryder's eyes, moving between them as my brain slowly caught up to what I was seeing.

No. There's no way. It can't be true.

"Gabriel, can we talk?" Elise begged, but I pulled my hand free of hers, my heart sinking like a brick in my chest as panic swallowed all the air around me and made it difficult to breathe.

Ryder and Dante started explaining, but I could hardly hear what they were saying.

"-you broke the Astral Adversary bond?" Leon gasped but I just kept closing the distance between us, staring at their eyes, finding an impossible reality mocking me.

It wasn't true. How could it be true? The Elysian Mate bond was for two Fae. Not more than that. But the truth was staring right back at me. Ryder and Dante had silver rings in their eyes and as Elise shot in front of me, planting a hand on my chest, I caught hold of her chin and examined the rings in hers. Nearly all of her green irises were now coloured silver, just a glimmer of it in the centre by her pupils.

"This is the best day of my life!" Leon cried, bounding around and grabbing Elise in a bone crushing hug as she tried to calm him down. He started throwing rapid fire questions at her while Ryder and Dante drew closer to them, seeming unable to keep their hands off of Elise as they kissed her neck and stroked their hands down her back.

"Elysian Mate orgy!" Leon announced, tugging at Elise's robe.

"Wait, Leo," she said breathlessly, but she was clearly captured by the desire following their mating too, her hands dragging over Dante's chest and Ryder's throat.

She hunted for me, but Ryder's mouth found hers and she was lost to the sea of passion that solidified their bond, everything else around her vanishing. Including me.

I backed toward the door, my world shrinking and a pit of jealousy and loss awakening inside me. I wasn't a part of this. I was an outsider, like I'd always been an outsider. She could never love me like she loved them, and maybe my love wasn't good enough for her anyway. It couldn't match that of her true mates.

"I have to go," I mumbled and Elise tried to look for me once more, but I was already stepping out the door, sliding a pouch of stardust from my pocket.

The door yanked open just before I threw it and Elise called my name in desperation before I disappeared into the stars. I wasn't even sure where I was going until my feet landed on a grubby street in the city and I realised I'd gone looking for Bill.

A Blazer girl screamed and fell on her ass in surprise at the sight of me appearing right in front of her, her pupils full blown and her hair wild. "Ah! It's a man with no friends! No friends at all!" She got up, stumbling away with another scream and I scowled after her as she hid behind a lamppost. She poked her head out to peek at me then ducked behind it again.

I strode down the street and through a little gate where Bill's home sat in the middle of a row of small houses, walking up to the door and knocking. No one answered, so I knocked harder, trying to ignore the Blazer as she started singing somewhere behind me.

"He had no friends that boy over there, maybe it was to do with his old underwear. Maybe his heart was as small as a pea, or maybe it was because of his bow-legged knee."

I ground my teeth, knocking harder as her voice drew closer.

"He had no friends that boy up the street, maybe it was because he had big hairy feet. Maybe it was because he had ears like Spock, or maybe it was because of his shrivelled cock."

"Bill!" I barked. "It's me, open the star damned door."

"Maybe at night he has horns like a ram, or maybe when you sniff him he smells like a clam."

"Bill!" I shouted louder, about to break the door down when it wrenched half open and he stuck his head out. He was sweaty and panting, his tanned, hairy chest bare and his eyes flaring with fire.

"By the stars, kid, do ya ever show up when I'm not balls deep in my favourite hooker?"

I growled in frustration, dropping my gaze from his as my jaw tightened. "Shit, sorry."

"What is it, are you alright?" he asked with a note of concern in his gruff voice.

"Billy boy, are you coming back to bed? I've spilled whipped cream *everywhere*," a woman's voice reached me and Bill looked over his shoulder with a noise of desperation.

"You okay?" he pressed and I slapped on a fake smile, meeting his gaze again as I nodded.

"Yeah, I'm good. I'll catch you later." I turned and headed off down the street, hearing him call after me as I took out the stardust and threw it over myself.

I wasn't sure where I was going, my mind focusing on one place to the next as the stars carried me along, waiting for me to decide. Whispers filled my head and suddenly I felt them guiding me somewhere, urging me toward someone. I was deposited in front of two glitzy gates with the words Zodiac Academy etched into them above a beautiful zodiac wheel.

I frowned, wondering why the stars had brought me to the posh kids' school when someone walked past me, turning to look at me curiously.

"Noxy?" Orion's brows shot up in surprise as he found me there and the knot in my chest eased a little.

"Hey er…" I ran a hand through my hair, feeling awkward as shit.

"You okay, man?" he asked, taking in my expression with a frown. He wore a silver and blue Pitball jersey with ZA on the front of it and his dark hair was pushed back in a casual way like he hadn't bothered to style it, but it had fallen perfectly into place anyway.

"I…no, actually. I'm having a shit day," I admitted, swallowing the sharp lump in my throat.

"You wanna hang out?" he asked like he was hoping for the company too and the breath went out of me in relief.

"Yeah, that'd be cool," I muttered and he nodded, leading the way through the gates onto the academy grounds. "Have you been out somewhere?"

He flicked up a silencing bubble as he glanced around. "Yeah, I was at the Acrux Manor. My mom works with them, so I'm always around there. And now my sister, Clara, does too…"

"How can you stand those Dragon assholes?" I asked with a grimace, realising I probably shouldn't have blurted that out, but The Sight said I didn't have to filter myself around Lance Orion. I could trust him, and the bark of laughter that left him confirmed it.

"I tend to zone out Lionel's grand speeches. Darius is cool. He likes to get away from his dickwad of a dad whenever he can and I'm all for helping him with that. Plus he's one of my only friends around here if I'm being honest. Is that sad?"

"You're the most popular guy at Zodiac, surely he's not your only option?" I questioned.

"Yeah…" He scrubbed a hand down the back of his head. "But I'm a Vampire anyway so being a loner is kind of my thing. Besides, once I made a name for myself in Pitball my first year, it was hard to tell the real friends from the groupies. But there's a girl called Francesca on my team who's cool. She's one of the few people at this school who I can trust since my sister graduated. With my connections to the Acruxes…well it isn't exactly easy distinguishing the power-hungry Fae from the genuine ones either. And the Fae at this academy are more power hungry than most."

"I doubt they're worse than Alestrians," I commented with a hint of a smirk. "But instead of fisticuffs at dawn like you guys have, it's bloody murder at any hour of the day."

"Nice," Orion chuckled as we headed along the winding path into the sweeping meadow of Aer Territory. "Don't go thinking the rich assholes here are any less bloodthirsty though. If the powerful scent blood in the water, they'll go at the weak like sharks."

"Guess that's life," I sighed. "Anyway, you're better off without many friends than having a bunch of shitty ones. I've lived most of my life with a single person I could rely on. It just means no one can slide a knife in your back while you're sleeping."

"Exactly," he agreed. "You wouldn't believe the shit that goes on in the shadows of this place."

"Like good little posh boys doing dark magic?" I jibed, knocking my shoulder against his and he smirked at me.

"Precisely. You can't trust anyone. Not even your own family." His eyes darkened.

"That sucks."

"Yeah, especially because Clara swore she wouldn't work for the Acruxes after she left Zodiac. She said she never wanted to be involved with them and now Mom keeps going on about how great she is doing with them like she can't wait for me to join them after I graduate this year. But I don't wanna follow in their footsteps and be Lionel Acrux's little bitch. I've got a real chance to join the Solarian Pitball League. Mom is just convinced I'm going through a phase." He rolled his eyes.

"I'm sorry, man. Maybe she'll come around?" I suggested.

He shook his head like he thought that was impossible. "Doesn't matter anyway, nothing's gonna stop me if I get selected. The Starfires are recruiting and I'm not gonna miss my shot."

My eyebrows arched. "I'd better get an invite to your first game." I grinned and he nodded. I fucking loved that team.

He smiled back, the light returning to his eyes. "Damn straight you will, and you'll be Pitside so you can see the carnage up close."

He led me to the huge tower which housed the air Elemental dorms and I gazed up at the immense spinning turbine at the top of the sheer white walls in awe. He cast air magic at the Elemental symbol above the entrance and led the way inside as the door unlocked. I followed him up a seemingly endless winding stairway that circled through the tower, each level heading off toward corridors full of dorms. My breaths came heavier as we made it to one of the highest levels and he led me down the hall with light walls and one door at the end of it.

"House Captain's quarters." He shot me a grin before pushing his way inside and I followed him into a huge room with a massive bed at the heart of it. A couple of armchairs sat by a stretch of floor length windows and Orion dropped down onto one, kicking his feet up on the coffee table between the seats and gesturing for me to take the other chair.

I sat down, looking around the massive room that was about three times the size of our dorm back at Aurora Academy.

"This is all for you?" I asked in surprised.

"Yeah." He gave me an awkward smile. "Fucking stupid, isn't it?"

"Moronic," I agreed with a mocking grin.

I picked up a box of protein balls by his feet, reading the name Proballs on the bright red box covered in Pitballs.

"You want one?" Orion offered. "They keep you building muscle up to three times longer after a workout."

"Seriously?" I snorted, pulling one out of the packet.

"Yeah, it's some organic elasto fruit thing from Baruvia," he said. "Totally above board. It's just a supplement. Coach gave them to me."

I tossed one of the fruity balls into my mouth and my eyebrows arched at the sweet, sugary taste of it as I chewed. I immediately ate another one and Orion laughed.

"They're good, right?"

"Really good." I ate a few more.

Orion reached out to take the box from me, but I hooked out another couple and kept it away from him. "Alright, calm down. Don't they feed you at Aurora?"

I shrugged, stuffing a few more between my lips before he shot forward and grabbed the box from my hand with a laugh.

"They're so moreish," I said through a mouthful of them.

Alright, so maybe I was emotional eating right now. And maybe I didn't give a fuck because these things tasted like a star damned rainbow and I'd had a shitty day.

A tingling sensation started up in my dick and I frowned as I swallowed the last of them.

"Do they normally make your dick feel weird?" I asked as the tingling spread all down the length of it and into my balls.

"What?" Orion balked. "No, what's it feel like?"

"Like pins and needles in my cock." I looked up at him, a weird swelling feeling taking the place of the tingling. "What the hell is in these, man?" I grabbed the box from him, turning it over to read the ingredients, but couldn't find anything strange among the list.

"Are you allergic or something?" Orion asked as my cock got a hundred percent hard. So hard it was fucking painful.

"I don't fucking know, Lance. Apparently," I snapped as my dick ground hard against the inside of my pants until I was sure it was gonna bust open. "Oh my stars," I gasped in fright, hurriedly unbuckling my pants and letting my zipper down. My dick kept growing and I was pretty sure my fucking balls were growing too. "What's happening?" I demanded of Orion in panic and he just shook his head at me in dismay. "Where'd you get these?"

"Coach," he confirmed. "Well, I mean, my friend delivered them to me from Coach."

"What. Friend?" I snarled as I fought to keep my dick contained within my boxers as it packed out the material and I winced as it started to throb painfully. "Orio, fucking help me."

Orion sprang to his feet, looking from the bulge of my ever-expanding cock to the box of Proballs. "Wait here."

He shot out of the room in a burst of speed and I groaned as my solid dick grew even bigger and suddenly split through my boxers, tearing them in half.

"No, no, no." Like a beansprout in the full rays of sunlight, it grew like a motherfucker.

I didn't wanna cast any spell in case I forever destroyed my dick so I just watched as it blew up like a fucking inflatable pool toy, growing straight up towards my face.

"Stop, for the love of the moon, please stop!" I grabbed onto it, getting to my feet and wrestling with the thing that was now the size of an elephant's trunk. I tried to push it back down, to hide it anywhere, but my pants were starting to rip now too with the weight of my ever-growing balls.

"Orio!" I cried, praying he hadn't abandoned me as visions of having to try and walk through campus like this flickered through my mind. *No, I won't do that, stars. I won't.*

I kicked off my shoes and torn jeans, giving up on trying to keep them in place. Then I cupped my huge balls in my hands as I ran across the room to a mirror on the wall. *Maybe it's not that bad.*

"Oh holy shit!" A strangled noise escaped me as I stood in front of my reflection, my dick growing right up and poking me in the chin.

It was now as thick as a watermelon and getting bigger by the second. My balls were like two bowling balls in my hands and terror ran through me as I thought about what might happen when they got too big. What if they popped? What if I was going to be a fucking eunuch because of this?

I sought out answers from the stars, but I swear they were laughing at me, offering me no solution and just giggling away up in the damn sky.

"Fuck you!" I shouted. "You couldn't have warned me of this? You can show me vision upon vision of Elise fucking other men, but giving me a heads up about this dicksplosion is beyond the realms of your power?"

Apparently today was the shittiest day of my life. My horoscope had warned me I'd be facing trials today, but it could have told me in plainer terms that my cock was destined to turn into a fucking giant balloon animal, couldn't it?

Footsteps pounded towards the door and panic flashed through me. I grabbed a blue blanket off the bed, wrapping it around my huge dick to try and hide it. It was fucking pointless but what else could I do? Just stand there like a huge-dicked idiot?

The door opened and Orion hurried inside, pulling a girl after him by the arm. She was wearing dungarees and had long dark hair, her eyes painted with eyeliner.

"So...this is Francesca," he said, his eyes moving to the huge cock hiding under the blanket. Not that it was hiding well at all.

"Why would you bring someone else here?" I hissed, trying to turn sideways to conceal it better. I didn't wanna show the girl my naked ass either, but maybe that was better than my monster cock.

"She's going to help," Orion promised.

Francesca burst out laughing and I shot her a glare so fierce she smothered it fast, sucking on both her lips to stop herself.

"Let me see the Proball box," she said as she composed herself and Orion shot over to pick it up and hand it to her.

"Who gave them to you, Orio?" I demanded.

"Well...Francesca did," he said awkwardly and I turned my rage on his friend.

"*You*," I snarled. "You fucking did this?" I gestured to my cock, but lost my grip on the blanket so it slipped down to the floor and revealed every huge, throbbing, veiny inch of my manhood.

"Oh my stars!" She fell apart in hysterics, clutching her sides and I bent down to grab the blanket with a curse.

My cock was so heavy that it hit the floor with a loud donk and I struggled to get back up again as it continued to swell. I managed it though, wrapping the blanket firmly around it, having to shift my huge shaft to one side so it could rest on my shoulder and continue to grow.

"Are you gonna help me or just stand there laughing? It'll be bigger than me in a minute!" I yelled and the girl pulled herself together as Orion looked uncertain of what to do.

Francesca took the Proball box from Orion, running her fingers over it and her two eyes suddenly slid together into one. She was a Cyclops, and she was clearly trying to pick up traces of a memory on that thing.

"What can you sense?" Orion asked urgently, his eyes whipping to the head of my cock as it poked its way out of the blanket and tickled my ear. *This is not my day.*

"Oh no..." Francesca sighed. "It's my friend Kelly, she er, had a moment alone with them while I went to the bathroom this morning."

"Who's Kelly?" I demanded at the exact same time as Orion did.

Francesca rolled her eyes at Orion. "You're such an asshole sometimes. You know Kelly, the girl you fucked last week and forgot to call?"

"I never said I'd call," Orion said simply and that was just a swell fucking answer right now.

"So this is vengeance for you being an asshole, Orio?" I growled, needing someone to blame who was in the room with me.

"Hey, I told Kitty-"

"Kelly," Francesca interjected sharply.

"Right yeah, well I told her what I tell every girl," Orion said, smoothing a hand over his hair. "I don't date. If I hooked up with her then she would've known that was all it was. I'm always straight with girls."

"*If* you hooked up with her? Do you seriously not remember? You don't even drink," Francesca said, punching his arm hard while Orion shrugged guiltily.

"How about we have this lengthy discussion over afternoon tea?" I snarled sarcastically. "Actually, we can have a sit-down meal and we may as well lay the table for four as my monster cock is about to walk off my body and start a life of its own any second!"

"Alright, calm down, Noxy. We'll fix this," Orion said reassuringly. "We just need to figure out what's in these so we can get an antidote." He took a Proball from the box, breaking it open and sniffing the contents. "The scent's covered with sweetener." He frowned, passing it to Francesca to sniff as her eyes returned to normal, but she came up empty.

I needed Ryder and his Order gifts to work out what was in it. I knew that, but I wasn't going to call the asshole who was in the middle of an Elysian Mate orgy with his new besties. No, I'd deal with my giant cock like a Fae.

"I'm gonna have to go and get Kimmie," Orion said.

"Who?" I growled.

"He means Kelly," Francesca said, punching him in the arm again. "I'll go get her, you just try and slow down the growth of that thing." She headed out of the room and my head spun as all the blood in my body headed off to fuel my huge dick. My balls were getting so heavy, I was gonna have to sit down soon, but I feared if I did that, I'd never get up again.

The tip of my dick was a foot above my head and my head kept swimming. Suddenly blackness curtained my vision and I stumbled forward, dropping the blanket once more. Orion shot forward to catch me and as if in slow motion, my huge cock swung sideways and slapped him hard across the face. He blinked in shock, processing what had just happened as I gaped at him and wrapped my arms around the veiny beast to try and wrangle it away again.

"I'm gonna pass out," I slurred, moving swiftly on from the cock slap I'd just given him, figuring it was best not to dwell on that. His cheek was red from it for fuck's sake.

He moved carefully around to my side, pressing a hand to my arm and using his water magic to draw more blood back up to my head. "I'm sorry, Noxy," he murmured.

"I'm never eating food gifted to you ever again," I said darkly.

"I made that promise too, man. Francesca's the only person I trust with giving me anything since…you know. The Oreos."

"Yeah," I muttered. "This is worse than that though."

"We'll get your dick back to normal," he promised, clapping his hand against my shoulder and I nodded at him as the vow flared in his eyes.

It would have been a nice bonding moment if I hadn't been hugging an enormous cock to my chest while it made a slow but determined path towards the ceiling.

The door opened and I cursed as Francesca returned with a petite blonde girl in tow.

"Did you have to actually bring her here?" I balked, trying to lean down for my blanket, but I couldn't reach it. You know what I could reach though? My balls. Which were now grazing the floor like two giant fucking pears hanging between my legs.

"Holy crap." Kelly at least had the decency to look horrified as she gaped at me. "How many did you eat?"

"I dunno, ten?" I guessed and she looked to Orion in horror who was offering her a death glare.

"You wanna explain yourself, Perry?" he demanded. He was just trying to get her name wrong at this point.

"I-I," she stammered then straightened her spine and pointed at Orion. "You're a fucking asshole. And I'm sorry about your friend but they were meant for *you*."

"Why am I an asshole?" Orion snapped. "Did I not tell you I don't date because I don't have the time to dedicate to a girl outside of my training?"

Kelly flushed, thinking on that for a second. "Well…yeah. But that doesn't mean you can just fuck me and not talk to me again."

"What did you expect? For us to be best friends?" he demanded.

Kelly shrugged. "You didn't have to be such an asshole."

"And you didn't have to try and blow up my star damned dick," Orion growled in fury.

"I know you're angry, man," I started calmly as I turned to him. "But you're not the one who has a whale dick right now that's about to punch a hole in the ceiling!" I bellowed.

Orion turned to me with an apologetic look then shot across the room and grabbed hold of Kelly, his fangs bared at her. "What did you put in them?" he snarled.

She quivered in his arms and Francesca planted her hands on her hips, clearly pissed at the girl too.

"I, um, mixed an engorgement potion with some Faeagra. I've been waiting for a chance to slip them to you and when Fran left her purse with me and I saw the Proballs with your name on them, well..." she trailed, her eyes wide as she gazed at Orion's sharp fangs. "You could use a withering potion to counter the engorgement but the Faeagra will last about an hour."

"Right, go get it," Orion commanded, pointing her out of the room then looked to Francesca. "Go with her and make sure she gets the right potion."

She nodded, leading Kelly out of the room and leaving us there once more, their giggles sounding back to me as I scowled.

"I don't like the sound of a withering potion," I said tightly. "I don't want my dick to wither."

"It'll be fine," Orion promised. "You can...use my bed to prop up your balls if you want."

"Thank you," I shuffled over to his bed, heaved them up and laid them on his mattress with a sigh of relief. "Fuck my life."

"Yeah, fuck your life," Orion sniggered and I cracked half a smile.

"You won't tell anyone about this, right?" I asked, looking at him imploringly as he picked up my cock blanket and brought it over to help cover me up as best he could. It was a true friend move.

"Course not," he said firmly, looking me in the eye. "I'd shake your hand and make a star vow, but I'm scared your cock might slap me in the face again."

I barked a laugh and let myself just fall apart as he did too, the ridiculousness of the situation too much. My cock brushed the ceiling and I groaned as my laughter died in my throat. "They'd better hurry up or whoever's in the room above yours is gonna get a nasty surprise."

"That's the Aer House common room up there so I really advise you to angle that thing elsewhere before it pops out of the floor in front of a hundred students," Orion said with a worried expression.

"Shit," I breathed anxiously, bending forward to give it more room, feeling like I was manoeuvring a tree trunk.

Francesca finally returned without Kelly, holding a potion in her hand and Orion snatched it from her, running over and holding it to my lips so I could drink it while still supporting my cock. I swallowed it down, laying my trust in it and my dick immediately started tingling.

"Oh thank fuck," I gasped as it began to get smaller.

It took a couple of minutes to shrink back down, but finally it returned to its normal size and I checked my balls over twice to make sure they were okay. The only problem was, I was still fucking hard.

"I'll er, leave you guys to it," Francesca said awkwardly and I glanced over at her, realising I should not have my cock out in front of her but I guessed she'd seen everything at this point. "Nice meeting you," she called, her cheeks turning rosy as her gaze dipped to my cock then back to my face. "Really nice. Not that *it's* really nice, I mean you are. I mean um, it's not small even now it's small, if you know what I mean? Oh that sounded dumb, um it's a nice big, cock." She cleared her throat, turned and marched out of the room, slapping her palm against her forehead and Orion started laughing.

"There you go, a little ego boost to brighten up your day," he said with a smirk then walked over to his closet, grabbing out some boxers and sweatpants before tossing them to me.

I pulled them on in relief, trying to ignore my throbbing cock, just thankful it wasn't permanently damaged from the experience. Traumatised, sure, but it looked like it had escaped unharmed for the most part.

I headed over to my torn boxers and jeans, picking them up and taking out the two stones that concealed the spyglass and Magicae Mortuorum book. They were the perfect subject changer, so I flicked up a silencing bubble and turned to Orion, clearing my throat. "Hey, any chance you wanna take a look at the Magicae Mortuorum for us? I'm getting nowhere finding anything in it to help with King and I'm pretty sure you're better at all this dark magic shit than I am."

Orion nodded. "Sure, anything, Noxy. I can't do it here though, I have a place I go if I need to do any kind of dark magic. I'll head there tonight." He took them from me, tucking them into his pocket. "So...there's a Starfire game on today. It's just about to start, did you wanna stay and watch it while your boner goes down?"

I snorted a laugh. "Yeah, that sounds kinda perfect actually." He switched the TV on and we moved to a couch at the end of his bed, his room a ridiculous size for one student, but I guessed House Captains and Pitball stars got perks here.

I'd talk to him about what had happened with Elise and the guys after the game. I could trust him. I just wanted to spend some time thinking about anything aside from the soul crushing possibility that Elise was never meant to be mine.

So I soaked up the Pitball match while my hard on finally sank and counted my blessings that Lance Orion would always have my back. Even when my cock grew into a giant anaconda.

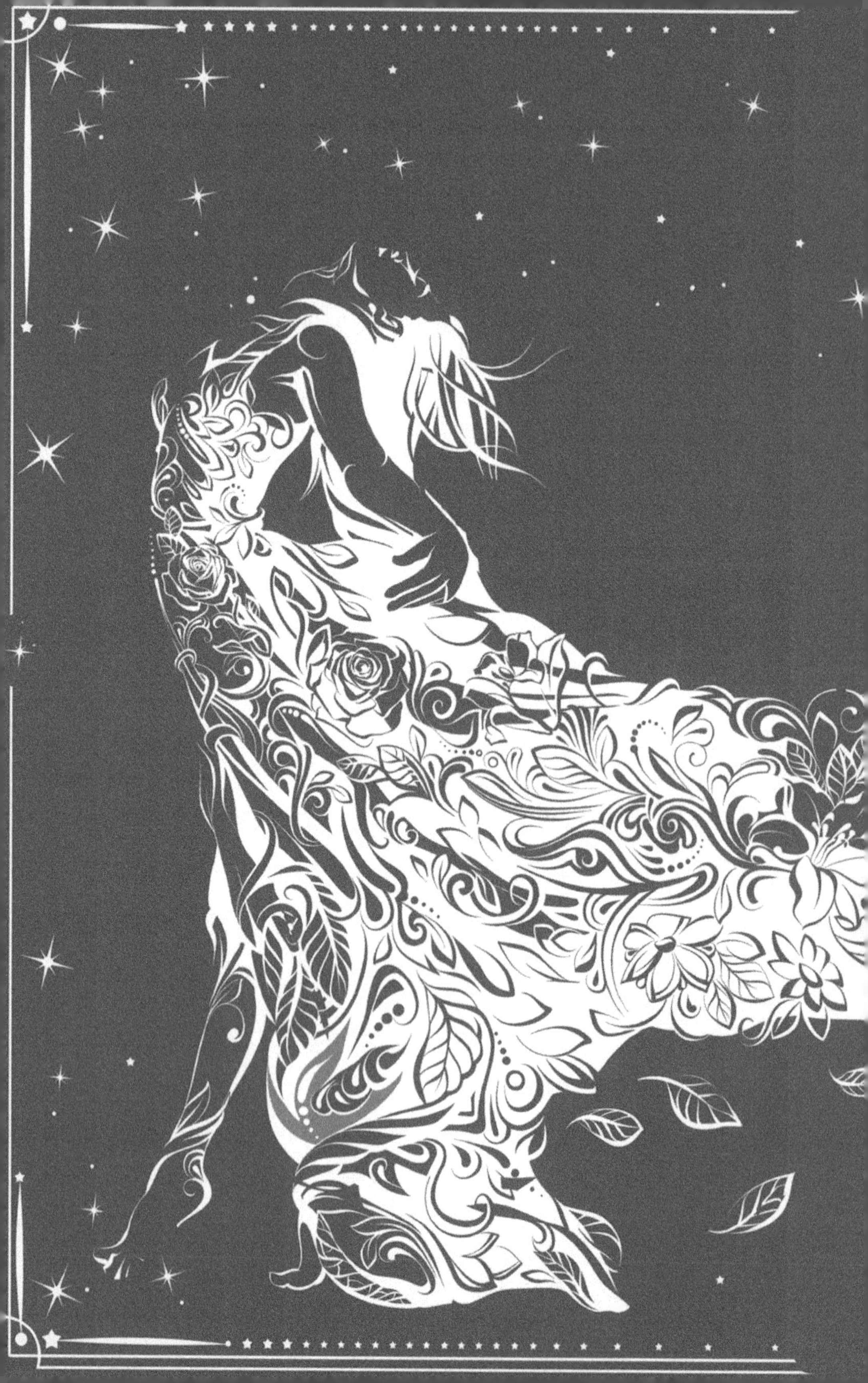

ELISE

CHAPTER TWENTY

We'd arrived back at the academy late last night and I'd snuck Ryder into our bedroom in his tiny snake form nestled between my cleavage.

Gabriel hadn't returned, messaging us to say he'd *seen* some things he had to deal with and for me not to worry. But I *was* worried. He hadn't answered any of my calls and I knew he was taking this new development between Dante, Ryder and I to heart.

I woke up sore in the most agonisingly perfect ways, my body spent from hours pinned between my kings who had been utterly insatiable until we'd eventually just passed out from pure exhaustion.

Dante and Leon had me pinned between them in the huge bed and Ryder had shifted into a Basilisk about the size of a python, curling himself around my thigh and resting his head on my stomach.

I stretched out, smiling as Dante murmured something in Faetalian and Leon purred in his sleep.

With a spurt of my speed, I shot out from between the three of them, placing Ryder down on my pillow and adding a tiny sailor hat to his head that

Leon had bought for him. Then I grabbed Leon's Atlas and took a photo of the three of them all curled up in bed for his scrapbook with a snort of laughter.

I sped around the room next, grabbing clothes and my wash stuff before shooting away to take a shower. But as I arrived in the shower block, I skidded to a halt, finding Cindy Lou holding court there with her friends Amira and Helga.

They stopped talking abruptly as they spotted me, and I narrowed my eyes at the bitch in the middle.

"Wow," I said, tossing my wash stuff down on a bench and cocking my head to one side as I gazed at her. "You really are as dumb as you look."

"What did you say?" Cindy Lou gasped, her nose wrinkling as she glared at me like I was something unpleasant on the sole of her shoe.

"I said, you really are as fucking dumb as you look, you stalking, piece of shit, psychopath." We hadn't had a lot of time for talking last night, but I'd heard enough to know that this skanky bitch had helped Bryce abduct Ryder before turning up at Dante's manor like a desperate bitch in heat thinking he'd give her his cock as a reward. She was damn lucky he'd been in such a hurry to get to Ryder, or she would have been fried with a lightning bolt. And yet here she stood, like she seriously hadn't realised that the kings of the two most notorious gangs in Solaria were out for her blood.

Amira and Helga looked between the two of us nervously as Cindy Lou raised her chin defiantly.

"I don't know what the hell crawled up your ass today, sugar, but-"

"Get the fuck out of here," I snapped at her friends, the air stirring around the room as my power rose to the surface of my skin. This bitch had tried to hurt my man and I was having a serious problem stopping myself from ripping her damn throat out right here and now.

Helga took a step forward to obey me and Cindy Lou stomped her foot, flames igniting around her hands as she moved into a fighting stance.

"Don't you dare listen to that whore," she snapped at her friends. "Even with an Elysian Mate of her own, she's still trying to sniff around my man. It's pathetic."

"*Your* man?" I asked, not bothering to hide the scoff in my voice as I looked at her. "Please tell me you're not referring to Dante, you deluded, desperate bitch."

Cindy's eyes flared with rage and she threw one of the fireballs at me with a shriek. But I'd been ready for her from the moment I stepped into the room and her pathetic attempt at an attack just collided with the air shield I'd erected before me and exploded into nothing in less than a second.

"Tell me you've got more than that," I purred. "Otherwise this isn't even going to be fun."

Cindy Lou's bottom lip trembled the tiniest amount, letting me see how concerned she was about that threat before she managed to tighten up her mask and stare me down.

"You know, I looked into you," she spat at me as her friends slowly began to shift away from her, like they could already tell which way the wind was blowing here. "I know you're the daughter of a whore. Is she the one who taught you how to bedazzle men into thinking your dried out pussy is the best thing since sliced bread?"

"At least I don't stalk men who have no interest in me and steal from them like some Dragon dick desperate wannabe," I replied icily.

My fingers flexed as I said those words and her gaze fell to my hand for a moment where she spotted the ring she'd stolen from Dante now sitting proudly on my thumb.

"Now who's been stealing from him?" she demanded, pointing at the ring while her eyes flashed with rage and jealousy. "Is that your mate's influence? Now that you're mated to a Night you've added stealing to your whoring repertoire? You bedazzle men into bed and then steal from them when they let their guard down?"

I laughed at her. Just fucking laughed in her pathetic, jealous face. And that was the last straw for her friends. Helga and Amira ran for the door, clearly seeing which way this was going to go and wisely deciding to jump ship.

I grinned demonically at Cindy Lou and she shrieked as she blasted me with as much firepower as she could muster.

I clenched my fists, grunting as the force of the blow struck against my air shield then flicking my fingers so that I could suck the air from her side of the room and gutter out her flames.

She stumbled back as I snatched the air from her lungs too, clutching her throat dramatically and falling against the row of sinks.

The door crashed open behind me and I spun around just as Dante strode into the room, electricity crackling off of his bare chest and sparking around the entire bathroom as a Dragon's growl rumbled through him.

"What are you doing here alone, bella?" he snarled, his gaze fixed on me as he closed the distance between us and caught my throat in his big hand, angling my face up so that I was looking him dead in the eyes. "You promised you wouldn't go off on your own."

"She stole your ring!" Cindy Lou cried. "And then she attacked me again like a total freak!"

Dante turned his head slowly to look at her, the sneer on his face so cold it made a shiver run down my spine. The good kind, the kind that gave me tingles because my man was freaking terrifying in all the best ways.

"Was I talking to you, puttana?" he spat in disgust, tossing a silencing bubble up to hide our conversation from prying ears. "I'll deal with you in a minute. Until then, keep your poisonous mouth shut if you expect to leave here with your life."

Cindy Lou sucked in a sharp breath and at first I thought it was in response to his words, but as she raised a shaking finger to point at him, I realised it was about something else entirely.

"Your eyes," she gasped, her voice catching on the final word. "They... they're..."

"I found my one true love," Dante said, raising his chin and owning the fact even though we had all decided that for now we would keep our newfound mate status a secret. I was guessing that he'd forgotten about casting a concealment spell over the silver rings in his desperation to find me though. And I couldn't deny the fact that I was loving watching this bitch break as she realised he would *never* be hers.

"Who?" she begged, a tear spilling over like her heart was actually breaking. Like she'd seriously believed that he might have been meant for her.

Dante's wicked smile turned even crueller as he looked at me, using his grasp on my throat to lift my chin even higher as he looked deep into my eyes. He didn't often go full Alpha on me like this, but when he did, I had to admit, it was damn hard not to just fall to my knees before him and give in to his every desire.

"Il mio dono dai cieli," he breathed, the words making the hairs stand up alone the back of my neck. "My gift from the heavens."

"That's not possible," Cindy Lou blanched, shaking her head as more tears fell, but Dante wasn't paying her the slightest bit of attention, his grip on me tightening as he yanked me forward and stole a brutal kiss from my lips.

Cindy Lou screamed like someone had just set her pubes on fire and an explosion of heat washed over us as she threw her power our way in a tornado of flames.

But as we broke apart with the intention to ward her off, the fire died out just as suddenly as it had begun and I looked around to find Leon striding into the room in a pair of maroon sweatpants with his long hair looking all kinds of just fucked.

"Oh hey, isn't that Cindy Poo?" he asked casually, a smirk on his face that was just two shades south of pure fucking evil. Shit, I loved when my laid-back Lion went all psycho.

"Do you know about this?!" Cindy Lou shrieked, pointing between me and Dante as he released me to face her again. "She's your mate but now...

now...they're saying that...that-"

"That Elise has now got three Elysian Mates? Although I personally believe it'll be four before long," Leon said with a chuckle that didn't reach his eyes.

"Three?" she echoed dumbly, shaking her head so that her sheet of black hair swayed around her.

"Oh sorry, did I ruin the surprise?" Leon grinned as he put his hand into his pocket and took a tiny black snake out of it, holding his palm towards Cindy Lou so that she could see it clearly.

The snake hissed aggressively before slipping off of Leon's hand, its body expanding to the size of a grass snake, a python, an anaconda. And then bigger and bigger still until me, Dante and Leon were backing up to make room for the giant serpent whose body was the width of a small car and longer than I could tell with the way it was coiled around itself.

Cindy Lou trembled with fear as Ryder reared over her, clinging to the sinks behind her and shrieking for help which wouldn't come. The silencing bubble Dante had cast held firm around the bathroom and before she could yell again, Ryder struck.

Cindy Lou screamed in agony as the Basilisk's giant fangs sank into her shoulder and a moment later, Ryder shifted back into his Fae form, laughing darkly as she stumbled and fell to the floor at his feet.

"I'd get that checked out if I were you," he said coldly as Leon tossed him a pair of sweatpants and he pulled them on. "Basilisk venom is lethal unless treated within fifteen minutes."

"It burns!" Cindy Lou screamed, clutching at the wound on her shoulder as she writhed on the tiles before us.

"Yeah," Ryder agreed. "That shit will burn right down to your bones within minutes and once it does that, it'll eat right into them - did I mention that there is no undoing the damage born of my venom either? So if it does get down to your bones you're fucked for life as far as that limb goes."

"Help me, Dante!" she begged, sobbing and panting and clutching her shoulder as we all just looked down at her in disgust.

"I should kill you for what you did to my fratello," Dante growled, stepping forward so his shoulder brushed against Ryder's.

"You're a real piece of shit, aren't you, Cindy Poo?" Leon added.

"You...you c-can't kill me!" she panted through the pain, her eyes wheeling between all of us. "People will find out it was you and-"

"I assure you, I am more than capable of destroying every piece of your body and making sure there isn't so much as a scrap of evidence left after you're gone," Ryder interrupted. "But I'm feeling generous today."

"You are?" I asked in surprise and he shrugged as he glanced over at me, the silver rings in his eyes making my heart leap.

"She's not worth the time it would take to mop up the blood," he spat. "So I thought I'd offer her a deal instead."

"W-what deal?" Cindy Lou begged, her skin looking decidedly green as the poison worked its way into her system.

"You're going to leave and never come back. You'll drink a memory potion and allow me into your head and I'll give you a dose of antivenom so that you can pack up your shit and fuck all the way off."

"But this is my home," she squeaked, looking over towards Dante like she seriously thought he might speak up for her worthless ass.

He spat on the floor before her, his upper lip curling back as he spoke. "I was all for killing you," he said in disgust. "But as Ryder was the one you fucked over like an unFae piece of shit, I decided to let him choose."

"Tick-tock, Cindy Poo, I think that venom is about to hit your bones," Leon taunted, making a dark smile spill across my face.

"Okay," she gasped in panic, looking back to Ryder and sobbing some more.

He crouched down before her and snatched her hand in his. "Swear it."

"I'll leave," she stammered. "I'll go far away from here and you'll never lay eyes on me again. I swear."

Magic clapped between their palms and Ryder yanked her hand to his mouth, sinking his fangs into her to deliver the antivenom and making her shriek in fright again.

The moment it was done, he snared her in his gaze and the two of them fell deathly still.

"I told him to make her dream of Dragon dicks every night for the rest of her life," Leon stage whispered excitedly. "But to piss herself if and whenever she actually comes face to face with a Dragon in real life. Actual *piss*. No Dragon will ever wanna fuck her that way and she will never get the Dragon D she dreams of."

"Shit, Leo, you're an evil mastermind," I said with a laugh just as Ryder stood upright and released Cindy Lou from his hypnosis.

Leon tossed him a small vial which I was guessing was the memory potion he'd mentioned and I watched as Cindy Lou drank down the lot, glaring at me the entire time.

Her eyes fell out of focus as she finished it and her gaze slowly shifted from me to Dante, a gasp escaping her as the crotch of her pale pink leggings suddenly grew very wet.

"What in the..." She stared down at the piss patch in total confusion and Leon whooped while Dante roared a laugh. Even Ryder broke a grin as Leon danced about, yelling excitedly about the fact that he'd actually done it.

Ryder reluctantly shifted back into a tiny snake again so that Leon could smuggle him out of the bathroom and we all turned our backs and left Cindy Lou there, sitting in a puddle of piss, never to be seen again.

By the end of the day, it had become clear that Gabriel was avoiding us and my heart twisted with pain for him as I left my Arcane Arts class and wondered where he was.

His Atlas had been going to voicemail all day and he hadn't shown up for any lessons. The only way I knew he was alright was from the single, clipped text he'd sent me saying he had some things to do today and would see me later, insisting I shouldn't worry. But since then, nothing.

"I have a cunning plan," Leon said in a low voice as he dropped an arm around my shoulders and tugged me close.

Dante moved to walk on my other side, his arm brushing against mine and sending a skitter of static across my skin.

"Oh yeah?" I asked, only semi-interested in what he was saying while my mind stayed wrapped up in my Harpy. "What for?"

"To get Gabe back." He smirked at me and I looked up at him hopefully.

"Really?" I asked and Leon grinned widely as he jerked me to a halt. We were only about a quarter of the way along the tunnel which led out from beneath the lake and the other students parted around us, heading away from the class with Professor Mystice among them.

Leon hesitated as our classmates wandered away, whistling sharply at Ryder as he stalked past too.

Ryder paused, narrowing his eyes our way and I found myself aching to see the ring of silver in them as I looked at their usual green colour. We'd all agreed that in the short term, while Dante and Ryder were working to uphold the peace between their gangs, it made the most sense to hide what we all were to each other. If it got out that the two of them were bonded via me, then it would open up the opportunity for their people to question whether it was the mate bond causing them to make these changes and no one wanted that. The gangs needed to see that this was the best thing for them and Alestria without questioning their leaders' motives. Not to mention the fact that if it got out that I was the first Fae known in history to claim more than one Elysian Mate, we could come under all kinds of scrutiny which none of us wanted.

Leon directed me back into the Arcane Arts classroom which was dark now that Mystice had extinguished the candles which had been lighting the space while we had our lesson on scrying.

My Lion threw a silencing bubble up around us and waited for Ryder to stalk back in too before tossing a fireball up to hang above our heads and illuminate our faces.

"Get in here for a pride huddle," Leon urged, wheeling me towards Dante and slinging his free arm around Ryder's neck as he tugged him in close too.

"Get the fuck off of me, Simba," Ryder hissed, shoving his arm back off and stepping aside. "I'm not in your damn pride."

"Okay, keep telling yourself that, Scar. But I'm gonna bet, when we have our next pride orgy, you'll be right there, whipping your trouser snake out and putting one of those cool hats on it for the party."

Ryder's eyes narrowed dangerously while Dante chuckled and I elbowed Leon to draw his attention back to the point in hand.

"What is your plan about Gabriel?" I asked, glancing up beyond the orb of fire to the dome of water overhead. It had been hard not to freak out over being back inside an amplifying chamber after King had kept me locked inside one for so many weeks, but Leon had held my hand throughout the entire lesson, reminding me that he was here and I wasn't alone and I'd managed to get through it. I was willing to bet the reason we were lingering here now was because Leon didn't want Gabriel using The Sight to *see* us coming.

"Okay, yeah. So, prepare to have your socks knocked off," Leon said enthusiastically. "Because I'm about to blow your damn minds with the amazingness of this plan."

"Spit it out, mio amico," Dante growled.

"Right. So the problem with Gabe, is that when he doesn't wanna deal with something, he just uses The Sight to go all incognito on us and then we can't even find him to deal with our shit. Like now, he's off somewhere, crying and hiding and let's face it - probably jerking off over the thought of how much crazy hot sex we've all been having without him while he vision pervs on us - but we can't go tell him to snap the fuck out of it because he'll just run away before we can get there."

"We already know all of this," Ryder said coldly, but as he folded his arms, I noticed him dragging his thumb over the Scorpio star sign he had tattooed onto his wrist for Gabriel and I knew he cared about his friend too.

"Side note - you need a Leo tattoo ASAP, Rydikins," Leon said, noticing the same thing I had. "And a Gemini for Dante and maybe a Libra for Elise, but I was also thinking we should all probably get her name tattooed on our cocks because she owns them. But then I thought it might kinda be like she was fucking herself every time one of us stuck our-"

"The plan, stronzo." Dante cuffed Leon around the ear to make him focus and he cursed as he massaged the place he'd been struck.

"Okay, okay. So, the plan is that Elise needs to give Gabe a branch for his nest. A super fancy, all the love, be-my-Harpy-mate-forever-I-want-you-and-your-mega-cock-just-as-much-as-all-of-my-other-dudes'-mega-cocks-and-hearts branch. Then he will swoon, they'll probably both shed a tear, some fucking will almost certainly occur, and we can all get back to being a happy pride once more."

"I like the sound of that," I admitted, silencing the protests I could see forming on Ryder's lips. "But every time I try to find a branch to give him, they just seem kinda shit. So how am I supposed to-"

"Ryder is going to make it," Leon announced excitedly. "Aren't you?"

"Fuck no. I'm perfectly happy mated to my girl," Ryder said. "I don't have any interest in mating with Big Bird next."

"That's why you and Elise will power share to make it. Aaaand, I think me and Dante should slip a little in too. So that it's from all of us. All you have to do is open up and let us drive some inside you. I promise you can take it."

"Why the fuck do you always have to phrase shit like that?" Ryder asked while Dante laughed loudly, his amusement making sparks fly from his skin and brush against the rest of us.

"Is that a no?" Leon asked, looking seriously disappointed in Ryder. Like shit, I wouldn't wanna be Leon's kid when he was disappointed with me because that look made me feel all kinds of crappy even though it wasn't aimed my way.

"Did I *say* no?" Ryder asked irritably before stepping closer and offering me his hand.

"You'll do it?" I confirmed, a smile lifting the corners of my lips.

"Don't go thinking I'm getting soft, baby," he replied, sliding his hand into mine and tugging me closer. "If this works then I'm gonna expect to have you on your knees while I fuck that pretty mouth of yours until you're choking on my cock."

"Sure," I agreed, having no objections to that and loving the way his eyes flashed with excitement at that prospect.

"And I'm going to watch," Leon announced happily while Ryder sighed.

"Let me concentrate," he said, his gaze fixing with mine as I felt his magic pressing against mine where our palms met and I let my barriers drop for him instinctively.

The dark and sinful nature of Ryder's power spilled into me in a heady rush, and I gasped as I opened myself up to it, loving the way it danced around my own, merging together and delighting in the company of one another.

Leon and Dante moved close behind me and while Dante took my free hand to press the roiling tempest of his magic into the mix, Leon slid his hand up the back of my skirt and gripped my ass cheek before adding the blazing heat of his power too.

A breathy moan escaped me as the combined power of all of our magic collided and ran through my veins, offering it all up to Ryder as he began to wield it into his earth magic to create our branch.

"Fuck," Leon groaned. "Next gang bang, we are power merging as we come. No arguments."

"D'accordo," Dante muttered, his accent making my cheeks heat with dirty ideas.

I watched as the branch formed in Ryder's hand, the bark a beautiful iridescent silver with little stones which seemed to wink and flash buried within the wood.

When it was finally done, we all drew back and Ryder handed me the branch, making me gasp at the solid weight of it.

"It's petrified," he explained as I felt the coldness of the wood in my hand and began turning it back and forth so that I could look at those gemstones more closely. "Each of those holds a drop of pure magic from each of our Elements," Ryder added as I inspected an orange stone which felt warm to the touch, clearly having come from Leon's power. Dante's stone was a deep grey with the smallest pulse of electricity locked inside it and Ryders was a dark and sultry green which made a sense of peace slip through my soul as I pressed my fingertip to it. The stone representing me was the biggest, white clouds seeming to twist and writhe inside it and the taste of freedom coating my tongue as I traced the shape of it. "I dunno if that's right, but it just kinda felt like-"

I leaned forward and stole a kiss from Ryder's lips, my smile wide against his mouth as my heart raced. "It's perfect," I breathed, holding the branch tightly and just knowing in my soul that this was the one.

"Great," Leon announced. "Then we need to move on to part two. I'm going to set Gabe's rooftop nest on fire."

"What?" I gasped, whirling back around to stare at him in alarm.

"He'll kill you for that, stronzo," Dante said, shaking his head. "You know how protective Harpies get over their nests. And that bastardo is one powerful motherfucker."

"It'll be fine," Leon said, waving him off. "Elise and I will shoot up to his rooftop at super speed so by the time he *sees* me coming, he'll have no choice but to turn up and stop me. And while he's freaking out and flapping his wings like an angry seagull, I need one of you guys to distract him so that I can hit him with a shot of Order Suppressant and force him to hang around to talk with Elise."

"Where are you going to get some Order Suppressant without leaving this room and giving him the chance to let him *see* you getting it?" Dante asked.

"I have some on me," Ryder interrupted, putting a hand into his pocket. "I've been carrying it since..." He frowned as he checked his other pocket and Leon started laughing as he presented the vial and syringe from his own blazer.

"I lifted it from you on the way into class," Leon explained.

"Why the fuck were you stealing from me?" Ryder hissed.

"Don't get salty over it. I've been lifting stuff from your pockets for months. Like literally every day since the first time I noticed that you were crushing hard on my girl."

"Bullshit," Ryder spat. "I've never lost a damn thing."

"Well I don't keep it," Leon rolled his eyes like Ryder was being dumb and I couldn't help but laugh. "You're my little pal. I don't steal from my little pal. But I do like to take a gander at what you keep in your pocketses before putting them back. Some of the stuff you carry around with you is seriously dark, Ryder. Though one time I found a pair of Elise's panties too and I got the biggest freaking hard on over it, then I had to try and hide it because it was during class and I got a Mindy to hold a potted plant over-"

"The plan, fratello," Dante interrupted while Ryder looked tempted to kill and Leon nodded enthusiastically.

"Oh yeah, right. So, Elise and I will shoot up to the roof, you two cause a distraction when Gabe arrives, I stick him with a dose of this and then Elise is free to give him the branch and bring him back to the pride, and all of my Lionesses will be happy once more." Leon beamed and I grinned too because his plan was actually pretty freaking good.

"What kind of distraction should I-" Dante began but Leon shushed him, pressing a finger to his lips and shaking his head.

"Don't plan it or he'll *see* it coming. Just do what feels right in the moment. Now go."

Leon wafted his hands at Dante and Ryder and I grinned as they headed out of the room, leaving us to wait while they got themselves over to the Vega Dorms, ready to cause the distraction when we needed it.

Leon grabbed me the moment they were gone, sinking his tongue into my mouth and kissing me like he would never get enough of doing it, like the world could end and fall away around us but we would still be here, locked together like this as it crashed and burned.

"You really are all in with this, aren't you, Leo?" I asked him as we broke apart and I looked into his golden eyes, watching the silver rings as they glinted in the light from his flames.

"It makes me so happy to have us all together," he agreed, leaning down to kiss my neck. "And I freaking love the fact that all of them are going to be mated to you too. It just gets me all warm and fuzzy on the inside. And all hard and thrusty on the outside. Not to mention how fucking much I love watching them with you."

"You're insatiable," I laughed, batting his chest with my hands and pushing him back as he tried to hitch my skirt up.

"Yeah. Maybe," he agreed, refusing to give up as he walked me backwards until he had me pinned against the wall and we were kissing once more.

My Atlas pinged just as I was starting to hope we might have time to fool around a bit and I groaned as I pulled back, my flesh all hot and needy. But I had more important things to do right now - like finding my Harpy and making sure he remembered exactly who he belonged to.

"Let's go," I said, turning my back on Leon so that he could hop on.

He giggled like an excited school kid as he did what I wanted, making me use my gifts to hold his bulk up as I gave him a piggyback. Once I was sure he was holding on tight enough, I shot from the room and raced towards the dorms.

The world whipped by and blurred around us. Leon laughed excitedly as I shot through campus, away from the lake and up the twenty flights of stairs along the new fire escape before skidding to a halt on the roof of the Vega Dorms.

Leon hopped down with a triumphant whoop and I chewed my lip nervously as he raised his hands and threw a ball of fire towards Gabriel's rooftop tent.

A whoosh of flames exploded across the side of it and I gasped as a figure shot down from the sky at an insane pace before landing between us with a yell of fury.

"What the fuck are you doing?" Gabriel bellowed, throwing water magic at the flames to douse them and shooting Leon with his power too.

Leon was ready for him though, throwing out a wall of flames to counter the water and their power collided with a heavy boom as they fought to force the other back.

A roar echoed through the sky and I looked up just as Dante flew past the rooftop and a bolt of lightning hit Gabriel in the ass.

Gabriel fell to his face, twitching and spasming from the shock while yelling furiously, lifting an arm to aim an attack at the enormous Dragon who dove out of sight beneath the edge of the rooftop again.

Leon darted forward and stuck him in the neck with the Order Suppressant the moment his attention was diverted. Gabriel's eyes widened and his wings shimmered out of existence as the suppressant took effect.

Gabriel whirled on him furiously, punching him in the jaw and the two of them fell into a fist fight while Leon giggled and warded off blows. Gabriel looked like he genuinely wanted to commit murder.

Leon managed to get to his feet between them as they rolled across the concrete rooftop and he booted Gabriel hard enough to send him flying away from him.

In the next breath, Leon was on his feet and sprinting for the edge of the roof. "Catch ya later, love birds!" he yelled before diving headfirst over the edge and damn near giving me a heart attack.

But a moment later, Dante swooped up towards the clouds from below and Leon whooped excitedly from his position on his back as they raced away towards the sky.

I heard Gabriel pushing to his feet behind me and turned to look at him with a nervous smile, my feet shifting awkwardly as I looked up at him and he glared back, looking as pissed as a duck with its tail plucked.

"So..." I began, wondering why I felt so freaking nervous as the branch in my inside pocket seemed to burn a hole in my blazer.

Gabriel's eyes glazed over for a brief moment and some of the anger slipped from his features as he blinked it away and looked at me.

"You got me a gift?" he asked curiously and I smiled shyly as I closed the distance between us, drawing the branch from my pocket and offering it to him.

Gabriel stilled as he reached for it and I couldn't help but smirk to myself, realising I'd actually surprised him for once.

"I love you, Gabriel," I said fiercely as he took it from me. "Please don't shut me out because the stars are determined to test us."

His eyes rose from the branch to meet my gaze and he slowly reached out to cup my jaw in his grasp, running his thumb across my skin and banishing the concealment spell I'd put in place to hide the new silver in my eyes.

"You know I love you too," he growled. "I just..."

"It will be us next," I swore to him. "I don't need The Sight to know that. I don't need a vision or anything like that because I *feel* it. Since the moment I first met you, I've felt it in my soul. Just like I felt it for the others. I've told you time and again how much I need all of you and this only proves it. We've all been wondering why the heavens chose Leon to be my one and only when it was clear I'd never love any of you any differently from one another. And now I know. He's not my one and only. It's all of you. Just like I've always said it was. And if the stars want to make us wait for our silver rings or even if they don't ever decide to give them to us, I still feel in my soul that your place is right here with us too. So I got you a branch because I want to be your mate. I want to do it the Harpy way and promise you forever at my side. Will you accept it?"

Silence hung thickly between us as Gabriel glanced down at the beautiful branch in his hand, his brow furrowing as he took in the details of it.

"I was supposed to be the one to give this to you," he growled.

"So give me one too," I challenged. "Give one to the guys as well if you want to. Because they helped me make that. They want you in this just as much as I do."

His lips parted on what I was certain was going to be a protest but as his thumb grazed over the stones set into the petrified branch, I knew he could feel the truth of my words and the power all of us had placed into creating it.

He released a breath laced with pain and dragged me towards him, his mouth finding mine as I sank into his embrace and my heart swelled with the depths of the love I felt for him.

I moaned as I wound my arms around his neck and he lifted me into his arms, carrying me back towards his tent and sighing my name against my lips.

"It's only you, Elise. Only ever you," he murmured, placing me down in the nest of blankets and quickly using his magic to remove all the water from the place as our kisses deepened and we peeled each other's clothes off.

I gave in to him as his weight crushed me beneath him and let him destroy my body and own my soul as we came together in the most beautiful, honest way I think we ever had.

I felt the power of the mate bond sliding around my being as I gave myself to him and I knew by the fervent look in his eyes that he could feel it too.

It didn't matter if his irises were silver or not. I was his and he was mine. That was all there was to it.

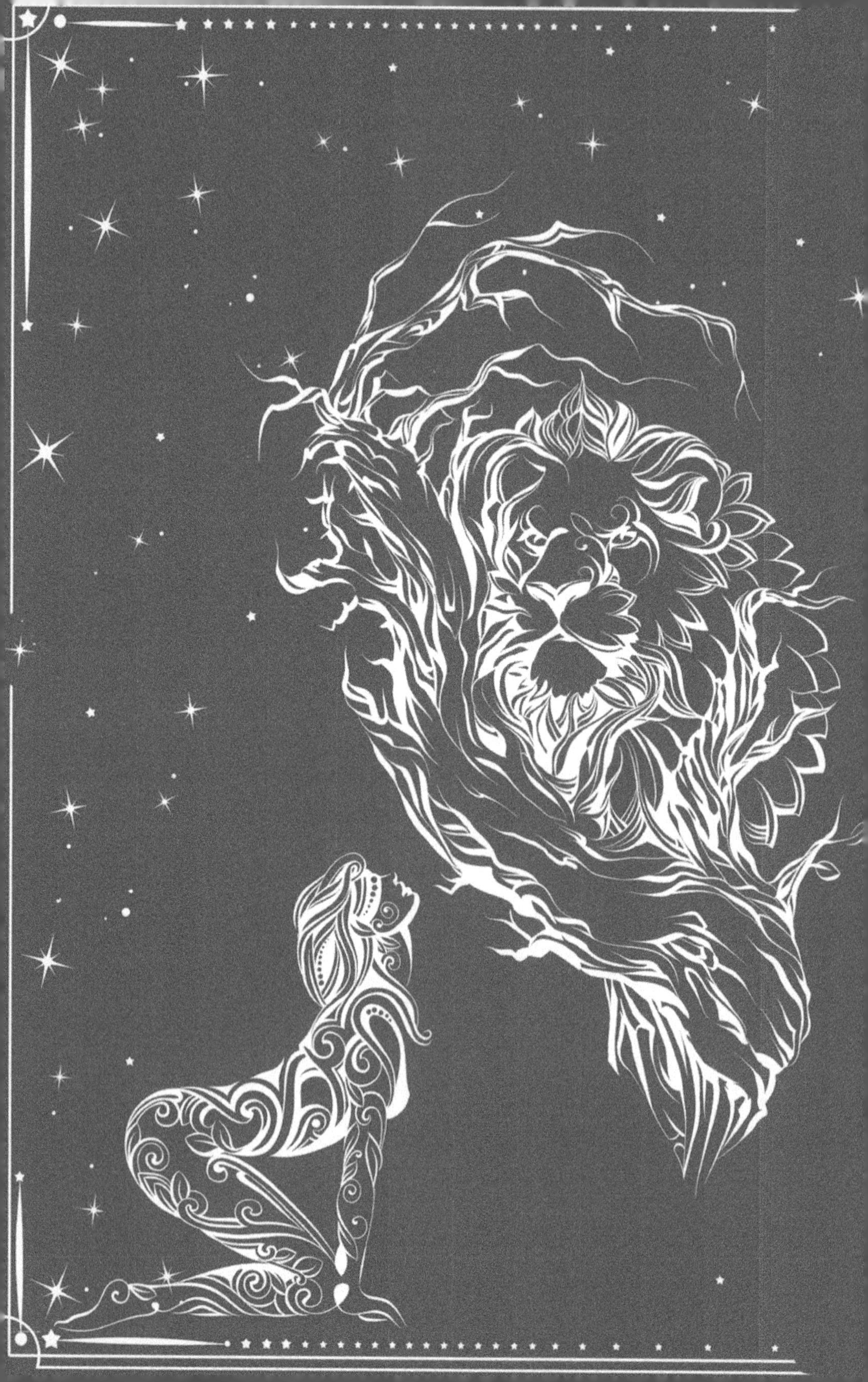

LEON

CHAPTER TWENTY ONE

The mark of a true Nemean Lion is to unite his pride harmoniously and with a balance that ensures each Lioness in the family unit is content. This, however, can be of greater issue when there is an imbalance of power within the pride. If a Lion mates with one or more Alpha Lionesses for example, tension may ripple throughout the family and unsettle the bonds which tie you.
Turn to page 54 for more information on understanding the needs of Alpha Lionesses.

I rifled through the pages of my special Lion book as I took a bite out of my morning toast in the Cafaeteria while Elise and Laini chatted opposite me. My eyes swung to Gabriel further down the table who was observing the room and everyone in it, hunting for any dangerous assholes that might have ties to King. I was beyond happy that he'd come to accept the idea that the stars might mate him to Elise as well. And I was certain that was the case. No room for error. Nothing. Nada. I mean, yeah, okay maybe it was one percent unlikely. Dante and Ryder had broken their Astral Adversary bond before their

Elysian bond had happened, so maybe that had triggered the whole moment or some jazz. But I wasn't gonna get all doubty on my dude Gabe. He was definitely going to join the silver eyes gang and I was going to prepare for it properly this time with balloons, matching t-shirts, confetti in the shape of silver rings, Party Rings which were painted silver. I had Mindys working day and night until their fingers bled to get the merch ready – all of whom had to take a memory potion at the end of their shifts so they'd forget about the whole four-way Elysian Mate thing.

Anyway, if we were gonna figure out this five-way situationship, all of us needed to get balance in our pride and find a way to live harmoniously together. I'd always seen that potential and now Ryder and Dante were besties, I didn't think it would be long to work out the final kinks.

The problem was, all of us were so headstrong, arguments broke out between us way too often. And so far, pushing each of the guys down beneath me as I tried to make them submit to my will hadn't been totally effective in stopping that. In fact, it seemed to just make them angrier. So maybe I was going about this the wrong way. I was basing it off of how my dad was with my moms. He was the Alpha of the group and they worked together to please him because it pleased *them*. Everyone in our pride was working to please Elise the most, making the whole thing competitive. But that wasn't how it was supposed to be.

I found the section about Alpha Lionesses and ripped through my fourth slice of toast as I started reading.

It is common for an Alpha Lioness to mate into a pride of submissive males and or females. She may become the centre of the group or she may take her place in the Ring of the Roar which surrounds the male if he is dominant. As this is the more common scenario, we shall start with this.

An Alpha Lioness has different needs to that of her submissive counterparts. She, like you, needs to feel like she is in control, holds power, and is heard. She will also wish to take the lead in many situations. This can cause a clash between the Alpha male and female if there is a disagreement on how to move forward. The same is true if there are multiple Alpha Lionesses in a pride- though this is largely uncommon, see page 57 for more details.

I flicked through the pages again and found the piece about multiple Alpha females as I washed my toast down with a swig of coffee and started on the Pop Tarts stacked up beside me.

A pride composed predominantly or entirely of Alphas is rare. However, few occurrences have been recorded in history, the most notable of which was Nigel Claw and his six Alpha Lioness mates. One of the Lionesses grew so vengeful in her bid to claim her Lion as her own, that she ate two of her wives-in-law and beheaded the other three. Nigel was so heartbroken that he had no choice but to avenge his mates' deaths and challenge his final Alpha female to a bloody match which resulted in both of their deaths.

A Pop Tart fell from my fingertips and plapped back onto the plate as I reread those words. "Fuck me…"

"What's up, Leo?" Elise asked and I looked up at her as she cocked her head questioningly.

My gaze flicked to Gabriel then to Dante across the room among the Oscuras. If they fought to take Elise for themselves, what would I do?

Kill them all.

The deep, instinctual voice resounded in my head and I cleared my throat. "Nothing," I told Elise tightly then went back to reading. *Holy shit, I have to make sure our pride is balanced.*

There is one lesser-known case of a pride built of an Alpha male and his three Alpha Lionesses which was successful, though likely an anomaly. Winston Hoghunter created a balance between his females by rotating the leadership of the Lionesses week to week whilst remaining as the head of the family himself. During a week, one Lioness would make the majority of the decisions for the group right down to sexual endeavours and the Alpha male would have their attention more often than the others to give them assurance of their importance and necessity within the group – both of which are intrinsic needs of an Alpha. This could also feed the possessiveness of an Alpha and allow them to exert their desire to claim their mate more fully. Winston reported that he spent more time with the mate whose week it was to lead the group, allowing him time to fully satisfy their Alpha needs.

I grabbed up my fallen Pop Tart, taking a savage bite out of it and thinking on that. Would Elise be up for a leadership rota? Could I convince the guys of it too? It seemed like a decent answer, especially when the alternative was me losing my shit and eating one of them for lunch. I'd eat Dante first. Nah, Gabriel. Ryder's muscles were constantly rigid so eating him would be like cracking through a pistachio with my teeth. But Gabe, he was always calm, composed. He probably did yoga at the buttcrack of dawn while he recharged his magic in front of the sunrise. He'd taste like a croissant, soft and sweet in the middle. Dante would be tougher to rip into at first, like a toffee with a gooey centre. Mmm, I'd do Gabe to start then finish with Dante. Maybe I'd rip my claws down Ryder's belly to crack into that nutty exterior of his after I'd had the others, then suck out his crunchy insides – *wait, what the fuck am I doing?! Oh my stars, I'm going to eat my boyfriends-in-law!*

Heat ran up my neck and I stuffed the book into my pocket, eating my way through the stack of Pop Tarts as I mentally beat myself up. *I've gotta work out the balance in the pride. And soon.*

I tuned in on Elise and Laini's conversation as I tried to stop salivating about how good Gabe would taste, working to block out those violent, delicious visions.

"-love that new book smell, don't you? Mmm, there's something almost sexual about it," Laini sighed wistfully and Elise laughed.

"I'm gonna equate that to the way I feel about blood. So yeah, it sounds hot if you're a Sphinx," she said with a grin.

"Listen up, Aurora!" a loud voice made my head snap around and my gaze landed on Eugene Dipper standing on a table wearing a dark purple cape clasped at his neck and billowing out behind him, little matching fingerless gloves and a gleaming silver belt with rats engraved into it. The guy had bully bait written all over him on a normal day, but what the hell was he thinking wearing that?

His white hair was styled to stand on end like petrified flames and I swear to the stars, he was wearing guyliner and it didn't look all that bad on him.

"The Fae at this school can be big, fat meanies," he snapped, placing his hands on his hips and stamping his foot.

I shared a look with Elise that said she was worried for his life and I couldn't help but respect the guy a little for this suicidal act. He was a dead Fae walking though so I whipped up a croissant, tearing into it with my teeth as I relaxed to enjoy the show.

"So I am officially setting up a new society!" Eugene whipped around, his cape floating out and showing the room the shining silver words across the back of it. D.U.D. "Join the Daring Under-Dogs now!"

"I'm surprised he's still breathing," I said through a mouthful of pastry as most of the room started laughing, taking out my Atlas and casually starting to record him.

"Oh Eugene..." Elise murmured anxiously under her breath. She really did care for the little rat boy and I didn't entirely hate him anymore. But I was still damn sure he wanted to get his tiny paws on my girl.

"Laugh all you want." Eugene whipped back around dramatically. "But

I'll show anyone who wants to take me on that I am a strong and powerful Fae. I won't let anyone flush me down the toilet or stuff me up a Griffin's butthole ever again! And yes, I'm talking to you, Ferdinand!" He pointed a finger at his old roommate who had scraggly brown hair and bushy eyebrows to match.

Ferdinand pushed out of his seat beside his friends, elevating to well over six feet in height as he glared at Eugene on the next table over.

"Yeah? What are you gonna do to stop me?" He smirked.

"Did that dude push Eugene up his own ass?" I hissed to Elise and her eyes widened.

"He told me he kept putting Eugene's socks in his ass crack, I didn't think things had progressed beyond that," she said in horror. "That's fucking sick."

"Yeah," I agreed, taking another huge bite out of my croissant. "The drama deepens." This was better than prime time TV, man.

"My head itched for three days after you put me in your butt!" Eugene squeaked furiously and gasps mixed with the laughter that kept ringing around the room.

"You crawled up there because you're obsessed with me," Ferdinand said cockily, shrugging his huge shoulders.

"I'd never crawl up anyone's butt!" Eugene shrieked, going ultrasonic. It was fucking epic.

"Then why'd you crawl up mine?" Ferdinand asked with a mocking laugh, looking to his friends for back him up but they wrinkled their noses.

"Why'd you shove him up your ass, bro?" one of them hissed at him.

"Because he deserved it," Ferdinand said with a smirk. "It was fucking hilarious." He barked a loud laugh, but his friends just shared a look of disgust and shifted away from him.

"I challenge you to a duel, Ferdinand Ferkins," Eugene shouted and my eyebrows shot up.

Holy shit, this was awesome. Eugene was definitely about to die, and I was gonna capture it right on my Atlas. *R.I.P. little dude.*

"Leon," Elise whispered sharply at me, narrowing her gaze at my Atlas.

"What? I'm documenting history, little monster," I said with an innocent shrug and she pursed her lips, turning away to watch again.

Ferdinand shed his blazer and rolled up his sleeves, marching confidently towards Eugene with a swagger in his gait. "Come on then, you turd hunter," he barked, opening his arms wide. "Fight me!"

Eugene dove from his table with a yell of defiance, colliding with Ferdinand who threw a hard punch into his face and knocked him flat on his back in an instant. I actually found myself rooting for the little guy as he squeaked in pain. Ferdinand went to kick him and Eugene slapped a hand down on the tiles, sending a shockwave through the floor that bucked Ferdinand right off his feet onto his ass.

Eugene dove on top of him, coating his hands in gleaming metal knuckle dusters and slamming them into Ferdinand's face left and right as fast and as furiously as he could. My face fixed into an astonished grin as he beat the hell out of him then Ferdinand smashing an ice coated fist into Eugene's side, sending him tumbling away across the floor.

He hit the legs of a girl with a skirt down to her knees, bright green hair and the largest blue eyes I'd ever seen. "Get up!" she squeaked excitedly in encouragement and Eugene scrambled upright, gazing at her for a long moment before running back into the fight. He freaking dropkicked Ferdinand in the chest, but the guy didn't move an inch and Eugene hit the ground again with a curse.

Ferdinand created a trident out of ice in his grip, laughing loudly as he cast a whirlpool of water around Eugene then stabbed it at him like he was Ursula and Eugene was the Little Mermaid.

"This is awesome," I laughed. "Go on Eugene! Show that rat stuffing ass bandit who's boss!" My voice filled the room and every Mindy in it was suddenly on Eugene's side, shouting out encouragements.

"That's it, little squeaker!" one of them screamed and a chant went up of *'little squeaker, little squeaker, little squeaker!'* making Ferdinand turn red with anger.

"Go on Eugene!" Elise cried.

Eugene suddenly dove out of the whirlpool and caught a vine as he cast it from the ceiling, swinging on it like Tarzan and slamming his feet into Ferdinand's chest. The Griffin staggered backwards and Eugene pressed his advantage. He wrapped Ferdinand in vines, binding his hands to his ankles so he was bent over before him and while Eugene swung on the vine, his foot collided with the Griffin's ass and sent him flying away from him with a yell of pain. Ferdinand hit the ground, struggling against the binds, but he couldn't get free.

Eugene landed on top of him and flexed his skinny arms like he was a bodybuilder and the green haired girl clapped and cheered furiously, making his chest puff out like a peacock.

"If anyone is being bullied at Aurora Academy, come to me and join the D.U.Ds!" Eugene cried. "I'll be teaching self-confidence lessons every Monday evening in Room 103 in Altair Halls, how to get out of a tight hole lessons on Tuesdays, unleashing your inner Fae lessons on Wednesdays and bully takedown practice Thursdays and Fridays." He whipped around, spinning his cape with a flare and jumped off of Ferdinand, heading over to the buffet line to fetch his breakfast as casual as fuck.

I banged my fist down on the table as I cheered and the Mindys went wild along with a bunch of other Fae who'd clearly earned his respect.

"Alright, it's official. I like the rat," I announced.

I uploaded the video on FaeBook and tapped out a quick post.

Leon Night:
@EugeneDipper just went Rambo on @FerdinandFerkins who allegedly shoved Eugene up his ass in rat form, making him the first rat on the poon.

The #poostranaut was defeated that day only to come back now and rise up as the official #backdoorconquistador he has longed to be ever since. Watch Eugene take down his bigassed nemesis right here. #Ferdtheturd #challengedtoapoo-ual #feararatinyourrear #paybackfromtheasscrack

Heather Altimus:
Now that's what I call a real Fae! #hecanmakemesqueakanytime
Janeen Smart:
Wow!! #dipyourdipperinme #eugeneismynewdream
Carla Dianne:
You could say that was #titfortatfromtheassrat
Holli Young:
He can explore my unchartered never regions whenever he likes #ratpacking

I looked up and Eugene appeared with a bowl of fruit and a large slice of frosted cake beside it.

I stood from my seat, forgetting everything he'd just done and pointing at the cake as Eugene was consumed by my shadow. "Where did you get that?" I said through a mouthful of my second croissant.

Eugene released a squeak then cleared his throat and pointed over at a group of Pegasuses who were eating their way through my cake. "They were giving out slices," he said.

"*Were?*" I growled, looking around and realising that every slice of cake was now in the hands of some greedy fucker in the room. "Give me yours," I demanded of Eugene, my Charisma washing from me. He might have beaten down Ferdinand, but I was a whole other level of Fae.

He started holding it out to me then blinked hard and yanked it away, hugging an arm around it and baring his teeth at me. "No. It's mine."

My eyebrows arched at his display of aggression and Elise looked up at him from her seat with a sideways grin.

"Give it to me, little mouse." I stepped up onto my chair then onto the table, my gaze locked on his cake as I wet my lips. "My cake. *Mine*."

"No!" Eugene squeaked, holding his ground as I glared down at him. "And I'm a Tiberian Rat, not a mouse."

"You'll be a squashed Tiberian Rat in a minute if you don't give it to me." My Charisma poured out of me, but I could see the little dude fighting it and I had to admire his tenacity. Since when had the rat boy grown such large balls?

I lunged for the cake, but he flicked a finger at the same time, catching my leg with a vine and uprooting me. My ass hit the table and I growled as he turned and ran away.

"I want cake!" I bellowed and Elise smacked my leg.

"Leo, you're acting like a two-year-old," she hissed and I pouted at her.

"I'm acting entirely appropriately for the situation, little monster," I insisted and she rolled her eyes.

I was suddenly accosted by Mindys, diving onto the table as they tried to hand me cake. Two of them were fighting over a plate of it, shrieking and slapping one another while others were racing around the room, fighting cake out of anyone's hands they could. Chaos descended and a grin split across my cheeks as I accepted every plate of cake handed to me, wolfing each one down and tossing the plates aside when I was done. Fuck. Yes.

When the final piece of cake was in my hand, the Mindys dispersed and I gazed down at the creamy filling of the sponge with a satisfied grin. Crumbs were scattered all over me and icing was smeared over my face as I brought it to my lips. Elise was staring at me with her mouth agape, like she'd never quite seen a display like this before. It must have been pretty impressive to her.

"Oh no," she breathed.

"Oh yes," I replied.

"Leo, wait," she demanded, reaching for my arm, but I leaned away from her, taking a slow and sexual bite out of the cake as I moaned. "You have an audience," she hissed.

I frowned as she jerked her head in the direction of said audience and I looked over, finding Middle Kipling watching me from the next table over. His eyes were wide, his dick unashamedly hard as he stood from his seat to get a better view.

"Oh shit, does he have a crush on me?" I whispered to Elise and she bit her lip, shaking her head, but it was pretty obvious he did.

I pushed the cake between my lips, chewing through the last of the soft cakeyness before sucking each of my fingers. *Delicious.*

Middle Kipling walked purposefully towards the restroom at the back of the hall, pushing through the door and slamming it shut behind him. *Oh my stars, did I just make it into his spank bank? Is he cashing in on the primetime Leon show right now?*

The Cafaeteria door suddenly banged open and I looked around, finding Ryder striding in with a large group of Lunars at his back. A collective inhale rang through the room as he walked over to the breakfast line and started grabbing food like this was just any old day. My heart beat excitedly as I glanced from them to the Oscuras in the same room, the barriers being forced down between them by their kings.

A ripple of tension ran through the atmosphere and as Ryder moved to sit on a table alone at the back of the hall, Dante stood up and walked over to talk to him. All eyes were on them as they had casual words with each other and slowly, the Lunars all got their food and sat down. They were on opposite sides of the hall to the Oscuras, but still, this was a fucking momentous occasion. And I suddenly realised something which was even better than the whole city being in a ceasefire right now. Surely if Dante was cool with closing the gap between the Lunars, that meant we could get some of them to try out for the school Pitball team!

"What are you plotting?" Elise asked, climbing out of her seat to sit on the table beside me and kissing away some frosting on the edge of my lips. My cock stirred to attention as I turned to her and rubbed my nose against hers.

"I just figured out a way to finally make our Pitball team the best in the academy league." I beamed then whipped up one of the plates beside me and jumped to my feet, cupping one hand around my mouth. "Ryder! Go long!"

I threw the plate like a frisbee, the thing tearing across the room towards him. He didn't even blink as he glared at me and it sailed over his head, smashing into a thousand pieces as it hit the wall behind him.

I burst out laughing and started pointing, using my Charisma to make all the Mindys in the room join in. Ryder's right eye twitched as I made a mockery of him, his hand tight around the spoon in his grip.

"Ha! You can't catch. Imagine him on the Pitball field? Good thing you're not on the team, buddy, it would be *such* an embarrassment. Can you imagine what Zodiac Academy would think if we put you on the field?"

I felt Elise frowning at me in confusion as I mocked Ryder and the Lunar King grew angrier and angrier.

"I could catch a fucking fly out of the air if I wanted to, Mufasa!" he bellowed back at me and I kept laughing, the Mindys still following suit with me.

"*Sure* you could," I taunted, whipping out my Atlas and picking up another plate. "Prove it then. Catch this. Hands only, no magic."

Ryder shoved out of his seat at the challenge and I casually used my fire magic to heat up the plate so it was red hot in my grip. *Prank time.*

I started recording on my Atlas as the whole school watched, looking from me to Ryder as they waited to see what would happen with bated breath.

I threw the plate hard and it whizzed across the room towards him. Ryder had to shove a freshman out of the way to get closer, knocking him onto his ass as he lunged up to catch the plate out of the air. He caught it between the tips of his fingers then cursed and instantly dropped it, the thing smashing against his feet.

His gaze turned venomous as he realised what I'd done and the whole school burst out laughing. He was suddenly charging at me like a rhino and I stole a kiss from Elise's lips in a dramatic goodbye before diving off the table, still recording over my shoulder as I ran for the door.

"You're dead, Mufasa!" he bellowed as I made it outside and started tearing along the path.

Ryder collided with me, taking me to the ground in a tackle that was as good as Dante's on the Pitball pitch. *Holy shit, I've found myself a rising star.*

Ryder started beating the hell out of me as I laughed and managed to roll over beneath him, throwing a few playful punches back at him too.

His hands locked around my throat, his muscles bunching as he bared his teeth at me. "You think you can make a fool of me and get away with it, Simba?"

"Just – a – prank – dude," I choked out and his grip eased a little as he frowned, processing that.

"You do that with Dante," he commented, seeming to think on something.

"Yeah, it's one of our favourite things," I said, sucking in some air as he released me and sat back on my stomach to keep me down. "I like to do it with my favourite people."

"Hm," he grunted. "Alright. You wanna prank me, Lion boy, then prepare to get pranked back in return." He shoved to his feet, yanking me up by the hand and I opened my mouth, on the verge of a squeal of excitement, but he shoved a palm over my mouth to stop me. "Don't be weird about it."

"Um, Ryder?" Eugene called and I looked over, finding Eugene walking towards the Lunar King, still wearing that long purple cape. Maybe I should get our pride matching capes...*Note to self: tell Mindys to add it to the merch list.*

Ryder looked like he was about to ignore him as he walked away from me, but Eugene leapt into his path to stop him. Dude's balls had apparently doubled in size lately.

"I heard a rumour that you killed Bryce Corvis," he breathed as I cocked my head to eavesdrop.

"And?" Ryder growled, trying to step past him, but Eugene dove into his way again.

"Well, it's just um, you…you saved me," he said, his eyes lighting up like two little shiny pennies.

"What?" Ryder hissed like he was disgusted at the idea. "I didn't do shit for you."

"You did though!" Eugene squeaked in delight, looking like he might actually shed a tear. "You freed me from the curse of seven years bad luck because of the star bond I broke with Bryce. He's dead so…it's gone." His face split into a wide, adoring grin. "All because of you."

Ho-ly shit. I was half tempted to start recording on my Atlas again, but I reckoned filming evidence of Ryder murdering someone wasn't the best idea.

"Great, now get out of my way," Ryder said, the rattle starting up in his body in warning.

Eugene blanched for a moment before throwing himself at him and hugging him tight, his thin arms tightening around Ryder's waist. It lasted all of one second before Ryder threw him off of him and Eugene hit the ground on his ass, continuing to stare up at Ryder like he was a star descended from the sky, here to walk among us. Ryder stormed off into the Cafaeteria and Eugene got up, smiling blissfully as he headed down the path and a bunch of giggling girls jogged after him. I noticed the green haired girl following too but from further away, biting her lip nervously.

"I'd snap him up quick if I were you, love," Ethan called to her as he walked past with a smirk on his lips.

She blushed, nodding and hurrying on down the path after Eugene but it looked like he was already surrounded by girls. Power really was the biggest turn on in our world. Hell, I was a little hard for him.

I snatched up my fallen Atlas from the ground, posting the video to FaeBook.

Leon Night:
Watch @RyderDraconis fail spectacularly as he fumbles an easy catch and shames himself in front of the WHOLE school.
Check my Mindys-only account for the slow-mo version, his face is priceless.
#Basiliskscantcatch #snakeittilyoubreakit #thereptilemissedbyamile

Emma-Leigh:
Hahaha oh my stars! How is someone so terrifying that cute??
#youcanfumblemeanytime

Amanda Olavessen:
Your Mindys-only account is a rip off these days Leon! I'm not paying fifty auras a month just to see you dance fully clothed and act out The Lion King scene by scene #bringbackthecumshots #thisMindyneedsherfix #Imissyourdickdance #whathappenedtofilthyfridays

Cynthia Rodriguez:
THROW ME NEXT TIME LEON #catchmeifyoucansnakeman #tossmeintheairlikeyoujustdontcare

Kendyl Barron:
I wanna come back as a plate in my next life #smashmeRyder #youbreakityouboughtit #gluemebackupandlickmycracks

The bell rang for the start of class and Elise suddenly shot to my side, tiptoeing up to kiss my cheek. "Fucking genius. Ryder just told me he's gonna try out for the Pitball team so he can beat your ass in public."

My jaw dropped and I picked up my little monster, spinning her around in excitement. She laughed as I hugged her then planted her back on her feet and slung my arm over her shoulder. "Yes!" I whooped.

Gabriel suddenly appeared beside her and my heart nearly leapt out of my chest. Dude could move like a ghost. His shirt was off, the inked symbols and markings covering his chest shining in the sunlight.

Hold the front fucking door was that a new tattoo? Was it about me? Hell to the fucking yes it was.

"You got one for me?" I asked excitedly, poking the new ink below his left pec (super close to his motherfreaking heart might I add) and read the words there aloud. "My Brightest Night."

"That's not for you. And it's not new. It's just something that won't leave me alone and-"

"Something with my name in it," I said.

"No, it's not Night it's night, like when the sun is gone and-"

"I thought the tats were for visions you didn't understand yet but were super, super, super important – like your love for me. And that's a big N not a little n," I said excitedly.

"That's a stylistic-"

"Oh my stars, you're so in love with me it hurts." I grinned big and Gabriel growled.

"I told you it's not-" he began.

"Shhh." I placed a finger to his lips and he narrowed his eyes at me while Elise giggled. "Let's all just feel the moment and not ruin it with words." I ran my finger down from his mouth to caress the tattoo and he batted my hand away with a frown before letting it go. Clearly because he knew deep down, I was right.

"You've got a Liaison," Gabriel announced just before Elise's Atlas pinged and she took it out, finding a message from Titan inviting her to his office because his schedule had changed. "Someone needs to go with you."

"Well which one of us should it be, Gabe?" I asked, using the tactics I'd learned in my Lion book over breakfast. I'd let Gabe make some decisions this week and see how that affected our little tribe. He narrowed his eyes at me like he knew exactly what I was up to, but I doubted even the stars could understand the inner workings of my conniving mind.

"You go," he decided. "I wanna do a circuit of the perimeter before class and I'll check out Titan's office on my way too."

"Good idea," I commented. "He's great at making decisions, isn't he Elise?" I nudged her and she frowned at me with a shrug.

"Sure," she said and I didn't miss the slightly smug grin pulling at Gabriel's lips or the way his chest puffed out ever-so-slightly. *Oh Gabe. You're gonna make such a good Lioness when I whip you into shape.*

She stopped him to say goodbye, looking desperate for a kiss from his lips and I flicked out my fingers, casting a ring of fire around us and making a couple of students scream in fright as they dove out of the way of my flames.

Elise laughed lightly. "Thanks, Leo," she said then dragged Gabriel into a passionate kiss, the two of them gripping each other so tightly I was half tempted to join in and turn this sad goodbye into a dirty hello. But then Gabe's wings burst from his back and he shot into the sky while Elise watched him go with an ache of longing in her eyes.

I let the flames fall away around us, taking her hand as we made our way to Altair Halls where Professor Titan's office was.

"You don't have to come everywhere with me, you know?" she said for the hundredth time this week.

"I know you can handle yourself, little monster, but I like handling you too. Especially your tits. I love handling them." I reached for her left tit, but she smacked my hand away with a laugh.

We reached Titan's office and she knocked on the door, a beat passing before he called out for her to enter.

"Oh, Mr Night," he said in surprise as I followed her into the room where Titan was sitting behind his desk.

"He's gonna sit in on our chat if that's cool?" Elise asked.

"Well, it's not really Elise," he said, wringing his fingers together as he looked at me. I may not have been a gang member, but he still let me get away with all kinds of shit in class because he knew I was best friends with Dante. "It's meant to be a private space for you to talk openly." He glanced at me with assessing eyes and for a moment I felt like I was being sized up by an overprotective father. Hang the fuck on, did he actually care about my girl?

"I can talk openly with Leo here," Elise said, shooting me a smile. "We're mates, there's nothing in the world I'd ever wanna keep from him."

Titan nodded, his shoulders relaxing a bit as he smiled. "Alright, sit down. I've never actually met anyone Elysian Mate bonded before you two, it's all very new to me. I'm so glad you have someone you can trust in this school though, Elise. The stars only know it's a Fae eat Fae world out there."

He cast a silencing bubble around us as we sat before his desk and I kept Elise's hand in mine, grazing my thumb over the chunky gold ring Dante had given her.

"So, I've been having a look over your grades. You're excelling in Elemental Combat, Astrology and Potions. But I think there could be some improvement on your Numerology scores and you need to work on your scrying abilities too, it's letting you down overall in Arcane Arts."

"Ergh," Elise groaned. "I hate numbers and trying to see things in water is just stupid. Gabriel's a Seer, if I'm going to get hit by a bus, he'll *see* it coming for me."

"Yes, well, you can't rely on your friendship with Mr Nox forever," he commented. "You will need to be able to keep an eye on your own fate if you're going to avoid straying down dangerous paths in future. It's very important, Elise. Have you been interpreting your Horoscopes each day and checking back to see if your assessments were correct? It's an essential life skill."

"Erm...no," she said, biting her lip guiltily. "I've just been kinda busy lately. Laini's been helping me catch up with the work I missed while we were on vacation and I've been prioritising valuable subjects."

"All subjects are valuable," Titan said a little sternly, but he didn't really pull it off. The guy was a sap, but he was a decent sap I guessed. "Anyway, I'm glad to hear you've been spending more time with Laini. It's important to create strong connections outside of your more intimate relationship." He glanced at me and I leaned back in my seat, balancing my ankle on my knee.

"Don't worry, my girl spends plenty of time creating strong, *deep* connections with other Fae, don't you little monster?" I said, a hint of teasing to my tone and she smothered a grin.

"Yeah. Me and Eugene are pretty good friends now," she covered for my implications and Titan looked between us curiously.

"Good. Eugene is coming on rather well since you befriended him, I'm glad to report. His grades have vastly improved in the last few weeks alone. I'm not sure what you've said to him, but whatever it is, keep doing it, Elise. It's wonderful to see him blossom." Titan smiled, resting his hands on the desk.

"I haven't said anything." Elise shrugged.

"He watches you like a hawk, little monster," I said with a smirk. "You don't have to say anything, you just breed badasses around you. It's one of my favourite qualities about you, that and how well you suck my-"

"Mr Night," Titan interjected sharply.

"Neck," I finished with a smirk. "She's a Vampire, remember? Get your mind out of the gutter, sir."

He blushed as Elise snorted a laugh. He could clearly see me toying with him, but if he was going to give me the assessment eyes and weigh me like a lump of meat to see if I measured up for his favourite student, then I was going to do the same to him. Elise had very few people she could trust in her life and if this guy wanted to look out for her then great. But I'd be doing a few background checks of my own before I let her skip off into the sunset with him.

Titan went through each of Elise's grades and wrote down notes for the areas she needed to improve on in her studies. I yawned, taking a nap beside her as he jabbered on about boring school things and I fell into a dream about me growing fluffy Lion wings and flying through a cloud. Dante soared along beside me, Elise rode on my back and Gabriel flew with Ryder in his pocket, wearing a tiny helmet and aeronaut goggles, his forked tongue flapping in the wind.

"Tiny hats!" I blurted as I woke up, feeling Elise squeezing my arm.

Titan was stacking up some papers on his desk and he waved his goodbye as Elise encouraged me out of my seat.

I grinned sleepily at her, pulling her against my hip as we headed out the door and I murmured in her ear. "I just remembered I bought another entire array of tiny little hats for Ryder in his smallest Basilisk form for our scrapbook photos."

She looked up at me with her lips wide and excitement twisted through her silvery eyes. "You did?"

"Yup." I grinned a Lion's grin. "Next time he passes out as a teeny weenie snake, we're doing a whole photoshoot."

"*Yes,*" she whispered conspiratorially. "Can we put him in a tiny bowtie too?"

"Little monster," I dropped my mouth to her ear. "You can put him in any tiny clothes you can dream up. I will personally make it happen."

"Are you shitting me, Leone?" Dante growled in my ear as we stood shoulder to shoulder on the Pitball pitch.

"Nope. This is happening. You wanted a peace deal, so the Lunars should be able to try out for the team." I folded my arms, staring at the Brotherhood members lining up for try outs, smiling from ear to ear as Ryder stood beside Ethan, looking uncomfortable as shit but determined as hell. He was in a purple Pitball kit that looked a size too small for him, clinging to his muscles, his huge thighs practically bursting out of his shorts.

"This is the best day of my life," I whispered to Gabriel on my other side.

"I think this might be the best day of my life too," he murmured back and the two of us started cracking up under our breath.

Elise wolf whistled and Ryder glowered at her with a promise of death in his eyes.

"He's gonna spank your ass raw for that, little monster," I muttered.

"Worth it," she sang as she tossed an airball up and down in her hand, spinning it on her finger with the gifts of her Element.

Mars looked like he was having an even better day than me as he eyed Ryder and Ethan like they were a meal laid out for a hungry dog. He'd wanted some Lunars on the team for a long ass time, but never in his wildest dreams would he have imagined the Lunar King himself would be lining up to try out.

We still needed a decent Waterback and our Earthbacker had dropped out a couple of weeks ago when Dante had shattered both of his kneecaps in practice and he'd decided the game wasn't for him anymore. That was the way of Pitball though. I'd sacrificed plenty of kneecaps and elbows in my time to get a ball in the Pit. It was the nature of the game. If you couldn't hack the broken bones and dislocated joints, then it probably wasn't for you. I mean, yeah it hurt like a motherfucker, but as soon as it was all healed up it was game on again, so what was the problem?

"Shadowbrook, you're up first," Mars beckoned him forward and Ethan jogged over with plenty of girls' eyes falling to his ass as he went.

His uniform was a little small too, but nothing like Ryder's. There wasn't much point in buying new ones out of the meagre school budget unless they made the cut though, and Mars always insisted they try out in the Aurora colours to get a proper feel for being a part of the team. I imagined it was only Ryder's stubborn determination to prove to me and the rest of the school that he could catch a ball better than anyone that he was standing here wearing that. But if I was going to get him officially on the team, I'd have to play my cards right – assuming he was actually any good. But his power level alone was enough to give him a decent shot. The rules could be learned, and he'd tackled me like a pro this morning so why wouldn't he be made for this?

Mars had Ethan try to score Pits while we all worked to stop him. He was one fast fucker, racing between us, even outpacing Elise at one point and slamming the ball into the Pit. We all cheered, because holy shit, that was the kind of talent we needed on the team. If he could score like that in a game against Zodiac, we were sitting pretty. Of course, he didn't get all the Pits. Me and Dante took him out so hard, he got a bloody nose but he didn't even bitch and whine about that as he waited for Mars to call time on us holding him down. I healed him before hauling him to his feet and he howled his joy to the sky.

"This is my game," he announced. "I was born to be on this fucking pitch."

"Yeah, yeah, stronzo," Dante muttered. "You're adequate."

"Was that a compliment to a Lunar?" I gasped in exaggeration, but Dante strode away, saying nothing. He might have been secret best friends with Ryder now, but he was still having a hard time cosying up to the rest of his gang. I couldn't really blame him on account of all the murdering of his family and all but as far as I knew, Ethan hadn't killed anyone he knew that well.

Ethan pushed his hand into his sandy hair, checking out our Fireside as she jogged by, her ass bouncing in her shorts.

I lifted my gold whistle to my lips and blew on it sharply, making him wince as he looked around.

"What the hell, man?" he balked.

"No perving mid-game. You don't screw the girls on this team. If you fuck and chuck my teammates and leave them pissy on the pitch, I'll make you regret it, Shadowbrook."

"That's rich," he scoffed. "I heard you threw a hissy fit because you had some drama with Elise at the last Zodiac game. You flushed the chance of the trophy down the shitter." Ethan arched a brow and I shrugged.

"That only proves my point," I commented and he rolled his eyes.

"Fine, I won't screw anyone on the team if I'm picked."

"Good." I grinned. "Mars will want you in, don't you worry." I clapped him on the shoulder then blew my whistle in his face again. "Now get off my pitch!"

"Asshole," he muttered before jogging away and I beamed at his back. *Ah, I love the smell of new best friends.*

"Draconis, you're up!" Mars called and to tell you I was excited was the understatement of the entire fucking century.

Ryder tugged at his shorts as they rode up his ass crack and I smirked as a bunch of girls here for the try-outs giggled and stared. The outline of his huge cock was so prominent I was pretty sure someone was in danger of getting their eye poked out.

I blew my whistle to get his attention and he glared at me, snaring me in his hypnosis. He showed me him ripping the whistle from around my neck and stuffing it down my throat until I choked on it. Then he released me from the vision and smirked challengingly at me.

"Right team," Mars called to us. "Draconis is trying out for defence, so you're all on offense. I'm going to shoot one ball onto the pitch and Draconis is going to try and get hold of it. Bonus points if you can get a Pit yourself."

Ryder grunted in acknowledgement of that and I chuckled.

"So just to confirm, we're playing piggy in the middle, sir?" I called to Mars and my team laughed.

"If you wanna call it that, Night, then sure," Mars answered, setting himself up at the side of the pitch to watch.

I snorted like a pig and a chorus of the same noise echoed around me from my team, Dante joining in with a bark of laughter.

Ryder's jaw pulsed with rage, but the focus in his eyes never wavered.

"Okay - three, two, one, go!" Mars bellowed and an earthball shot out of the hole in the earth quarter. Everyone raced that way, but Ryder just stood there as Dante scooped up the ball then threw it over Ryder's head to me. I caught it, tossing it to Elise and she leapt into the air to catch it while Ryder just remained there like a pissed off statue.

"Mr Draconis!" Mars called. "You need to try and get the ball."

"He can't catch, sir," I shouted back. "I think that's the problem."

I caught the earthball as it was tossed my way again and Ryder's eyes locked on me. He started running, tearing along the pitch, sand kicking up behind him as he raced for me like a bull with a rocket up its ass. I lifted the ball above my head to throw it to Gabriel, but Ryder cast a huge net of vines behind him, towering up into the sky to block my opening to any other players. I turned and ran, tucking the heavy ball under my arm and racing for the Pit instead.

Well if you can't pass it, score it.

His furious footfalls came behind me as I sped towards the middle of the pitch and my whole team started shouting encouragements at me to score.

The ground shook beneath my feet and I stumbled, nearly dropping the ball and cursing under my breath as I kept going. Screams sounded out behind me and I threw a look over my shoulder, finding the whole team falling into a huge fissure opening up in the ground.

The fury in Ryder's eyes made adrenaline stab through me and I gritted my teeth as I focused, closing the distance to the Pit and lifting my arm to launch it in.

I was snared by a vine around my ankles, dragged into the air at high speed and I tossed the ball at the Pit with all my might, a shout of excitement pouring from my lips. It sailed toward the hole on a course for victory, when another whip slapped it back into the sky towards me. I reached out to try and catch it, my fingers just grazing it before I was slammed back down onto the ground on my back with a pained groan as the air was forced from my lungs. I lifted my head as Ryder casually caught the ball out of the sky with one hand and dropped it into the Pit with a flick of his wrist, staring at me the whole time to capture the moment he proved me wrong. But he had no idea that I'd planned this whole thing and just shown the entire world that Ryder was a killer Pitball player.

Mars cheered enthusiastically and I joined in, pounding my fists in the sand and Ryder came walking over, standing above me so I was sitting in his shadow.

"I *can* catch, Mufasa." He kicked sand at me then strode away across the pitch, mending the fissure in the ground and spitting all the other players back out of it. Elise was floating up on a gust of air as she watched him, calling out his name. "That was insane! Did you see that, Professor?"

"I sure did. You're on the team, Draconis," Mars announced.

"No thanks," Ryder said, tearing off his too tight shirt and causing a bunch of girls in the line-up to practically swoon over his scarred and tattooed body. "I just came here to prove a point."

"Yeah, he's too chicken shit to actually play on the team. He'd totally crack under the pressure against Zodiac," I said, cupping my head in my hands and flopping back onto the sand. "Let him go, Professor. He'd never be able to hack it."

A thumping of footfalls sounded my way again and suddenly Ryder was on top of me, wrestling me in the dirt as he punched me. I rolled him over, throwing wild punches as we fought like cubs and my Rydikins tried to kill me. It was so cute how much I got under his skin.

He rolled us once more and my head fell backwards into the Pit, his hand slamming over my face as he pushed me down. I bucked my hips hard and he went shooting over my head into the Pit but I caught his hand before he fell all the way, rolling as I grabbed onto him with my other hand too.

He snarled, trying to shake me off, clearly not caring if he dropped to the bottom of the ten foot hole.

"It's like a backwards Lion King moment," I cooed.

"Let go of me you piece of shit," he snapped.

"So you can fall down there and cry about being too scared to play Pitball?"

"I'm not scared of anything. Games are for children," he spat. "I'm not gonna waste my time on one."

"Suuure," I said, winking. "That's why you won't play. I'll keep up the story, don't worry."

"There's no story," he snarled and I winked again. "Stop winking."

"I'm not winking." I winked.

"Fuck you and your stupid game," he growled.

"Yeah, it's so stupid running around using magic to fight other Fae, beating down another team and getting victory blowjobs from my hot mate. She gets so horny after a game. A stupid, stupid game."

He went quiet, glaring at me for a long moment. "Pull me up," he commanded and I did, yanking him to the top of the Pit and hauling him over the edge. He pushed me aside as he got to his feet, running his tongue over his teeth. "I'm gonna join your little team, Lion. Because every time we practise, I'm going to see how many of your bones I can break." He strode off to tell Mars and I shared a triumphant look with Elise who did a backflip in mid-air to celebrate.

Mars practically jumped for joy when Ryder delivered the news and I whooped as I got up, my heart swelling. Because now we really did have a chance to defeat Zodiac Academy. And even better than that, every single one of my boyfriends-in-law were on my team.

Best. Day. *Ever*.

We finished up the try-outs but no one shined like Ethan and Ryder had and Mars soon called them over to sign them up officially. I ran to Elise, tugging her against me by the ass and whispering in her ear. "Wanna torment our little snake friend?"

Her eyes sparkled and a savage grin pulled at her lips. "I'm in."

Everyone was heading off the pitch to the locker rooms while Mars kept Ryder talking and I took Elise's hand, jogging toward the bleachers. She giggled loud enough for her voice to carry and as I glanced over at Ryder, his eyes locked with mine. I smirked challengingly at him, pressing my tongue into my cheek while raising my fist to the opposite cheek and giving him a blowjob gesture. *I'm gonna get some, Rydikins. Buh-bye.*

Elise towed me behind the bleachers and we peered through the gap in the seats, watching Ryder as he fell for my trap, marching this way as Mars headed off to the locker rooms with Ethan.

"Why is that tight ass uniform so hot on him?" Elise murmured under her breath.

"Because his buttcheeks are like two slabs of iron and we never get to appreciate that enough," I answered simply.

"We?" she chuckled and I snorted.

"Hey, I can appreciate the male form," I said.

"Oh yeah? Can you appreciate it on your knees with your mouth around his cock because I'd love to see that," she purred in my ear.

"I'm way too sober for that, little monster, plus I'm about to dom you so hard you'll cry," I taunted.

"You couldn't dom me if you tried," she said challengingly and I knew exactly how much she liked to be pinned down and fucked by me, so she was asking for trouble.

A Lion growl escaped me. "I could dom you *and* Scar if I wanted to."

She grinned mischievously. "I dare you to try. You couldn't make Ryder do anything you say."

My brows arched. "You're on. What do I get if I manage it?"

"What do you want?" she asked flirtatiously.

"Titty rights," I decided instantly. "For a week. The other guys can't have them, just me."

She laughed. "Fine, but if you fail, I get breakfast in bed every morning for a week."

"You're on." I shoved her to her knees and she gasped in surprise as I rolled my zipper down and smirked at her, fisting a hand in her hair. "Show your Pitball Captain a good time, sweetheart."

She gave me the come-fuck-me-eyes and I slid my cock between her lips as she parted them for me, making her moan. She fucking loved when I went all Alpha on her. She swirled her tongue around the head of my dick and I groaned while her skilful mouth got to work as she started to pump the base of my cock.

"Fuck, what game are we playing again?" I muttered, lost to the feel of her already.

She laughed and her throat tightened around the head of my cock as I thrust deeper in to feel it.

My gaze flicked to a shadow moving in my periphery and I found Ryder standing there, his shoulder leaning on one of the metal struts that held up the bleachers, his arms folded and his eyes dark. *Time to dom the dom.*

There was only one way I was going to get Ryder to do anything I said, but I was a master of manipulation and he wouldn't be able to resist what I wanted. Because he'd think it was the exact opposite of what I *really* wanted.

"Fuck off, dude," I told him. "We're busy."

He hissed angrily at that, stalking towards us and I fought a grin. *Here snakey, snakey. Come right into my trap and get dommed.*

Elise slid her lips off of my cock and I kept my hand in her hair as she looked to Ryder, her eyes bright and hungry as she reached for his waistband too. I tugged on her hair, keeping her away from him. "She's mine right now," I snarled possessively and Ryder practically spat venom. "Only Pitball Captains get post game blowjobs." I tugged up my shorts and my boner strained against the inside of them.

"Bullshit," Ryder snapped. "You want me too, don't you baby?" He slid his hand under Elise's chin and she nodded keenly, biting her lip.

"If you get your cock out, Ryder, I'm gonna be so pissed," I said and he shoved his tight shorts down, smirking at me in a challenge as he freed his hard dick.

I glared at him then pushed Elise's head towards his cock, moving a step behind him and controlling her as she took him into her mouth.

"Fine, hurry up then." I moved her head up and down and Ryder grinned like he'd won something as I used our girl to mouth fuck him. *I'm the dommiest dom in the world. No one can outdom me.*

After a minute, he shoved my hand off of her head like he'd just realised what was happening and held onto her himself. I stayed close behind him, gazing down at Elise over his shoulder as she took him in deep and her eyes lifted to meet mine. I pretended to lick Ryder's ear, wiggling my brows at her and she nearly choked on his cock as I mouthed *my snakelet* at her.

Ryder jerked around and I acted totally casual, narrowing my gaze at him. "Are you just here to ruin my post game high, asshole?" I asked him. "You'd better hurry up and finish then you can leave me to enjoy her pussy in peace."

His jaw flexed and he drew his cock out of Elise's lips. "Get on your knees, baby," he told her and I fought a smirk as she did as he said and he dropped down behind her, running a hand over her ass.

Well look at the two of them kneeling for me.

I walked around in front of Elise, my cock aching for attention as I played my little game and watched the Lunar King tugging down her shorts and panties. He looked me right in the eye with a smirk as he drove himself into her, taking her doggy style as he claimed her pussy to spite me.

"*Ryder,*" Elise moaned loudly and I enjoyed the show for a moment, running a hand over the bulge in my shorts and squeezing the base of my cock.

Fuck me, this was hot.

"So you're just gonna stay in that too tight shirt looking like a dipshit forever, are you Rydikins?" I mocked and he tore it from his body, tossing it aside with a snarl. Man, this was too easy.

I circled around them and Elise's eyes followed me, the want in her gaze clear. I moved behind Ryder again and she looked over her shoulder at me while I pretended to hump his head and made exaggerated sex faces. A laugh burst from her but it was lost to a loud moan as Ryder drove harder into her.

His head snapped around to look at me and I immediately flattened my expression to a scowl.

"You done yet, buddy?" I snipped. "Or do you need to be prodded gently with a needle or some shit to finish?"

"Pah, gently? That word's not in my vocabulary," he scoffed. "I could come while I was being flogged and choked to death, Mufasa," he laughed obnoxiously and I smirked darkly as I moved closer behind him.

"Bullshit," I said simply, stepping past him and inspecting my nails. He was playing so easily into my hands, it was fucking beautiful.

"Oh you don't believe me?" he growled, slowing his pace as Elise clawed her hands across the dirt in frustration and pressed her hips back in a demand for more.

"Ryder, come on," she snarled.

"No, I don't," I said lightly. "Now are you quite done with my girl yet, because she looks like she's getting bored."

"Fuck you," he hissed, his eyes spewing venom. He cast a long vine whip in his hand and tethered another one around his throat, tossing me the end of it. "Whip me and pull that as tight as you like," he said in a challenge and I bit down on the inside of my cheek as I fought the smile itching to pull at my lips. This was too damn easy.

I shrugged, snatching the whip from his hand and taking hold of the tether around his throat too. I moved behind him, yanking the choker tight before whipping his back hard. He laughed through the pain, driving into Elise in furious thrusts that had her crying out and I wondered vaguely if we should put a silencing bubble up. Meh.

Elise looked over her shoulder again, her eyes wide in disbelief at seeing what I was doing. Ryder's back grew red from my strikes and I tried to hook my Atlas out of my pocket to take a photo. *One for the scrapbook.*

"Oh fuck," Elise moaned as Ryder increased his pace and groaned low in his throat, spanking her ass hard. Elise screamed as she came and Ryder cursed, trying to hold out on his own release. But I snapped the whip down hard across his ass cheeks, forcing him to still as he gripped her hips and came with a deep growl at my command. *Well hot damn, I just dommed him so hard he came for me.*

"Oh shit, sorry, boss," a voice made us all pause and we looked over to find Ethan Shadowbrook standing there with damp hair and sweats on. "I heard screams and thought...I dunno what I thought."

"This isn't what it looks like," Ryder snarled, looking back at me in realisation and I smirked widely. Ryder flicked a hand and a wedge of earth jutted up from the ground to hide Elise from view and Ethan took a step back.

"It's cool, boss. Each to their own. No judgement here." Ethan continued retreating, a shit eating grin forming on his lips and Ryder pulled out of Elise, tugging his shorts up and marching toward him. Except he got yanked back by the choker I had hold of and I snorted a laugh as he dissolved the magic so the vines disappeared.

"You didn't see anything," Ryder spat at Ethan and he nodded quickly.

"I won't say a word about you being a sub," Ethan said seriously and I burst out laughing, earning me a furious glare from Ryder and Elise supressed her laugh as she scrambled back into her panties.

"I'm not a fucking sub!" Ryder bellowed, striding towards Ethan and grabbing a fistful of his shirt.

"Sure you're not. It's cool though, man. Some Alphas like to experiment."

Ryder swung a punch at him and Ethan took it like a trooper, stumbling back a step and rubbing his reddened jaw.

"If you say a word about this, you're dead," Ryder warned.

"I won't." Ethan offered him his hand for a star vow and they made one quickly before Ryder sent him on his way then turned to me with rage in his eyes.

But I was already busy dropping down behind Elise and drawing her hips back to line up with me.

"You're an asshole, Leo," she laughed and I smirked.

"A winning asshole," I reminded her. "Titty privileges are *mine*."

Ryder strode back towards us and I held up my hand for a high five. "No hard feelings, right dude? It was just a little game." He punched me in the head and my vision swum for a moment as adrenaline burst into my veins. "Low five?" I wheezed out, offering my hand lower instead.

"Face five." He slapped me hard across the cheek while a smile played around the corner of his lips and I knew we were bros again. Best bros.

I looked down to my little monster, desperate to unleash the tension in my throbbing dick and cursed as I found her gone. She was fully dressed, tossing her hair as she looked back at me.

"You took too long, Leo," she said in a teasing voice. "I wonder if Gabriel's busy." She shot away in a blur of speed, her laughter carrying to us and I tipped my head back with a groan.

"Queens don't wait around to be fucked by peasants, Simba," Ryder taunted and I sighed heavily as I looked down at my hard dick.

I knew who the real dom was in this five-way relationship. And it sure as shit wasn't any of us guys.

"Hey, I think I just figured something out." I jumped to my feet as Ryder walked away and I jogged after him, wondering why he was moving so fast.

"You call me Mufasa when you're angry at me and Simba when you like me."

"No," Ryder answered.

"Sure you do," I pushed, but he just quickened his pace.

"So do you wanna come back to our room and watch The Lion King with me?" I asked.

"No, Mufasa," he growled, striding off ahead of me.

"See! Now you're mad again. I've got you figured out, Scar!" I called after him, but he didn't reply. Aw, I loved our bromance.

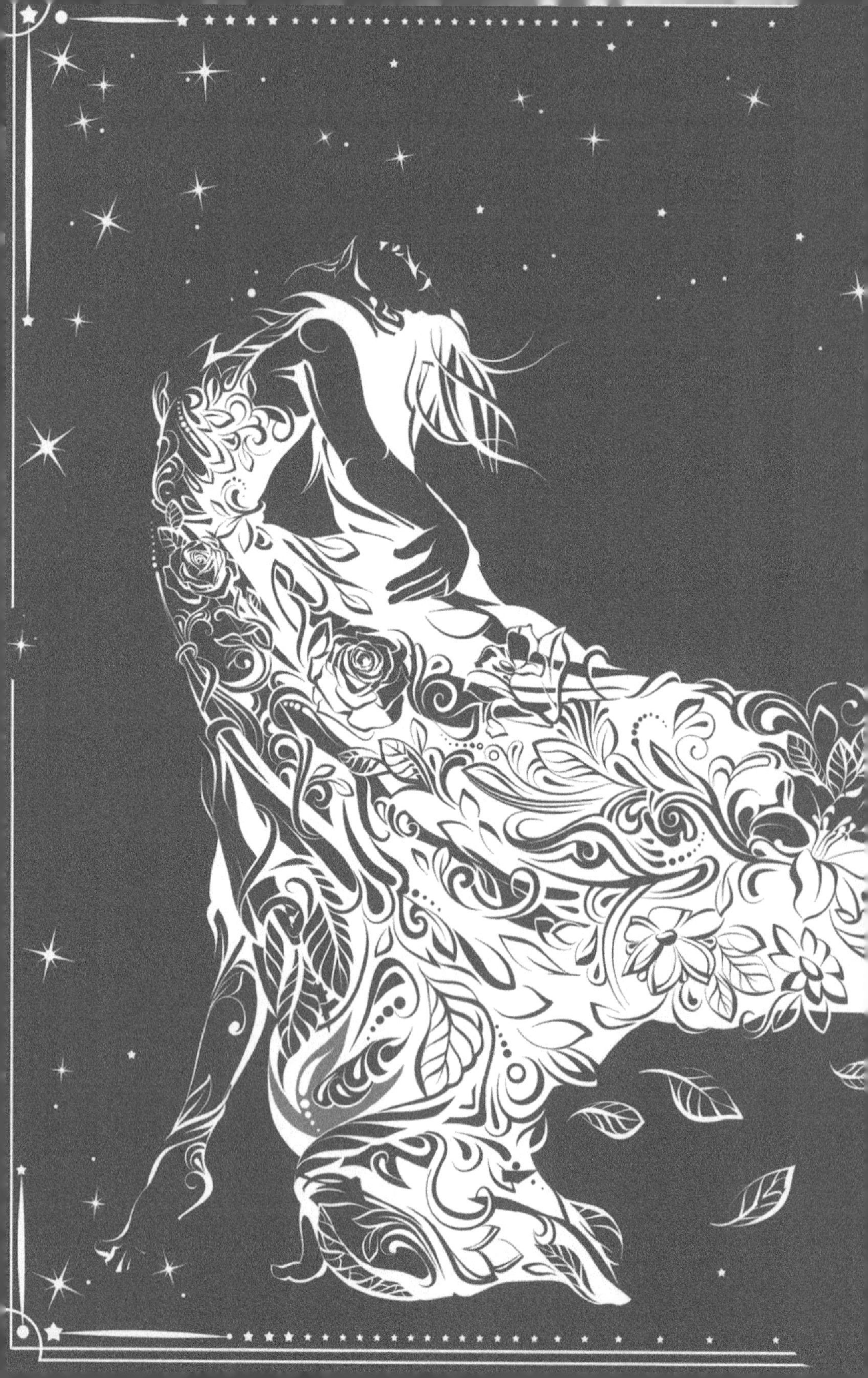

ELISE

CHAPTER TWENTY TWO

I woke on February eighteenth with an ache in my soul and pain in my heart, slipping out of the bed I'd been sharing with the others and darting away from them before the sun even rose.

I hadn't told them that today would have been Gareth's birthday. I wasn't even sure why I'd kept it to myself, but for some reason, every time I'd made an attempt to mention it, the words had just stuck in my throat and lodged there.

We had so much to deal with at the moment. Ryder and Dante were constantly away trying to navigate this fragile new peace between the gangs and Leon's family were still grieving the loss of Roary to Darkmore Penitentiary. Not to mention the fact that the deadline Lionel Acrux had set for Dante to impregnate his niece was fast approaching and we hadn't had five minutes to try and concoct a plan to get him out of it. Then of course there was King and our continued investigations into what the hell he or she was up to and what we could do to stop them. I was still under constant guard too, my boys not wanting me to be alone anywhere just in case King tried to take me again as their official blood donor.

But I just *needed* to be alone today. Not for long. I only needed some time away with no one but my brother for company and my grief to occupy me. We'd never had the money to go all out for birthday celebrations, but I always used to cook him breakfast and we'd spend the day together doing something. Since he'd emerged as a Pegasus, he'd often taken me out for a ride and we'd find somewhere remote to just hang out and forget about our problems for a while. Then we'd eat cake and talk shit and spend the evening watching old movies, just the two of us until Mom got home from her shift and joined us for a slice, picking all the frosting off and leaving the actual cake.

I ended up down by Lake Tempest, looking out over the water as the sun rose and gilded it in golden tones.

I made myself focus on all of the good things we'd shared, all of the love and happiness and laughter. Tears carved a path down my cheeks, but I just let them fall, Gareth's journal held tight in my grip as I tried not to let myself think about the possibility of him still being alive somewhere.

It was such a pretty fantasy and I'd been indulging in it far too often since I'd discovered the fake papers Gareth had had made for me and Mom. Was I holding the answers to his whereabouts in my hands right now? Was there some code hidden within this journal which would lead me back to him?

I was caught between the desperate desire to scour each and every page for even the slightest hint and the clutches of an unthinkable fear of not finding anything if I did.

If I gave into the desire to hope, then I knew I wouldn't be able to stop until I found him. And of course if he really was out there somewhere, hiding, waiting, wishing he could spend his birthday with me too, didn't I need to do everything I could to track him down?

But what if he wasn't? What price would I pay for giving into the sweet dream of hope?

I closed my eyes and begged the stars to give me some sign, some symbol of what I needed to do to get the answers I craved. Should I just let myself fall for the bait that had been laid out for me? Because if I didn't, I was just going to be left with the endless question of what if...

"You shouldn't be out here alone, bella," Dante's voice came from behind me and I looked over my shoulder to find him striding down the beach towards me in nothing but a pair of sweatpants.

I must have been really zoned out to have missed a Dragon landing nearby, but I wasn't really surprised by that. My head was so full of loss and pain over my brother that I could barely draw breath, let alone pay attention to my surroundings.

"I know," I breathed, an apology in my tone even though I knew I'd have done the same thing all over again if I could go back in time. I just needed this, some peace with my memories and time with my grief.

"Come." Dante held a hand out for me and I slowly took it, letting him pull me close and burying my face against his chest. He smelled like a storm and the crispness of the air just before the heavens broke apart and unleashed their fury on the world.

He lifted me off of my feet, cradling me against him as he walked across the stones towards the boathouse. But instead of heading into it like I'd expected, he just kept walking, carrying me back towards campus and murmuring some song in his native tongue beneath his breath.

My tears fell still as we walked, but I didn't move my mind away from the memories of my brother, wanting to bathe in them, soak them into my skin and devour them. I never wanted to lose a single one of them. Never wanted to hesitate to think of his face or his laugh or the way I'd always felt when I was with him.

"Come on, amore mio, time to go," Dante said softly and I looked up at him as he opened his car door and set me down on the passenger seat.

He buckled my seatbelt for me and I looked up at him in confusion just as he closed the door and left me inside, trying to figure out where he was taking me.

He hopped into the passenger seat and started the engine without a word, but I couldn't help my curiosity as I spoke up.

"Where are we going?" I asked, unable to hold the question back.

"To visit the dead, bella. You need to be with your brother today."

I frowned at that strange reply but just settled back into my seat as we headed down the street away from the academy and towards the outskirts of town. I didn't know how Dante had known that I was falling apart over Gareth, but I was starting to feel really grateful that he had.

We stayed silent for the journey, but I was just happy to have him beside me while I grieved, to know I wasn't as alone as I had been when Gareth had first been taken from me anymore.

When we pulled up outside the cemetery, I wasn't even surprised, but a frown still tugged at my brow and I shifted in my seat.

"Gareth isn't here, Dante," I said in a soft voice, shame filling me because I hadn't even been able to give my brother this much. "It costs a lot for a plot here and I-"

"The four of us paid the fees for you, bella," he said, cutting me off. "Each of us bears a certain level of responsibility for the things that happened to your brother before he was taken from this world. And I for one wish that I could go back and see things differently with what I know now. Leon and I were both his friends once, we should have realised he needed help-"

"Don't," I whispered, shaking my head. "None of it was your fault. Just like I've had to accept that none of it was mine. I loved my brother with the fiercest, most beautiful kind of love, but he lied to me. And I understand why. I get it. But if he'd just been honest then everything could have been different in so many ways. There are so many times when his fate could have changed and yet it didn't, and there isn't any point in any of us feeling guilty over that anymore. All we can do is focus on the choices left to us now."

"Here." Dante reached into the back of the car and grabbed a box before handing it to me.

I opened the lid curiously and swallowed thickly as I found Gareth's ashes inside along with a small birthday cake and a candle.

"You don't have to scatter them today," Dante said as tears pricked the backs of my eyes again. "But if you like the plot we found for him then you have the option."

"What if he isn't really dead?" I asked, unable to hold back the question which had been burning inside of me.

"Then...we should take the time to investigate that possibility fully. You can't be left with what-ifs, bella. But I think that for today you should let yourself grieve. And tomorrow we can give hope a shot."

I bit my lip and gave him a nod. Dante got out of the car and headed around to the trunk, giving me a few minutes of silence to just process this as I looked into the box and brushed my fingers over the urn which may have contained all that was left of the boy I'd grown up with.

My car door was pulled open a moment later and I looked up at Dante who had changed into a smart pair of trousers and a white dress shirt, complete with shiny shoes and a tie. He leaned down, pressing a kiss to my cheek and I let him unbuckle my belt before stepping out.

"We knew what today was, so Leon's moms sent a dress and some shoes for you if you want them, but it's up to you," he added.

I glanced down at my less than totally clean sweats and snorted a laugh.

"That might be a good idea," I agreed, letting him lead me around to the back of the car so that I could get changed too.

It was still stupidly early so the parking lot outside the cemetery was abandoned and with a flash of my speed, I changed into the figure-hugging white dress and killer heels before tossing my baggy sweats in the car.

Dante picked up the box containing Gareth's ashes and the cake then offered me his other hand as he led the way up to the imposing stone wall which encircled the graveyard.

Heavy iron gates barred the way inside and a guard sat in a little hut beside them, but as his gaze met Dante's, he just gave him a nod and the gates swung wide to admit us.

"Perks of being the Oscura King?" I guessed.

"The dead here have all been cremated," Dante replied with a shrug. "So it's not like there are any bones which could be stolen to use for dark magic anyway, but there's a theory that even ashes could hold some power so they still guard this place. But like you said, I'm not just some random Fae and the men here know to let me in when I come to visit mia famiglia."

My grip on Dante's fingers tightened and a pang of guilt crept through me as I realised I'd been so caught up in my own pain that I hadn't even considered the fact that Dante would have loved ones here too.

"How many members of your family are resting here?" I asked as we started down a long path pebbled with white stones which led into the graveyard. All kinds of trees and beautiful flowers filled the space surrounding us, interspersed with regular white headstones marked with the names of the Fae who had passed.

"Too many to count," he replied. "The Oscuras have lived in this part of the kingdom for generations, and we have always been a big and violent family. My papa is here and his papa and his papa too. Maybe even further back than that. Not, many of them died of old age. One day, my remains will join them here as well."

"Not any time soon though," I said firmly and he gave me a soft smile in reply.

"I hope not."

Dante led me deeper into the graveyard and I couldn't help but feel calmer the further we walked. This place was beautiful. There were little streams and tiny bridges to cross them, countless flowers and trees so full of life and vitality that it didn't even seem like a graveyard at all. The air was crisp and fresh and little everflame candles burned before shrines and in crevices while birdsong coloured the air.

We began to head up a hill and Dante led me down a path which turned away from the main track until we headed through a beautiful white stone archway with the name Oscura carved into the rock.

I stayed quiet as we moved between the graves of Dante's family and he reached out to brush his fingers over headstones, murmuring greetings to the people he'd loved and lost, and I took in the weight of all the grief my brave Storm Dragon held in his heart.

The path took us between the trailing fronds of a stunning weeping willow and in the shade of the tree, a huge headstone carved with a statue of a Wolf baying to the moon beside it stood bearing his father's name.

"I brought someone to meet you, Papa," Dante said, giving me a warm smile as he led me up to the headstone and the ring on my thumb seemed to hum with power as we drew closer to it. "This is Elise. She's my un vero amore."

I smiled hesitantly, reaching out to touch the head of the enormous Werewolf statue and brushing my fingers over the cold stone. "Hi," I breathed as the ring heated further and I was filled with the strongest sense that Micah Oscura really was here, watching us, standing close to his son.

The wind suddenly picked up around us and a handful of pink blossoms swirled on the breeze as it sped around me and Dante, lifting my hair and filling me with a sense of love and lightness as a surprised laugh escaped my lips.

"I think he likes you, amore mio," Dante purred, leaning down to steal a kiss from my lips and making my heart race.

"Do you always feel his presence so keenly here?" I asked, my voice low in case I disturbed the magic that was keeping Micah so close to us in this moment.

"Not always. I have to pique his attention. And between bringing you here and the peace deal I've made with the Lunars, I'm willing to bet today has him very interested. And I want to tell him all about it. But first let me show you the spot we found for Gareth."

I nodded my agreement, glancing at the Wolf statue once more as I left Micah's grave behind and we kept walking back out from beneath the weeping willow and up to the top of the hill where the trees receded. The morning sun was shining down on a beautiful, grassy spot surrounded by wildflowers with a tiny burbling stream running past it.

Dante led me straight over to the simple white headstone there and I sucked in a breath as I read the inscription on it.

Here lies Gareth Tempa, a soul too good for this world.
May the love he held in his heart be spread wide in his death and may he enjoy freedom in the sky for all of time.

I looked up at the wide, open sky above us and smiled as I watched the clouds slipping by overhead.

"If it's not right, we can change it," Dante said. "Leon made the everflames and Gabriel and Ryder infused the ground here with life so that the flowers will blossom here all year round."

"It's perfect, thank you," I breathed, chewing on my bottom lip as Dante placed the box containing the cake and Gareth's ashes down on the ground.

He took my hands and turned me to look at him.

"What is it, amore mio? I can tell something is eating at you besides your grief."

I hesitated for a moment, not sure if I should really voice what I was feeling, but needing to say it so desperately that the words were burning in the back of my throat.

"I feel guilty, Dante," I breathed and he shifted closer to me, his fingers brushing down the back of my hand before he wrapped it in his.

"Why?" he asked in a low voice.

"Because when I first came to Aurora Academy, I was willing to do anything and everything it took to uncover the secrets around my brother's death and to fight with all I had to get justice for him. I wanted revenge. I wanted the Fae who stole him from me to die at my hands and I didn't care if it killed me to achieve that. But now..."

"Now what?" he asked.

"Now I know that I don't want to die. I don't want to give my life for this because now I have so much to live for and I'm afraid that that will mean I don't achieve what I set out to in the end at all."

Dante tugged me around to look him in the eyes, cupping my cheek in his hand as he gazed down at me intently. "This is what Gareth would have wanted," he said firmly. "All that he did before his death, all the risks he took and sacrifices he made were to protect you and give you a better life. All he wanted was for you to be happy, amore mio. The best way that you can honour his memory is by doing that for him."

I nodded my agreement and let him pull me close so that I could take some comfort from his embrace.

I inhaled deeply and breathed in the heady scent of the storms which always seemed to cling to his skin.

"We can look into the idea of him still being alive out there somewhere another day," Dante said in a low voice. "Today just let yourself grieve and spend his birthday with him. There's no rush to get back and there's nothing else you need to be thinking about other than this."

"Okay." I stepped back, wiping the tears from my cheeks and exhaling slowly.

"There's something else that you should have," Dante said, reaching into his pocket and taking a thick envelope from it which I was surprised to find was addressed to me, though the address on it wasn't mine.

"What is this?" I asked curiously as I opened it and Dante waited while I pulled the covering letter out and looked it over. "This...I don't understand. Why is my name on something about the ownership of a club?"

"That is the official transfer of ownership documentation for The Sparkling Uranus, though I think it could probably do with a new name personally."

"But how-" My words cut off as I turned the page over and found a list of figures that stole my breath away.

"That's the average income from the club on a monthly basis leading up to the end of Old Sal's ownership of it," Dante explained, pointing at it. "And that is the increasing bottom line which has been rising since I placed some of my people there to oversee it. I think that it could double that turnover with a bunch of renovations and some new headline acts. I'd be willing to front the cost of those improvements which could be paid back to me over the course of the next five years, or I would be happy to negotiate a partnership deal instead if you'd be interested in that. You could even be a silent partner if you prefer. I already have people who can take over the day to day running of it on a more permanent basis so you wouldn't even have to be involved in it at all if you didn't want to be. Alternatively, the figure at the bottom is what I would be happy to purchase it from you for. I took into account the value of the property and business and added a sweetener on account of the money I expect the place to earn me if you choose that route."

My eyes widened as I stared at that figure. At all of the freaking figures. There was an insane amount of money laid out on this piece of paper, but I was struggling to understand what the hell it had to do with me.

"I don't understand-" I began, but Dante cut me off.

"What do you remember about the things that happened when Old Sal and that bastardo doorman of hers tried to take advantage of you, bella?" he asked me softly.

I wet my lips, my mind travelling to that day and what they'd tried to do to me. What I'd been so close to doing with Petri while that bitch had used her Siren gifts to manipulate me. A shudder ran down my spine and I had to fight against the urge to block out those memories, which was what I'd been doing with them for the most part since then.

"You killed them for me, Drago," I murmured, reaching up to hold his cheek in my hand. "You rescued me."

The hint of a smile graced his lips and he brushed his fingers through my lilac hair as he leaned down to press his forehead against mine. "I will always rescue you, amore mio. Though I wish you didn't require so much rescuing."

"I do not," I protested, pulling back and Dante smirked as he caught my waist to stop me from retreating.

"Well, you're right. I did help to set you free from that spell and I beat that figlio di puttana to death with my bare fists for daring to even think about laying his filthy fucking hands on you. And then when I'd sated my rage a little in spilling his blood, I made that cagna sign over the club and all of its assets to you."

"You did...what?" I breathed, a frown tugging at my brow as I took that in.

"I knew that you weren't in the right frame of mind to discuss it right then and I meant to have this conversation with you before now, carina, but recently there has been so much going on that it slipped my mind. But that woman was the reason Gareth took the risks he did. She was the one holding that debt over your head and his. I made her suffer before she died, and I wanted you to have the club which caused so much of this pain for your famiglia."

"I don't know what to say," I murmured, looking down at the figures again. Was it right for me to take this? Or was it like accepting blood money if I profited from the very place which had been the beginning of our misery and the reason for Gareth's lie?

"Then don't say anything." Dante took the paperwork back from me and placed it in his pocket. "That money is yours. You can use it for anything you want to or even give it away to charity if you'd prefer. But if someone was going to profit from that bitch's death then it had to be you, bella. I'll keep this safe and the business thriving for you until you make up your mind on that."

My lips parted but I didn't know what else I was supposed to say about that, so I just nodded mutely. Dante bent down to the box we'd brought with us, taking the little birthday cake from inside it and handing it to me before using a tiny spark of electricity to light it.

"Happy birthday, Gareth," he said in a low voice. "I hope you don't mind that I'm here with your sister. If it makes you feel better, she's the one who pursued me, stalking and pestering me until she managed to lock me down and-"

A laugh spilled from my lips as I gave Dante a playful shove and smacked his chest to tell him off for that bullshit. "Whatever you wanna tell yourself, Drago."

"I'll leave you two to talk," Dante said with a chuckle, pressing a kiss to my hair. "Papa wants to hear all about you anyway, and I have plenty of other family members I can call on. Take as much time as you want."

He strode away from me back towards the weeping willow as I set my eyes on the little cake and slowly sank down to my knees to spend some time with my brother. We had a hell of a lot to catch up on after all and if he really was here listening, then I was pretty sure this conversation could last a while.

I placed the cupcake down on the edge of his headstone and fought against the lump in my throat as I considered how much this plot must have cost my kings and how much effort they'd gone to to make sure it was perfect.

"Well, Gare Bear, I'm not actually sure where to begin," I muttered as I took the simple urn from the box and turned it over in my hands.

There was a trowel sitting beside the grave for me to use, so I picked it up and began digging a hole in the soil, ready to place the ashes inside it. I may not have been entirely certain that my brother's remains really were in that box, but if they were then this was the perfect place to lay him to rest.

I wet my lips and slowly lifted the urn containing his ashes into my hands again before emptying it into the hole I'd dug for him. Just as I started to swipe the soil back into place on top of the ashes, the light caught on a white stone in the centre of them and I gasped as I plucked it out. I'd almost forgotten all about this strange crystal I'd found amongst his things, but as I held it in my hand, I swear I felt closer to him somehow.

I slipped the stone into the pocket of my dress then pushed the rest of the soil into position over his resting place.

The sun climbed steadily through the sky as I sat talking to my brother, telling him about my kings and the things we'd been doing to figure out what the hell had happened to him. I bitched him out for his lies and cryptic bullshit and cried so much that I stopped trying to wipe my tears away. I laughed over old stories and the candle on his cake burned all the way down to the frosting before going out then I ate it for him, teasing him about being too slow to claim it for himself.

There was something cathartic in just letting the words spill from me. In saying all of the things I wished I'd said to him while I had him and in exposing all of the lies and secrets he'd kept from me. I complained about the journal and begged him to give me some more clues to help figure this whole mystery out, but I got nothing in return.

I didn't feel his presence here the way I'd felt Dante's father's. And the longer I stayed sat there, talking to him about everything and nothing, the more that treacherous hope grew in my chest. I knew I shouldn't have been letting myself give into it, but it was so hard to resist. If I didn't feel him here, then wasn't it conceivable that he wasn't here at all? That he wasn't dead?

When my throat was raw from speaking so much and the sun was beating down on me overhead, I finally pushed myself to my feet again, releasing a long breath and brushing my fingers over Gareth's headstone as I said goodbye to him. Hours had passed and though my grief had poured freely, and my heart felt tender and raw, I also felt lighter, freer. My mind was less clouded, and I was filled with a drive to get to the bottom of this freaking mystery once and for all. I was going to figure out who King was, make them pay and find out exactly what had happened to my brother.

I turned and started walking back towards the weeping willow where Dante had disappeared, but as I pushed through the trailing fronds, I didn't find him there.

I opened my mouth to call out for him, trying to remember which way he'd said all of the other Oscura graves were housed, but the graveyard had officially opened to the public now and it didn't feel right to start shouting while people were here visiting lost loved ones.

It didn't really feel right to shoot around using my Vampire speed either, so I brushed my fingers over the Wolf statue adorning Micah's grave then moved out from beneath the weeping willow once more on the far side of it.

I looked left and right, spotting headstones with the name Oscura carved into them in both directions and frowning as I strained my ears to listen out for my Storm Dragon. But I didn't catch any sounds from him, so I took a guess and turned right, moving between towering trees and crossing the burbling stream using a little wooden bridge.

I turned a corner and found myself walking down a narrow path between two high, white stone mausoleums. I very much doubted there were any actual corpses in there anymore what with the laws concerning the care of dead bodies to protect against the use of their bones in dark magic, but some parts of this graveyard were old enough to outdate those restrictions. The names carved into the faces of the stone were weathered, so I couldn't be sure that they were still Oscura graves, but the path seemed to curve up ahead, turning back the way I'd just come, so I stayed on it.

The tracking bond Leon had given me told me Dante was close by so I decided to keep exploring until I found him.

Moss covered statues were set between the trees beyond the mausoleums and my gaze trailed over the figures of Centaurs, Griffins, Pegasuses and more, every Order represented one after another with small name plaques all around them and I realised that these were sites dedicated to Fae of certain Orders whose ashes had been scattered amongst others of their kind.

It was so peaceful here that although I was still hunting for my Storm Dragon, I found myself moving slower, drinking in the sights and the calm feeling in the air. It was a beautiful place to find eternal slumber.

A little gravel path turned off between the trees, looking like it might lead me back to the Oscura area again so I turned down it, my high heels struggling on the uneven ground. I could see the sunlight spilling in between the trees up ahead and as I stepped out into it, my gaze fell on a man who was kneeling before a small headstone, clutching a teddy bear in his hands. I'd been using my enhanced senses to listen out for Dante, so I caught some of his words without meaning to.

"I never can decide if I should bring you gifts for the age you were when I lost you, or be trying to find something you might have liked now if you were still with me," he murmured and I stilled as I recognised his voice, flicking my gaze back to him. His back was bent, his head lowered which was why I hadn't realised who he was at first but as a shuddering breath escaped him, I recognised my Potions professor and fell still.

Titan seemed lost in his grief and I didn't want to disturb him, glancing around to pick an exit route so that I could leave him in peace. But as I turned, my foot slipped in the gravel and at the crunch, he looked around, his eyes finding mine and widening in recognition.

"Elise?" he breathed, rocking back to sit on his heels as I gave an awkward half smile and a vague, hand flap wave thing.

"Err, yeah. I was just here visiting my brother," I explained. "I didn't mean to disturb you, sir, I was just taking a little walk before I leave. So I guess I'll see you-"

"It's alright," Titan replied, pushing himself to his feet and dusting the mud from his knees. It didn't really work, but I had grass stains on my new white dress from sitting with Gareth so who gave a shit? "I didn't know you had a brother resting here."

"Umm..." I trailed off as my pulse spiked. I'd been so careful in keeping to my cover story and I was almost certain I'd never let it slip in front of Titan before. No one was supposed to know about my connection to Gareth and now I'd just gone and blurted it out like a fucking moron at the slightest prompting.

"I told you about my daughter," he went on, not seeming to notice my momentary panic as he looked back to the little headstone, his fist tightening around the teddy he still held. "She was my whole world..."

I could feel his grief filling the air that surrounded us and a lump rose in my throat at the thought of the little girl who had clearly been loved so dearly, taken from this world too soon.

I stepped closer to him, laying a hand on his arm as he stared down at the grave. "I know it doesn't make it better or anything, but I'm so sorry for your loss," I murmured, my throat thickening on behalf of a girl I'd never known.

Titan placed a warm hand over the top of mine where it rested on his arm, his grip tightening over my fingers as he spoke in a rough voice.

"They tell you it gets easier, but that's not true, is it? You just get better at compartmentalising. You learn how to function around it. But any time you step back into that place of grief and think on the love you lost, it's all there waiting for you. The pain, the love, the what ifs-" He broke off as a sob caught in his throat and he pressed a fist to his lips as a tear slid down my cheek for him.

"Sometimes I think the stars are the cruellest creations in this entire universe," I breathed. "Taking the lives of innocents, dealing them the worst fates."

"While those who deserve such fates live on without care or consequence," he spat. "Like the Fae responsible for taking my child from me."

"You know who it was?" I asked in surprise. "Weren't they punished?"

Titan turned to look at me, fury and pain burning in his eyes as he parted his lips on a response, but a frown pulled at his brow instead. "Your eyes are so incredibly silver in this light," he murmured. "I could have sworn the ring was only thin before, but now I can hardly see any green at all."

I blinked a couple of times, wiping the tears from my cheeks and releasing my hold on him as I half laughed that comment off and half panicked about the fact that I'd clearly forgotten to place the concealment spell over the new rings in my eyes this morning. Apparently I was just spilling all of my secrets to Titan today, not that he seemed to be particularly interested in them, his gaze moving back to the grave before us.

I muttered some vague explanation about them seeming brighter in sunlight and when I was crying, but he didn't even seem to be paying me much attention anymore.

"Did you make any promises to your brother before he died?" Titan asked softly, leaning down to place the teddy before the grave alongside a collection of other toys which were already there.

"Not before. But since. I've made promises in his name," I said, not that I could really get into the oaths of bloodshed and vengeance I'd made on Gareth's behalf.

"I think that those promises are the only reason I find to wake up in the morning some days," he said with a nod. "I think they give our grief purpose."

"Then I hope you manage to fulfil them," I said and I was crying again, unsure why I was even bothering to wipe the tears away at this point.

Titan's arms moved around me and I fell against him, burying my face into his chest and taking some comfort from him as he hushed me, rubbing soothing circles against my back. I'd never had a father, never felt an embrace like this from someone who wanted nothing more than to help drive my sorrows away. I wasn't sure why I kept having feelings like that towards him, but we had formed a bond which went beyond student-teacher. Most likely because of our shared grief - and I had no doubt that I had Daddy issues too.

I'd always wondered what our lives might have been like if mine had stuck around. But that was just a pretty fantasy, not any kind of reality for me.

"If you want to talk some more, we could go and grab a coffee or a bite to eat," Titan began, but he was interrupted by the call of Dante's voice.

"There you are, bella. I was beginning to worry," he said and I looked away from Titan to smile sheepishly at my Storm Dragon. "I thought we said no wandering off alone?" He was trying to keep his voice casual, but I could see the underlying panic in his gaze. He'd clearly been freaking out that I was missing and guilt twisted in my gut as I moved towards him, my hand outstretched. I dropped it again quickly, remembering that I couldn't let Titan see that we were more than friends, but I gave an apologetic smile.

"I'm sorry, Drago, I was looking for you. But I think I got a bit turned around in here," I explained. "And then I ran into..." I glanced back at Titan, wondering what his first name was and if it was weird of me to want to know. I didn't really want to call him *professor* here. What we'd just shared had had nothing to do with school.

Dante seemed less concerned about touching me in front of witnesses and he slung an arm over my shoulders as he looked at our Potions professor, his gaze flicking to his daughter's headstone as he nodded in greeting.

"Sorry for your loss, mio amico," Dante murmured. "But I need to get this one back to her mate."

Titan looked a little torn and I felt bad, wondering if I should tell Dante that I wanted to go grab that coffee. But I knew my Storm Dragon wouldn't leave my side, especially if we left this place and it was pretty clear from the stiffness in Titan's posture that he wasn't as comfortable with the Oscura King as he was with me.

"Maybe we can catch that coffee another time?" I asked, feeling weirdly hopeful about that and berating myself internally for it.

He's not your freaking dad, Elise, stop getting crazy ideas about making him into one.

Titan almost looked like he was going to protest but then a family of Fae walked around a corner and drew his attention, and by the time he looked back to me he was just shrugging, turning back to his daughter's grave.

"I'd like that," he told me. "Have a good weekend."

I bid him goodbye and let Dante steer me away towards the exit.

"What was all that about, bella?" he asked.

"He's just sad, Dante. Like me."

Dante placed a kiss in my hair and led me back to the car. Then he drove us into town, picked up a load of takeaway from a drive-thru and took me on a drive up into the mountains that lined the eastern outstretches of Alestria and found a beautiful lookout spot for us to park.

We spread ourselves out on the hood of the car, eating our food and watching the view while exchanging countless stories about our lost loved ones. And by the end of the day, I was able to smile over some of the good times instead of just sobbing over all the grief.

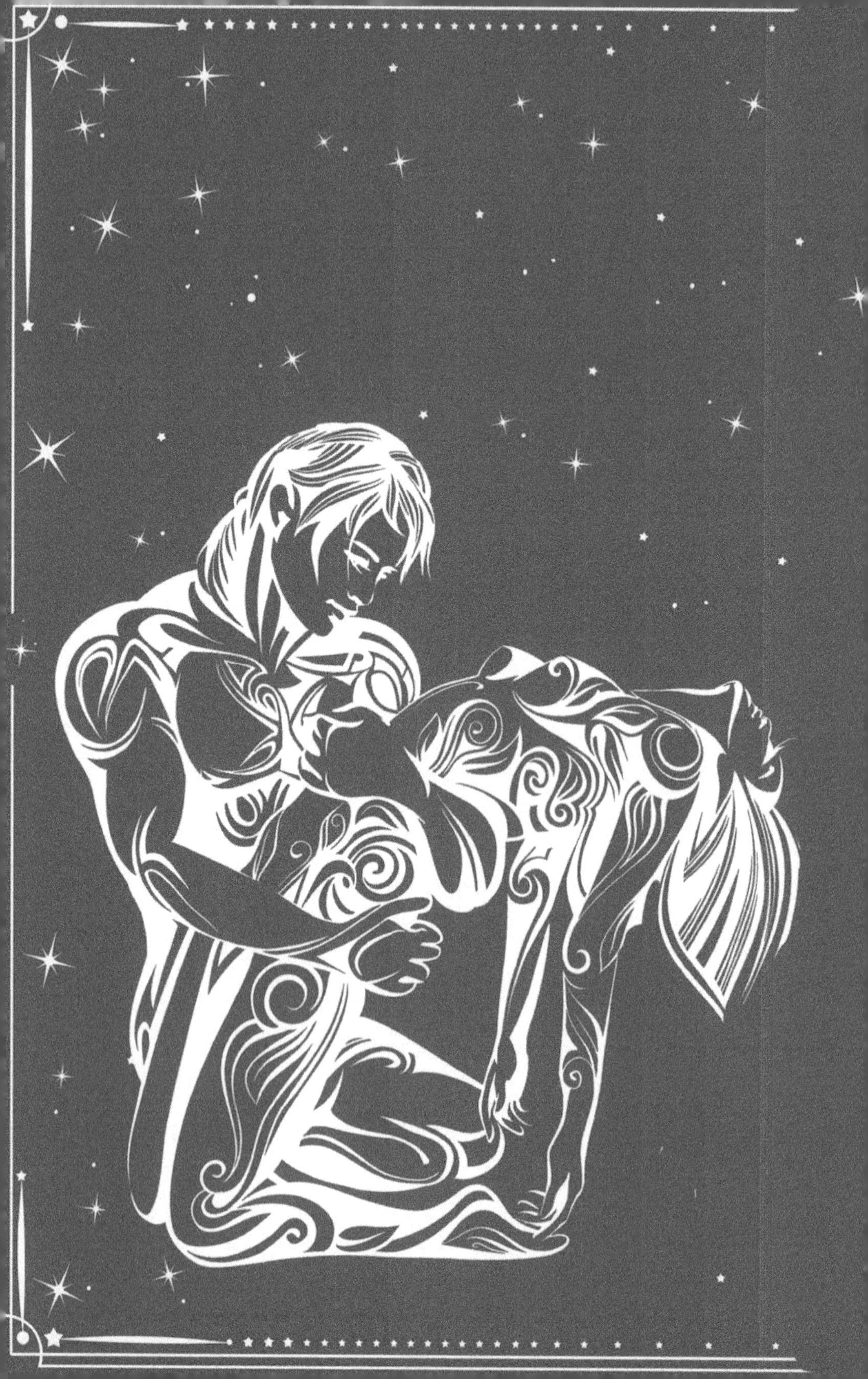

RYDER

CHAPTER TWENTY THREE

Since the stars had broken the bond between me and Dante, I was drawn to him in a way that could mean only one thing. We were Nebula Allies. And that shit rocked the foundations of just about every rule I'd ever lived by in my life. One above them all: to do whatever was necessary to wipe out the Oscuras. And he wasn't just any Oscura, he was *the* Oscura. But any hatred that had clung to my soul like mould over him had vanished as if it had never been there. I remembered what it was like to despise him, but I couldn't conjure any of that acidic anger which had lived in me for so many years whenever I'd even thought of him in the past. It was freeing, an unbreakable chain finally releasing me. And I had no fucking clue what to do with this new version of myself.

It was made slightly easier by the fact that Inferno and I had to keep pretending we were just in a truce for the sake of our gangs, but I didn't know how we were going to make it work long term. Was I going to have to pretend my whole life that I wasn't in a relationship with Elise because the Lunars could never accept me being with the same woman as Inferno? The thought made me sick to my stomach. No, there had to be another way. I just couldn't see it yet.

I headed out into The Iron Wood during the breakfast hour, feeling like a kid up to no good and not entirely hating that as I walked to the boulder that divided the Oscura and Lunar territories out here. Elise had been feeling down this week over her brother and Dante and I had something planned to cheer her up this morning. She hid it well around others, but she could never hide her pain from me. My beautiful girl wanted to sit in her suffering and ride out the storm as she remembered the brother who had loved her unconditionally. It was the only way she would be able to heal in the long term, so whenever she needed me there, I sat at her side and suffered with her.

"Are you sure about this, serpente?" Dante's voice reached me from the shadows to my left and he stepped out from between two tall trees, his eyes sparkling with mischief, letting me glimpse the silver rings in them for a moment before he concealed them again.

A smirk pulled at my mouth as I reached out to him and he slid his palm into mine in a handshake, connecting the marks that the stars had branded on our flesh. Together they made the infinity symbol and where our palms touched, power rang between us, the strength of our new bond like Sun Steel chains locking us together. They were unbreakable, gilded in starlight and forged of our souls. There was no point in our future where hatred could live between us anymore. The stained slates of our pasts had been wiped clean and I never wanted them to be tarnished again.

"Remind me how dangerous it is." I grinned as I released his hand, my smiles becoming far more frequent than I was used to around him.

"It's so fucking dangerous," he said mischievously and my grin grew.

"Perfect." I looked around for our girl as my heart beat a little faster. "Where is she?"

Dante's lips parted but Elise suddenly dropped out of the canopy above, falling onto my shoulders in a crouch and leaning down like a flexible little gymnast to sink her fangs into my neck. I groaned at the kiss of pain, her lilac hair brushing against my cheek as she fed and I gripped the back of her head to hold her there. When she pulled her fangs free, she sighed and did a back flip off of my shoulders, landing gracefully with the assistance of her air magic. I turned around and Dante's arm brushed mine as he moved toward her. We were two wild creatures captivated by one enchantress and I didn't care if I remained under her spell forever.

"What are you guys waiting for?" she asked with a slanted smile and Dante pulled his shirt off, starting to unbuckle his uniform pants. The weight of her pain had eased today, but there was still a tug of grief beneath it all. I hoped we could distract her enough to banish it completely for a while.

"We don't have long, bella," he purred as she eye fucked Inferno's naked chest.

"Then you'd better hurry up," she encouraged and I waited as Dante stripped off and placed his clothes on a rock.

He walked away from us where the trees widened out then leapt forward, his skin splitting apart as he shifted into his huge Dragon form. Electricity crackled along my skin and the bite of it made me growl. I enjoyed that far more than I liked to admit.

Elise held out a hand for me and I took it, letting her lead me over to Dante as he flexed his wings and watched us with one large brown eye. Elise released my hand, throwing me a wild look before climbing up onto Dante's back and settling herself behind his shoulder blades.

"Come on," she called excitedly and a ripple of anticipation ran through me. What the actual fuck was I doing right now?

I stepped forward and placed my hands on Dante's toughened navy scales and electricity trickled over me, raising the hairs all across my body but not hurting me in the slightest. I started to haul myself up, my foot hitting his wing and he grunted as I fought to get higher but didn't get anywhere.

"Bend at the hip," Elise called. "By the stars, why is your body so stiff?"

"It's not," I hissed, kicking Dante's wing again and Elise started laughing.

"You'll regret that laugh when I get up there," I huffed at her.

"Which will be when? Sometime next week? You might need to make an appointment, I could be busy by then."

"Very funny," I growled then gave up with this bullshit, casting a pillar of earth up from the ground, letting it carry me to the top of Dante's back and stepping off of it to drop down behind Elise. I yanked her back against me, pushing her hair aside and biting her earlobe hard enough to make her gasp.

"You need to do some yoga to loosen yourself up," she teased.

"Alright, you get in the downward dog pose and I'll practice the stiff snake from behind you," I said in her ear and she released a wild laugh.

"I love when you make jokes," she whispered, turning her head to try and steal a kiss but I didn't let her take it.

"I don't make jokes, I'm always deadly serious." A smirk played around the corners of my mouth as I breathed in her sweet cherry scent and let my fingers wander down her thigh to where her dark purple skirt met milky skin.

"You make the best kind of jokes." She pressed her lips to mine and Dante shifted impatiently beneath us.

I ignored him, sliding my fingers under her skirt and wrapping my other hand around her throat as I kissed her greedily. I was just growing hard when a zap of lightning shot directly into my balls, making me swear loudly and release her. I may have liked pain, but that shit was too far.

"Asshole," I called to him and he released a growl which sounded a lot like a laugh.

He flexed his wings in preparation of taking off and Elise cast a concealment spell around us to keep me hidden from any gang members who might look too closely once we were in flight.

I held onto Elise tightly, anticipation racing through me as I prepared to do something I had never once in my life considered doing. Most Dragons forbid anyone riding on them regardless, it was some sacred law that had something to do with a Dragon's pride. I had always secretly admired the fact Dante flouted that law with his family and friends, giving no shits what the world thought of him for it. But I'd never imagined I'd be one of them. I'd once have cut my own heart out before that happened. Now, the stars had bound us, and I wasn't going to fight them on it because it felt so right, so damn good, even if it was unfamiliar and fucking strange.

Dante lifted his head then took off into the sky with a huge leap that left my stomach on the ground. Elise whooped, her fingers clasping mine over her waist as Dante raced towards the sun. Lightning flashed in the gathering clouds and he tore into them, making my pulse quicken and the best kind of fear run through me.

Dante climbed and climbed until we were so high, the white mist of the clouds hung thickly around us. He suddenly broke through it all and the sun spilled over us like molten gold and Elise inhaled a sharp breath.

I clutched her tighter, gazing across the beautiful landscape above the clouds, the world just an endless expanse of blue above a swirling white sea. Dante sailed lazily towards the sun as we drank in the warmth and the clouds below us darkened to deepest grey. Thunder rumbled beneath us and I knew we were caught between two worlds, one of light and the other of dark. It was a haven, a place I had never seen but it was instantly one I wanted to return to again and again.

"See that endless horizon?" I purred in Elise's ear and she nodded, a breathy noise escaping her as I pulled her tighter against my chest. "That's how far my love goes for you, baby. On and on into fucking eternity."

She turned her head, her silvery green eyes locking with mine as her lips parted and I felt her love for me rushing out from every pore in her flesh. The world was so quiet with her this close, the torment that had lived in my head for as long as I could remember no more. All my demons had fallen in love with her too, and when she was here they sat still and quiet, tamed by her and no one else. It was peace unlike anything I'd ever known.

As she leaned closer to speak to me, Dante nosedived and I nearly flew off of him except Elise grabbed hold of his scales and I kept hold of her. He started spinning as we crashed into the clouds and rain pounded down on us in a torrent as we tumbled into the darkness.

Thunder boomed in my head and I roared a laugh as adrenaline swept through my veins. Dante kept falling and falling, racing toward the earth before breaking out of the clouds below and rain flooded over us. The lake was a sea of wild ripples as the rain hit the water like bullets and Dante sped low over its surface as fast as he possibly could. His tail carved a path through the water before he took off back towards the raging heavens and all I could see was a spiderweb of lightning as it lit up the whole sky.

He crashed back through the clouds, flying upwards so fast that everything became a blur and all I could hear was the bellow of thunder and Elise's whoops of excitement calling back to me.

He broke through the top of the clouds once more, continuing to climb as the wind whipped over us and Elise flicked a finger to dry us off with her air magic, the sun bleeding into my skin and warming my blood too. I felt alive, every cell in my body buzzing with the high of adrenaline and I never wanted it to end.

When it seemed like Dante would fly us right to the stars, he flipped over backwards and suddenly we were falling, tumbling right off his back. I held onto Elise with all my strength as we plummeted through the sky, my instincts telling me to keep her safe.

"Let go, Ryder!" she called, no hint of fear in her voice, but I wasn't going to do any such thing. I clutched her even tighter as we spun upside down, faster and faster as we fell like a missile.

"Trust me!" she called and I swallowed the lump in my throat as I did as she said, slowly loosening my grip on her.

She kept hold of my arms as we levelled out and suddenly we were falling horizontally, gripping each other's wrists as we sped towards the dark clouds below. But it didn't feel like we were falling anymore, it was more like floating even though we must have been moving at speed.

Dante swept along far below us, disturbing the clouds and casting a huge shadow across them. They split apart, opening up and up until we could see right across campus from the glistening lake below to the sweeping Iron Wood that spilled out around the edge of Alestria.

My heart pounded powerfully as I tore my eyes from the view below to my whole world in front of me, watching as her lilac hair blew wildly and her eyes lit up with eternal life. I couldn't stop staring at her like that, so alive that it made me burn. I wanted her to look like that every day, like nothing was impossible. Her pain was beautiful, but no pain existed in her at all in that moment. She was pure light, joy filling every inch of her soul. It was how she deserved to feel every second of her existence.

Dante roared loudly as he flew up toward us and I held Elise's wrists tighter, refusing to let the wind pull her from my hands even though I knew she'd be safe with her air magic no matter what happened. Dante suddenly shot beneath us and we hit the leathery surface of his left wing, bouncing and rolling across it until we lay side by side on our backs panting.

"Fuck," I laughed, the rush still buzzing through my body. Elise rolled over and kissed me as Dante sailed along on an updraft and I fisted my hand in her hair, tasting the sweetest creature on Earth and bathing in the knowledge that she was *mine*. My tongue stroked against hers and her hand fisted in my shirt as she drew me as close as she could.

When we broke apart, she guided us onto Dante's back with her air magic and I held her waist as he slowly circled down to the ground to land among the trees.

His taloned feet hit the earth with a boom and Elise sprang off of him with a whoop, speeding around to his nose and placing a kiss on it. "That was incredible, Drago."

I used my earth magic to get down, still grinning as my feet hit solid ground and Dante shifted back into his Fae form.

He pulled on his clothes, smirking like an asshole. "So we're all agreed Dragons are the best Order?"

"Pah," Elise scoffed and I sniggered.

"You're third best," I decided. "Basilisks, Vampires, then Dragons."

"Na-ar, Vampires are first," Elise said firmly.

"Then?" Dante and I both demanded.

"Then Pegasuses," she said with a smirk and I thought of her brother with a tug in my chest.

"Alright, but then what?" I pushed.

Dante finished buttoning up his shirt, moving to stand beside me and folding his arms as he waited for her answer.

She tapped her chin as if she was thinking then the bell rang in the distance. "Oh, time for class. See ya." She saluted us and shot away into the trees in a blur of movement.

I cursed and Dante released a low laugh.

"We'll get it out of her," he said.

"When she chooses my Order, I win her to myself for a night."

"When she chooses my Order, I will ensure she enjoys that night with me far better than she would have with you, serpente."

"Wanna bet?" I shoved him in the shoulder and he shoved me back with a smirk.

"Yeah," he agreed. "I do."

I ruffled his stupid quaffed hair and he yanked my tie tight around my throat until I half choked.

"See you in class, Inferno." I headed away, glancing back as he gave me a sideways grin and I fought mirroring it, but lost that fight.

I fixed my tie as I headed through the trees, using the paths that led through Lunar Territory to head to my first class.

Magical Beings was being held on the Empyrean Fields today as Professor Meteoris wanted us to have some hands-on experience. I couldn't see myself working with animals though. Most of the ones I'd had to handle for classes didn't much like me, and Meteoris had said I had a dark aura which they could sense. Apparently I needed to work on that, but I also apparently didn't give a fuck.

A fenced perimeter had been set up on the grass with little pens for the different animals like some kind of petting zoo. Elise was crouched with Leon in one of the pens as they cooed over some tiny fluffy things I had no interest in.

Meteoris called us to her as everyone arrived and I gravitated towards Gabriel who was holding a horned Elixis piglet with black and white spots all over its body. He absentmindedly stroked its head and its eyes hooded with happiness as it grunted softly and fell asleep. I guessed Gabriel had that calming energy thing going for him. The second I got close though, the piglet woke up and squealed, trying to fight its way out of Gabriel's hands.

Gabriel blinked out of some vision and turned to me in surprise. "Oh hey. Why are you startling my pig?"

"I dunno, ask the pig," I tossed back, folding my arms as Meteoris started introing the class. She kinda looked like a child with her tiny frame and blonde pigtails, but she must have been in her thirties.

"Why are you startled by the big, tattooed Basilisk who looks like he'd eat you whole?" Gabriel whispered to the pig as it started to relax in his hands again. The piglet's eyes whipped to me and back to Gabriel again like it wanted me to leave, and I took a pointed step away with a murmur of annoyance.

"Animals don't like me," I said with a shrug.

"That's right, everyone pick a creature," Meteoris called. "Today we're going to attempt to Familiarise. You must be bonded with a creature to exert your will over it. The key is to establish a strong connection with the animal. This can be achieved by petting it and speaking with it until you earn its trust.

If a magical being deems you trustworthy, then it may offer you up its star-given name."

"Are you called Fluffy Fluffikins?" Leon cooed loudly as he snuggled an Ignitious kitten with red fur against his chest and Elise gazed at them both with eyes the size of dinner plates. Cuteness really wasn't my thing. So this class was getting a firm no from me.

"How will we hear its name? Will the animals speak?" Eugene asked as he tried to grapple with a scaly Terris weasel which was scratching and biting at his neck as it tried to break free from his grip. He was bleeding quite badly actually.

"You will hear it whispered from the stars," Meteoris said excitedly. "It can take quite some time to bond with an adult creature, but younger animals are more impressionable, so we are working with babies today and we'll work up from there after a couple of weeks. Off you go."

Gabriel brushed his fingers over the piglet's head again then his eyes brightened. "Oh, hello Nuvis."

"That's it?" I said incredulously. "You got its name already?"

Gabriel shrugged innocently and I scowled.

I looked between the pens from the little stripey pink Soaris foals to the rainbow coloured Arcus iguanas. Maybe I'd bond better with a reptile…

I walked over to the pen and scooped one out which promptly bit my thumb and drew blood. I gritted my teeth as the pain ran through me and the beast worked seriously hard to get free so I let it go and moved on, feeling Gabriel following me.

"This is pointless," I muttered.

"You'll find one," he urged.

"Which one? Have you *seen* it?" I asked, glancing back at him but his awkward expression said he hadn't.

"Just keep trying or you're gonna fail this class. I have *seen* that," he said real helpfully, but I guessed he was right. I didn't wanna fail this shit, even if it wasn't worth my time.

I picked up a spiny Vertix badger cub which whined and yelped like I'd broken its damn leg. I put that one back and moved to the Soaris foals which whinnied, rearing up and kicking their silver hooves at me while flapping their wings. I felt the professor's eyes on me and ground my teeth as she drew closer.

"Oh dear, your aura is always so dark," she tutted. "Didn't I tell you to work on that?"

I drew a slow breath in through my nose as my irritation rose. "I don't do light auras."

"Nonsense," she clipped. "Keep trying, Mr Draconis." She waved me past her towards a couple of Aquis chicks with golden beaks and black feathers that shone like stardust. They didn't like me one bit, the first trying to peck my eyes out while the second seemed to attempt suicide rather than stay in my company by running at the fence post and nearly knocking itself out.

Gabriel chuckled behind me and I spun around to glare at him, finding the piglet upside down in his arms, snoozing soundly.

"Teach me," I demanded. "What are you doing to make the pig thing do that?"

"You just need to be gentle and approach it with good intentions," he said like it was so simple. "Here. Try and stroke him."

He offered me the piglet and I reached out to touch it, but it squealed before I even got close and Gabriel clutched him back against his chest.

I folded my arms, glancing over at Leon and Elise who had Ignitious kittens with fiery tails running all over them. Dante moved to join them with a couple of young Severis crows on his shoulders and my frustration grew.

"This one's Bethany, and that's Hector, this is Lewellen," Leon said, pointing at each of the kittens as Meteoris clapped enthusiastically and awarded him rank points. "The crows are Kyle and Phillip." He pointed at the birds on Dante's shoulders who he hadn't even touched yet. How the fuck did he manage that?

"He has an affinity with animals because of his Charisma," Gabriel explained, clearly reading the question from my expression.

"Well whatever the opposite of Charisma is, that's what I have," I said. "This is pointless. Like I said, animals don't like me."

"That one does," Gabriel said just as a wet nose butted against my hand.

I looked down in surprise, finding a ghost hound there, beating its three tails as it gazed at me with bright, adoring eyes. And if I wasn't going entirely crazy, I could have sworn it was *the* ghost hound. It wasn't in a pen either and it definitely didn't look like a puppy. I hadn't seen it since that day it had helped me out against Bryce and I had to admit I'd wondered about it a time or two.

"What are you doing here?" I muttered. "Scram."

Gabriel jabbed me in the ribs with his elbow. "What are you doing, idiot? Talk to it."

I glanced at him, shaking my head. "This one isn't part of the class. It keeps following me. I think it's brain damaged or something."

He looked at me in that all-knowing way of his. "It's not brain damaged. Pet her. She wants you to."

"She?" I murmured.

"Yeah, it's a girl. Can't you tell?"

"No," I grunted as the hound sat watching me, its head cocked to one side. Well, it'd probably help me pass this class I supposed.

I reached out to touch it and Gabriel shoved my shoulders. "Kneel down, get on her level."

I muttered angrily under my breath but did as he said, kneeling before it on the grass and its – *her* – tails beat harder.

"Hello," I mumbled, feeling like a complete moron as I reached out and vaguely ruffled the soft blue fur on her head.

She pushed her head into my hand and her wet tongue ran over my palm. Something hard and cold melted inside me and I kept stroking her, gazing into her large eyes which were tinted darkest navy. I supposed she was sort of nice. And she had bitten Bryce pretty damn good. I could admit I liked her just from the single act alone.

"What are you doing here?" I murmured and Gabriel knelt down beside me, reaching out to stroke her too. She let him for a moment before nuzzling back against my palm and climbing straight into my lap, curling up in a tiny ball that seemed impossibly small for her size.

"Err, what now?" I looked down at her as she tucked her nose under her tails and fell right asleep.

"Now cuddle her," Gabriel urged and I gave him a deadened stare.

"I don't cuddle."

"You cuddle Elise," he whispered and I gritted my jaw.

"That's different."

"No it isn't," he countered.

"Oh my stars, look at you guys," Elise suddenly cooed and I looked up, finding her standing there with her hands clasped over her mouth as she looked down at me and Gabriel with the little animals, seeming on the verge of combusting, or maybe crying. Whatever it was, it was weird.

"What?" I grunted.

"It's just so *cute*." She practically bounced up and down before Leon arrived covered in fluffy kittens, two sticking out of his pockets, one poking out the top of his collar, three more balancing on his arms and one on his damn head.

"Where'd you get a ghost hound, dude?" Leon gasped.

"A what?" Meteoris flipped around from behind him, her eyes landing on the blue ghost hound in my lap, her mouth opening and closing like a fish out of water.

"Mr Draconis! Do not move. I shall remove it from your person. Hold very still." She closed in on me as students turned to look and a couple of them shrieked.

"What? It's fine. It's just lying there," I growled.

"Ghost hounds are one of the most dangerous creatures in Solaria, their poison can work itself into the brain and shut down all cognitive abilities within a few hours," she gasped.

"I can't be poisoned." I shrugged.

"But they are most volatile, Mr Draconis. She could go on a rampage and bite every student in this class within minutes. They cannot be captured by anything but fire and even then-"

"I'll take her elsewhere then." I stood up, bundling the beast against my chest and Meteoris screamed, fire blazing in her palms as fear daggered through her eyes.

"Even an experienced trainer should not handle a ghost hound like that! They do not offer their star names to anyone," she cried in fright. "Put it down and step away."

"I'm not gonna do that," I deadpanned, and Gabriel snorted a laugh.

"He's clearly handling her fine," he said, but that didn't seem to calm Meteoris down even a little bit.

The hound lifted her head and rested it on my shoulder and I stiffened awkwardly, looking at Gabriel for advice which he didn't give. "What's it doing?"

"Oh my stars, it loves you," Leon gasped and I shot him a scowl.

"No," I rejected those words. "Don't be ridiculous. Something's wrong with it."

"Oh dear, I may have to put the poor thing down," Meteoris said sadly and I hissed at her venomously, clutching the animal to my chest.

"You'll do no such thing," I snapped as Leon slid his Atlas out of his pocket and very unsubtly took a photo of me.

"One for the scrapbook," he breathed to Elise like I couldn't hear and she snorted a laugh.

I clenched my jaw as Meteoris stared at the beast in my arms like it was a bomb about to go off.

"I'll take it off campus," I announced, turning my back on the bitch who'd threatened to kill it and striding away across the Empyrean Fields towards The Iron Wood. By the time I made it to the tall fence marking the boundary of Aurora Academy, the hound had fallen asleep against my shoulder.

"How odd."

"Very strange."

"Never seen something like that before."

I turned at the voices, finding the three Kipling brothers sitting on branch in a tree like that was a totally normal thing to do and I offered them a blank stare.

"He's noticed us," Kipling Senior commented.

"Clearly," Kipling Junior replied.

"How much do you want for it?" Middle Kipling asked, eyeing the creature in my arms. "Two hundred auras?"

"She's not for sale," I gritted out.

"Shame," Kipling Senior remarked.

"Pity," Junior agreed.

Middle Kipling took a cupcake from his bag and slowly pushed it down his pants, his hand moving up and down within them.

"By the stars." I turned away from them, heading to the X which marked the concealment magic in the fence where I could get out.

I slipped through the seemingly solid fence onto the other side and placed the ghost hound on its paws. She wound herself around my legs like a cat then leapt away and climbed a tree with her sharp claws, watching me from a branch above my head. She was perfectly silent as she moved and as she jumped up onto another branch, she walked straight into the tree trunk and disappeared.

"Good riddance," I muttered, turning back, but then a voice sounded in my head I couldn't ignore.

"Periwinkle."

I halted, looking back up at the tree, finding the ghost hound poking its face back out of the trunk and looking down at me with bright eyes.

"Didn't hear that," I muttered then hesitated, flicking a finger and using my earth magic to overturn an old log on the ground, revealing all kinds of bugs and slugs. The ghost hound leapt down onto the feast with a yip of excitement and I strode away through the fence that led back to campus, finding Middle Kipling licking frosting from his fingers in the tree while his brothers chatted casually about the weather.

I turned away with a grimace and headed back to class, a blur of motion tearing up to me as I headed across the field. Elise grinned as she stopped a foot in front of me. "Professor Meteoris says you have to pair with me and Leon for the rest of class so we can show you how to bond with the Ignitious kittens." She smirked at me and I rolled my eyes.

"Fine."

"How did you tame that ghost hound?" she asked as we started walking back to class together.

"It's broken," I muttered dismissively.

"Because only broken things could possibly like you, right?" She arched a brow and I nodded slowly.

"Yes."

"Including me?" she whispered.

"You're the most broken thing in my collection and my favourite," I murmured and she smiled widely at that.

"What other things are in your collection?" she teased.

"My soul and now the hound." I shrugged.

"So you're keeping her?" she asked excitedly.

"I was joking."

"Boo." She pouted. "Leon's already named her."

"She doesn't have a name," I growled even though she did. *But she definitely doesn't have a name given to her by someone else.*

"Where did you put Miss Snufflington?" Leon asked sadly as I arrived and the rattle went off in my chest.

"*That* is not her name," I hissed.

"Yes it is," he said tauntingly. "The stars told me."

"No they didn't," I growled, unsure why that pissed me off so much but it did. She wasn't called Miss fucking Snufflington.

He rolled his eyes. "Alright, they didn't. But it totally suits her, right? Miss Snugglebunny Snufflington."

"No," I snapped.

"Why are you getting so angry about it? Do you luuurve her?" He grinned, his eyebrows wiggling and I punched him in the gut. He wheezed out a laugh. "You definitely do."

"Shut up. Show me this kitten taming thing," I demanded to change the subject and Leon plucked a furry red kitten from inside his blazer and held it out to me. As I went to reach for it, it hissed angrily and Leon withdrew it.

"Oh, it's your aura," he said with a frown. "It's too dark."

My jaw flexed in annoyance. "What does that even mean?"

Elise moved up just close enough for our arms to brush and I looked to her, my gaze following the line of her little pixie nose then down to her full lips which I wanted to brand as mine over and over again. I hadn't had nearly enough time alone with her lately.

"That's better," Leon said and my head snapped around.

"What?" I grunted.

"Your aura is brighter with Elise near you like that." He placed a kitten on my head and I stilled so it didn't fall off.

"Take it off," I commanded, but Leon just backed away, pressing his finger to his lips.

"It likes you," he whispered.

"It doesn't," I growled, reaching for it and taking the little thing into my grip. It didn't bite me, so I guessed that was something. I lowered it down to cup it in my palms and it looked up at me nervously before nuzzling into my thumb.

"Ooh, it does like you," Elise said excitedly and her smile made my heart lift as I watched her get pleasure out of this.

"Oh yeah?" I muttered.

"Yes," she whispered, inching closer and running her thumb over the kitten's head. It mewed softly and I gently brushed my thumb over its little leg as its eyes flashed with tiny flames.

"Lewellen," the stars whispered in my mind and I jolted, looking to Elise in surprise.

"Did you hear that?" she asked and I nodded as a grin split across her beautiful face.

The bell rang in the distance for the end of class and I let Elise take the kitten and place it back in its pen. I hounded after my girl towards the edge of class where Leon was being reprimanded by Meteoris as he tried to smuggle several of the kittens away under his blazer. He huffed every time she took one out of his pockets and looked heartbroken at having to say goodbye to each of them.

"You'll see them next lesson, now move along, Mr Night." Meteoris ushered him away before grabbing a final kitten out of the back of his waistband with a tut.

"Not Gregorius," Leon groaned as the kitten was placed back with its siblings.

"Gregorius needs to go back to his mother for a while, you can see him next time," Meteoris said sternly and Elise jabbed Leon in the back to get him moving.

My gaze fell to Elise's ass as I walked behind her, her skirt lifting up a little in the wind and almost giving me a view of her panties.

"I think Ryder's gonna turn into a complete softy one day," Leon murmured to Elise. "He's gonna be all about cuddles and rainbows."

"And teddy bears," she added with a light laugh and a growl built in my throat. "He's gonna be so into warm hugs, we'll end up calling him Olaf."

My teeth gritted and I fisted a handful of Elise's hair, yanking hard and making her bend right over backwards so I was glaring down at her. "The only thing I have in common with that snowman is that my heart is made of ice. And you'd better remember it, baby."

Her throat bobbed and her chest heaved as I held her there, her lips parting and her eyes filling with lust.

"By the stars, he's watched Frozen," Leon whispered mostly to himself and I bared my teeth at him.

"Fuck off," I growled. *That's it, I want her to myself. And I want her now.*

As the rest of the students disappeared down the pathways towards their next classes, I threw an elbow into Leon's gut then picked Elise up under one arm and strode away with her while she tried to wriggle her way free, though I got the feeling she wasn't fighting all that hard.

"Hey!" Leon called as I walked off at a fierce pace, rounding the library and pushing a window open on the bottom level. "It's not your special week, I don't wanna eat you, Scar!" his voice carried to me.

I didn't know what the hell that meant and I didn't care to know. I tossed Elise into the library and dove after her, shutting the window and slamming a hand over her mouth as Leon went running by. Her eyes were alight with lust as I bore down on her in the dark corner of the library behind a long stack of books.

"I think you need a reminder of who I am, baby," I hissed, casting a silencing bubble around us as she shifted onto her knees beneath me.

Her hair was fucked up from where I'd fisted my hand in it and I reached down to smear her candy pink lipstick too. I liked when she looked like the broken girl she was. I wanted her pain painted on her skin today, not hidden beneath it. Dante might have distracted her in the skies earlier, but I could feel the ache in her returning again and maybe it was time she embraced that pain and dealt with it a different way.

"Come on, Ryder," she said tauntingly. "We both know your heart is as sweet as an apple pie." I could see the challenge in her eyes as she goaded me, knowing exactly what she was doing.

"You're playing a dangerous game today, Elise," I warned, casting a vine which slid around her wrists, drawing them behind her back and tightening sharply enough to make her wince. "I'm your Elysian Mate which means you're made for me in every way," I said with a dark smirk. "But you've never had me at my worst, baby. So I say we test the bond the stars gave us and see if you can handle it."

Her slender throat bobbed and I watched her pupils dilate as I stared down at her all tied up for me.

"I can handle anything, Ryder," she said in a growl that spoke of her power and it felt even better to have her like this, knowing I had a wild creature at my mercy right now.

I slid my fingers under her chin, gripping tightly as I leaned down to speak to her. "I think you might just regret those words, Elise."

"I think you're underestimating me. I could handle ten of you without breaking a sweat," she said, that tongue of hers asking for trouble.

"It's going to hurt."

"I'd be disappointed if it didn't. Question is, how far do you really think you can push me before your heart softens and you can't go any further?" she taunted and the words set off the rattle in my chest.

"You think I've been holding back on you?"

"I know you have," she said, raising her chin defiantly and it brought out the Alpha in me, the challenge too much to ignore.

I released a slow breath, brushing my fingers down her neck and ripping open the top buttons of her shirt to see more of her pale flesh. I'd hungered to make it red from the day I'd first met her and now she was down on her knees, daring me to do it. Sure, I'd put her down there, but that was even better. I didn't like women who begged or drooled over me. Before Elise, I'd liked them quiet and submissive. But this girl needed pain almost as deeply as I needed it. She wanted to hurt because her agony was her greatest strength. And all of that emotional pain inside her needed to spill out from time to time in the form of something far more physical. But she didn't like to make it easy for me, which was even more of a turn on.

"Safe word," I demanded of her and she wet her lips as she thought on it.

"I won't need one," she said huskily, those words alone making my cock as hard as iron. "You could peel the skin from my bones and I wouldn't breathe a single word in refusal."

"You're a little danger whore, aren't you Elise?" I said heavily, pushing my thumb into her mouth and letting her slit it open on her fangs. She sucked my blood greedily and a groan left me at the feel of her wet, hot tongue against my skin, aching to feel it on my cock instead.

I unzipped my fly with the intention to give myself just that, but she released my thumb from the grip of her teeth and levelled her gaze on me.

"I'm going to fight back," she announced. "You can have me at your mercy, Ryder, but only if you make me bend to your will."

I chuckled darkly, flicking my fingers to release the vines binding her wrists. "You really are my perfect match."

"We'd better go somewhere we can cause utter devastation without being disturbed," she said with a smirk and I nodded.

"The basement in the Vega Dorms," I decided and no sooner had I said it than she shot away with her Vampire speed and I was left with my cock hard and aching for release.

I slipped back through the window and headed across campus at a fierce pace, knocking students aside when they weren't quick enough to get out of my way. I was on a war path, my bloodlust rising, my need for pain almost as keen as my need for pleasure in that moment. If there was ever a time when I was just the sum total of the words inked on my knuckles, it was now.

I headed straight for the Vega Dorms as my heart beat harder and harder and I thought over exactly what I was going to do to her. When I reached the entrance, I ran my tongue piercing along my teeth as I slipped inside and pushed through the door that led to the basement. I shut it firmly behind me and sealed it tight, welding it in place so no one could get in and more importantly, my girl couldn't get out.

I shed my blazer, leaving it on the floor as I walked down into the basement and headed along the passage towards the boiler room where I held my gang meetings. All was quiet, but I knew she was here, her ears trained on my approach.

I slid the buttons free of the shirt cuffs on my wrists, taking my time to roll up my sleeves then loosening a button at my throat too. I stepped into the boiler room and didn't bother to look for my girl, knowing she was hunting me like a predator with the gifts of her Order. I wouldn't find her if I tried, but she would come to me hungry for a feast and I intended on giving her one. But she was going to have to work for it.

I moved to the centre of the room and quietly laid a trap for her with my earth magic, softening the ground all around me in a circle as I waited for her to attack.

"Why are you hiding, baby?" I smirked, my eyes trailing from the large boilers to the stacks of old boxes in the far corner. "Are you afraid?"

Silence. My little hunter was taking her stalking seriously.

"I thought you wanted me at my worst," I goaded her. "Do you need that safe word after all?"

A blur in my periphery made me twist around and Elise came at me with bared fangs, but as her foot hit the floor beside me, she fell with a yell, tumbling down into a concrete pit of my creation. I cast vines over the top of it as she lunged up to get out then hardened the ground around me once more.

I grinned down at her in my snare as she bared her fangs at me in a snarl. I crouched down, gazing in at her and casting a sharp curved silver blade in my hand. "Are you hungry, bad girl?"

She nodded slowly, her throat rising and falling as she stared at my wrist and I pressed the tip of the blade there, scoring it up my arm and grinning through the pain. My blood dripped down on her and she opened her mouth, drinking it like it was rain and my cock grew rock hard for her as I watched. I gave her just enough to set her bloodlust alight then healed the cut on my arm and stood up, twisting the blade between my fingers.

"Let me out," she demanded.

"I'm not sure you can handle this game," I taunted and her eyes narrowed.

"You think you're so dark, Ryder, but I'm your mate. That means my dark side is just as dark as yours."

I considered that, running my tongue over my teeth, hungry to drag it over her. "Let's test that then, shall we? Let your mental barriers down, baby."

She raised her chin and did as I said as I cast away the vines trapping her beneath me. Her eyes locked with mine and I cast a vision in our minds, coating the walls in blood and filling the air with chilling music that sent a ripple of anticipation down my spine. I pulled her out of the trap, tugging her up in front of me and holding both of her wrists in one hand while I placed the blade under her chin.

"The vision is fake, but we're not," I told her. "My touches are real." I dragged the knife down to her throat, grazing her skin but not cutting her as a shiver gripped her.

She reached out to open my shirt buttons, seeking out the X on my chest and carving her fingers over it.

"Are my touches real?" she asked and I nodded, stepping closer to her as I skated the knife down to her shirt and slid it beneath the material.

She wet her lips and my cock throbbed at the sight before I slashed the knife down the middle of her shirt, tearing it to shit and exposing her black push up bra beneath. I placed the knife between my teeth, walking her backwards as I dragged her blazer and shirt from her body, tossing them aside and clawing my hands down her bare sides, over her skirt and beneath it to clasp her hips in my hands. I spun her around with a jerk of strength and she spun like a ballerina before me, her skirt spinning out in a fan before I tore it off of her and threw it on the ground.

I admired her ass in the little matching black thong she wore and let my gaze travel down her toned legs to her high heels. She glanced back over her shoulder at me, her lilac hair slipping across her skin and grazing the base of her neck. I moved forward, shifting it aside and taking the knife from between my teeth, pressing the tip of it to the top of her spine and running it all the way down the length of it, the sharp point kissing her flesh but never breaking it. She'd bleed for me by the time I was done, but I wasn't going to rush the show.

When I reached her little thong, I kicked her legs wider apart and she gasped as I slipped the blade under the material, grazing it between her ass cheeks and along to her soaking wet slit.

"Ryder," she moaned, reaching behind her to grasp the back of my neck and draw me closer. I leaned in, but didn't press my body to hers, grazing my teeth along the shell of her ear as I slid the blade back and forth in her arousal.

"I'll never beg," she said huskily and I chuckled darkly.

"I don't want you begging, I want you screaming." I changed the shape of the blade in my grip into a thick metal dildo, shoving it inside her without warning. A gasp of fear escaped her as she expected the slice of the blade and I laughed harder, shoving her head to one side for me and biting into the fleshy patch behind her ear. "As if I'd cut up that pretty pussy of yours, baby."

She moaned as I drove the metal in and out of her, her nails tearing into the back of my neck.

"So you do have some limits?" she teased breathily and I ran my tongue over the mark I'd left behind her ear, making her shudder from the sudden coldness of my tongue piercing.

"Only when it comes to you. Do you want to hurt for me, baby?" I asked and she nodded, her chest heaving as I worked her pussy in deep, forceful movements of my hand, making the metal expand and hit her g-spot in the perfect way. She cried out, grinding into my palm every time she took the full length of it and my cock twitched needily for her as I held her at my mercy.

When she was on the verge of coming, I pulled it out and bent her over in front of me, my hand splaying across her back as I cast away the metal in my palm and created a wooden paddle instead. Better than that, there were small spikes across the middle of it in the shape of the Capricorn symbol – *my* symbol. I spanked her ass with it and bloody pinpricks of the symbol appeared there as she screamed. A deep, animal growl left me as I waited for her to tell me to stop, but she just looked back at me with hooded eyes and breathed, "More."

I groaned at that single word, striking her ass in a new place to brand her with my sign, again and again, hitting her upper thigh and colouring her whole ass cheek red. I cast the paddle away, smearing my hand through her blood and making her moan for me once more.

"You're looking a little uneven, baby," I said with a smirk, palming the milky whiteness of her unmarked ass cheek.

"Sounds like you've got work to do then, Ryder," she taunted in breathless voice, moving to stand upright, but I fisted a hand in her hair and pushed her down again. She ground her ass into my crotch and I stole a moment of pleasure as my cock rubbed against her. I was desperate to get inside her, but not until she'd hurt for me, then come for me.

"Hold your ankles," I commanded and she folded at the spine, doing as I asked and giving me the best view as I knelt down behind her.

I cast the silver blade in my hand again, slicing it through her thong and tugging the material away from her bare pussy, loving how wet it was in my palm. I pushed it into my pocket before running the edge of the knife up the inside of her left thigh, my gaze locking with hers as she watched me through her legs. Her pupils dilated as I dug the blade in deeper, making a small cut that spilled blood down the inside of her thigh.

She gasped as I dropped down to her ankle before the droplet spilled onto the floor then ran my tongue all the way up the inside of her leg and devoured every drop of it, making her suck in another breath as I made it to the apex of her thighs. I didn't stop there, burying my face in her pussy and driving my tongue into her tight hole. She moaned loudly and I blindly slashed my wrist open with the blade, offering it to her lips and her fangs drove hungrily into my flesh as I dropped the knife and used my free hand to squeezed her ass, devouring every drop of her sweet taste.

Her thighs quivered as she fought to stay in the position I'd put her in while her body came apart and I laughed against her flesh as I slid my hand between her thighs and gave her clit some much needed attention. Two strokes of my fingers had her coming for me and I pushed three fingers into her pussy to feel her as she rode out her orgasm.

When she was done, I dragged my tongue up between her ass cheeks, feasting on her and making her mine in every way. I leaned back and bit deeply into her unmarked cheek and she moaned in pleasure, feeding on my wrist more fiercely and I groaned as she stole away my magic. It felt so fucking good to be drained by her, feeding my queen and gilding her strength with my own. But she was getting greedy and I still needed some magic to finish what I'd started with her. I yanked my wrist free from her lips and stood up, gripping her hair and tugging her upright as I walked around to stand in front of her.

Her eyes were full of lust and she looked a little power drunk as she stood before me in nothing but her bra and those sexy ass high heels. I recast the blade in my hand once more and slid it between her cleavage, cutting away the fabric so her tits sprang free for me and she shrugged out of the material, throwing it away without care.

"Is that all you've got?" she asked huskily even though I could see how much I'd affected her already.

I laughed deeply and beckoned her closer with two fingers. The moment she took her first step, I lunged for her, tossing her over my shoulder and carrying her to the wall. I threw her against it, capturing her wrists with two vines and stringing her up for me. Her arms went taut as she used her strength to fight them and they snapped, her feet hitting the ground before she grinned and shot around behind me, tiptoeing up to speak in my ear.

"I told you I was gonna fight," she purred and my cock jerked in my pants.

She gripped my shirt from behind and tore it to shreds, ripping it off me as I whirled around to catch her, but she shot away before I could. She came at me in a blur, gripping my belt, undoing it and tugging it off of me as I swung out an arm to try and catch her. She evaded me once more and the belt whipped down across my lower back as she tore past me once more, making me bark a laugh.

"Seems a little unfair to play with your Order gifts, baby," I growled, kicking off my shoes and tearing off the last of my clothes. "But if you wanna play dirty then so will I." I shifted into a huge snake, filling the entire room and coiling all around the edges of it as I trapped my Vampire within the centre of the space.

She sped around in an attempt to escape but I closed the gap, trapped her in the middle of my scales and squeezed. She gasped as I wrapped myself all around her, lifting my head to her ear, my tongue flicking out mockingly and making her curse. I shifted down to the size of a large python, still locked tightly all around her naked body as I slithered around her and my rough scales grazed all over her flesh and pert nipples.

"Ryder," she panted in surprise at liking this and I hissed a laugh, using my hypnosis to steal away her sight. She growled, blind as I shifted back into my Fae form and grabbed hold of her arm.

She swung out to strike me, but I caught it easily and shoved her back against the nearest wall, my solid cock pressing to her stomach as she fought to get free and I refused to let go.

"I wanna see you," she snarled as I tugged her lower lip between my teeth.

I drove my tongue into her mouth, unable to resist another taste of her as I returned her vision to her and kissed her fiercely. She tore at my back and I groaned at the slice of pain, slamming her more fiercely against the wall to try and hold her there. She shoved me away, spinning us around with a whirl of her speed and throwing me against it instead. I hooked her thighs up around my waist, kissing her possessively and aching for the feel of my mate around me. I lifted her hips, guiding my cock to her entrance, but she broke our kiss and tried to get away, a challenge in her gaze. And if she wanted me to force her hand, I was more than willing to comply. I gripped the backs of her thighs and threw her onto the ground, following her down and pinning her beneath me against the rough stone as I used my hypnosis to make blood shower down on us from the ceiling. Her head tipped back as she gazed up at her perfect fantasy as I gripped her throat and drove myself inside her.

Her eyes snapped back to mine and she moaned beautifully for me as I thrust fiercely into her pussy, not giving her a choice but to keep up with me as I stole what I wanted from her tight body. She squeezed her tits and arched her back as I fucked her mercilessly and drowned in the feel of her pussy tightening around my cock.

I gripped her throat tighter to cut off her air supply and she scratched her nails over my hand as a snarl of delight left her and her hips moved faster to chase the movements of my own.

"*Mine*," I growled against her lips, loosening my hand on her throat just as she came and her screams wrapped around me.

I exploded inside her at the sound, spilling every drop of my cum just for her and groaning through my release as her nails drew blood on my hand.

I fell still as we panted together and she turned my hand over, licking away the blood before healing it with a swipe of her thumb. My forehead fell to hers and I smiled at my dark queen, seeing every one of my broken shards reflected in her eyes. And I realised together, we made something entirely whole.

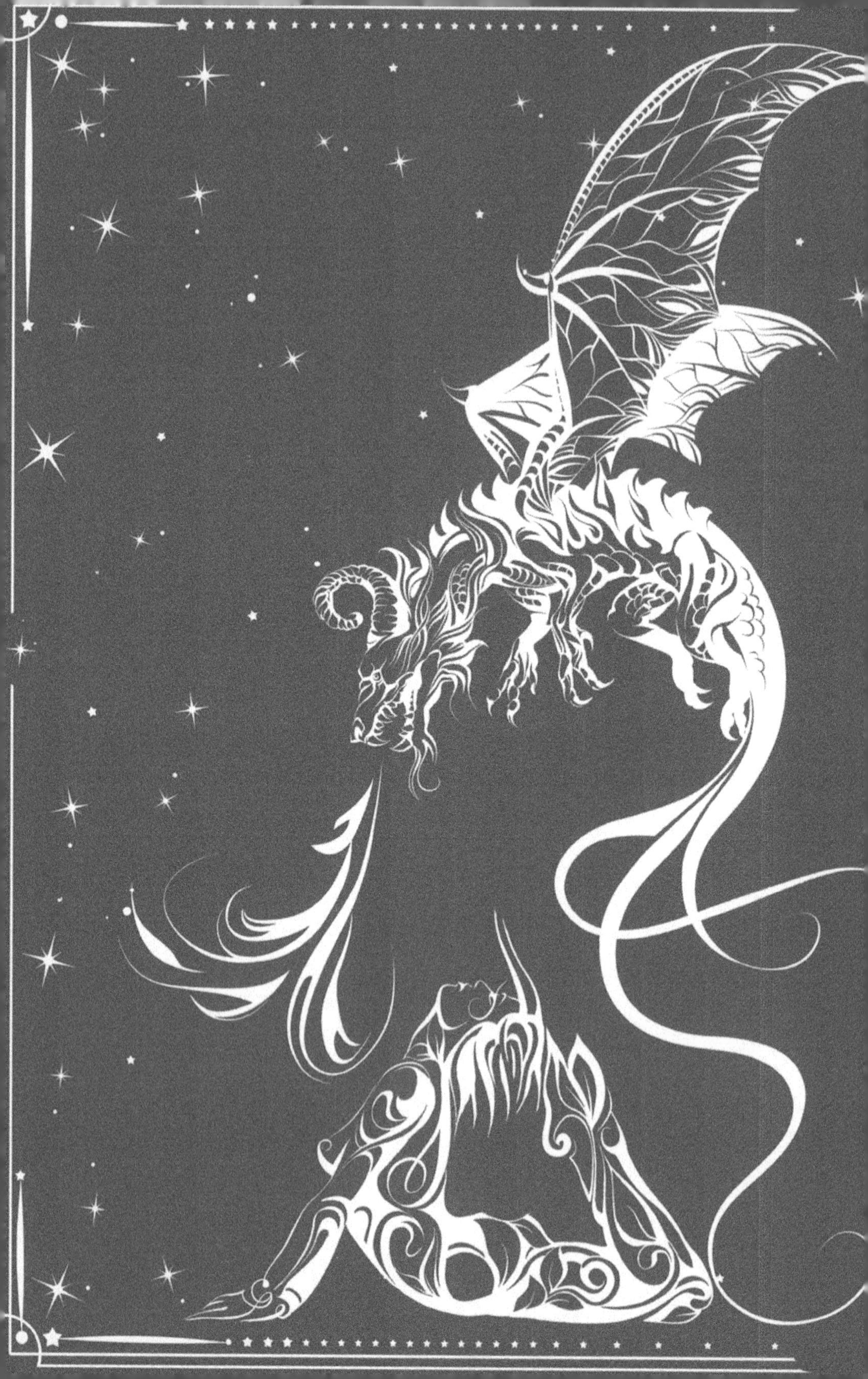

DANTE

CHAPTER TWENTY FOUR

I drew Elise back against my body by the hips, her soft curves moulding to me perfectly beneath my Pitball shirt which she was sleeping in. I had her all to myself, the bed at Gabriel's feeling large for once, though I didn't seek out any more space, wanting to hoard my vampirina like a pot of gold.

"You're crushing my ribs, Dante," she murmured in her sleep and it wasn't that easy to make my muscles loosen around her. I needed to refuel my magic and I always got extra possessive when it ran this low.

"Sorry, bella," I chuckled, slipping out of bed in my boxers and heading over to the treasure chest I'd brought here.

Gabriel hadn't complained about me bringing it, so I'd slowly been filling it with new gold items and now I had a sizeable collection waiting for me inside. I draped a few golden necklaces and medallions around my neck, the weight of them settling against my chest and sending a slow trickle of magic into the well inside me. I missed my Oscura medallion, but Leon still refused to give it back even though it had been a parting gift in death. A death he had not followed through on. So the gift was now void and I'd tried on more than one occasion to steal it back, but stealing from the best thief in

Solaria was unsurprisingly difficult.

He was currently out on a job thieving some artwork from a wealthy Monolrian Bear Shifter in the next town over. His mom Safira adored the artist of the piece he was after and it was her birthday next week, so he was determined to get hold of it.

Ryder was off dealing with a couple of rebels in his gang – which were becoming more and more common lately. He had to deal with one every few days and I had the feeling that this problem wasn't going away. But anytime I asked Gabriel about it, he just shook his head and said we didn't need to worry right now. And that wasn't particularly comforting. I liked to be prepared for fights, so if some of the Lunars were planning to rise up, I wanted to be ready. But in true Gabriel fashion, he wouldn't give me any details and told me to place my faith in his visions. I had come to trust his Sight, but it was still frustrating being unable to *see* what was coming for myself.

He was currently out circling the skies and bathing in the rising sunlight to restore his magic. Spending so much time here made me realise how protective Harpies were. He was constantly watching out of windows and securing the place with magical locks and alarm spells that allowed only the five of us to pass through them undetected. I got the feeling if anyone else walked in here without our permission, they'd be blown to pieces before they could even say hello. I wasn't against that in the slightest though, because it meant Elise was safe. Gabriel provided a kind of security that I'd only ever felt at my family home before now. This place had become that too, a little haven above the entire city that no other Fae could reach.

"Come back to bed, Dante," Elise groaned sleepily as she tried to hide from the golden light slipping in through a crack in the blind.

I put on some gold rings, a couple of heavy bangles and a gold belt around my waist which was cool against my flesh then climbed back under the covers and captured my girl beneath me. She wriggled, gasping at the coldness of the metal kissing her body and I grinned down at her as I kept her trapped.

"I have you all to myself for once and you expect me to let you sleep, carina?" I teased, nipping at her jaw as I knocked her thighs open and rested my weight between them, instantly growing hard for her.

"I don't do mornings," she groaned, closing her eyes again but a playful smile pulled at her lips.

If she wanted me to work for her attention, I was more than happy to play her game.

I worked my mouth up her jaw to her ear, making her shiver beneath me as I took my time. Then I spoke to her in my native tongue, knowing how it affected her as she guessed at all the filthy things I might be saying. "Hai bisogno di un promemoria che sei mia."

She released a breathy noise, turning her lips toward me to claim a kiss, but I didn't give her one on her mouth. I lowered my head to kiss her throat, then her collar bone, moving down between her breasts as I pushed the Pitball shirt up to gain access to her bare skin. I ran my mouth down her stomach to the edge of her tiny little panties then tugged the material of them between my teeth.

"Gabriel," she gasped and I growled.

"Dante," I corrected sharply, electricity tumbling off of me and zapping her for that slip.

"Ah!" she yelped then kicked me. "No Drago, Gabriel's here."

The covers whipped off of us and I turned my head with a curse, finding Gabriel perched in the windowsill with his wings folded behind him and a bemused expression on his face. A vine of his making coiled around the covers as they tugged them fully off the bed then disappeared

"Good morning, Elise," he spoke to her with the Devil in his eyes and I growled as I pushed myself up to kneel.

"She's mine this morning," I said firmly.

"Says who?" Gabriel asked tauntingly.

"Says me," I growled, ready to fight this stronzo and push him out the window if I had to. We'd come to an arrangement over Elise, but we'd never fully seen eye to eye. I liked him much more than I used to, but I felt far closer to Leon and now Ryder too.

"I thought you were busy taking an important phone call," Gabriel said casually just as my Atlas started ringing.

I glowered at him then whipped it off the nightstand and my gaze fell to Lionel Acrux's name. Well, it fell to the name I'd saved him under on my phone which was Dragon Bastardo.

I huffed out a breath, figuring I couldn't ignore this call. He'd been trying to contact me all week and I'd evaded him, but I knew I couldn't do it any longer.

"Ciao?" I answered coolly.

"Hello Dante," Lionel's deep and commanding voice filled my ear as Gabriel slipped off of the windowsill, cast a silencing bubble around my girl, lifted her up and pinned her to the wall.

I tried to ignore that little display of dominance as my hackles rose and I focused on the call.

"You've been avoiding me," Lionel stated.

"I've been busy, Papa D," I tossed back.

"Of course. I heard about the little gang peace treaty in Alestria. How very civilised of you. The next thing you know, the Fae of your city will stop defecating in the streets and hunting for their food with their teeth."

A growl built in my throat. "Alestrians do not shit in the streets and hunt their food like animals." Not all of them anyway. I'd seen plenty of Blazers squatting down back alleys and trying to dive on pigeons for food, but I wasn't going to tell Lord Stronzo that.

My eyes flicked to Gabriel and Elise again and my jaw tightened as he kissed her and she wrapped herself around him like she was desperate to get closer.

I turned my back on them as Lionel went on.

"I'm calling to invite you to my manor today. You would have had advanced notice if you'd responded to my secretary's calls, however, you have forgone any such courtesy and I am now ordering you to attend. My niece, Juniper, will be here too and I will expect you to spend some time impregnating her if you want to uphold our arrangement of me allowing you to reside in Alestria. I want Storm Dragon heirs in her belly before the weekend is up."

Every drop of blood in my body ran cold and I fell entirely still.

"And if you refuse, I will ensure you are moved to Tucana within the next week and will remain under my constant watch within my home. You will be transferred to Zodiac Academy and you will never see your little Vampire whore again. And I will get my Storm Dragon heirs either way, so the choice is yours."

My breaths came in deep, uneven pants and my throat wouldn't give up the words he wanted. Because agreeing to that was unthinkable. And yet I already had. The bells of fate were tolling and I had to answer their call.

"I expect you here by noon. Do not test me, boy." Lionel hung up and I was left in the wake of his words like a bomb had just gone off in my face.

I sank down onto the edge of the bed, my Atlas going slack in my grip then it slipped from my fingers entirely and hit the floor.

I felt Gabriel's silencing bubble drop then Elise shot to my side, gripping my hand. "Dante, what is it?"

I turned to her, taking in her beautiful silver ringed eyes and the worry burning in them. I reached out to cup her jaw, my thumb grazing along her flesh. I'd do anything to keep her.

"Muoverei il sole, la terra e ogni stella nel cielo per te," I told her. *I'd move the sun, the earth and every star in the sky for you.*

Gabriel's shadow fell over us as he moved in front of me and I was surprised when he pressed a hand to my shoulder. I looked to him with my fate closing in on me on all sides and latched onto the single glint of hope in his gaze.

"Lionel Acrux wants him to impregnate his niece," Gabriel told Elise and she cursed his name with every insult she knew.

"No," she spat, gripping my arm. "I won't let that happen, Dante."

"He must be provided with the Storm Dragon children he craves for his fucking empire," Gabriel said heavily. "There's no way around that."

My heart sank like it weighed a ton and thunder boomed overhead as my storm powers leaked out of me in rage.

"No," Elise growled again, looking to him. "There must be a way around this."

Gabriel fell quiet for a long moment and all I could feel was the rising panic in the room.

"It's okay, amore mio," I told her gently, but she shook her head in refusal as tears built in her eyes.

"Gabriel, please," she begged, reaching out to grab his hand and he jolted out of a vision.

"There's a way," he said on a breath of hope and I was surprised to see how worried he was about this. "You need to tell Lionel that you've mated to Elise. You need to take her with you and show him both of your eyes."

A breath lodged in my throat and I looked to my girl, seeing her willingness to do that for me as my heart began to race. But we were doing everything we could to hide this fact. If word got out that she had more than one mate, it would draw the attention of the press.

I guessed so long as Ryder's mate bond remained a secret, it was worth the risk though. And maybe Lionel would keep the secret as it wouldn't serve him any purpose to out it. If he did though, I could handle the press, but the idea of having to fuck some random girl was unthinkable. There was no way I'd even manage it.

"Lionel may accept that as enough of a reason to stop harassing you on the matter of providing him with more Storm Dragons," Gabriel continued thoughtfully as he sought out more answers. "But not necessarily." He frowned and I felt my fate being weighed and measured by the stars. "So you'll need a backup plan too."

"Like what?" Elise asked desperately, her fingers sliding between mine.

Gabriel's nose wrinkled for a moment then he nodded with some decision. "You need to go to the Kiplings and pay them for...sperm."

"Dalle stelle," I sighed as Elise groaned.

"If you can sneak it into the Acrux manor and Lionel insists on heirs even after you show him your eyes, then...that's the answer. He will accept that you aren't physically able to have sex with anyone aside from your mate and will opt for an insemination option." Gabriel gave me an apologetic look, but this was far better than actually having to go through with getting Juniper pregnant.

"Where are we going to find the Kiplings this early on a Saturday?" Elise asked, chewing her lip anxiously.

"They'll be at Aurora," I said. "They're orphans, so they usually stay at the academy on the weekends instead of their shitty foster home."

"Aww," Elise said. "If they didn't creep me out so much, I'd wanna hug them for that."

I snorted a laugh, getting to my feet and pulling her up with me.

Gabriel let us pass as we headed to the bathroom to shower and get ready for the day. Sadly, my dick wasn't in the mood for claiming my girl anymore, it was too horrified by the idea of going anywhere near Juniper so it was playing dead in case she was lurking nearby.

It's okay amico, I'll never put you in another girl. I'm going to fix this shit. Today.

We found the Kiplings sunning themselves out on the Empyrean Fields, all of them lying on a blanket with their muscular, deeply bronzed chests bare as they read facts out loud from a couple of thick encyclopaedias. Griffins recharged their magic by acquiring new knowledge, which seemed like the dullest thing in the world to me, but I supposed they loved it like I loved gold. *No one will ever steal my gold.*

"Ciao," I called as we approached.

Elise was wearing a skimpy, pale pink dress which showed off her long legs, but they didn't even spare my hot as fuck girl a glance as they looked up in unison.

"Good morning, Dragon," Kipling Senior said blandly. "How can we help you?"

"I need to buy something from one of you," I said, casting a silencing bubble around us and feeling awkward as shit.

"Everything has a price," Kipling Junior said.

"What are you looking to purchase?" Middle Kipling asked. They all looked eerily similar despite their different ages, their hair and eyes dark, their height and frames nearly exactly the same.

"Well..." I shared an awkward look with Elise and she moved closer to my side. "I need some sperm."

"What kind?" Kipling Senior asked immediately, not missing a beat. "I have some Manticore and Harpy in stock. We can acquire all other Orders, but we'll need extra time for Basilisks, Dragons and Cerberuses. If you acquire sperm from a specific Fae, we will need their address and time to organise a kidnapping."

"We can manage it without taking the Fae hostage, but that will incur more fees," Middle Kipling added. "Memory eraser potions are extra if they become necessary."

I ran a hand over the back of my neck. "Actually, mio amicos, I was informed you might be able to supply me with one of your own, er, samples. But the thing is, it's to impregnate a woman..."

The three of them all held out their hands in unison. "A star vow,"

Senior offered.

"To ensure we will not discuss anything about this transaction," Junior finished for him.

I took a moment shaking each of their hands to seal the vows, finding their lack of reaction to this strange despite the fact that I'd spent a lot of time dealing with them in the past.

"So you'll do it?" Elise questioned when it was done.

"Of course," Kipling Junior said. "There will be a sizeable fee owed to the one of us who will volunteer." They looked between each other, then nodded like they'd just made some decision and Middle Kipling pushed to his feet and started walking away.

"Who is the woman? We'll need a name and details of the situation so we can ensure the child born to the mother is kept tabs on," Kipling Senior stated.

"We like to ensure our seeds are kept track of," Kipling Junior added.

"Merda santa, you've done this before?" I balked.

"No," Senior and Junior said at the same time.

"O...kay," Elise said as the two of them fell back into reading facts to each other from their encyclopaedias and we stood there awkwardly waiting for Middle Kipling to return.

"A gruffelephant weighs up to eighty four tons and grazes exclusively on neverleaves on the Shimmering Islands of Sandoom," Junior told Senior who nodded.

"Quelliot trees are infused with the magic of a powerful Fae tribe who went extinct on the land of Lerubia thousands of years ago. The forest is four thousand acres in size but is under threat since it was discovered that the bark of the trees can heal many, previously untreatable Fae diseases."

"Is he um, going to be long?" Elise asked.

"How long is a piece of string?" Senior asked.

"As long as you cut it," I said with a shrug.

"Then there is your answer," Junior said and they returned to reading from their books.

Dalle stelle...

Middle Kipling finally returned carrying what looked like a birthday cake which still had the candles on it.

"Oh no," Elise breathed, tugging on my sleeve in urgency.

"What is it, carina?" I murmured as Middle Kipling dropped down onto the blanket at our feet.

"He has a thing for cakes," she whispered, a note of horror in her voice.

"All inanimate objects have the ability to turn me on if they're sexually stimulating enough," Middle Kipling said matter of factly. "I currently am particularly aroused by Victoria Sponges. I shall simply borrow this one momentarily and return it to the birthday party in the Cafaeteria when the task is complete." He unzipped his fly, taking out his large dick and jamming it into the bottom of the cake in one fluid thrust.

My jaw dropped and I stood transfixed as he started thrusting up into the cake while his brothers continued reading facts out of their books, having absolutely no reaction at all to their brother fucking a sponge cake beside them.

"Per il sole e tutte le stelle, cosa sta succedendo?" I breathed in disgust.

"We'll just come back in a bit to collect the um, thing." Elise snatched my hand, trying to tow me away, but my feet were rooted to the ground. It was awful, yet I couldn't seem to look away.

"I'm almost done," Middle Kipling said frankly, his brow pinching in concentration.

He pulled out of the birthday cake, placing it carefully down beside him and Kipling Senior tossed him a specimen cup out of nowhere. He finished in it with a long groan then clipped the cap onto it and took a little paper bag from his pocket, placing it inside like a gift before holding it out to me.

"That will be a thousand auras," he said slightly breathlessly, tucking his dick away while I stared at the bag and nodded mutely before taking it hesitantly between my thumb and forefinger.

I cleared my throat. "I'll transfer it to your account."

"Thank you for you business." Middle Kipling stood, picking up the cake and heading back in the direction he'd come from and I had the horrible feeling he really was going to return that cake to the party.

"Let's go," I said hoarsely, taking hold of Elise's hand and marching her away from the Kiplings with a feeling of being eternally changed by that experience. *Dalle stelle, I'm never going to recover from this.*

"It's better than you giving your sperm to Juniper," Elise muttered after a long stretch of silence.

"I suppose that was the price I had to pay, I just wish you hadn't been there to see it, bella."

"I've seen it before," she said, her nose wrinkling and she started recounting the time she'd gone to them and Middle Kipling had just been finishing up with a cake before serving it up to his brothers.

I didn't know whether to laugh, vomit or cry. I hadn't cried since my father had died, but somehow this seemed to warrant it. "I don't think I'll ever eat cake again and that's a damn shame, carina, because my mamma makes the best cakes in Solaria."

"Maybe the disgust will pass after a few years," Elise said hopefully.

"No, amore mio, I believe I am forever scarred." I folded the bag around the cup and placed it in the pocket inside my blazer, trying not to think about it too much as its presence haunted me.

We made it to the front gate, heading out beyond the boundary of the school before I took a pouch of stardust from my pocket and pulled Elise to a halt. We shared an intense look as we readied to walk into the Dragon's den together before I threw the stardust into the air and we were torn away across the kingdom.

We landed outside the immense gates of the Acrux manor and a couple of guards let us in. I swear it took us ten minutes to walk up the huge driveway to the massive gothic manor house which could have contained three Pitball fields.

We walked up the steps where the golden door stood, large enough to allow me to walk inside in my Dragon form if I wanted to. But I imagined only a pretentious stronzo would want to enter his own home like that.

We were let inside by a frowning butler who glared at us like a couple of rats who'd just wandered into his master's home. The entrance hall was glitzy, adorned with gold and full of enough priceless shit to buy a whole private island. It was a shame I'd had to make Leon give back everything that he'd stolen from Lionel to cover taking the spyglass. Apparently it had worked though, because old Asscrux hadn't noticed that the dark artefact had gone missing and I hoped it stayed that way because we needed it.

Lionel appeared at the top of the stairs in a smart white shirt and chinos and the butler bowed so low his nose almost touched the floor.

Lionel swept a hand over his light blonde hair as he moved down the stairs at a slow and measured pace like we were now operating on his time and he had plenty to spare.

"I see you brought the Vampire girl," he commented in a way that said he wasn't pleased about that at all, yet the politeness never left his tone. It was something to do with his piercing eyes, the way they assessed Elise as if she was a creature unworthy of being in his home. It made my hackles rise and electricity danced along my skin, a fact he quickly noticed and assessed.

"Don't waste that lightning of yours, boy, you will need to provide plenty of it to me today to make up for your insolence of late." He reached the bottom of the stairs then snapped his fingers at the butler. "Fetch Juniper."

"That won't be necessary," I said sharply, walking closer with my hand firmly around Elise's. "I can't provide heirs for you, Lionel. The stars called Elise and I together and mated us." I stared him dead in the eye, giving him the truth which I prayed would be enough to make him back off on this Storm

Dragon babies ideas altogether. But if not, my inner pocket now contained our backup plan. *The lengths I will go to to stay away from this fucking bastardo.*

"I'm afraid his dick won't work for any other girl now," Elise said lightly, shrugging.

Lionel's jaw locked tight as he approached, grabbing hold of my jaw and staring right into my eyes where my silver rings were on show. Smoke plumed from his nostrils as he looked to Elise, his upper lip peeling back at the sight of her Elysian rings before he quickly composed himself. Unless he cared to check the Elysian mate register, he wouldn't know that she was mated to Leon too, and I didn't imagine he was interested in much outside of himself to bother.

"Well…how convenient," he said tersely. "I suppose congratulations are in order, Dante. How pleased you must be that your future children will be mutts."

I lunged at him, those words tearing at something deep inside me, but I hit a shield of air so solid it felt like colliding with a brick wall. "If anyone's a mutt, it's me, Lionel. Don't you forget I'm from a long line of Werewolves."

"How could I ever forget?" he said dryly, picking an invisible piece of lint from his sleeve like I was boring him. "Regardless, you will find a way to impregnate my niece, or I shall make your life terribly uncomfortable."

I realised the butler had left and that Lionel had cast a silencing bubble at some point anyway. He was no doubt used to being subtle when it came to being a complete controlling stronzo. I wondered what the rest of the kingdom would think if they knew this manipulative psycho was ruling them alongside his pals.

"I'll give you a specimen," I offered, raising my chin. "You can inseminate Juniper. But I'm not fucking her."

Lionel released a weary sigh. "*Fine.* Follow me." He turned and led us upstairs while Elise and I shared a relieved look.

My heart pounded with the excitement of tricking this bastardo. He was going to get heirs alright, but they sure as shit wouldn't be Storm Dragons.

Lionel led us to a bathroom the size of my entire bedroom back in Alestria, the taps gold, the bathtub big enough to swim in and a walk-in shower that was basically a whole room of its own. Everything was tiled with cream marble that had gold rivers running through the grain.

"Wait here. I will have Jenkins bring you a cup." Lionel scowled then headed out the door and I grinned at Elise, flicking up a silencing bubble.

"You owe Gabriel big time," she said teasingly, straightening out a crease on the dark blue shirt I wore.

"I'll give him a thank you blowjob later," I joked and she laughed.

"Maybe leave the blowjobs to me, you'd be no good at them, Drago."

"Don't challenge me, bella, my Alpha nature will urge me to prove you wrong and I really don't want to suck him off for the sake of winning."

"Hmm, I think I'd enjoy the show, so maybe I *should* goad you." She wiggled her eyebrows and I chuckled as I pulled her against me.

"You wouldn't dare, amore mio."

"Oh wouldn't I?" She tiptoed up to speak in my ear. "You couldn't give a good blowjob to save your life."

"Daddy, where are you?" a husky female voice called and the bathroom door swung open.

I looked around to find a pretty girl who was around our age standing there in lacey black underwear, her lipstick smudged. She had light brown hair and freckles across her nose, her eyes deep and dark. She might have called for her Daddy, but she was definitely not Lionel's daughter, so that only left one really fucked up option.

"Oh shit, sorry." She backed up in alarm. "By the stars, you didn't see me, okay?"

"Clara," Lionel barked as he appeared in the doorway, pulling her out of the room by her arm and giving her a stern look.

He threw us a glare as a growl left him then dragged her away down the hall. We both poked our heads out to gaze after them down the hall, finding Lionel pushing the girl into a room and talking to her in a low tone.

"You're not to wander around the house when I have guests," he hissed.

"Sorry, Daddy," she purred, reaching out to caress his chest and he let her hand linger there, lust filling his eyes. She could only have been a couple of years older than us and Lionel was at least in his forties, plus married with kids. *Fucking pervertito.*

"Stay in here, I'll be back soon. This won't take much longer," he said, his voice becoming low and hungry.

"Ew," Elise whispered in my ear and we quickly ducked back out of sight as Lionel turned to look our way.

Elise stifled a laugh against my shoulder and when Lionel's footsteps headed back towards the bathroom, we started making out to cover for the fact that we'd been spying on them. Not that it wasn't obvious anyway.

"You did not see Clara Orion in my house, understood?" Lionel snapped and we broke apart, giving him innocent ass looks which clearly didn't wash with him. "If you breathe a word to anyone, all arrangements we have are off and you will be moved to my corner of the kingdom where I can keep constant tabs on you."

"I got it," I snarled, my amusement dying just like that. "I won't tell anyone. I don't give a shit who you stick your dick in." I thrust out my hand and he slid his palm into it to make a star vow before doing the same with Elise.

Jenkins suddenly appeared with a golden cup, handing it over to me and Lionel nodded stiffly backing out of the room and gesturing for Elise to follow him.

"I can't come without her," I said instantly and he scowled.

"Yup, he's as flaccid as a wet fish without me," she said, smiling adoringly at me.

"I hardly think that's true," Lionel growled.

"Oh is it different with you and *your* Elysian Mate?" Elise asked him sweetly and he glared at her as she mocked him over not having one.

"Fine." Lionel shoved her into the bathroom with me. "I shall be out here and you will cast no silencing bubbles so I can ensure you don't come up with any foolish plans to pull the wool over my eyes," he said with a sneer twisting his lips.

"Enjoy the show then, my Lord," Elise said dramatically, batting her lashes as she swung the door shut in his face and locked it. I slid my blazer off, hanging it on the towel rack beside the sink and checking the Kipling cup was still secure.

Elise turned to me with mischief in her eyes, coming at me fast and starting to slide my shirt buttons free. My heart pounded at the wildness in her gaze and I grinned darkly as I caught on to her plan to make Lionel Acrux as uncomfortable as Faely possible.

"Give me that dirty talk I love so much, bella," I purred loudly and she swallowed a laugh.

"I need to be ravished by you, big boy. I need your Dragon dongle in my Pit hole right now."

It took everything I had not to laugh, but as she yanked my shirt wide and dragged her nails down my flesh, the hunger in me rose up like a beast and swallowed my amusement whole. I reached for her dress, but she danced away, standing up on the edge of the bathtub and taking hold of a shower hose attached to the golden taps.

"Make me as wet as a waterfall, Dragon beastie. I want to come all over your face!"

I stalked toward her as she lifted the shower hose above her head, flicking the water on with her foot so it rained down on her, turning her light pink dress transparent. She wasn't wearing a bra and electricity sparked over my flesh at the sight of her nipples hardening through the material. *Merda santa...*

"Oh Dante!" she gasped as she let the shower run all over her head and douse the floor too, so it washed over my feet. I kicked off my shoes, unbuckling my belt and whipping it through the air so it made a loud snapping noise.

"Oh!" she cried. "Whip me with your Dragon dick again!"

I bit the inside of my cheek on another laugh and whipped the belt across her thighs, making her gasp in real pleasure this time. The water kept running over me and little flashes of lightning burst through it, making her pant and moan as it shocked her. I moved before her, pushing up her dress and shimmying her panties down her thighs as I kept my gaze on hers, not giving a fuck that that stronzo was listening. If he was going to determinedly stand out there then we'd give him a show he wouldn't forget.

I slid my hand up between her thighs and felt the soaking heat of her waiting for me, a wolfish grin pulling at my mouth. I slid two fingers deep into her pussy, watching her expression as she tipped her head back on a sigh.

"Oh my stars," she gasped. "I don't even know how you can carry those shifted Dragon balls between your thighs in Fae form. Rub them on me, Dante. Rub them everywhere."

"Dalle stelle," I stifled my laugh as I pumped my fingers in and out of her, making her moan as she started to squeeze her own breasts. She was perfect. My little Vampira all wet and taunting the big, bad stronzo just for me.

I brought electricity to my fingertips within her and released controlled sparks of it that had her pussy clenching hard for me. She gasped and forgot to taunt Lionel as she rode my hand, a growl leaving me as my cock swelled and pressed firmly against the inside of my pants.

I leaned in to taste her, dragging my tongue over her clit and sucking as electricity poured from me, making her fist her hands in my hair and breathe heavily as she drew closer and closer to the edge I was going to launch her from.

One more flick of my tongue had her coming apart for me and I watched her fall to ruin in the most beautiful way as she clamped down on my fingers and rode the high I fed her. I drew out the pleasure in her body, sending lightning skittering through her flesh as she continued to moan my name.

Her eyes were hooded as I finally pulled my fingers free of her and sucked them clean, tasting my ragazza dolce on my flesh. But it wasn't enough. I needed more of her and as the water continued to wash over my feet, I grabbed her hips and threw her over my shoulder, slapping her ass hard and making her scream in delight.

"You've got the biggest Dragon dick I've ever seen," she gasped and I smirked, not hating that compliment at all.

Of course, she'd probably never seen another Dragon dick considering we were pretty rare, but I knew I had nothing to worry about in that department.

I knocked all of the toiletries off of the vanity unit, sending them flying across the room as I planted her ass down on the surface. A savage grin pulled at my lips as I hooked her leg over my shoulder and freed my aching cock, lining myself up with her pussy and driving myself into her with one fierce thrust.

"Ah!" she cried as my forehead pressed to hers and I slammed into her tight body with punishing force. I was gonna fuck my girl on every surface in this room and leave it in the biggest mess I could possibly make.

I pressed one hand to the mirror above her head, bracing myself as I pounded into her clenching pussy and groaned with the perfect feel of her.

"It's so big!" she cried then moaned loudly in a way that was one hundred percent genuine, making me smirk widely. "I can't take it!"

"You're going to take it here and then you're going to take it on your knees like the dirty girl you are," I said loudly, and her eyes lit up as she enjoyed my words.

"Treat me like your little Vampire whore, Drago," she begged. "Get me on my knees for you, big boy."

I carried her across the room, throwing her against the door and pounding her against it for a good few minutes, making the whole thing rattle while Elise screamed. I sucked her nipple through her dress, growling like a beast and just letting myself go fucking wild as I claimed my Elysian Mate in the most animal way I knew. Then I pulled out and pushed her down to her knees, her soaking lilac hair clinging to her cheeks as she took hold of my shaft and started pumping it in a locked fist.

I swallowed the rising lump in my throat, resting one hand on the door as I stared at this beautiful creature who had captured my heart in its entirety. She sucked the tip of my twitching dick between her lips and I groaned, my fist banging against the wood as she flicked her tongue over it and sent lightning daggering off my body and blasting holes in the tiles on the walls. She laughed headily as she took me deep into her mouth and the sound made my whole cock vibrate.

"Guardami, bella," I commanded in a rough voice and she seemed to understand as her eyes lifted to meet mine.

I thrust my hips as her hand slid down to squeeze and massage my balls, making me grunt and growl loudly as she took complete possession of my cock. There was no other girl in this life or the next who I would ever want like her. She owned every piece of my flesh and she knew exactly how to break me.

My air magic whipped around me and where I normally would have reigned it in when I was feeling this out of control, I let it run free, tearing around the room in a tornado and ripping everything to shreds in its path. The pane of glass in front of the huge shower exploded in a shower of jagged shards and I cast an air shield to keep us safe while Elise kept sucking my cock like it was her favourite flavoured thing in the world.

Thunder boomed beyond the window and rain thrashed against it wildly as I let my magic flow out of me and wreak havoc on Lionel's house. I could hear tiles being ripped from the roof, feel the walls trembling under my absolute power.

This. Was. Fantastico.

Pleasure collided with a rippling wave of ecstasy inside me and I cursed loudly as I came.

"In the cup," I managed to grit out loud enough for Lionel to hear, but Elise ignored that lie of a command as she swallowed down every drop of my cum and my head spun with satisfaction.

She slowly drew her lips off of my cock and I let the storm die beyond the room, but not before I pelted hailstones hard enough at the bathroom window to leave a huge, jagged crack down the middle of it.

Elise got to her feet, leaning in for a kiss as I rearrange my pants and laughed headily into her mouth.

"You're my fucking queen," I told her and she dropped her lips to my neck, sliding her fangs in to feed from me.

I clutched her to me by the small of her back as she groaned over the taste of me, using my air magic to dry her dress so her tits weren't on show, but I left the rest of us wet as a final fuck you to Lionel when we dripped water through his fancy halls. When Elise was finished feeding, I picked up my blazer from the towel rack and hooked out the pot of Middle Kipling's sperm, looking to the golden cup Lionel had provided.

"You do it," I mouthed to Elise as I held it out to her and she wrinkled her nose, shaking her head violently and pushing my hand back towards me.

"No way," she hissed.

I cursed under my breath then popped the lid off and poured it into the cup, quickly putting the lid back on the empty pot and pocketing it.

"Merda santa," I breathed as I realised there were a few cake crumbs floating in it, but what the fuck could I do about that now?

We headed to the door, unlocking it and swinging it wide where Lionel stood with his arms folded and his lips pursed. His eyes flipped from our soaking hair to the destroyed bathroom beyond us as I held out the little golden cup to him in offering.

"Was that performance really necessary?" he growled in irritation.

"I don't know what you mean, Papa D," I said innocently.

"We always have sex like that. I guess it's an Elysian Mate thing." Elise shrugged and Lionel's eyes narrowed but he said no more even though his anger at the wrecked bathroom was clear. I guessed he thought he'd gotten what he wanted though.

He beckoned Jenkins closer and had him take the specimen from my hand, Lionel's eyes not leaving mine as the butler walked away.

"You will learn not to mock me, Dante," he warned. "I am satisfied for now, but believe me when I say, you do not want to know me when I am displeased. Come, you will provide my lightning now." He turned and marched down the hall and we followed at a slower pace.

Relief swept through me because I'd once again evaded being tied fully to the Dragon Lord, and if Juniper got pregnant from that insemination, then I guessed I didn't have to worry about anything until her kid Emerged in their Order form, which for most Orders wouldn't be until they were teenagers. And that seemed like a lifetime away. Besides, so long as Gabriel had my back, we'd always be able to *see* a way around it. And I made a mental note to thank the stronzo for that.

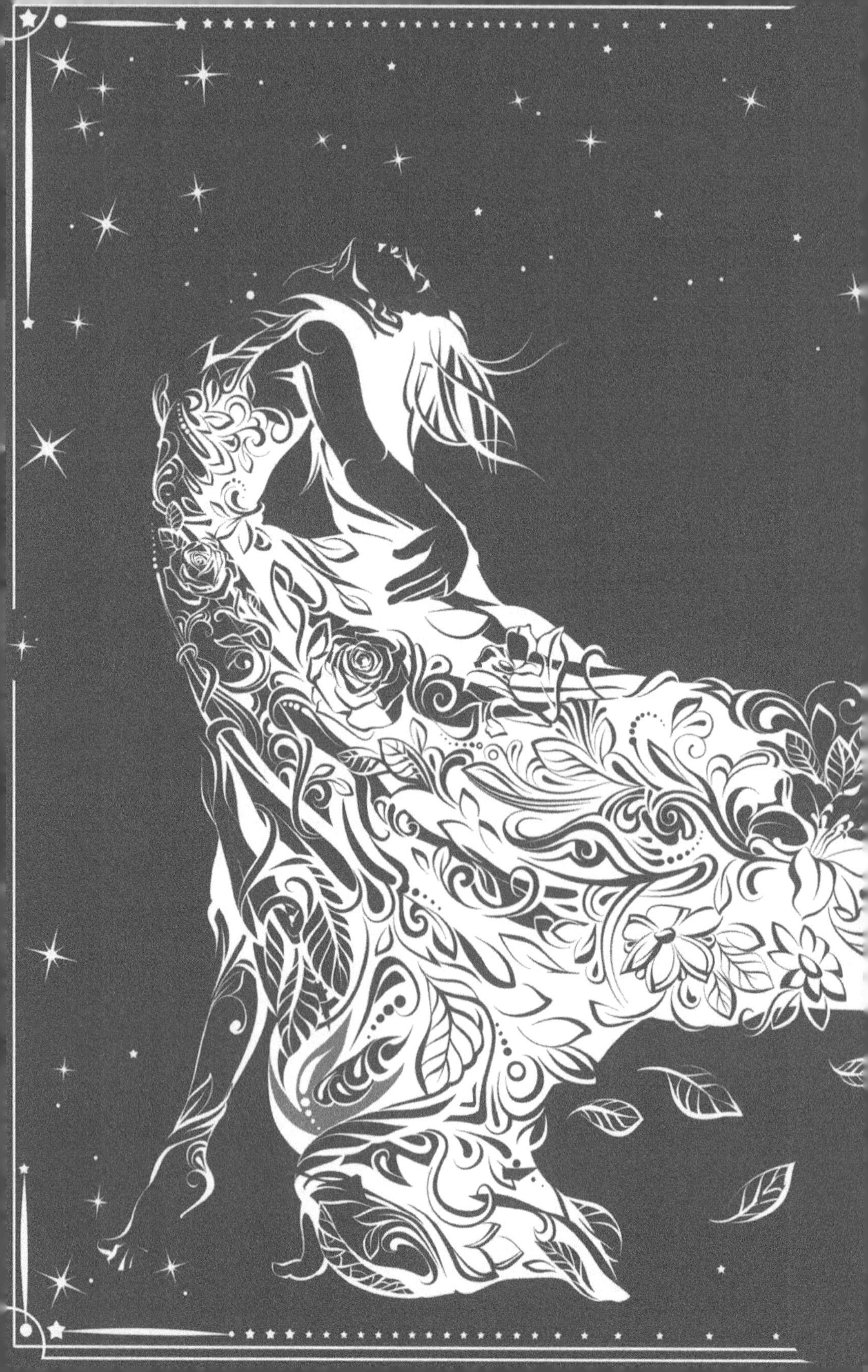

ELISE

CHAPTER TWENTY FIVE

I sat in the library with Laini and Eugene, working on our Astrology homework and feeling all kinds of overwhelmed. My workload was stacking up higher and higher by the day while I scrambled to do all of it plus the work I'd missed while I'd been held hostage by that fucker King.

I was also on edge all the damn time, fighting against the constant fear of someone trying to grab me again as well as losing sleep over it. And if I wasn't losing sleep over that then one of my guys usually made sure I lost it for a better reason. Or two of them, or three...

"What's the sex face for?" Laini asked, arching an eyebrow over her astrology chart and giving me the 'don't bullshit me' look.

I rolled my eyes and pointed at the book in front of me. "Neptune makes me dreamy." I replied.

"Oh no, if you wanna get freaky with a planet, you should give Jupiter a bit more of your attention - she's a real whore."

I laughed and Eugene joined in, though his ears turned red with embarrassment.

Gabriel glanced over at us from his oh-so-subtle babysitting position by the window where he was doing his own work and making sure no one turned up to kidnap me. I was caught between loving that my guys cared about me enough to want to babysit me and this clawing need for some alone time which I was pretty sure was just my inner rebellious brat throwing a tantrum and wanting to prove I could look after myself.

But I guessed they had good reason to want to protect me and I knew just as well as they did that I was no match for King if they tried to take me again. But then, neither were any of my boys. Not with all the stolen power King held. And yet here I sat, prime for the picking, practically begging for an abduction while nothing happened. What the hell was that about? It had been clear that King needed me for that twisted spell - or at least that they needed my blood, so why hadn't they come looking since my escape? Had they found someone easier to subdue to take my place?

But Gabriel was certain that an abduction wasn't planned for my near future and I had a life I wanted to live, so I was going with the whole denial thing coupled with a healthy dollop of caution.

I turned to Eugene, opening my mouth to beg him to help me out with this stupid chart, but before I could get the words past my lips, Gabriel got to his feet and strode over to me.

"We need to go," he said in a no arguments tone, his eyes glazed as he focused on something behind my head and a vision captured him.

"What is it?" I asked, reaching out tentatively and circling my fingers around his wrist, touching the tattoo which said *we fall together* and was so similar to my own.

Gabriel said nothing for several long seconds and Eugene sucked in a gasp.

"He's *seeing* the future, isn't he?" he squeaked. "Is it bad? Is it to do with me? Should we run? Or get ready to fight? Or do you guys wanna come hide out in my nest? Dante got some lovely soft new boxers the other day which really add to the cushioning and-"

"The Vampire we dropped to the hospital has finished his first round of rejuvenation treatments," Gabriel said, his gaze moving to meet mine. "He's been kept in a sedated state for the most part while they worked to bring him back to health and figure out what he knows, but he's not been well enough for a Cyclops interrogation because it's so intense and his mental state isn't great."

"Okay..." I said, unsure where he was going with this.

"But Basilisk interrogation isn't the same at all. Cyclopses force their way into a Fae's psyche a bit like a battering ram slamming down the door before ripping through the contents and stealing everything they want to know. But a Basilisk is much more subtle, they can slip inside, bypassing most mental barriers unless someone knows to actively anticipate their intrusion and they can navigate the mind in a much less invasive way. But seeing as they're a near extinct Order and the FIB don't currently have any in their employment to use for cases like this, no one has attempted to reach into the Vampire's mind that way."

"And the stars have told you that we should?" I asked, my pulse picking up in anticipation as I thought about that. "Do you think he knows who King is?"

"I'm not sure," Gabriel replied. "I don't know him, so I can't really *see* anything about him as such, only that you need to see him and hear what he has to say. And that it will change your fate to hear the truths he knows."

"Then let's go." I jumped up, using my speed to toss everything into my bag as I hurried to get ready to leave and Gabriel frowned, catching my arm to slow me down.

"Changing your fate might not be a good thing," he warned in a low tone. "All I know is that if we choose to go and see this guy, the path we're all on will change. Your path in particular. Drastically. But I'm not getting any real sense of whether that's a good thing or a bad thing or a seriously fucked up thing and I-"

"He might have the answers we need about King," I replied firmly, looking at him so that he could see I'd already made my mind up on this. "That's all I need to know to make this decision. We have to go and see him, and we have to go now. It can't wait. Gareth has already waited too damn long for me to figure this out."

Gabriel sighed and nodded. "I can *see* that you're on this path now whatever I say anyway, so we might as well get going."

I quickly gave Laini and Eugene goodbyes, promising to meet back up for more studying as soon as I could and begging them not to give me up for a lost cause as they waved me off. Eugene even took my half-completed star chart back from me as I went to stuff it in my bag and promised to take a look for me which I knew was code for 'help me fix all of my fuck ups on it' and I beamed at him.

I walked at Gabriel's side as we headed for the exit and the few inches of space we left between us made my palm itch. I wanted to tell the whole world he was mine. I didn't care if it went against everything Elysian Mates were supposed to do or the way I was expected to behave, I loved Gabriel and I hated having to pretend I didn't, like he was some dirty, little secret.

As we stepped outside, the heat of the sun washed down over me and I groaned as I tilted my head back, shrugging out of my cardigan and just enjoying that feeling on my skin. Was there anything better than soaking in the warmth of the sun after months of winter clouds and dark days? Leon was definitely on to something with all of his sunbathing crap.

"Ryder is just pulling into the parking lot," Gabriel said, taking his shirt off and making my mouth dry out as I drank in the sight of all of his tattoos.

"You got a new one," I said, pointing at the small throne on the side of his ribs. "What vision prompted that?"

"One I only get flashes of. I don't really understand anything from it, but I've seen countless blood spilled over that throne and as far as I can tell, there's no stopping that fate. When it comes, I think the entire kingdom ought to be afraid."

"You think it's *the* throne?" I asked, dropping my voice in surprise. No one had really sat on the Solarian throne since the Savage King and his family had been murdered by Nymphs all those years ago, though I guessed the Celestial Councillors had kept it warm. But seeing as the four families were equally matched in their power, none of them had the potential to rise up above the others and claim it for their own.

"I don't know. But if that shit comes to pass, I plan on being well away from it."

A shiver ran down my spine at the dark look in his eyes and he shook his head, reaching out to brush a hand over my arm in a comforting gesture. "Like I said; I can't *see* a whole lot about it, so don't let it worry you. It's definitely not in the near future anyway. So for now I say we focus on the problems at hand."

"Yeah," I agreed. "We've got plenty of those."

"Go on, if you shoot there, you'll meet Ryder as he pulls in and he can take you to the hospital on his bike. I'll race you from the sky."

I grinned at the challenge in his eyes then shot away at full speed, zipping through campus before he could even take off and skidding to a halt in the parking lot, right beside Ryder as he pulled up on his bike.

I leapt on before he could get off and he stiffened in surprise as I wrapped my arms around his waist before he realised who it was.

"What are you up to, baby?" Ryder asked, turning to look at me over his shoulder.

"Gabriel says we need to head downtown to the hospital where we dumped that Vampire King had been holding in the tunnels," I said. "He thinks you'll be able to sneak into his mind and get us some answers that will change my fate."

"Hold on tight then," he said, just like that. My Basilisk really was one of a kind. His trust in me and my word went without saying and I loved him for not even needing to question me before pulling away with a roar of the engine and making me squeal excitedly as we raced back out to the street.

Ryder rode like a man possessed, zigzagging between traffic and doubling the speed limit as we shot through town and I clung on tight. It was exhilarating, a breath of fresh air shot straight into my lungs and even though a more sensible Fae might have been afraid, I was confident in my ability to catch us with air magic if we crashed. Plus we'd be able to heal ourselves, so the fun seemed worth the risk.

When his bike roared up outside the hospital and he put a foot down to hold the bike upright, a couple of nurses screamed in surprise and darted back inside.

Ryder ignored them, turning on his seat so that he could wind an arm around my waist and tug me close for a kiss while my heart was still racing. It was risky for us to do that out in public like this, but with the nurses out of sight, there wasn't anyone else close by to see us and he was just too damn hard to resist.

Gabriel dove from the sky as Ryder's tongue pushed into my mouth and we broke apart to look at him.

"Do you really think we're gonna get some answers from that fuck up in there?" Ryder asked him as Gabriel let his wings shift out of existence and tugged his grey t-shirt back on.

"Don't call him a fuck up," I chastised, slapping Ryder's shoulder to tell him off. "If I'd been left thirsty like that for years, I'd be just as feral."

"Oh come on, Elise, you're feral even when you aren't thirsty," Gabriel teased.

"Yeah, you're a damn animal, baby," Ryder agreed as he climbed off of the bike and offered me a hand to tug me after him. "And when you *are* thirsty..." He let out a long, low whistle and I narrowed my eyes.

"Fucking terrifying," Gabriel agreed.

"Alright, alright, I get it, you two are little besties now so you think that means it's cool to rib on me. But don't think I couldn't get the two of you to turn on each other in a flash."

"Oh yeah? How would you do that?" Gabriel asked.

"By promising to suck the dick of whichever one of you won in a fight," I replied simply, and they cut each other a challenging look.

"*Or*," Ryder said thoughtfully. "We could just team up, overpower you and take what we want from that sweet body of yours anyway."

Gabriel grinned at him and I couldn't help but smile too. They really were little besties and it was too freaking cute. I swear I was going to get hearts in my eyes if they started joking about and teasing each other anymore.

"Fine," I sighed. "But if you start braiding each other's hair, I want in."

I turned and headed towards the entrance to the hospital and the two of them moved to walk at my sides as we strode towards the doors.

"I'll handle getting us in there," Gabriel said in a low tone just as we pushed inside.

The place was fairly quiet seeing as it was a long-term care facility and we'd turned up outside of visiting hours and the woman behind the front desk looked up at us with pursed lips and a hell no expression on her face.

"Visiting hours are between-" she began but Gabriel cut her off.

"Hi. We're not actually here to visit anyone," he said, smiling in the face of her cat's ass lips. "We have actually come in hope of getting a tour. Our brother Leon is in serious need of some help with his delusions and the doctor he's been seeing suggested this might be a good place for him to get some treatment. But he wasn't totally sure what the facilities were like here. Money isn't an object; we just want him to have a nice place to stay while he gets the care he needs."

"Is he violent with the delusions?" the woman asked, seeming more interested in us at the mention of money.

"Nah," Gabriel replied. "He just thinks he's able to become all kinds of Order forms, so he does a bunch of crazy crap-"

"Like that time he thought he was a Griffin and did a shit in that woman's purse," Ryder supplied and I almost choked on a laugh.

"Yeah, and he thought he was a Minotaur once and tried to head down to one of their maze runs but obviously he was too slow so he just got trampled," Gabriel added.

"And I'll never figure out where he got all of that glitter when he was convinced he was a Pegasus and kept sneezing it at people," Ryder said thoughtfully.

"O...kay." The woman got to her feet and ushered us after her. "I can give you a quick tour, but please be sure not to disturb any of our patients as they are easily upset by changes to their routines."

She bustled over to a security door and placed her palm against it so that it could get a read on her magical signature before striding off down a long corridor with us trailing right behind her.

She started waffling on about the various kinds of treatments they offered here and the therapy rooms they had and I looked around curiously, wondering what Gabriel's plan was from here.

As we moved into the residential section of the hospital and Gabriel continued to ask a bunch of questions about the place, he held a hand out in front of me and pointed at a closed door.

I looked up at him in surprise and he smirked at me as he used his magic to conjure an illusion behind the woman's back so that it looked like me and Ryder were still right there walking beside him and I gawped at the perfection of the cast.

Ryder was either less impressed or just more interested in finding out what was behind that door because he grabbed my hand and tugged me over to it, tossing a silencing bubble around us just before we slipped inside and Gabriel and the woman walked away.

The room was pretty plain, just the hospital bed in the centre of it, set up with a view out the window over a green landscape. The bottom half of the walls was painted a gross salmon colour and there was a general smell of pine disinfectant in the air.

"Who are you?" the man in the bed gasped, sitting upright, his eyes wild as he looked between the two of us, raking a hand through his messy blonde hair. He'd had it cut since being here though and his beard had been shaved clean too. He was probably in his late forties and handsome, though his complexion was gaunt and there was a hollowness to his cheeks which hadn't filled out yet, not to mention the darkness in his eyes. "Wait...you're the ones who pulled me from the dark place," he whispered.

"Err, yeah, I'm Elise and this is-"

"It was dark down there, dark, dark, dark in the dark place. Screams bounding off the walls and men in white suits come to pick my bones clean. Avast! You won't stop me now!" He tried to leap up, but a metallic click sounded as cuffs held him on the bed and he fell back down against the covers again, kicking and screaming and losing his damn shit.

I glanced back at the door nervously as Ryder stepped closer to him, though I knew that with the silencing bubble up, no one would hear the commotion.

As the Vampire's gaze fell on Ryder, his fangs snapped out and he lurched towards him, but before he could get close, his eyes glazed over and he slumped back against the pillows instead.

"Come here," Ryder bit out, glancing my way and extending a hand. "His mind is like water, I can't hold him for long without going deeper. If you want to see it too then it's now or never."

"I'm in," I agreed, stepping forward to take his hand and letting him drag me into the hypnosis too until we found ourselves standing in a room full of doors with a little boy with blonde hair hammering on them one after another in a frenzied state.

"That's him," Ryder explained to me. "And behind the locked doors are the other pieces of him."

"Why is it like this?" I breathed, glancing around the space and finding very little here with us.

"It's just a simple way for the brain to visualise it. But as far as I can tell, someone has been fucking with his head, making him forget things, lose his mind."

"King," I growled, because who else? "But let's hope that that was because he knew too much."

Ryder nodded before taking a large key from his pocket and stepping forward to put it in the lock of the door the kid was hammering against.

He turned it with a grunt of effort and I moved closer, laying a hand on his arm as he began to push at the heavy wooden door. I could tell that unlocking it was nowhere near as simple as the visual representation made it seem, but with a growl of determination, Ryder forced it wide and a blinding light washed over us from the other side of it.

The kid ran through it with an excited cry and I exchanged a glance with Ryder before we stepped inside behind him.

The brightness of the light faded and I was hit with a surge of love and emotion which I knew belonged to the Vampire as he unlocked memories of his past, his family. He had an older sister with long, blonde hair and parents who both loved him and pushed him in hopes of getting him to achieve greatness. He'd grown up surrounded by powerful people and had attended Zodiac Academy and his name was...Marlowe Altair.

"Holy shit," I breathed, watching as the child before me began to grow into a version of the man we'd just seen laying in the hospital bed. But this version of him was younger, probably in his twenties instead of his forties and his physique wasn't thin and wasted, it was strong and muscular. His hair was a lustrous blonde in a mess of curls which had been styled almost as carefully as his facial hair and he oozed power the way Fae born to it always did.

Altair was the name of one of the ruling families of Solaria. Melinda Altair - this dude's freaking sister - currently sat on the Celestial Council alongside Lionel Acrux. She was one of our rulers, one of the most powerful Fae in the whole star damned country.

"Are you sure we want to mix it with these people?" Ryder murmured as Marlowe looked around in awe, inspecting his hands and fine clothes and drinking in his memories which had been lost to him for so long.

"I think it's a bit late for that," I whispered back. "Besides, what are you gonna do, just lock the poor guy's memories away again?"

Ryder shrugged like the idea of that didn't sound so bad and I smacked his arm to tell him off.

"Don't be an asshole. His fate could have just as easily been mine if King had managed to keep hold of me. Or if you guys hadn't come to my rescue."

"Never," Ryder growled. "We would have torn the world apart to find you."

"I need more," Marlowe said suddenly, shooting towards us with a spurt of his speed and Ryder raised a hand, taking control of the vision and halting him in place. "Give me back the rest of it."

Ryder looked to me, letting me make the choice, but it didn't matter to me if this guy was wrapped up in a powerful family or any of that. He needed help and as far as Gabriel had said, only a Basilisk could provide that help. I didn't even know if there were any more of Ryder's kind out there and besides all of that, this man may well have knowledge locked away inside his head which would lead us to King and ending this whole mess.

"Do it," I commanded and Ryder bowed his head with a hint of mocking, but did as I said.

We headed back to the room filled with doors and Ryder moved to the next one, finding it even harder to unlock as he grunted from the exertion. I moved to take his free hand in mine, lending him my power.

I knew that Order gifts didn't really work in the same way as magical strength, but as the barriers between us fell away and our power merged, the door broke apart and Marlowe stepped through with an audible gasp.

Beyond this lock on his memories, there were later years of his life. He'd travelled after graduating and had done charity work all over Solaria. My heart pounded as I watched him moving to a street in Alestria not too far from where I'd grown up - though the apartment he purchased was pure luxury in comparison to my old home.

He started working in community centres set up to help with people who were victims of poverty and gang violence. I watched with my heart in my throat as he met with a man or...no, was it a woman? Their image was blurred and kept changing and as my pulse spiked, I just knew that this was King. But I didn't think they'd been hiding their identity from Marlowe when they first met, the block on this part of his memories felt more forced, like magic was the reason he couldn't put a face to the person from his past. Probably the dark kind.

"You did this to me," Marlowe gasped, images zipping past us so fast that it was hard to take them all in, but I grasped most of it.

Marlowe and this person had shared a lot of feelings about the ways the gangs were destroying Alestria and how they were the root of all the problems here. Marlowe had even gone out and tried to help fight back against them on several occasions - he was one of the most powerful Fae in the country so he was able to do so, but any time he defeated a gang member or even got them sent away to Darkmore Penitentiary, three more gangsters just took their place.

Marlowe and his friend came to the conclusion that gangs were like a plague and though they'd attempted to go after the leaders of the Oscura Clan and the Lunar Brotherhood separately, they'd been impossible to locate. And neither of them had been convinced that assassinating key members would work either. The problem with this city was that the gangs ruled it with an iron fist. There were just too many of them for Marlowe to take on even with his high level of power.

He'd gone to his sister, Melinda, and begged her to bring the Councillors and the Savage King to Alestria to deal with the problem. But she had just laughed at the suggestion, telling him that so long as the gangs didn't try to claim any more power than they had, that they were welcome to rule this forgotten part of the country. It was just the way of Fae – the powerful rose to the top.

Marlowe and his friend had been angry at that, discussing their outrage about the way the Councillors dismissed this city and its people, claiming that they didn't deserve to own their seats on the Celestial Council if they didn't believe in protecting all of their people equally.

They'd talked in great depth about the way that the country should be run and how someone more honest and deserving should be the one holding all of the power if the Councillors and the Savage King weren't willing to wield it wisely.

Time had passed after that and they'd gone back to their work, helping the people most in need, but then one day, Marlowe's friend had appeared with a book.

I sucked in a sharp breath as I recognised the Magicae Mortuorum, watching in horror and fascination as the person who was clearly King took a blade and cut their palm open so that they could offer the dark thing their blood in payment for reading from it.

We watched as they found the spell that King had been using on the full moon and Marlowe gave him some blood to use in it willingly, clearly on board with being the Vampire blood donor in those initial days.

But as time went on and King's power began to build while he took sacrifices from suicidal Fae, Marlowe started to question what they were doing. He'd met someone, a woman who he wanted a life with, and he didn't feel like the way to improve this city was by stealing the magic from hopeless Fae anymore.

But King was drunk on the power they'd already stolen and corrupted by the darkness of the Magicae Mortuorum. The more blood they offered it, the darker their intentions seemed to get, and their thirst for power grew until the purity of their initial motivation became twisted up with this desperate desire for power. Marlowe had watched it happen and tried to intervene, claiming King was more interested in becoming the most powerful Fae in Solaria than they were in saving the people of Alestria anymore. The two of them fought, getting into a magical battle that came damn close to seeing both of them dead before King managed to use their stolen power to win.

When it was over, Marlowe was dragged down into the tunnels beneath the academy and he'd been stuck down there ever since, slowly being driven mad by the thirst and the lack of magic in his veins. Used as a living blood bag for King whenever they needed more Vampire blood for their dark magic.

I was pretty overwhelmed by the info dump but just as I turned to Ryder, meaning to ask him a question, I caught sight of something that stole my breath right out of my lungs.

"Wait," I gasped. "What was that memory? Who was that woman?"

Marlowe looked at me with a frown, his thoughts slipping and flowing around us like water and seeming to be completely out of his control as he tried to figure out the way they were meant to fit inside his head.

"Woman?" he asked me.

"Yeah, the woman you were kissing, the one in the little apartment with the baby boy in a crib-"

The memories flashed to life all around me then and my heart began to race as I looked around at memory after memory of him and my mom. They'd met while she was working in The Sparkling Uranus and he'd become somewhat obsessed with her, paying for private dances night after night before finally plucking up the courage to ask her to be his. She'd been heart broken when they'd met after Gareth's father had left her for his Elysian Mate and she'd been left to raise a baby all alone, but then she'd slowly fallen in love with this man. A man who had the same golden hair as I had naturally. A man whose penetrating gaze was running all over me like he was noticing the same similarities I was.

"That woman is my mother," I breathed. "And my father disappeared before he ever even knew she was pregnant with me-"

A loud bang jolted my attention away from the images I'd been staring at and I screamed as I was wrenched from the hold of the hypnosis and fell back into my own mind with a hard smack, finding myself restrained by an angry looking FIB agent while a second man snapped a pair of magic restricting cuffs onto Ryder.

"Do you want to explain what you're doing in here harassing this patient?" the dude holding me barked and I gaped up at him, my mind whirling with everything I'd just learned and trying to get my head around the insane idea that had just presented itself to me. Was this Vampire seriously my dad?

"Keep quiet, Elise!" Gabriel called from out in the hall and I instantly sealed my lips, knowing better than to question him at a time like this. "We just have to go with them, and this will all resolve itself later!"

The officer who was holding onto me sneered as a doctor ran past us, trying to calm Marlowe down as he thrashed and yelled.

"Call my sister!" he bellowed. "Call Melinda Altair!"

But before I could see whether or not anyone was listening to what he had to say, I was towed out of the room between Ryder and Gabriel and we were whisked into an FIB car and driven away.

I sat alone in a cell in the FIB station, waiting for fuck knew what for fuck knew how long while they put me through 'processing' which seemed to mostly amount to just leaving me to sit here bored off my ass.

Eventually at half past who-even-fucking-knew, the door swung wide and a tall, blonde woman strode into the room with a click of killer heels and a long, white coat which was tailored so specifically that it perfectly outlined the curves of her figure.

A ball caught in my throat as I looked up at this woman who I'd seen on TV and in news reports countless times throughout my life.

Melinda Altair was stunningly beautiful as well as incredibly powerful and as she regarded me, I had to fight the urge to fidget in my seat - which was actually more of a bench with a waterproof mattress thingy on it.

"By the stars, it's true, isn't it?" she breathed, her navy blue eyes raking over me as she closed the door behind herself and stepped into the room. "Marlowe was raving and screaming by the time I got to see him, but the one thing he was adamant about was you."

"I..." I began, feeling at a total loss for words because I'd been sitting in this place for hours now and I still had no fucking clue what to make of the idea that that dude had to be my honest to shit sperm donor.

I mean, I hated my so-called father. It wasn't something that I even gave much thought to or made me feel sad or any shit like that, it was just a fact. The guy had left my mom, broken her heart for the second time so that she was never really quite right again after it and had left me to grow up without a dad. I'd never been particularly upset over it because I'd never known any different. But had I been bitter? Hell to the fucking yeah, I had. And now I was trying to grasp the concept that he'd never been a deadbeat at all. Had never *chosen* to leave. That my mom hadn't been delusional about him having been kidnapped or whatever the fuck she thought had happened to him and...yeah... head fuck.

"There's a simple way for us to be sure, if you don't mind me taking a drop of your blood?" Melinda asked, moving closer and lowering herself onto the bench beside me. How she managed to make it look like a throne was beyond me, but I knew I wasn't pulling that shit off.

"Err..." Wow, words had escaped me. Really great impression I was making. But I couldn't help but feel a little hesitant about someone taking my blood after being locked up at King's mercy for weeks while he drained me regularly.

"It's nothing, really. I can go first to show you." Melinda pulled a small bottle from her pocket and un-stoppered it, holding it up to the light so that I could see the clear concoction glimmering faintly in the light. "If we are blood relatives then it will turn white when our blood mixes within it. If not, it will turn black and no harm done. But I'm afraid I have to insist you do this. You can imagine that with a family such as mine, it isn't beyond the realms of possibility that someone might try to lie about such a thing and as Marlowe had no recollection of your mother being pregnant..." She trailed off, waiting patiently for me to produce a full sentence and I let out a slow breath.

"Yeah. I get it. I'm having trouble believing in it myself so, let's get a solid answer and then, well, then we can just see." I shrugged and she beamed, her fangs snapping out and making a prickle run down my spine as I fought the urge to shift further away from her.

I held my ground. But the Vampire in me was warning me that this right here was a fight I couldn't win. I just had to hope she didn't get any ideas about claiming my Sources from me because I was pretty sure I'd die if I had to fight her for them.

I watched as she pricked the tip of her finger on one fang and let a bead of blood drip into the potion before healing the small hurt away then I followed suit myself.

My gaze stayed fixed to the potion as the drop of my blood fell into it, the two red dots swirling around and around each other in a circle instead of dissolving into the rest of the liquid. Then the whole thing began to grow brighter and brighter until it shone with a white brilliance that almost made my eyes hurt to look upon it.

Melinda moved so quickly that I hardly even knew what was happening as I heard glass breaking and her arms wound around me tightly as she crushed me against her in an embrace that was punctuated by a soft sob.

"Oh, my sweet girl," she breathed into my hair as I belatedly returned her hug, feeling all kinds of weird but sort of warm inside as well. "You were lost, and we never even knew to look for you."

She held me like that for several long seconds before pulling back with a sniff and clasping my face between her hands so that she could look at me more closely.

"What's this?" she asked curiously, staring into my eyes and no doubt seeing the silver hiding within them.

"Oh, yeah I found my Elysian Mate," I explained, thinking of Leon and hoping he wasn't freaking out right about now. Did he and Dante even have any idea where we all were?

"I can see that," she replied. "But why is there a concealment spell clinging to you?"

"Wait," I gasped as I felt her magic brush against mine, but it was no good. She was too powerful and too well trained, and she demolished my work in less than a heartbeat, sucking in a sharp breath and clutching her chest as she stared at me mutely.

"There are three rings in your eyes," she murmured, half to herself, a frown forming between her brows as she tried to put the pieces together. I was surprised she could make out the three individual rings as no one other than me had realised they weren't just one solid block of silver yet. But I guessed that as she was a Vampire too, her eyesight was as sharp as mine.

"It's not what you think," I began, even though it absolutely was, and she released me as she sat back, her frown deepening like she didn't appreciate me lying to her. But what was I supposed to do? I couldn't risk the fall out that could come down on Dante and Ryder's heads if their gangs found out about us, especially while the peace between them was so tenuous.

Melinda reached into her inside pocket and held out another small vial of potion for me to take.

"Drink it," she commanded, her voice thick with Coercion so powerful that as her magic slammed against my mental barriers, it smashed them down and I found myself swallowing down the contents of the potion before I could even think to try and fight her off.

She released me from her hold on my mind as quickly as she'd taken control of me and I leapt upright, stumbling away from her as I clutched at my throat.

"What the hell was that?" I demanded. "Did you poison me?"

I always wore the necklace Ryder had given me with his antivenom in it in case anything like this ever happened to me. But the fucking FIB agent had taken all of my personal shit from me before locking me up in this damn room, so I was helpless against whatever she'd just forced me to drink.

"Calm down. It's nothing like that. It's simply an honesty potion. You must understand. I am the head of one of the four most powerful families in the entire kingdom. You are one of us now, which means you represent us. I need to know if that's going to cause me any grief or if you can be trusted to wear our name with pride."

"You want honesty?" I asked incredulously, thinking of the many lies I'd been telling ever since my brother's death and wondering if she would care about any of them or not.

"Yes. So tell me, Elise, why are there three silver rings in your eyes?" Melinda fixed me with an intrigued look and my tongue began to move without me giving it permission, telling her all she wanted to know and more. I was pretty sure this kind of magic was illegal, but who was I going to tell about it? She was one of the rulers of the fucking Kingdom for fuck's sake.

"I have three Elysian Mates. Everyone knows about my first - Leon. We registered our mating and everything. But the second and third only happened recently and we all decided to keep it a secret for now."

She gasped, her mouth agape for a long moment at that impossible news. "By the stars. *Three* mates? That's unheard of, how can it be?"

"Because they fit me in every way. I could never have had just one of them," I said simply, the truth pouring out of me which I'd known long before the stars had decided to mark us for it.

She stared at me in awe, her gaze roaming over my eyes in delight. "Why did you hide this?" she asked, looking like she couldn't understand that at all.

"Because two of my mates come from rival gangs. And because we knew this had never happened before and we were afraid of what it would mean for all of us if it came out-"

"That's nonsense. This is wonderful news! And no one cares about silly gang culture, Elise, really. You need to get out into the world. Away from this...place. Would you like to transfer to Zodiac Academy? I could have you in class there by Monday if-"

"No," I gasped. "I want to be here with my mates. I have no desire to change schools."

"Well, I suppose we can put a pin in that idea," she said with a shrug. "It must be a lot for you to take in all at once, finding out not only that your father is alive but also that you're a member of one of the most powerful families in the Kingdom. But you really mustn't be silly about this mate thing being kept a secret. This is a truly amazing thing that has happened to you. It is a sign of real power and the favour of the stars upon our great family! If anything, people would only think more favourably of the Altairs, knowing that one of us was the only Fae in history to claim multiple Elysian Mates. Think of the positive reaction we'd get from the polyamorous Orders - oh the more I think on it, the better it gets!"

Melinda hopped to her feet, clapping her hands together excitedly and beaming at me.

"I seriously don't want this secret coming out," I reiterated.

"Okay, okay," she replied dismissively. "We can talk about it when you and your mates come for dinner with the family next week - sorry it couldn't be sooner, but I had to cancel a meeting with the leader of - oh, actually that's confidential, but you get the gist. Just tell me this, what are your intentions towards me and my family?"

"Intentions?" I asked blankly. "I have no intentions – I just found out about you. I guess it might be nice to get to know you but that's about it."

"And you aren't after any kind of financial gain?" she asked.

"No," I replied with a frown, though I guessed I could understand why she needed to hear these answers.

"And you have no intention of betraying us, spying on us or hurting our family in any way?"

"What? No. Why the hell would I-"

Melinda swept me into another hug and beamed at me. "I just had to be certain. I'm so glad we found you, Elise, and I can't wait to know you better."

The pure honesty in her words knocked me for six and I was left speechless as she released me, wondering what all of this would mean for me long term. But I couldn't help but feel a little hopeful. She was my blood after all and here she was, claiming me as one of her own without asking me for anything in return as far as I could tell.

Melinda swept towards the door, knocking on it and stepping out as an FIB agent opened it for us. He handed me a bag with my personal effects inside it but before I got the chance to thank him, Melinda had already started walking away.

"I'm sorry we can't chat for longer, but the FIB have been informed of the great service you and your friends have done my family in finding my baby brother after all these years and no charges will be pressed. I have to get back for a Council meeting in ten minutes I'm afraid, but don't worry, I'll be telling them all about the long-lost Altair baby girl and we can figure out a press release once you've had a few days to get your head around everything."

She was talking a mile a minute and walking fast despite her heels and it was all I could do to just keep up with her as we headed through the precinct and made it out of the front doors where I spotted Ryder and Gabriel waiting for me.

"Wait, you're going already? But I need to talk to you about the Fae who was keeping your brother captive all this time. I think that they pose a real threat to the kingdom and they've been using dark magic to-"

"Oh, sweetie, don't worry yourself about that too much. I've got my top agents working with Marlowe now to bring back the rest of his memories and to help us track down the culprit. Besides, a bit of dark magic does not make a regular Fae a match for me and the other Councillors." She chuckled like I was amusing her then pulled a pouch of stardust from her pocket and swept forward to place a kiss on my cheek in farewell.

"*Wait,*" I said again, realising she was going to leave already, my head whirling with everything I hadn't said. "You swear you won't tell anyone about my mates, right?"

Melinda laughed, tossing her blonde hair and beaming at me. "You're an Altair now, Elise. Nothing can touch you. *Nothing.* Don't you worry your pretty head about a thing. I'll be in touch about lunch soon." She wiggled her fingers at me in a wave as she tossed the stardust over her head and before another protest could escape me, she was gone.

"Was that Melinda Altair?" Ryder asked me, his brows up like he hadn't expected her to show her face even if her brother had just been found and I was her secret niece.

"Err, yeah," I agreed, still coming to terms with it myself.

"What did she want?" Gabriel asked, frowning as he tried to force a vision, but clearly coming up short.

"Well," I said, stealing myself for the insanity that was about to pour from my lips. "Apparently, I really am an Altair. So maybe my fate really will be changing after all."

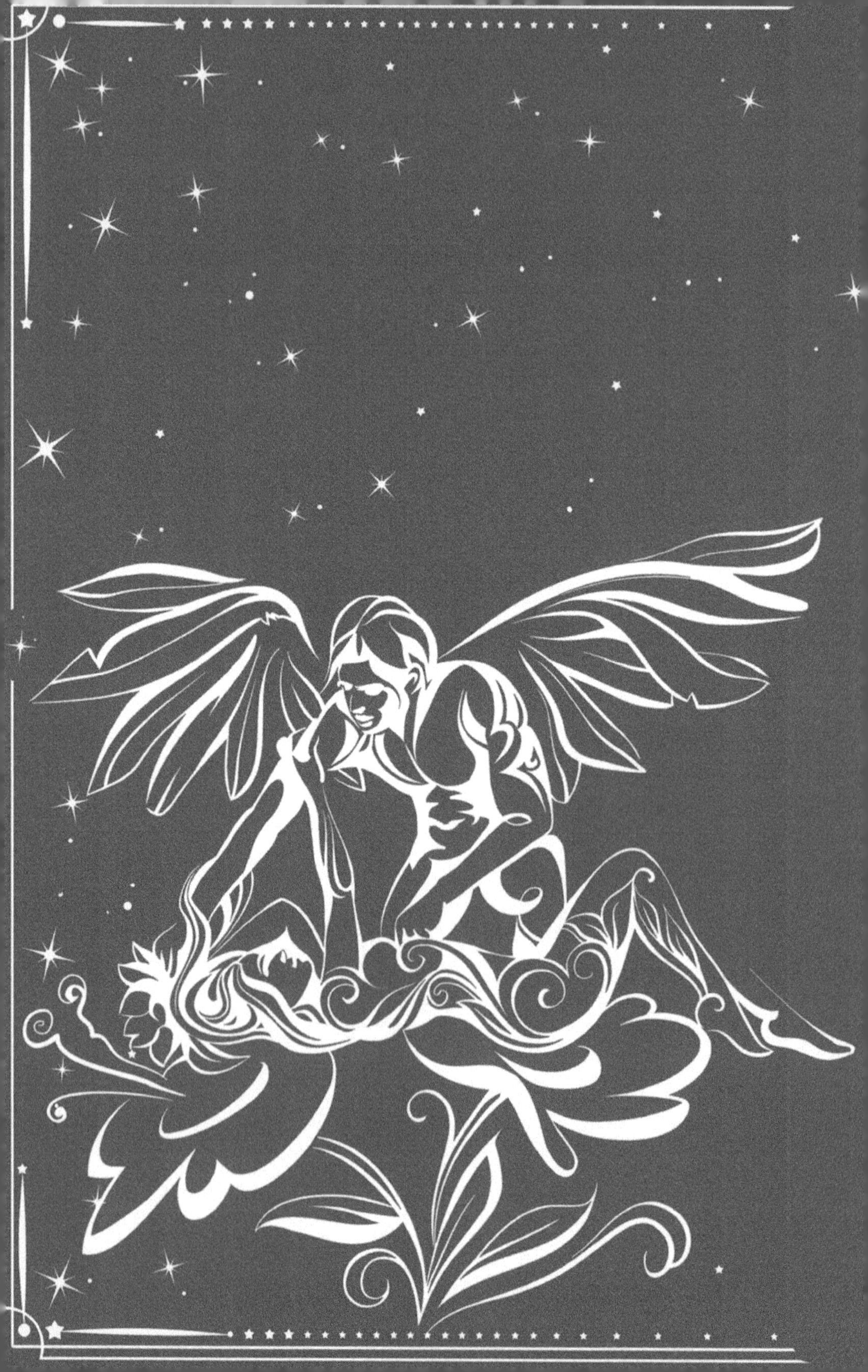

GABRIEL

CHAPTER TWENTY SIX

With two weeks off for Spring Break, I'd expected to spend the first morning of the holidays buried in my girl and making her scream for me. Unfortunately, Dante had whipped her away to spend some time among his family last night and Leon had stayed at my place, saying something about it being 'Dante's special week'. Whatever that meant. Ryder stayed too and though the apartment was a decent size for one or two Fae, I was starting to think we were going to have to sort out something larger long term if we were going to continue living together outside of school. I hadn't really questioned the strange arrangement we'd all fallen into it, it just felt natural. And whenever I called on The Sight to give me answers about our future together, the stars were vague. All I knew was that so long as we were together, we could make Elise happy and that was always my priority these days.

I got up before dawn to await the sunrise, switching on some TV in the lounge and thinking over the news that Elise was an Altair. The Sight hadn't let me in on that little secret and I was unnerved by how something as life altering as that could have slipped past my radar. I just had to have faith the stars wouldn't leave me high and dry if her life was ever on the line, or any of her mates' lives for that matter. I'd had no more flickers of visions lately around Ryder dying so I hoped I'd managed to steer him off that path. I'd been nudging him any and every way I could to try and keep that fate from materialising, and I prayed I'd done a good enough job. I didn't want to discuss it with the others in case I twisted fate once more and threw him more forcefully back onto that path somehow. For now at least, the stars were quiet on the matter.

I was surprised when Ryder and Leon appeared in the room, looking kind of lost as they joined me on the couch in their boxers.

We watched some Pegasus racing while Leon ate his way through everything in my kitchen - except the Mino Pops which Ryder hoarded like they were rare diamonds. If he thought we had no idea he got up in the middle of the night to munch on them, he was fucking deluded.

"I'm booooored," Leon groaned after the third race we'd watched and the sunlight was just beginning to peek through the gap in the blind. It was only ever worth watching the qualifiers of this sport, any Pegasus in Solaria was allowed to try out which meant it was a complete shit show. Their tails got set alight when they flew through the flaming rings, some of them got high in the rainbow fields then bashed into every other obstacle to the end of the race, while others flew into the invisible walls or ended up stuck on the sticky tunnels that ran through Sugar Mountain. Seeing a Pegasus do the whole course without error was exciting once then boring as shit after. I wanted carnage, dammit.

My Atlas buzzed on the arm of my chair and The Sight showed me a flash of the message before I picked it up and read it.

Bill:

Hey kid, wanna go for a walk with me?
I'm waiting on a call from an informant and have some time to kill.

I pushed out of my seat, surprised he was up this early. "I'm going out."

I strode from the room, showering, getting dressed in some jeans and tying a sweater around my waist before heading to my bedroom to use the window. I found Leon there dressed in jeans and a gold and black Skylarks t-shirt, his eyes as wide as Puss in Boots'. Ryder was beside him in dark clothes, leaning against the wall and glancing over at me with a decision in his eyes.

"Can we come too?" Leon asked hopefully. "I wanna meet Bill."

"How did you know I was going to meet-"

Leon took my Atlas from his pocket, apparently having swiped it from me and I scowled. "Bill will like me. I'm a great boyfriend-in-law."

"No," I said, shaking my head, but The Sight was niggling at my brain, showing me visions of Leon bounding around Bill and licking his face while my P.I. laughed. "No," I told the stars, heading to the window and snatching my Atlas from Leon's hand.

"I should talk to him about his search for the Lunar traitor," Ryder said casually, but as I looked over at him, I didn't buy that. He'd never asked to see him personally before now.

Leon side-stepped into view beside him, nodding keenly. "Yeah. *See*. Ryder needs to talk to Bill about official business. And I do too. You can't keep Bill from us, Gabe. Come on. We know he means a lot to you. You don't even mention your adopted parents, you just say Bill did this and Bill did that. Well I wanna see what Bill did, Gabe. Let me see."

I growled in frustration then shrugged like I didn't care. But maybe some part of me wanted Bill to meet them. I'd told him about our arrangement as I knew he wouldn't breathe a word to anyone, and all he'd said was that I should be careful so I didn't get my heart broken. He was too good of a guy. The only Fae who'd ever given a damn about me my whole life. The one person who I'd want them to meet if things really were forever between us all. I didn't know if that was the case, but I wanted to believe it was. I felt a sense of home among Elise and her men like I had never felt anywhere in my life. Admitting that however, was difficult for someone who'd spent their entire life shutting people out.

"Fine," I decided, stepping away from the window and grabbing a pouch of stardust out of the drawer by the bed.

"Yes!" Leon roared, gripping Ryder's shirt in his fist and tugging him away from the wall. "Did you hear that? He said we can go."

"I heard him just fine, Simba, I'm not deaf," Ryder growled, shoving his hand off of his black shirt.

They followed me out of the room to the front door and we slipped into the hall beyond the stardust boundary I'd cast to make the apartment more secure. Bill had sent me his location, but I hadn't even checked the message, seeing it in my mind's eye anyway. I threw the stardust over us and we were dragged away to New Moon Park where I'd taken countless walks with him in the past.

The rising sunlight glittered through the trees around us, making magic grow and multiply inside me as I soaked in its rays. There were a few morning joggers out, a couple of Centaur girls cantering along the path in their shifted forms chatting breathlessly as they fuelled their magic by running. A group of Sirens were swimming in the lake, their scales glittering on their skin whenever their heads broke above the surface. A scruffy looking Werewolf was passed out on a bench behind us, his tongue lolling out of his wide jaws which were missing teeth and his grey coat was matted and patchy. There was a sign propped up by the foot of the bench with words written across it in scrawling handwriting. *The Nymphs will take over the world. The end is nigh. Save the children!*

I'd never even seen a Nymph, they lived on the fringes of society and the FIB killed any when they were sighted. They were a weird ass species who stole the magic of Fae by using sharp, probed fingers to suck it out of our hearts and kill our kind in the process. But I imagined if one stumbled into

Alestria, it would rue the day it had made that decision.

I spotted Bill walking up the path out of a group of trees and my stomach knotted at the thought of introducing him to Leon and Ryder. I didn't know why that made me nervous, but it did. Maybe they wouldn't like each other. I called on The Sight for answers, but it gave me none, so I just raised a hand in greeting and he nodded as he strode toward us.

Leon flew past me, racing down the path and I cursed, my hands tightening to fists as I let this shit show play out. He collided with Bill, hugging him and knocking the cigarette from his hand while licking his fucking moustache.

"Leon!" I barked. "Down. *Now*."

He nuzzled into Bill's head, purring loudly as I jogged over and Bill tried to fight him off.

"Fucking street kids," Bill snapped, fire flaring in his palms.

"It's alright," I called. "He's with me."

Leon stepped back, purring loudly as I reached his side and Bill swiped a hand over his large moustache with a look that said he'd never been touched like that in his life.

I cleared my throat as Bill looked to me for an explanation and I pushed my fingers into my hair as I stalled for time. "Um, sorry to spring this on you, Bill. But this is Leon-"

"Gabe's boyfriend-in-law," Leon finished for me and I growled.

"That's not what he is," I muttered as Bill's eyes widened in realisation.

"Well fuck me sideways. Hello." Bill held out his hand and Leon shook it vigorously.

"Gabe talks about you a lot, like a *lot*," Leon said excitedly and my neck started to burn. "He looks really happy when he mentions you too, so I know how important you are to him, Dadsy."

"Dadsy?" Bill balked.

"Yeah, do you not like that? I call my own dad, Dad, so that doesn't work. And Father seems a bit formal. You look like a Dadsy, but we could go for Pa? Or Papa?" Leon offered.

"Bill is just fine," he said with a confused look, glancing at me for an explanation I didn't have. "Who's the statue?" He jerked his chin and I looked over my shoulder, finding Ryder still standing a hundred feet back where we'd left him. He'd cast a concealment spell to hide his face from the surrounding Fae, his hair appearing longer and darker.

I beckoned him over and he walked stiffly towards us, looking like he was half regretting this decision to come. I let him into my silencing bubble and he lowered the concealment spell so that the three of us could see him properly, but I imagined no one else could. Bill sucked in a breath of shock, which was saying something for him. I wasn't sure I'd ever seen him surprised in my life. I'd told him about my friendship with Ryder, but he'd always been sceptical about him being a true friend.

"Hello," Ryder grunted and Bill assessed him, slowly taking out a cigarette and lighting it up.

"Hi," Bill replied. "Your reputation precedes you, kid."

Ryder nodded. "Gabriel told me you're the best P.I. in Alestria."

"Did he now?" Bill smirked, looking to me and I shrugged.

"You are," I said simply.

"How many Lunar throats have you squeezed for information in your time?" Ryder asked and Bill took a slow drag on his cigarette.

"As many Lunars as I have Oscuras," Bill replied on a breath of smoke.

"Good answer." Ryder smirked and Leon looked between them, practically bursting with the excitement he was fighting to contain. "Any P.I. who can successfully conduct investigations right under both gang leaders' noses without his name ever reaching my ears has gotta be worth his salt."

"Well that's a fine compliment coming from the Devil's tongue," Bill said and my senses prickled with the tension passing between them for a moment. He held out a hand and Ryder gripped it, respect for each other shining in their eyes.

"Bill Fortune, Cyclops, fifty three years old, oh you live on Capricorn Street? My cousin Pawl lives right around the corner from there," Leon said, looking up from the I.D. he'd clearly stolen from Bill.

"By the stars, I didn't even feel you lift it," Bill gasped, patting his pocket as he realised his wallet was gone. "Where's my damn Atlas?"

Leon slipped it from his back pocket, spinning it between his fingers. "I've saved my number under Leon the Leo Lion if you ever need me. And if I call, the ringtone will be The Lion Sleeps Tonight by The Tokens. Oh and I added a little profile picture of me with that passed out hobo Wolf over there, isn't it great?" He turned the Atlas around to show us the photo and I literally had no idea when he'd slipped off to take it. He'd put his head inside the wide jaws of the Werewolf, his eyes on the camera as he grinned and put his thumb up.

Leon handed Bill's stuff back over and he stared at him in surprise as he puffed on his cigarette.

"I'm gonna need some lessons on pick pocketing like that, kid," Bill said and Leon beamed.

"Of course, Dadsy."

"Don't do that," Bill grunted.

"Pa?" Leon questioned and I punched him in the arm.

"Bill," I growled. "I don't even call him Pa." The words slipped out before I could stop them and Bill gave me a glowy eyed look that brought heat to my cheeks. I cleared my throat and looked away. "Are we walking, or what?"

I turned and led the way down the path and the others moved beside me, the two of them flanking Bill. Leon asked him endless questions which he happily answered, glancing at me occasionally and giving me a bemused look. Ryder chipped in from time to time, clearly interested in Bill too and he had plenty of questions for them in return. I didn't say much, just quietly enjoying them bonding with the most important guy to me in the world. It made me wish Elise was here more than anything.

After a while, Bill's Atlas buzzed and he excused himself to go and speak with his informant while Ryder, Leon and I all sat on the lake's edge and watched the Sirens playing in the water.

"Bill's great," Leon said with a wide smile.

"Yeah." I picked a blade of grass by my leg. "He is."

"Gabriel!" Bill barked from behind me and I twisted around just as flashes of The Sight accosted me.

Ryder was being dragged through a crowd, all of them jeering and booing. He was being beaten and cut, his face bloody as they started slicing pieces off of him. I felt myself shouting in terror and as The Sight spat me back into the real world, that same sound left me now.

"No!" I roared, seeking out Ryder and gripping his arm to reassure myself he was there and he was alright.

He looked at me in confusion and I shook my head in apology, getting up and backing away.

Bill took hold of my arm, pulling me away onto the path, his eyes filled with darkness. "I've got a name," he growled. "Is this the right time to tell him?"

My head spun as I panted, fear still clutching my heart from that vision. I'd *seen* it before, but this time it seemed more certain, more impossible to change. And that terrified me more than anything.

"Tell who what?" I asked, trying to focus, but I kept seeing flashes of Ryder in a pool of blood, his roars of pain echoing through my head then his head being cut from his shoulders and his death tainting the air.

Bill shook me and I blinked hard to try and concentrate.

"Kid, I've got the name of the Lunar traitor," he hissed and my mind finally sharpened on those words. He held out his Atlas, showing me a video that played through the eyes of a Fae and I realised I was watching a recorded memory. Scarlett Tide stormed through a door with a letter clutched in her hand. She looked younger, her dark hair longer and a keen kind of pain in her eyes. "The Oscuras want peace? Where was my brother's peace when they cut pieces off of him and left him for the crows to finish?" she spat, crushing the letter in her hand and tossing it into the fireplace. She turned to whoever I was seeing this vision through and held out her hand.

"You saw nothing. Make a star vow with me or I'll gain your silence with your death," she hissed and a male hand reached out, gripping hers.

The vision ended and my throat thickened.

"Do you want me to tell Ryder or do you wanna tell him yourself?" Bill asked with a frown.

I glanced over my shoulder at Ryder as Leon told some story with dramatic arm movements and Ryder watched him with a slight smile playing around his mouth.

"I'll tell him," I said breathlessly.

Ryder had told me about his suspicions over Scarlett, but the confirmation was like a gong ringing in my head. I knew it would change everything. The depths of this betrayal would shake the foundations of the entire Brotherhood. She had withheld the letter from Ryder that should have ensured peace between the gangs years ago, so who knew what she would do now to thwart the deal again.

I walked over to Ryder, crouching down and resting a hand on his shoulder. He turned to look at me and I was sure he could see the seriousness in my expression before I even spoke the words.

"It's Scarlett," I said, handing over Bill's Atlas to show him the video.

His eyes became hard, steely and murderous as he watched the evidence play out before him. Then he stood up as Leon took it from his hands, his own features falling into something dark and forbidding as he watched.

"I'm going to The Rusty Nail," Ryder hissed.

"We're going with you," I said immediately, The Sight urging me to do so, but I didn't even need its encouragement. I wasn't going to let him face this alone.

He thought on that for a moment before nodding and in those few seconds, I saw Ryder dying in a hundred ways before my eyes. I rubbed my eyelids with a growl, seeking out the ways to avoid each and every death that lay before him today. I wouldn't leave his side for a second. I'd be his guardian, his protector. There was no way in Solaria I'd let the Lunar King meet his end under my watch.

I took the stardust from my pocket and turned to Bill. "I'll message you soon."

"If you think I'm gonna let you walk into a fight in Lunar territory alone, you've lost your damn mind, kid." He rolled up his sleeves like he meant business and strode over to stand at my side.

"Dadsy's gonna give her what for," Leon breathed excitedly and I stamped on his foot.

"He's not your Dadsy."

"If you're up for it, old man, I could use your Cyclops powers to extract all of her memories and make copies of them like that video. I need the whole Brotherhood to see the evidence so there's no denying it," Ryder said and Bill nodded, darkness swirling in his eyes. He'd always had a flare of psycho in him, but I'd never actually seen him interrogating marks for his investigations. His informants always seemed scared shitless of him though, and I guessed I was about to find out why.

I threw the stardust over us and we were transported across Alestria, planted on the street where The Rusty Nail sat in the shadows, the morning sunlight blocked by a towering building on the next road over.

"Read all about it!" a newspaper delivery boy called as he strolled along the sidewalk, shoving the rolled papers into people's mailboxes. A vision burst through my head and I cursed, hearing the news before it poured from the guy's lips, my chest tightening with concern. "The Lunar King has been bonded by the stars in an Elysian Mate foursome including the Oscura Dragon King!"

"No," I snarled, my head filled with too many flashes of the future, all of it jumbling together. I should have *seen* this coming. Why didn't the stars warn me? It must have been leaked by someone I wasn't keeping tabs on, but who could that possibly be?

Ryder strode over to the newspaper kid as Bill gave me an intense look and Leon carved his fingers through his long hair anxiously. Ryder snatched a paper from the boy's grip, striding back over to us as he stared at the front page in horror. I moved beside him as he re-joined our group and Leon pressed right up against his other side so he could look too.

There was a photo of Elise standing between Dante and Leon, all of them smiling widely at the camera with the silver rings in their eyes gleaming. Beside them, Ryder had his arm around Dante, smiling wider than I'd ever seen him smile.

"That isn't me," Ryder spat in disgust.

"This photo's from my FaeBook profile, but you're not in it and Dante's eyes definitely don't have silver rings in them," Leon growled as my heart warred in my chest.

"They've used some fucking photo manipulation to add me into it and make me *smile*," Ryder snarled, his fingers tearing into the paper and ripping his fake face right out of it.

I grabbed it from him before he could tear it to shreds, reading some of the article under my breath. "The Lunar King has broken the code of his people after the stars mated him to Elise Callisto alongside Storm Dragon, Dante Oscura, and Nemean Lion, Leon Night. High Lord Melinda Altair confirmed this incredible revelation late last night with this telling photograph which is set to shock the nation. Not only that, but Elise Callisto has been announced as the long-lost niece of Melinda and daughter of her missing brother Marlowe Altair who has reappeared after twenty years lost in the jungle. Melinda is overjoyed that Elise has become the centre of the first ever recorded polyamorous Elysian Mate bond, but the news in Alestria is expected to cause uproar among the Lunar Brotherhood and the Oscura Clan just weeks after a fragile peace treaty was formed. No doubt the members of the gangs will now all be asking themselves, was this peace intended for the greater good or just a way of manipulating their people into accepting this new bond between them?"

"Fuck," Leon croaked, snatching the paper from my hand to read it himself.

I looked at Bill as he lit up a cigarette, his eyes saying we were fucked. Visions flashed through my head of Ryder walking into The Rusty Nail, all of them ending in his death, but as I turned to tell him we needed to leave, I found him burying the newspaper boy's papers in the ground and barking at him to go and fetch every single one from the mailboxes he'd delivered them to.

The boy trembled beneath him, stumbling over his own feet as he hurried to comply and I jogged over to Ryder, turning him around to face me.

"We have to go," I hissed. "If you walk into that bar, there's a hundred ways you could die."

He sneered. "You think I'm going to run from my own gang like a coward?" he growled, trying to get past me but I blocked his way.

"I think you're going to get yourself killed if you act like the big man right now," I hissed, my chest hitting his.

"I'm not afraid to face my own death, Big Bird," he snarled. "Do you *see* a fate where I walk out of there as their king?"

I looked for it and though there were countless deaths on this path, there were a couple which led to him living another day. I was about to lie and say there was none in an effort to protect him, but he saw the truth in my eyes before I could form the words.

"I'm going in. The rest of you fuck off home," he demanded, striding across the street towards The Rusty Nail.

"Ryder!" Leon called after him in a panic.

"Kid's got a death wish," Bill muttered, looking to me. "What's the plan Gabriel?"

"The plan is not to die. Stay close to me," I said firmly, leading the way after Ryder and Leon and Bill kept to my back without a word of complaint.

I didn't like walking either of them into this place, but I could *see* ways to protect them and according to the stars, without them, Ryder was fucked.

Ryder yanked the front door open and an ice blade slammed into his chest. He cursed, throwing out his hands to fight, but more and more shards blasted at him, ripping down the middle of him and as fast as I ran, I couldn't get to him in time. He hit the pavement, his eyes already lifeless as Leon's yells of terror rang in my ears.

I blinked out of the vision, diving at Ryder and yanking him away from the entrance.

"Take the back door," I demanded and he looked at me with a frown before nodding stiffly and heading that way.

I kept close to his side, The Sight on hyperdrive as I foresaw so much death that it made me ill. I needed to keep him alive at any cost. I couldn't let my concentration waver for even a second. One wrong move and his fate was sealed in blood.

We walked down the dark alley and Ryder pulled the side door open, stepping inside and I followed, keeping to his back as he walked up to the door that led into the bar. He pushed through it and jeers rang out as he was spotted.

"Traitor!" someone yelled as Ryder rounded the bar and flames burst towards him. He threw up a wall of dirt to block them, but the fire curled around him swallowing him up and burning into his flesh until he roared in pain. Leon blasted the man responsible with his own fire magic and I tried to douse the ones surrounding Ryder in water, but it was too late as his body charred and he fell to the ground in a broken heap at my feet.

"No!" I bellowed, reaching for him as he twitched and died before me, making pain wash through me in a wave.

I blinked out of the vision and tugged Ryder back a step. "To the left of the bar," I muttered in his ear and he nodded stiffly, stepping to the left where two unFae assholes dove at him, fighting him with blades of ice and metal. Ryder fought back, snapping one of their necks, but the other one slit Ryder's throat, making me yell in fear. He choked on his own blood, sinking to his knees as he fought to heal the gaping wound while Leon dove on his attacker with a roar of rage.

"Go left, should he Gabriel!?" Leon tossed at me as Ryder hit the ground in a pool of blood and death.

I blinked out of the vision with a curse, grabbing Ryder's arm and steering him behind the bar, placing myself half a step in front of him as a shield.

"You're not my bodyguard, Big Bird," Ryder grunted, nudging me aside as a barmaid stared at Ryder with wide eyes, the heckling in the bar growing to a loud din.

Bill toked on his cigarette as he took in the scene, seemingly unphased by the throng of angry Lunars. He'd always had a steely heart, but this was a surprise even to me.

"You sure you wanna be here, Bill?" I murmured.

"I trust your visions, kid. I won't die," he said with a shrug and I groaned at the weight of that responsibility.

"Gabe's like our layer of cotton wool, aren't you Gabe?" Leon said.

"Don't call me Gabe," I grumbled.

"Scarlett Tide!" Ryder bellowed to the room and quiet fell. "I accuse of you betraying the Lunar Brotherhood, of thwarting a peace deal set in place by Dante Oscura and my father years ago!"

"Fuck you and your peace deal!" an ugly motherfucker shouted from the crowd and they all broke into shouts again.

Ethan Shadowbrook suddenly pushed through the room and climbed up onto the bar, his pack clustering close by his feet.

"Scarlett, come and answer to your king!" he roared.

Scarlett appeared at the back of the bar, standing on a table with her face fixed in a sneer as she glared at Ryder. "You've gone too far, Ryder. You've bonded with an Oscura. The only traitor in this room is you!"

A cry of ascent went up from around half the Lunars and I tried to weigh our odds as The Sight kept feeding me visions of blood and terror. I had to keep a clear head. I had to protect Ryder, Leon and Bill. That was the only thing I could focus on.

Ryder pushed past me, climbing up onto the bar himself and pointing at Scarlett. "You lied to me when I escaped from Mariella Oscura. You told me the Lunars marched with my father and watched the Oscuras murder him, but that wasn't what happened!"

"Your father died to save us, and this is how you repay him?" Scarlett said coldly, holding a hand to her heart in feigned shock, but it looked like a lot of people were buying it.

"I'll cut out your tongue for daring to wield it against me, to feed lies into my head. You took the letter sent to me from Dante Oscura after my father's death and I have proof!" He held out his hand to Bill who passed his Atlas over.

"Are you really going to believe this bullshit?" Scarlett scoffed as furious eyes turned on Ryder.

Ryder cast a projecting spell as he played the video and it was cast onto the entire ceiling for everyone to see.

Ethan Shadowbrook and his pack howled angrily as they watched, but there was still doubt in too many eyes.

"That doesn't prove anything," Scarlett said lightly.

Ryder tossed Bill his Atlas when it had finished playing, pointing at Scarlett. "I challenge you to a fight, Fae on Fae."

A metal pinging noise sounded as someone threw a fire magic grenade and I lunged for it half a second before it went off at Ryder's feet. I wasn't quick enough and he exploded with the blast, blood splattering everywhere as my hand was ripped to shreds too and any Fae in the blast zone around us lay screaming and wounded. Pain and terror rained down on me as I cried Ryder's name, tasting his blood on my lips.

I blinked out of the vision and cursed, diving up onto the bar, creating a wooden baseball bat in my grip from my earth magic as the grenade came flying toward us. I hit it with one good whack and it sailed back towards the man who'd thrown it. He screamed and his little friends scattered before it smacked him in the back of the head and he was blasted to pieces.

"Holy shit," Ryder breathed as chaos descended in the bar, blood covering anyone who'd been near enough to the blast as I propped the bat over my shoulder with a smug smile.

"I've got your back. Just stop moving before I tell you to," I hissed.

The screams died down and Ryder pointed at Scarlett once more. "Answer my challenge. I will strip your title from you in blood before all of my people."

"We're not your people!" a woman spat in the crowd below us, throwing out a palm and sending a huge blast of air magic at us. Ryder was thrown backwards off of the bar and slammed into the wall, impaled on a pair of razor sharp Elsian ram horns which hung above the bar, his head hanging forward as he died.

"Noooo!" Leon screamed, his grief scoring down the middle of me as I felt it too.

I blinked out of the vision, casting a blade in my hand in place of the baseball bat as the woman opened her lips to shout at Ryder, wrapping her in vines and tying her to a chair with a gag in her mouth. *For the star's sake, will everyone stop being such a murderous dick for five seconds?*

"I won't fight you Fae on Fae," Scarlett called to Ryder. "Because your fate is already written. Get hold of him!" she cried to the Fae surrounding her and they surged forward, making my heart stammer.

Ethan's pack and a bunch of Lunars still allied to Ryder closed ranks to hold them back, colliding with them with battle cries.

A brutal fight broke out which made my heart pound and Leon climbed up to stand beside Ryder, his hands raised as flames coiled around them. Bill hauled himself up to stand beside me and a vision of his powers rang through my mind. I could get us out of here using him. But as I turned to face Ryder, vines wrapped around him from several earth Elementals and he was yanked forward off of the bar. He battled the vines as Leon burned the Fae who held him down, his teeth bared and fury in his eyes. I severed as many vines as I could while Ryder tried to fight one hand free, but before he could, a water Elemental gripped his head and froze it solid, silencing Ryder's shouts of rage forever as he ripped his head right off of his neck.

Terror filled me as I watched the horror show, helpless to it as I fought to destroy as many of the assholes who'd killed my friend as I could.

I blinked out of the vision with a curse, throwing a series of carefully aimed rocks at the heads of the earth Elementals who had been going to pull Ryder from the bar and knocking them out cold before gripping Bill's arm. "Use your Cyclops' screech on every enemy Lunar in this room."

"That's a big ask, kid," he said, but his jaw grit in determination of pulling it off. "I'm gonna need a minute."

"Alright," I said, turning to my friends just as Leon dove off of the bar to engage another fire Elemental, his flames burning his opponent and making him scream.

Ryder blocked every attack sent his way with a shield of wood on his arm whilst throwing axes back at them with shouts of fury, casting them again and again in his palm. He split a man's skull in half like a fucking watermelon and the woman beside him wailed in grief, throwing a torrent of water from her body in a huge tsunami. We were all washed backwards over the bar and I pushed the water away with my own magic as it twisted around us in a whirlpool. Ryder went under and I dove down to get him, but the woman's magic had gripped his body and blood was pouring from his eyes, nose and mouth, every drop of it rushing out into the water around him as he died and colouring my whole world red.

I blinked out of the vision as the man died beside his furious wife and I threw out a palm, casting her hands in blocks of ice, before wrapping a vine around her throat and snapping her neck. It was fucking brutal, but it was the only way to save Ryder and there wasn't a thing I wouldn't do to keep him alive today.

Ethan charged through the crowd beneath us with a howl of excitement, casting ice blades in his grip to stab any enemy Lunars that tried to take him down. But it was fast becoming clear that Scarlett had the majority on her side and Ryder's allies were started to get overwhelmed.

Magic rang everywhere in the room, huge holes carved through the walls and a groaning noise above said the roof was in danger of falling.

"Bill!" I shouted at him where he was taking shelter behind the bar, his fingers on his temples as he focused on the immense power he needed to conjure for the task.

"Couple more seconds," he rasped out.

A huge wooden beam was struck by a rogue fireball and it snapped above us, tumbling towards Ryder and crushing him dead before I could even get my hand up to stop it.

I blinked out of the vision, catching his arm and tugging him toward me a split second before the beam smashed down onto the bar.

"Cover your ears!" Bill roared and I pulled Leon out of the crowd below, slapping his hands over his ears before I covered my own.

Ryder did the same, whistling to Ethan and he quickly got the word out to his pack as they covered their ears and Bill's power exploded out of him. We were thrown from the bar, the screeching noise cast by the power of his mind filling the whole room. The enemy Lunars were screaming and though it hurt like a bitch, I knew it was nothing in comparison to what they were feeling.

Bill ran to us, shouting something I couldn't hear before he tugged the stardust out of my pocket in a clear demand. Ryder directed Ethan and his pack out of the bar and they nodded, pouring outside into the morning light and dragging any of their allies with them.

Leon climbed onto the bar, snatching the stardust from Bill and throwing it over us. We were ripped away from the carnage and relief filled me as we finally left the danger behind and the stars seemed to whisper my praises in my ears.

We hit the ground, so disorientated by the Cyclops screech that we all landed in a heap of limbs and my head hit a solid chest. Ryder grunted beneath me, scruffing my hair.

"I have a feeling I'm still alive because of you," he said in a low tone.

"No shit, Sherlock. Don't ever dive into a bar full of enemies again," I growled, trying to push myself up but finding the weight of a huge Lion Shifter holding me down. Bill was sprawled on the ground a foot away face down, his head lifting as he tugged his box of cigarettes from his pocket and pushed one between his lips.

Leon reached over, offering him a flame on his fingertip and Bill nodded to him in thanks.

Leon rolled off of me and I got up, pulling Ryder after me and finding us standing before a large fence that parted us from across a sprawling vineyard.

"Where are we?" Ryder grunted.

"Ummm, nowhere," Leon said lightly just as I got a flash of the truth from the stars and I chuckled darkly.

"What a choice, Leon," I muttered.

"It'll be *fine*," Leon said, waving a hand.

"Where. Are. We?" Ryder demanded, looking to me for an explanation and I hesitated before answering, *seeing* the punch I was going to get for my answer.

"Well, I think I've had enough fun for one day. I'm gonna go celebrate with Brandy and Cherry," Bill said, brushing down his knees as he got up. "Any chance I can borrow some more of that fancy stardust to get myself home, kid?"

I walked over to him and wrapped him in a tight hug, clapping his back. "You saved our asses, Bill."

Leon's arms suddenly wrapped around us too. "You really did, Dadsy."

"Stop that," I muttered, but didn't shove him off because it looked like Bill kinda liked the attention.

"I didn't do nothin'," he said dismissively, but a smile played around the corners of his mouth as we released him. I passed over the last of the stardust and he smirked as he took it. "Stay outa trouble, kid."

"You know I can't promise that," I replied and he chuckled as he threw the stardust and vanished before my eyes.

I turned to find Ryder who scowled intensely. "Where are we, Gabriel?"

I sighed. "The Oscura stronghold," I said with a slightly concerned look, though I was far enough away now that I'd avoided my fated punch from him.

Ryder nodded stiffly then turned around and started striding off up the road, apparently planning to walk anywhere else in favour of staying here.

"Are you gonna get him, or am I?" Leon murmured.

"I'll do it. He'll only punch you in the face right now," I said and he snorted.

I jogged off after Ryder, seeking out advice from the heavens on the best way to handle this. The stars were telling me we needed to stay at Dante's house whether he liked it or not, because it was the only place in the city that Ryder was safe right now. So somehow, I was going to have to convince Ryder to stay in the home of the people he'd once sworn to destroy.

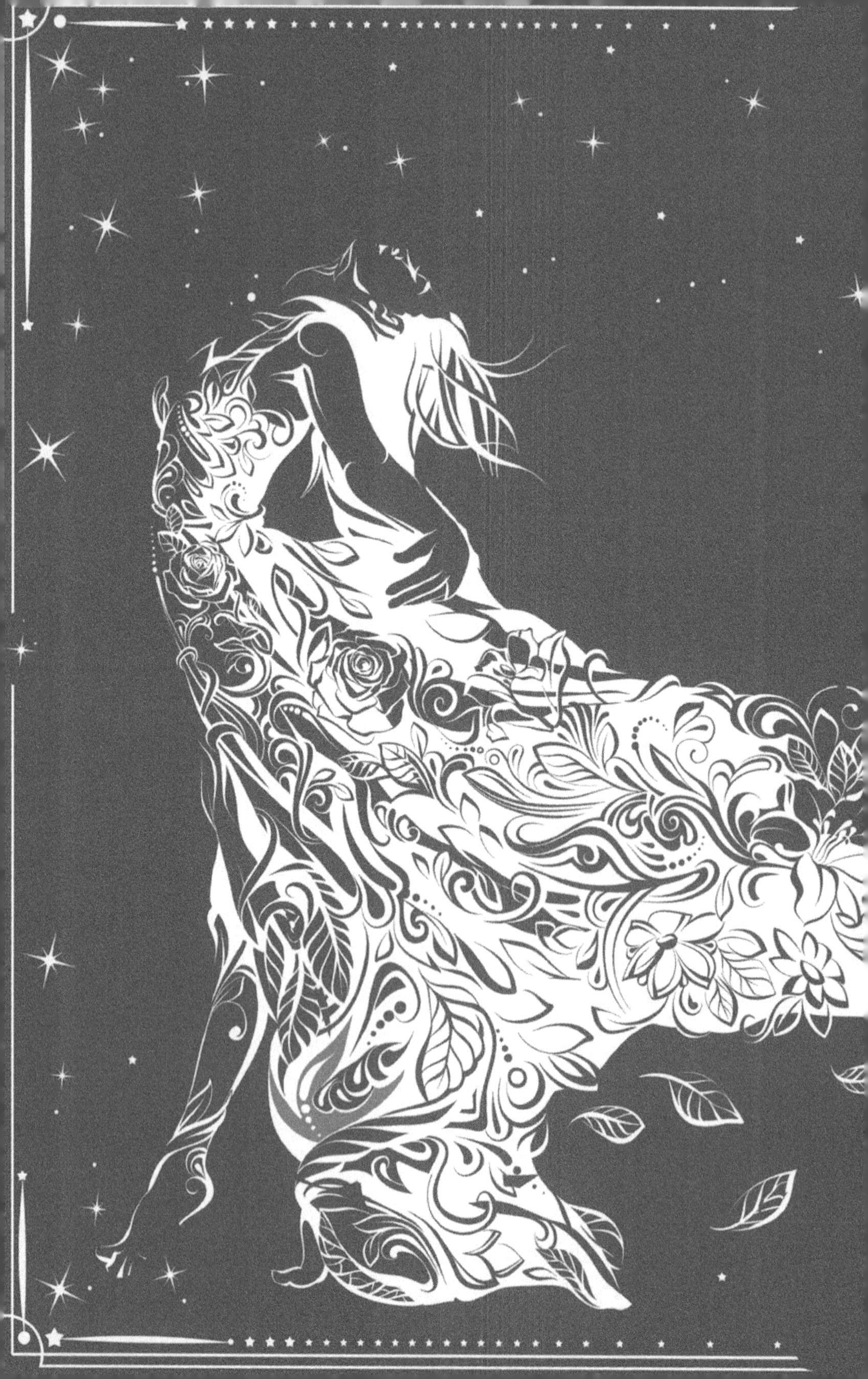

ELISE

CHAPTER TWENTY SEVEN

The Oscura household was the kind of crazy that you just couldn't help but want to dive into. It was loud, vibrant, full of playing children and howling Wolves, hungry mouths and so much love that I swear you could feel it as you walked through the gates.

So far, since we'd arrived, we hadn't quite made it inside yet, instead getting dragged into a game of hide and seek with Dante's younger siblings and cousins. Their magic wasn't Awakened yet so they couldn't cast silencing bubbles to help them hide and as soon as they'd remembered that I was a Vampire, they'd begged me to play, wanting to see if they could beat me with my gifts.

I got done counting to a hundred and shot into the vineyards, following the sounds of hushed giggles and stifled breathing as I found all of them one by one, making them squeal as I appeared so suddenly and laughing with them before speeding away to find my next target.

It was easy to locate all of them with my gifts but with the sun shining down on them and their laughter colouring the air, I was pretty sure I would have been happy playing this game all day.

When I'd finally rounded them all up, I paused, looking around in search of my final prey, my senses on high alert and eyes narrowed. Dante wasn't playing by the rules. I couldn't hear him anywhere which meant he was using a silencing bubble.

I pursed my lips, looking around and turning to face the big white mansion which was the beating heart of the Oscura Clan.

Movement caught my eye from the right corner of the house just as someone ducked out of sight. Someone stupidly tall and unbearably attractive.

Got you.

With a smirk on my lips, I took off running, speeding up the hill between the grape vines to the house and around the corner so fast that I kicked up a trail of dust behind me.

I skidded to a halt as I paused to look at the quiet courtyard to this side of the house. Beautiful, wrought iron patio furniture sat alongside a burbling water fountain and two big lemon trees towered to either side of the space, just starting to blossom and fill the air with their scent.

My skin prickled with the touch of electricity and my fangs snapped out.

"Come out, come out, wherever you are, Drago," I purred, knowing he was here and narrowing my eyes at my surroundings as I tried to spot his concealment spell.

I checked between the shadows and behind the thick trunks of the lemon trees. Just as I was about to move on, a breath of awareness danced along my spine, giving me half a second's warning of Dante's attack. But half a second may as well have been a whole minute for me as with a burst of my speed, I leapt aside before shooting around in a circle and pouncing at Dante's back as he dropped the concealment spells which had been hiding him in shadow.

He turned just before I hit him, catching me in his arms and whirling me around before driving me back against the trunk of the lemon tree. A Dragon's growl rumbled in the back of his throat and he wrapped a hand around my neck to pin me in place.

I bared my fangs at him, my heart racing and a mixture of playfulness and genuine bloodlust filled me as my gaze caught on the thump of his pulse in his neck.

Dante managed to catch my hands in his, pinning them to the tree above my head and leaning in with a dark smile on his face. "Maybe I can't run from you, bella. But I think I can fight you off."

"Not likely," I disagreed, arching my spine so that my hips brushed against his and he growled again.

His grip on my neck shifted until he was drawing me closer instead of pinning me down and his mouth found mine in a rush of heat and passion that set my whole body screaming with the demand for more.

I moaned into his kiss and he bit down on my bottom lip, tugging it between his teeth and growling too.

Then his mouth moved from mine, painting a trail of kisses along the side of my jaw and up towards my ear before he tilted his head to the side to give me the access I craved.

My fangs sank into his flesh and electricity crackled all over the two of us as I drank down the sweet poison of his blood, grinding my body against his again, his thigh slipping between my legs and making me ache for more.

The sound of a door banging caught my ear half a second before a tirade of Faetalian words spilled over me and I gasped as Dante pulled back suddenly. He couldn't have dislodged me if I hadn't let him, but I withdrew in the same moment, my cheeks flaming as his mom laid into him and I turned into an awkward pear at a strawberry party, not knowing what the hell to do with myself.

The back and forth between them got more heated, though every word continued to be spoken in Faetalian so I didn't know what they were saying, but I could hazard a guess that it was about me. And from the look on his mom's face, she wasn't very happy with me.

"Enough," Dante snapped, the ring of an Alpha to his tone making his mom stop talking instantly and her eyes widened like she hadn't been expecting that. "Elise, I would like to tell my mamma more about our bond so that she understands-" He was cut off by a panicked howl and a rush of footsteps pounding this way and all three of us looked around just as a pack of Wolf pups hurtled into the courtyard, yipping and snapping at one another in their race to be first.

Several of them shifted back at once, showing lots of nudey Wolf butts to the world but that was clearly such a common occurrence around here that none of them cared.

"Alpha!" a little boy who I was almost certain was one of Dante's brothers said urgently. "Leon Night just showed up at the front gates looking like death warmed up and he's got-"

An older girl gave him a shove and spoke over him. "Ryder Draconis is with him!" she gasped and the pups all started howling as Bianca began murmuring in Faetalian and looking up towards the heavens, like the stars might have some answers for her.

The pups all began asking questions at once and the clamour of noise made my head spin as concern for the others filled me. Ryder wouldn't have chosen to come here willingly, even with the peace deal in place, this was a massive step. One that I hadn't even expected him to take at all, let alone now when the dust hadn't even settled between their gangs.

Dante whistled sharply to disband the noise and silence fell instantly.

"Mamma, can you assemble everyone who's here for a pack meeting. I'm going to go and greet our guests and then I have some things I need to tell all of you."

Bianca nodded, barking orders at the pups to get inside the house and all of them went running after her with their tails tucked between their legs as they fell to the command of their Alpha.

I exchanged a worried glance with Dante and he jerked his chin towards the front of the house before striding away.

But there was no way I was going to walk all the way down to the gate at the edge of the property. It was over a mile away and Dante just moved too damn slow for my liking.

I shot after him, grabbing hold of him and throwing him over my shoulder before racing away down the hill while he growled at me and made half-assed complaints, but we both knew this made the most sense.

It didn't take long for us to reach the gates and my eyes widened in surprise as we found a pack of around thirty full-grown scary as fuck looking Werewolves all shifted into their Order forms, snarling and pacing before the gates.

I dropped Dante onto his feet and the Wolves all looked around at us in surprise as we started forward.

"Move aside," Dante called, striding between the Werewolves who parted to make space for us, leaving a route to the iron gates free for us to walk through.

Beyond the gates, Leon was grinning and waving at us while Gabriel stood a little way back with his arms folded across his chest. Ryder was the furthest back of all of them, staring right at the gates with a cold, hard look in his eyes which practically begged the Wolves to attack him.

"By the stars," Dante muttered irritably as he fell still on our side of the gate.

Silence rang out for several long seconds until Leon burst it as expected.

"Come on, dude, open up. We have news and we're tired and hungry and I know your mamma will have lunch ready soon and I really need to wrap my lips around her lasagne like yesterday and-"

"Go back to the house," Dante barked in a loud, commanding tone which made all of the Wolves surrounding us snap to attention. They looked between the new arrivals and their Alpha in shock, clearly not wanting to leave him here and he growled at their hesitation. "Now!" he snapped, that

Alpha tone back in his voice and all of them turned tail and ran.

Well, all but one. A huge Wolf with fur the colour of molten silver moved closer to him, growling low in its throat as it looked between Dante and the others, its ears flat and tail low. And though it had clearly been affected by his command, it clearly hadn't been forced to follow through on it the way the others had.

Dante sighed, reaching out to ruffle the Wolf's ears before nodding once and stepping between it and the other guys' line of sight.

The Wolf shifted back into Fae form and I arched a brow as Rosalie appeared before me, my gaze catching on the myriad of silver scars which crisscrossed her left side from her thigh all the way up to her neck.

She stiffened as she caught me looking, her hand opening and closing and her posture tensing like she was almost tempted to try and hide them, but her pride was fighting a battle against showing her discomfort.

Dante kept himself between her and the others and tugged his shirt off before offering it to her. It didn't seem like the Wolves gave much of a shit about nudity in general, so I wasn't sure if that was more to do with the scars or her privacy, but she tugged it on quickly and was soon swamped in the material.

"What happened?" Dante asked, turning back to face the others. "Why are you here?"

Leon launched into a seriously graphic explanation while Ryder continued to stand there rigidly, saying nothing, his eyes void of emotion even though I was sure it had to have hurt to have the gang he'd ruled over for so long turn on him like that.

When Leon was done describing a decapitation in great depth, Gabriel interrupted him for the first time.

"It's safe for him here," he explained. "For all of us, if we can stay for a few days. After that, the hunts will have died down and we'll have more options."

Dante sighed, running a hand over his face before looking up again and nodding. "Fine. But I'm not going to lie to my famiglia about it. If you cross this threshold, they are going to be told the truth of what you are to me."

His words were for Ryder and my gaze was on my Basilisk too, waiting for him to say something or do something or even just freaking blink.

"I guess we're about to find out how loyal your Clan really is then," he said eventually, looking like he would literally rather be anywhere in the world but here.

Rosalie growled a low warning, baring her teeth as her long, black hair slid forward over her shoulders. "You should be thanking my cousin, not offering up veiled insults," she hissed and Ryder's gaze moved to her slowly.

"I'll make up my own mind on how I address him or anyone else, little pup. Don't presume to tell me otherwise. My crown might be slipping right now, but I'm still a king."

Dante placed a hand on Rosalie's shoulder to stop her from responding to that and I shifted from foot to foot as he took his sweet time opening the gates.

I could feel the magic sparking in the air around me as Dante manipulated the protection spells cast around the place and told them to accept Ryder. It took several minutes which I was guessing was because he had specifically designed a lot of this protection to keep Ryder out and I held my breath as I watched this shift take place.

This act of trust between the two of them - Dante for allowing his once hated enemy into his home and Ryder for walking into a place filled with people who had wished for his death for years - was incredible to watch.

The gate finally swung open and Dante gestured for all of them to step inside, his gaze fixed on Ryder.

"Welcome, fratello," he said in a serious tone. "It looks like it's time for you to meet the rest of your family."

"Family?" Rosa questioned, arching a brow at Dante as she tried to keep her face blank. "What the hell is going on here, Dante? I can feel a new bond between you now, just like I can feel how your bond with Elise has strengthened and it seems like you're keeping secrets."

"I have been," Dante replied. "But I'm ready to tell them to all of you now. Do you trust me?"

Her gaze slipped from him to Ryder and back again. "Yes," she agreed finally. "I guess I'll go make sure the others are waiting for you then."

She turned away without another word, tossing the shirt Dante had given her back over her shoulder before shifting into an enormous Wolf and racing away up the drive towards the house which we could just see in the distance at the top of the hill.

"Are you sure this is a good idea?" Ryder asked, staring after her.

"What's the matter, fratello? Are you afraid of the big bad Wolves?" Dante teased.

"My people just turned on me for less than this. You're about to march a man who has been their sworn enemy for years straight into the heart of their stronghold. Are you really so confident that they won't turn on you? Or are you still hoping I might die after all?"

That last part was said with a hint of humour to it, but the cold look in Ryder's eyes said he really did expect this to go to shit.

Dante just laughed though, clapping a hand against his shoulder. "I think you're about to learn a whole hell of a lot about what it means to be an Oscura, serpente. Come. Let me show you what true loyalty looks like."

Ryder scowled like he still had objections and I moved to take his hand, winding my fingers between the letters that spelled out the word *pain* on his knuckles.

"You're safe here," Gabriel added in a tone that said it was a fact.

Ryder sighed and nodded. "Fine. But I'm not sleeping in a fucking dog pile."

Leon whooped excitedly and started ripping off his clothes, tossing them at Gabriel who caught everything automatically.

"Let's arrive in style then!" Leon said before shifting into his gigantic Lion form and dropping down low before wriggling his big furry ass at us and looking over his shoulder with the pleading eyes.

"No," Ryder said the second he realised what Leon wanted.

Dante just laughed and jumped on and I rolled my eyes at Ryder before grabbing him and using my strength to toss him up onto Leon's ass.

He hissed at me irritably, but as I leapt up to squeeze in between him and Dante, I pressed a kiss to his mouth to keep those pissy protests inside.

Gabriel took off, calling out a challenge for Leon to race him and Ryder lost his opportunity to get back down as Leon leapt up and began running up the drive at full speed.

I laughed as I gripped my thighs around his broad frame and Ryder wound his arms around me, pulling me tight against his chest.

He still didn't seem to have much to say so I just leaned against him, letting him know I was here for him and silently promising to get some time alone with him later so that he could talk about this shit with his gang.

When we made it to the front steps of the house, Gabriel was waiting by the front door, his wings gone already and a smirk on his face as he lorded his win over us. We all hopped down and Leon shifted back, pouncing on Ryder and licking his face before doing the same to Dante then running away before either of them could do anything about it.

"Your fucking cock just slapped my leg," Ryder growled.

"Oh come now, Ryder, we all know how much you love my cock really," Leon called back just as Dante's mom opened the door.

Bianca's face paled as she stared at Ryder and I stifled a laugh as Leon apologised for his cock comment and the fact that he was butt naked, but she just kept her eyes on the Lunar King.

"This will all make sense once you hear what has happened, Mamma," Dante promised her, moving up the steps and laying a hand on her arm as she forced herself to look up at him instead. "Do you trust me?"

"Of course, Dolce Drago," she replied in a low voice. "But this...he...he is the image of his father. The man who took your papa from this world. It's all I can see when I look at him."

"It used to be all I could see too. But things have changed. Come." He steered her back into the house just as Leon finished pulling his clothes back on and the four of us followed somewhat hesitantly. Ryder was stiff as he moved and I kept my hand on his arm to remind him I was here and I'd have his back if anyone turned on him.

We strode through the enormous house, passing by the kitchen and following Dante out onto a huge terrace that looked out over the view of the valley and the vineyards beyond.

The rest of the Wolves were all out there already and they were talking loudly between themselves. But as we stepped out, silence fell and all eyes either shifted to Dante or Ryder who stepped out behind him.

"I know that this peace deal is new and that the wounds of our past still burn like they're fresh at times," Dante began. "But I need all of you to pay attention to what I am going to say and what I am going to show you so that you can understand how solid this bond between me and Ryder truly is now."

Silence. The Wolves all waited to hear him out with bated breath, none of them daring to interrupt their Alpha while he was addressing them.

"For the last year, since Elise came into our lives, me and the three men standing here beside me have been drawn to her - and to each other in turn - like moths to a flame. The stars have pushed and prompted all of us into each other's company and though our relationships had varied between non-existent to pure, venomous hatred before we met her, time and again we have found ourselves coming together surrounding her."

"It's true," Rosalie said from her place at the front of the pack. "I can feel the bonds between all of them, though I can't figure them all out..."

Dante ran his fingers over his hand and removed the concealment spell he'd placed there to hide the mark which bound him to Ryder before holding it up for them all to see. The Wolves shared looks and shuffled closer, seeming torn between excitement and fear.

"A few weeks ago, Ryder's life was in danger and I went to his aid. We fought side by side and defeated those who had meant him harm and when it was done, the stars drew us together to ask us if we wanted to end the feud between us. The stars gave us the chance to change our bond - and we both decided to end the hatred. We are no longer Astral Adversaries. The stars rewrote our fate."

Gasps and murmurs broke out between the crowd as they looked between Dante and Ryder, their eyes wide with fascination and more than a little hope.

"I promised all of you peace and I meant it. In the last year, I have seen more to Ryder Draconis than I could even explain to you now. He is a good man at heart, and I can promise you that this choice was the right one. Now we are bonded in a new way. I don't even know if there is a word for it, but we were both marked." Dante indicated for Ryder to reveal the matching mark on his own hand too and he did, though his expression remained guarded.

More gasps and exclamations filled the air and Dante raised a hand to halt them.

"Following this decision, the stars called Elise to us and we were offered the chance at another bond."

This time when Dante removed the illusion from his eyes to reveal the silver rings there, every Wolf in the place actually seemed to hold their breath, their gaze dancing between him, me, Leon and back like they couldn't figure out what he was saying. Which wasn't a surprise because as far as anyone knew, this had never happened before.

I quickly dropped the spell concealing the additional silver in my eyes too and Leon leapt forward to remove the spell hiding Ryder's when he took too long to follow suit.

"What is this, Dante?" Bianca demanded, staring between all of us while she tried to figure it out.

"The stars offered both me and Ryder the opportunity to be mated to Elise and we took it. She's our Elysian Mate. Which makes him my family."

The silence rang out for three, two, one - and then an enormous cheer erupted from every Wolf in the vicinity. They howled to the sky and leapt up and down, rushing all of us and dog piling everyone as we were nuzzled, licked, hugged and squeezed by so many arms that I had no chance of keeping track of it all, laughter bursting from my lips.

Ryder looked more than a little freaked out by all of it and eventually, Dante whistled sharply to get them all to move back.

"We need to celebrate!" a man cried.

"Let's get the rest of the famiglia here!" another woman yelled.

And the Wolf pups all started chanting "Party, party, party!"

Dante chuckled affectionately and ushered the four of us back inside while the pack began rushing about, getting things ready, finding food and tables and decorations.

Ryder looked like he was at an utter fucking loss as to what was going on.

"What just happened?" he hissed. "Did one of your cousins just lick me?"

"Me too!" Leon said much more enthusiastically.

"I'll make sure they all understand that this includes you too, falco," Dante said, gripping Gabriel's face between his hands and pressing his forehead against his. "We all know you'll be next."

Gabriel's eyes flickered with doubt at that suggestion, but he gave Dante a warm smile, gripping the back of his hair for a moment as he held him close, and my heart just about burst with love for all of the men in this room.

"I still don't get it," Ryder said, drawing our attention back to him as he gritted his teeth in frustration. "Did they all seriously accept that? Just like that? You turn around and say 'oh hey, the guy who we've all hated since the dawn of time is my friend now' and they're just cool with it?"

"Of course they did, dude," Leon laughed, though I noticed his attention wavering as he looked towards the kitchen and I just knew he still had that lasagne on his mind. "Dante is the Alpha of the motherfucking pack. What part of 'his word is law' don't you get?"

"So now I'm...what? Welcome here?" Ryder still seemed totally dumbfounded and I moved to take his hand again, pressing a kiss to his cheek.

"Now everything between all of us will just keep getting better and better," I promised him.

"You just became an Oscura, mio amico," Dante teased, slinging an arm around his neck and tugging him close. "Your life will never be the same again."

The door swung open and Bianca walked in, shooing a few Wolf pups away as they tried to follow. "I need to understand all of this, Dante," she said, her gaze skipping between the five of us and her brow creasing a little as her focus landed on Ryder.

"Of course, Mamma," Dante replied. "Come talk to me in my office and I can explain all of it to you while the others set up the celebrations."

Leon started bouncing on his toes as he reached out towards them like he had something to say and Bianca laughed indulgently, patting him on the arm. "Go look in the kitchen, Leone," she whispered affectionately, glancing at Ryder once more before following Dante out of the room.

"Come on!" Leon said excitedly, grabbing my hand and Ryder's arm and dragging us out of the room at a run.

Ryder dug his heels in so Leon let him go and I laughed as he dragged me after him as fast as he could. I glanced back over my shoulder finding Ryder grumbling curses as he and Gabriel were forced to jog after us or risk being left alone in the Wolf den for anyone to find.

We skidded to a halt in the enormous kitchen where the delicious scent of herbs and pasta filed the air. Leon charged to the fridge, ripping the door open and groaning as he grabbed what looked like a freshly made vegetable lasagne out in a wide, terracotta dish.

He hurried to the kitchen island and the scent of melted cheese filled the room as he used his fire magic to reheat the dish before setting it down and quickly plating himself up a huge portion.

Leon instantly started shovelling the food into his mouth, slamming an arm down onto the counter around his plate and snarling through mouthfuls like he thought we might be about to steal it from him.

I rolled my eyes and grabbed three more plates out of the cupboard Leon had left wide open then dished out a portion each for me, Gabriel and Ryder.

Gabriel pulled up a stool as he started on his meal and a groan escaped him as the taste of Bianca's cooking flooded his tastebuds.

Ryder was still lingering like an awkward duck and I gently guided him to take a seat at the enormous breakfast bar too. Honestly this place was insanely big - there were ten stools here as well as a dining table big enough for twenty on the far side of the room and this wasn't even where the family generally ate. But I guessed with how many siblings Dante had and the fact that every other distant family member seemed to show up here at least three times a week, they needed the space.

"I'm not just gonna help myself to his mom's food," Ryder grunted. "She clearly doesn't want me here and I-"

"Don't try to tell me your mouth isn't watering at the smell of this lasagne," I teased. "Besides, I can guarantee you that Bianca would be more insulted if you don't eat than if you do." I raised a forkful of delicious, cheesy pasta and roasted vegetables to his lips and he caved, opening his mouth while giving me a flat look. But as he began to chew, I saw his eyes sparkle with just how freaking good that was and I knew I'd won.

I dropped into the chair beside him and started on my own meal, barely taking a few mouthfuls before Leon was licking his plate clean like a savage. He grabbed the terracotta dish the lasagne has been in and gasped in horror as he found it empty even though I'd seen him dishing up the last of it for himself while I was trying to tempt Ryder to eat more, but he wouldn't.

"Which one of you took my last bite?" he demanded, dropping the dish back down on the counter with a clatter as he began to prowl around the breakfast bar.

Gabriel started eating faster as he speared the last of his food onto his fork and grabbed Ryder's uneaten plate of food, devouring that too, leaving Leon's predatory gaze landing on me.

"Bad Lion," I warned, turning to try and block his access to my food.

"Share, little monster, don't be greedy," Leon replied, his eyes going over my shoulder to my plate.

"Says the dude who just popped his belt open to make room for all the food in his gut," Gabriel teased and my gaze fell to Leon's open belt with a chuckle as he squared his shoulders.

"That's not the point," Leon said firmly and he lunged at me so suddenly that I barely managed to stay between him and my plate.

"Stop!" I gasped as he wrapped his arms around me and tossed me over his shoulder, clamping a hand down on my ass to hold me in place while he dove on the last of my food.

I laughed as he demolished it in two big bites before leaning forward to lick my plate too.

Leon sighed in satisfaction as he dropped me back on my stool and placed his hands on the breakfast bar either side of me to box me into the cage of his arms.

"Who's been a naughty little monster?" he asked in a low growl, his brow furrowing as he looked into my eyes.

"What do you mean?" I asked, reaching up to wipe some cheese sauce from the corner of his lips which he promptly licked off of my fingers.

"There's something seriously wrong with you, Simba," Ryder muttered as he leaned back in his seat to look at the two of us.

"Shh," Leon said, ignoring Ryder as he kept his focus on me. "Do you want to tell me where exactly you found my Heart of Memoriae crystal, Elise?"

Leon slowly lifted his right hand before me and held up the crystal I'd found amongst Gareth's possessions and I gasped.

"Stop pick pocketing me, asshole," I said, slapping his chest. "Give that back."

"No can do. This is mine," he replied and I frowned.

"No. It was Gareth's," I said angrily, reaching out to snatch it from him and feeling that warm hum of power swirling within it. "And I feel closer to him when I have it with me."

"Wait a minute," Leon said, pointing at the crystal as he stood upright again. "I asked Gareth to look after that for me. It's really valuable and the FIB were looking for it but I bit this dude's arm off so I had to go all incognito until the heat died down and I never got around to asking for it back-"

"You did what?" Gabriel asked while Ryder chuckled darkly.

"Never mind that. Point is, a white jasper crystal can be used to store memories. And you just said you feel close to Gareth when you hold it, so what if-"

"How do I access them?" I demanded as my heart beat faster, staring down at the crystal in my hand as it seemed to heat even more, and I wondered if I might have been holding some answers in my possession this whole freaking time.

Leon reached out to take it from me and I handed it over, hope building in my chest. "You just have to push your magic into it and- oh." He frowned down at the crystal, sighing in disappointment.

"What is it?" I demanded.

"I'm sorry, little monster. But there's a catch – if the person who places their memories inside it doesn't want other Fae accessing them then the crystal can place a block over them and it looks like that's what Gareth did. I can't see anything and if I try to force it to reveal its secrets, it will destroy everything hidden within it."

"So that's it? There's no way around it?" I demanded, taking the crystal back and frowning at it in frustration.

Leon sighed. "Only the person who placed the memories into it can unlock them again if they choose to put the block in place. It needs their blood to open it. There's no other way."

My chest deflated as fast as the hope had risen in me and I looked to Gabriel desperately, hoping he might be able to *see* some other way for me to unlock the secrets held inside.

"Can I have a look?" Gabriel asked, reaching out for it and I passed the crystal to him, my heart racing as I held my breath, waiting for his gifts to give us some answers.

Ryder reached out and took my hand, squeezing my fingers in a silent gesture that helped calm the aching need in me.

"Sorry, little angel," Gabriel sighed. "I can't *see* you unlocking this. If Gareth did leave any memories in there then he would have to be the one to unleash them again."

I blew out a breath, trying not to let the disappointment of that fact crush me as I nodded. It hadn't changed anything really. Just left me in the same position as I'd been in before I knew what the crystal could do.

"Here." Gabriel used his magic to make a clasp around the crystal and constructed a delicate silver bracelet to hang it on before offering it back to me. "If you feel closer to him while you hold it then you should keep it close all the time."

Leon took the bracelet from him and fastened it around my wrist. "If the cops ask, you found this somewhere far away from me, okay?" he whispered conspiratorially and I couldn't help but breathe a laugh as the warmth of the crystal fell against my wrist again.

Somewhere outside the house, a chorus of howls broke out, growing louder and louder as they announced the arrival of what sounded like an enormous Wolf pack.

"What the fuck is going on now?" Ryder growled, his entire body tensing like he was expecting a fight.

"The rest of the Oscura Clan just showed up," Gabriel said with a grin. "And we're all about to find out just how hard they can party."

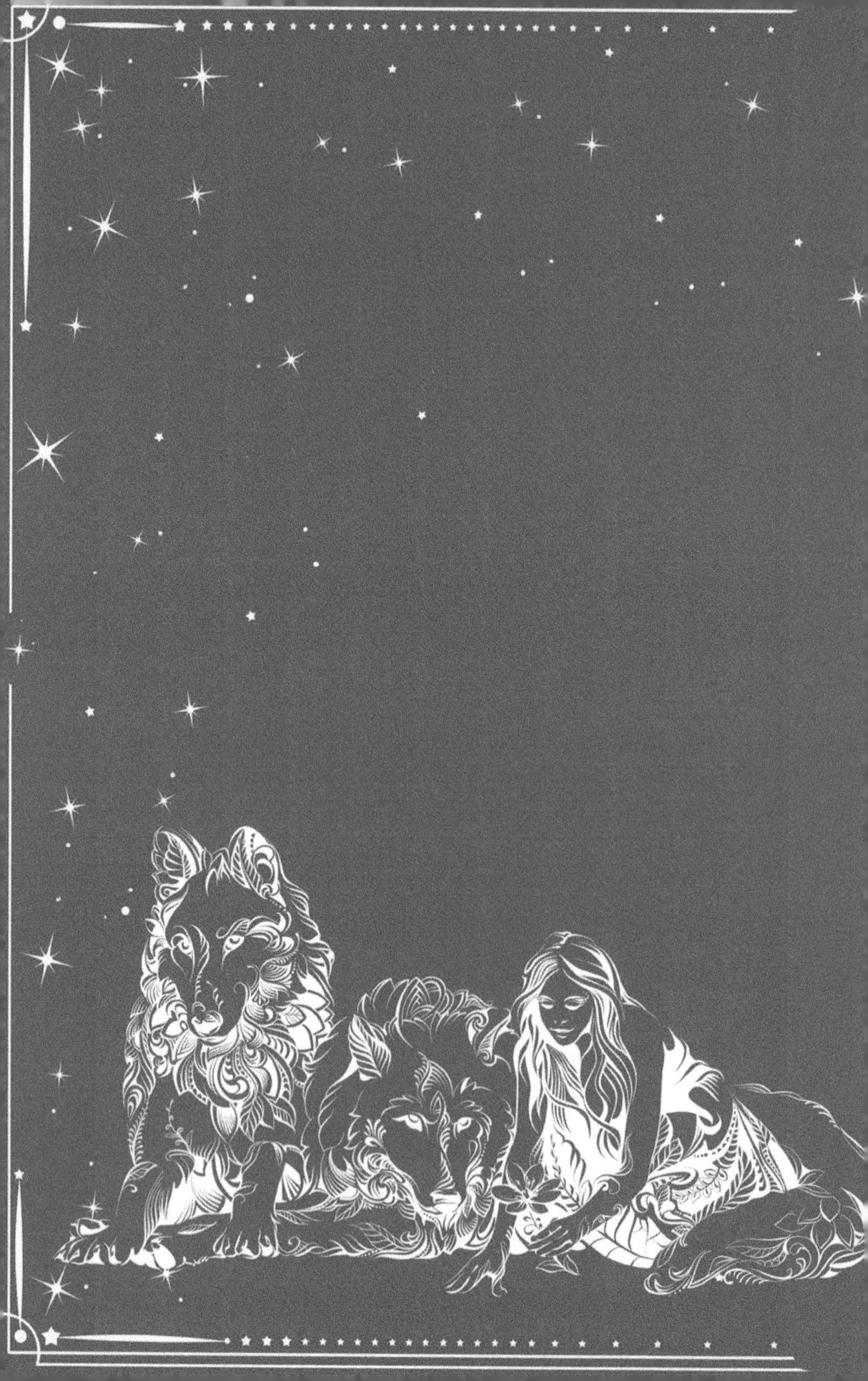

ROSALIE

CHAPTER TWENTY EIGHT

The partying was going on long into the night with my Uncle Claudio getting shit faced and diving into 'the pool' from the end of the huge table that had been set up on the lawn for all of us to eat around. 'The pool' was actually just a hole that my cousin Tula had dug using earth magic filled with water my cousin Loui had conjured. It had been about three feet deep max and it was a damn miracle Claudio hadn't broken his neck. Funny though. Especially when he'd been dragged out of the thing by his ankle, covered in mud with his pants falling down to bare his hairy ass to the world.

But no matter how much my famiglia laughed and celebrated, I found it hard to fully give in to the fun.

My heart was broken. And I couldn't even tell anyone about it. And aside from the guy I'd fallen for being way too old for me, I'd also been the reason he'd been sent to Darkmore Penitentiary for the rest of his fucking life. Roary wouldn't entertain the idea of me visiting him or calling or anything at all so I knew he hated me, and I couldn't blame him for that, but it hurt.

It hurt almost as much as the scars on my body when I woke in the night reliving the torture my papa had put me through and the searing agony of each and every slice he'd carved into my skin.

But I was pretty certain that this pain in my heart was worse, because unlike my body, the scars wouldn't heal over. I couldn't imagine any end to this suffering or any resolution to it. I'd sworn to do whatever it took to release Roary from that hell, but I couldn't come up with a single plan that might actually work to do it.

Dante swore that once the Dragon bastardo, Lionel Acrux, got what he wanted from him then he'd honour his word and have Roary set free, but I had a feeling in my gut that that wasn't true.

So I needed to come up with a way to free him myself and I was determined to figure it out, no matter how impossible it may have seemed.

I'd slipped away from the party when I couldn't keep the smile plastered to my face any longer.

I was happy for Dante, truly. I'd sensed the connection between him and Elise with the gifts of my Moon Wolf and I hadn't been able to figure it out since she'd been mated to Leon instead. Maybe I should have just trusted my gut and seen it coming, but it had seemed so impossible that I'd been thrown off by it.

Anyway, it had worked out for them and I had been right. I guessed I needed to learn to trust those instincts more, but there were so many mysteries surrounding all of the gifts I supposedly had from my rare Order that it was hard to be certain which might be real, and which were just myths.

I sighed as I looked up at the moon, feeling my power surging inside me even though I hadn't had my magic Awakened yet. I was sitting on the grey tiles of the roof outside my bedroom window. It was on the opposite side of the house to the party which meant the sounds of the ongoing celebrations were muffled.

"Is this where everyone goes to escape the mayhem?" a rough voice asked, making me flinch in surprise and I looked around to find Ryder Draconis standing in my room, looking out of my open window at me.

"I'm the only one who needs the escape," I said with a shrug, my posture stiffening as the old hatred that had been bred into me made my muscles tense. But Dante had told us he trusted this man and I was devoted in my love for him, so I forced myself to stay where I was.

"Until now," Ryder replied. "But don't worry, I'll find somewhere else to steal a beat of silence."

He turned and started to walk away and my skin tingled as my gifts tried to get my attention, the moon seeming to shine brighter for a moment and the strongest sense that I might be about to miss out on something important filling me.

"Wait," I called before I could second guess my instincts. "There's only one roof after all. I don't mind sharing it."

Silence followed for several long seconds then Ryder reappeared, climbing out of the window with considerably more difficulty than it gave me. But then he was about four times my size so that was hardly a surprise. Hell, he could probably snap my neck with one hand if the notion took him.

He moved to sit on the other side of the window to me, propping his back against the slanted roof which ran up behind him and breathing out slowly.

"How did you find me?" I asked curiously, because I was certain I'd closed my door behind me and I'd been quiet out here.

"Your pain called to me," he replied simply, like that made perfect sense.

I didn't reply to that because that would undoubtably lead to questions which I didn't want to answer plus pitying looks and all of that shit I just wanted some reprieve from.

The minutes ticked by and he didn't ask though, so I slowly relaxed again, wondering if he might actually be different to the rest of them.

"Are you certain you don't mind my company?" he asked like he was fully expecting me to bolt at any moment. But I was Rosalie Oscura, and I didn't run from anything. Not anymore. I'd already seen more than enough of the worst the world had to offer and if I'd learned one thing then it was to always stand my ground and know my own mind. I wouldn't cower for anyone ever again.

"Dante trusts you, so we all trust you. What's there not to understand about that?" I asked with a shrug, forcing myself to relax.

"A whole hell of a lot," he muttered. "No one I have ever known just blindly follows orders like that unless they're terrified of the consequences of failing the person who gave them."

I tutted, rolling my eyes at him and looking to the moon again. "Well then I feel sorry for you. None of us are afraid of Dante - we don't need to be. He would only ever hurt one of us if we betrayed him and we'd sooner die than do that. We love and respect him and he has proven he is worthy of that over and over again. He's earned his position as our Alpha through a lot more than just being the biggest, baddest, most powerful one among us. No one would even consider going up against him, no one would even want to."

"Not even you?" Ryder asked, his eyes alight with knowledge and I laughed him off.

"Not even me. I may have been born to be an Alpha in my own right, but Dante has never tried to deny that or clip my wings. He's helping me to learn what it is to be a good and true Alpha and when my time comes to form a pack of my own, we'll figure it out."

"So you won't just try to take this one from him?" Ryder pushed.

"Wow. You really have a lot to learn about family," I muttered.

He considered that for a moment then nodded. "Maybe you're right."

We sat there in silence, looking out over the distant, starlit hills for several more minutes until I couldn't take it anymore.

"Aren't you going to ask then?" I demanded.

"Ask what?"

"About...me, my pain, what it is and why I'm feeling it. I assumed you came looking for it because you wanted to give me the whole 'it'll be okay in time' speech that I've been hearing daily from my aunt and everyone else who thinks I need their opinion. But you're just sitting there saying nothing, so..."

Ryder scoffed softly, shaking his head.

"I can literally taste the pain on you, pup. And as much as I may find you to be one of the least abrasive Wolves I've ever met, I have no interest in discussing why a little girl has a broken heart."

"I'm not a little girl," I growled, his words making me think of Roary and how pathetic he must think I was. Just another little idiota with moon eyes over him. But it wasn't like that. The pull I felt towards him wasn't just because he was hot and kind and funny and...well, I mean yeah those things *helped*. But I felt it. I felt the pull between us with my gifts and I just knew that he could be the one for me. But I also wasn't foolish enough to think he'd be interested in a girl ten years younger than him, let alone one who had ruined his life, so I was resigned to nursing my broken heart and keeping my secrets over it.

"Yeah. And I'm not a fucked-up shell of a man who barely knows how to handle emotions beyond the two I have scrawled on my knuckles," he replied.

A smile tugged at the corner of my lips at his teasing, and I glanced at his hands where they hung over his knees. The word lust was looking back at me from his left hand and as he saw me staring at it, he turned his right knuckles my way too. *Pain*. Made sense.

"Where did you get all of your tattoos done?" I asked him curiously, spying some more peeking out from beneath the edges of his clothes.

"Depends. I do a lot of them myself. They all have meaning to me even if it might not seem that way at first glance."

"Like what?" I breathed and he shrugged.

"Some of them remind me of the things I stand for, others remind me of the things I've lost." He rolled his shirt sleeve back and pointed out a Basilisk coiled around the Lepus constellation. "Those are to represent my parents. Some of the designs don't have meaning in themselves but the painful act of their creation is reason enough."

"What's the Scorpio sign for?" I asked, pointing to the star sign lower down his arm and he grimaced.

"That was fucking Gabriel being a dick. He pretended The Sight had shown him that it was really important for me to get that tattoo but all he did was trick me into marking my body with his fucking star sign." Ryder tutted, swiping a thumb over the mark like he meant to wipe it off, but he totally could have had it magically removed if he really wanted to. It was a pain in the ass, but possible over several sessions. Which meant he'd made the decision to keep it.

A laugh escaped me as I imagined how pissed he must have been when he realised that he'd been tricked and Ryder arched a brow at me.

"I can feel the bond between the two of you, so maybe it has meaning too," I added with a shrug.

"Well don't tell him that because as far as he knows I'm still pissed over it. That said, he is probably the only friend I've ever had so maybe you've got a point. But now Leon keeps going on and on about me getting a Leo tattoo for him, like my body is a fucking doodle pad for all of them to mark however they want." He rolled his eyes.

"Maybe you should do it," I suggested with a shrug. "I can feel the connection between you and him too. And you share a mate now so doesn't that make you like... boyfriend-in-laws or something?"

"Oh for fuck's sake, not you too. Don't call me that. Not now, not ever."

"I think it's cute. Go on, Paulo has been trying to learn how to tattoo as one of his latest hobbies so all the stuff you'd need is right here. Plus you'd be doing it a kindness to use it for decent art - don't tell Paulo but he gave my cousin Greta a Pegasus tattoo on her back the other week and its horn looks like an honest to the stars cock. Seriously - it's even got veins. The rest of us are all taking bets on how long it will be before she manages to get a better look at it in the mirror or in a photo and realises what he's done. It's going to be freaking epic when she does."

Ryder breathed a laugh and I realised I was actually enjoying his company.

"You know what's weird," I said. "I was raised by a man who told me nothing but horror stories about you. He warned me of all the awful things you'd do to me if I ever got this close to you and yet in the end, here I am sitting beside you with all my limbs attached while he...he..."

I trailed off, my mind filling with the memories of all the fucked up things my papa had done to me over the years, all of the pain and fear and terror he had subjected me to which was supposedly to 'make me stronger'. I'd lived in hell for the years I'd spent trapped at his mercy before Dante and my Aunt Bianca had found out about me and demanded I be allowed to come and live here. And they didn't even know a fraction of what I'd lived through with him. It wasn't that I'd wanted to lie to them about it, more like the pain of those memories hurt too much to share them. And what would the point be now anyway? He was dead, gone, all I had left to remember him by were the scars in my heart and the ones on my flesh.

I ran my fingers over the lines of ruined skin on my right side and Ryder's gaze dropped to take in the movement.

"You hate your scars?" he asked, though it was more of a statement than a question.

I looked at him, eyeing the tiny line of silver skin showing above his shirt and he nodded.

"I know the feeling." He pulled his shirt up to reveal the myriad of scars coating his chest and I swallowed thickly, knowing he'd suffered even worse than me. Ryder dropped his shirt. "Or at least I used to. I used to think they were a sign of weakness, a reminder of the time I'd spent at that bitch's mercy and of the way she'd overpowered me...all of that shit."

"But now?" I asked, a hint of hope to my tone which I wasn't sure I even wanted to admit to. But I didn't know another person who had scars like mine. A few of the other Oscuras had survived a bit of torture, but not at my age and not like I had. The years of psychological abuse and captivity in my papa's home had been almost as impacting on me as the final act of violence that had marked my body for life. Ryder's torture may not have come from a parent, but it was still from someone he was forced to live with for months, he knew what it was like to be a captive and at the mercy of a powerful Fae.

"Now I know better than to try and define myself by my weakest moments," he replied with a shrug. "It took a while and years of doing everything I could to try and prove to myself and the world that I was untouchable, unstoppable, fearless, but in doing that I forgot to live at all. Elise was the one who really showed me what I need to be happy and how I should define myself."

"And how's that?"

"By the things that matter most to me. By the things I would live and die for." He held his knuckles out to me again and flicked his fingers like he'd shake the tattoos off if he could. "Not this. But this." Ryder tugged his shirt up and showed me a black X which had been inked right across his heart and my pulse quickened as I felt what it was to him. That was her. And everything she'd given him. And the power of it awoke my gifts and made my skin tingle.

"My family are everything to me," I breathed. "I wish I could just make this scar represent them, but all it does is remind me of him and what he did to me."

"So change it," Ryder shrugged, dropping his shirt again. "I certainly didn't change over night and I wouldn't say I'm even close to done learning about the person I can be instead of the one everyone expects me to be. But I have decided not to give a fuck about what anyone else thinks anymore. I can follow my own path and know that by the time I reach the end of it at least I lived my life following the way I wanted my fate to play out."

I thought about that as I turned back to look up at the moon, silently asking her to help guide me in this, to help me figure out what I needed to do.

I wasn't sure how much time passed before I made my decision and I turned to look at Ryder again.

"I want you to cover it up for me," I said firmly. "I'll go get Paulo's tattoo equipment and I want you to cover my scars in ink."

"Hiding them won't make them go away," Ryder said slowly.

"I know it won't," I agreed. "That's not why I want to do it. Right now, whenever I look at myself in the mirror, I see those scars and I see the face of the man who gave them to me. I see the frightened little pup he tried to force me to become. But that's not me. I'm not a girl who shies away from shit when it gets bad and I'm definitely not the kind to cower before anyone. Not anymore. So when I look in the mirror, I want to see a reflection of all the things that give me strength. I want you to cover it with a rose vine and each bud and flower on it will represent a different member of my famiglia. The vine will be our love for one another which will always keep us connected. And before you try to object because I'm too-"

"Fine," Ryder cut me off before I could start up on my super reasonable arguments for why it was cool for me to get a massive tattoo at the age of fourteen with approximately thirty minutes of snap decision in the lead up to making it.

I gaped at him for a beat then I grinned widely and leapt at him, throwing my arms around his neck and squeezing tightly. Ryder froze then gave me a vague pat on the head before I bounced off of him, leaping through the window and racing through my bedroom before darting down the hall to grab all the things he'd need.

By the time I returned with it, my grin was so big it cut into my cheeks and I dumped the tattoo gun, ink and all that crap down on the end of my bed with an excited squeal.

"Where do you want me?" I asked, rocking on the balls of my feet while Ryder looked somewhere between tempted to change his mind and being amused by me.

"The bed is fine. How big is the scarring?"

I yanked my shirt off to show him and he wrinkled his nose, grabbing a bed sheet and tossing it at me.

"I don't need to see you naked, pup," he grumbled.

"I've got a sports bra on," I protested, wrinkling my nose right back. "Besides you're old. And a Lunar. And Dante's boyfriend-in-law so eww."

Ryder snorted a laugh while I tried not to think about Roary who was most definitely older than him and who I had no problems fantasising about whatsoever. But that was cool, I could own being a hypocrite inside my own head and I stood by my assessment of him anyway.

I dropped my pants too, standing there in my boy short panties and showing him how the scarring descended halfway down my thigh, turning so that he could see where it curved around my ribs on both the front and back of my body.

"Well by the looks of that scarring, you're going to need hours of work done to cover it. And it will hurt like a bitch. I mean, I guess I could heal you as I go but I usually don't do that until the ink is finished and I'm setting it into the skin so-"

"No. I don't care about the pain. In fact, I want to feel it. I want to write over the agony of the scars with it and keep the people it's representing in mind as it happens," I said firmly.

"Good," Ryder replied, surprising me again. He didn't act like most of the older Fae I knew, and I suddenly realised what was different about the way he was treating me. He was accepting that I was my own person and that I knew my own mind. He wasn't telling me I was too young or that I'd see things differently as I grew up. He didn't try to tell me that he knew better or any of that shit. Because he got it. People like me and him didn't get to be kids. We never had the chance to be too young for shit because that was stolen from us. And if I was old enough to have survived the things I had, then he trusted that I was old enough to make my own choices now. I just wished he could convince my Aunt Bianca, Dante and the rest of the pack to understand that too. Holy shit, they were going to lose their fucking minds when they saw this tattoo. "We can make a start now and when you can't take it anymore, I'll heal you and finish up another day."

"No," I replied with a bit of bite to my tone. "I can take it. I want it finished tonight. The whole thing. I'm ready to start living my life again, Ryder."

His gaze moved to my scars again and the amount of flesh they covered down the left side of my body and I knew he was thinking that it was going to take a hell of a long time, not to mention the pain. But I was guessing he could also see that my mind was made up, so he nodded and indicated for me to move onto the bed and with a dark smile, I did so.

Tonight was the last night when anyone would see me as a pup or pity me for my scars. When it was done, my famiglia would see this tattoo, freak the fuck out then learn that I was done playing by anyone's rules but my own. I was an Alpha in my own right. And I was ready to take up that role.

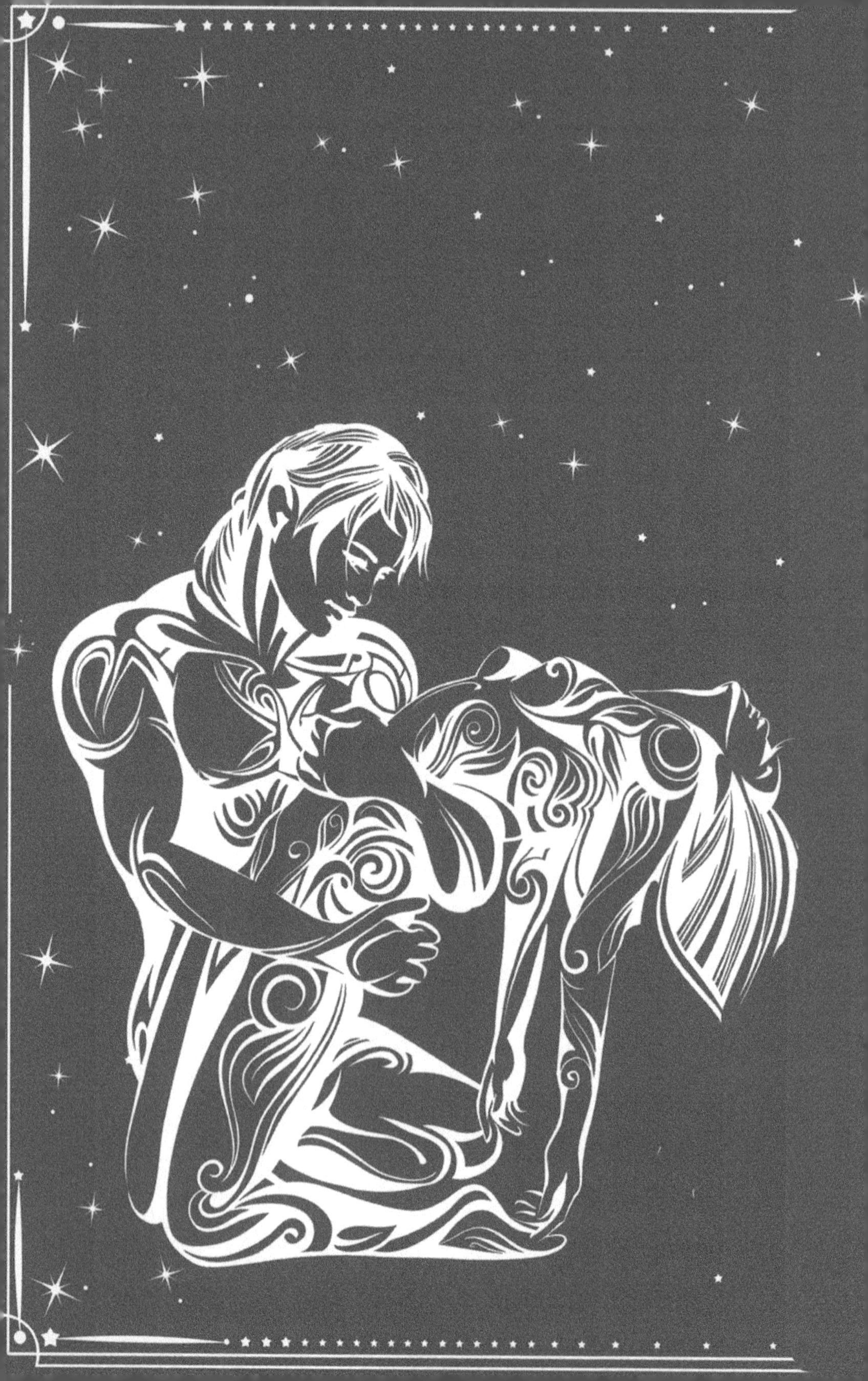

Ryder

CHAPTER TWENTY NINE

It took me a good few hours and a lot of magical ink, but Rosalie's tattoo was finally done and I healed away the last of the wound, cleaning away the blood with an alcohol wipe. She slid off of her bed, pulling her crop top back on along with her boy short panties. I'd hardly given a shit that she'd been naked for half of the work, it was necessary to cover the full extent of her scars. And I was pretty sure she felt this weirdly platonic bond we were forming too.

I guessed it was vaguely similar to how I might have felt toward a sibling. Not that I could ever really be seen like that to her or anyone in this family besides Dante. They'd go along with their Alpha's orders, but without him I was just an outsider. One who'd hurt their family, killed people they loved. There would always be blood on my hands when it came to the Oscuras and I found that unsettling since the stars had broken mine and Dante's Astral Adversary bond.

I turned my wrist over, eyeing the new ink I'd added just above the Scorpio tattoo on my wrist of the Leo symbol. I didn't know why I'd decided to do it, but while Rosalie had taken a break from her session, I'd marked it on my skin without much thought. The lion had a few flames curling around it too and I knew this meant something more than I'd ever admit out loud.

"Oh fuck," Rosalie gasped.

"What? Did I screw up that final rose?" I got up, moving over to where she stood before a long mirror and inspecting the rose that sat just above her collar bone.

"No, Ryder...it's perfect. It looks badass!" She wheeled around, throwing her arms around my neck and I stilled in her hold as she squealed her excitement in her ear.

"It's nothing," I grunted.

"It's *everything*," she snarled as she released me, her eyes flaring with power for a moment. Shit, when this girl was Awakened, she was gonna be a force of nature. I could feel the weight of her pain lifting from her and was sure she'd be far stronger for this experience overall. Life handed out pain in droves in Alestria, but Rosalie Oscura was a survivor. She'd be one of the few who thrived because of her suffering. Like my girl Elise.

"Well...good," I muttered.

"Is there anything I can do for you in payment? We've got stardust, or auras or-"

Rosalie's door burst open and a bunch of young kids spilled in, diving on Rosalie and licking her madly.

"We missed you!"

"Where've you been?"

"Oh wow, look at that tattoo!" one yelled and they all fell on her, checking out every inch of it while I tried to slip out the door. Before I made it to freedom though, one of the small people spotted me.

"Oh my stars, the Lunar King's here!" one little girl cried before diving at me.

I was accosted by tiny Wolves as they climbed me, licked me, pawed at me. "Argh." I tried to shake them off, but they were clingy little motherfuckers.

"It's Dante's boyfriend!" a girl yelled.

"I'm not his fucking boyfriend," I blurted and all of them shrank away like I'd struck them, gasping dramatically.

"He swore!" a small boy breathed. I couldn't have guessed any of their ages, all I knew was that most of them didn't come above my hip bone in height.

"Fuck!" a girl squeaked then all of them giggled

"Fuck, fuck, fuck, fuck!" another boy took up the chant.

"Oh shit," I muttered.

"Shit!" another boy yelled and I figured that was my cue to stop talking.

"Shit, fuck, shit, shit, fuck!" the tallest boy shouted then led a charge out of the room as they all echoed him every time he swore.

I ran a hand down the back of my neck, looking to Rosalie as she snorted a laugh.

"Aunt Bianca's gonna have your balls for that," she said with a grin.

"Well do you still wanna pay me? Because if you do then show me somewhere I can really hide in this house."

"Okay." She smiled and beckoned for me to follow her out the door.

"Are you not getting dressed?" I asked and she shook her head, throwing a wicked grin back at me over her shoulder.

"I'm going to show my whole family how Alphas wear their scars." The confidence in her expression made my heart do something weird, like it was getting bigger for a moment.

I was fairly sure this was pride. I remembered the day I'd branded my knuckles with the two defining emotions I lived between. It had felt like reclaiming a piece of control, setting boundaries that made sense to me so that it was wasn't just chaos in my mind anymore. But this was better than that, because Rosalie had branded a permanent reminder of the love and good in her life over her scars, reminding her what really defined her, what she had to live for. I'd had no one but a gang of cutthroat Fae when I'd escaped from

Mariella. And the only dream I'd wanted to pursue was vengeance. If it hadn't been for Elise, I would still be that lost, violent creature with nothing and no one to live for now.

We passed by Wolves who cooed and gasped at Rosalie's tattoo, a mixture of horror from most of her older family to jealousy and amazement from her younger ones.

"You wait until Bianca sees," one aunt called after her, but Rosa just tossed her hair, giving no fucks. And I liked her even more for it.

She eventually led me through a gate into what appeared to be a private quarter of the house.

"These are Dante's rooms," Rosa explained and I looked around at the gaudy gold ornaments placed on plinths and a couple of treasure chests along the walls.

"Makes sense," I said with a smirk.

"Mamma wants him to be able to have his privacy. As a Dragon, he needs his alone time and sometimes our cousins need to be locked out, so they don't start a cuddle party without his consent."

I released a low laugh as she led me into an enormous room with a dark furniture and massive bed beneath a golden chandelier. There were treasure chests and paintings of different Wolves on the walls and one with a Storm Dragon flying through the clouds, plus the large Oscura emblem painted over his bed. It was sort of…quirky and I didn't entirely hate it.

"Here you go," Rosalie announced. "Hole up here all you like."

"Thanks," I murmured and she turned to me, leaning in and hugging me with her ear to my chest.

"No, thank *you*, Ryder. You've given me more than you will ever know," she whispered and as she stepped away, I was pretty sure there were tears in her eyes. But it wasn't pain she was feeling because I would have been able to sense it if it was.

"Wear your pain as armour, Rosalie," I told her firmly. "There is nothing more frightening in this world than a Fae who can bleed in front of their enemies without flinching."

A smile lit her lips and she nodded, a promise in her gaze as she headed to the door and waved goodbye as she slipped out into the hall. The door shut, leaving me in the dark and I didn't bother to turn the light on.

I released a heavy breath, moving to sit on the end of the bed, listening to the party raging on beyond Dante's quarters. It must have been well past midnight but I was still wide awake, my instincts burning with the feeling of being surrounded by so many Oscuras. It was confronting somehow, seeing his family up close like this and I quietly longed for a family I'd lost years ago.

I took a razor blade from my pocket, twisting it between my fingers as I used my hypnosis to conjure my mother and father in my mind, my abilities allowing me to ensure I never forgot them. Though it had been months, possibly more since I'd let myself see them like this. Their faces always came with a weight of guilt in my gut, the knowledge that I wasn't the man they'd wanted to raise. Mariella had ensured I was forged as a monster and my life was split in two because of that. Before her, and after.

I used my hypnosis to see them in this room, walking along together hand in hand, smiling, laughing, loving each other. That was how I remembered them. I didn't let myself think too much about the pain in my father's eyes after she'd died. He had never been the same, withdrawing into himself, from others. I'd been the only one he'd smiled around. He'd kept me in a bubble of safety and loved with me with his whole heart, maybe even more than that, like he'd been trying to make up for the love I'd lost when my mom had passed.

After an hour or so, voices carried down the hall and I stiffened as I recognised Dante and his mother.

"-don't be ridiculous, Dolce Drago," she hissed. "The boy is in my home, I will see him if I want to."

"He needs some time to adjust to the idea of this," Dante reasoned and

I could almost picture him trying to bar Bianca's way to his room.

"He had plenty of time while he was tattooing my fourteen-year-old niece without my permission," she growled and I shifted the razor blade in my grip, the old habit soothing my anxiety as I let a little blood fall from my thumb and fed on the pain.

"Come dance, Dante!" Leon's voice carried from further away.

"Yes, go and be with your Leone," Bianca encouraged.

"He's not my Leone," Dante muttered. "Just leave Ryder alone, Mamma."

"I'm only here to bring him some food, he may be Vesper Draconis's son, but I do not allow empty bellies in this house." The sound of heels clipped up to the door and I stiffened as it opened and Bianca appeared there in her long, dark green dress with Dante peering over her head from behind, an apologetic look on his face.

"Why are you sitting here in the dark, nuovo figlio?" she demanded, switching on the light and I winced against the brightness. She shrieked and I was about to defend myself from an attack when she ran forward and grabbed my hand, turning it over to see the cut on my thumb. "No, no, no." She tutted, tugging hard as she placed a platter of food down beside me on the bed.

"What are you doing?" I asked in confusion, looking to Dante.

"Taking you to the bathroom," she said sternly and I frowned as I followed her into the en-suite where she rinsed the cut under a tap. "Dalle stelle, il ragazzo si taglia? Non va bene."

"It's fine," I grunted, tugging my hand away but the woman was surprisingly fucking strong. She ran her thumb over the cut when the blood which was coating my palm was washed away and healed it in a flash.

"He's a Basilisk, Mamma, he needs pain to rejuvenate his magic," Dante said in exasperation from the doorway to the en-suite and I threw him a look asking for help. I could kill a man with nothing but my bare hands, but I had no idea how to disarm this bustling little woman. What did she want? I had no idea of her intentions.

"Dolce Drago, get out of here." Bianca wafted a hand at him. "I want to speak with Vesper's son in private."

I begged him with my eyes not to leave, but the traitorous bastard shrugged and headed away, leaving us to it.

"Now," Bianca huffed, straightening as she stared up at me. For someone so small, she sure had a big backbone. "You will not bleed in my home, nuovo figlio."

"Why'd you keep calling me that?" I frowned.

"It means new son. The stars have bound you to my Drago which makes you mine too, you see? Nuovo figlio." She turned sharply around and marched back into the bedroom. "Are you coming?"

I drifted after her, feeling lost and confused as I waited for her to throw insults at me and curse me over her dead husband's grave.

"Come here into the light. I want to look on your face so I can get used to it." She beckoned me under the large golden chandelier above Dante's bed and I stood there with my arms hanging awkwardly at my sides. She lifted her chin, inspecting me closely, reaching up to grip my jaw and turn my head left to right.

"Mmm," she hummed disapprovingly. "Why do you have to look so much like your papa?" she murmured. "Your mother was fairer, lighter eyes. Though now I'm looking, I can see some of her in you too…it's hidden deeper though."

"You knew her?" I rasped, unsure what to make of any of this. I was just surprised she wasn't trying to rip my heart out of my chest right now.

"Yes, a long, long time ago. We attended Aurora Academy together. We weren't close, but we had the same classes. That was before she was Lunar allied." She smiled slightly at some memory. "Oh come cambiano le cose…"

I cleared my throat. "I'm sorry if I'm making you uncomfortable in your own home, Mrs…Oscura," I said, awkward as fucking anything as I addressed this woman who had hated me and the Lunars with a passion for her entire life.

She swatted my arm and I flinched, about to defend myself and not wanting to kill Dante's mother, but nothing else came of it.

"Ragazzo sciocco," she scolded. "Call me Aunt Bianca or Bianca at least."

"Okay," I grunted.

"Now, come on and eat. I cannot stand a hungry pup."

"I'm no pup," I growled.

She eyed me curiously. "I will be the decider of that, nuovo figlio. Did Vesper Draconis raise a boy or a man I wonder?" She sat on the bed, patting the space between her and the huge platter of bread and cheeses she'd brought for me.

I dropped down next to her and she pointed at the food, but when I didn't pick it up, she reached over my lap, grabbing a hunk of bread and splitting it in half. "Share it with me, Ryder, as a sign of our new alliance."

She offered me half the bread and I took it, breaking a piece off about to push it between my lips before she shrieked like her ass was on her fire. She grabbed a small bowl of oil from the platter and held it out for me. "Dip it in this. I made it myself from the olives we grow in the southern grove."

I dipped the piece of bread in it, unsure why the fuck a bit of oil would make the bread taste any different but as I pushed it between my lips, every tastebud in my mouth went off like a fucking firework.

"Holy shit," I growled, tearing off another piece of bread and coating it in more of the oil. Bianca watched me with her eyes brightening, passing me more bread when I finished the piece in my hand.

"Bene, yes?"

"Very fucking bene," I agreed around a mouthful of it. "You really made this?"

"Yes," she chuckled. "You act as though you've never had homecooked food before."

"I haven't, well, not since I was a kid anyway. And I don't really remember that." I cleared my throat, swiping the bread around the last of the oil in the dish before devouring it. "Oh, I ate it all."

She slapped my arm again in that way that made me think she was about to fight me, and magic shot to my fingertips in response. It seemed to be some kind of friendly gesture though as she just laughed and stood up, barely taller than me on her feet than she was sitting down.

"Come with me." She headed to the door and I got up hesitantly. "A growing boy like you needs something better than oil and bread."

"There's something better?" I murmured hopefully.

"So much better." She shot me a mischievous grin and I followed her into the hallway, the sound of laughing and singing coming from somewhere in the house and my muscles tightened.

"You have nothing to fear in my home, nuovo figlio," Bianca said firmly, sliding her arm through mine so I was suddenly escorting this Oscura queen along the halls of her own house. "My Drago says you are family, so that is what you are."

I nodded mutely as she led me back into the house and I was thankful that most of the party had stayed outside, so we slipped past unnoticed into the enormous kitchen and through to a large larder. Shelves filled the whole room, bursting with tins, jars, linen bags, this place holding enough food to feed an army. And I guessed that was exactly what it was for.

Bianca released my arm, grabbing a bottle of red wine out of a rack and tiptoeing up to try and reach a tin on a shelf too high above her head. I moved forward, hooking it off for her and passing it over. She patted my arm with a warm smile. "Grazie, ragazzo dolce."

I remained silent as she fetched a couple of glasses from the kitchen, filling them with wine before passing me one. I took it, bringing it to my nose and inhaling to check its ingredients.

She laughed, slapping my arm. "You think I would try and poison you? Seems a fairly foolish way to try and kill a Basilisk, no?" She beckoned me after her to the kitchen as she carried the tin and her own wine then gestured for me to sit at the island.

She grabbed a light blue apron off of a hook with the words *Alpha of the kitchen* curling around a wolf in a chef's hat in the centre of it. She tied it in place then grabbed some food out of the huge refrigerator and started cooking something on the stove. My wine sat untouched for a while, but eventually I took a sip. It ran over my tongue and I tasted the summer these grapes had ripened, tasted the earthiness of the cask the wine had sat in for years, the fruits added to sweeten it from cherries to a hint of orange. I released a noise of satisfaction that had never left me before. I'd never drunk wine in my life, it had represented the Oscuras for one and I'd never seen the point of it for the other. The alcohol couldn't affect me unless I let it, but this was far more than just a means to get drunk.

Bianca turned to me with a knowing look. "Good?"

"It's…incredible," I admitted, taking another swig.

"That's from the year I married il mio amore scelto dalle stelle." A sad look entered her eyes and I frowned as I focused on the silver rings in them, my heart crushing in my chest as I tasted her pain on the air. Her Elysian Mate had died at the hands of my father. Anger curled through my veins at the thought, the idea of losing Elise to anyone enough to make me want to go on a killing spree of every shady asshole in the city just to make her death less likely.

"I'm sorry," I grunted, jerking my chin at her eyes as her pain continued to flow into me and her lips parted as she felt my power at work.

"Sorrys are for the living," she said simply, returning to her cooking so quickly that I was sure she was trying to hide her grief. But there was no hiding that kind of agony from me.

"You are the living," I remarked and she released a sorrowful sigh.

"My husband made his own choices," she said. "Grief is a fact of life. It is why mia famiglia celebrate whenever they have a reason to. Who knows when the sunrise could bring your last tomorrow?"

I drank more of the wine, thinking on that. "If it helps your pain, then maybe you'd want to know that I spent a hundred percent of my days in misery after my father died. Until Elise…"

She snapped around again, sniffing as she wiped tears from under her eyes. "You think it pleases me to know you have suffered, nuovo figlio?"

"Yes," I replied firmly.

"Well, you are wrong. I have lived this way of life because it is necessary. Death has become a constant foe which I have been forced to let into my home time and again. But I do not take pleasure in my enemies suffering because of that. I have wanted a peace deal since the beginning, but my husband was as stubborn as your father and their fathers before them. There is no force on earth which can break an Astral Adversary bond, it breeds violence and death and destruction. There is no answer to it until one or both of the bonded dies. At least that is what we believed until now. There was an answer all along, and you and my son were the ones to discover it. The bond has been broken by love. You placed your destructive needs aside in pursuit of one girl." A note of adoration filled her tone. "A girl who is a gift from the stars to my famiglia and the whole of Alestria. A girl who has captured the hearts of two enemies and saved our city because of it."

A smile quirked up the corner of my lips. "They made her too perfect for either of us to resist. The stars are conniving little fuckers."

"Language, nuovo figlio," she scolded, whipping a tea towel at me and I smirked as she cracked a grin. She shook her head, turning back to making me whatever delicious smelling meal she was cooking up on a pan and my stomach growled loudly. She tutted, muttering under her breath, "Detesto uno stomaco vuoto."

She soon served up a steaming hot plate of spaghetti and meatballs and I fell on it like a ravenous wolf – which was fucking fitting I supposed. Between that and the wine, I was in heaven. It was the best food I'd ever eaten and I just wanted to keep eating it even when I'd finished every last scrap.

Bianca sat opposite me drinking her wine, satisfaction filling her eyes as she watched me. When I was done, she snatched up the plate and refilled my glass.

"Go and enjoy the party," she encouraged and my eyes flicked to the clock on the wall. It was almost three in the morning and the celebrations were still going strong. My gaze moved to the window where I could make out the flames of a bonfire in the distance and the silhouettes of dancing bodies. Some of them were definitely naked. When the Oscuras partied, they did not hold back.

"Thank you for the food," I murmured, slipping out of my seat and taking my glass of wine with me. I was just going to head back to Dante's room and wait for Elise to get tired enough to join me.

"Ryder?" Bianca called as I made it to the door, and I glanced back with an arched eyebrow. "Don't slink off back to bed, give mia famiglia a chance, they might surprise you. And dalle stelle, let down your Order gifts so you can enjoy the true effects of Oscura wine." She winked, ushering me away and I slipped out the door, considering her words.

My gaze fell on the open patio doors that led onto a large, decked area with a huge hot tub. Elise was in it in a little pink bikini with Leon and Dante beside her shirtless, all of them staring up at something above them as they grinned and cheered.

"Go on Gabe!" Leon shouted, slapping his hands down in the water.

"I've *seen* that this is gonna go really well!" Gabriel called back from somewhere and curiosity got the better of me as I drifted to the patio doors.

I walked out onto the decking and tipped my head back, finding Gabriel up on the roof barefoot in just his jeans with his wings outstretched behind him. He had a stupid look on his face that said he was wasted.

"Gabe, Gabe, Gabe!" Leon started chanting and Elise and Dante joined in.

"Land right here," Elise called, pointing at the water in front of her.

"But not before the two aerial backflips you promised, falco!" Dante shouted.

"I'll give you three aerial backflips and a pirouette before I land," Gabriel said cockily, shrugging like it was nothing.

He took two running steps towards the edge of the roof and jumped, his wings failing to open as he flipped over backwards and slammed face first down onto the decking with a loud thwack.

I roared a laugh and all eyes whipped onto me.

"Scar!" Leon cried excitedly, diving out of the water, jumping over an unconscious Gabriel and leaping at me, nearly knocking the wine from my hand. "I went looking everywhere for you, but then Dante said you wanted to be alone and forbade me from finding you." He pouted, nuzzling the side of my head and I batted him off as I flattened my smile.

"Ah!" Elise shrieked and we both turned to her in alarm, finding electricity bouncing off of Dante through the water as she started climbing out of the tub. "You're electrocuting me, Drago." She kicked at him and he smirked headily.

"My bad, bella." His eyes were hooded as he stared at her ass.

She climbed out, shooting over to Gabriel and rolling him over. His eyes were open and a dreamy smile was on his face which was covered in blood from his broken nose. "Hello, angel."

I guessed he was just fine.

Elise giggled as she healed his nose and he used his water magic to wash away the blood, using a little too much so it came out of his palm in a torrent, but he didn't seem to give a shit.

"Told you I could do it," Gabriel said smugly and Elise laughed harder.

"Come on, we're playing the Oscura-Obbligo game." Leon grabbed my hand, towing me toward the hot tub. His foot slipped on the wet decking and he nearly pulled me over as he tripped. I held him upright, pushing him along to the tub while he gave me the big eyes that said I'd just saved his life.

"Stop looking at me like that, Mufasa," I muttered.

"Like what, Rydikins?" He cooed, batting his damn lashes.

Gabriel rushed over and climbed in ahead of us, smirking. "I win."

"It wasn't a race," I growled.

"But if it had been, I would have won," Gabriel said smugly.

Elise came up behind me, leaping onto my back and biting my earlobe. "I could eat you up, you're so scrummy."

Leon dove into the hot tub backwards, sending a huge splash out around it and I grinned, turning my head to look at Elise as she released my ear. She kissed me sloppily and I laughed into her drunken kiss, tugging her under my arm and dropping her into the hot tub.

I lifted my wine glass to my lips as I watched them, but Dante pointed at me.

"Stop," he commanded and I frowned as I did. "Let your Order gifts down before you drink that, fratello. That's a dare."

"Yay!" Leon beamed and I shrugged as I did then swallowed the entire glass of wine, the alcohol fizzing through my veins and giving me a kick.

"Your turn, Ryder," Elise said excitedly. "You've got to dare one of us."

"I don't play games," I said dismissively.

"Oh come on, yes you do, Scar," Leon said, pushing his wet hair away from his face and Elise's eyes trailed over his muscular shoulders.

"No," I replied simply.

Dante plucked up a bottle of wine from a table beside the tub, plucking the cork out with his teeth and holding it out to me. I offered him my glass to fill, and he kept pouring until it was spilling right over the top of it.

"Then drink with us until you're feeling playful, fratello." He smirked.

"I could drink ten bottles of wine and I still wouldn't be 'playful'. That word doesn't apply to me." I drained half the glass in one long drink and Elise leapt to the edge of the tub, tugging at my shirt.

"Get in," she urged, taking the glass from my hand and I indulged her as I pulled my shirt over my head and tossed it aside. My beautiful Vampire sat at the edge of the tub, watching me unblinkingly like she didn't wanna miss a second of this show. And far be it from me to disappoint my baby.

I unbuckled my pants, dropping them and kicking off my shoes and socks so I was just in my dark grey boxers. Elise gripped the hem of them, peeking inside for a second before snapping them back against my skin with a giggle. Her lilac hair was sticking to her cheeks and I wanted to bottle the light in her eyes and keep it forever.

"You having fun, baby?" I murmured and she nodded.

"Especially now we're all together," she said, shifting aside in the tub to make room for me to get in.

I climbed into the hot water, sitting down between Elise and Gabriel as my girl passed me back my drink. Her hand landed on my thigh beneath the water as the wine started to have an effect on my head. My thoughts grew fuzzier and any concerns I'd had about joining the party ebbed away. There weren't even any Wolves out this way, it was just us. And that was how I liked it.

Gabriel's hand landed on my other thigh and I turned to him in surprise. "Dude," I growled, but his eyes were glazed in a vision.

He started laughing as he snapped out of it then lunged forward and kissed me hard on the mouth, his stubble grazing my jaw. He pulled back as I went to punch him, and I missed by a fraction of a hair.

Leon and Dante burst out laughing, bouncing up and down in the water.

"He actually did it," Dante boomed, apparently having concocted this dare while I was distracted by Elise.

"Gabe's wild when he's drunk," Leon said, grinning like a kid as Gabriel laughed and chugged another glass of wine like it was water.

"Mmm," Elise hummed. "I like it when you guys touch each other."

"I'll suck any of their dicks for you, little monster," Leon said instantly. "Just pick a dick, any dick."

"If you try to put your mouth near my dick, Mufasa, I'll strangle you with your own hair," I said casually.

"Yeah, I love you, Leone, but I only want our Vampirina's mouth on my cock." Dante smirked darkly.

Gabriel leapt out of the water, perching on the edge of the tub beside Leon and nearly falling off the back of it. "I'll do it," he slurred.

"You're drunk," I told him as Dante filled up my glass again and I realised I wasn't far off drunk myself.

"Naaah." Gabriel waved me off. "I'm soberly total. No, I'm totably sobal. Oh, you know what I mean."

"I'm gonna do it for my mate," Leon decided, moving in front of him.

"You're gonna suck off Gabriel in Dante's family home in front of anyone who happens to walk by?" I deadpanned.

"Yeah," Leon and Gabriel said at the same time.

"For Elise," Leon added and Gabriel nodded, his eyelids drooping. Man, he was fucked.

"Look at me, angel, I need some help getting hard," Gabriel asked, dropping his glass in the water and vaguely trying to reach for it as it floated away.

I should probably stop this.

Dante filled my glass again as I finished another one and Elise whipped off her bikini top, arching her back against the tub so Gabriel could see her perky little tits.

I should definitely do something.

My gaze snagged on Elise's tits again and I forgot what I'd just been thinking. Something about cheese? Dante's mom had so much cheese in that larder. *I'm gonna go and eat some later.*

I leaned in to suck one of Elise's nipples into my mouth, making her moan loudly.

"If I tip my head down like this, you can pretend I'm a girl," Leon told Gabriel matter of factly.

"A girl who's not Elise sucking my cock is as unappealing to me as a guy doing it," Gabriel said thoughtfully, nearly falling off the edge of the tub again, but Leon caught his arm. "I'll just watch her."

"I know! I'll make a video so Elise can watch it whenever we're not around," Dante said excitedly like this was the best idea ever as he swiped up his Atlas from the table.

"Ooh, can I be in it?" Elise asked and Dante turned the camera on her as I toyed with her nipples and made her pant for me. I rubbed my face between them too because…tits.

"Are you watching, little monster?" Leon demanded, looking over his shoulder as he rested his hand on Gabriel's inner thigh.

"Yeah," she said, sitting more upright so her tits went under the water and I was left pouting without a toy. "Are you guys really gonna do that for me?"

"Yeah," Leon said with a wide smile. "I'd do anything for you."

"I'd fly to the moon and bring back a piece of it for you," Gabriel said. "By the stars, do you think I could actually do that?" His eyes glazed for a moment then he frowned. "Apparently I'd die. But I'd die for you, Elise."

"I'd die for her harder, stronzo," Dante said firmly.

"I'd have all of my skin peeled off while I was still alive, *then* die for her," I said smugly, slinging an arm over the back of the tub behind her.

"Aww you guuuys," Elise cooed.

"Right, I'm gonna do it, Gabe. Prepare yourself for the best blowjob of your life," Leon said, gripping the hem of Gabriel's boxers. I probably should have looked away or some shit, but I was kinda interested to see if they were actually gonna go through with it. Dante got in close like a fucking porno director with his Atlas in his grip and Elise craned her neck to get a better look.

"Hurry up, I can't keep hard with you looking at me like that, Leon," Gabriel growled, holding a hand below his face to block his view of Leon down there.

"You're not even hard at all, man. How am I supposed to work with a banana skin for a dick?" Leon complained.

Gabriel started hiccupping. "I – *hic* - am hard. Oh no, wait, I'm – *hic* – not."

"Make room, make room," a female voice called from behind us and Gabriel fell into the water just as an old woman appeared in a very revealing silver swimsuit that was not age appropriate for her in any way. It had cut out areas over her stomach and breasts and her tanned, wrinkled skin was on full display for us all. Several necklaces hung around her neck full of charms and they jingled as she walked shakily along.

"Aunt Lasita, I thought you were in bed," Dante balked.

"Cosa?" she snapped.

"I thought you were in bed," he said slower and louder.

"Cosa?" she cried again, waving a long stick in her hand and prodding me and Elise in the heads with it. "Move aside, I'm coming in."

Elise dipped lower beneath the surface as she scrambled back into her bikini top. I slid down the seat as Lasita climbed into the water and settled herself between us.

"Ah, bellissimo," she sighed contentedly, resting her stick against her shoulder. She looked to me, her eyes roaming over what she could see of my body then smiled coyly. "Oh hello sprite, you've come for me at last, have you?"

"Er, what?" I frowned, looking to Dante who took a gulp of wine out of his golden chalice.

"You're the sprite I made the deal with for my pixie dust protection medallion." She shook a charm at me on one of her necklaces which looked like a small bicycle bell. "You were disguised as a grubby little man before, but I see you've come to me as a true tempter of the night at last." Her hand gripped my knee under the water and I jerked it off with a grunt.

"Dante," I barked as he whispered in Elise's ear beside him, clearly distracted by her.

"Lasita, that's Ryder Draconis," he said loudly. "He's mated to Elise like I am."

"Cosa?" Lasita snapped. "Speak up, you talk as loud as a mouse, ragazzo Drago."

"Ry-der Dra-co-nis," Leon boomed as he sounded out my name.

"Oh it's the Leone with the mindworts," she said, waving her stick threateningly. "They've eaten the plaps in your brain, I see, it's made you talk very slowly. Quite unfortunate."

She leaned in close to my ear and whispered, "Where will you take me for our night of romping? To the barn?"

"Dante," I barked again, shifting a few more inches down the seat so I was pressed up against Gabriel who'd passed out, his head hanging backwards over the edge of the tub. He hiccupped in his sleep, his whole chest jerking.

"He's not a sprite, Lasita," Dante said in exasperation.

"Cosa?" she called and Dante growled in frustration.

A chorus of howls suddenly went up from the dancing Oscuras out by the bonfire and the pounding of bare feet sounded across the decking. Rosalie appeared in her boy shorts and sports bra, her tattoo on full display still as she grinned at us.

"We're all going for a run, we thought you might lead the way under the moon, Drago?" she asked hopefully.

Dante stood from the water with a wide smile. "Yes, I want to fly." A bolt of lightning shot off of him, hitting the fairy lights around the patio and short-circuiting them. "Maybe it's time to sober up a little though." He pressed his hand to his forehead, casting some healing light and standing up slightly straighter though he was clearly still far from sober.

"I'm coming too," I said, standing as water streamed off of me and Lasita clapped excitedly as she stared at my abs.

"Is it time, sprite king?" she asked, squeezing my calf and I awkwardly climbed out of the tub and onto the decking.

"You just, er, wait here," I told Dante's aunt and she nodded eagerly.

I slapped Gabriel in the face, making him wake with a jolt and Elise's name on his lips then I healed him enough to clear his head.

"Oh shit..." he groaned, rubbing his eyes as he followed me out of the tub and Leon and Elise climbed out and ran onto the grass, chasing each other in circles as they laughed, trying to slap each other's asses.

"Did I almost let Leon suck my dick?" Gabriel hissed at me, gripping my arm so hard the pain gave me a little shot of magic.

"Yeah," I answered with a smirk.

"By the stars," he cursed.

"Are you coming?" Rosalie called to us. "You can ride on my back if you want to, Ryder?"

"I think you've touched my little cousin plenty tonight," Dante said sternly.

"He's just going to *ride* me, Dante, calm down," Rosalie said, planting her hands on her hips.

"Stop saying that," he growled.

"What's wrong with him riding me?" she taunted and electricity crackled along his skin.

"Stop it," Dante snapped.

"Ride me instead, Ryder," Leon called as he stripped out of his wet boxers and bared his dick to the world.

"Yay! We can ride together," Elise cried and I nodded, heading over to join her as Gabriel followed a step behind.

"Oh hey, Gabe's awake," Leon said with a grin, lifting a hand to his head and healing himself. He burst out laughing, pointing at Gabriel. "I totally would have sucked your dick, dude. Isn't that cool? This is the best night ever!"

Elise fell into hysterics and I took a moment to heal her, pulling her against my chest as she sobered up a bit and stole a kiss from my lips.

"Mmm, you taste like wine and sin," she purred.

Leon shifted into his huge Lion form and Rosalie shifted beside him, lifting her furry silver head to the moon and howling keenly.

Elise shot up onto Leon's back and I started to follow, trying to use Leon's front leg to get a foothold. My foot slipped on his silky fur and I fell back down to the ground. A wet nose pressed to my back and I glanced over my shoulder, finding Rosalie pushing me up with her head. *Oh for the love of the stars.*

She shoved me hard and Elise caught my hand, yanking me up beside her and I grumbled as I settled myself behind her.

"You're the most awkward cutie I know." Elise kissed me hard which helped take the sting out of those words. I was not a fucking cutie.

Dante shifted into his Dragon form ahead of us then fell over and crushed a shed at the edge of the vineyard. I roared a laugh as he kept rolling, his huge taloned feet waving in the air before he got himself upright again and shook his head.

Elise laughed wildly as Dante flapped his wings and took off into the sky, sailing kind of wonky for a moment before straightening out and roaring at the moon. Every Wolf in the Oscura household answered his cry in a piercing howl that ran right down to the depths of my soul. Leon roared too, his whole body vibrating beneath us and I held onto Elise as he reared up like a horse and raced after the Wolves tearing through the vineyard ahead of us. Gabriel flew with Dante, soaring and wheeling around him as he rode the wind.

Rosalie ran so fast, she was like a silver bullet, tearing to the front of the pack as she led us all after Dante in the sky. Leon charged along with them and my stomach lifted as adrenaline washed through my veins. I held Elise tighter as a boom of thunder cut through the air and another howl went up from the Oscura Wolves.

Elise answered it with her own and I found myself howling too, lost to the power of this pack and the feeling of being right where I was supposed to be. As part of a family I never should have belonged in.

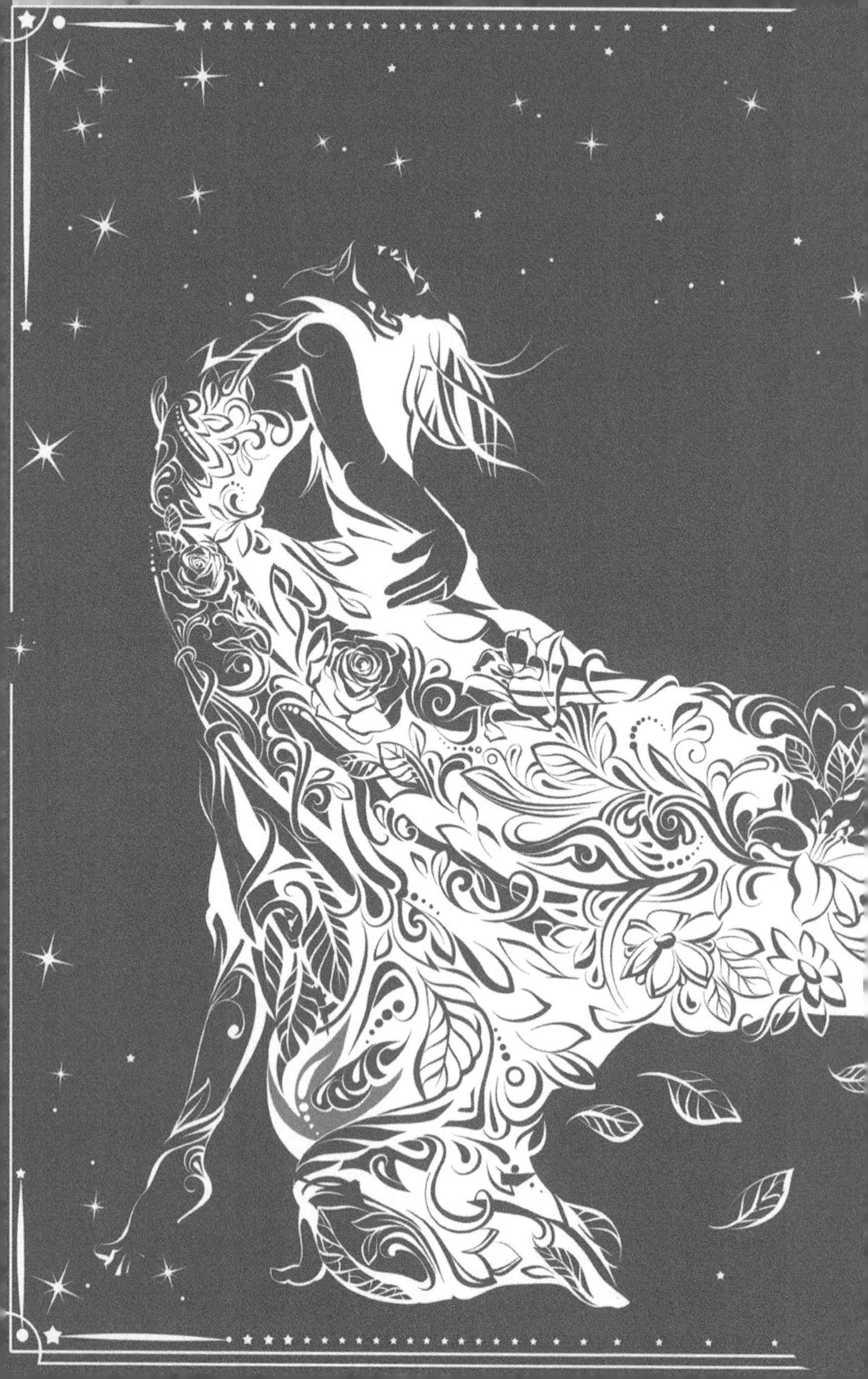

Elise

CHAPTER THIRTY

"*That's Orion's Belt,*" Gareth said, pointing up at the stars which sparkled overhead as we lay on the beat up old couch on the roof of The Sparkling Uranus and listened to the thump of music sailing up to us from the club below.

"*Are you sure?*" I asked him, squinting at it as I took another swig from the bottle of Vodka we'd swiped from downstairs. It was cheap and nasty and burned all the way down as I swallowed but it was a Saturday night and we had nothing better to do, so half-drunk star gazing had won. "I think that's part of the Little Dipper…"

"*Oh, err, yeah. I was looking at it upside down,*" Gareth replied and I sniggered.

"*I thought you were meant to be the smart one?*" I teased. "There's no way you'll be getting that scholarship spot at Aurora Academy if you can't even find basic constellations in the sky.*"

"*Funny you should say that…*" Gareth pushed himself upright and leaned down to grab something from his school bag before tossing the thick envelope into my lap.

I pushed myself up too, swiping strands of long, blonde hair out of my eyes as I tugged the contents out and my heart began to race as I read the words there.

Dear Mr Gareth Tempa,

We are delighted to inform you that you have been selected to become this year's scholarship student at Aurora Academy. An allowance has been granted to provide you with your uniform and basic supplies so we look forward to seeing you on the first day of term on September first. Please remember that this is a full board academy so come with clothes to wear outside of classes and anything else you may need during your personal hours.

I dropped the envelope into my lap and squealed as I launched myself into Gareth's arms.

"You did it!" *I gasped, tears prickling the backs of my eyes as I realised this was really happening. All of the dreams and prayers we'd had for as long as I could remember were actually coming together. Fate was on our freaking side for once.*

"Yeah," *Gareth said slowly, not sounding anywhere near as excited as me and I jerked back, scowling as I looked at him and pointing my finger in his face.*

"Don't start doubting now," *I growled.* "You know that if you really want to be able to get the kind of job you'd need to get yourself out of this dump, then you're going to need that fancy ass diploma from an honest to shit academy."

"I know, Ella, I just..." *Gareth sighed, his gaze bouncing between mine.* "I don't want to leave you here alone with Mom. She's going through another bad spell of luck and-"

I punched him in the chest and glared at him. "You seriously think I can't handle Mom on a bender?" I demanded. "By the stars, Gareth, this is your whole future we're talking about here. I don't need you to stay behind and hold my fucking hand. I'm a big girl and you'll be back to visit plenty."

"*Our* future," he growled in a promise I knew he'd keep and my heart swelled, knowing he was doing this for me just as much as him.

"All the more reason for you to go, Gare Bear." I looked down at the acceptance letter again and pulled out the class itinerary and campus map that had been included. "Look at this freaking place! You're going to have the best fucking time. I want you to promise me you will."

"While I know you're stuck back here getting a shitty high school magical education?" he asked with a frown. And yeah it sucked that when I turned eighteen and my power was Awakened I wouldn't be able to go to an academy like him, but I'd make the best of staying on in our admittedly shitty high school and learn the basics at least.

"Fine. Teach me every single thing you learn then. I won't even complain about it," I teased. "But you have to go, Gareth. Promise me you won't let anything fuck this chance up for you, least of all me."

Gareth sighed, looking down at the map and his fingers trailed over it for a moment before resting against the Pitball pitch. His lips curved up into a smile and I could see just how excited he was about this prospect despite his concerns for me.

"Are you sure?" he asked.

"Certain," I swore. "And once you graduate, we can pack up our shit and move across the kingdom to some place by the sea like we always dreamed of."

"You can count on it," he said, grabbing me and pulling me into a bear hug as tears pricked the backs of my eyes again and I breathed in deeply, savouring this moment in his arms.

I was going to miss him so fucking much while he was gone, but I knew in the end it would be so worth it if we really managed to make our dreams *come true.*

The incessant ringing of my Atlas made me groan as it woke me up and I rolled out of my spot in Gabriel's makeshift nest on the roof above Dante's room with a scowl as I hunted for it beside us.

My dream had been so vivid that I swear I could almost feel my brother's embrace lingering around me as I breathed out slowly and let the moment fade away once more.

I was alone in the bed now, the rays of sunlight which shone in around the edge of the canopy letting me know that it was dawn and explaining where my Harpy had gone. He often liked to soar through the sky while he replenished his power in the morning and I was left to stretch out in the bed in the extra space.

My Atlas rang out just as I located it and I groaned again as I squinted at the screen, seeing it was just after five in the morning. Who the fuck would be calling me this freaking early?

I glanced at the unknown number then tapped on my horoscope with a sigh, wondering if I'd be able to crash out again now or not. It was that annoying kind of early where I probably wasn't tired enough to just drift back off, but if I'd never been disturbed I'd have probably slept for another few hours.

Good Morning, Libra! The stars have spoken about your day...
With Mars shifting into your chart for the foreseeable future, you are
bound to feel the effects of the chaos it brings with it. Your future has many
possibilities right now so it's important you make each decision with care.
Don't just follow your heart, because your head will help you see things
more clearly. Venus is once again sending lots of attention your way and you
are making great steps towards juggling it nicely, but don't forget to take
time for yourself too.

My Atlas started ringing again and I scowled at the unknown number, half considering cutting it off, but curiosity got the better of me and I answered instead.

"Who is this?" I asked, rolling onto my back and looking up at the canvas roof of the tent.

"Elise, sweetheart, it's your aunt," Melinda Altair chuckled. "You should save this number - I don't just go giving it out to just anyone you know."

"Oh, er, sure. I'll do that," I said, sitting up and suddenly feeling all kinds of weird.

I hadn't really processed this whole *being an Altair* thing yet, let alone the fact that I actually had a dad out there. I probably should have called my mom to tell her, but after the last time we'd talked at Christmas it had been radio silence between us again and I was getting sick of being the only one of us who ever bothered to make an effort to break it. I still got updates from the people managing her care and I'd let Leon talk me into letting him pay for her to stay on there for the foreseeable future. I just wasn't sure what it would do to her to find out about Marlowe. I mean yeah, he was alive and he'd never chosen to walk out on her, but he was hardly in any state to come see her or reunite or whatever the fuck she might want. Melinda had sent me an update a few days ago via email – not that I had any idea where she'd gotten my email – but she'd explained that Marlowe was still struggling with a lot of his memories and it was going to take him a while to adapt to using his magic and just functioning like normal again. Mom might even spiral worse when she found out where he'd been all this time, that he'd been trapped and alone and needing help...yeah, I was gonna keep putting that shit off. Especially while there was no chance of him being able to contact her or anything himself. Because he was clearly no more up for that than she was.

"So how are you? Are you excited for our lunch today? I thought you might be looking for a more extensive update on Marlowe and I just know he will be so excited to meet you properly once he's recovered."

I blinked a few times, realising it was my turn to talk then nodded. "Right. Lunch. Mmmhmm." I wasn't really sure what I was supposed to say to that. The last time we'd met it had been brief, but she'd still managed to steal a secret from me before going on to sell it to the press after I expressly asked her not to, so lunch had not been on my agenda at all.

"Is this a bad time?"

"No, sorry. I literally just woke up and my brain is trying to catch up." I kinda wanted to chew her out, but I'd learned a few lessons about the Celestial Councillors following our run ins with Lionel Acrux and I didn't want to make an enemy out of another one of them if I could avoid it.

"Silly me, I forgot about the time differences between Alestria and the capital," Melinda said and I frowned because she was only an hour ahead of me which still made this a weird as fuck time for a chat. But I guessed as one of the Celestial Councillors she was pretty busy, so maybe this was the only free time she had.

"You do know that my mate was almost killed because of that story you gave the press about us, right?" I demanded, unable to hold it in a moment longer.

"Well I trust he was strong enough to deal with any fallout, sweetheart. A man mated to an Altair wouldn't be just anybody now, would he?" she asked sweetly like this was a non-issue.

"So you assumed he'd be strong enough to look after himself? Does that mean you knew you'd be putting him in danger then?" I demanded.

"Danger?" Melinda tittered a laugh. "From a few jealous thugs? I'm afraid in our family, you have to expect that kind of attention from time to time. People see our power and convince themselves that they can take you on. I presume that your mate is well and good now and that he has reminded them of why it was a bad idea to try and mess with him in the first place?"

I chewed my tongue, not really having a good answer to that which wouldn't sound like I was whining about the situation. Did I trust that Ryder was strong enough to deal with this and survive it? Yeah. But that still didn't make it okay.

"I asked you not to tell anyone about me having three mates," I said instead. "I trusted you with that information." Not that I'd been given much choice in that.

"Really? Why?" she asked, her voice laced with confusion like she didn't even remember me saying I wanted it kept secret. "It only shows everyone else how powerful you are. I just wanted the article about you to reach the widest audience, to spread far and wide and show everyone how proud we are to be welcoming you home."

I cleared my throat, unsure what to say to that. She'd somehow spun my whole outraged thing into me feeling weirdly proud of myself. How had she done that? Damn politician, she'd just talked me out of my own thoughts.

"Anyway, I wanted you to know that I secured you that place at Zodiac Academy like we discussed. They're expecting you on Monday and I can send someone to come pick up your things via stardust before you head over for lunch later. Do you know roughly how many bags of luggage you'll be bringing with you, or-"

"Wait," I interrupted, regaining some of my momentum. "I thought I told you I'm not interested in moving schools. I like it here. This is my hometown. My mates go to school with me here too and I really don't think I'd fit in at that fancy pants academy of yours. Thanks for the offer and all, but I'm doing just fine here."

"You are?" Melinda asked, sounding unconvinced. "But it's Alestria. Wouldn't you rather be away from there?"

My skin heated for a moment and I closed my eyes. It had been mine and Gareth's dreams to escape this shitty town and start over somewhere else. But that was before. And as much as I still intended to leave at some point, right now my life was here and I wasn't going to be moving away without finding out the truth about what had happened to my brother.

"Look, I really do appreciate it, but nothing has changed just because I found out I'm related to you guys. I think I'd like to try and build a relationship with you because I've always wanted a bigger family, but I've also always wanted to make my own way in life and to get myself out of the place I grew up in. I'm not looking for handouts, but it would be nice to hang out or whatever." I shrugged because I wasn't entirely sure what I wanted from her, but I did like the idea of getting to know the side of the family I hadn't even realised I had.

"Well, you may not be looking for handouts and I admire that sentiment, Elise, but I hope you realise that our family has an obligation to you. There's a trust fund in place for you - for all Altair heirs - and now that we have officially recognised you as a part of the family, we are legally bound to honour that."

"Are you saying I've got money?" I asked with a frown, unsure how to feel about that.

"Oh, sweetheart, you really are that innocent, aren't you?" Melinda tittered. "Did it seriously not even occur to you? Not even after you realised who you are?"

"No, not really," I replied honestly. "I've mostly been reeling over the fact that my dad isn't some deadbeat and that I've even got some other family."

"Well, not to worry. You'll get used to all the things it means to be an Altair soon. I was just calling to check in about lunch. You're still on for two?"

"Oh, I hadn't realised that was an actual arrangement we had, but yeah. Sure. Yeah. I can do that."

"And bring your mates," she added.

"Well, Dante and Ryder are actually working on a bunch of gang stuff today and they're not around..." Not to mention the fact that they were both still super pissed over the whole newspaper article bullshit and there was no way they'd be talked around as easily as I had just been. Not that I was totally won over by her, but she was kinda hard to stay mad at.

Melinda sighed. "Fine, fine. I suppose it will be simpler to meet them one at a time anyway. Someone will meet you outside the academy gates to collect you at two."

"Wait, I'm not at the academy," I said quickly, sensing she was about to end the call. "I can send you my location though."

"Perfect," she replied.

"Okay, I-"

The line went dead and I just kinda stared at it. Melinda Altair was...a lot. Mostly nice, I was pretty sure. But a lot. She was clearly more than used to getting her own way and I got the feeling I was going to have to be sharp on my reflexes if I wanted to make sure I didn't accidentally agree to anything I wasn't certain on with her.

But as well as feeling more than a dollop of anticipation over meeting her and the rest of her family, I actually felt kinda excited too. This was a big deal. I'd never really had anyone to go visiting with for Sunday lunch before and now I was bringing Leon to meet them too.

I had an actual, for true, lunch date to meet the family to bring him on. I wondered if Gabriel would want to come too. He was my mate just the same as the others even without the silver rings in his eyes and he was probably more capable of being pleasant than Dante or Ryder would be with the Altairs right about now.

My Atlas pinged and I looked down at it again, spotting a message from my Harpy.

Gabriel:
Thank you for thinking of me, angel, but I need to go and see Bill this afternoon. Take Leon, have fun and don't sit beside the fireplace.

I frowned at the weirdness of that last sentence but filed it away in my brain because I knew better than to disregard his advice then I rolled over and closed my eyes, deciding the best thing I could do right now was try and get some more sleep in.

"Little monster." Leon's lips brushed against my ear and I moaned sleepily as the warmth of his body shifted over mine. "Wakey, wakey."

"What time is it?" I mumbled, reaching out to push my fingers into his hair without opening my eyes.

"Almost time to go," he replied, leaning in to press a kiss to my neck which had me arching against him and drawing him closer.

I mumbled some response to that, but as Leon began to move his mouth down my body, I forgot all about it and concentrated on the feeling of his lips on my flesh.

His fingers curled around the straps of the silky teddy I'd slept in and I let him drag it down, freeing my breasts so that my nipples peaked in the cold air.

Leon growled a low, deep sound in the back of his throat as he licked his way towards my left nipple, swirling his tongue around the flesh surrounding it but denying me the satisfaction of actually touching it.

I cursed beneath my breath as he moved away from my aching breasts, his head moving down my body and kissing and licking his way to my navel as he continued to roll the silky material off of my body.

I lifted my hips for him, letting him slip it over my ass before pulling it down my legs and tossing it aside, leaving me bare beneath him.

"Leon," I moaned as he moved his mouth to my left knee and pushed my thighs apart, his heated gaze fixed on my centre as he skimmed his fingers back and forth over my legs without once touching me where I really wanted him to.

"Are you hungry, little monster?" he asked me, his eyes burning as he dragged them up my body to meet my gaze.

"If you're about to ask if I'm hungry for your cock then just save us both the jokes and put it inside me already," I growled, pushing up onto my elbows and reaching for him.

I grabbed the front of the smart grey shirt he was wearing and yanked him towards me, wondering why he was wearing so many star damned clothes. They were in the fucking way.

Leon gave me a dangerous smile before snatching my wrist to make me release him then pinning it to the blankets at my side.

He gave my body a hungry look before shifting back onto his heels and tossing my legs over his shoulders.

"We have to go if we don't want to miss lunch with your fancy new aunt," he said, looking up at me with his mouth hovering mere inches from my pussy which was throbbing with need right about now.

"What?" I gasped, pushing up onto my elbows again and frowning at him. "No, that can't be right. We don't have to be there until two and it's only..." I looked up at the sun which was blazing overhead and frowned in confusion.

"Well, it's actually like ten past," Leon said, giving my pussy a wistful look. "Gabe asked me to come up here and snuggle with you about four hours ago when he left to go see Bill and couldn't keep an eye on you anymore. And then when I got here you were all cute and sleepy and I was in a napping mood myself so instead of waking you, I just used a silencing bubble to sneak in with you. And I might have cast a restfulness spell on you too, because I know you haven't been sleeping all that well recently so I just wanted you to get your snooze on while you could."

My lips parted on what I had intended to be some kind of admonishment for him making that choice for me, but then he dipped his mouth low and ran his tongue up the centre of me, making my head fall back as I moaned.

Leon lapped at my clit for several blissfully perfect seconds then shifted back suddenly, shaking his head as if to clear it.

"No can do, little monster. You can't be late. Come on, let's go."

"I thought you said I was already late?" I growled, bucking my hips in a clear demand. "And I swear, Leo, I'm so turned on right now I'll be coming on your face within about thirty seconds. Please, just give it to me."

"Hmm..." Leon propped himself on one elbow and ran two fingers down the inside of my thigh, keeping up a perfectly slow pace until he reached my entrance and sank them into me.

My moan that time was even louder, and he smirked at me as he drove them in deep, feeling my pussy clamp tight around him before pulling them back out again way too soon.

"Nope. I can't do it, little monster. You need to go meet your fancy new family and I can't be the reason you're late." He shoved my legs off of his broad shoulders and grinned at me as I gaped at him.

"But you *are* the reason I'm late - you spelled me to keep me asleep!"

"Yeah, but it just seems a bit full on to tell them we're late because I was fucking you blind, doesn't it? Saying you overslept isn't half as bad."

"But I have no plans of telling them that, Leo. I just want you to make me come. Right now."

"Nope." He hopped up and tossed a dress at me as I tried to grab hold of him. "Come on. And I promise I'll get you off so good later that you'll forgive me for leaving you hanging and then some."

I narrowed my eyes at him then blew out a harsh breath as I gave in.

"How about this then," I suggested as I stood up, keeping the dress in my hand but making no move to put it on. "Let's play a game. We'll see which one of us cracks first."

Leon's eyes flared with excitement as he unashamedly stared at my tits.

"You think you can make me give in and fuck you?" he teased like he doubted it, but I was pretty sure we both knew who was going to lose here.

"I think that you will before I do," I replied with a smirk before shooting away from him, leaving him in Gabriel's rooftop nest and speeding down into Dante's room where I tossed the dress aside and quickly found another one.

By the time Leon had caught up to me, I was dressed in the tight black thing which clung to my skin and made my tits look stupidly good. I'd done my hair and makeup too, opting for a lipstick the colour of black cherries before placing a pair of killer heels on my feet.

Leon groaned, running a hand through his flowing golden hair and I grinned at him in challenge.

"What happened to the frilly, flouncy dress Dante's mom bought you?" he asked, looking like he couldn't decide if this was better or worse - probably because he'd just realised I was most definitely going to win.

"I think I should keep that for dinner with the family tonight, don't you?" I asked innocently. "Don't you like this one?" I turned to give him a view of the back which was open to reveal my spine and had a slit up the back of the skirt which flashed a few extra inches of thigh when I walked.

"Err, *like* isn't the term I'd pick," he said, taking a step forward before halting suddenly and frowning at me. "But it doesn't matter how shit hot you look, little monster, I'm still not gonna crack."

I shrugged a shoulder innocently, popped a stick of cherry gum between my lips and headed for the door.

Dante's mom waved us off, calling out about some boy who had been left to wait around for us by the gates for almost twenty minutes now and my heart leapt as I wondered who Melinda had sent to get us.

As we stepped out into the sunlight beyond the front doors, one of the older pack members just so happened to be trundling by on the drive in one of the little vans they used in the vineyards and I shot forward before leaping onto the back of it.

Leon broke into a run to catch up with the van, hopping into the back beside me with a grin and standing at my side as I held onto the roof of the cab to make sure I didn't fall out as we headed down the drive towards the main gate.

"Are you worried about today?" he asked me, leaning in close so the scent of summer washed from his flesh to caress my senses.

"A little," I admitted. "I mean, you can't really get much further from my upbringing to the kind of place we're heading to right now and as much as I like the idea of bonding with these people, I'm not convinced blood is all it will take for that."

"Don't worry about that," Leon replied with a shrug. "We made it through that party at the Acrux place."

"Up until our antics got us thrown out," I reminded him, wondering if Melinda would remember me from that night and cringing a little.

Leon just laughed it off though, shrugging his big shoulders like that didn't faze him in the slightest.

"You can't force people to like you," he said. "That's the long and short of it. No matter who you are or where you're from there will always be some asshole who wants to take a piss in your rainbow. But fuck them. Because for every miserable bastard who can't appreciate the way you shine, there are a hundred who would count themselves blessed to bask in your glow. So focus on those people. They're the ones who matter. If it turns out these fancy fuckers don't like us, then fuck them. Blood is all well and good, but family means a hell of a lot more than DNA and you just so happen to have found yourself plenty of love either way."

I bit my lip as I smiled at that assessment, glad Leon was coming with me for this headfuck of a lunch. I needed his casual disregard for other people's bullshit judgements today and he was right. All I could do was be myself and the rest would fall the way it would. Only one way to find out anyway.

As the van reached the gates, it drew to a halt, but before Leon could make a move to jump down, I leaned in close to him and whispered in his ear. "Oh shit, I just realised, I totally forgot to put any underwear on."

Leon gaped at me, his eyes moving down my body as I gave him a wink and shot away, slipping through the gates before the van driver had even managed to get them halfway open.

There was a boy waiting there, sitting on a low sandstone wall to the side of the drive and I sucked in a surprised breath as I recognised him. Caleb Altair, Heir to Melinda's seat on the Celestial Council - as in, future leader of our freaking kingdom and apparently my cousin now too - arched a brow as he spotted me too.

"Are you always this late or is it a one off?" he asked casually, pushing a hand through his curling blonde hair and getting to his feet. "'Cause it's cool either way, but next time I'll bring snacks for the wait if it's a habit."

I broke a laugh, moving closer to him then pausing at an awkward distance. We'd gotten along well enough when we'd met before but that was without either of us knowing we were related and all that jazz, and now I was feeling fifty shades of awkward. Did we hug? Do some kind of cousin fist bump? Shake hands? Do the cheek kissing thing? Fuck if I knew.

"Sorry," I said, opting for the awkward, standing-a-little-bit-too-far-away-and-not-knowing-where-to-put-my-arms thing. "I overslept."

Caleb laughed, closing the distance between us and pulling me into a hug.

"I figure this is weird whatever way we do it, but seeing as we've missed out on years of making mud pies and all that shit, a hug is the least we deserve," he explained before releasing me again. He may have been a few years younger than me, but somehow he didn't really seem it. He was as tall as me and his body had a noticeable amount of muscle even if it wasn't quite as much as my guys. But at only fourteen years old, he certainly had the look of a man about him more than a boy and I had to wonder if he'd ever really made mud pies or if he'd spent his entire life training to be the man he'd been born to become.

Leon caught up to me and wrapped his arms around us too, purring loudly as he nuzzled against me and Caleb while his hard dick less than subtly pressed against my ass.

"Let's get going then, my man, my girl woke up hungry, didn't you, little monster?" Leon said, nipping at my earlobe.

I released Caleb and stepped back, but Leon kept his arms draped around me from behind, placing a kiss on my cheek and flexing his hips so his cock pressed even firmer against my ass. *Damn him.*

"Sounds good. Mom will have lunch ready by half past, so we won't have long to wait." Caleb took a pouch of stardust from his pocket and held it ready for us.

"I didn't realise your mom cooks," I said, my stomach grumbling at the thought of food after my mega snooze.

"Fuck no, of course she doesn't. I meant the staff will have it ready for her." Caleb burst into laughter as he threw the stardust over us and we were whipped away by the stars before he managed to get control of himself.

We landed heavily outside the gates of a house which looked more like a bank. And not the kind of bank I'd bank at. The kind of bank with fancy men to open the doors and bow and give you champagne as you headed in to store away your bars of gold. But like, even fancier than that.

It was all marble everything. There were pillars either side of the gate which were made from the stuff in a whitish colour with gold veins running through it then a low wall lining the driveway made from even more of it. The gates themselves were silver and I wasn't totally convinced that they weren't genuinely silver like the precious metal instead of just coloured like it.

Leon let out a low whistle as the gates parted and a dude in a fancy little hat drove up to collect us in a golf cart.

Caleb just hopped on like this was totally normal and I could practically see Leon calculating the value of everything surrounding us as he stepped forward, giving me his hand so that I could climb into the cart.

The moment we were all on board, the driver whipped us around and we whizzed back up the drive towards the...house? I wasn't totally sure houses were supposed to blot out the sunlight like that beast was currently doing, but sure, I'd go with house.

Caleb chatted about the family, dropping names and descriptions so fast that they all went right over my head and I just nodded along, feeling more than a little overwhelmed by the time we made it to the front door.

We followed Caleb up a set of marble steps to the marble building and I was surprised to find the door was made out of plain old wood. Well, plain old mahogany inlaid with an inscription in some language I couldn't read, but still, it wasn't marble for a change.

Once we were inside, we picked up the pace while Caleb pointed out various rooms and I just nodded along, not really seeing anything beyond the echoing space and money dripping from the walls. It probably wasn't really any more lavish than the Acrux Manor, but I guessed it was just the fact that I knew I was related to these people that had me thrown. Walking through the Dragon Lord's fancy pants house was so far detached from me that I could just kind of laugh at how absurd it was. But this place was somewhere I could have been familiar with. It was somewhere I could have played as a child or might spend a lot of time at in the future.

Leon's fingers wound between mine and I released a slow breath, taking comfort from his steady presence at my side before we stepped into a dining room which was thankfully a pretty normal size. I mean, it still had a table big enough for ten to sit around it, but as far as this house went, that was small.

"Elise!" Melinda cooed as she hopped to her feet, arms open wide as she moved forward to embrace me, kissing me on either cheek before turning her attention to Leon. "And the dashing Leonidas," she said, a slight but noticeable flirtatious lilt to her tone. It didn't set my hackles off though, it seemed more like her general way than an actual advance and for some reason I wasn't threatened by her.

"You can just call me, Leon, Mrs A."

"Of course," she replied, stepping back so that a tall man could approach next who I recognised as her husband from the newspapers. "This is Oscar, my husband and your uncle, Elise," she said. "And that's Caleb's younger brother Hadley." She pointed to a boy who looked strikingly like his brother but with darker hair like his father's. "And the girls, Iris and Jenna," she added, pointing me towards two blonde haired cutie pies who were looking up at me with wide eyes.

"You never said her hair was purple," Iris breathed in astonishment.

"I want my hair to be purple," Jenna added with a grin and suddenly the tension I'd been feeling burst, and a laugh escaped me.

"You want to hear the story behind me dying it this colour?" I offered, moving to take a seat opposite them before realising that was right beside the fire and moving around to sit beside Jenna instead as Gabriel's warning rang in my memory. I assumed he'd *seen* me dropping food down myself in that chair or something and I was more than happy to avoid the embarrassment of that.

"It's a good story," Leon added enthusiastically, taking the seat beside me and leaning back in it with his legs spread wide and his arm around the back of my chair like he was perfectly at home here. "It involves her thinking me and her other mates might have been bad guys and disguising herself so that we didn't catch onto her secret identity."

The girls bounced in their seats, squealing with excitement as Leon made my life sound way more interesting than I could have managed and I flashed him a smile before trying to figure out how to tell that story without getting too deep into the fact that my brother had been murdered and everything that went with that. I was perfectly happy to tell Melinda and the older people at the table those details because hell, they might even be able to help me find some answers, but it seemed a little heavy to lay on the kids at our first meeting.

We all fell into conversation as starters were brought out for us and Leon made the adults laugh at least as often as the kids with his crazy tales and outright bullshit. He casually avoided any mention of what his family did for a living, and I never went into too much detail about Dante or Ryder's gang lives either. Funnily though, I got the impression Melinda already knew all about that and gave precisely zero fucks about it. That said, I was going to be checking Leon's pockets before we left here because there was no way in hell that I'd be risking him stealing from another Celestial Councillor after what had happened to Roary.

Just as our starter plates were being cleared away, the door burst open and I squealed in alarm as a Vampire shot into the room and the empty chair beside the fire exploded into flames.

Leon was on his feet between me and the newcomer in a flash, a snarl of warning escaping his lips as flames ignited coating his fists in the same instant.

"It's okay!" Melinda called, jumping up too and dousing the chair with water to put it out, allowing me to get a better look at the Vampire so that I could recognise him.

"Oh," I breathed as my gaze fell on my father and his on me.

"Marley," Melinda chastised as she moved over to her brother and laid a hand on his arm. "What did I say? You still aren't used to having your magic back. I think this is a bit too much for you, I wanted to bring Elise to you alone after your nap. Remember?"

Her tone was firm but her eyes were soft and as she stroked a hand along his cheek, I felt a tug in my gut that reminded me of my own brother. She'd known the same loss as I had. Her brother had disappeared and she'd had no idea where he was for years. Then when she was finally given her answer, she found out he'd been living in conditions which were arguably the worst imaginable for all of this time. I just hoped that he'd been so lost to the thirst and the insanity brought on by being denied magic for so long that he hadn't even been fully aware of the time passing him by.

"It's okay," I said, laying a hand on Leon's shoulder and prompting him to relax his stance as he banished the flames he'd conjured. "Erm, Marlowe, right?"

"Dad," he growled and I swallowed thickly.

"I, ah, never had one of those." I shrugged and his eyes crinkled with pain which made my gut twist guiltily. I knew now that that hadn't been his choice, but it was still the truth and I wasn't exactly a kid needing her daddy anymore. But I guessed I still wanted…something with him. If we could figure it out.

Melinda sighed, patting his arm sympathetically as I tried to decide how that word might taste on my tongue. I knew it wasn't his fault that I'd never known how it would fit there, but that didn't make it easy for me to just open my arms out wide and start calling him Dad.

"Maybe we could try and catch up on the last twenty years a bit over lunch?" I suggested, somehow feeling stupidly awkward all over again.

I wasn't sure why it was so different with him. Maybe because Melinda and her family seemed to only want to know me. With Marlowe I couldn't help but feel like he wanted so much more than that. He wanted back the life he'd had stolen from him. Which meant he wanted those twenty years, the birthdays and the Christmases and everything in between. But I wasn't going to be able to give them to him. For a start, they belonged to Gareth and now that I didn't even have him, offering up the memories I'd shared with him seemed so much more invasive. And this man, no matter what he might have wanted to be to me, was a stranger.

"Tell me," Marlowe growled, taking the seat opposite me and staring without blinking.

His skin was pale, no doubt from all of those years underground and I could see that he was more than a little unhinged by what he'd endured down there. But as I struggled to come up with the words he wanted to hear from me, I saw that hunger in his eyes, that pain, and I just knew I had to try.

"Okay then, where do I begin?"

After three hours, four more courses and more laughter than I would have expected with such heavy subject matter, Marlowe had clearly reached the end of what he was able for.

He'd eaten his food - mostly because Melinda kept reminding him to - and had listened to every word I had to say with rapt attention. He didn't seem massively capable of stringing long sentences together which Melinda had explained was due to the trauma he'd endured, but I just knew that he understood everything I told him.

His eyes glistened with pain when I spoke about my mom and when I'd had to admit to the heartbreak she'd suffered over him leaving her he'd actually shed a tear which had cut into my soul.

He hated that he'd done that to her. To us. I could see it in his eyes and feel it in the way he'd gripped my hand across the table. My heart hurt for him and for me, my mom, Gareth. How different would our lives have been if he'd been there to love all of us? I hadn't been able to bring myself to break the news to him about Gareth's death in the end and though I was trying to convince myself that that was because I didn't want to lay too much on him all at once, I knew it was partly because I hoped it wasn't true.

No matter how much I fought against the urge to hope, I knew I was already losing that battle. Which meant it was time I started searching for him.

Melinda eventually led Marlowe away to his room after I'd sworn I'd come back and visit him again soon and we'd been given over to my cousins so that they could take us on a tour of the house.

Jenna and Iris shrieked in excitement as they raced up the stairs toward their rooms, begging me to see theirs first and I couldn't help but smirk at Hadley as I watched him battle against the desire to race them too or play it cool. Ah the joys of being a preteen.

"So, I read in the papers that Marlowe has been 'lost in the jungle' for the last twenty odd years," Leon said casually to Caleb as we walked and my cousin snorted a laugh while I frowned in confusion.

"Yeah, well, Mom would hardly let the story get out there that some psycho managed to lock him up in a tunnel for all of that time, now would she? Imagine how that would look. An Altair overpowered and kept prisoner like that while none of the rest of us noticed? No fucking way." He chuckled like the idea was too absurd to even contemplate and I exchanged a glance with Leon.

"So what does that mean about King?" I asked. "She told me the FIB would investigate."

"The guy who was holding Marley captive?" Caleb confirmed and I nodded. "Right. Yeah, Mom won't let him get away with that shit. The agents she sent are special ops. In and out, assassin style. They'll sort him out."

"We don't even know if it is a him," I pointed out, the tension rising in my body at the casual disregard they seemed to hold for this threat.

"Okay then, him or her. Don't worry about it. I promise you, they're probably dead already." Caleb shrugged dismissively but that didn't ease the knot in my stomach at all.

They weren't taking this seriously. Not the way they needed to be. King had been stealing power for years now and after that shit they'd been pulling beneath the ocean with the multiple sacrifices, who knew how powerful they might be? Those FIB agents might be good, but I still had doubts. Serious doubts. Though I really wished I could have Caleb's confidence in them being able to do away with him or her once and for all.

Before I could push him any further on the subject, we made it to Iris's bedroom and I was engulfed in so much princess pink regalia that it made my eyes sting.

The girls stole my attention as they showed me their things and we explored the rest of the house then I agreed to go and explore the gardens with them when it was done.

But just as we stepped out into the beautiful gardens beyond the back of the manor, a voice called out to us and we turned to find Melinda approaching with a whole camera crew and a woman I didn't know in tow.

"Elise, Leonidas, this is Portia, she's a reporter for The Celestial Times and has come to do a quick interview with us about you being reunited with the family after all of these years," Melinda said, flashing us a stunning smile as I took in the costume change she'd pulled off since lunch. She was wearing a navy-blue dress which was slightly more formal than the previous one and her hair looked freshly styled too.

The girls both groaned while Hadley rolled his eyes, but Caleb flashed a bright smile like he was more than camera ready at all times and I had to wonder if he was faking it or if he genuinely didn't mind having random photoshoots sprung on him. I guessed that was always going to be a part of his life in his position though, so it made sense for him to accept it easily.

"Shall we run?" Leon teased in a low voice, dipping his head so that he could speak in my ear and I breathed out a laugh as I tipped my chin to look up at him.

"And where would we run to, Mr Night?" I purred, laying a hand on his chest and allowing my fingers to slip inside the open shirt buttons at his throat.

"I'm sure there are plenty of good hiding places around here, little monster," he promised, his arm coming around me until he was gripping my ass and pulling me closer.

A camera flashed beside us and I flinched as I looked around at the photographer who'd just stolen that candid shot as he promptly took a second photo with absolutely zero shame.

"How about a group shot?" Portia called out, ushering us towards the rest of the family and we were corralled together.

I didn't really know what to say about all of this and I certainly wasn't sure I liked it, but I went along with it, allowing them to rearrange us and take more and more photos.

Every time I was in a shot beside Leon, his fingers brushed against my skin, touching my arms, my bare back, my neck. All subtle touches of his skin against mine, but I knew full well what he was doing. He'd remembered the game we'd been playing before coming here and the more he did it, the more I grew achy for the touch of his flesh.

But I wasn't the type to lose easily.

So as the photographer repositioned us again, I made sure my back was pressed to his front and pressed my ass against his crotch before throwing a silencing bubble up around the two of us and speaking in a low, sultry tone. "When you give in and take me, Leo, do you want my ass or my pussy?"

I dropped the silencing bubble, grinding my ass back against his hardening cock and smiling for the camera just as a low growl escaped him.

Melinda and Oscar glanced his way while I pretended not to notice and shifted my hips so that I rubbed against him again and he cursed under his breath.

Portia shot a few random questions at me about where I lived and how I'd grown up, but Melinda fielded them with some bullshit fluffed up version of me living a quiet life and being a studious girl. I didn't feel like contradicting her. I had no shame about where I'd grown up, but I knew if I mentioned The Sparkling Uranus or offered up more details on my mom's profession it would only lead to more questions, not to mention an article about it and that shit wasn't anyone's business but my own.

We moved to take more photos and Leon's hand shifted between the slit at the back of my skirt, his fingers brushing up the backs of my thighs and making me stifle a gasp as he grazed them over my ass.

Maybe the no panties thing had been a bad idea.

Leon grinned for the camera then turned and pressed a kiss to my neck and I had to fight a moan.

It didn't take much longer for the interview to wrap up and Leon quickly pointed out the time, reminding me that we'd promised to be back at Dante's for dinner tonight.

I was way past the point of protest and pretty certain that I was happy with losing the game now and I had to battle my libido back down to make it through the round of goodbyes.

Caleb escorted us back to the gates, but when we got there, Leon informed him that he had his own supply of stardust and that we didn't need the ride. Caleb seemed intrigued by that, but just said goodbye and watched as Leon threw a handful of the glittering black powder over our heads and we were swept away into the grip of the stars.

The moment we were spat back out again, I knew we weren't anywhere near the Oscura stronghold and I looked around at the stunning array of sports cars surrounding us in surprise.

"Where are we?" I asked and Leon grinned darkly as he grabbed my hand and led me over to a stunning black sports car which was parked to the far end of the lot.

"I got a tip off that the owner of this beauty was having dinner here tonight and I thought you might wanna play thief with me, little monster," he explained. "I've been studying all of the alarm systems on it and I'm pretty sure that given about three minutes I can-"

I shot away from Leon while he was still talking, a grin on my lips as I raced towards a little hut where the valets clearly kept the keys to the cars parked up down here. Beyond it, high up on the hill, I could see a beautiful, exclusive looking restaurant with views out over the lake and the sound of music and laughter reached me from inside.

I made it to the little hut and paused as I felt the tingle of a detection spell brushing against my skin. It was subtle and pretty cleverly done, but I was becoming something of an expert with this kind of magic after uncovering so many of Gareth's secrets, so it didn't take me too long to manipulate it to let me through.

Then I just waited until the valet inside hung a set of keys on one of the hooks then took off back up the gravel drive towards the restaurant to collect another car.

The moment he was gone, I shot a bolt of air magic at the camera in the corner of the room, knocking it aside so that it was facing the wall then sped inside and snagged the key to the sports car.

I raced back to Leon's side with a wide grin, tossing him the key and the smile he gave me in return was all animal as he caught me around the waist and stole a filthy, adrenaline fuelled kiss from my lips.

"Do you wanna drive?" he offered as we broke apart and I laughed.

"No, Leo. I want you to drive. Fast."

His smile widened and he unlocked the car, opening the door for me to hop in before rounding the hood and getting in behind the wheel himself.

The smell of fresh leather enveloped us as the doors closed and Leon started her up with a deep purr of the engine – a purr he echoed in his own chest.

I waited until he'd sped us past the restaurant and whooped as we zipped out onto the highway, Leon taking me at my word and hitting the gas hard.

He chose a route which led towards the mountains which I recognised from being at Dante's house and I guessed we were heading back there like he'd said.

As we turned off of the highway and onto a winding mountain road, I reached over and slid my hand up his thigh, smiling darkly as he shot me a hungry look.

"What are you doing, little monster?"

"Playing a new game," I replied, glancing at the speedometer. "Keep the car above ninety and I won't stop."

"Won't stop what?" he asked as I slid his fly open and pushed my fingers inside it to caress his hard cock, letting him know exactly what.

"So what happens if I slow down?" he asked, his gaze bouncing between me and the road and I knew this was dumb as fuck, but I was high on the thrill of it plus high on him and I trusted his driving well enough to chance it.

"If you slow down, then I stop. And you have to give me what I want instead," I purred.

Leon was nodding before I'd even finished talking and I smirked at him before pushing his boxers down and releasing his hard cock.

I groaned with need at the sight of it, my pulse thumping as I leaned down and ran my tongue along the length of his shaft with a throaty moan.

Leon hissed between his teeth and I felt the speed slowing a little, causing me to raise my head and check the speedometer. We were still above ninety. Just.

"Losing so soon, Leo?" I teased.

"No fucking chance," he growled in response and my smile widened as I wrapped my hand around the base of his cock before leaning down and closing my lips over the head of it.

Leon groaned as I worked my way down his shaft, taking him right to the back of my throat and loving the way he tasted in my mouth as I worked my tongue over him.

"Fuck," he breathed, the car swerving around a bend and making me grab a fistful of his shirt to keep my balance.

I pulled back and checked the speedometer and he cursed again, managing to keep it over ninety so that I carried on.

I sucked and teased him, my tongue ravishing him as I moaned my own desire around his solid length and his cursing got more and more frequent as I felt him thickening in my mouth.

But before I could bring him to ruin, the car swerved hard to the left and I was almost knocked clean off of him.

The car jerked to a halt and I lifted myself up to see why we'd stopped, but Leon's mouth collided with mine before I could get a look out of the windows.

His hands were in my hair and all over my body and I moaned loudly as I began to unbutton his shirt in a frenzy of heat and need.

He grasped the shoulder of my dress and yanked it down, quickly followed by the other one and as I started to push the rest of the fabric off of me, his mouth fell over my nipple and he bit down in the most delicious way.

Leon sucked and teased my breasts, his touch rough and demanding and making me so freaking wet that I was panting for him as I shoved my dress down over my ass then kicked it off, leaving me in nothing but my heels.

With a growl, Leon gripped my waist and yanked me into his lap, turning me so that my back was to him and he shoved me forward over the steering wheel.

I could feel the heat of his cock between my thighs without actually pushing into me, my wetness drenching his shaft as we ground against each other and the head of his dick rode over my clit in a way that made me gasp and beg for more.

His big hands wrapped around my hips and he lifted me just enough to give him the room he needed. I wound my fingers around the steering wheel a second before he thrust his cock inside me, making me cry out as I closed my eyes and just focused on the feeling of him filling me.

"Your pussy, little monster," he growled, taking hold of a fistful of my hair as he drove into me even harder the second time. "In case me slamming my cock into it wasn't a clear enough answer to your question from earlier."

"Show me you own me, Leo," I begged and he growled in satisfaction as he took up the challenge of doing just that.

Leon released my hair, shoving me forward to give himself more room and crushing me against the steering wheel as he gripped my ass and began to bounce me up and down on his huge cock in time with the punishing thrust of his hips.

Words escaped me as I gave up control of my body to this king of beasts and he slammed into me over and over and over again until my pussy was squeezing tight around his dick and I was coming all over it with a scream of pleasure.

He didn't even let me finish riding it out before picking me up and separating our bodies as he pushed me onto my hands and knees on my own seat, though I had to grip onto the door to maintain the position in the small space.

"*And* your ass," he said in a wicked tone and I looked over my shoulder at him with wide eyes as he used my own wetness which was coating his cock as lubricant for taking my ass next.

He wasn't gentle with me or slow, giving me exactly what I'd asked for and using me in the exact way he desired and as he seated his huge cock fully inside my tight hole, I found myself breathless and shaking beneath him.

Leon shifted his fingers onto my clit then gripped my hair with his other hand and began to move again.

My whole body was buzzing with the fullness of him inside me and I gasped and panted for him, moaning his name over and over again as I gripped the door like it was a freaking lifeline.

Leon growled as he reared over me, his pace merciless and grip tight while he thrust in deep and kept his fingers moving over my clit the whole time so that I was panting with the need for release.

The car bounced beneath us and the windows fogged until every piece of my body seemed to explode with pleasure all at once. I came so hard that my breath caught in my lungs and a choked cry escaped me. My muscles squeezed, clenching tightly around him and he pulled out of me with a growl before coming all over my back.

I sagged forward, the most deliciously spent feeling taking over my limbs and a soft laugh left my lips as Leon slapped my ass cheek playfully.

"Fuck, I love you so much, Elise," he purred, sliding his open shirt off of his shoulders and using it to mop his cum up before I moved to sit upright.

"I love you too, Leo," I replied, still breathless, my chest heaving and drawing his gaze to my tits again.

I glanced out of the window, my eyes widening a little as I realised we were literally on the side of the road with plenty of cars speeding past us no more than a few meters away. I'd been so dick blinded that I hadn't even noticed them while he fucked me senseless in full freaking view of everyone who had passed us by.

"Shit, Leo, anyone could have seen us," I gasped, moving to cover my very on display nipples with my hands, but he just grinned at me.

"Maybe I wanted the world to see that you're mine," he replied darkly, letting me know he'd been getting off on the idea of people seeing us. "And I really love your tits, so don't go hiding them before I'm finished having my fun," he added, giving me a grin which said he wasn't totally done with me yet.

I began to shake my head, my gaze flicking to the passing cars again, but he knocked my hands aside before I could protest any more, leaning down to savage them with his mouth.

I really wanted to tell him to stop, but that felt so fucking good that the words weren't quite making it to my tongue.

Leon raised a wrist to my lips in offering as I moaned softly and I cursed because he had me there. There was no more fighting what my body wanted so I just gave in.

The moment my fangs drove into his skin, he slid his fingers between my thighs again and started to rub at my clit, the combination of his power flooding into me and my already overly sensitive flesh, dick blinding me all over again.

Leon moved his mouth down my body, pushing his fingers inside me as his tongue took over the work on my clit and I wrapped my thighs around his neck, fucking his hand and his face for all the world to see.

I was his anyway. So at the end of the day, who really gave a shit?

And as I came even harder than before, grinding my pussy against his face and drinking his blood deeply, I knew that I didn't. Not one shit. Because I was in motherfucking heaven.

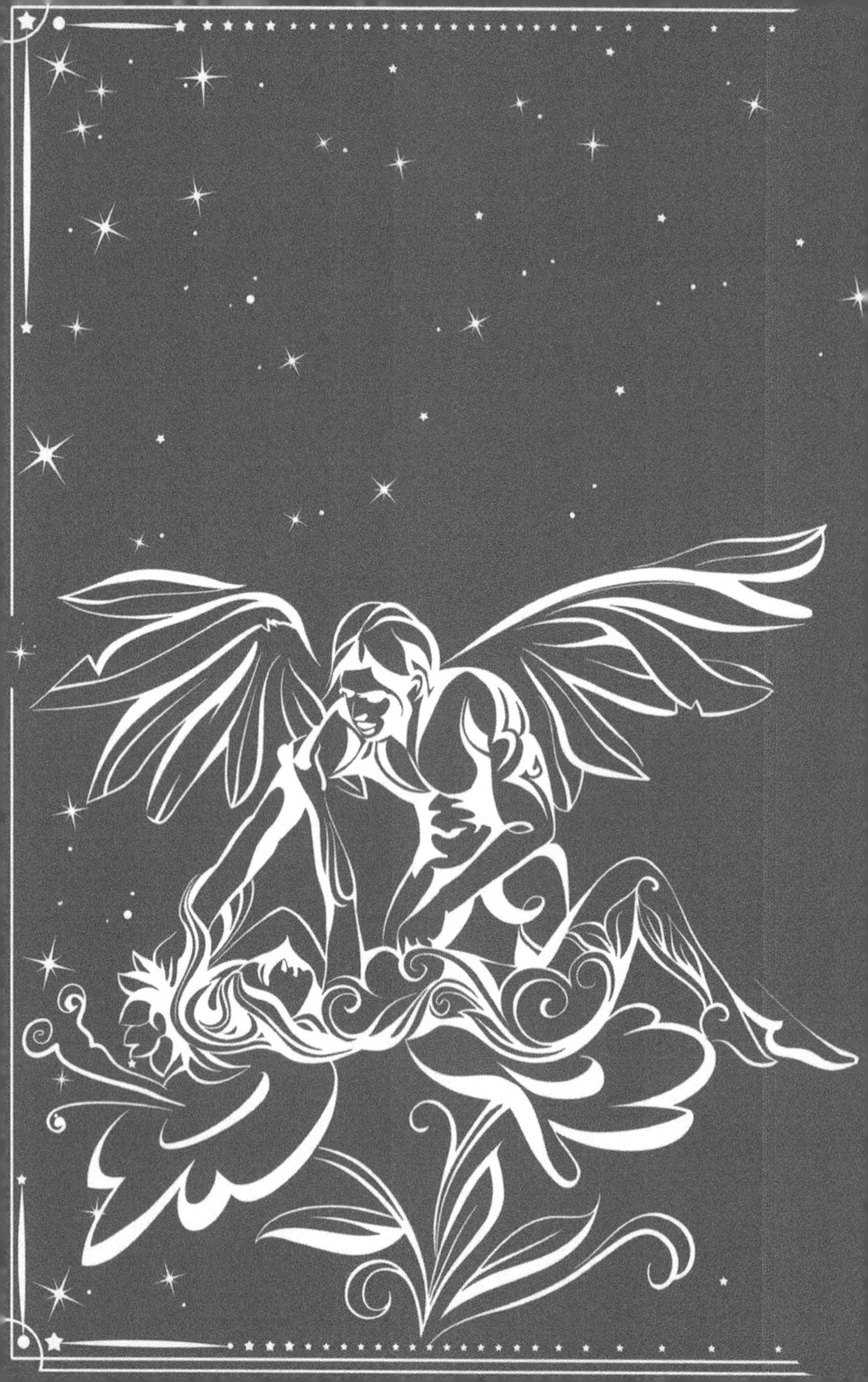

GABRIEL

CHAPTER THIRTY ONE

"I can't believe you," Leon grumbled angrily as we arrived at the winter cabin where we'd spent Christmas, the stardust depositing us right on the doorstep.

Snow covered the roof and surrounded us in a world of white while little flakes fluttered down in a gentle breeze. We wanted to have a few days alone together before the end of Spring Break and to give Dante's mom a rest from cooking and cleaning for us. I'd helped her out as much as possible, but the woman was determined to mother us. And as sweet as that was, after so much time in her household being jumped on by Wolf pups at every opportunity, we all needed a bit of a breather. Especially after a pack of pups had broken into the bathroom where Ryder had been taking a shit this morning. He had not been pleased, though it was funny as fuck.

"Oh get over it already, *stronzo*," Dante said to Leon in exasperation. Dante had taken back Leon's medallion while he was passed out drunk last night and he was pissed as hell about it.

"It. Was. *Mine*," Leon growled.

"No, it's mine and you took it," Dante growled as Leon worked to break down the concealment and alarm spells on the cabin door before throwing the door open with a bang and marching inside.

Elise shared an awkward look with me. "Any chance you can *see* a way out of his mood?" she whispered.

"I heard that!" Leon called in anger and Elise sighed in frustration, heading inside after Dante.

Ryder held back at my side, his toleration for drama set at absolutely zero. His arm brushed mine and I frowned, sensing the edges of a subtle concealment spell on him.

"What are you concealing?" I murmured, taking his arm and trying to turn it over to see his wrist.

"Nothing." He yanked his arm away as I caught sight of the Scorpio tattoo I'd tricked him into getting, sure there was something else there which he was hiding. But The Sight gave me no clue of what it was and Ryder's face said he absolutely wasn't in the mood to tell me, so I had to let it go.

I kicked the door shut as we walked inside, asking the stars for a bit of guidance on our angry Lion, but they were silent and I swear I felt their amusement. They were little assholes sometimes.

"Stop it, stronzo," Dante barked as I rounded into the lounge and found Leon throwing things out of Dante's travel bag in all directions.

"Where did you hide it? I'll find it, you know I will," Leon snapped, looking up at Dante with a narrow eyed glare. "I'm the best thief in Solaria."

"Well now you're the second best." Dante smirked and I sensed the impending explosion before it came.

"You stole from me when I was passed out in a ditch drunk – I could have *died*, what if the bears had come and dragged me off into the forest to eat me?" Leon roared.

"That wasn't a ditch, Leone, it was a fire pit two feet from my house which you crawled into while it was still burning because you said your feet were cold," Dante snapped. "And half my pack slept out there with you anyway."

"Pah, you don't know anything," Leon said dismissively. "Just give it back. It was a gift." He held out his hand in a demand.

"I gave you my medallion because you died," Dante said darkly. "And you are not dead. So unless you want to drive a dagger into your chest right now, then I'm not giving it back."

Leon gasped in horror, holding a hand to his heart. "Oh, now you want me to kill myself?" He swung around to look at Elise. "Did you hear that, little monster? He told me to drive a dagger into my chest!"

"Leo…" Elise said in exasperation. "It's Dante's medallion, you're overreacting."

"Overreacting?" he gasped, grabbing the coffee table and throwing it across the room where it smashed against a wall. "How am I overreacting?!"

"I'm gonna take a shower," Ryder muttered, slipping away through the bathroom door to escape.

"Because you just threw a table at the wall," Elise said, pointing at the destruction with a pout.

"Oh, so now I can't get upset when my best friend – my *best friend* – tells me I should kill myself?" Leon bellowed.

"That's not what I said, stronzo!" Dante bellowed and electricity zapped off of him at Leon, making him yell as it struck him.

"Did you see that?" Leon gasped. "He tried to finish me himself!"

"I've had enough of this," Dante muttered.

"Well I'll just go and *die* then, shall I?" Leon huffed, storming into the bedroom and slamming the door so hard the cabin shuddered. I released a weary sigh.

"How do we calm him down, Gabriel?" Elise asked me again and I concentrated on the furious Lion, the stars giving me a glimmer of an answer.

"Well…you can give him back the medallion, Dante-"

"No," he clipped.

"Or…" I frowned, shaking my head. *Not worth it.*

"What?" Dante pressed and I folded my arms.

"Or we can all sing Hakuna Matata, but if it doesn't include Ryder then it won't work and there's one in a million chance of him going along with it. Which is just a little more than it would take to convince me to do it too, so I say you give him back the medallion." I tossed my bag onto the couch and hooked my arm around Elise's waist, pulling her down onto my lap in an armchair. She grinned, running her fingers down my chest in a soft caress and I already felt the tension in my limbs easing.

"Dalle stelle." Dante rubbed his eyes. "Won't he just calm down on his own if we give him enough time to chill out?"

"Um…no," I said assuredly as I checked with the stars. "He's set to be in this mood for two weeks at least."

"Even if I go and get naked for him and cover myself in chocolate sauce?" Elise suggested and I squeezed her ass through her jeans as I smirked.

"Even then, but if you do that for me, I promise you'll forget all about his mood," I said in low tone and she grinned mischievously.

"No one's fucking anyone until the Leone is dealt with," Dante said decisively. "I'm not spending the next however many days with devil Leon. He's a fucking nightmare to be around when he's like this."

"Well I gave you your options," I said simply, my fingers sliding up the back of Elise's cami to stroke her silky skin.

I didn't like being told not to do something, and I especially didn't like being told not to fuck my girl. She smirked, leaning down and pushing my head to one side.

"You hungry, angel?" I asked breathily as her fangs snapped out.

"Starved," she breathed then bit deep into my neck, drawing a groan from my lips.

Ryder stepped out of the bathroom pulling a shirt on over his jeans, his short hair damp and the scent of soap carrying from him. "Has he calmed down yet?"

"No, but how do you feel about singing Hakuna Matata to him?" Dante asked seriously and Ryder barked a dry laugh.

"I'd sooner pluck my own eyeballs out, Inferno." He headed to the kitchen, picking up a jar of dry pasta and pouring a bowl of it before tossing one in his mouth and crunching through it.

"By the stars," I cursed as Elise withdrew her fangs from my neck and healed the bite away. "I'll make us breakfast."

"Oooh, pancakes?" Elise asked hungrily.

"Whatever you want, angel." I placed her on her feet and headed to the kitchenette, snatching the bowl of dry pasta from Ryder's hand and shaking my head at him. "If you wanted me to cook, you just had to ask."

"I'm perfectly happy eating that."

"You don't even know what it is, do you?" I narrowed my eyes.

"It's cereal," he said with a shrug.

"Not even close." I tossed the pasta back into the jar and took what I needed from our cooler bag, sensing a curious little Storm Dragon drifting closer while Ryder went to sit with Elise.

I taught Dante how to make pancakes while he chopped some banana to go with them, taking his sweet time as he cut them perfectly then looked at me for approval. The Wolf blood in him was showing as he gave me little doggish smiles every time I praised him. I stacked up pancakes on five plates, drizzled them in syrup and left Dante to arrange his specially chopped banana on each of them as I headed to the bedroom door.

I knocked softly but Leon didn't answer. "I've done breakfast," I called. Still no answer so I shrugged and headed to the kitchen island where everyone was gathering to eat.

Elise sat beside me, devouring her meal with noises so sexual that my dick jerked hopefully in my pants.

"You keep that up and I'll stuff something else in your mouth, baby,"

Ryder taunted before pushing a massive bite of pancakes and banana between his lips. It was hard not to think of the fuck fest that we'd all been a part of the last time we were here at Christmas, and I shared a look with Dante and Ryder that said they were thinking the same thing.

A knock came at the door and we all looked around in confusion.

"Who the hell is that?" Elise questioned just as The Sight gave me a vision of who it was.

I slid off of my seat, my expression stern as I yanked the door open and found Leon outside carrying a large pile of wood in his arms, snow on his shoulders and a woolly hat on his head.

His golden eyes fell on the pancakes and horror crossed his features. "I climbed out a window and went chopping wood to keep us all warm, and you've been here eating breakfast without me." He threw the wood blocks at my feet and stormed past me with a snarl. He strode into the bedroom again and slammed the door hard. He was asking for drama, the guy was a fire Elemental for the star's sake, we didn't need wood.

"That fucking Lion needs to grow up." Ryder pushed out of his seat, his fingers curling into fists as he strode toward Leon's door. I moved into his path before he could get there and he snarled at me.

"Get outa my way, Big Bird."

"No." I folded my arms. "You'll just make things worse if you go in there."

"Well what are we gonna do?" he demanded.

"There must be something, Gabriel?" Elise asked hopefully.

"Unless Ryder's up for singing…" I started but the look Ryder gave me said that was never going to happen and the possible fate dissolved before my eyes.

"I'll do anything but sing," he hissed and I felt a new path opening up before us.

"Oh," I breathed then starting laughing. "You really will do anything."

"What's that supposed to mean?" Ryder growled.

"You're going to let Leon do a photoshoot of you in those tiny hats he bought for you."

"What tiny hats?" Ryder spat.

The door cracked open behind me and Leon peered out through the small gap. "What's that?" he asked curiously.

"Ryder's going to let you do a snake photoshoot with outfits and shit," I said and Leon considered that.

"With the backdrops too?" Leon asked through a pout.

We all stared at Ryder hopefully and his lips pinched together in anger.

"He isn't gonna do it," Leon muttered, about to shut the door again.

"Oh for the love of the moon," Ryder hissed. "Fine. You can have ten minutes with me in my Basilisk form and if any of you breathe a word of this to anyone else, I'll gut you." He pulled his shirt off, tossing it angrily away from him and Elise shot over with her speed with a squeal of excitement. She unbuttoned his pants for him, dragging them down to his ankles with his boxers and he shifted into a snake the size of a python.

Leon came running out of his room and scooped Ryder up in his hands, draping his tail around his neck and holding his head up to speak to him.

"Smaller," he commanded, his brows tugging sharply together.

Ryder flicked his tongue out at him furiously then shrunk to half his size.

"Small-*er*," Leon enunciated grumpily and Ryder hissed, but shrank down to his smallest size and curled up in Leon's palm. A smile bloomed across Leon's face and he passed Ryder carefully to Elise then jogged away into the bedroom with a laugh. "I'll get the costumes!"

"Don't forget the pirate one," Elise called and I chuckled as Dante roared a laugh.

"This should be interesting." Dante grinned, throwing himself down on the couch to get a front row seat to the show.

I fixed the shattered coffee table with a wave of my hand and we soon all gathered around it as Leon set up an entire miniature backdrop of a pirate ship before placing a tiny pirate hat on Ryder's head and sticking a little peg leg to the end of his tail.

Leon snapped countless photos while Elise changed out the backdrops and switched up Ryder's outfits. He had to sit on a little plastic horse while wearing a cowboy hat, curl up on a scrap of fake grass surrounded by easter eggs while wearing bunny ears. Then there was the little fire truck with the yellow helmet and real working hose, the deck chair with a floppy sun hat, the cupid set up with a love heart hat and tiny golden bow and arrow. My favourite was probably the astronaut helmet with a backdrop including all of the planets and a tiny rocket and of course the miniature sleigh, Santa hat and gifts which was set up with a bucket of snow Leon grabbed from outside. I laughed so much I nearly busted a lung then after ten minutes exactly, Ryder shifted back into a huge ass naked man, tearing a sparkly hat from his head and crushing it in his fist.

"Happy now, Simba?" He grabbed his boxers from the floor, pulling them on while Leon beamed from ear to ear.

"Very. I've got twelve set ups ready and enough shots to make a calendar out of them every year for at least the next ten!" He turned his gaze on Dante. "I'll get that medallion back, buddy. Game on."

"There's no game, Leone," he replied darkly. "It's mine."

"Sure." Leon winked. "There's 'no game'." He air quoted the words with another wink and Dante scowled.

My eyes glazed as a vision took hold of me and I saw Orion arriving here at the cabin. As I blinked out of it in surprise, a message appeared on my Atlas from him and I picked it up, reading the words.

Orio:
I think I've found something that might help your royal problem.

My heart raced and I quickly showed Elise the message as the others gathered around to read it too.

"Invite him here!" Leon cried excitedly, snatching my Atlas and pressing call on Orion's number before holding it to his ear. "Guess whooo?" He hit the speakerphone button so Orion's dry tone came down the line.

"Is it my best friend?" he deadpanned and Leon clutched the phone to his chest as he whisper shouted to us.

"Did you hear that? He called me his best friend." He held the phone back to his ear with a cattish grin on his face then leapt onto the couch face down, kicking his legs up behind him and swinging them back and forth.

"Is Noxy there?" Orion asked.

"Sure is, dude," Leon purred. "And Elise is here too. You know, my mate with the come fuck me eyes and pouty lips. She's hot right?"

"Sure," Orion said suspiciously. "So can you pass me over to Noxy?"

"She has a tiny little lacy one piece I bought for her. It's lilac just like her hair and see through as hell, wouldn't you like to see her in it?" Leon asked.

"*Leo*," Elise snarled, kicking him in the ass but he just shhed her.

Ryder's rattle went off in his chest and electricity sparked in Dante's eyes.

"She'd look so good spread out on a bed of man chests. Four of them. While I record the whole thing," Leon growled. "You in?"

"For fuck's sake, Leo." Elise snatched the Atlas from his hand and tossed it to me. I caught it smoothly and held it to my ear, still scowling at Leon.

"Sorry about that," I muttered, switching off the speaker phone. "Any chance you can come over? I'll send you the location."

"Yeah sure, just so long as your Lion friend doesn't try and invite me to any more orgies. Also, I've tried unsubscribing to his newsletter, but it just keeps popping up every week. Do you know how I can get rid of it? I can't escape it, man."

"What newsletter?" I muttered, glancing over at Leon who just smirked at me.

"It's called the Weekly Orgy," Orion said. "It's mostly pictures of Elise in skimpy underwear, but sometimes there's columns on the pros of polyamory and the health benefits of orgies for Pitball players. It's er, pretty intense, Noxy. I assumed you got it too."

My hand clenched around my Atlas as my gaze narrowed on Leon. "No, but I'll make sure you don't ever get another one," I said through my teeth.

"Appreciate it. Shoot me the address and I'll be over soon."

I hung up and strode over to Leon, grabbing a fistful of his shirt as I yanked him to his feet so he was nose to nose with me. "You've been sending photos of our girl in her underwear to another guy?" I snapped, fury pouring through my chest.

"What the fuck?!" Ryder roared as Elise shot to my side with a gasp and Dante cursed colourfully in his language.

"Leo?" she demanded. "Is that true?"

"Well, it's not *not* true," he said, deflecting as he gave her a guilty ass look. "But hear me out, little monster. Lance Orion could bring a lot to our harem. He's hot as fuck, obviously, he's gonna be a Pitball star so we'd have loads of extra money, *plus* he'd be able to get us seats to any pro games in The League – The *League,* Elise. I've interviewed a bunch of girls he's fucked and they said he made them come so hard they couldn't breathe. He likes it rough and he's a biter too. You guys have got that whole fang banger thing going on, imagine the sexy blood party you guys could have together?" Leon's eyes sparkled with the idea and I growled possessively over Elise.

"You think I'm gonna let any other guy lay a finger on her?" I snarled. *It's a miracle I let all of them do it.*

"You think any of us will, Leone?" Dante snapped.

"I don't want anyone else," Elise agreed in a growl. "I want you four and that's it. You can't just recruit Fae to my harem, you idiot," she snapped, slapping him across the cheek, but it didn't do anything to wipe the smile from his face. I shook him, making him look me in dead in the eye and the grin finally slipped from his lips.

"If you send a newsletter with photos of Elise in it to anyone outside of this group, I will break your arms, then your legs, then every one of your fingers," I warned as Ryder came up beside me with a dark intent in his eyes.

"And I'll be right there waiting to flay you alive afterwards," Ryder agreed.

Leon looked between us, guilt falling over his features at last. "*Fine*, I'll cancel Orion's subscription to the Weekly Orgy, but only if you guys sign up instead. I need an audience for my material."

"When do you even get time to put a newsletter together?" Elise demanded. "You're with us all the time and sleep twelve hours of the day."

I released Leon's shirt from my fists and he shrugged like he didn't know. But he sure as shit did.

"Oh for the stars' sake, it's the Mindys, isn't it?" Elise snapped and Leon shrugged again. "Isn't. It?" she pressed and he sighed.

"I just send them voice notes for content in the magazine and they transcribe it and put it all together with the photos I send them." He gave her a guilty look and she growled.

"If you wanna send a newsletter of me in my underwear to our harem, Leo, then fine. But you do it yourself. I don't give my permission for you to send photos to a bunch of random Fae."

"They're not random, they're Mindys," he defended himself.

"You don't even know their real names," Elise hissed. "Name one Mindy's full name and I'll let you do whatever you like." She folded her arms and waited and Leon's brow pinched.

"Pfft, easy," he said then paused, clearing his throat, his eyes roaming over all of us. "Dan..tryder...Gabel...ise," he said. "She's foreign from a faraway...place."

"Dalle stelle, you could have made up any name, but you went for that?" Dante sighed, shaking his head at his friend.

"Fiiine," Leon gave in as Elise arched a brow at him. "I'll do the newsletter myself."

Leon pulled Elise in for a kiss and she melted against him as they made up but I wasn't feeling so forgiving. What the hell was he thinking sending pictures of our girl to another man?

"Not good enough," I said darkly and Ryder nodded his agreement, closing in on Leon.

"You need to be punished," he growled.

"Pfft, what are you gonna do, Rydikins? Spank me?" Leon laughed.

"It'll be worse than that, Leone," Dante warned, scowling at his friend.

Leon went to move as we closed in on him, but found his feet frozen in place as I used my water magic to hold him there. I let the ice creep up his body higher and higher and his eyes widened. "Um, guys?" He looked to Elise for help, but she just folded her arms and watched the show.

"I say you freeze him solid and leave him out in the snow for the day," Ryder said to me and I smirked cruelly.

"I could cast a bolt of electricity into the shell of all that ice too so it bounces around in there with him all day," Dante added.

"Come on guys," Leon tried. "Let's just hug it out."

"I know what we'll do," I said as an idea struck me, talking to the others and ignoring him. I drew a silencing bubble around me, Ryder, Dante and Elise, telling them the plan and Elise laughed wildly before shooting away to Leon's bag and finding the lilac one piece he'd bought for her. She shot back over to him, dangling it from her finger in front of his face as I dispelled the silencing bubble.

"You're gonna put this on, Leo," Elise purred and his eyes widened.

He huffed out a breath, looking between all of us. "If I do that, will you all be happy then?"

"Yes," we said in unison and he shrugged, grabbing hold of it and I released him from the ice so he could strip out of his clothes and struggle his way into it. And he really did struggle. The thing was tiny and I hurried forward before he could rip it, casting an enlargement spell on it so it doubled in size. He still had to squeeze in, but the material was stretchy enough to let him into it and when he was done, he looked like a drunk man's whore.

"Perfect," Ryder laughed as we all fell apart too. I walked over to Leon's clothes, taking his Atlas from his pocket and holding it up to take a photo.

"Smile, Leon," I mocked.

He rolled his eyes then smiled big and wide for me as I snapped the picture then blurred out his cock before posting it to his FaeBook account. The guy could front out anything, he literally gave no shits.

Leon Night:
Felt cute might delete later.
#itreallypushesupmyballsnicely #ilovethewayitwedgesinmyasscrack
#iwanttofeelthisfabulouseveryday
#doesitmatterthatmynipplespeekoutthetopofit

A stream of comments came in instantly and I cursed in surprise at the amount of followers he had, clearly all subscribed to his updates.

Laura Metz:
WOW! You're really rocking it, my king! It's #purrrfect
Bree Graziano:
I'm going to buy you this in every colour so you'll have one for each day of the week, Leon! #rainbowLion
Tasha Mcgookin:

I didn't know you were so progressive, Leon, it's so swoon-worthy. I'm going to buy my boyfriend a whole range of these! #mencanbeprettytoo

Well that sort of backfired.

I looked up to find Elise tweaking Leon's nipples and squeezing his pecs.

"You like that, little monster?" he asked in a growl and I had no idea how he managed to pull off that shit, but she actually blushed.

"Alright, alright, enough of seeing your cock packed into that thing, Leone. Take it off," Dante commanded and Leon laughed before he stripped out of it and pulled his clothes back on.

I shot our location to Orion and a beat later, a knock came at the door. I moved to answer it and grinned at him as I let him inside. "Hey man."

"Hey Lance!" Leon ran over and I slammed a hand to his chest to stop him from licking Orion, making him purse his lips at me.

"Hello Leon," Orion said tightly. "Let's respect everyone's boundaries today, yeah?"

"Sure, sure," Leon agreed then grabbed his hand and dragged him across the room, pushing him down onto the couch as the others greeted him too. He grabbed a cushion and plumped it up before pushing it in behind Orion's back. "Do you need anything? A coffee? A chocolate bar? A vein to suck on?" He offered his wrist and Elise snarled ferociously, diving in front of him and baring her fangs at Orion.

"I'm good," Orion said firmly, offering Elise a smile. "I just fed, savage girl."

"Good, because I'll have your balls if you try it." She backed down, but her eyes were still narrowed on him in warning.

I loved when my little angel turned into a possessive beast, it was so fucking hot.

"Give me your Atlas," Leon suddenly growled at Orion, starting to pace back and forth behind Elise.

"What?" Orion frowned.

"Give it to me, man, I dunno what I'll do if I don't get it," he said through his teeth and I *saw* him going psychotic if he didn't get it, my brows arching in surprise.

"It's okay, give it to him," I told Orion firmly and he frowned, placing his trust in me as he handed his Atlas over to Leon.

Our Lion friend tapped through it then sighed in relief and tossed it back to Orion with a bright smile. "All your old copies of the Weekly Orgy are gone. Now I don't have to kill you."

"What?" Orion balked. "*You* sent them to me, and I tried to delete them but there was some magical coding on them that stopped me."

"Well now the problem is solved and you need to never look at our girl in her underwear again. You're not a part of this harem," he growled in warning and Orion bared his fangs in anger.

"I never wanted to be a part of-"

"Shhhh," Leon hushed him, his features softening. "It's alright. You can still be my best friend. I forgive you."

Orion opened his lips to protest but I cleared my throat to draw his attention, giving him a shake of the head. Handling Leon's wild mood swings was an art in itself, and Orion didn't need the headache of attempting it right now. He blew out a breath of annoyance, trusting my judgement and dropping the line of conversation as he took the Magicae Mortuorum book and the spyglass from his pocket in their concealed rock forms, placing them down on the coffee table.

"Anyway..." Orion gritted out as Elise pulled Leon after her, pushing him down into an armchair and sitting in his lap in a clear move to protect her Source. "I've got some news."

"What did you find, Vampiro?" Dante asked, sitting down beside him while Ryder drifted closer.

"So first I spent ages looking at one page which has clearly been read a lot, but I don't think it's relevant. Thought I'd check and see if you have any thoughts though as you've been around King up close." Orion took the concealment spells off of the stones and the Magicae Mortuorum appeared. He flipped it open, thumbing through the pages until he reached one and pointing at an image of a man with three faces. "This spell here is about concealment, but it doesn't seem to be the same one King is using from what you've described. It's more like…creating a whole new identity. But what's fucked up is that whoever's face you take has to die."

"Merda santa," Dante cursed as Elise moved to take the spyglass and looked at the page through it and I knew what she was thinking as hope crossed her features. Gareth had had this book.

"Why do you think this page has been read a lot?" she asked curiously and Orion pointed to a black, five pointed star drawn at the top of the page.

"That's a marker," he said. "If you run your thumb over it, you can feel how many times this page was read." He guided her hand up to it and Leon growled in warning, making Orion release her and offer him a look that said *really?* Apparently he'd fast changed his mind on Orion joining the harem now he was actually here near our girl. I could see the desire to kill in his eyes and released a breath of amusement at the dumbass. I understood that look though, the five of us were it. I didn't know why it felt right, but it did. The thought of anyone else joining us now was abhorrent.

"Oh, that's a lot," Elise breathed as she brushed her thumb over the marker. "And what's this?" She tapped her finger on some numbers scrawled beneath it.

"I don't know," Orion said with a frown. "It's written like a date, but the numbers don't make sense."

She leaned in closer, reading them and her eyes widened as she sucked in a breath. "It's not a date. It's a clue." She shot across the room in a blur of motion, opening her travel bag and ripping stuff out of it as she hunted for something. My gut knotted and I shared a look of concern with the other guys. I wanted to believe more than anything that Gareth was out there somewhere waiting for Elise, but if that was true, why wouldn't he have shown up to find her by now? Why hadn't he reached out at all? The idea of my girl getting her heart broken all over again was unthinkable. But I also knew that if there was even the tiniest possibility of him being alive, I would do anything and everything to help her find him. I just wished The Sight would be more useful in the matter because so far it had offered me nothing.

Elise shot back to the couch with Gareth's journal in her hand, flicking through it until she paused on a page near the end of the book. She had a pen in her hand and I moved behind the couch, looking over her shoulder so I could see what she was doing.

There were eight square boxes drawn on the page and nothing else, but at the top of it there was a written line. *Beneath the star, you'll find the way.*

Elise wrote a number in each box, copying them from the Magicae Mortuorum. I held my breath as everyone crowded closer, the eight boxes dissolving on the page to reveal a long list of names I didn't recognise. There was an Oscura on it though, so I looked to Dante as Elise's head whipped around too.

"Who is that?" She passed him the journal with desperation in her eyes and Dante frowned as he read the name.

"A cousin, he died a long time ago, I barely knew him, bella."

"Do you recognise any of the other names?" Elise pushed and Dante read each one slowly before shaking his head and passing the book to Ryder. We took turns to study it, but all of us came up blank on the other names.

"Here, let me Faegle some of them," Orion offered, raising his Atlas as he took the journal from Leon.

We waited in silence and Elise chewed her lip as she sat close to Orion so she could watch him entering the names into the search engine.

"They're all dead," Elise breathed in realisation after he'd entered a few.

"She's right," Orion said and Elise released an excited laugh, pointing at the open page in the Magicae Mortuorum book.

"He was trying to get a new identity from someone who was already dead," she said in realisation, her eyes brimming with tears.

"Elise…" I said gently, terrified of her getting her hopes up only to see them dashed, but I couldn't deny that there was a trail here, even if it was unlikely. Could he really be out there somewhere? Maybe this spell was the reason I couldn't *see* him. "We don't know enough yet."

"But we know *something*," she pressed. "We know my brother was trying to run, and this proves he was trying to hide really well too."

"Even if he pulled this off, he'd have a new name, we wouldn't be able to look him up, little monster," Leon said. "So how can we find him?"

"What about blood magic?" Ryder demanded of Orion. "I've heard there's ways to spy on people if a blood sacrifice is given and you have an important object belonging to the one you're seeking."

"Yes…" Orion said slowly and Elise gazed at him in hope as my gut clenched. "But it's dangerous, and you're not trained. I couldn't do it for you because you have to be connected to the person, so…I just don't think it's viable. You could die if you attempt it, Elise."

"But-" she started and I cut in.

"No," I snarled. "You're not risking your life for this, angel. Blood magic is no joke."

"I didn't say it was," she sighed, but Leon squeezed her arm to get her attention.

"Please, little monster. Don't do that. It's too dangerous. I can't lose you. None of us can."

She melted under his gaze, nodding as she gave in and the knot in my chest eased.

Elise clawed a hand into her hair. "Maybe Gareth's waiting for me to figure something out. Maybe there's more answers, a trail I'm supposed to find," she said in a tumble of words, getting to her feet and beginning to pace. "And this makes so much sense. If he assumed the identity of someone who died in Alestria, then of course he couldn't stay in the city. And he wouldn't be able to come and get me because someone could recognise him."

"That wouldn't stop him making a phone call or sending an email or even using concealment spells while he came here in person," I said, my brow pinching.

"Why are you so against it being true?" She rounded on me in anger and I looked to the guys for help.

"It's not that, angel..." I trailed off, not wanting to go against her. That wasn't what I was trying to do, I just feared how little evidence we really had. And if she started chasing after shadows, where would it end?

"He's worried about you getting hurt if you're wrong, baby," Ryder stepped in and she turned her glare on him instead.

"But if he's out there I have to find him, you get that right?" she demanded.

"We all get that, amore mio," Dante said softly. "And we'll do whatever we can to follow this trail, but if it doesn't lead to him..."

"But what if it *does*?" she snapped. "He wouldn't have given up on me if he thought I was out there waiting for him, so I won't give up on him. And what if there's a reason he can't come to me? What if he's in trouble?"

"She's right," Leon said firmly. "Gareth might need us, and we can't let him down like we all did when he needed us most."

I hung my head, the shame of what I'd done the last time I'd seen him alive weighing heavily on me. I wasn't sure I'd ever really get over the guilt of it, even though Elise had forgiven me for it. I just couldn't shake the sense of regret over knowing her brother knew me as a monster and nothing else. A guy who should have been a part of our lives now, someone I could have grown close to and loved as a brother of my own and he'd only ever felt hatred towards me.

"Give me the names," I said decisively. "I'll send them to Bill. He'll find out if there's been any reports of disturbed graves or stolen papers to do with these Fae."

"Thank you." Elise snapped a photo of the names on her Atlas and forwarded it to me and I spent a moment typing out a message to Bill as I sent them to him. I moved toward her, wrapping her in my arms and kissing her on the head as she took a shuddering breath.

"If he's alive, we'll find him," I promised her and she nodded, taking a moment in my embrace before she recomposed herself and looked to Orion.

"So what else did you find?" she asked and he smiled sadly, looking back to the book.

"Well, once I gave up on examining this page, I decided to go back to the spell King has been using for their sacrifices." He flipped through the pages then paused on one with the image of the four Elemental triangles surrounded by symbols which were impossible to read.

"The answer to undoing King's power is here." Orion pointed to a piece of text at the bottom of the page which had always been undecipherable regardless of the spyglass. "But…" He sighed. "It requires a sacrifice to read it."

"No one's giving blood," I said immediately. That thing could take a piece of someone's soul if we gave it the chance, and I was not risking that with anyone in this room.

"No, it's not blood it wants," Orion said, but his eyes were still dark. "It's the pain of a woman suffering under the power of the four Elements. I used a couple of dark spells to reveal that much, but I couldn't go any further."

"That's horrifically specific," Leon muttered.

"I'll do it," Elise said simply, getting to her feet.

"No," I snapped the same time as Leon and Dante did.

"It's not an option," Elise snarled. "I'll do anything to defeat King, and

I've faced far worse pain in my life. This will be a small sacrifice to make." She looked me in the eyes, willing me to back down, but how could I? I couldn't cast my power against her. I wouldn't.

"She can handle it," Ryder said in a low voice, walking over to her side and taking her hand, placing a kiss on the back of it. "Our girl could walk through the fires of hell and reach the other side in one piece. This is child's play for her."

"I'm not hurting her," Dante growled.

"Why this of all things?" Leon groaned, looking to Orion. "Isn't there another way, dude?"

"No," Orion said with a frown then looked to Elise. "I'm sorry, but this is the answer if you want to find the way to undo King's power."

Elise pulled her shirt off and grabbed Ryder's hand, pressing it to her chest above her pale pink sports bra. "Hurt me," she commanded and he immediately obeyed. A vine coiled out from his palm, winding around her arms and legs, tightening over her flesh until she winced. "All of you," she insisted, looking from me to Dante to Leon. "I can handle it. I'm telling you to do it."

"That was an order from your fucking queen," Ryder barked and my hands tightened into fists as Leon walked over to her, kissing her firmly on the lips in an apology before opening his palm and letting flames roll across her body like a second skin. She cried out and the noise made my heart pound and terror race through me. I ran forward to fight them off, but her eyes turned on me in a desperate plea.

"The faster you do it, the sooner it will be over," she hissed then Dante stole her voice away with his air magic and she choked, her eyes watering as he drained every ounce of oxygen from her lungs.

"Now, Gabriel," Ryder snarled and Leon looked at me pleadingly, wanting this to be done.

I cursed, raising my hand and hating myself as I cast ice across her arms and hands, a freezing, biting cold cutting into her.

Pain flared in her eyes and Orion shot forward with the book, taking her hand and pressing it to the page. I watched in agony as the seconds ticked by, but suddenly the text unmasked itself, visible to us all.

I dropped my hand, dissolving the magic the exact moment the others released her from theirs. I caught her as she sagged forward with a moan of pain and rested my hands to her bare back. Leon, Dante and Ryder's hands all joined my own on her skin as healing magic flared between us and we stole away all of her pain as fast as we could.

"I'm sorry," I breathed in her ear, kissing her as the hurt of what I'd done left a mark on my heart. I knew she was strong, but turning my magic against her made me sick to my stomach.

"You have nothing to be sorry for," she panted as her skin healed and she stood upright, brushing her hands over each of us as she smiled. "Thank you."

"This is it," Orion breathed and we turned to read the words as he held out the book.

A spell was laid out to strip the newly acquired Elements from King, the answer right there before us. We needed Vampire blood to pull it off as part of a potion which Ryder immediately started writing down the ingredients to. To speed the process up, a Vampire could feed on the vessel once the Elements had been stripped away while the spell was being chanted to draw the stolen magic out of them faster, but it wasn't necessary. But if a Vampire didn't do that then it would take a lot longer to rip the stolen magic out of the host and that would give King more time to fight back. One glance at Elise told me she was fully planning to drain every last drop of stolen power out of King the moment she could and I swallowed down the fear that sparked in me.

"There's a warning here," Orion said gravely, pointing to a small footnote at the base of the page. "It says that though a Vampire can drain the stolen power faster, they must act quickly to release it into the sky where it belongs. If not, the power will work to corrupt them, feeding into their bloodlust and making a demon out of them."

"We shouldn't risk it," I said, reaching for Elise's hand. "We can just contain King and use the spell to force the magic out of them without you draining it."

"And what if that takes too long?" Elise demanded.

"Our girl won't be corrupted by the power," Leon said confidently, reaching out to brush his fingers through her hair.

"I just have to release it the moment I steal it. Simple," she agreed but as I cast a look at Orion he didn't seem at all convinced.

"Dark magic lures you in unlike anything you could possibly understand without having experienced it," he warned. "I'd think very carefully about doing this before you charge in and attempt it."

"Okay," Elise agreed, raising her hands in surrender. "I won't bite the fucker to drain them unless everything starts going to shit and I don't have any other choice."

"I think that's for the best, bella," Dante agreed.

Ryder remained quiet and it was hard to tell what he was thinking.

"Good," I said firmly. "That's decided then. We'll rip the stolen power out of King together using the spell."

Everyone nodded their agreement and I sagged in relief. I would do everything in my power to make sure it played out that way. And I'd be damned if I let Elise get that close to the bastard unless we couldn't help it.

"I guess we know why the asshole never wanted any Vampires joining the Black Card then," Ryder muttered. "You're King's kryptonite, baby."

Elise grinned like she didn't mind the sound of that at all then swung around and hugged us all tightly. "This is our answer. We can defeat King with this."

I held her close, meeting Orion's gaze over her shoulder and giving him a firm nod of thanks.

"Now all we need is an opportunity," Dante said, his eyes sparking with anticipation.

"If I could just *see* King better, get a glimpse of his movements..." I trailed off in frustration as Elise stepped back and took the book from Orion to reread the passage.

"You know what you need, bro? An amplifying chamber. A really awesome one," Leon said with a grin that said he was up to something. "So I say we build one right here."

I created a dome out of ice beneath a frozen lake beside the cabin and Ryder wielded his earth powers to make criss-crossing arches of metal to support it in a honeycomb shape. He coated the floor in moss while Leon cast everflames around the edges of the chamber and I built a seat out of intricate wood at the centre of it which reclined to allow me to gaze right up towards the stars. Elise and Dante worked to cast concealment spells outside the dome, so it was invisible to anyone but us.

I could already feel the power of this place as the water within the ice amplified the celestial signals surrounding us. This was possibly Leon's best idea ever. Between the snow and ice and the fact that there were no other Fae for miles in every direction, this place was perfectly tuned to the stars. There were no magical signatures but ours to interfere with The Sight and the amount of water in this place made the perfect conduit for messages from the stars. And I was so accustomed to our group now that I knew how to easily tune out their signals to focus on the visions gifted to me from the heavens.

"Do you think you'll be able to *see* in here?" Elise asked hopefully as she slipped through the ice door and smiled around at the place.

"I can hardly keep the visions out already," I said with a grin. Not to geek out or anything, but this place was fucking awesome. It was like a playhouse for my damn gifts and it was taking everything I had to keep myself in the present moment right now.

"Then let's go," Ryder said, beckoning everyone out of the chamber into the tunnel of ice that led back to the surface. "He needs to focus."

"I'll just sit in the corner quietly," Leon whispered.

"No, Mufasa," Ryder growled, walking over to him and tugging him toward the door.

"Ohhh but I'll be as quiet as a mouse," Leon promised, looking to me with big eyes.

"You couldn't be as quiet as a mouse if I bet you two million auras to do it," Dante laughed.

"I could be quieter than an ant's fart for two auras, dude," Leon said with a smirk, but Ryder shoved him out the door ahead of him.

Elise shot up to me, grasping the back of my neck as she tiptoed and kissed me hard. "Find that asshole," she whispered against my lips and I nodded, pressing my forehead to hers for a moment before she shot away out the door and shut it tight.

I moved to sit on the wooden chair which was really more of a throne because why the fuck not? Then I lay back and gazed up at the glistening frosty ceiling and let my eyes become hooded as I focused. It took no more than a couple of seconds for the stars to descend on me and I sucked in a breath as I was torn into a swirling mass of uncontrollable visions, stretching out way into the future, then tomorrow, next week, a month, a year. It was a blur of everything and a thousand paths which had the potential to be followed, some of it more set in stone than others, the uncontrollable haze of fates making my mind spin wildly.

I worked to focus and *saw* a huge stone throne made of snarling Hydra heads on long necks, all winding together into a monstrous being that almost looked alive. Blood coloured it red and in flashes I saw Fae after Fae sitting on it from the Savage King himself to each of the Councillor's Heirs as grown men, to Lionel Acrux, to two twin girls with deep green eyes, their hands clasped in one another's. Then the throne split apart, cut in two and crumbling to pieces as the vision shifted, making my gut clench and my heart race.

Orion was older, fighting enemies I couldn't see with a silver blade in his hand and Darius Acrux flew over him in his golden Dragon form. I saw the twins once more, bullied and broken by the Heirs. I felt their pain. I heard them suffering and *saw* their worlds fall to ruin before suddenly they were rising up in a roaring tower of flames which blinded me.

I tried to focus, grasping onto my gifts and forcing them in the direction I wanted to go as the future kept spanning out in too many directions. I *saw* the world falling to ruin and death and destruction sweeping through the kingdom like a plague. I felt loss and heartache and I couldn't tell if it was mine or the twins', Orion's, Darius's, Lionel's, or the whole world's. There were so many paths, so much pain and death, just glimmers of hope along the way and I shattered in the despair of it all, trying to seek out the light.

In the pressing dark, I found it, a veil seeming to lift as I sought the paths through the grief to the shining possibility of a sweet, peaceful future beyond. But then it was gone and I was blind once more, dragged into the depths of so much darkness, I couldn't *see* anything at all. It felt like standing before an impenetrable wall, blocking my gifts, something I couldn't perceive right before me. All I knew was that it was immeasurably powerful, destructive, terrible, a bringer of complete and utter doom that could twist all of our fates into it and never let go.

I begged the stars to bring me back to the now, feeling like I was being thrown into the pits of death where I could never return, and they finally gifted me that desire.

I nudged the stars gently and found them more responsive to my whims as I angled them towards King. And finally, they let me *see* them. They were just a blur of shadow, but I knew it was them from the cold feeling sweeping through my bones. They stood as a dark lord in Alestria, the streets red with blood as magic swept into their body and made them into a creature of impossible, terrifying power.

I *saw* the throne once more, the shadowy form of King claiming it as Fae wound through the entire palace around him, offering up their lives, their power. King fed on it all, becoming the most powerful Fae to ever walk the land. They ruled with an iron fist, crushing any who turned against them, wielding the masses of the Black Card to control the kingdom. There were curfews and hooded guards patrolling the streets, watching every Fae and making sure they abided to King's laws.

I tried to force the stars to show me King's face and the shadows began to peel back as I watched the monster sitting on their throne. Lionel Acrux stared at me from within their hood and my heart juddered, but their face changed just as quickly, showing me people I knew hiding behind the mask of shadow. From Orion to Eugene, Greyshine, Scarlett, Mars, Titan, Cindy Lou and finally…Gareth. His mouth was moving in words I couldn't hear and I tried to get closer, his face contorted as he screamed and screamed and suddenly his voice boomed in my head. "Save her, Gabriel – save her – the power will destroy her and all that she loves, let her bite you, it's the only way!"

I tried to answer, but my voice wouldn't work and I reached out to him, wanting to beg for his forgiveness, but his face disappeared into shadow once more, consumed by the dark within the hood. I didn't understand what he meant, but I committed the words to memory, sure they were important somehow. Then I turned my power his way, trying to seek him out for my girl, but the stars wouldn't show me him no matter how hard I tried. I just wasn't connected to him enough to find him and it hurt me as I failed my girl and was wrenched away into another vision.

I was standing in a parking lot, the roof above me cracking and splitting apart, the place about to collapse. The roar of a crowd sounded from beyond the building and I ran to a barred window, looking outside where the Lunar

Brotherhood were rioting. Ryder was being dragged through them and I fought with the bars to try and get out, my magic failing me as I bellowed his name. They stabbed him, shouting *traitor* as they made him bleed, dragging him to a huge stone statue of a Centaur rearing up and pointing to the stars. They wound a vine over its outstretched arm and strung Ryder up and the mob worked to rip him to pieces in a bloody execution.

"No!" I cried, panic consuming me as I sought out other paths, ways to avoid this fate, but they were closing in, so many of them curving back onto this one.

"How do I save him?" I demanded of the stars as I tried to find a way out.

"This day will come," they whispered inside my head.

"How do I stop it?" I begged.

"You cannot," they answered.

"Please, I'll do anything," I said in desperation.

"You will see this come to pass, Gabriel Nox, son of fate," they answered.

"I can't, I won't let it happen," I insisted as my heart began to crack in my chest. "How can I make sure he doesn't die?"

"You ask the wrong questions," they answered, their voices seeming to slip away into the distance.

"What's the right question?" I begged, feeling them leaving me behind with the weight of this unthinkable destiny laid out before me. They disappeared from my mind like a dying wind and my anxiety flared.

"How do I save him?" I cried, but they were gone and I stood alone in an endless expanse of white, too bright to see anything beyond it.

I squinted against the light, struggling to focus and suddenly the world shifted.

I stood at the base of a dark mountain in Alestria and up ahead of me was a hooded figure leading the Black Card behind them up a rocky path. I could sense the very time and date this would happen. It was one week away on the full moon. King was going to hold a ritual larger than they ever had before. And that would be our chance to strike. But if we failed, I didn't hold out much hope for the people of Solaria.

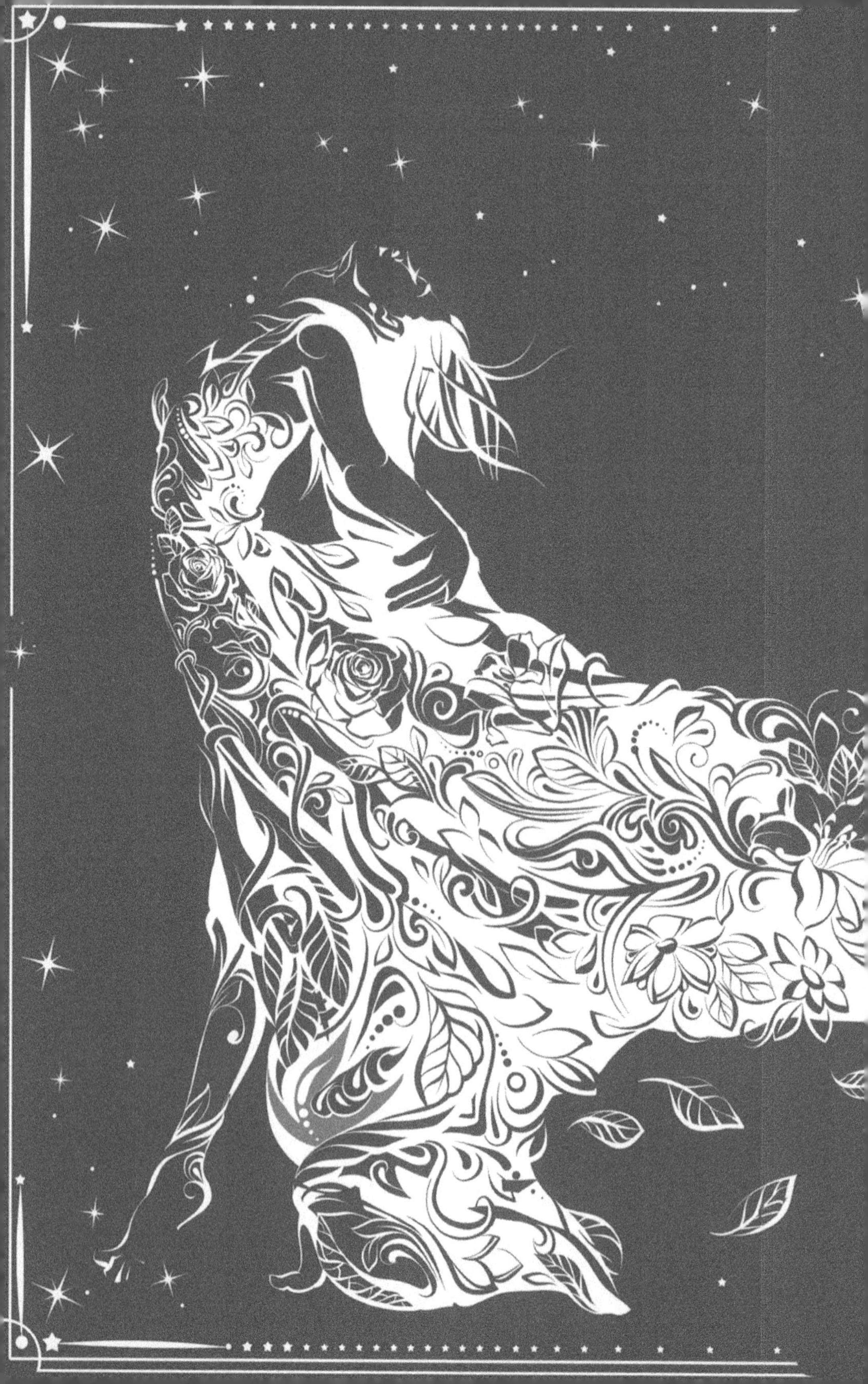

Elise

CHAPTER THIRTY TWO

"Come on, Ella, we're going to miss it," Gareth hissed, clutching my arm and giving me a shake to get me to wake up.

I groaned and shook him off, pulling a pillow over my head to try and shield myself from the world, but of course he wasn't having that.

"I heard Talia has that client with the candy fetish coming in tonight," he added temptingly and my stomach rumbled.

Dinner tonight had been leftover pizza from last night, which mom had called back to us before heading out for her shift at the club. Of course, last night we'd eaten almost the whole damn thing so that had left me and Gare Bear with precisely one cold slice each. Not nearly enough.

"You're sure this is going to be worth it?" I asked, peeking out from beneath my pillow shield.

"Yeah," he grinned. "I saw her practicing for it the other day and it looked so cool. We have to go see it in person."

I giggled and let him yank me out from beneath the covers, hastily braiding my ass length blonde hair and pulling on the sweater he offered me.

It was old and well-worn but still soft and warm, plus it smelled like him which meant it smelled like home to me. Neither of us mentioned the fact that Mom had promised me a new sweater of my own two days ago when my last good one had gotten ruined. Not that I was going to be bringing it up. The only reason it had ended up half shredded and no use was because I'd been fighting with Terrence Patrius again. Mom had screamed at me for about an hour straight and when I eventually told her that he'd been calling her a cheap and dirty whore while offering to pay me one aura to suck his slimy dick, she'd just snapped and told me I should have asked him for five and then I might have been able to buy my own clothes.

That was when Gareth had jumped in to my defence and of course Mom had just thrown her hands up in the air and headed out for a shift, yelling something about having to swallow a dick herself now to get me a new sweater.

There hadn't been any new sweater though, so who could say if there had been a dick to swallow, but I was fourteen and as much as I respected the things our mom did to pay the bills, I was never gonna live that life. Especially not for one measly aura from gross Terrence.

Gareth had been fuming after she'd left then he'd gone and taken this sweater from his closet and leant it to me. We both knew he only had two of them to offer from and that this was the nicer one, but I knew better than to try and refuse him when he was looking out for me. It only made him mad. And then sad. Sometimes he said things about the life we should have been living but I just shrugged it off. I wasn't one for dwelling in misery. I was just pinning my hopes and dreams on the escape we were gonna make one day in the future. Gareth had been studying his ass off to try and get a scholarship to Aurora Academy and if by some miracle he got it, our fates were gonna change once and for all.

"I heard Terrence Patrius ended up in the nurse's office at school today," I said casually as I slipped my battered sneakers on and followed him out the front door. "Apparently someone jumped him, tied him to that big tree

in the middle of the school yard then forced him to deepthroat one of those gross, inedible hotdogs from the canteen."

"Is that so?" Gareth asked, the corner of his mouth twitching with amusement.

"Yeah. And then they pinned a note to his chest saying, 'I owe you one aura' and signed it from Mr H Dog."

Gareth snorted a laugh, losing it as I'd expected and I grinned at him, flexing my fingers as I felt the sting of my cracked knuckles alongside the memory of me punching that asshat's smarmy face in. Of course, the school nurse had healed his face right away, but I'd been left to suffer. Not that I was bitter over that or anything.

"I heard the note also included a performance review," Gareth added casually. "One star - for such an almighty cock, you sure aren't good at sucking one. Poor effort - would not recommend."

I burst out laughing just as we made it to the foot of the stairs in our apartment block and quickly slapped a hand over my mouth to stifle it as Gareth shot me a warning look.

We really shouldn't have been heading out onto the streets after dark around here and we both knew it. We were unAwakened and had no magic to protect ourselves and neither of us had emerged into our Order forms yet either. So this was definitely a bad idea.

But Ginette had been practicing this move all week as well as bragging about it to everyone who would listen, and we hadn't been able to resist the urge to place bets on what would happen when she performed it for her client. My vote was that the john would jizz his pants the moment the glitter hit his face. Gareth was betting on the dude actually getting busy with his dick before he finished - but only for like ten seconds.

Winner got bragging rights and boy, did I love to brag and smoosh my brother's face into the knowledge of my victories.

Gareth cracked the door open and we both held our breath as we peered out into the dark street beyond. The streetlight just outside our building had died a couple of months back and there was no sign of anyone coming to fix it.

It was pretty quiet outside - still plenty of noise of city sounds, cars blasting horns and people laughing and yelling, but no sign of magical explosions or angry voices or fearful screams. Hopefully that meant the gangs were busy terrorising some other parts of town tonight.

Gareth took my hand and I let him because I knew it made him feel better to know he had hold of me. But we both knew that if things went south out there, the only thing we could do was run and hope not to die.

"Last one there has to tie one of Mom's nipple tassels to their school bag as an accessory," I teased before darting forward and dragging my brother out into the night with me.

We sprinted down the street, hugging the shadows and racing along the few blocks that separated our apartment building from The Sparkling Uranus before diving down a side alley that stank of piss and cheap sex. We weaved around the homeless dude who was sleeping by the row of dumpsters then skirted the couple rutting in the shadows against a dirty wall before finally making it to the side of the building where our mom worked.

We raced around the back and found the door wedged open with a brick as usual and quickly slipped inside.

Gareth gave me a grin which I knew meant 'yay! The gangs didn't kill us tonight' and I gave him the same one right back.

One of the bouncers saw us slip in and rolled his eyes at us as we jogged down the short corridor and Gareth opened up the hidden door set into the wall there. It wasn't exactly the best hidden door in the world, and you could totally see the outline of it when the lights were up, but the voyeurs liked the thrill of convincing themselves that no one knew they were here.

We shuffled along the narrow, hidden corridor and Gareth quickly opened the private room there before slipping inside and locking it behind us the moment I followed him.

There was one chair in the small room, set up beside the little table which offered a selection of lubes, masturbation aids and an emergency call button - just in case any of the johns who like to self-asphyxiate got into a bit of trouble.

Neither Gareth or I took that chair. We both knew that the cleaning staff did the bare minimum around here and I had no intention of getting manticrabs or syphfaelis from sitting on one of the surfaces.

We moved to stand before the one-way mirror on the wall and I cursed as I realised we were late.

Ginette was already in there, dancing her tits off to music we couldn't hear while the john stared at her with want in his eyes and his hands rubbing up and down his thighs.

I shuddered and Gareth smothered a laugh while not for the first time, I wondered why we subjected ourselves to this shit. But it was hard to have hobbies around here for two broke kids, and it gave us a laugh if nothing else.

But as Ginette moved to dance with her ass shaking in the john's face, my heart beat a little faster in anticipation of the big finale and the glory I was certain to receive when I won the bet. The beat dropped, Ginette fell forward to touch her toes and let it rip, farting right in his face and setting off an explosion of Pegasus glitter from her ass which completely coated the dude's face and upper body.

The guy groaned, doubling over so that his face almost got jammed in her ass crack and he clutched at the crotch of his pants as he made a right old mess of them.

"Yes!" I exclaimed as a laugh tore from me and Gareth's eyes widened in alarm as the couple in the room we were spying on looked our way. Oh shit.

Gareth snatched my hand, unlocked the door and in less than a heartbeat, we were racing away down the corridor, choking on our laughter and panting as we pushed our legs as hard as they would go.

We sped out to the bar and Gareth dragged me down to hide beneath it before anyone could spot us.

"I win," I goaded, holding my hand up for a high five and he rolled his eyes at me.

"Yeah, yeah. You win."

His palm slapped against mine in acknowledgment of my victory and I jerked awake with a gasp, bolting upright as I stared down at my still tingling palm.

I took in several shudderingly deep breaths, my heart racing with the remembered adrenaline of running at Gareth's side and the memories of that night clinging to me so fiercely that it was almost as if it had literally just happened.

I felt the warmth of his sweater caressing my body, heard the sound of his laughter ringing in the air and as I closed my eyes, I felt almost like I could turn and reach out for him.

The white jasper which hung from the bracelet on my wrist felt warm against my skin and I looked down at it, turning it over with a frown. Leon had been certain that we couldn't unlock its secrets without some of Gareth's blood, but I was sure that memory had at the very least been boosted by the crystal.

My hair shifted against my ear and I realised belatedly that Ryder was loosely coiled around my neck in his Basilisk form, his head lifting slowly before he brushed his scaly nose against my cheek.

I reached up to run my fingers down his spine then slipped out of bed, climbing over Gabriel's legs and smirking at the sight of Leon spooning Dante.

I moved across the room silently to avoid disturbing them and took Gareth's journal from my things at the foot of the bed before padding across the room and taking the small, curving iron staircase up to the hatch in the roof. When I stepped out into the cool air above the Oscura stronghold, I found the sky paling with the approaching sunrise in the east and birds singing in the vineyards which stretched out in all directions for miles surrounding us.

We'd headed back here from the cabin last night and Dante's mom had done all our laundry and cleaned the entirety of her son's quarters while we were gone. She definitely didn't need to dote on us like that, but I couldn't deny it felt kind of nice to be mothered.

I grabbed a warm blanket from a pile Dante had left up here and curled myself in it as I took a chair with a view. Ryder stayed coiled around my neck as I began to leaf through the well-worn pages for the hundredth time and I was glad to have him with me for support. His skin had warmed against mine so he was like a little scarf containing our combined heat.

Aside from the clues we had unlocked at the cabin, it had been months since I'd discovered anything new in the countless doodles, sketches and notes which filled the journal, but that dream had made me feel so close to my brother that I was just consumed with the need to try again. Maybe unlocking the page referring to the identities he might be using now would open up another secret for me to discover.

I scoured page after page, my fingertips tracing drawings and words while I silently begged my brother, or the stars or any fucker out there who might have been paying attention to give me some more clues in this.

Just as I turned the last page in the journal, the sun crested the horizon and the first rays of dawn spilled over me, making me lift my head to look at it.

Ryder shifted in my hair, a low hiss escaping him as he slid around my neck. I glanced back at him as he moved towards the journal and my breath snagged as I looked down at the page I was holding open.

On it had been nothing but a faint sketch of the ocean and a view out over the horizon before, but as I watched, golden ink began to paint patterns on top of that image, the lines slowly forming a map of the whole of Solaria right before my eyes.

I gazed down at it, wetting my lips as I drank in the names of cities, towns and villages all over the map, carefully scrawled in Gareth's handwriting.

I skimmed my fingertips over the golden lines with my pulse hammering and as I traced across a spot in the centre of the page, a brush of my brother's magic touched my skin.

I closed my eyes in concentration, untangling the careful concealment spells and using my power to call on the thing which was hidden from me there. As I broke them apart, a solid cube fell from the page and only the speed of my gifts let me catch it before it could fall to the floor.

I opened my fist and frowned at the golden dice, recognising it as one of the ones we used in Arcane Arts to try and predict the future sometimes. Casting with a dice meant following the call of fate and not influencing it at all, and my heart raced as I gazed back at the map, finding words scrawled along the bottom of it.

Fate will guide me.
Long may it hide me.
Until my angel can find me.

Ryder slid from my body, shifting back into his Fae form as he hit the ground and taking the journal from me in silence. He moved closer to the edge of the private balcony Dante had created for himself up here and held the book up in the sunlight.

I stood too, letting the blanket pool at my feet and turning the dice over between my fingers thoughtfully.

"Do you think this means he really ran?" I breathed, hope clutching my heart in a vice as I couldn't help but look towards the horizon and wonder if my brother was out there somewhere, watching the same sunrise as me and waiting for me to find him.

Had he seen the articles about me in the papers? Did he have a few clues about my life now to hold onto while he continued to hide from the monster who had tried to cage him?

"I think it means he planned to," Ryder hedged, never one to rely on something so intangible as hope and I bit my tongue as a few tears escaped me and ran down my cheeks at his words.

Ryder turned to me sharply, feeling the stab of pain he'd caused with his doubt and frowning at me as he caught my hand and tugged me closer to him. I was wearing nothing but his shirt from the day before and the cool air was chilling my bare legs, but I didn't care about that, needing to see if he might believe me on this. If he would be with me on it.

"I just don't want you to lay all of your hopes and wishes on this, baby," he growled. "Not when there's no evidence that he managed it."

I nodded silently, trying to swallow back my tears but as Ryder's grip tightened on my hand, he drew that pain out of me instead of allowing me to retreat from it.

A shuddering sob rattled through my chest and he leaned in, kissing the tears from my cheeks and tasting my pain.

As his mouth found mine, the connection I felt to his power almost consumed me as my grief rose up like a tide in my chest, so powerful that I feared it would destroy me.

But as Ryder's tongue swept across my own and he moved his hands to encircle my waist, I felt grounded by him. That kiss was filled with so much hurt and suffering which both of us had lived through, but it was also filled with love and hope and the promise of a life for us no matter how this all played out.

The sound of the hatch opening drew my attention as I wound my arms around Ryder, but I didn't pull back until I felt another set of lips grazing my neck and strong arms winding around my waist from behind.

Gabriel flexed his wings behind us as the three of us stayed close like that for several long seconds, casting us all in shadow as he drank in the power of the rising sun.

"Show me," Gabriel murmured, his voice rough with a lack of use after his sleep as his lips grazed against my ear.

I broke away from Ryder, turning between the two of them and handing him the journal, where the golden map still sat on full display.

Gabriel took it and the gold dice from me, laying the journal flat on the small wrought iron table as he stepped away from me.

He closed his eyes, his breaths coming slow and deep as he called on his connection with the stars to guide him before he rolled the dice.

I watched while holding my breath, Ryder's grip tightening around my waist as he held me against the hard plains of his body and we watched the dice roll.

It tumbled over and over, seeming to move at random like expected before suddenly jerking to the left and stopping so abruptly that it didn't look entirely natural.

I hurried forward, Ryder keeping pace with me as the three of us peered down at the number five which sat solidly on the city of Destinelle.

"What does that mean?" I breathed. "Do you think he could be there, or-"

"One roll doesn't mean anything," Gabriel replied. "Not for sure." He plucked it up again and rolled once more, Ryder and I staying silent to preserve his concentration.

Again, the dice seemed to jerk in an unexpected direction, but this time it landed on the city of Goliath. Once again, the number five stared back at us though.

Gabriel silently rolled again. And again. He repeated it over and over while the dice jerked to a halt on countless different towns and cities, never once landing in a dead zone of farmland or jungle or desert. Always some form of civilisation and always the number five.

It had to mean something, but I just couldn't figure out what and the lump in my throat was only growing thicker as Gabriel continued to roll the dice.

But as the sun crested the horizon, the golden ink began to fade away and I gasped as I lunged for the journal, willing it to stay and give us longer to figure this out. Before I could even lift it into my hands, the dice sank back into the page, the five dots the last thing I saw then nothing but the original sketch of the horizon looked back at me once more.

"Gabriel?" I asked, afraid to say a single word more than that and begging him to *see* something else.

He turned his steely grey eyes on me, a frown tugging at his brow as he reached out and cupped my cheek in his large palm, his thumb skimming across my cheekbone and pain in his eyes.

"I can't *see* him," he breathed, and I could tell it pained him to say those words almost as much as it pained me to hear them. "I've tried all I can, but there's no answers there for me."

I shook my head in fierce denial. "No. There's something here. Some answer. That note was clearly about me finding him. He obviously had a plan and he left that for me so that I could find him. It's a map, Gabriel, that has to lead to him!"

I could hear my voice raising in pitch as desperation clawed at me and Gabriel's eyes flashed with hurt as Ryder tugged me around to look at him.

"He's doing all he can. You losing your shit won't help anything," he growled at me like I was some dumb kid and my hand crashed against his cheek before I could even think about what I was doing.

Ryder snarled at me, his mouth pulling into a dark smile as he moved right into my personal space, pressing his forehead to mine. "You wanna act out?" he challenged. "You wanna hurt someone? That's fine, baby, I'll be your punching bag if that's what you need. But it's not gonna make any of the answers you're seeking appear for you."

My fists curled tight with the desire to lash out at him again like he was offering and my fangs snapped out as anger coiled in my gut, but before I could give in to it, Gabriel caught my arm and made me look at him instead.

"The number five was consistent," he said, like that might offer me something. "It means freedom and a sense of adventure. If that number has an affinity to Gareth, then maybe that's because he really is out there somewhere experiencing those things."

I gripped onto the idea of that with all I had and nodded, trying to remember if a five had been one of Gareth's numerology numbers or not. It did ring a bell, so maybe, but my general hatred for all things which relied on fate too heavily meant I wasn't sure. I'd never paid a whole lot of attention to anything that claimed to be in control of our destiny because I'd always been determined to be the master of my own. And I really sucked at Numerology.

"Sometimes The Sight is a curse as much as a blessing. It won't work on demand. It won't always give us the answers we need. And some of the answers it does provide are so terrifying that I wish I didn't even have to know what was coming." Gabriel's gaze cut to Ryder and his brow pinched before he looked back to me. "I won't stop hunting for the answers we need, but sometimes our fates are out of our hands. All we can do is pray to the stars for a reprieve, even if those prayers fall on deaf ears."

"I won't just accept that," I growled.

"Neither will I," he swore. "I just wish I could *see* more."

"Do a sacrificial reading," Ryder suggested firmly and Gabriel's eyes widened as they shot to him.

"No," he replied instantly.

"Why not?" I demanded, though I knew why he was hesitant, but I'd give anything to find Gareth.

"Because that's dark magic and it's incredibly dangerous. Even if it wasn't, I'd need blood and stuff from you as well as myself and then it would require a draining dagger because it's not like you can just do it with a kitchen knife. I don't happen to be in possession of anything like that and I have no interest in being sent to Darkmore Penitentiary for getting my hands on one either," Gabriel said firmly.

"But you'd be able to *see* him then, wouldn't you?" Ryder pushed, ignoring the flash of rage in Gabriel's eyes as my chest swelled with hope at the idea.

"Stop putting those kinds of ideas in her fucking head," Gabriel hissed like he was wishing he could exclude me from this conversation. "Besides, I don't know shit about dark magic or the way it can be used for divination like that. All I do know for sure is that people who fuck around with the Shadow Realm without knowing what the fuck they're doing can get dragged inside and have their souls ripped right out of their fucking bodies."

My eyes widened and I looked to Ryder, wondering if he'd known about that and he only shrugged, confirming he had. "So maybe we need to find someone who knows how to fuck around with it already," he deadpanned but Gabriel was already shaking his head.

"No. No fucking way. You know, Ryder, sometimes I let myself forget what a psycho you really are, but in moments like this, I remember exactly why I used to think you were no good for our girl."

Gabriel pressed a brief kiss to my forehead then took off towards the sky without another word, speeding away so fast that he was nothing but a dot in the heavens within seconds.

I turned to Ryder, chewing on my bottom lip as Gabriel's words of warning warred with the desperate desire in me to do whatever it took to reunite with my brother again, no matter what it cost me.

Ryder's eyes were dark with what I could have sworn was more than just rage for several long seconds - like Gabriel's words had actually just pierced the hard shell of his heart and cut him open. But in the blink of an eye that look was gone again, and he cupped my cheeks between his hands, moving his face so close to mine that our lips were brushing as he spoke to me.

"I am a psycho, baby," he growled. "And unlike your other boyfriends with their moral high grounds and lines they refuse to cross, I want you to know that there isn't any depth I wouldn't sink to for you. I'm willing to trade my soul for you. I'd do anything to anyone. Don't ever make the mistake of thinking I wouldn't. So if it takes a sacrifice to find your brother and heal that hurt I feel in your heart then consider it done. No matter the cost, I'll pay it. Even if I have to cut my own throat and bleed out at your feet, I'd die happy knowing it had been for you."

His mouth crushed against mine before I could respond to that, and he kissed me in a hard, brutal, demanding way which tasted of his devotion and the sins on his soul. He was still very much naked since he'd shifted and he clearly had no shame about that, driving his hard cock against me forcefully in a way that reminded me in no uncertain terms that I was his creature now.

But before I could give in to the demands of his body for mine, he broke away from me again just as suddenly and strode back down into Dante's room without a backwards glance, leaving me to reel over everything we'd just discovered and grieve over the fact that it didn't change anything. Yet.

We were all tense as we arrived back outside the gates of Aurora Academy for the first day back at school, the five of us pulling up in Dante's truck with him and Ryder sitting together in the front seats.

This was it. We had to front it out, own what we all were to each other and hope that the remaining hostile members of the Lunar Brotherhood didn't come to kill us all. And I wasn't even going to let myself think about King, The Black Card, my missing brother, the vague threat which still hung over Gabriel's head from his past, our issues with Lionel Acrux or this shit show which was my family drama - and no, I still hadn't called my mom about Marlowe's reappearance, but like a snakey bitch I had confirmed with the wellness centre that the residents didn't get given access to the national news. So yeah, I was using a mixture of avoidance and desperation to get me through the days, topped off with a dollop of impending unavoidable doom from countless sources, but apparently that was our standard now. *Peachy.*

Before we even got out of the car though, the Oscura Clan came racing out into the parking lot, howling and whooping excitedly, cheering for us to join them like it was a damn coronation or something. Not far behind them, Ethan Shadowbrook and the loyal members of the Lunar Brotherhood appeared too, though they were careful not to mix with the Oscuras directly all the same. There may have been peace now, but they were still separate gangs. Still rivals, just - hopefully - without the bloodshed involved anymore.

"Are we good to go, Gabe?" Leon asked, bouncing in his seat beside me excitedly like he couldn't wait to get back to school.

Gabriel frowned in concentration for a moment then nodded finally. "Don't call me Gabe," he muttered automatically and we all sniggered at his expense before he went on. "As far as I can *see*, the disloyal members of the Brotherhood who attended the academy are now gone thanks to Ethan and his pack. There shouldn't be any direct threats here today. But stay close to me all the same. I don't trust this peace."

"I got us something to help," Leon said suspiciously as he lifted his ass off of the chair and rummaged around to pull a small bag from his pocket.

He sat back down heavily, tipping the contents into his palm and grinning as we all looked at the crystals in his hand.

"What is that?" Dante asked him and Leon grinned like the cat who'd gotten the cream.

"Midnight Amethyst crystals - as in motherfucking luck in a rock."

"Oooh," I cooed, reaching out to take one of them from him and holding it up so that I could watch the way the colours shimmered in the light.

"I got us one each and two for Elise because without her there is *way* too much sausage in this sandwich and as much as I would be down for sucking a dick or two in the right circumstances, I just feel like we need to extra protect our only pussy."

"Wow Leo, I feel so touched by that loving declaration," I said, fanning my face like I was warding off tears.

"Don't talk about her like that, asshole," Ryder growled, even though he knew Leon was only teasing.

"Oh, I'm sorry Rydikins, I didn't mean to hurt your feelings. How about we all just get together later and watch Frozen? Because I know you've seen it, but I'm wondering why?"

"What are you talking about?" Ryder grumbled, pocketing his crystal while the others accepted theirs too.

Dante snatched the biggest one with a wild glint in his eyes that was all Dragon and promptly gave his full attention to inspecting his new piece of treasure.

"I'm talking about the way you told us you can only reference kids movies because after you were kidnapped and all that cheese, you never watched TV again. *But* you also referenced Frozen while trying to insult me the other week. And Frozen came out after you'd escaped Mariella's clutches which means-"

"It doesn't mean shit," Ryder snapped, reaching for his door handle and getting out before Leon could finish his grand reveal.

Gabriel chuckled and Dante grinned as they climbed out too. Leon rolled his eyes at Ryder's back through the window before unhooking a couple of my shirt buttons and casually slipping my second lucky crystal into my cleavage. He kissed the curve of my breasts one after the other and re-buttoned my shirt while I giggled at him.

"You're not going to drop this, are you?" I asked him.

"The Frozen stuff?" he questioned, a mischievous gleam in his eyes. "Oh hell no."

Leon hurried to get out of the car and I followed him, catching up to the others so that we could all walk into the academy together, surrounded by the mingling crowd of our supporters.

"So tell me, Ryder," Leon pressed as he jogged forward and slung an arm around the Basilisk's neck. "Are you team Anna or team Elsa?"

Ryder growled and shoved his arm off as he started to stride towards Ethan. "I'm not having this dumb as fuck discussion with you, Simba," he said in a firm tone. "Just let it go."

Leon's mouth fell open in shock and he turned back to face the three of us while Ryder kept walking away and I couldn't help but laugh.

"Did you hear that?" Leon gushed. "He told me to *let it go*. Oh my stars he's so fucking in love with me *and* Frozen!"

We all started heading for our first class of the day, trying to ignore the whispers, stares and several assholes who were full on recording us on their Atlases as we walked, but the sound of Dante's Atlas ringing made us pause outside the Cardinal Magic classroom.

The others all hesitated as he lifted it from his pocket, but he waved them off and they headed inside among the rest of the class. I lingered despite his dismissal, spying the caller ID and moving to stand toe to toe with Dante as he threw a silencing bubble up around us.

He waited for all the other students to leave before answering and I trained my gifts so that I could pick up the words on the other end of the line.

"Congratulations, Dante," Lionel Acrux cooed as the call connected and Dante frowned.

"What for?"

"Juniper just found out that she is pregnant. It looks like your seed is just as virile as all Dragons'. So hopefully there will be more of your kind in the world before long."

"Great," Dante deadpanned, but I could see he was trying to smother a snigger. The only baby that bitch would be having was the love child of an emotionless Griffin - which happened to be one of the most common Orders there were - and a birthday cake who got more than a candle jabbed into it. I wondered if the kid might be born with icing for hair and clapped a hand over my mouth to hide my own laughter.

"It is," Lionel agreed in the smuggest fucking voice in the world. *Gah,* someone really needed to kick that dude in the dick.

"So will you hold up your end of the bargain?" Dante demanded, his humour slipping away. "And release Roary Night from Darkmore Penitentiary."

"Hold your horses, Storm Dragon," Lionel replied wearily. "I'm hardly going to hand over my only bargaining chip for nothing more than a bit of DNA mixture and some jars of lightning. No, no. Don't be so hasty."

"You swore that once you got what you wanted from me, you'd-"

"What I want is more Storm Dragons," he hissed. "So until this child - or one of the many others I expect you to sire Emerges as said Storm Dragon, there will be no pardon for the Lion thief."

"Wait a minute, stronzo," Dante snarled. "You swore to set him free once I got that cagna pregnant. And now she is. So give me what you promised me or I swear upon all the stars in the sky that I'll-

"I would choose your next words very carefully indeed," Lionel cut over him. "Because I have it within my power to order that Lion and anyone else who may have been involved in the break in at my home to be executed. Don't forget I know all about the little Wolf bitch too. So allow me to be frank with you. You seem not to understand this deal we have struck, so I will make it binding to stop these incessant demands for a change to the terms. I will make the Lion's sentence irrevocable by pain of death. All I need do is obtain some of his blood and bind his life to the terms of our arrangement. I'll tie him to it in a star-bound death bond. Roary Night will never have his sentence lessened or revoked by my hand or any other unless one of the offspring you provide me with Emerges as a Storm Dragon. And if he doesn't agree to the bond, I'll make sure your cousin Rosalie pays for the crimes she committed against me."

"You can't do that," Dante snarled viciously. "There's no reason for any of us to believe that I will be able to pass on my Order form to any child. I'm born of generation upon generation of Werewolves! I am the only member of my famiglia to Emerge as anything other than a Wolf in over eighty years!"

"All the more reason for you to give my niece more children then, to stack the odds in our favour," Lionel purred as my mind whirled in panic and my heart shattered for Roary, stuck all alone down in that dank, miserable hell.

"*Please*," Dante said, his voice cracking as rage fell to desperation. "Don't do this. I will do anything and everything you ask of me, but this bond you speak of placing on him will ensure he is trapped in Darkmore for the entirety of his sentence. Don't steal his life from him because of me. I'm begging you."

I reached out and clasped Dante's hand in mine as I felt him shattering over this. I knew him soul deep. I knew him to his core, and he would never beg for anything unless it was for the love of his family. But Lionel had clearly already figured out that this was his weak spot, and I could tell before he even answered that he wouldn't be turned from this path.

"Perhaps now you will learn to respect my commands. And the next time I ask you to do something for me, you will do it without any of your less than charming snark and attitude. Or I may end up punishing someone even closer to you - like your sweet little Elysian Mate for example."

Lionel cut the call and a roar of rage exploded from Dante loud enough to rattle the walls and break a few windows. He launched his Atlas across the corridor so hard that it shattered into a thousand pieces then he turned and started storming towards the exit.

I made a move to follow him then realised that there was something more important than that right now - we had to warn Roary not to let that motherfucker get hold of any of his blood or be blackmailed into agreeing to that fucking death bond over Rosa.

I shot into Cardinal Magic, ignoring the alarmed gasp from our professor, and speeding straight towards Leon before throwing him over my shoulder and shooting back out of the room again.

As soon as we were back out in the corridor, I dropped Leon to his feet and snatched his Atlas from his pocket before shoving it into his hands and throwing a silencing bubble over us.

"Call Roary," I gasped as Leon looked at me with wide, concerned eyes.

"Why? What's wrong?" he asked, already dialling Darkmore without waiting for my answer.

"Lionel. He...Juniper is pregnant, so Dante tried to get him to release Roary like he'd promised but then he flipped out saying he won't let him go until one of the kids becomes a Storm Dragon. Long story short, he's going to bind Roary's life to that deal and if he doesn't agree, he's going to make sure Rosa gets charged for stealing from him. He wants to make a mother fucking death bond with him. That means he won't ever be able to be released early unless one of those kids turns out to be a Storm Dragon and between the fact that she's pregnant with a freaking Griffin/cake baby and that even *if* Dante were to be a real sperm donor in the future, there's like only the tiniest chance for him to pass on his Order-"

The call connected as Leon's eyes filled with the same panic I was feeling. I shut up so that he could speak to the woman who had answered the call, using my gifts to listen in.

"Darkmore Penitentiary, how can I-"

"I need to speak to an inmate urgently," Leon cut her off. "Roary Night, inmate number Sixty-Nine. There's a family emergency and I really need some information from him or someone might die."

"Oh. Erm, that's quite...hold please."

Leon ran a hand through his hair, fisting it roughly and I wrapped my arms around his waist, squeezing him tight and laying my head against his racing heart.

The classroom door banged open behind us and I looked around as both Gabriel and Ryder stepped out.

"I'm sorry, Leon," Gabriel breathed, his brow pinching as he stepped into our silencing bubble. "But I can't *see* any way to change this fate. I think they've already-"

"No," Leon snarled, lurching towards Gabriel and forcing me to use my gifted strength to shove him back a step as he bared his teeth at him. "Don't fucking say that. Roary has his whole fucking life ahead of him. There's no way he's going to miss out on it stuck in that fucking hell hole!"

"Hello?" the woman on the other end of the line asked as she returned.

"Where is he?" Leon snarled.

"An officer is just escorting him to the phone now, please hold and you'll be connected shortly."

Gabriel opened his mouth again, but Ryder stepped forward and elbowed him in the ribs. "Let him try, Big Bird," he growled. "He needs to fucking try."

Gabriel nodded slowly, glancing towards the door where I knew Dante had disappeared to, his eyes full of a sad, hopelessness that carved me open because I knew what it meant. He'd already *seen* this play out. He knew what was going to happen and he knew there was no stopping it.

"I'll go and talk to Dante," he muttered, laying a hand on Leon's shoulder briefly before heading for the exit.

Ryder stayed right there beside us and one look at him had my heart breaking even more for Leon. Because I knew why he was here with us. He could feel Leon's pain and he knew it was going to get worse too.

"Hey, Leon, what's going on?" Roary asked hurriedly as the call finally connected and Leon gasped in relief.

"Roar, don't let any of those fuckers take you to meet with Lionel Acrux or a lawyer or anyone like that," Leon said in a rush.

"Why? What's-"

"It's fucked, Roar. So fucking fucked. That bastard has threatened to place a death bond on you and he's going to hang Rosa's freedom over your head to make you agree. He's saying that unless Dante gives him a kid who actually Emerges as a Storm Dragon then you'll never be let out of there before your sentence is up. No pardons, no early release, no parole, fucking nothing. He'll make you rot in there for each and every one of those twenty-five years and-"

"Number Sixty-Nine, you have to come with us," a gruff voice sounded in the background of Roary's call and my eyes widened in alarm as I looked up at Leon.

"No," Roary replied instantly, the fear in his voice clear as he realised where they were going to take him.

"It wasn't a request," the man who I assumed was a guard barked. "The High Lord has demanded you report for an assessment on your case."

"I won't go," Roary said firmly but then shouts rang out, a Lion's roar following them and the distinct sounds of fighting, kicking, punching.

Leon yelled his brother's name over and over, but it was no use. After a few minutes, the sounds on the other end of the line moved away then the line cut off abruptly.

"It's already too late. I know he won't put Rosa's freedom in jeopardy, he's only in there anyway because he protected her before," Leon breathed in despair, sinking down onto his knees and clinging to my legs as he buried his face against my stomach. A mournful, hopeless sound escaped him and the pain of it tore me apart as tears fell freely down my cheeks.

Ryder stepped up behind Leon, laying his hands on his shoulders and looking into my eyes as he did what he could to try and relieve him of some of his pain, but I knew it was no use.

Leon's last hope of seeing his brother released from that hell had just been stolen from him and the only way out of it was an impossible task. Even if Dante agreed to give Juniper his own children in future there were no guarantees, not to mention the fact that Dragons usually Emerged when they were teenagers. Whatever way this played out, there wasn't a happy ending for Roary. His life had been stolen from him and now the rest of us would have to live with that too.

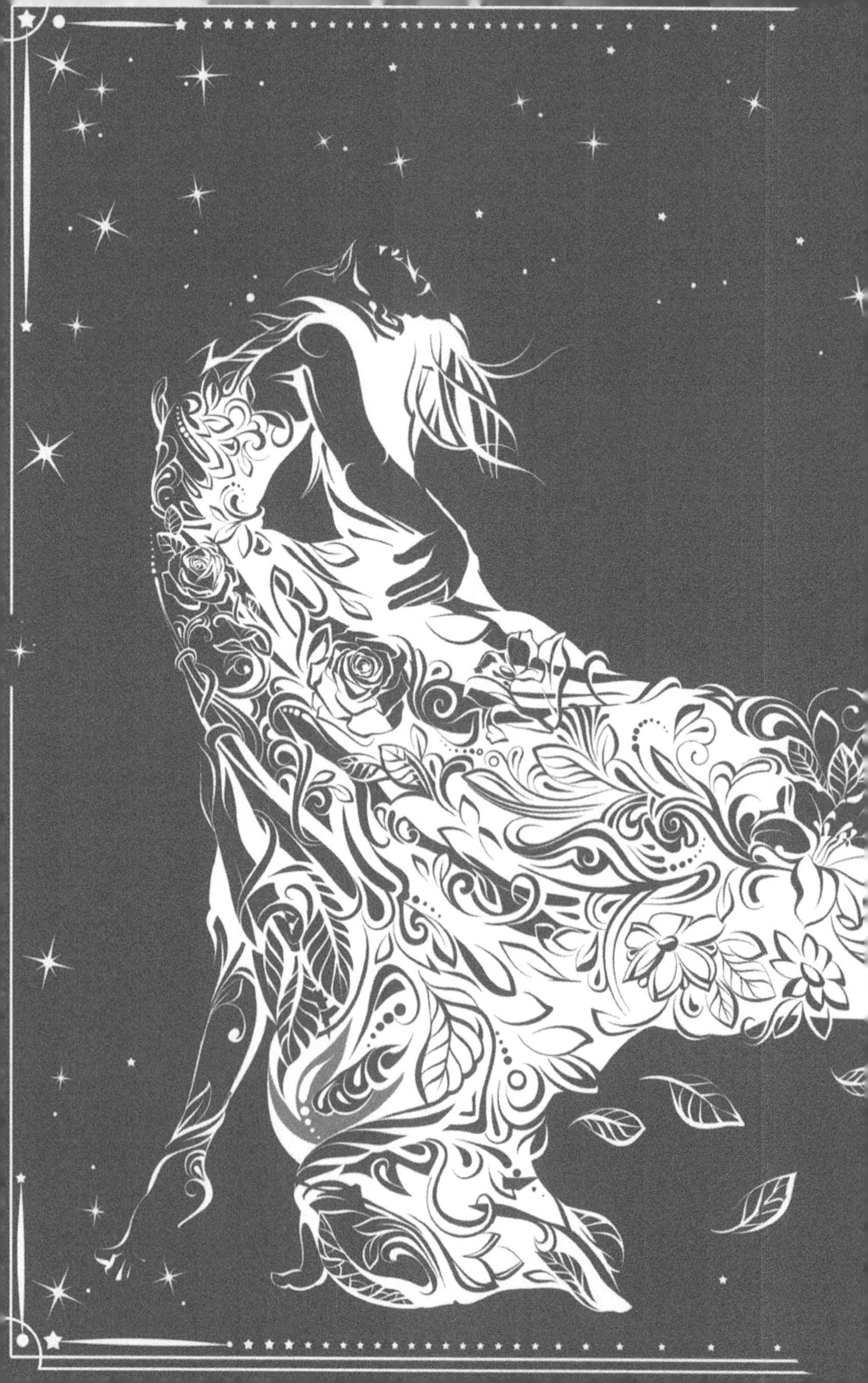

ELISE

CHAPTER THIRTY THREE

The rest of the week passed too slowly. Dante and Leon didn't return to classes, the two of them too lost in their grief and guilt to be able to face it. I only attended because Gabriel insisted that he stay close to both me and Ryder so that he could keep an eye on all of us easier. Dante had been willing to give his own sperm to Lionel the next time Juniper needed impregnating so that there was at least a small chance for Roary to be let out if the baby Emerged as a Storm Dragon, but Gabriel had looked into that future and swore it wouldn't work. And I had to admit I was relieved by that. I hated the idea of some other woman carrying Dante's child, not to mention the fact that I was certain it would have destroyed him. Dante's family were his whole world. He wouldn't have been able to cope knowing a child of his was being raised by Lionel fucking Acrux.

As our final class ended on Friday and everyone began to head to the Cafaeteria to get dinner, I let the crowd sweep me along and found myself walking with Eugene.

"Hey, Elise, how's things?" he asked me with one of his exuberant grins and I gave him my best attempt at returning a smile.

"Leon got some bad news from home this week, so it's been a bit of a tough one," I said to explain my clearly poor mood. "I don't really wanna get into it though. How are you?"

"I'm good," he replied, nodding his head over and over while rummaging in his bag for something. "Super busy with all of this Daring Underdogs stuff, you know? And I'm starting to receive some backlash from some of the assholes in this place who don't like me helping their victims to fight back."

"I hope you teach them a lesson the way you did with Ferdinand," I said. The Griffin had been suspiciously absent ever since his public beat down and I'd heard a rumour that he'd taken some personal time out from school.

"Oh for sure," Eugene agreed, finally pulling his purple cape from his bag and throwing it around his shoulders before fastening it in place. "But the purple cape of justice can be a heavy burden to bear. I'm having to fight to maintain my position as the DUDs defender pretty much daily and it's not just about my pride anymore. I have other Fae looking to me and needing me to prove to them that we really can stand up for ourselves and change our fates. One spill of bad luck could be the end of my reign before it's even begun."

"We can't have that," I agreed as his mention of bad luck made me think of the crystals Leon had given me in hopes of keeping luck in my favour. "And on that note, I have something I wanna give you."

"A gift?" Eugene squeaked, giving me the big eyes as we stepped inside the Cafaeteria together and the rest of the students hurried to the line forming for food. "Is this how I officially get accepted into the harem?"

"By the stars, Eugene, you have to stop with that," I laughed, taking the midnight amethyst crystal from my pocket and holding it out for him. "My harem is full. I got the whole set, and I seriously am at my cock limit."

Eugene's cheeks burned cherry red and I breathed a laugh as I took hold of his wrist and made him take the crystal from me.

"Wow," he breathed, his gaze falling from my face to the crystal and his eyes widening in awe as he tested the weight of it in his hand. "Is that midnight amethyst?" His nose began to twitch like crazy and I nodded, grinning at the look on his face.

"Yeah. Solid luck, or so they say. Leon got me two because he's a flashy asshole and as much as I appreciate it, I feel like one lump of luck has to be more than enough. And after the shit you went through when Bryce dicked you over and the stars cursed you, I figure you deserve a little weight in your corner so far as luck goes."

"You had two?" he asked me, blinking rapidly. "You gave up on double luck, for me?"

"I dunno if having two really gave me double luck. The way I see it, you're lucky or you're not." I shrugged.

"Oh no, I disagree. I think two would give you double luck and three would be triple and four would be-"

"Dude, don't make this weird," I said, nudging him playfully and he grinned widely as he clutched the crystal to his chest.

"I'll treasure it forever," he breathed, giving me the heart eyes and I shook my head, unable to stop smiling at his dopey look.

"Excuse me," a girl's voice interrupted us and a bag smacked into my arm as she came to stand so freaking close to me that she was practically on my feet, forcing me to step back and leave her standing closer to Eugene. I eyed her green hair with interest as I tried to figure out if I knew her and she turned a shy look my way before addressing Eugene. "I was just going to ask if you'd like to join me for lunch, Genie."

It took me a beat to realise that Eugene was Genie and that she was stepping up to claim him.

I smirked at Eugene over the top of her head as I backed up a couple more paces, allowing her to have the stage. "No worries," I said. "I was just leaving. Enjoy your lunch, Genie." I winked at Eugene who looked totally confused and the girl swooped forward, kissing him right on the cheek and taking his hand in a bold move, even though a blush lined her cheeks. She guided him away before I think he'd even realised what was happening, but a bright smile split over his face.

I glanced at the huge line for food and sighed, realising my dawdling had just cost me any chance at a decent choice for dinner and taking a piece of cherry gum from my pocket as I considered just ditching out on the meal altogether. Coming in last meant getting a few scraps of the crappiest food on offer and I didn't care enough about going hungry to eat like that tonight after the week I'd had.

I lifted the gum to my lips, starting to turn away but before I could, Ryder's sharp whistle caught my ear and I looked around, finding him striding straight past the queue of people towards the front and jerking his chin at me in a clear command.

I arched a brow at him which he knew damn well was in reply to the whistling and the corner of his lips hooked into a smirk as he clicked his damn fingers at me instead.

Oh hell no.

I made a move to turn away but came face to chest with Gabriel who just grinned at me and spun me back to face Ryder again, stealing my unchewed gum from my hand and giving me a nudge to get me moving.

"If you don't go willingly, he's going to bind you in vines and swing you over there like a pretty little piñata," he said, his eyes flashing with amusement at that vision and I growled beneath my breath.

"Well maybe you wanna step in and save me from that fate?" I suggested.

"Nah. I'm gonna get us a table and wait for the two of you to grab our food."

He gave me a little shove and I huffed irritably before zipping to Ryder's side where he was now standing at the head of the line, holding everyone else up as they waited for me too.

"Well, this is incredibly rude of you," I teased, picking up a tray and pushing it into his hands.

"I thought I'd let you pick out dinner to make up for it," he replied, his gaze raking down to my bare thighs and back up again slowly.

"Hmm." I looked across the array of delicious looking dinners then shrugged. "Nah. I've given you all the training you need at this point. I think you're capable of picking out the good stuff for yourself now."

I started backing away from him as he placed the tray down, arching a brow at me like he didn't agree at all before reaching for a bowl of plain freaking rice and taking it for our dinner.

"Ew." I scrunched my nose up at him as he followed that up with some plain boiled potatoes and more veg - all without seasoning and I sighed as I resigned myself to a boring ass meal filled with nutritional value. *Yuck.*

Ryder continued to make bad choices and my Atlas buzzed in my pocket, giving me an excuse to look away from the shit show of a dinner he was selecting as I answered it without bothering to check the ID.

"Err, oh howdy-doody, Elise," Principal Greyshine's voice came down the speaker and I cursed beneath my breath. I'd been working to avoid him ever since the first time he'd tried to get me to come have a little chat with him, but he seemed determined to get me alone for some reason.

"Hey," I replied slowly, moving along as Ryder continued to gather up our dinner and I stopped paying any attention to him.

"I was hoping you could stop by my office for that chateroo before your liaison with Professor Titan? I'm afraid if you don't, I'll have to start looking at your place in this academy, Elise. You've missed a lot of classes and unless I can go over a few things with you then I'll have to assume you no longer meet the criteria for your scholarship placement."

"Fine," I snapped, hearing the extra bite in my tone and cringing a little - that wasn't exactly the best way to keep him on side if my place here really was at risk. "I'm just having my dinner and then-"

"That'll be dandy. I'm in my office. Come alone. Don't tell anyone."

"What? Why not?"

"Oh, ah, I just mean, there's no need to. Nothing to see here. Just you and me having a good old chin wag, no need to bring anyone else along or any of that jazz...ahem, anyway, I'll catch you on the flip."

Greyshine hung up on me and I frowned at my Atlas as I shoved it back into my pocket before turning to look at Ryder again just as we made it to the end of the serving line.

He had a second tray now too, this one stacked with four boxes of pizza as well as a handful of candy and a plate of sugar-coated doughnuts.

"Ooooh, look who finally figured out how to eat like a king," I teased, reaching out to take a tray from him but he kept hold of both of them, rolling his eyes at me.

"You won't be so pleased about it when I lose that V you love licking your way down so fucking much," he teased me right back, making my eyes fall to his waistband where I sadly couldn't even see a peep of abs, let alone the very tempting V he'd mentioned.

"Well maybe for dessert I'll make you work up a sweat to burn the calories back off," I suggested, following his lead as he crossed the room and took a seat on the table Gabriel had picked out for us.

No one else had dared join him, despite the fact that the place was crowded and I hopped up to perch my ass on the end of the table so that I was sitting between the two of them. Eyes followed us everywhere we moved and whispers were exchanged. We'd been getting eyeballed constantly since we arrived back at the academy, the news about me and my mates still the hottest topic of discussion everywhere we went. I didn't really give a shit what they thought of us and imagined their lives must have been pretty damn dull to take such an interest in ours. But whatever. Gabriel was doing a great job helping us dodge calls from the press and had even directed us into the Iron Wood to hideout yesterday lunchtime when a reporter had somehow snuck on campus to try and get an interview. I wanted to discuss my personal business with the world about as much as I wanted to jam a pineapple up my ass.

Ryder eyed me for a long moment then caught my waist and dragged me off of the table so that I fell into his lap. I gasped in surprise and turned my head to look at him, a question in my eyes which he leaned in close to answer, his words low and just for me.

"I've had to pretend you weren't mine in front of people for a long fucking time, baby," he growled, his hand moving onto my thigh beneath the table before his thumb tracked a line beneath the hem of it. "I'm done with that bullshit. I want every motherfucker in here to look and see who owns you. I don't want any of them getting any crazy ideas about the fact that I share you meaning I might be willing to let them get so much as an inch closer. You've got the four of us and that's it. We own you. I own you. And I want to make sure every single fucker who lays their eyes on you knows it."

"Show them then, baby," I breathed, my eyes meeting his in a clear challenge and he didn't waste a single second in capturing my lips with his, the harsh bite of his kiss taking me off guard as his hand came up to clasp my chin and hold me in place exactly where he wanted me.

I gave in to him, loving when he owned me like that and letting him take what he wanted from me as the cold stud of his tongue piercing swept across my tongue.

Just as I felt myself melting into a puddle for him, Ryder turned my chin away from him, using his grip on me to make me face across the table to Gabriel instead as he began to move his mouth down my neck, sucking and biting.

Gabriel's eyes lit as he stood, placed his palms flat on the table between us and leaned across to kiss me savagely too. For a few bliss-filled moments, I forgot about the room full of students surrounding us and came undone between them, moaning into Gabriel's mouth and tasting him hungrily.

When the two of them drew back, I opened my eyes to find pretty much every student in the room gaping at us and silence filling the air. A blush heated my cheeks a little at all of the attention but I resolutely ignored it, reaching out to grab a pizza box and flipping the lid open as I snagged a slice.

Well, if there had been any doubts about Gabriel being involved in this relationship too, there weren't now.

I concentrated on eating as the noise around the room slowly picked up again and by the time my gaze emerged from the half empty pizza box, almost everyone had gone back to focusing on their own business. I snagged a perfect, sugary doughnut from the plate to round off my meal and leaned back against Ryder as I began to devour it slowly, sighing in satisfaction at the sweet taste on my tongue.

The three Kipling brothers approached us as we were finishing up our meals and Kipling Senior handed Ryder a sealed envelope without saying a word.

"Anything else I should know about?" Ryder asked them, dropping the envelope into his pocket without any comment on it.

"All seems fairly calm within school grounds," Kipling Junior replied with a shrug. "Our ears will remain open as usual."

"Good," Ryder grunted. "Give my girl an orange soda."

Junior handed one over so fast he must have had it ready.

I grinned as I grabbed the can, cracking it open and taking a long swig of it before sighing in appreciation. "Thanks. You want a doughnut?" I held the plate out to them, and Middle Kipling's face flickered with rage for what I was pretty certain was the first time I'd ever seen any emotion on it.

"You can keep your carb filled whores, thank you very much," he bit out before turning sharply and stalking from the room.

"He's not a fan of food with holes," Kipling Senior commented like he was discussing the weather.

"Too provocative," Junior agreed.

"Practically begging for it," Senior said with a nod.

"Especially if there's a glazed topping." Junior nodded at the doughnuts and the two of them turned and walked away without another word, leaving me to spit my fucking doughnut out with a shudder.

"By the fucking stars," I groaned while Gabriel laughed at my expense before snagging himself a doughnut and happily biting into it.

His gaze slid to Ryder's and I could tell there was still a little tension between the two of them over the ideas Ryder had had about using dark magic to try and track Gareth down, but thankfully neither of them had felt the need to argue it out again since.

"Well, as much as I'm enjoying this, I have an appointment with Greyshine," I sighed.

"No," Ryder growled. "I've got to have a meeting with Shadowbrook and the others about the rebels and-"

"So go," I replied. "You know I love that you all wanna keep me in sight at all times, but I also can't keep hiding out forever. King hasn't made any attempt to snatch me again and I think they'd be pretty dumb to try now. Not only do I have four, crazy, possessive, murderous mates who would come to avenge me, but I'm also an Altair."

"Speaking of which, any word on whether or not your fancy new family have managed to track the motherfucker down or not?" Ryder asked, the sneer in his voice clear for all of us to hear.

"No," I sighed. "I spoke to Caleb last night and he said there weren't any updates but he kept going on about the fact the FIB agents who've been dispatched to deal with it are special ops and all that shit, so he's confident they will."

Gabriel's eyes clouded with a vision and I gave him a moment to *see* it through, but he just shrugged. "I can't *see* you getting the news that King has been caught. So let's assume that's not going to happen any time soon and just keep to our plan of sticking together. I can take you to see Greyshine then to your Liaison with Titan tonight. Leon is going home to speak to his parents about Roary, and Dante has gang business too."

"Okay," I agreed with a sigh, getting up and pressing a kiss to Ryder's cheek in goodbye before he turned and headed away to where Ethan and his pack were sitting.

Gabriel took my hand as we walked out, and I tried not to drag my feet as we made our way to Greyshine's office.

I knocked on the door as we arrived and Greyshine tugged it open almost instantly, his eyes wide with relief which quickly fell away as he spotted Gabriel there too.

"Oh, ah, Mr Nox. What, what, what are you doing here?" Greyshine wrung his hands together as he looked between us and I shrugged.

"Is there any reason for him not to be?" I asked.

"Well, yes, I really need to speak with you alone. In private. So er, perhaps Mr Nox you could just pop on back to your dorm and-"

"I'm staying," Gabriel said firmly and Greyshine withered a little before him then quickly nodded as he stepped back to let us in.

"What's this about?" I asked.

"Oh just, some, ah, forms you need to sign." He bustled over to his desk. "And I just wanted to make sure you're not struggling in any subjects after your missed classes."

"You didn't ask *me* to come in and discuss the classes I missed. And that was weeks ago so I don't see why it's an issue now," Gabriel said, moving to stand behind me as I took a seat in the only chair available on this side of the desk which wasn't stacked high with books.

"No, well, ummm... Miss Callisto is held to different standards than you are, Mr Nox, because she is here on a scholarship basis which has certain requirements. One of those is that she is present for a minimum of ninety four percent of her classes and after missing an entire month I'm afraid she now cannot fulfil-"

"Wait," I interrupted him. "You're not seriously saying you might kick me out, are you?"

My heart began to race as I looked at him with desperation in my gaze.

With the million and one things I had to think about at the moment and worry about and freak the fuck out about, the last thing on my mind had been the fucking scholarship rules.

"You can't kick her out," Gabriel snarled fiercely. "She had to take that time out because you couldn't keep this academy safe from the fucking gangs. When people sign up to come to this place, one of the key things the academy guarantees is that there are magical wards and locks in place to keep us safe during our training. So don't try and bullshit me or her by saying she hasn't stuck to her end of the deal when you sure as fuck haven't stuck to yours."

Greyshine fell back down onto his seat with a solid thump, blinking up at Gabriel through watery eyes and clearing his throat several times as he shuffled some papers on his desk.

"No, no, I didn't mean to imply that she will lose her place...extenuating circumstances and all. But I, ah, needed to just check that she-"

"I'm right here," I said, waving a hand in annoyance to bring his attention back to me and away from the brooding Harpy who was leaning over my shoulder. "Don't talk about me like I'm not in the room."

"Of course not!" Greyshine gasped, noticing my fangs which had snapped out in my irritation and seeming to remember that I was pretty freaking powerful in my own right. And a goddamn Altair too come to think of it. "I just need to know if you're struggling at all or would like to request some additional help from your teachers or even some one-on-one time with a study buddy or a tutor?"

"I'm doing okay," I replied, though I knew that was a bit of a lie. I had fallen behind while we'd missed so many classes and I'd pretty much been behind since joining the academy anyway. I found it damn hard to concentrate lately with everything I had going on too so that really hadn't helped the situation.

"I'd be happy to tutor her," Gabriel added as Greyshine's brow furrowed like he wasn't sure he believed me.

"You would?" Greyshine asked hopefully. Gabriel was the top ranked student in our class after all so I guessed I couldn't do much better than him for a tutor.

"Yes. I'm interested in teaching as a possible profession anyway, so it would be a good practice for me to see if I really enjoy it or not," Gabriel replied.

"Wonderful!" Greyshine announced, clapping his sweaty hands together then glancing at me again hopefully.

I looked up at Gabriel and flashed him a smile in thanks. "If I say yes, does that cover it? Am I good to assume my scholarship is fine and my place here is secure then?" I asked.

"Yes." Greyshine nodded profusely, mopping at his forehead to swipe a bead of sweat away and from the way he kept looking at me, I could have sworn he had something else on his mind.

"Are you feeling nervous, sir?" I asked him curiously, training my gifted hearing on his heartbeat and finding it racing.

"No, no," he denied quickly. Too quickly.

I glanced up at Gabriel again, wanting to check if he'd *seen* anything for us to be concerned about, but he only shrugged, clearly as in the dark as I was.

"Okay, well you said about me signing something?" I added and Greyshine paled before nodding again and rummaging around.

Eventually he found a sheet of paper and shoved it at me, keeping his hand flat over the page and leaning in as he offered me a pen.

I reached forward to take it and frowned as I felt myself slipping into a small silencing bubble which he'd clearly thrown up hastily to exclude Gabriel.

"I need you to come and find me alone as soon as possible," he hissed but the bubble fell away before I could question him and I frowned harder.

Greyshine jabbed the piece of paper to remind me to sign and my confusion only grew as I found the entire page blank. I sure as fuck wasn't signing anything I couldn't even read. Though I didn't get the impression this was a concealment, more like it really was just some scrap of paper he'd found. I glanced up to ask what the hell was going on but he looked so freaking nervous as he just pointed at the page again, so I quickly signed it. My name sure as fuck wasn't Admiral Hardcock though so it wasn't going to bind me to anything.

"Okay, thanks. Buh-bye now." Greyshine snatched the page away then ushered me and Gabriel out of his office with much hand flapping.

The door slammed and locked behind us abruptly and I turned to Gabriel who looked just as perplexed as I felt.

"He just got me to sign a blank piece of paper then used a silencing bubble to ask me to come find him alone. Is he planning something dodgy or is he just a fucking weirdo?" I asked Gabriel and a low growl left him as he absorbed that information.

I gave him a moment to try and *see* something that might explain our Principal's strange behaviour but after a few minutes of trying he just shook his head.

"I've got no idea what that's about. I can't *see* anything to worry us though. But you're not meeting up with him alone. Maybe he's under the influence of King or working for them and using some kind of dark magic to block my visions. I'm not taking any risks with you."

"Okay," I agreed, taking his hand and leading the way down the long corridor toward Professor Titan's office for my Liaison session. "Soooo, you never told me you wanted to be a professor before."

Gabriel actually looked kind of embarrassed for a moment and my smile grew as I gave his hand a squeeze in mine.

"It's not definite," he replied with a shrug. "I just needed a lot of help with The Sight and Mystice made a huge difference to me. He taught me about how to live with it, unlock it, understand and interpret it, and I thought it might be cool, maybe, one day, once I've got an even better understanding of my own gifts, to help others learn about them."

"You want to make a difference the way he did for you?" I asked, tugging him to a halt outside Titan's office. We were early and the door was ajar, showing me that he wasn't here yet.

"Maybe. I dunno. I don't really fancy making a living by touting visions to the highest bidder and I've never really felt a pull towards any other career. The Sight is such a big part of who I am, it just made sense to focus on those skills somehow." He shrugged, looking more than a little uncomfortable and I grinned at how freaking cute he was being.

"So that's why you want to be my teacher then?" I asked. "It's got nothing to do with playing out some naughty schoolgirl fantasy or anything?"

Gabriel's eyes ran down my body and his smile turned about three shades dirtier. "I mean, that hadn't been on my mind. Until now..."

He tugged me towards him, making me squeal like a freaking idiot as he yanked me close and lowered his mouth towards mine.

But of course, before we could even begin to live out a little bit of that fantasy, Professor Titan rounded the corner and cleared his throat loudly.

I broke away from Gabriel with a sigh, following Titan into the room and seeing his gaze sweeping over my uninvited shadow.

"I know that Mr Night insisted on being here for your previous sessions, Elise, but I really don't see the need for yet another student to be sitting in on them now too," Titan said, sounding tired and I paused before me and Gabriel could take our seats, glancing up at my Harpy as guilt twisted in my chest.

"He does have a point," I said slowly, wondering if I could maybe get Gabriel to back off just a little. "Would you mind, maybe waiting outside for me instead of sitting in? It's not like this is particularly interesting for you anyway and..." I trailed off, shrugging and not wanting to say out loud that I actually enjoyed my little chats with Professor Titan. Because yeah, I had realised that I was kinda falling into this role of relying on him and I kinda enjoyed having this father/daughter relationship with him, even though I knew I really should have been pursuing that with my DNA dad and all that. But with Titan it was just easier somehow.

Gabriel hesitated, considering me for a moment then finally nodded. "I'll be right outside," he said and I knew he got it more than the others did because he had a similar kind of relationship with Bill. "No silencing bubbles."

I grinned at him as he leaned down to take a quick kiss from my lips then he stepped out into the corridor and closed the door behind him, leaving me to give Titan an awkward smile as I plopped down into my chair.

"I've missed-" Titan cut himself off as his Atlas began to ring and he gave it a quick glance before silencing it with an apology to me.

"I've missed you too," I blurted and he gave me a blank stare for a moment before chuckling.

"Oh, I was just saying I've missed Mr Pluto's latest update on your progress in your counselling sessions," he explained and my face heated as I realised what I'd just said to him like a fucking creeper weirdo.

"Err..." I sucked my lips between my teeth and begged the couch to swallow me but of course it didn't like a total asshole. I didn't even have anything to say to that because I hadn't had a single session with Mr Pluto thanks to Ryder paying him off for me, so now I was just staring.

"But I have missed you too, of course," Titan said, putting me out of my misery though now I knew it was just to try and make me feel better which was even more mortifying.

"I dunno why I said that," I muttered, looking at my shoes and hoping to the stars that Gabriel wasn't actually listening in on this shit show.

"Well, I think I do. I know that it's my job to attend these sessions and to look out for you, but the two of us have formed a...kindred connection if you will. Bound by our grief and more than a few common interests beyond just our teacher/student roles. I'm very fond of you too and it makes me glad to hear that you feel the same."

For some fucking reason, my eyes prickled with tears at his words and I shuffled like an awkward duck as I tried to figure out what to do with them.

"So," Titan went on, saving me from having to come up with some response to that because I was fresh out of anything to say. "A lot has happened since we last had a proper meeting like this. You're mated to two more Fae and have played a major part in the overhaul of the gang culture in Alestria which has the potential to massively alter the way everyone in this city lives from day to day. That's pretty huge, Elise. Not to mention the fact that you found your father. And that you're a member of one of the most powerful families in the entire kingdom now."

I breathed a laugh and shifted a little uncomfortably in my seat.

"Did you want to talk about that? I take it from the photographs I've seen all over the newspapers that you've been engrossing yourself within your new family."

My mouth opened and closed like a fish several times then I suddenly burst into tears, burying my face in my hands.

I tried to hide from the world as my walls imploded and all of it just kind of hit me like a ton of bricks. This was exactly why I'd been holding back from Marlowe and the rest of the Altairs. They were my new family. But I wasn't ready to let go of my old one. Why did it feel like the one thing was so intrinsically tied to the other? Like allowing myself to fall into the idea of being an Altair, of having more people who might give a shit about me or want to be something to me meant letting go of Gareth and everything he'd been.

He hadn't even had the same father as me, so he was nothing to them. Literally. Just some sad story about a boy they'd never known who they only even heard about via me. Sure, they might feel sad for me, but that was about it. And I wasn't ready to leave him behind to throw myself into their world.

The couch dipped beside me and Titan tentatively wrapped an arm around my shoulders, patting me gently as I fell against his chest and just let myself cry.

I hadn't ever really been held like that before. Not by someone who was only interested in my welfare. Someone who didn't want anything from me other than for me to feel better. Of course I had my kings, and Gareth had always comforted me when I'd been feeling sad. And my mom used to cuddle me when I was a little kid, but as I'd gotten older a distance had formed between us which hadn't allowed for that anymore. She'd always called me tough and joked I didn't need anyone. But that wasn't true. I'd needed a parent. I just hadn't known how to ask her to be more of one to me when she was clearly struggling with so much of her own pain. Gareth had always been the one who looked after me really. Ever since we were little kids. But it never should have been his job.

"Marlowe seems nice," I breathed, once I managed to rein in the crying enough. "I mean, he's not altogether recovered from his time…lost in the jungle." the lie tasted bitter on my lips, but I couldn't exactly go spilling the truth to Titan about where he'd been or who had found him. The official line was that Marlowe had known my mom was pregnant before he'd gone missing which was how they'd discovered me. "But he just wants a lot from me. All at once. Like he wants to reclaim all of that lost time or something, but I can't exactly just hand it over. And I can't just pretend that growing up without him meant nothing even if he hadn't intended to walk out on me like I'd thought…"

Titan sighed heavily, holding me just tight enough that I knew he wouldn't let go until I moved away, but not squeezing me too tight either.

"After my daughter died…" He cleared his throat then went on. "I made the decision not to have any more children. Of course, I knew I'd love them if I did and that it wouldn't have been replacing her, but…" He blew out a long breath. "It felt like doing that would have meant moving on with my life, leaving her behind. And there's nothing wrong with that of course in some ways. Life does go on, the world keeps spinning and we can't only live for our grief, but it isn't easy to make the choice to start something different when you know it won't ever include them."

I nodded, staying where I was, leaning against his chest and knowing I should move away, but I was stealing some comfort from him and I wasn't capable of making that choice right now.

"It's not like I don't want to get to know them," I said. "It's just a lot. And they're strangers to me. Melinda and Caleb and the rest are all fairly low key about it, acting normal and stuff. But Marlowe is so intense, and I feel like he's already got an idea in his head about all the things I am or will be to him and I'm never going to be able to live up to that."

"I'm sure he will love you no matter what," Titan assured me but I shook my head a little.

"I don't know. Melinda got him an Atlas and he's been messaging me non-stop, but..." Guilt twisted in my gut because I currently had over fifty unread messages waiting for me, some of which I'd seen flash up in my notifications and knew were asking about things like the food I enjoyed or books I read along with the answers to those questions from him. It was just so much all at once and I knew that I was only running away from my problems by ignoring them, but I didn't know what else to do. I wasn't ready. I hadn't even processed this yet and Marlowe wanted me to call him *Dad*. "I feel closer to you than I do to that stranger," I whispered and Titan stilled.

"I feel...very protective of you too, Elise," he murmured after a few moments where I felt so much heat rising in my cheeks that I was surprised I hadn't set him alight. "But we've had time to form that bond. And we have shared grief. No doubt I'm projecting some of my wishes for my own child's stolen life onto you and you have always been without a father, so..."

Neither of us said it but we knew that was what it was between us. We filled a certain amount of the voids we each held, but was that really a bad thing? Titan got it. He got me. It was easy and had happened naturally. I wanted this with the man who had contributed his DNA to my creation in some ways, but what if it didn't come so naturally with him?

It wasn't like I was some kid needing a Daddy. I was a grown ass woman who had survived countless things he couldn't understand and who was perfectly capable of choosing my own fate now. I didn't know what that was going to mean after I graduated, because my focus was still on bringing down King and finding out what had happened to Gareth, but after that I would make my own mind up. What I wanted from a father was...this. Someone who gave a shit, who I could unload on and who just got me. Did I really need to try and force that with a stranger when I'd found it already?

"How about I make you a promise?" Titan offered, leaning back a little and I sat up too, wiping my tears away and giving him an embarrassed smile as we shifted apart.

"What promise?"

"I think you should attempt to connect with Marlowe Altair. The man has clearly been through a lot and I understand that he's overwhelming you, but I get the feeling you've gone your whole life missing the love of a father and now he's right there waiting for you. If the texts are too much then tell him so, you don't have to ignore all of them. Maybe just reply to one and explain that you need some time to adjust before answering all of them."

"Maybe," I mumbled, fiddling with the hem of my skirt and avoiding his gaze.

"And my promise to you is that...I'll still be here. I care about you Elise, and I'm not going anywhere. All the time you wish to have a relationship with me like this, I will welcome it. I don't know why, but I feel like you and my daughter could have been friends and I see a lot of her in you. I feel a lot of fondness towards you for that...but I am not your father. No matter what either of us may wish. So...I'm still here. But I don't want you to miss the opportunity to connect with the man who really is your blood because of me."

"Okay," I breathed, managing to look up at him and giving him a rueful smile. "But I know he won't be as cool as you."

"Oh-ho, I'm cool now, am I? Well bless the stars, perhaps I should be throwing some kind of party in celebration of that!"

I snorted a laugh and he chuckled, gripping my shoulder briefly and nodding towards the door.

"You believe Gabriel Nox will become your Elysian Mate in time too?" he asked but it was more of a statement.

"I love him just as fiercely as the others," I replied. "Silver rings or not. He's mine and I'm his."

Titan let out a low whistle. "And they're really good to you? All of them? Even Dante Oscura and Ryder Draconis?"

"They are," I agreed firmly. "They're better men than most people could ever realise."

Titan absolutely did not look convinced by that statement, but he just blew out a breath and shrugged. "I feel a stern talk brimming in my gut, so perhaps it's time we called it a night on this session?"

"Okay," I said, pushing to my feet. "We don't need to end up with me screaming in defiance and slamming the door in your face."

"Fates forbid," he agreed with a chuckle.

I moved to the door, my fingers curling around the handle before I glanced back over my shoulder at him as he took his place behind his desk once more.

"Thank you," I breathed. "And for what it's worth, I think your daughter was really lucky to have you while she was still alive."

Titan smiled sadly at me, his eyes brimming with tears for a moment before he nodded and bid me goodnight in a gruff voice.

I stepped outside into the corridor and the moment I closed the door, Gabriel's arms were around me and I was breathing in the delicious fresh scent of his skin as I released a slow breath.

"I *saw*," he explained. "And I think you needed that."

"I did," I agreed.

"So what now?"

"Now, I think I'd like to go somewhere quiet and answer one of

Marlowe's messages."

Gabriel pushed me back gently and placed a soft kiss on my lips. "Then let's go, angel." He took my hand and led me away down the corridor and I felt lighter for the first time in a long time as at least a few of my worries seemed to slip away.

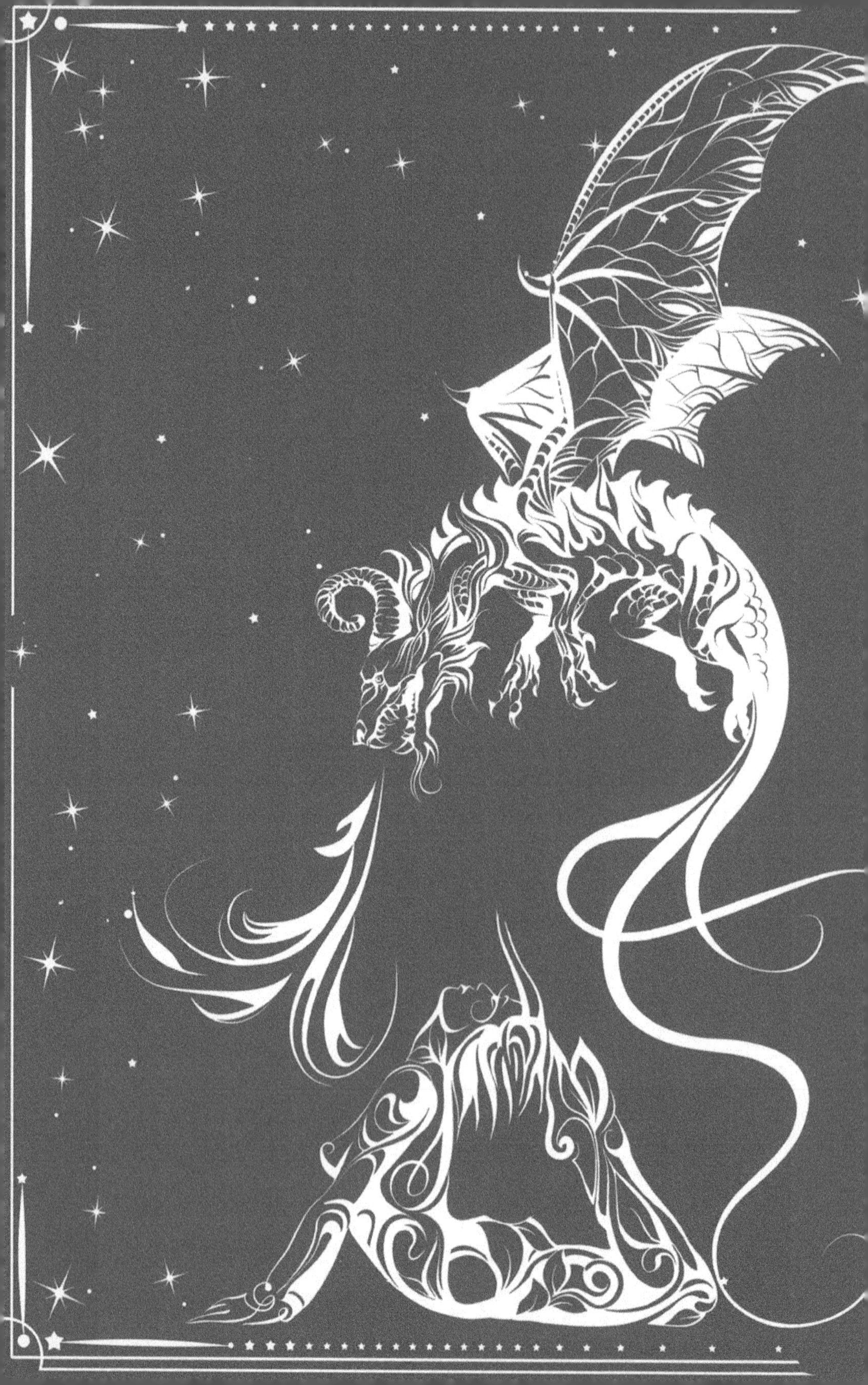

DANTE

CHAPTER THIRTY FOUR

The moment finally came when we could strike at King and I for one was desperate to see him pay for all the bloodshed he'd caused. There was a steely darkness in Elise's eyes too and I knew she was thinking of her brother tonight, his loss a weight we all seemed to carry.

We followed a narrow, winding track up into the mountains, the full moon bright and burning in the starry sky above. Gabriel led the way in the dark, none of us casting a single Faelight to see by, the silvery glow of the moon enough to illuminate the path. I'd suggested I fly everyone up the mountain in my Dragon form, but Gabriel said we'd be spotted, so we were reduced to walking instead.

"We should be able to see the main path from up here," Gabriel said in a low voice even though we had a strong silencing bubble cast around the five of us. There was a note of concern in his voice like he was worried about what we were going to see, and I crept closer behind him as we reached a cluster of boulders to the right of the track.

Gabriel scaled one, laying down on the top of it to peek over and I followed him up as Elise joined my other side, her breaths uneven as we gazed down at the wider path that wound toward the heart of the mountain. Fae walked mindlessly along it, seeming to be in some trance, nonsense pouring from their lips as they walked at perfect intervals from each other. There was no misinterpreting what they were. Blazers.

"Dalle stelle," I breathed. "There's so many."

"Why are they walking like that, where are the Black Card to escort them?" Elise asked, a note of horror in her voice at the sight of so many Fae walking to their deaths.

"It must be some kind of summoning spell," Gabriel said darkly. "King's found a way to call his victims to him."

"Is that a guess or can you *see* it?" Leon asked from Gabriel's other side.

"I didn't *see* it," Gabriel said simply.

"Sooo, it's a guess?" Leon pushed.

"Obviously," Ryder answered for Gabriel next to Leon, elbowing him in the side. "But it's pretty clear that's what's going on here."

"There must be hundreds of Fae heading to King tonight," I said as my upper lip peeled back. In just the few moments we'd been here at least fifty had passed and the line seemed endless. Was this why King hadn't come for my girl again? Had they allowed the full moons to pass by while building up to this enormous ritual or whatever the fuck they were planning?

A rustling noise sounded behind us and I jerked my head around, ready to go into battle but Gabriel rested a hand on my arm as my gaze narrowed on the little bush that was shaking by the track.

"It's just an animal," Gabriel said and my heart rate settled as I looked back at the mass of Blazers walking by.

"Heads, shoulders, fleas in bows, fleas in bows. Heads, shoulders, fleas in bows, fleas in bows," one guy sang mindlessly as he went. "And flies in ears and mouth and nose. Heads, shoulders, fleas in bows, fleas in bows."

Leon snorted. "Awesome," he murmured to himself.

"Come on," Gabriel said, climbing back down off the boulder and we all followed as he continued up the path we were following. It was far steeper and narrower than the one the Blazers were on, but that meant it would cut a quicker route to wherever King's victims were heading. I just hoped we could spring our attack before this many sacrifices were made and their magic was given to King. Besides the loss of life, if he took this much power, I feared for the whole of Alestria. Maybe even the whole of Solaria.

We eventually reached the summit of the steep path and followed it around some large rock formations through thick, thorny foliage. Ryder and Gabriel used their earth magic to bend the prickly bushes away from us and widen the track beneath our feet whenever it became too steep. As we rounded the huge rocks, I got a view of the sheer valley running away beneath us and the track that weaved like a snake within it, climbing toward a gaping dark cave mouth that led into the belly of the mountain.

"Air magic?" I offered, spinning up a small gust in my palm.

"If we use air magic we'll be spotted," Gabriel said, shaking his head, his eyes saying he had some other plan. The ground was near vertical where it sloped away from us towards the rocky tracks below though and I couldn't see many other options.

"What's the plan then, falco?" I asked as Elise pressed to my side, looking down at the obstacle before us.

"To get into that cave," he answered mystically and I sighed, hating being out of the loop with him and the stars sometimes.

Ryder worked to gather more shadows around us to conceal us against the rocks then slit his thumb on a razor blade to restore his magic. We needed every drop at our disposal tonight. We'd fed Elise as much as she could take and not let her use a single bit since without giving her more blood to replenish it. All of us had spent the day charging our magic to the absolute max, but only Ryder and I could actively create it now that we were here, and Elise would be able to steal it once we inevitably ended up fighting the Black Card. I wore as much gold as I could manage without it hindering my movements despite having to put up with Leon's gangster jokes all the way here.

"Hey, little monster," Leon breathed. "Where do Faetalian gangsters live?"

I rolled my eyes. Apparently he wasn't done with the jokes even now.

"Where?" Elise whispered.

"The spaghetto," Leon said then fell into silent chuckles at his own joke as he looked at me.

Elise cracked a smirk, shaking her head. "Not the time, Leo."

"Alright, alright, just one more. What do you call a gangster Dragon?"

No one answered, everyone waiting anxiously while Gabriel's eyes glazed with a vision.

"Al Dragone," Leon said with a suppressed laugh, poking Ryder in the ribs. "Get it? Like Al Capone? Only it's Dragone."

"I get it, Mufasa," Ryder snapped. "Now shut up or I'll rip your tongue out."

Gabriel blinked out of the vision and looked to us with a decision in his eyes. "We can walk inside with the Blazers, but we need to change our appearances."

"That's strong magic, bro," Leon said thoughtfully, focusing properly at last. "We're gonna waste a lot of power doing that."

"Which is why Ryder's going to cast it," Gabriel said, giving him a dark look.

"I'd need a painful death to recharge from that," Ryder said and Gabriel's dark expression said one was coming. "Alright." He cracked his neck and stepped up to Elise, holding out his palm and starting to run it over her as he created an illusion to change her appearance. He made her hair appear long and dark and shadowed her eyes to a deep brown colour, the rings within them completely hidden. Then he worked through the group, making Gabriel seem blonde with pale skin, giving me blue punk rocker hair and a multitude of piercings then finally gave Leon short hair and spotty skin. The concealments would be detectable up close but as it was dark and no one would be looking too closely at us, they'd probably hold up long enough for us to get in the cave.

"This is so not cool," Leon complained. "I wanna look like an ex FIB agent with a dark, mysterious past, a scar running through his left eye and a glint in his gaze that says he's seen things."

"Oh, you mean like this?" Ryder said, then held a hand to his own face to cast another illusion spell, making his hair thick and black and added a huge scar to his right eye. If you looked closely at any of us, it was clear who we were, but I doubted King would be out here searching for us.

"Yeah, I want that!" Leon said excitedly.

"Tough shit." Ryder smirked and Leon growled angrily.

"Stop fighting," Elise hissed, turning to Gabriel. "How are we getting down to the path?"

"We're going to make a tunnel," Gabriel said simply.

"Why don't we just tunnel directly into the cave?" I suggested, jerking my chin at it.

"Because there's wards around it. The only Fae getting through there are ones high on Killblaze or members of the Black Card," Gabriel said simply. "King's clearly not taking any chances since we smashed up his underwater palace."

"Then how-" Elise started but Gabriel reached into his pocket, taking out a vial of Killblaze in answer.

"We only need a little in our system to fool the wards," Gabriel said, his brow pinching. "And I'll be able to remain sober as I'm technically still in the Card."

Elise eyed the vial with a look of horror in her gaze and I moved forward, taking her hand and turning her to look at me.

"It's okay, amore mio. Gabriel will look after you, won't you falco?" I looked at him and he stepped closer to Elise.

"I'm not afraid," she said, glaring at the vial again. "I just don't want the shit that killed Gareth in my body ever again."

"Ryder's antivenom will heal you of its effects once we're all beyond the wards," Gabriel promised then slipped something else out of his pocket. "He made this for tonight." It was a hard, silver flower with four sharp petals.

"It has my antivenom in it," Ryder explained, apparently having known about this already.

Gabriel always had to hold back details on his visions when we made plans, but it was frustrating being left out of the loop most of the time. My instincts burned at me to take the lead, but as he knew the future, it was pretty impossible to state any kind of case against him being in charge.

Ryder reached out, pressing his finger to Elise's chest and painting a cross there.

A small smile pulled at her lips and she nodded decisively. "Okay," she said, reaching for the vial of Killblaze. "Let's just get it over with."

She shook the vial to activate the crystals and we all stepped forward, Ryder taking a moment longer than the rest of us as he forced his Order gifts to recede, allowing himself to be poisoned by this shit. Elise plucked the stopper from the vial and me, Leon and Ryder all pressed closer to her as the four of us breathed in the drug. There was no immediate effect, but my head started to feel lighter as we inhaled the last of it and Elise tucked the vial into her pocket.

"Hold onto me," Gabriel commanded and we all clustered tight around him as Leon started giggling.

"The moon just told me I'm pretty," he whispered right in my ear and I found myself laughing too.

Gabriel suddenly cast a huge hole in the earth beneath our feet and my back hit soft earth as we shot down a tunnel in the ground. His magic made the whole thing smooth so we slid down together at a furious speed while Leon whooped and laughed.

We came to an abrupt halt and were suddenly stepping out of small cave as Gabriel directed us into a gap in the line of Blazers. I marched a couple of feet behind Leon as I tried to focus on what we needed to do, but merda santa, the sky was so sparkly. The stars all winked at me and I heard them giggling as they flirted. Leon could have the moon, I was going to fuck every glittery little star in the sky.

"I'll fly up there for you. Whoosh, here I come." I flapped my arms but only seemed to fly horizontally and that was no fun. "Oh ciao, bella," I purred as I spotted a rock that looked just like Elise. It even had her pixie nose. I picked it up and stroked her hair. "Amore mio, I have been looking for you." I looked around then slowly slid my zipper down and pushed Elise into my boxers before doing my pants back up.

"Hey Leone," I hissed, cupping my hand around my mouth and he looked back at me with a wide smile.

"I have a rock with my cock," I told him and he burst out laughing.

A low giggle came from behind me too and I glanced back, finding Ryder there with a stupid smile on his face. But wait, was that his face? Or was it the face of a man? An FIB man. I looked away quickly, upping my pace. I was being hunted. He was going to take me to Darkmore Penitentiary and never let me go.

"Oscuuura. Oscura. Oscar Oscura," the FIB agent said loudly and I cursed under my breath.

"Oh no. He knows who I am," I muttered in fright.

"What a stupid name," the agent said. "Too many Os and Ps. Draconis. Now that's a name. A name for a king." He laughed in his deep tone and I looked back, catching the eye of Elise behind him.

"Help me," I mouthed.

"What?!" she shouted.

"Help. Me," I mouthed slower.

"I'm going to eat twelve pies," the agent decided. "Each a different fruit. Lots of sugar. Love sugar."

"Merda santa, he's going to bake me in a pie and eat me," I gasped.

"Who told you about me wanting to eat my boyfriend-in-laws?" Leon suddenly hissed, twirling around and leaping like a frog along the path then laughed wildly. "Where's that croissant man with his feathery, fluffy, pastry wings? Nom, nom, nom, I'm coming for you pastry bird."

"Have you seen the moon?" Elise called. "It's so big and round. Do you think I could climb up there?" She tried to climb the air in front of her and stumbled over her own feet. A tall man helped her up. A tall man I knew. It didn't look like him. Well it did, except this man was blonde and paler than a ghost, but it definitely was him under all that papery skin. Gabby.

"Hey Gabby!" I shouted, waving as I smiled. "Gabby, it's me! Oscar!" *Oh no, the agent will have heard me.* I quickly looked away and found Leon picking up rocks in front of me, stuffing them into his pants.

"I've got them too now. All the cock rocks," he sang. "You can't take them from me, they're *mine*."

"What?" I frowned. He wasn't making any sense at all. He must have been on drugs. Fucking Blazer.

I glanced over my shoulder as the agent got closer and I let out a girlish yelp. "Stay back!" I slapped him in the face and his head wheeled sideways then he burst out laughing.

"My face hit your hand," he chuckled.

It *was* kind of funny actually. *Funny, flunny, flumpy – what was I saying again?*

I straightened my spine, putting on a posh voice. "Ah yes, Mr Lionel Acrux I'm afraid we'll have to remove your balls with a hack saw. No healing can be done at all while you're undergoing the surgery unfortunately. It will be quite horrific. We're going to record it for the news, is that alright? There'll also be a Griffin taking a shit on your face simultaneously. All above board. Nothing untoward. Hey that rhymed," I said, twisting around and finding the agent stalking me again.

"I'll boil those balls when you're done with them," the agent offered.

"I don't know what you're talking about," I lied, glancing around nervously. *He's onto me.* "I don't know anything about any balls."

"The Dragon Lord's balls," the agent said, roaring a laugh. "I'll feed them to a rat, then feed that rat to a cat, then the cat to bat."

"You wouldn't do that," I gasped.

Leon started singing Hakuna Matata loudly and Elise sang the Circle of Life even louder, trying to cancel him out.

"I would do it," I said.

"Do what?" the agent whispered. "I like Lions."

"What kind?" I asked to keep him distracted.

"Simba. Not scar. Scar's a stronzooooo," he howled like a wolf. "*I'm a stronzo.*" He hung his head and I dropped back to pat his arm.

"You're *my* stronzo," I whispered and he held my hand as we approached the tunnel ahead of us.

Leon kept picking up rocks and stuffing them in his pants while singing louder and louder. There were strange people in these parts of the woods.

We reached the huge cave ahead and I squeezed my new friend's hand as we stepped inside, looking up at the arching stone ceiling above us where sharp stalactites glinted and glittered. A warm glow shone up ahead of us and I followed all my new friends towards it as we headed around a corner into a huge cavern with a massive fire pit at the heart of it, flames all twisting and dancing and swirling within it. A mass of hooded Black Card members were gathered around it all chanting excitedly. I was excited too. *I love parties.*

Someone grabbed my arm and I was suddenly yanked away from the friendly fire into a dark alcove. Something sharp drove into my flesh and I growled, twisting around to attack the spikey thing, but my mind suddenly cleared and I fell still as the floaty feeling in my head receded.

I turned to Ryder beside me and he jerked his hand out of mine with a grunt, rubbing his eyes as Gabriel cast a tight silencing bubble around us, sticking the others with the antivenom flower Ryder had given him.

Elise sighed in relief as she was healed from the Killblaze's effects and Gabriel kissed her cheek, his own relief clear at having us back.

"By the stars," Leon cursed as he started fishing rocks out of his boxers, tossing them onto the floor. I reached into my own pants, taking out the lone rock in there and dropping it into the pile with a frown. Had I really thought that rock looked like Elise?

"We need to wait for the final Blazers to arrive," Gabriel said in a low voice.

"When's my kill getting here to recharge my magic?" Ryder murmured.

"Three, two, one," Gabriel murmured then a Black Card member came striding along, dragging a Blazer behind him.

"Please don't hurt me!" the Blazer wailed as the guy shoved him onto his ass right in front of our alcove. The hooded pezzo di merda started kicking him with a smirk on his face and Ryder lunged out of the darkness like a viper striking its prey, slamming a hand over the guy's mouth and yanking him into the cover of the shadows. He cast dirt down the Black Card member's throat to silence any noises leaving him, binding his hands in the same movement to stop him using his magic. Ryder cast a blade in his grip and made a bloody mess of the guy as he fed on his pain while I casually braced his victim for the blows he delivered.

When he was dead, we cast away the concealment spells on our flesh and waited in the dark as the last of the Blazers filed inside. Elise stared at Ryder with her fangs digging into her lower lip and utter lust gleaming in her eyes. She loved when he went mega psycho.

"Everyone ready?" Gabriel breathed and we all nodded.

We'd gone over this part of the plan a thousand times and there was no room for error. King was going to meet his end tonight. And we were going to make him suffer for Gareth before we sent him beyond the veil.

Elise lengthened her fangs, cutting her palm open on one of them as we prepared to do the spell laid out in the Magicae Mortuorum book that could strip King of his newly acquired Elements. We'd drain him dry and expose the pathetic Fae he was beneath it all before finding out how well he could fight against one of us without his stolen magic to aid him.

Gabriel took the potion Ryder had brewed from his pocket, each ingredient in the small bottle bought and paid for from the Kiplings in preparation for tonight. Elise added a few drops of her blood and a line of smoke coiled up from the contents. Gabriel took a sip then passed it around the group for the rest of us to do the same.

I felt a strange burning feeling in my throat as I swallowed a mouthful of the tangy liquid and the sensation sank deep down into my stomach.

"You remember the chant?" Gabriel murmured and we all assented. "Okay…" He paused, listening for something as quiet fell out in the cavern and King's voice filled the air.

"Brothers, sisters, we are all gathered here tonight for the largest ritual in the history of our great movement. The time has come to seize my final gifts of power so I can gain control of Alestria and expand our influence across the land," King's ever-changing voice called.

"Not on our watch, asshole," Elise hissed, her eyes sparkling with the desire to kill. It was hot as fuck and sent electricity buzzing through my veins.

"Let's end him for Gareth, bella," I said, pulling her close to place a burning kiss on her lips.

As I released her, fire flared in her eyes. "For Gareth," she agreed and the others all echoed those words.

I knew there was a great risk involved tonight, Gabriel had told us himself that there were many paths that could lead to our deaths on this mission. But not one of us was fazed by that. We would do whatever it took to destroy King. Our girl deserved that and far more for what they had taken from her. So if my life was the price of justice for Elise and her brother, then I would gladly hand it over to the stars.

"A morte e ritorno," I growled as Gabriel led the way out of the dark into the burning light of the fire pit in the cavern.

"A morte e ritorno," Ryder growled low under his breath and I looked to him in surprise, my heart rising in my chest as he shot me a look and shrugged. Merda santa, I loved that serpente.

"Magicae retro dare tibi," Gabriel started chanting and we immediately took up the chant too, keeping our voices low as the magic began to build in the air. I doubted we'd remain unnoticed for long, but we'd get a small head start at least.

"Magicae retro dare tibi," I said with the others and the power grew around us as the spell worked to loosen King's grip on their stolen Elements.

King paused mid speech where they stood up on a raised area of rock and they brandished a silver blade in their grip. They gazed through the crowd of Blazers with a flicker of worry crossing their currently female features and I smirked at seeing them so unsettled.

"Stop!" King suddenly cried to the Black Card and their own chanting fell dead on their lips.

Our words rang out in the cavern and we raised our chins, calling them louder so they filled the entire space. I cast a fierce air shield around us to keep us all safe as King's eyes turned our way, squinting to see us beyond the fire. Elise took hold of my hand and her magic mixed with mine as she added her own power to the shield and I smiled at our combined strength flowing between us.

"Who's there?!" King bellowed, but we just responded by chanting louder and louder, the words tumbling from my tongue over and over again. "Stop them!"

Ryder threw out a hand the same time Gabriel did and a huge net of vines fell down on the Black Card members, tangling them together as they added thick, sticky sap to the net, making it harder for them to fight their way free. Magic was thrown at us in huge pelts of fire balls, ice blades and spears and I braced for impact with my heart pounding fiercely in my chest. The force of the combined magic hammered against our shield in furious waves, but Elise and I held strong, keeping us safe from the unFae stronzos who worked to try and destroy us together.

King threw out their palms, sending an explosion of fire towards us like a meteorite.

"Focus!" Gabriel roared.

We all stood our ground as Elise and I kept the shield strong and we continued the chant. The fire slammed against it in a flaring wave so hot it burned even beyond the dome of air we were protected within. Gabriel cooled the air with his water magic and Leon worked to extinguish the billowing flames that blocked our view of the cavern.

My breaths came heavier and I shared a determined look with Elise beside me as adrenaline surged into my blood.

The moment the flames cleared, the Black Card were upon us, colliding with our shield and battering it with their own power.

We kept chanting as I sent all of my magic out into the shield to keep it strong, the hooded Black Card members swarming around us like a dark sea.

"Keep going!" Elise cried in encouragement and we spoke louder still, making King curse in fury.

They were clearly struggling against the power of our spell as they cast huge blasts of air at our shield, trying to punch holes in our defences. I growled, clenching my teeth as I fought to heal up any weak spots, determined not to let the bastardo break through.

"Motherfucker," Ryder snarled through his teeth as he shot spikes out of the ground beneath the Black Card members, then fell back into the chant with the rest of us.

King catapulted spears at us next, the power of them like missiles as he battled to cut into our shield and I yelled out a warning as one sliced through the barrier. My heart lurched as it shot directly at Elise and Gabriel's hand flew out, throwing it off course with a blast of water so it hit the ground and smashed to pieces.

"Holy fuck," she breathed, looking to him with big eyes as I sealed up the hole.

"Keep chanting," he demanded and we all shouted out the spell as Elise and I kept the shield in place once more.

I could feel my magic pouring out of me and didn't know how much longer I could keep it up. The thought of letting down my famiglia made my heart thump with terror and I gritted my jaw as I worked to keep it in place for as long as I possibly could. But there was a time limit on our defences and we all knew it.

King froze over our entire air shield with a roar of defiance, turning the whole thing to frosted ice. A shiver fled down my spine as the temperature plummeted by fifty degrees and Leon countered the deadly air with heat pouring off of him in molten waves of power.

"Time to move," Gabriel announced then cast a huge hole beneath us and we fell into a dark tunnel.

Ryder cast a Faelight above us and we all ran along behind him as he and Gabriel blasted a path into the rock. I could see the effort it took them as they worked together to break the solid ground apart and I feared how much magic we were burning through already.

"Leon, hurt me," I demanded as Ryder panted and strained to cut through the earth.

"I don't wanna," Leon growled.

"Do it, stronzo!" I commanded and his hand slapped onto my arm, scalding me so badly I roared in pain, letting Ryder feed on it and swell his magic reserves.

"Thanks, Inferno," Ryder panted.

Gabriel suddenly carved a path upwards and we spilled out on the other side of the cavern behind King. They spun around with a snarl, casting huge chunks of ice at us like cannon balls. Elise threw out a palm, sending them flying back at King on a furious wind so they were forced to shield themselves from her attack.

Gabriel took up the chant once more and we all fell in with it. King groaned, trying to cover their ears as the Black Card all swarmed toward us once more from the opposite end of the cavern. The Blazers were scattering, all confused and frightened in their drugged-up state and I knocked a few aside with a blast of air to keep them out of the firing line.

"Stop!" King screamed in a woman's voice. "Enough!"

We pressed on with the chant and King wailed as we weakened them further, but the Black Card made it to us once more and we were forced to shield again from their onslaught of magic. My power grew weaker and Elise called out to me, "I've got the shield, Drago. Use your storm!"

I reluctantly let her take over the shield, building electricity around me that sparked off of my skin before blasting it at one Fae at a time among the crowd. They died with cut off screams as they faced my wrath, and chaos reigned as others tried to escape the terrifying power of a Storm Dragon.

King pelted huge boulders at us and Elise cried out in warning just before her shield fell. I gasped as we broke apart to avoid the falling rocks and Leon and Ryder dove forward into the fray, killing Black Card members one by one.

"King!" I bellowed to force their attention onto me then blasted lightning at them that slammed into their chest and sent them sprawling backwards onto the ground.

"No!" they wailed, fighting to heal themselves and get up.

I shoved through the crowd, struggling to get to the bastardo as a blur of motion shot past me. Elise made it up to the raised area of stone where King was, but the asshole was already on their feet as she arrived and the two of them started battling with furious magical attacks.

My gut clenched with fear as she used her speed to avoid the terrifyingly powerful blows that came her way and all I could do was fight any stronzo who came at me and continue our chant. But the Black Card weren't fighting fairly and we were fast getting overwhelmed.

I struck down my opponents with lightning to try and get through them faster, but three suddenly came at me together and I cursed, battling to defend myself.

"No – no!" King wailed and I glimpsed them dropping to one knee, fire curling around their body defensively so Elise couldn't get close.

I threw my hands out, slamming a wave of air magic at my enemies to blast them aside and finally broke through the crowd, sprinting over to join her before the fire pit on the raised area of flat rock. A growl rolled through my throat as I built lightning in the air, about to smite King and destroy them for good.

King groaned under the influence of our spell, the power of it working to strip away their stolen magic. And now they were at my mercy, there was no chance I'd be letting them walk away. I cast my lightning down on them in one furious blast, a yell of effort leaving me as I raised my arms. It hit an air shield surrounding them, bouncing off it in a shower of huge sparks and I cursed, bringing more and more of it down on them, electricity flying everywhere as I battled against their immense power. We all managed to keep chanting, the importance of that immeasurable even when we were in combat.

King shouted out for help and I swore I could have recognised the male voice they used for a moment, but my mind wouldn't fix on a name.

A cry of pain caught my ear and I turned to look for my brothers. Leon and Ryder were fighting for their lives in the crowd, a long cut running up Leon's arm and bleeding profusely. Panic tugged at my heart as Elise sped away to help destroy the bastardos around them and I was left to bring the full fury of my power down on King. Gabriel fought like a warrior just beyond them, swinging a spear in his hand and slamming it into any Fae brave enough to take him on. But more and more of the Black Card were closing in and as I battled to break King's shield, I knew we didn't have enough time.

Come on, stronzo, die for me quicker.

Leon shouted out as he was thrown across the cave and hit a wall with a hard crack. Panic rushed through my limbs as Gabriel tried to get to him, his eyes full of some terrible fate that awaited our Leone as Black Card members swarmed toward his still body. Elise fought to get there too as Ryder killed his opponents with fierce strikes of his metal coated fists, but Ryder was suddenly lost within the sea of robed bodies.

"No!" I cried, abandoning King and racing into the crowd to help my famiglia.

As I made it into the throng of bodies, something sharp tore across my back, then my thigh, my arm. Blood spilled and I roared in desperation as I battled toward the glimpse of lilac hair ahead of me.

"Elise!" I cried.

"Get out of there!" Gabriel bellowed at her, his wings shredding through his shirt as he tried to take flight and get to her.

But too many Fae caught hold of his arms, his legs, yanking him back down and tearing at his wings. My breaths became frantic and our advantage seemed to slip away just like that, our fate turning on a dime.

An ice blade sank into my arm and I whipped around with a snarl, blasting the Fae who'd struck me with lightning so they turned to dust before my eyes. But five more took their place, rushing at me with blades of ice, wood and silver in their grip.

I knocked the first Fae to the ground with a hard punch from my gold ring clad hand, but the next stabbed their ice blade into my gut. I tasted blood in my mouth, felt the hands of death slip gently over my shoulder and draw me into their arms.

"No," I gasped.

I hunted for Elise in the crowd of bodies, desperate to see her one last time as a silver blade drove up beneath my ribs and pain daggered through to my core. Gabriel bellowed a battle cry as he broke through the ranks to my right, killing the stronzo in front of me as I hit the ground, the pain in my body inching deeper.

Gabriel fought above me, keeping me safe from anyone else who drew close and a vague smile pulled at my lips as I watched this man I'd once despised battle for my life. His wings were battered, cuts lined his flesh and all I wanted to do was get up and help him. But I was getting too cold and my limbs wouldn't respond to the commands I gave them.

"Amore mio," I begged the stars to bring her to me. "Let me see her again."

"Don't give up," Gabriel called to me in desperation, but the look on his face said he had *seen* my fate. It was written. So I prayed for this one last wish to be granted.

She broke through the crowd, suddenly there, leaning over me, her hand on my cheek, her eyes brighter than every star in the sky.

A smile pulled at my mouth as she spoke words I couldn't focus on and green light swept from her hands as she pressed them to my body.

Darkness pulled me down into its embrace, but her voice found me there, calling me back.

"Dante!" she begged in a broken voice. "Don't leave me. I need you. Please come back, Drago."

I fought to be with her, shaking off the cold clutches of death, desperate to stay at her side forever.

"Wherever you go, I'll be there, amore mio," I told her, though my eyes were still too heavy to open.

Heat filled my veins as her healing power swept through me and my eyelids finally became light enough to lift.

The stars had let me go, giving me another day at her side and I would thank them for every day after this that they gifted me. She hugged me close, her air shield wrapping around us as Black Card members slammed into it.

But I realised that they weren't fighting to get in though, they were bodies, pilling up and up, cut to ribbons by piercingly sharp vines.

Elise arched over me, fighting back the weight of the bodies and I found the strength to move once more. I reached up to push my fingers into her hair and she lifted her head with a choked noise escaping her.

"I'm here," I said and she kissed me hard for one desperate moment before looking up at the bodies surrounding us.

"What's happening?" she gasped as the last of the light was blotted out by the mounting bodies.

"I don't know, bella," I whispered, pushing myself up and she groaned with effort as she used her air magic to force the bodies to fall away from us. We stood among the massacre and she sagged against me, the last of her magic failing and leaving us entirely exposed.

"Go and feed, Elise," I commanded, but she clung tighter to me, clearly not wanting to leave me alone without protection for even a second.

Gabriel clambered over the pile of bodies, bloody and his eyes full of worry as he reached us, crushing us into his arms. Leon made it to us next, the huge cut on his arm still bleeding and fear in his eyes, then Ryder appeared soaked in blood as he reached the middle of the bodies and all of us closed ranks. Gabriel healed Leon's wound, but I sensed that was the last of his magic as he cursed beneath his breath.

"Ahhhhhhh!" a voice shouted and I turned, finding Eugene there chasing the last of the Black Card toward the exit.

There was an enormous chasm in the ground which most of the remaining Card members in the cavern had fallen down and they were struggling to get out as I looked to Gabriel in surprise.

"Did you know he was coming?" I asked.

He nodded, a glint in his gaze. "He followed us here. I just couldn't tell if he'd arrive in time or not."

I hunted for King among the Blazers who were running out of the cavern, screaming wildly and bumping into each other in their confused panic.

"There." I pointed him out as King staggered along among them with flames still swirling around their cloaked body.

"We have to finish the spell," Gabriel snarled, lifting his head and beginning the chant again.

Ryder joined him, chanting loudly as a dark determination flashed in his eyes. I drew on what little power remained in my body as I began chanting too, hoping I could pull enough from my gold to sustain the magic long enough to end this.

Eugene yelled out in panic and I gasped as Elise shot away from me suddenly, her fangs bared and hair flying around her.

"Wait!" I took a step to follow her but Gabriel caught my arm and shook his head, the command in his gaze clear as I began chanting yet again.

The ground trembled as King tried to wield earth magic against us from the far side of the gaping chasm, but as the power of the chant took root in them they stumbled, cursing as they fought to remain upright.

"We can do this," Leon snarled determinedly, laying his hand on my shoulder and dropping the barriers around his power. The flames of the magic burning within him was near extinguished but as my magic swept between the two of us, he was able to take up the chant too.

King yelled at us as they threw a handful of ice daggers our way, but Ryder blasted a wall of rock into their path to shield us before they could hit.

An ear splitting scream made me whirl around and my eyes widened as I spotted Elise ripping her fangs into the neck of one of the remaining members of the Black Card like some kind of wild beast.

Three more of them turned her way and fear spilled through my chest, gripping my heart in a vice as they aimed their attacks at her while she was feeding. But before I could even make a move to protect her, Eugene was there, looking like some kind of bog monster as he dove before her, his flesh coated in what looked to be armour built from rock and dirt.

Gabriel chanted louder and Ryder dropped the wall of rock which had been protecting us so that we could lay our eyes on our prey once more.

King had dropped to their knees mere feet from the exit tunnel, their head bent and hidden within the folds of their hood as their entire body shook from the power of our spell driving into them.

My heart soared with hope as Elise shot back to join us, her voice raised as she began chanting too, her hand grasping mine while blood ran freely down her chin from her feed and her magic now replenished.

King roared in agony, throwing their hands up and making the entire cave tremble so violently that I almost lost my footing as I fought to continue our chant.

Their body was definitely masculine now and once again the sound of their voice had recognition prickling at my senses.

Embers were cascading from his flesh as he fought to turn his magic against us once more, the little flames sizzling out in the air one by one like they were fading from existence altogether. And as the last of them went out, King fell to his knees, cursing us with a scream of fury as the power of the spell we were casting flared through my limbs and I was suddenly certain we'd stolen the fire Element from them.

The cavern trembled even more violently as he turned his magic on us with furious determination and as a huge lump of rock fell from above us, we were all forced to leap aside, falling to the ground as the chants escaping our lips faltered.

King turned to look at us as he managed to regain his feet, his hood falling back and the concealment spells flickering.

My breath caught in my throat and Elise gasped in horror as his face was unveiled for a split second, his identity revealed at long last.

"Titan," Ryder spat as the bastardo got his concealment spells back in place within the blink of an eye.

He threw his arms out and the cavern trembled so violently that I stumbled to one knee, my eyes darting up to the crumbling roof above us again as I feared the entire thing caving in on our heads. As I looked back across the gaping chasm, I swore, catching a glimpse of Titan's robes as he made it to the tunnel and raced away among the Blazers.

"It can't be," Elise said in refusal, gripping my arm in an iron hold as we all got to our feet. "He wouldn't. He's a good person, he…"

"It's him," Gabriel growled. "I can *see* the truth now as plain as anything, the stars confirmed it."

"No," Elise's voice broke and I pulled her against me, resting my chin on her head.

"I'm sorry, amore mio," I said, knowing our Potions professor had become important to her. That stronzo would pay for this pain in her. I'd make it so.

Eugene ran over to us with anxiety in his eyes. "Hello?" he shouted. "We need to go, guys, where are you? Eugenie is here to save the day!"

"We're right here, dude," Leon called and Eugene snapped around in confusion, seemingly looking right through us.

"What? Where?" he asked, running towards us with a frown.

"Oh shit," Ryder murmured. "I think I'm doing it."

"What, fratello?" I asked.

"The Basilisk camouflage thing," he said.

Leon stepped away from us, clambering over a few bodies and his eyes widened as he looked back. "You are! I can't see you at all. You're camouflaging all of them, Scar."

Ryder stopped touching us and Eugene's eyes widened in amazement, clapping his hands in excitement. "You did it Ryder!"

"Yeah, yeah," Ryder muttered. "Come on, we need to get out of here."

I pulled Elise closer who was still clearly in shock over discovering King's identity. My head was spinning too, but all I could think of was getting her out of here and making sure she was safe.

"Are you okay, amore mio?" I breathed and she shook her head as she gazed up at me with tears in her eyes.

"Why him?" she whispered.

"He was in the perfect position to pull it off," Ryder said in a deep voice.

"I trusted him," Elise choked out, burying her face in my chest and I lifted her into my arms, cradling her against me as we all started walking for the exit.

"Follow me. There's another route out of here. I'm not risking bumping into Titan again tonight. We don't have enough power to fight him now that he's broken free of the spell. We'll have to finish him another time," Gabriel said darkly, leading us across the cavern.

Elise was quiet and her features tight, so I held her close and whispered a promise in her ear. "Ti darò la sua morte, mio unico vero amore. E ogni stella del cielo verrà a vederlo soffrire per mano tua." *I will deliver his death to you, my one true love. And every star in the sky will come to watch him suffer at your hands.*

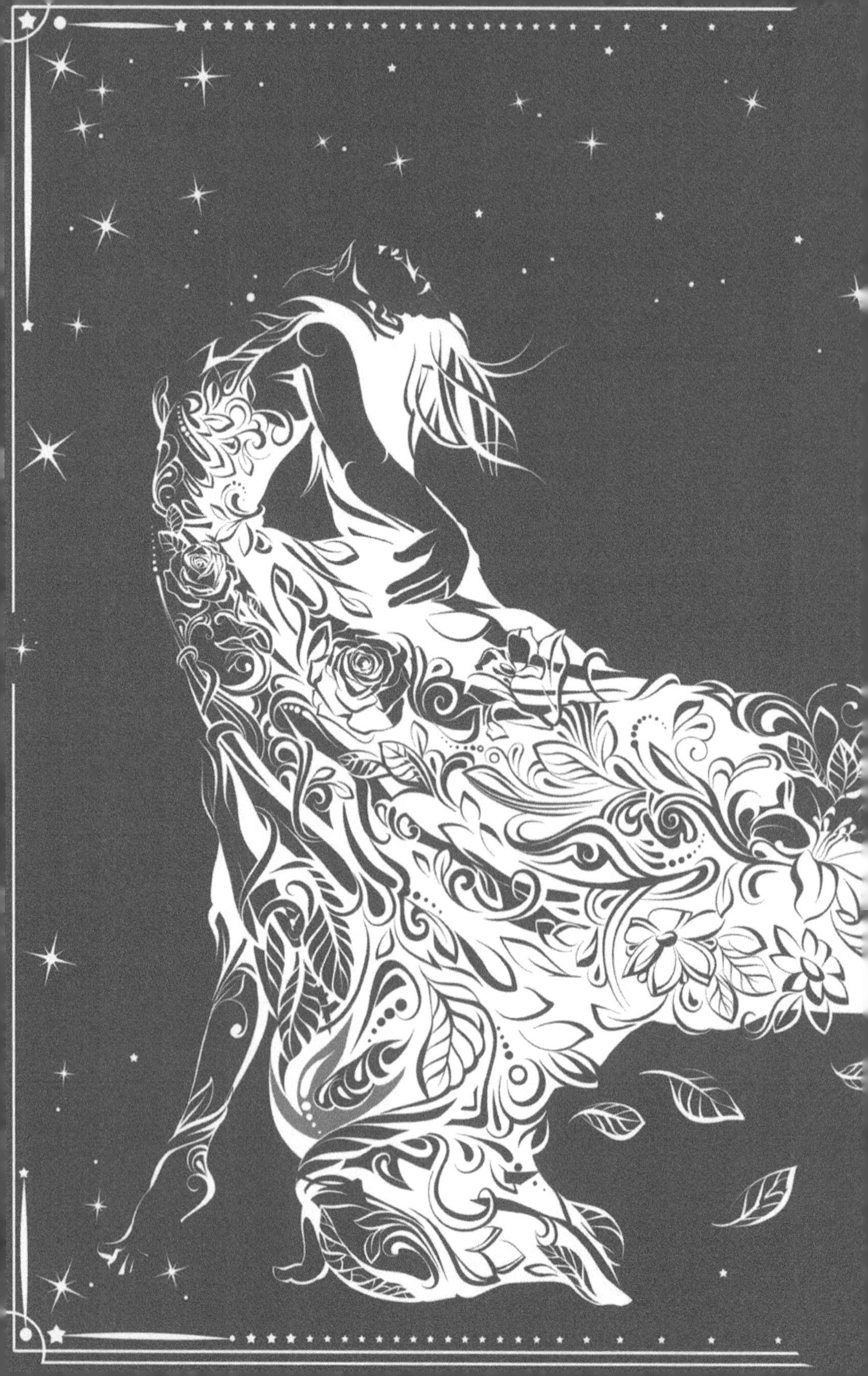

Elise

CHAPTER THIRTY FIVE

I wasn't supposed to be awake. I wasn't supposed to be lying there with my eyes closed while pretending to be asleep. But I was. Not because I still believed it was Santa who snuck in here during the night to leave me gifts. But because I knew it was so much better than that.

I couldn't resist the urge to peek, my eyelashes curtaining my view of the dark room me and my brother shared as I watched him cross the space between our beds.

He crept over to his secret spot in the far corner of the little bedroom and carefully eased the loose floorboard up before reaching into the space below it. He didn't think I knew about that spot, but I did. I never peeked though. That was his and that was okay, but he didn't keep secrets from me not even when he thought he did.

I fought the urge to lean to the side and take a look at what he was placing inside the pillowcase he'd stripped from his bed and just lay there as he placed the items inside. But the longer he took, the harder it was to resist and I cracked my eyes open again just a little.

He turned slightly and I caught sight of something pink, my heart leaping as I spotted the tutu skirt on the ballerina doll just before he slipped it into the pillowcase and out of sight. A few weeks ago, I'd been sad because the other girls in my class had all started bringing their favourite dolls to school with them. I'd told them all I hadn't been able to pick a favourite, but the truth was that I didn't own any dollies.

I hadn't told him though. Gare Bear hadn't known about it. But that had definitely been a ballerina - I saw it!

A grin bit into my cheeks and I couldn't fight it off before Gare Bear stood upright and moved towards my bed.

I scrunched my eyes up tight so he couldn't catch me looking and felt the soft press of the pillowcase full of little presents falling onto the bed by my feet.

I was so excited I wanted to squeal. But I had to hold it in tight. So tight I held my breath too, keeping our secret and pretending I didn't know it was him and not Santa.

"Love you, little angel," Gareth whispered, moving to stand over me and gently pushing my hair away from my face.

My heart squeezed at his words and I felt them all the way down to my toes. He loved me and I loved him. My big, unstoppable brother who always knew what I needed even though I never asked for anything. I wanted to say the words back. But I had to keep up the act.

I knew I'd never sleep now though. I'd lie here all night long and wait and wait and wait until he woke up and then I'd jump up and yell to tell him that Santa had been this year. Then he'd smile so big it would light me all the way up from the inside out. We both knew it wasn't Santa. It was him. The only person I'd ever really need. But we'd both keep the secret and I'd hold my dolly tight and when I went back to school after the holidays, all the other girls would be so jealous it would burn them up inside.

Gareth's fingers ran down my cheek before he placed a kiss against my skin and my heart swelled with love for him. He was all I really wanted for Christmas anyway. Just my big brother with his big heart and a million adventures waiting for us in the future...

I gasped as I woke, the feeling of Gareth's fingers running down my cheek so real that I reached up to caress the spot, finding only tears there instead of him. I smiled a little at that memory. Of how much I'd loved that freaking ballerina doll. I never did tell him that all the other girls hadn't brought dollies to school anymore after Christmas. They'd all been given some new Pegasus teddies with rainbow hair and glittery eyes and they'd laughed at me with my ballerina. I didn't care though. I didn't want a stupid Pegasus teddy and I didn't want them to be my friends either. I didn't need them. I only needed Gare Bear and I'd always have him. Or so I'd thought...

Leon reached for me and tugged me closer to him in the darkness and I curled myself up into a ball as he wrapped his arms around me, my knees pressing to his stomach while I hugged my arms around my chest. I squeezed hard, feeling like all of my pieces were trying to fall apart as my pain over losing Gareth crippled me for several achingly long minutes.

Leon pressed his forehead to mine, a soft, pained growl escaping his lips and drawing my gaze up to meet his, the golden colour seeming to swirl in the silver moonlight which made it in through the window. I hadn't meant to wake him and I was surprised I had considering how deeply he normally slept, but I guessed he'd known I needed him in that moment.

"I should have been a better friend to him," he breathed, his voice laced with guilt. "I shouldn't have let him push me away. I should have noticed something was wrong. Really wrong. Maybe then I could have-"

I pressed my lips to his as a sob tore at my chest and he pulled me closer as he slowly kissed me back. It wasn't a lust filled exchange, more like shared grief and lost hope, but it helped me pull the shattering pieces of my heart back into one place.

"If we don't find him, I don't know if I'll survive it," I breathed, my eyes stinging and my limbs trembling as I admitted that. "I've only coped at all until now because I could focus on figuring all of this out. On revenge and making someone pay. But now I know that King is Titan and I thought he was my, my...I thought he *cared* about me. I thought maybe he even loved me, just a little, Leon. I know it's stupid to feel so betrayed, but he was the first adult in all my life who made me feel like I mattered beyond what I could give them. I thought..."

A sob caught in my throat again and the bed dipped behind me as Ryder shifted back into his Fae form, his body curving around mine from behind as he placed a kiss on my neck and wound an arm around my waist.

"You have us, baby," he promised. "Fuck Titan. Fuck anyone else aside from the five of us. We all have more love for you than you could possibly need, and no spineless motherfucker is going to get away with hurting our girl like this."

Leon growled his agreement and I nodded, not having words for the way I was feeling and just missing my brother so fucking much that I didn't know what to do with it.

Neither of them pushed me, they just stayed there, arms wrapped around me, holding me tightly and letting me grieve.

We were in Dante's bed back at the Oscura stronghold which had become our new go-to place at the weekends since we needed to avoid the Lunar Territory where Gabriel's apartment was. As I finally managed to get my tears under control, I lay in their arms, listening to the sound of Wolves howling while they ran beneath the moon. Dante was out there with them, leading the pack and flying through the sky, the distant sounds of thunder drawing closer as he built a storm above our heads.

Gabriel had wanted to fly with him tonight too and I knew he was beating himself up for not figuring out King's true identity sooner, but I didn't blame him for that. None of us had seen it coming. He'd been so inoffensive, so sweet. But as I lay there between my men and let my mind turn over everything that he'd said to me both in his role as my professor and when he had held me captive while disguising his identity, things started to click together.

He'd told me he was sorry when he'd taken me. He'd tried to get me to understand what he wanted to do to Alestria. Why he was doing what he was doing. And in a twisted, megalomaniac kind of way, I could see exactly where he was coming from.

He'd loved his daughter fiercely and gang violence had stolen her life from her. His entire vision was based on the idea of overthrowing the gang leaders and even the Celestial Councillors in the name of stopping those kinds of atrocities from happening, thinking he could protect everyone if he just ruled with an iron fist.

But he was hurting way more people than he ever might have helped to achieve it and I couldn't understand why he didn't see that. He was preying on the vulnerable, encouraging them to give their lives up for him. The whole Killblaze situation was just so fucked up. He was pushing it out onto the streets everywhere, getting the most vulnerable Fae hooked on it with no care for the repercussions of those addictions. The crimes committed in aid of getting another hit, the families hurt or torn apart by it. Let alone the most helpless Fae of all who ended up taking their own lives because of it. And yet he still had himself convinced that what he was doing was for the greater good.

I lay there, unable to sleep for I wasn't even sure how much longer until eventually, the sound of Dante and Gabriel landing on the rooftop drew my attention.

I strained my ears, listening to the rumble of their voices as they teased each other over which of them was the better flyer and I managed a small smile as they laughed. It was just a stolen moment of happiness amongst the dark, but knowing that the two of them were getting closer and enjoying each other's company soothed my soul a little.

This bond between the four of us, it wasn't just about me and each of the guys. They had been in need of each other just as much as they were in need of me. They'd needed the love and trust which was growing between all of them, and I was starting to feel like the stars really had known what they were doing when they'd chosen us for each other.

The hatch opened and I looked over as the two of them walked down the spiralling iron staircase in the corner of the room, Gabriel removing the water from their flesh with his magic as Dante snagged a pair of boxers and pulled them on.

Ryder pressed a kiss to my neck before shifting into his Basilisk form, his smooth scales sliding across me as he wound his way over my body to make more room in the bed.

Gabriel dropped into his place a moment later and Dante fell into the space beyond Leon, moving up close to him and laying an arm over his sleeping form so that he could tangle his fingers with mine.

"Sleep," Gabriel breathed in my ear as he spooned me, and a moment later he spread the huge span of his right wing across the bed, concealing us all beneath it. "Sleep, little angel."

I released a long breath, letting my eyes fall closed once more and taking comfort from the touch of all four of my kings surrounding me. I may have been lost and grieving all over again. But no one could take this from me. The five of us right here were it. Family. One we'd built for ourselves and which no one could ever steal from us. Five broken, hurting souls who had needed each other so much that despite the many obstacles placed between us, we'd finally figured out where we belonged in the world.

And that was right here. Together.

When I woke the next morning, I found myself alone with Gabriel and my eyes puffy from tears once again. He wasn't asleep and his wing still cocooned us beneath it as he gently stroked his fingers through my hair and watched me with that hawk like gaze of his which always saw so much.

"Morning," I mumbled, rolling in his arms so that I was facing him properly.

"Good morning," he replied, his voice rough from sleep.

"Where's everyone else?" I asked.

"Ryder insisted on heading out to try and find Scarlett again even though I told him he won't be able to. He said Ethan Shadowbrook was waiting for him and I guess he wants to make sure the loyal members of his gang don't forget who their king is. Dante and Leon went looking for food, but I told them not to disturb you by bringing anything back here. I'm sure they will have saved you some though if you're hungry."

I shook my head, not feeling any kind of appetite whatsoever as my pain and grief rose up in me again. I wished I could have just kept sleeping so I didn't have to feel like this.

"I think it's time we did more about searching for Gareth," Gabriel said abruptly, pulling me out of my spiral before I could even really start down it.

"What do you mean?" I asked because I knew he'd been using The Sight to hunt for him as much as he could, and I'd been scouring the journal as well as using the map and dice at sunrise as often as I possibly could too, but we hadn't turned up a single new lead.

"We should go and see Bill. We've been coming at this like it's a magical problem, one we can find a hidden answer to or one we can *see* the answer to. Maybe it's simpler than that. If Gareth ran then we know he must have used a fake name, or even one of those identities Bill has been looking into, but he still might have left a physical trail. Bill might not have turned up any leads based on the list of names we gave him, but he is the best at what he does, and I think that if anyone stands a chance of tracking Gareth down for you, then it would be him. So what do you think? Shall we get him looking into this from all angles?"

My eyes widened at that idea and I found myself nodding as I reached up and dragged my fingertips down the inside of Gabriel's wing. He groaned, a shudder of pleasure rolling through his body and I bit my lip as I raked my eyes over his tattooed flesh.

Gabriel sighed as he closed his eyes for a moment, and I continued to caress his wings.

"That feels so fucking good," he murmured. "But Bill isn't going to be around later, so if we want to go see him, we need to cut this short."

I smiled, running my fingers onto his arm instead where I brushed them over a tattoo of a Cyclops who was carrying the weight of the world on his shoulders.

"Is this for him?" I asked and Gabriel nodded.

"One of the earlier tattoos I got before I met him. The stars clearly knew he could help me and at first, I assumed that was because he was a P.I. But of course he ended up helping me in so many more ways than that."

"You love him," I stated and he only hesitated for a moment before nodding.

"For the longest time, he was all I had. Even if we didn't need his help with this, I'd really like you to meet him."

A smile tugged at the corners of my lips and I leaned in to kiss the tattoo. "Then let's go," I agreed.

I hopped up and shot away to dive into a hot shower, needing a few minutes alone to compose myself and get my shit together. I couldn't let this news over Titan break me again. I'd already suffered too much and too long after losing Gareth and though this had struck a fierce blow to me, it was nothing compared to that agony. His betrayal wasn't even a true betrayal. He'd clearly just been using me since the very first day we met, trying to manipulate me and make me feel sorry for him when all he really wanted was my blood.

Though as I considered the many times I'd been alone with him and he'd done nothing at all to hurt me, I wasn't certain I was right about that. Not that it mattered. Whatever I'd thought we shared was clearly done now and

I wasn't even certain why I was surprised. Every parental figure I'd ever had had chosen to use me or check out on me in the end. Hell, Titan had been the star damned reason for my father's disappearance.

I scrunched my eyes closed and scrubbed at my body until my flesh was pink and by the time I stepped back out again, I'd forced all of those feelings into a little box in the back of my brain where I could just forget about them. For now. No doubt I'd be sobbing the night away again later, but as of this moment, I was donning my big girl panties and sucking it the fuck up.

I shot around in a blur of motion, using my air magic to dry myself and tame my hair and painting on some makeup before grabbing a pale blue halter dress from my things and pairing it with some strappy white heels.

I snatched my Atlas into my grasp and read over my horoscope with a vague tinge of interest, hoping today would be a better day.

Good Morning, Libra, the stars have spoken about your day. Today is a day of adjustment and reassessing. Some ugly truths may have come to light, but the path to new connections and happiness are open to you if you just allow yourself to embrace them. Don't allow one bad experience to damage relationships you could well come to treasure.

I gave that a couple of minutes to sink in then clicked on my messages, opening the newest one.

Marlowe:
My favourite Pitball team are the Skylarks, but I tried to watch a game today and realised none of the players I know are even playing anymore. Caleb mentioned you're on your academy team, maybe I should start following your league instead?

My heart twisted guiltily as I read that over. He'd sent it yesterday and I hadn't even read it until now. I was just so nervous of this new connection with him that I was fretting over how to proceed. But after a night spent mourning the true identity of King and realising the man I'd been using as a substitute father figure was actually the one who had robbed me of my real dad, I found I wanted to work harder at making this connection.

Elise:
I'm a Blueshines fan myself. Maybe I can help catch you up on all the new players at some point? And yeah, I love playing Pitball. I'm the team Airstriker and I'm damn near unstoppable. I could forward you the link to watch all of our recent games on the academy FaeBook page if you'd like?

I didn't even manage to slip my Atlas away again before his reply pinged to it and the hint of a smile tugged at the corner of my lips as I read it.

Marlowe:
I would love that! I used to be the Airstriker myself back in the day at Zodiac Academy! Maybe we could play a few rounds next time you come for a visit??

Elise:
That sounds great :) I'm forwarding you the link now…

Marlowe:
Got it! I'll watch them all today and let you know my favourite highlights!

I smiled a little more as I read that. There were hours of gameplay there for him to watch so no doubt he wouldn't really sit through all of it just to see me play, but I couldn't deny that I liked the fact that he wanted to.

I paused to check myself over in the mirror, and I was damn pleased to see I looked pretty freaking presentable, so I sped back out to find Gabriel waiting for me by the door.

He looked edible in a pair of black jeans, his chest still bare and wings on display as he held a white shirt in his hand.

"I told the others where we're going," he explained. "And I thought we could fly if you want to? Save some of the stardust for when we need it."

"I'd like that," I agreed and he broke a smile, reaching a hand out for me.

I placed my palm in his and he drew me up the spiralling staircase that led to the private roof terrace above Dante's room.

The day was picturesque and the sky brightest blue with the sun beating down on us and heralding the signs of the summer to come.

Gabriel snatched me off of my feet as I was distracted by the view and I squealed, wrapping my arms around his neck and looking up at him excitedly as he spread his wings wide. He leapt into the air and my gut plummeted as we shot skyward, my grip on him tightening as he chuckled and before I knew it, we were racing towards the horizon.

The wind whipped around us and I used my air magic to create a spearheaded shield in front of us, allowing us to cut through the sky even faster while saving my hair from slapping me in the face a million times.

It was exhilarating, racing across the sky just as fast as I could run with my gifts on land and watching the world zip by beneath us.

Before long, we were passing over the city and Gabriel plummeted from the sky without so much as a warning, tearing a scream from my lungs as I clung on tighter.

Despite his insane speed, when his feet hit the ground, I was hardly even jostled, but when he set me down on my feet, I felt the world tilting beneath me as I struggled to regain my balance.

I caught hold of his belt as I stumbled back a step and suddenly he was pressing me back against a cold wall, his lips on mine as the rush of the adrenaline pulsed through me and I was moaning as I tugged him even closer.

Gabriel's forearm landed on the wall above my head and his wings flexed to block out the world beyond him as his other hand moved to my thigh and pushed up beneath the hem of my dress.

His tongue pressed inside my mouth and I felt his kiss right down to my toes. That kiss said everything there was between us. It was deep and heated and touched in pain, but it was brutal and honest and demanding so much more. It told me I was his and he was mine, no matter what the stars had to say about it. This right here wasn't something that could ever be undone and neither of us was going anywhere.

The sound of a man clearing his throat drew my attention, but Gabriel seemed so lost in me that it took the dude actually calling his name to get him to pull back.

Gabriel turned around, letting his wings shimmer out of existence as he took his hand from my leg and snagged my hand instead, tugging me to his side so that I could see the guy too.

Bill was pretty big, probably in his fifties with a handlebar moustache and a cigarette jammed into the corner of his mouth which trailed smoke towards the sky. He was wearing faded jeans and a white wifebeater, a few old tattoos showing on his arms but nothing that looked gang related.

His eyes slid over me appraisingly, but not in an unfriendly way. More like he was surprised to see me. Though I could tell he knew exactly who I was.

"Elise," he said, nodding to me before looking back to Gabriel who was pulling his white t-shirt on. "To what do I owe this pleasure? When you said you wanted to meet, I assumed it was for work. But this is a nice surprise."

"Well, technically there's a side of work to it," Gabriel hedged. "But, I did wanna bring Elise to meet you too. I figured the two of you might be sick of hearing each other's names without having faces to put to them."

"Alright then. Shall we get some grub?" Bill indicated the diner we were standing beside and Gabriel led me after him as we headed inside.

We took a booth by the window and as Gabriel began to fill Bill in on the things that we'd discovered about Titan and the rest of it from within the confines of a silencing bubble, I excused myself to the bathroom.

I lingered in there for a little while, fixing my slightly smudged lipstick and fiddling with my hair before hearing a ping on my Atlas.

Marlowe:

That pit you scored at the 4:59 count had my heart in my throat! I thought it was gonna explode on you for sure!

Marlowe:

I've never seen a run as good as you made in the 5th round against that mammoth of a Waterback!

Marlowe:

Boy oh boy, I forgot how much I love this game! And it's even more exhilarating watching my girl play!

Marlowe:

Ho-ly cow, I couldn't watch when the Fireside took you out in the 7th round! But you came back strong, my girl!

I couldn't even deny the grin that was stuck to my lips as I read his messages. He really was watching my games and the pride in his tone made me feel all kind of…warm inside.

Elise:

You might wanna look away for the 10th round – I was knocked out cold and had to sit the 11th out *laughing emoji*

Marlowe:

I'll take note of the name of the little fucker who did it and go pay him a visit when I finish watching the game x

I snorted a laugh, assuming he was joking, then remembered how unstable he still was and sent Caleb a heads-up message just in case he wasn't. Either way, I'd never had a parent give a shit about someone being mean to me before though, so I was pretty sure I was cool with it if he went and hunted that asshole down. It had been a dick move of a tackle anyway.

By the time I returned, food and drinks were already laid out on the table.

I dropped into the vacant seat beside Gabriel and Bill cast his eyes over me with interest as I inhaled the scent of coffee and my stomach rumbled at the sight of the veggie burger and fries Gabriel had ordered me.

My appetite had died at some point yesterday, but I couldn't resist the call of the food now and I had to fight the urge to dive in headfirst. Gabriel pushed a black cherry milkshake towards me, and I really did groan as I lifted the straw to my lips and drank a healthy, sugar-filled, icy cold, delicious mouthful of it.

"So," I began, hunting around for some interesting subject matter. "I bet you've got some pretty embarrassing stories about Gabriel you could share with me?"

Bill grinned and leaned forward like we were sharing a secret. "Did he ever tell you about the time he asked me to teach him how to throw a punch? I took him to this underground fighting ring and there was this little girl there-"

"She wasn't that little," Gabriel grumbled, looking torn between allowing me to hear this story or not.

"She was eleven and you were fourteen," Bill sniggered. "Anyway, Gabriel got all defensive about going in the ring with her, kept saying he wouldn't hit a girl and silly nonsense like that. Of course, the girl got fed up waiting and cracked him right in the nose."

"What did Gabriel do?" I asked, grinning between them while my Harpy groaned.

"He bitch slapped her so hard he left a hand print and she ran off crying to her momma."

"You missed the part where she tried to knee me in the balls," Gabriel grunted.

"And you missed the part about boxing requiring a closed fist," Bill tossed back, making me giggle.

My Atlas pinged again and I glanced at more messages of excitement from Marlowe as Gabriel looked at me curiously.

"My err, Marlowe just found out about me playing Pitball and he's gone a bit crazy over it," I explained, unable to hide the fact that I was actually pretty okay with that. "He's watching some of my old games and sending me his reactions."

Gabriel gave me a wide smile, taking hold of my hand and squeezing.

"Gabriel tells me you're shit hot on the Pitball field," Bill commented, seeming genuinely interested in that too and I grinned as I glanced at my Harpy for a moment before setting my drink down to reply.

"Fuck yeah I am," I replied. "And now that we've got him and Ryder on the team, we're gonna be unstoppable."

"I didn't realise you were playing too," Bill chastised, looking to Gabriel.

"Well, yeah. But I'm not pro material like Elise," he said, nudging my arm.

"You think I could go pro?" I asked him, arching a bow.

"Hell yeah. More than half of the pro players these days come from too much money and fancy ass academies. They need players with grit like you to remind them what the game is really about."

"Oh yeah, I'm sure they'd love to see me brawling for the ball like a true Alestrian," I teased and Gabriel shrugged.

"You know you could take down half of those polite motherfuckers in your sleep. Don't go getting all coy now, angel."

"I'd love to come watch you guys play," Bill said. "Always did love the atmosphere at a match."

"Really?" Gabriel asked, seeming a little surprised by that.

"Of course I would. Make sure you tell me when the next game is and I'll be there front and centre. I might even bring Ginger - sports get her all kinds of hot."

"Okay, okay, enough about that," Gabriel said with a grimace as Bill just chuckled.

"You could invite your Marlowe too, Elise," Bill suggested, teasing me over the way I'd explained who Marlowe was to me though I was sure he knew via Gabriel or the papers.

"Umm, yeah." I nodded. "I think I'd like that." I glanced down at my Atlas and Marlowe's horrified reactions to my take down and quickly shot him a message to invite him to my next game before I could chicken out of it. We had to start somewhere, right? And if the hundred freaking out with excitement messages Marlowe sent in reply to that invitation were anything to go by, I had to assume he agreed.

We fell into more conversation about Pitball then started talking about other things in our lives and Bill regaled us with funny stories from his P.I. work. Most of the best ones included him being hired to figure out if someone was cheating on their partner and him having to gain photographic evidence which put him into more than a few precarious positions.

I demolished my food and Gabriel got me a second cherry shake and after a while I was just smiling and enjoying our time together while Gabriel seemed to come alive with energy, clearly loving the fact that we were all getting along so well.

When the conversation finally turned to the search for my brother, Bill didn't scoff or offer up platitudes like I'd been worried he might. He didn't make any promises either, but he listened to everything we knew about Gareth's plans and showed him the passports which I'd found with new identities for me and Mom. He took notes and asked some questions I hadn't expected, like details about the way my brother looked in his Order form and information on things he liked to do and the kinds of places he enjoyed visiting.

By the time we left, my smiles didn't even feel forced anymore and I was left feeling more than a little optimistic about what he might find as Gabriel launched us back into the sky and we headed back toward the Oscura stronghold and the others.

Returning to the academy after finding out King's true identity had left me reeling. It still didn't sit right in my head. It couldn't. Wouldn't. Titan was my friend; he was kind and caring and just about the only adult I'd ever met who simply gave a shit about me because they wanted to. I'd needed him. But he wasn't him at all anymore. And the weight of that discovery had struck me like a knife to the chest.

The official line was that Professor Titan had suddenly been called away on a family emergency and for the time being, Potions classes had been suspended.

After putting it off for the entire weekend, I'd eventually called Melinda and told her that we knew King's identity in the hopes that she could send the FIB his way and arrest that son of a bitch after all. My grief and heartache over finding out that it had been him this entire time had begun to turn into something dark and hateful as my need for vengeance built with every passing minute and I knew I was getting close to cracking over it.

He knew how much I'd been hurting over Gareth. He fucking *knew* and he'd comforted me, but he was the reason I'd lost him at all. Not that he could have known that, as I was fairly certain he still knew nothing about my connection to Gareth. But I just didn't understand how he could spout that shit about wanting to stop the gangs and save Solaria while hurting people and stealing lives himself. He was no better than any of the powerful Fae in this kingdom and nothing at all would change with a tyrant like him seizing power.

I needed to unwind. I was seriously close to losing my shit altogether and it wasn't going to be pretty when I did.

I walked down the corridor after class, heading away from the Cafaeteria a few steps behind Leon. He was engrossed in getting the Mindys to help him out with some prank he was planning, so he didn't even notice when a door burst open beside me.

I almost blasted the asshole who had attempted to kill me with a door using my air magic, but I managed to hold myself back as I spotted Principal Greyshine at the last second.

"What in the-"

"Elise, I must talk with you!" he demanded, his eyes whipping around fearfully, before he ushered me into the empty classroom with him.

I already knew he wasn't King, and I was getting seriously tired of trying to swerve him all the damn time. So with a huff of frustration, I stepped into the room.

"What's up?" I asked, constructing an air shield around myself just in case. I may have been almost certain Greyshine was harmless, but I wasn't an idiot.

"It's about Dante," Greyshine blurted, his eyes swivelling to the door as the sound of Leon calling for me came from beyond it.

"What about him?"

"He...I need you to please acquire a piece of footage he obtained of me in a, err, compromising position."

"You mean the one of you getting railed by that stripper with a massive Dragon dildo?" I asked, tension falling from me as I realised that was all this was about.

Greyshine paled, his mouth opening and closing like a fish as he gaped at me in alarm.

"Don't worry," I said quickly. "I'm the only one who's seen it. He's my mate after all and he wanted me to know what collateral he had on people. Seriously dude, that tape is tame compared to some of the dirt he's holding over other Fae."

"But I can't sleep at night, knowing he has it, that he might release it into the world or-"

"Are you planning on screwing him over or betraying him in any way?" I asked as Leon yelled for me in a more panicked tone and I took a step towards the door.

"No! I would never-"

"Then stop worrying about it. I swear to you, Dante will never release that tape or any of the others he has in his possession unless he is given no choice. Don't fuck with him and it will stay buried. And I promise you, every single professor in this place plus more than half of the most powerful Fae in the city have way worse secrets than you. You should see the sex tape he got of Lionel Acrux fucking a girl in her shifted form."

"What's that now?" Greyshine asked, perking up considerably and I shuddered, wishing I hadn't mentioned that one to the guy with the Dragon fetish. "Was the girl a Sphinx by any chance? A masculine Sphinx with a receding hairline and a-"

"*Point is*, you don't need to worry," I reiterated, cutting him off before tugging the door wide and shooting down the corridor to catch up with Leon.

I jumped onto his back and laughed as he flinched in surprise, a growl escaping him a moment later as he snatched my arm and dragged me over his shoulder. He caught me in his arms and frowned down at me seriously while holding me to his chest.

"You scared the crap outa me disappearing like that," he said, his eyes full of fear and making my gut twist with guilt.

"Sorry. Greyshine caught up to me for that word he's been desperate for." I reached up to smooth the creases out of Leon's brow and he sighed.

"So what did he want?"

"That sex tape Dante made of him," I replied with a shrug. "What are you up to now?"

"I've got detention," he said with a pitiful expression. "Apparently it's not cool of me to hide nitter critters in the toilets and record people's screams when their asses get bit. Especially when those people include Coach Mars."

I laughed and he broke a smile. "So what are you up to now?"

"Gabriel is playing tutor for me," I replied. "He's gonna help me catch up on the classes I missed to make sure I can keep my scholarship spot."

"So you're gonna be his naughty little school girl?" Leon asked, his eyes brightening at the idea of that.

"Do you like that visual?" I teased.

"I'd like it even more if you made me a tape of it," he said, purring excitedly.

"I'll see what I can do," I agreed as we made it back to our dorm and I checked my Atlas to see if Gabriel was ready to meet me yet or not.

"Oh no, you won't just *see*," Leon disagreed, taking my hand and dragging me inside and I was surprised as a petite girl slipped into the room behind us before the door could fall shut.

"Here you go, Leon," she said breathily, offering up a folded uniform which he took from her with a grin. "Can I grab your laundry while I'm here?"

"Thanks Mindy," Leon replied, vaguely patting her on the head as he grabbed the uniform from her without even looking her way. He hurried over to our closet and started rummaging around inside while the Mindy quickly grabbed every piece of dirty laundry she could find as well as stripping the bed.

"What's wrong with the normal laundry service?" I asked even though

I knew I was wasting my breath.

"Err, they don't fluff and de-crease the way I can," Mindy replied almost sounding offended.

I shook my head as she hurried out of the door then moved over to Leon just as he spun to face me with a fancy black gift bag with the words *Medusa's Secret* scrawled across it in pink lettering. There was a pink bow tying it closed and I untied it curiously before pulling out the new lingerie he'd bought me. The set was black and lacy complete with a garter belt and stockings and Leon practically bounced on the balls of his feet as he told me to try it on.

I used a flash of speed to get myself into the expensive set in the blink of an eye and Leon groaned, biting his knuckles in an over exaggerated way as he fell back onto the bed before holding out the uniform Mindy had given him.

"She's like a foot shorter than you and two sizes smaller," he explained as I looked at it in confusion. "But please, please, please, don't let Gabe know the plan. Just, hide the camera and act natural like you wear your uniform like this every day. I wanna see his face and I'm gonna get Dante and Ryder to place bets on how long he holds out before he's inside you."

"You're crazy," I laughed as I pulled the small uniform on. The skirt didn't quite conceal the tops of my stockings and the buttons over my cleavage in the push up bra absolutely wouldn't fasten.

Leon hopped back up to do my hair for me and he grinned like a maniac as he tied my lilac strands in pigtails.

"Seriously?" I questioned, wondering what the hell Gabriel would think of this and getting pretty into the idea of the game myself.

"Oh yes." Leon backed up to appreciate his work. He took a few snapshots then dragged me in for some more selfies before sending them on to Dante and Ryder, asking them how long they thought it would take Gabriel to crack.

Before he could start taking any more photos of us, I tossed him over my shoulder and shot out of the room, racing back across campus in a blur of speed so that nobody would see me dressed like this. I was all for it with my kings, but I wasn't going to be giving anyone else an eyeful if I could help it.

I skidded to a halt outside the classroom Greyshine had assigned for me and Gabriel to use for our tutoring sessions and Leon dragged me inside the second I placed him back down on his feet.

"Have I told you lately how much of a turn on I find it when you toss me over your shoulder like that, little monster?" he teased as he flicked the lights on and hurried across the room to set his Atlas up to record. I spotted Dante and Ryder's replies on it - Dante saying he believed Gabriel would hold out for half of the hour we had scheduled in here while Ryder demanded to know where this tutoring session was being held.

"I've lost count of the amount of things that turn you on, Leo," I teased, moving to take a seat at the professor's desk where there was enough room for me and Gabriel to work together.

"That's because anything to do with you is a turn on," he replied.

I yelped in alarm as a series of pops sounded around the room and almost all of the overhead lights went out, leaving on a single spotlight over the desk I was sitting at, it's light warm and muted.

"Mood lighting," Leon explained with a grin as I turned to arch a brow at him.

Before I could point out the fact that Greyshine would know exactly who had been in here when half the light bulbs in the room had been destroyed with fire magic, the door swung open and Gabriel stepped in.

"Hey," he said distractedly, his brow furrowed in a way that told me The Sight was niggling at him while Leon practically jumped up and down with excitement in the far corner of the room.

"I'll be off then," Leon said loudly. "Catch you guys after my detention. Don't do anything I wouldn't do." He winked at me from behind Gabriel's back before tugging the doors closed and leaving us to it while I had to stifle a laugh.

Gabriel dropped into the Professor's chair on the opposite side of the desk to me and grabbed his Astrology books out before looking up and giving me his full attention. I made sure not to think about Leon's plan but of course the moment I did, my attention shifted to the new underwear I was wearing. Gabriel's gaze sharpened as I was certain he caught a glimpse of a future where he got a damn good look at it.

I smiled sweetly before he could say anything about it though and opened my own books, pointing at the star chart I'd been working on most recently and sighing.

"I know I've been getting the planets wrong on this," I said. "But I can't figure out why I keep doing that and obviously the whole thing is wrong if I can't even figure out where Venus is or what Mars is up to."

Gabriel smiled and reached out to take the chart from me, explaining what I was doing to fuck it up so spectacularly and leaning in to show me where he would start.

I leaned closer too, the scent of him wrapping around me as I let my gaze travel from the page between us and over the thumping pulse in his neck. I licked my lips and gave into the idea of biting him for a few long moments before forcing myself not to act.

Gabriel's eyes met mine and he tilted his head to one side. "Are you thirsty?" he asked, clearly having *seen* where the future might take us, but I just shook my head innocently, wondering how far I could push him by messing with his visions.

I popped a piece of cherry gum into my mouth and diligently fixed my star chart, using the plotting method he'd explained and was relieved to find the rest of it fell together easily after that. As I was finishing up on the alignments, I let my mind wander, picturing myself dropping to my knees beneath the desk and wrapping my lips around Gabriel's solid cock, taking him all the way in to the back of my throat and-

"Elise?" Gabriel grunted and I quickly changed my mind about doing

that, focusing on the next issue I was having with my work as I looked up at him innocently.

"Yeah?" I asked, watching the heat in his eyes flaring as his gaze rake over me in the too small shirt and I blew a bubble with my cherry gum.

"Were you just planning to…" he trailed off as I gave him a blank look and I had to fight off a laugh at his confusion.

The bubble popped and I turned my chart towards him for inspection. "I'm getting a little lost here," I said, pointing at the outer edge of it. "I know I need to plot this constellation, but I feel like the positioning is off or something."

Gabriel looked down at my chart, pushing his fingers into his dark hair as he tried to concentrate, and I crossed my legs beneath the table. The toe of my shoe ran up the back of his calf where his long legs were extended towards me and he stilled.

As he looked up at me, my gaze fell on a pencil which was sitting precariously close to the edge of the desk and I made the decision to knock it off before bending over to pick it up again and flashing him a look at my new panties beneath my short skirt. In my fantasy of course he couldn't resist me and promptly started fucking me on the desk, but before I could get too carried away with that line of thought, I changed my mind, snatched the pencil into my grasp and went back to concentrating on my work.

I could feel Gabriel staring at me as I fixed the chart the way he'd explained, and I slowly lifted my eyes to his.

"What next, Professor?" I asked in a low voice.

Gabriel cleared his throat as I diligently thought about all of the help I needed with my tarot predictions instead of thinking about sex again, and he adjusted himself in his chair.

"Tarot?" he offered, pulling a smile from me as I left my star chart on the desk and grabbed my Arcane Arts notes out next.

Gabriel grabbed a deck and started dealing it while I filled my imagination with countless filthy plans, deciding to act on them then changing my mind as soon as he got a vision. When he finally flipped over The Lovers card, a dark growl escaped him.

"Are you doing that on purpose?" he asked me slowly, steely grey eyes meeting mine.

"Doing what?" I took the gum from my mouth and tossed it in the trash while I held his gaze and fiddled with the collar of my shirt, no doubt showing off even more cleavage as the button forcing the tiny item closed across my chest strained in protest.

Gabriel narrowed his eyes and finished dealing the deck, but as he opened his mouth to explain something about the lay of the cards, I made sure I focused on the feeling of his cock driving into me as I imagined up more ways that he might destroy me in this room.

The thought of the others watching the tape of this crossed my mind and I bit my lip at the idea of that, causing Gabriel's gaze to snap across the room to where Leon had left the Atlas recording us.

"Deal for yourself and tell me what you *see*," Gabriel commanded suddenly, scooping the cards up and shuffling them before placing them in my hands.

I shuffled them some more myself, feeling his gaze crawling all over me before I dealt my cards face down onto the desk.

I flipped the first over, finding The Empress there and glancing up at Gabriel, expecting him to give me his insight into it.

"I want to hear your thoughts first," he said as he sat back again, his voice taking on a dangerous tone which made a shiver run along my spine.

"Oh, sure...so The Empress can mean femininity, motherhood and stuff like that. So maybe this is something to do with my Mommy issues," I suggested with a shrug.

"Maybe," he replied, leaning back in his chair and owning it like a motherfucking throne. "It can also mean sexuality, wild pleasure and confidence. She can represent female empowerment and even self-pleasure as well as fertility. Tell me, sweet angel, how are you feeling right now? Because if your body is in need of a release, maybe the cards are telling you to do something about that."

"Well...that's not the interpretation Mystice usually talks about in class," I replied, his intent look making me feel all kinds of flustered as he smirked at me.

"Let's see the next card then."

I flipped The Devil over next, my eyes raking over the demon sitting on his throne with two chained and naked Fae stood waiting by his feet. My mind whirled with a mixture of the things I remembered from my classes on this card and the scalding hot look in Gabriel's eyes, and I tried to force myself to think of the ways it could be interpreted.

"Err, ambitions and addiction-"

"It can also encourage us to explore how good it can feel when we're bad," Gabriel interrupted. "The Devil's energy can encourage all kinds of deviant behaviour."

"Is that so?" I asked, my lips tipping up at the corner as I saw what he was trying to do here. He thought he could play me at my own game and win. Well game fucking on. "So you think I might be a deviant then, *sir*?" I asked, playing up to this teacher thing he had going on as I leaned forward on the desk, giving him a clear view down the front of my shirt.

"Next card," Gabriel growled and I flipped it over like a good girl, revealing The Seven of Swords.

"Secrets," I said huskily. "Solitary plans."

"The nature of the secrets is key," Gabriel replied, not missing a beat. "It can refer to a hidden kink and the thrill of doing something you know you shouldn't while keeping it secret."

"Like someone who was screwing their professor might feel then?" I asked, running the toe of my shoe up the back of his leg again as a smirk pulled at his lips.

"Next card."

I turned The Magician over, wondering how he was going to make this one dirty as I recited what I knew about the card for him. "Hmm, isn't this one all about male power?"

"It could imply taking control," he replied. "Confidence in claiming what you want."

I moved my foot up over his thigh and he caught it between his hands, holding me still and halting my progress as his own fingers began to skim upwards from my ankle over the silky fabric of my stocking.

I didn't wait for him to tell me to turn over the next card, flipping The Sun over and trailing a finger over it. "Positivity, joy-"

"Orgasms." Gabriel growled, tugging on my foot sharply so that my chair slid closer to the desk and his hand could move up and over my knee. The feeling of his fingers on my flesh was making my whole body quake with need and I suppressed a moan as heat built in my core. "Let's see the last card then."

I licked my lips and flipped over The Ace of Wands. "Enthusiasm." I smirked at him and the look he gave me in return made my toes curl.

"It also looks kinda like a cock, wouldn't you say?"

I breathed a laugh and Gabriel suddenly dropped my foot, gathering the deck back up as he pushed a piece of paper in front of me.

"Write this down as I dictate it," he said, getting to his feet and slowly beginning to shuffle the deck as he walked away from me with measured steps. "Tarot cards hold messages from the stars."

I played along and started writing, resisting the urge to hound his steps with my gaze as he headed away from me towards Leon's Atlas.

"Today, the cards told me to explore self-pleasuring, deviant behaviour, a new kink..."

His footsteps moved behind me and my senses prickled as I felt him drawing closer, but I fought off the urge to look around, writing down every word he spoke instead.

"Claiming what I want. Orgasms and..." Gabriel moved right up close behind me, his hand coming down on the desk beside the piece of paper I was writing on as he leaned down over me and his mouth came close to my ear. "My professor's cock."

I bit my lip at his words but like a good little girl, I wrote every last one of them.

Gabriel dropped Leon's Atlas on the desk on my other side, caging me in from behind for a long moment that made my thighs clench together before he shifted back just slightly. He swiped a card from the deck and slid it down the front of my shirt, careful not to let his fingers brush my skin.

I carefully tugged it out again, knocking the straining button undone in the process and looking down at the card. The Eight of Swords looked back at me, a woman bound and blindfolded in the centre of it.

"Looks like the cards are up to no good tonight," Gabriel commented. "Kind of like my naughty student. Were you really planning on making a sex tape of us?"

I tipped my head back slowly until I was looking right up at him so I knew he had a perfect view straight down the front of my shirt then I shifted my legs, parting my thighs so that my skirt rode up to reveal my garter belt as I spoke. "Yes, Professor Nox."

Gabriel growled as he leaned down to kiss me, his hands grasping the back of my chair as his mouth moved against mine upside down. I moaned into his mouth, sliding my hands down my body to relieve some of the ache in my hardened nipples before pushing them between my legs.

"Fuck," Gabriel groaned as he broke the kiss, his gaze moving to my hands as I hitched my skirt higher and dragged my fingers up my inner thighs.

I leaned even further back in my chair, moaning as I slid my fingers over my throbbing clit through the lacy black fabric and Gabriel started kissing my neck while watching the show.

He tossed the deck of cards down onto the desk before us where they fanned out across it, our fate already decided. His hands moved around my body and he unhooked more of my shirt buttons as I moved my thighs even further apart and slowly pushed my fingers inside the top of my panties for him.

Gabriel sucked and bit my neck, no doubt marking my flesh with hickies and teeth marks, but I was okay with that. As he tugged my bra down so that my tits spilled over the top of it, I pushed two fingers inside myself with a soft cry.

"You are such a bad girl, Elise Callisto," Gabriel purred as he moved his hands to my nipples and began to tug and squeeze in a way that had my pussy throbbing even more needily.

"If these are the kinds of detentions you offer out, then I think I'm okay with that, Professor Nox," I said breathily as I circled my clit for him, and my back arched against the chair.

"Only for my favourite student," he replied, turning to kiss me hard, his tongue driving into my mouth.

One of his hands slid from my nipples and moved down my body and I gasped as he met my hand with his, pushing two long fingers deep inside me and making me cry out.

Gabriel leaned right over me, pumping his fingers and curling them just right while I continued to work my clit and within moments, I could feel the orgasm building in my body.

"I love you so fucking much, dirty girl," Gabriel groaned against my lips and as he pushed his fingers into me again, I came for him, my pussy gripping him tightly and my moans of pleasure colouring the air.

While my body was still pulsing with pleasure, Gabriel yanked me upright, forcing my shaky legs to hold me in my heels as he pushed me face down over the desk and kicked the chair out of the way.

I braced myself against the hard wood as he yanked my panties down, not even bothering to remove them completely and leaving them around my ankles as he rolled his zipper open to free his solid length.

His hand cracked down against my ass cheek and I gasped at the bite of pain as he slid his cock into my still throbbing pussy.

I groaned some garbled version of his name into the mess of homework and tarot cards beneath me as he seated himself fully inside me, pausing there for a moment as he flipped my skirt over my back and caressed the roundness of my ass.

"Do you like that?" he asked me roughly, his fingertips digging in as he took a firmer grip of my hips and I knew in that moment that he was going to destroy me.

"Yes," I gasped, feeling so full of him that it was hard to get the word out.

"Good girl." He spanked me again and I sucked in a sharp breath as he tugged his cock back out of me before slamming it in again so hard that my hips smacked against the edge of the desk and a delicious bite of pain reached me.

That was all the warning I got before he started to take what he wanted from me, his solid cock slamming deep inside me over and over again while his fingers bit into my hips and his balls crashed against my clit in the most amazing fucking way.

I grasped the far side of the desk to brace myself, pushing my ass back into the thrusts as he used me for his pleasure and I loved every fucking second of it.

My nipples dragged back and forth across the papers and cards on the desk, the roughness of them sending even more pleasure radiating through my body as Gabriel thrust in and out of me like a savage.

My pussy gripped him tightly as I fought to keep up with him and just as I started to wonder how much more I could take, pleasure crashed through me like a tsunami and I cried my orgasm to the walls.

Gabriel finished with me, his hot cum filling me up as he fell over me, panting in my ear and keeping us locked together while we rode out the last of it with heaving chests and tingling flesh.

"I love you, Gabriel," I mumbled, turning my head to seek out his lips and he gave them to me with a low growl.

"You'd better. Because there's no way in hell that I'm ever letting you go."

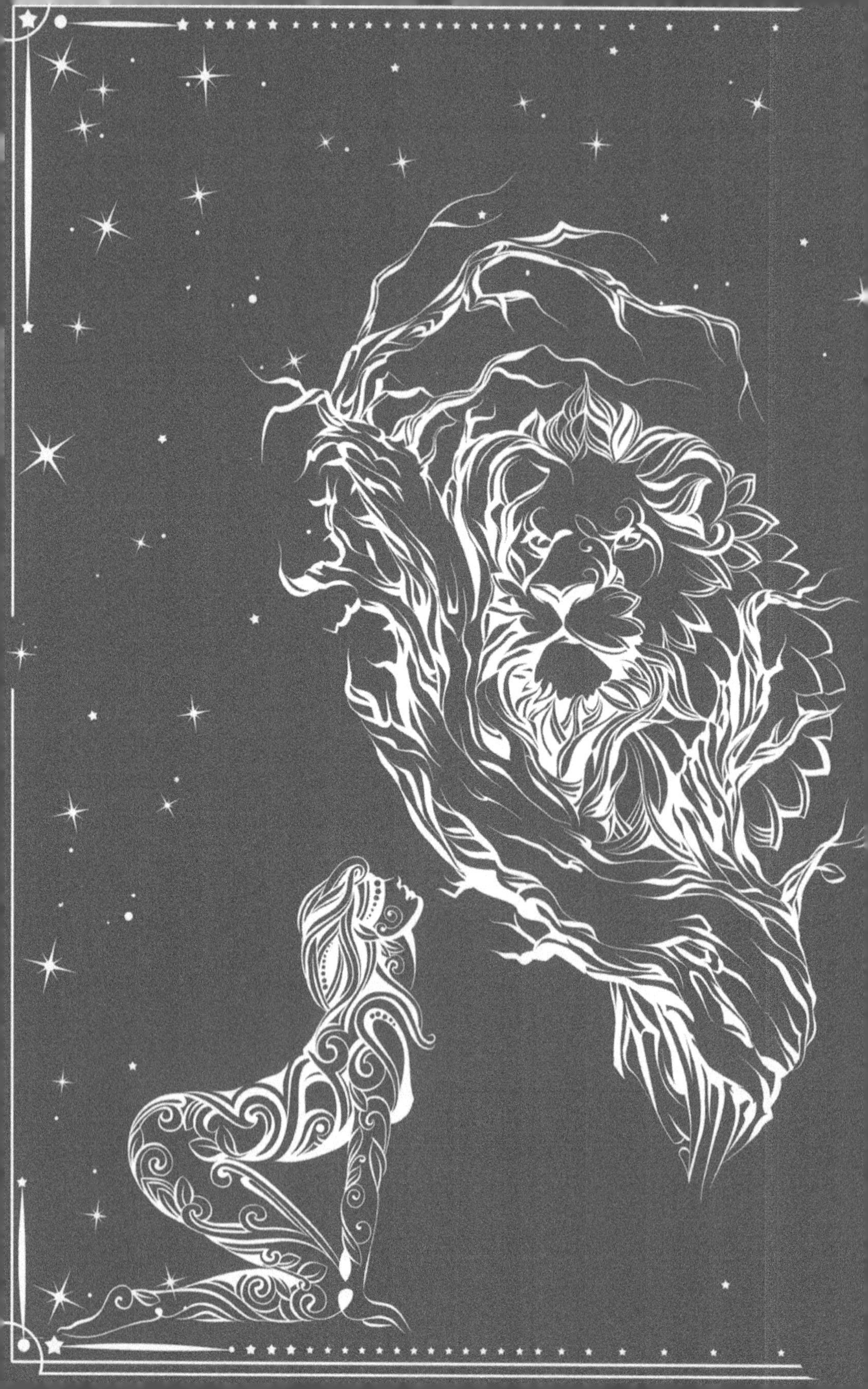

LEON

CHAPTER THIRTY SIX

This week had been a shit pit of mass proportions. Titan had gone to ground and no matter how hard Gabe tried, he couldn't figure out where he was. On top of that, Dad had gone off on a rant when I went home for dinner last night after I'd told him to go and visit Roary. It was the first time he'd acknowledged his existence for weeks, and I was hella pissed with the words that had come out of his mouth about Roary being the black sheep of our family. It was fucking bullshit.

For the most part, I didn't let myself think about the fact my brother was going to be in Darkmore for a long ass time. I slapped on my usual pretty smile and wore it like armour against the pickaxe of life which was trying to chip away at my chest and carve a hole out of my heart. I sent Roary care packages as often as I could and whenever I visited him, I snuck in contraband via the guards' pockets too. They didn't even know it was there and Roary lifted it the moment he got close to them after I left. I wasn't giving up on him, and in the meantime, I was gonna make sure he at least had some small home comforts like decent shampoo for his mane.

The Kipling brothers had turned up at my dorm one day and laid out all the laws of Darkmore and all the possible loopholes in the death bond Lionel had forced on him – I guess I had Dante to thank for sending them to me. But the long and short of it was, Roary couldn't be released from the bond by Lionel Acrux, the only other way he was getting out of that place before the end of his sentence was if one of the kids Juniper gave birth to Emerged as a Storm Dragon – which Gabe said wasn't gonna happen – or by breaking out. A feat which was fucking impossible, and he'd probably end up dead trying. If there was any way to help him do it, I'd lay my life on the line to pull it off. But Darkmore was unbreak-outable. No one had ever achieved it and anyone who tried either ended up killed in the attempt or back in prison with an even bigger sentence hanging over their heads. Aside from that, Lionel had locked him in tight with this death bond bullshit. Even if Lord Asscrux himself up and died, or we managed to get a different Celestial Councillor like Elise's fancy new aunt on side, no one else could pardon him either, because Roary would still be bound by the terms of it.

The worst thing was, Roary had accepted his fate. He'd halted his appeal and whenever I saw him now, he just wanted me to go through everything I'd been up to down to the finest detail. My big brother was living vicariously through me and as much as I hated that that was his fate, the desperation in his eyes told me he needed every word I had to give. So I started jotting down my best stories for him in letters so that he'd have something to keep him amused between our visits. The only good thing that had come out of it was that Roary and I had never been closer. The bond we'd formed as kids was now fiercer than it ever had been. But the price of that was far too high. I wanted my damn brother in my life, and I couldn't have him. It was the cruellest fate I'd ever had to face.

I was currently taking a nap in Arcane Arts, my head propped up on the cushy pillows laid out for everyone to sit on. A couple of Mindys had given me theirs too to prop up my legs and I got some shut eye while Gabriel and Elise worked beside me with pendulums.

It was Gabriel's special week with Elise so I was making sure to distract Ryder and Dante as often as possible, keeping them away from her from time to time so Gabriel could have her to himself. It was hard work, man. I'd had to get real creative to avoid Gabriel *seeing* what I was up to, making all of my decisions spur of the moment. Of course, that was my usual style anyway. No one could predict my moves. I was like the wind, blowing one way then – bam! – blowing another. The perfect assassin.

Last night, I'd set myself on fire to keep Dante and Ryder's attention away from Gabriel for an hour. And when we'd gotten back to our dorm – which had now been officially reassigned to all Elysian Mates in our group and had a new triple king sized bed (sorry Gabe) – Gabriel had Elise pinned beneath him with a big ass smile on her face. I was so proud. *That's my Lioness.*

He was still being a little negative Nancy about the stars mating him to Elise, but I knew it was gonna happen any day now. I had so much merch ready for the party, it was gonna blow his mind. I'd made sure the Mindys were fully in charge of the preparations so Gabe couldn't peek on my plans. It was gonna be epic.

The bell rang, sounding the end of class and even better than that, lunchtime.

I yawned widely as Elise pushed her fingers into my hair and I opened my eyes as she leaned down to kiss me. But before she could, I grabbed hold of her cheeks, squeezing to squish out her lips.

"Hey, little monster." I turned her head towards Gabriel.

"Leo," she growled, trying to push my hand off.

"Pucker up Gabe," I demanded and he looked over at me as I offered our girl's lips to him.

She fought my hand off and bit my finger in revenge. "What the hell are you doing?"

I shrugged. *It's Gabe's week.*

Maybe I should have told them about how I was balancing out our pride and making sure no one ever became possessive enough to kill the rest of the harem, but the guys seemed to get so grouchy whenever I brought up the fact that they were my Lionesses that it put me off sharing my magical plan. I mean, you'd think they'd be happy. I'd had Mindys fight to the death to get a piece of me in the past. The literal death. And I was spread out on a cracker for these dudes like cream cheese. Why'd they have to be so aggravated by it all? It must have been so much effort fighting the pull of the pride and my animal magnetism.

"You're an idiot," Gabe commented before leaning in and kissing Elise and she grinned, melting against him while I smirked victoriously. *I have you right where I want you, little Lioness. Stick your tongue in my Nala and make her purr.*

Someone kicked me in the side and I looked around to find Ryder there beside Dante.

"You coming, or what?" Ryder growled and I smiled wider. *Look at him coming to pick me up from class like my boyfriend here to take me to prom.*

"You bet your ass I'm coming," I said, shoving to my feet. I was gonna get a burger with fries, a side of onion rings, a bowl of coleslaw, extra cheese, extra sauce, extra mashed potato - and a side salad as I didn't wanna jeopardise my immaculate body.

Mystice was waiting to lock up, but he had a patient smile on his face as he watched us all together, the five of us heading to the exit.

"What are you smiling at, sir?" I asked as I slung an arm over Dante's shoulders while Ryder flanked his other side and Gabriel and Elise walked beside me.

"Forgive me, guys," he chuckled. "I don't mean to stare, but I've been obsessed with fate my whole life. I've met plenty of Fae mated by the sun, the moon, or both, but I've only ever met a couple of Elysian Mated Fae. And never in all my teachings would I have suspected this was possible."

"It's beautiful, isn't it sir?" I said with a smirk. "Take it all in."

Mystice's eyes slid to Gabriel and his smile slipped a bit. "Feel free to tell me if I'm overstepping, but you're a part of this group too, Gabriel, that's as clear as day. Are you expecting to…I mean, have there been any signs that you might also become mated just as you thought previously?" His eyes sparkled with the idea and I looked over at Gabriel, seeing the doubt in his eyes.

"I don't know," he said honestly, a heavy weight to his tone.

"He will be," Elise said firmly, her hand against Gabe's chest and Mystice studied her for a moment with a look of fascination on his face.

"I do hope so," he said with a warm grin.

"I'll be hers no matter what," Gabriel said, his jaw flexing and my chest swelled.

But I knew he was destined. Call it feline intuition, but me and the stars were good little pals most of the time and I knew they'd do me this solid. *Especially as you owe me over Roary, don't you starsholes?* I glared up at the domed glass ceiling that gave a view into the dark water of the lake, narrowing my eyes in the direction of the sky. Yeah, they knew they owed me.

Mystice waved to us as we headed out of the room and we walked up the long tunnel and out into the sunlight on campus. It was the perfect day, a hint of summer in the air and everything seeming just…right for once. There was so much shit going on lately that I just wanted to enjoy it and make my pride smile.

"Oh hey!" I broke away from the group, pulling out my Atlas and flicking on the selfie mode. "We need a picture together. We don't have one and none of you have any excuses to say no." I grabbed Elise, positioning her in front of Gabriel and Dante, shoving their shoulders together behind her. Then I pushed Ryder up against Dante's other side as he scowled then squashed myself in beside Gabe and angled the camera at us.

"Everyone smile!" I commanded and they all did, except Ryder who stared impassively at the camera. "Ryder, smile dammit."

"I don't smile," he hissed.

"Oh come on, yes you do. I've seen you smiling at Elise's tits plenty of times. Elise get your tits out."

"I don't want to put a photo on our wall with my freaking tits out," she laughed.

"Fiiine, Dante tickle him," I called and Dante actually did it, but Ryder just arched an eyebrow at him. *For shit's sake, of course he's not ticklish.*

Gabriel leaned forward and whispered in my ear, "You need to punch Dante in the face."

That sounded like a message direct from the stars to me. I wheeled around, clocking Dante on the chin and he cursed, his lightning zapping me immediately in retaliation. Ryder cracked a grin and I quickly whipped around to look at the camera and snapped the photo. Everyone was smiling, it was fucking perfect. The best photo ever.

"Yes! Last one to the Cafaeteria is a rotten Griffin shit!" I cried, running away from them all and Elise flew past me in a blur, her laughter calling back to me.

I glanced over my shoulder, finding Gabriel casually shedding his blazer and unbuttoning his shirt, taking his sweet ass time. Ryder and Dante were running behind me with determination in their eyes, but I'd gotten a decent head start. Ha, suckers, I was gonna be the king of the boyfriend-in-laws.

I hit a wall of air and fell to the ground on my back with a growl. Dante leapt over me with a laugh and I lunged upwards to try and catch his ankle but he was too fast. Ryder charged past me next with Dante in his sights and I narrowed my gaze, taking out my Atlas and calling in reinforcements on FaeBook.

Leon Night:
Calling all Mindys! Stop Dante Oscura and Ryder Draconis from reaching the Cafaeteria before I get there!

#Mindysassemble #Mindymob

Brianna Hayes:

On my way! I will tear down the Cafaeteria before I let them in it, then rebuild it for when you arrive. #dropadragon #stopasnake

Gemma Guinan:

I just dove out of a top floor window in Altair Halls, broke my leg and healed it. Worth it for you Leon. I'm coming! #sticksandstonesmaybreakmybonesbutonlyfailurecanhurtme

April Hatcher:

We will build a Mindy wall and they'll never get through our impenetrable love for you, my king! #walloflove

Kaysie Ward:

A feast shall be waiting for you when you arrive with your queen @EliseCallisto!

Erica Collins:

I was off on a run in my Lioness form, but I'm coming for you now, Leon! Watch out for me – I'm the naked girl clasping her bosoms with your beautiful Lion face shaved into my lady hair. #theybounceforyou

Telisha Mortensen:

@EricaCollins if you were naked in the woods, where were you keeping your Atlas to see this post??? #toomanyplotholes #theresonlyoneplacewithspace #Lionessesbecrazy

I shoved to my feet and raced after Dante and Ryder with a wild laugh as Mindys poured into their path to block their way, forming a barricade right in front of them. They were forced to slow and suddenly a Mindy caught my hand and tugged me sideways into the bushes. She was very, very naked and definitely had my lion face shaved into her pubes. *Awesome.*

"This way, my king," she hissed, dragging me along down a track behind the bushes then we cut through a group of Mindys who all cooed and stroked my back as I went. I tossed them a thanks and a wink and they all swooned, melting into puddles on the floor.

"You're a cheat, Mufasa!" Ryder roared from somewhere behind us as Mindy pulled me back onto the path and bowed low to me.

"Thanks Mindy!" I called as I ran up the path toward the Cafaeteria where my little monster was perched on a small ledge above the door, swinging her legs back and forth, blowing a bubble with her cherry gum.

I powered toward the entrance and Gabriel casually landed in front of me, sweeping a hand through his hair a second before I got there. He opened his arms for Elise and she jumped down into them, kissing him passionately as I huffed out a breath.

"No fair," I growled. I knew it was his week and all, but this was *my* game and I deserved to win it.

"Seems perfectly fair to me." Gabriel smirked, placing Elise down on her feet.

Dante and Ryder came up behind me and Ryder punched me in the kidney, but a faint smirk lined his lips.

"You play dirty, Lion boy," he growled.

"Dante used magic first," I pointed out and Dante shrugged.

"No one said it was against the rules," he said and we all headed into the Cafaeteria where eyes followed us and people unsubtly snapped photos.

We were still the talk of the whole school and the whole city too. Newspaper articles were constantly coming out about us and my secretary Mindy was declining requests for interviews every day. We'd probably have to face the press eventually, and I was all for soaking in the sunlight of fame, but the others didn't seem so keen, so I could respect that. Mostly. I may or may not have been in negotiations with *Roarsome News* about a nude photoshoot with a silver and gold background to bring out my fancy eyes. It'd be totally tasteful though so it was all cool.

We sat at our favourite table in the middle of the hall where the Mindys had already laid out a feast for us.

"You've really gotta stop them doing this shit, Leo," Elise said as she sat down and I moved behind her, massaging her shoulders.

"Relaaaax, little monster. I'm taking care of you. And they wanna take care of you too," I purred and she tried to bat me off for a couple of seconds before giving in to my incredible massage skills.

I'd gotten my masseuse Mindy to teach me how to give Elise the best massage of her life. My Mindys were a fountain of knowledge when it came to pleasing my pride. Dante had reluctantly let me practise on him and told me I had raw talent. Well, he hadn't said those words exactly, but I'd translated the way he'd groaned when I got deep into his neck muscles to mean just that.

"Oh my stars," Elise murmured, letting her head hang forward as I rubbed my fingers in firm circles over her shoulder blades. "That's actually really fucking good."

"See," I said proudly. "I can be your Mindy." I leaned low to her ear. "If you wanna call me Mindy in the bedroom sometime, I wouldn't mind that. You can make me do anything you want." *Oh man, I should definitely Mindy it up for my pride sometime.*

She shrugged me off suddenly, her head snapping around with narrowed eyes. "Is that what you used to do with them?"

"Well…" I swallowed the razor blade in my throat.

"Hey guys!" Eugene appeared in his purple cape and matching fingerless gloves. *Saved by the rat.* The green haired girl followed behind him, smiling at him with large eyes.

I latched my gaze on this random Rhonda. She was my perfect distraction from Elise's death glare and the questions she wanted to ask about whether or not I'd fucked my Mindys in the past. I'd friendly it up with this girl and Elise would forget allllll about my dirty past by the time I was done.

"Hey, I'm Leon." I held out my hand to her, sending out a flicker of

Charisma to see how she reacted, but despite the hint of a blush, her gaze moved back to Eugene promptly. Aww, little rat dude had a girlfriend.

"Sally," she said. "And I know who you are." She smiled awkwardly and sidestepped closer to Eugene.

"What's your Order?" I asked as I dropped into my seat next to Ryder. Elise was already losing interest in me. I was so cunning, it should have been illegal.

To be fair to the rat dude, Eugene had earned my respect big time since he'd saved our asses and actually, I was gonna get him laid as a thank you. I was nice like that.

"Um, I'm a Questian rabbit," she said with a smile and Elise's fangs snapped out, making Sally back up with a gasp.

"Oops, sorry. Prey Orders bring out the hunter in me." She hid her mouth with her hand and I barked a laugh. "I swear I'm well fed and don't crave anyone's blood but my guys'."

Sally laughed nervously, moving closer to Eugene again and their hands brushed. He didn't even seem to notice the opportunity that was right there. I mean, come on dude.

"I bet you'd eat up a juicy rabbit shifter, wouldn't you Ryder?" Dante mocked and Ryder hissed loudly in anger, making me turn to him in surprise.

"Questian Rabbit Shifters have more to them than being prey Orders," he snarled and my eyebrows took a one way ticket towards my hairline. What in the twelve star signs was that reaction about? He liked Rabbit Shifters? There had to be a reason for it, but what?

I lost complete interest in Eugene and Sally, narrowing my eyes as Ryder gave me a death glare which told me to back off. There was no chance of that though. I was on the scent of something delicious, and I wasn't gonna let it go until he gave me my answer.

"Do you find them hot?" I asked and his nose wrinkled.

"No," he snarled.

Interesting.

"So…your favourite Disney character is Thumper?"

"No," he snapped.

"Hmmmm." I stroked my chin dramatically and he elbowed me in the ribs.

"Drop it, Simba."

"No, I don't think I will. Is it because you've got cutsie bunny blood?" I teased and he grunted, swiping up a pain au chocolat and tearing into it.

Oh.

My.

Stars.

All the pennies dropped in my head, rattling around in my brain as excitement tore through every piece of me.

"I know what it is!" I yelled, bashing my fist down on the table, making Eugene and Sally scamper away. That was cool, they'd played their distract-my-mate-from-my-previous-Mindy-whoring-ways parts well.

Ryder grabbed me by the collar of my shirt, yanking me nose to nose with him. "You don't know anything. Now shut your mouth."

"I know," I whispered, barely opening my lips and his eyes narrowed as he tried to snare me in his hypnosis, but it wasn't going to happen. I didn't keep secrets from our pride. It was already too late. I was going to tell them all because it was the best news I'd ever had ever.

"I will gut you, Simba," he hissed, but it was a risk I was gonna take as I flicked a finger to cast a silencing bubble around our table then wheeled towards the others.

"Ryder's m-"

He attacked me, wrapping a vine around my throat so hard I choked. "Quiet."

No one could silence me though. I was unsilencable. I cast a fire at his vine, snapping it and gasping down air as I leapt out of my seat and slid across the table, dropping down beside Dante.

Ryder jumped out of his seat too, snarling at me with a threat in his eyes. "One more word and I'm gonna make a winter coat out of you."

"But I wanna hear," Elise complained, pouting at him. "Come on, Ryder, we don't have secrets. It can't be *that* bad."

Ryder ripped his gaze from me onto her and I could see his hard exterior melting slightly. "I'll tell you in private, baby."

"I already know, I just *saw* it," Gabriel said casually, tossing a grape into his mouth with a smirk.

"Well I'm not being left out." Dante folded his arms and Ryder hissed furiously.

"Pleeeease, Ryder," Elise asked, batting her lashes at him and he threw his hands up in fury, dropping back into his seat.

"Fine," he snapped. "But if the four of you tell anyone else, I'll make you regret it."

"Firstly, you should totally be proud anyway, dude," I said. "And secondly, you can trust us. We're your boyfriend-in-laws, if that doesn't count for something then I don't know what does."

That didn't seem to comfort him, but he just returned to eating his pain au chocolat and ignored me.

"What is it, Leo?" Elise asked excitedly.

I shot a glance at Ryder, grinning widely and waiting a few more seconds to build the suspense. "Ryder's mom was a Questian Rabbit."

Everyone gasped, looking to Ryder for confirmation, but did they really need it? This explained his fluffy little heart and tiny button nose. "Doesn't it make so much sense? Like, *so* much sense."

Dante burst out laughing as Ryder slammed his hand down on the table. "What makes sense about that? I'm nothing like the Questian Rabbit Order."

"Oh my stars, it really does make sense," Elise said, diving at him and squeezing his cheeks. "Look how bunnyish your cheeks are."

"Do you need a reminder of how cold my blood runs, baby?" he growled in warning and she bit her lip.

"I wouldn't mind one," she purred then looked to me. "This explains why the bunny filter on the Snapdragonchat app looked so good on him."

"Wait a second," I gasped. "You have a photo of Ryder in the bunny filter? I need to see that this second!"

"Traitor," Ryder growled at Elise, curling a hand around her waist as he yanked her against his hip in a tight hold.

"Well, it's on Ryder's Atlas, he's got the only copy," she sighed then turned to him. "Buuut, if you let the other guys see it, I'll make it worth your while…"

"How?" Ryder murmured and she leaned up to whisper in his ear, making a dark and hungry look cross his features.

"He's definitely gonna say yes," Gabriel muttered just before Ryder snatched his Atlas out of his pocket then tossed it across the table to me.

I pounced on it like a cat catching a butterfly and Dante laughed as he leaned in to look at it too. Elise was taking the photo of the two of them and Ryder looked mildly surprised over his pink bunny ears, cute little nose and whiskers to match.

"This. Is. Everything." I forwarded the photo to myself then Gabriel swiped the Atlas from my hand to see, chuckling before tossing it back to Ryder.

"Happy now?" Ryder growled before leaning in to kiss Elise's neck.

"You have no idea," I said. *One for the scrapbook.* "So what was your mom like?" I gazed at him with a wistful smile, cupping my chin in my hands, but he stiffened in his seat and suddenly looked all emotionally uncomfortable.

"You don't have to answer that, fratello," Dante told him.

"It's fine," Ryder muttered. "It's not like I'm ashamed of her. She was a better Fae than most."

Elise watched him closely, her fingers winding between his as we all waited for him to go on. Gabriel had a sad look in his eyes and my heart tightened as I worried that we were gonna hear something we didn't like. But whatever it was, Ryder deserved to have a safe space to say it.

Ryder cleared his throat, clearly not liking being the centre of attention but he didn't try to change the subject. "She was…a good mom," he said stiffly. He wasn't much of a storyteller, but I still hung on his every word. Ryder rolled his eyes at my intent expression and let out a long breath. "She used to call me her daredevil because I liked jumping off stuff, trying to do backflips and all kinds of stupid shit. She said she knew I'd be a Basilisk like Dad because I never cried when I fell and hurt myself." He shrugged and my heart turned into a molten lump of goo.

"I used to do shit like that too, it gave my mamma a heart attack," Dante said with a chuckle.

"My mom had air magic, so she just let me do what I liked. But she only caught me if it looked like I was gonna break my neck. She said people who don't learn to fall never learn to get back up again." He smiled slightly like he'd only just remembered that.

"How old were you when she died?" Elise asked softly.

"Six," he grunted, brushing his thumb over the word *lust* on his knuckles, Elise's fingers still intertwined with them. "She'd think I'm a fucking idiot for this. Pain's important to me, but lust?" He shook his head at himself. "This is some broken boy's way of hiding from the world. Pretending there's nothing but these two emotions and living a life based entirely between them…it's like building a house around yourself with no windows or doors." He looked to Elise, bringing her hand to his mouth to kiss the back of it. "You let in the light, baby."

She melted and I did too, leaning my head on Dante's shoulder as I gazed at them. "It's so romantic," I whispered and Dante snorted a low laugh.

"You shouldn't be branded with anything that's not important to you, Ryder," Gabriel said and Ryder turned to look at him, his brows knitting together. He looked down at the word *lust* again and nodded decisively. "I'll change it."

"To Leon?" I asked hopefully and Ryder gave me a dry look.

"No," he deadpanned.

"Oh come on, you got a mark for Gabriel, why not me, bro?" I pouted at him and he rolled his eyes.

"I already did." He ripped his sleeve up and turned his arm over, making my heart beat out of rhythm.

He ran his thumb across the skin above the Scorpio tattoo, revealing an intricate Leo mark just for me with curling flames around the lion's face.

I sucked in air so hard I nearly choked on it. "Rydikins! How long have you had this?" I half dove across the table, grabbing his arm to inspect it. It was purrrrfect.

"A while," he muttered. "And don't go thinking too much into it, my head was in a weird place that night."

"I love it and it means *so much*," I said with a bright smile then sank back onto my seat. "Now you need to get one for Dante and then you need to ink all five of our star signs on me – is it weird if I get them along my cock? Nah, that's cool actually. It'd be cool, wouldn't it?" I looked around for their agreement, but their expressions said it would not be cool as Elise laughed. *I'll convince them when I'm driving my star-signed cock into our girl and fucking her for all of us.*

"So what are you gonna change the word lust to?" I pressed Ryder for an answer. "Oh man, I just realised it's gonna mess up how I remember which tattoo you have on which hand."

"What do you mean?" Elise asked with a frown.

"Lefty lusty, righty fighty," I said like it was obvious. Which it was, duh.

Elise laughed. "Hmmm, it needs to be a good four letter word," she said as Ryder watched her with a smirk.

"Leon is the obvious one," I pushed and Dante elbowed me in the gut.

"He's not getting your name, Leone," he said with a grin. "If he gets anyone's name it'll be Drago."

"You wish, Inferno," Ryder laughed.

"Gabe?" I suggested.

"Don't call me Gabe," Gabriel said flatly.

"Well, what do you suggest?" I demanded in frustration.

"I've already *seen* what he's going to get," Gabriel said with a light shrug. Damn bro was such a future hogger sometimes.

"Well what is it then?" I pressed. "Lion? Gold – like my eyes? Meow like-"

"Dalle stelle," Dante cut over me. "Let Ryder answer."

Ryder shrugged, but a little smile was playing around his mouth as he unlinked his hand from Elise's then rubbed this thumb over the knuckles of his left hand, manipulating the ink within his flesh with some spell and changing the word *lust*. I tried to see it before he was done but Elise moved in closer so I couldn't and I bounced impatiently in my seat.

"Let me see," I begged.

"It's perfect," Elise whispered, kissing Ryder on the lips and as he reached up to grip her hair to hold her in place, his knuckles were angled at me with a word that made my heart squeeze with happiness for my snake bestie. *Free*.

I walked along the path towards the Vega Dorms at the end of the day, reading from my book *A Pride To Be Proud Of* as I looked forward to seeing my pride. I'd been held back after Elemental Combat class by Professor Mars to discuss final tactics for the upcoming Pitball game tomorrow.

We were facing Omega Academy and if we beat them, we were one step closer to going up against Zodiac in the final. I was so ready. Readier than a lubed up whore. We were gonna motherfucking win this match then we were gonna smash Zodiac Academy into the ground and claim our trophy. It was my dream, man, my *dream*. We had to do it. But Omega were fierce competition and Mars had gotten word they'd been training with the freaking Neverlights from The League because Rue Comet's daughter was on their team. It was shady as fuck and I wasn't gonna stand for it. Aurora Academy never got a scrap of funding, but Omega were almost as well funded as Zodiac and now they were getting inside tips from the freaking League? Grrr, if we just won the Pitball cup one time, Aurora would get an injection of money and our whole pitch would get a revamp. Someone from The League would have to come and visit us to present us with our trophy, there'd be a ceremony and cake and celebrations, and the whole kingdom would see how worthy we were. It was our year, our time to write our names in the stars. And I needed to make sure my best players had the most relaxing night of their lives tonight so they'd be on top form for tomorrow. So I was about to Mindy the fuck outa them.

I read over a passage in my book that I'd highlighted and left notes around.

A Lion may show his deep and unending affection to his pride by occasionally allowing them to exert their Charisma over him. It takes a great deal of trust indeed to allow your strong mental barriers down to let your Lionesses' Charisma affect you, but the results can be most rewarding. Alpha Lions may struggle with this most, but if achieved, the bond between Lionesses can be intensely strengthened. A Lion may also derive satisfaction from pleasing his pride and making sure each of his Lionesses are cared for, pampered and shown they are deeply loved. Examples of pleasing your Lionesses may include buying them their favourite foods, running them a relaxing bath, hosting a night in with their favourite movies, touching them in ways that shows your adoration like massage or hair brushing.

I bumped into someone who gasped and I lowered the book in my hand, finding a bright eyed, red haired Mindy looking up at me.

"Oh sorry, Leon," she said as a blush ran across her cheeks. "I got overexcited. I just wanted to show you how we're getting along with the merchandise. I made you a catalogue." She offered up the binder with a silver cover.

"Shit, not here Mindy." I grabbed her, knocking her into a bush and diving in after her to hide as I peeked up through the leaves at the sky. "Gabe's always watching."

Her lips parted in concern as she hugged the binder to her chest. "Do you think he saw us?"

I pressed my finger to her lips. "Shhh, Mindy."

I needed to do something unpredictable to throw Gabe off the scent if he happened to be looking my way with his third eye.

"Destroy all the merch and start all over again, I can't be involved!" I forward rolled out of the bush and sprang to my feet, swinging a punch at a freshman. They screamed and ran for their life and I chased after them a few paces with a roar.

No one can predict me, I'm a wild man.

Principal Greyshine appeared, hurrying down the path with his head low as he tried not to be noticed and I ran up behind him, leaping onto his back and holding on tight. "Yah!" I cried.

"Mr N-Night," he stammered in surprise, trying to shake me off but I held on even harder.

"Go Shiner, go!" I cried, pointing to the Vega Dorms up ahead.

"Oh, I, um. Alrightaroo then." He moved forward on stumpy little legs and I clutched onto my tiny principal as he staggered his way towards the dorms, grunting and wheezing as he went.

"You need to work out more, sir," I said in his ear. "Never skip leg day."

He tried to answer but he was panting too much and he was sweating like a waterfall. He managed to get me to the door and I dove off of him, kicking it open and ninja rolling my way inside before kicking it shut again.

My Atlas pinged in my pocket and I took it out as I stood up, satisfied that I'd thrown Gabe off with that little display.

Scar:

We're going to watch Frozen. Are you coming back to our room?

My lips parted and utter excitement ran through me. I shoved my Atlas back into my pocket and started running up the stairs, taking them two at a time. He'd finally dropped his walls, he was allowing me to peek into his heart and see the Disney princess living in there. Was it Belle? Aurora? Ariel? *Of course* it was Ariel. He'd been waiting to get his legs for years and live above the sea. We needed to have another movie night. Maybe he'd wear Mickey Mouse ears if I bought them for him. We could get matching ones for the pride. Different colours for each of us.

I made it to our floor, racing down the hall and shoving the door open with a grin.

Every cell in my body froze to ice and horror tore through me right down to the pit of my soul. There was blood everywhere. So much blood.

Elise lay on the bed gutted, her hands locked with Gabriel and Dante's, their eyes lifeless and blood still dripping to the floor around them. It was a massacre, a horror show.

I ran forward in complete panic, my hands shaking and fear possessing every inch of me.

"Elise!" I cried, grabbing her hand which was so, so cold. "No, no, no." I reached for Gabriel, feeling the frozen stiffness of his cheek, then Dante whose throat was slit and eyes were so dead it made me ache everywhere.

"*Dante*," I choked out, shaking him then falling down on my girl as my world shattered and my heart fell to ruin. I was nothing without her, *nothing*. I was half aware of screaming for help while the rest of me broke and sobs shuddered through the centre of my being.

"Please no, please," I begged of the stars, burying my face in Elise's neck.

A cold, dark laugh sounded from behind me and I whipped around, ready to destroy whoever had done this. I'd make them hurt and scream as I tore every one of their organs from their body and made them suffer at my hands. Then I'd follow my sweet Elise into death and find her among the stars.

Ryder stood there, his laughter growing to a boom and I blinked in shock, trying to process what I was seeing.

"Your fucking face," he wheezed, pointing at me and realisation hit me as I whipped around to face the bed again. The illusion was gone, my family no longer dead and bleeding in front of me.

"You…faked it?" I rasped and Ryder nodded, still laughing harder than I'd ever seen him laugh.

"I told you I'd get you back for pranking me," he said, grinning like the Devil.

My jaw dropped and I slowly wiped the fucking tears from my cheeks. "That was too far, Ryder!" I bellowed, running at him and slamming my shoulder into his gut.

He hit the wall and I punched and punched him while he laughed and took every blow. We slammed into the floor and I wrapped my hands around his throat, choking him as he still tried to keep laughing and I snarled like a beast.

"You. Don't. Joke. About. My. Mate. Dying," I hissed through my teeth and he finally stopped laughing.

The door swung open and Elise slammed into me with the strength of her Order, knocking me flying and I hit the floor.

"What are you doing?" she gasped and I snarled, the beast in me still raging.

"Ask *him*," I spat, jerking my chin at Ryder as he shoved himself up and healed the wounds I'd left on him.

Elise looked to him in surprise, her eyes wide as Dante ran through the door, chasing after her.

"What's wrong?" Dante demanded as Gabriel casually swept into the room, moving to me and hauling me up by the hand.

"Not cool, man," he said to Ryder who rolled his eyes, shoving to his feet.

"What did you do?" Elise pressed, grabbing a fistful of Ryder's shirt.

"I just pranked him that's all. He can dish it out, but he can't take it," Ryder said with a shrug.

"He cast an illusion of you all dead with blood fucking everywhere," I snapped, my heart still pounding furiously in my chest.

"Oh come on, Mufasa, it was just a joke," Ryder growled.

"By the stars, Ryder," Elise cursed. "That's not okay."

Ryder's face fell and he chewed the inside of his cheek as he finally seemed to grasp the fact that he'd gone too far. My heart tugged as I realised this really had just been his way of trying to play a prank on me. He'd planned the whole thing out, lured me here and had the illusion already in place. No one had ever played games like this with him before and he had no idea what the boundaries were. I didn't wanna make excuses for him, but dammit he looked like a naughty school kid right now and it was too freaking adorable.

I sighed, rubbing a hand over my face. "It's fine, dude," I said. "It was just a joke. It was funny I guess, like, for a psycho."

Ryder ran a palm down the back of his neck. "No…maybe it was a bit too far now I think about it."

Elise walked over and kissed me, settling my panicked heartbeat at last. I pulled her closer, needing to feel how real she was as the fear of losing her still clung to me. "Fuck, little monster. I thought I'd lost you. It was the most terrifying thing I've ever experienced. If you die, make sure you buy me a ticket to go with you."

"Aw, Leo," she said sadly, kissing me again and I tasted her cherry sweetness with a groan.

I started laughing and she stepped back, smirking at me as I lost it, clutching my stomach as I fell apart.

"It was pretty funny, man," I told Ryder. "Like, never do it again bro or I'll incinerate you, but ha...yeah it was a pretty good prank."

Ryder cracked a grin and I walked over to hug him, clapping him on the back and he did the same to me, making my heart lift. That was the first hug he'd ever reciprocated. Did we just become official best friends? I looked down at my left hand as we stepped apart but there was no fancy mark there like he and Dante had for each other. I pursed my lips in frustration. What did I have to do to get myself a star tattoo? Wasn't I friendly enough? Didn't I deserve a best friends' mark like them?

Well at least I'm not completely unbonded like Gabe.

Aw, poor Gabe. I'd give up my friend mark for you to get your silver rings, dude. Nah, I wouldn't. Dammit, I would.

"Well I guess you owe me now, buddy," I told Ryder, throwing myself onto the bed and cupping my hands behind my head.

"It was tit for tat," Ryder scoffed.

"You made me think my Elysian Mate and my best friends were dead, that's not tat. That's fucking rat-tat-tat-tat." I fired a fake machine gun at him and he smirked.

"He's right, you totally owe him, Ryder," Elise said lightly, flinging herself onto the bed beside me and I nuzzled into her with a purr.

"Fine, what do you want?" Ryder demanded and Gabriel tried to cover a laugh with a cough, clearly *seeing* what I was gonna ask. Ryder shot him a glare that said he knew exactly what that had been and Dante openly laughed.

"Wellll, I was planning a whole pamper night for you guys tonight. I was gonna be your Mindy to get you all relaxed in time for our Pitball game tomorrow morning," I said as Elise ran her hand down my chest.

"And?" Ryder growled.

"And, now *you're* gonna be our Mindy instead," I said with a wide smile.

"Fuck off," he balked. "I'm no Mindy."

"You are tonight, Mindy," I said. "Unless you wanna sing Hakuna Matata for me instead? Those are your only options."

"Ha, you're screwed, Mindy," Dante chuckled, slapping Ryder on the arm and Ryder glowered.

"I'm not singing," Ryder snarled.

Gabriel dropped down onto the edge of the bed, kicking off his shoes. "Come here and give me a foot massage, Mindy."

Ryder hissed through his teeth.

"Then you can do my back." Dante whipped off his shirt and Ryder gave him a cold look.

"I'll massage Elise then fuck her raw, that's my final offer," Ryder said and I snorted a laugh.

"No way, dude. You owe me," I pushed.

"Yep," Elise agreed. "In fact, you can't touch me until you make it up to Leon."

"*Baby*," he snarled and she grinned.

"You'd better get massaging Gabriel's feet," she taunted and Ryder's eyes turned to pitch as Gabriel took off his socks and wiggled his toes at him.

"No," Ryder snapped.

Dante fetched a bottle of argan oil from the bathroom, holding it out to Ryder.

"No," he hissed again, knocking it out of his hand.

"Okay well...I guess you're not gonna be able to touch me for a loooong time," Elise teased and Ryder's jaw flexed in frustration as he stared at her.

"Fine," he gritted out and we all waited in anticipation, looking from him to Gabriel's feet. But then, the best thing that could ever have happened to me happened. Ryder started saying the Hakuna Matata lyrics. I mean, it wasn't singing, but it was so fucking close that it made my life complete.

"Sing it," I demanded and he vaguely changed the way he said the words, the slightest lilt to his tone but it was enough to make me grin from ear to ear. I interjected with Simba's parts of the song so we rocked out together and he glared the whole way through it. But it actually happened and I just wished I'd managed to record it. I dove off the bed and hugged him again, having completely forgiven him. Then I shoved him into my spot beside Elise where he preceded to grab her, squeeze her ass and kiss her like she'd made him spend a year away from her rather than two minutes.

I ran to the closet, whipping the door open and taking out the huge pamper box I'd had a Mindy stash there along with a cooler bucket full of beer.

I grabbed the argan oil from the floor, pulled my hair up into a bun and knelt in front of Gabriel, grabbing one of his feet.

"I was joking, man," he said, but then I started kneading oil into his feet like a fucking pro -thanks to masseuse Mindy – and his eyebrows arched.

"Okay, fuck it, go ahead," he said and Elise laughed.

I smiled, a purr resounding in my chest as I gazed around at my perfect pride. "I'm gonna be the best Mindy that ever Mindied."

I woke among a tangle of bodies with Dante's silky soft hair brushing against my chest. I'd put a treatment in it and brushed it good, just like I'd done for all of my Lionesses. Ryder had taken some convincing, but I'd managed it while Elise had sat in his lap feeding him chocolate as we all watched Frozen.

Every one of my pride were now primped and preened to the max. And then obviously the argan oil had gotten places that it wasn't meant for and we'd all ended up in a slick, messy mega orgy that ended in us competing to see who could give Elise the most orgasms. I'd won because after they'd all fallen asleep, I'd stayed up eating her out until she gave me my win. I was the king of this pride after all, and I was more than happy to make sure she knew it.

The Pitball game wasn't until eleven am so none of us were in a rush to get up as we snuggled in bed together. Ryder was in his Basilisk form and was the size of a large anaconda, his head on Elise's belly while his huge body curled all around the rest of us, stealing our heat. Did he even know he was cuddling us or was he just subconsciously doing it in his sleep?

Gabriel held Elise against him while my head lay on her tits on top of my Pitball shirt which she was wearing and Dante spooned me, his hand clasped with hers on my hip. This was happiness at its purest. My favourite place in the world.

A soft snoring sound drew my attention to the end of the bed and I frowned as I lifted my head, gasping as I spotted Ryder's little ghost hound.

"Miss Snufflington!" I cried, waking everyone up including the foxy looking creature which raised its head with a wide yawn.

Ryder shifted back into his Fae form, landing on top of me and crushing me to the mattress. "That's not her name," he snarled then shoved off of the bed, grabbing some boxers and pulling them on before approaching her.

"Aw, she's so cute," Elise cooed, sitting up and reaching for her and the hound let her stroke her pointy ears.

"Why does it keep showing up around us?" Dante asked.

"I dunno," Ryder grunted, pointing to the wall. "Go." He wafted his hand.

"No way," I snapped. "She wants to stay."

"She's going to stay," Gabriel added and I grinned at him.

"She is?" I asked excitedly.

"Yeah." He reached out to stroke her head and she licked his palm. "She's Familiarised with Ryder."

"I didn't Familiarise with nothing," Ryder muttered, though his eyes kept straying to the hound like he wasn't so sure about that.

"You're here to stay?" I cooed at the creature, scooping her up in my arms and cuddling her to my chest. "Ohhh you're the cutest, snuggliest, buggliest thing ever, aren't you Miss Snufflington?" I baby talked her and Ryder strode over, yanking her out of my arms.

"Don't talk to her like that," he grumbled.

"Well you'd better let everyone know her real name soon, Ryder," Gabriel said. "Or Leon's one is gonna stick."

"Fine, she's called ghost hound," he said and I tutted.

"No she's not," I insisted and Elise chuckled.

"I like Miss Snufflington," she said.

"No," Ryder hissed.

"Come on," Gabriel pushed. "The stars already gave you her name, didn't they?" He smiled like a mystic man then walked off into the bathroom.

"They did?" I asked excitedly.

"No." Ryder looked at the ghost hound in his arms and I was sure he was lying.

"Fiiiine, be that way." I slipped off the bed, grabbing my Pitball uniform from the closet before heading into the bathroom. I stripped out of my boxers and got into the shower with Gabriel who rolled his eyes as I grabbed the shower gel from his hand.

"So have you *seen* who will win the match today?" I asked hopefully.

"It could go either way," he said thoughtfully. "Omega Academy are bringing their A game."

"But so are we, right?" I elbowed him as I lathered up my junk and he smirked.

"Yeah, still too close to call though. And even if it wasn't, if I told you we'd win you'd change your whole attitude on the field and we might lose."

"Good point, dude. Don't tell me shit. I wanna be as ignorant as a lost llama out there today."

He stepped out of the shower to get dressed and I was soon exiting the bathroom too in my Pitball uniform.

It wasn't long before we were all ready for the game in our matching attire and I picked up my little monster, throwing her over my shoulder as she squealed and I slapped her ass as I ran out the door. The guys followed and we all made our way across campus to the pitch with the little ghost hound trotting at Ryder's heels.

"Are you gonna tell me her name now?" I asked Ryder as I placed Elise down beside me and his jaw flexed.

"Fine," he grunted.

"So what is it?" I demanded.

"Periwinkle," he said and I swivelled around, scooping her up and cuddling her tight.

"Hello Winkle," I cooed, tickling her chin and her back leg started kicking as I hit the perfect spot. Man, I was good with animals. I was like a hot Dr Dolittle.

"Periwinkle," he reiterated in a growl.

"Yeah, yeah. But she needs a nickname, and she looks just like a Winkle, don't you Winkle?" The little creature wagged its three tails as I rubbed my nose against hers.

"No." Ryder snatched her from me. "If she's going to have a nickname it's Peri, not fucking Winkle." He sneered and I rolled my eyes. Winkle was way cuter than Peri.

As we approached the pitch, I realised the whole of the school were already gathered in the stands, plus a mass of supporters for the Omega team in their green and white colours.

As we headed into the changing room, Ryder put Periwinkle down and she immediately ran off through a wall and vanished. We found the rest of our team dressing for the match while Coach Mars barked out reminders of how we were gonna play this game. Our team had a seriously strong defence, but Omega was reputable for their defence too, so it was gonna be a bloodbath out there. We were going to focus on brute force in the first half of the game to save as much magic as possible for the second round.

"Callisto, I want you shooting Pits whenever you get the chance," Mars ordered and I nodded my agreement as I headed to my locker, popping it open and taking out my special Pitball Captain whistle.

"Yes, sir," Elise said brightly. "And if I can knock a few teeth out along the way I will."

"That's the spirit," Mars said with a grin.

"Shadowbrook, I want you shadowing Callisto whenever she's going for the Pit," Mars commanded Ethan. "If she gets overwhelmed, you need to do anything you can to get your hands on the Pitball and score before Omega's defence turn on you."

"Sure will." Ethan smirked cockily as he looked at Elise. "Just pass me the ball if you get tired, love."

She flipped him her middle finger, smiling challengingly at him. Dante moved to her side, resting a hand on her back and murmuring something in her ear that she grinned darkly at.

"It's rude to whisper, Oscura," Mars barked. "If you've got something to say you can share it with your team."

Dante looked around with his eyebrows arching in surprise. "I just promised Elise if she scores more than five Pits today I'll ti farò venire sul mio cazzo di Drago," he said with a chuckle.

"In a language we all understand or I'll dock rank points," Mars growled, folding his huge arms.

"I'll make her come on my Dragon cock," Dante said and the team burst out laughing while Mars scowled.

"Minus two rank points, get your head in the game Oscura," he snapped and Dante shrugged.

"She's my motivation," he said simply and Mars rolled his eyes.

"Night, get over here and do your pep talk," Mars commanded and I jogged over, climbing up onto the bench beside him and blowing my whistle loudly to get everyone's attention.

Dante stared at my golden whistle like a magpie with a twinkle in its eye, but he wasn't gonna take this from me like he'd stolen my freaking medallion. Not that I was still salty over that or anything.

I did my speech which blew everyone's minds then led the team out onto the sandy pitch where the Omega team were already lined up to play us. They looked as hungry as we were for the win with their shiny ass, extra grippy shoes and their smug little fancy fucker faces. Their captain was the smuggest dickwad I ever saw with his gleaming rich kid hair and sparkly rich kid eyes. *Well you know what I'm gonna do with that silver spoon that you were born with in your mouth, Captain Trellis? I'm gonna shove it up your ass.*

"Go on Elise!" someone cried and I turned, spotting Marlowe in the stands next to Bill, the two of them clapping and cheering us on. Behind them were my moms and Dad, all wearing Aurora Pitball jerseys with my number and our surname emblazoned across them.

"Hey!" I waved at them and they jumped up and down, crying my name.

"Go on Gabriel!" Bill called and my little buddy's chest swelled out.

"Hey Dadsy!" I called and Bill frowned at me, but I continued waving until he waved back then grinned at Elise. "Marlowe came to watch you, little monster."

She blushed, toeing the sand at her feet as she gave Marlowe a small wave and I purred loudly. Anyone who showed up for my girl was worth their salt in my books. Except fucking Titan. Who'd been there for her like a snake nursing a mouse back to health so it could eat it for lunch. I'd never forgive that asshole for gaining her trust only to betray her like he had.

But I wasn't going to focus on him today. It was our time to shine. To thrash our enemies and show them we were a team to be feared. Elise needed this win more than any of us, so I'd work my ass off to hand it to her.

I stepped up to where the referee held the first Pitball of the game. Captain Trellis stood opposite me and I gave him my most psychotic smile to make him shit himself, and a flicker of uncertainty passed through his gaze. The ball was tossed into the air to start the game and I cast fire behind Trellis before kicking him squarely in the chest, narrowly avoiding his fist as it came at my face. He stumbled backwards, burning his ass on the fire with a yelp and the crowd burst out laughing as I snatched up the Pitball and tossed it over my shoulder toward Elise. She caught it and raced down the pitch towards the Pit while our defence slammed into the Omega team to hold them back, blood and magic flying as everyone collided with roars of determination.

An almighty cheer went up and I turned, finding Elise circling the Pit with her arms in the air in celebration, the first Pit of the game already scored.

"Fuck yes!" I whooped, racing over to her and picking her up in the air as she laughed. Marlowe went mad, snapping photos on his Atlas and cheering like crazy while my little monster smiled from ear to ear. Ryder crashed into me, slapping Elise's ass in celebration and I laughed as I placed her down and we all readied ourselves for the next round.

The Omega team looked unsettled and they sure as hell should have been. We were a force of nature and they couldn't handle us.

The next two rounds were brutal, the Omega team fighting back hard and scoring both Pits. I set my sights on Captain Trellis again and again, satisfied every time I took him to the ground beneath me and made him grunt in pain. I was his nemesis, his demon in the night and he couldn't escape me.

Ryder was like the wings of death as he cut down his opponents, working seamlessly with Dante to round them up then taking it in turns to knock them down. Gabriel used The Sight to get in the way of any asshole who blocked

Elise's path to the Pit and throw them into the waiting arms of the defence. The game was so fast that he couldn't always predict the oppositions' moves, but when he did, it gave us one hell of advantage. And although people with The Sight weren't allowed to go pro, he sure as shit could play in the academy tournaments, so ha ha fuckers.

Omega gave us a serious run for our money but by the second half, we were in our element, scoring over and over. I even managed to pull off a double backflip score when Elise threw me on a gust of wind towards the Pit. Ka-blam, right in the belly of the beast. It was fucking poetry. This was my favourite thing ever after sex with Elise and snuggle piles with my pride.

In the final round, Ryder blasted half the pitch apart with his magic and I knocked Trellis into the hole he created with a good punch to the gut. Elise was blocked by a ring of Omega assholes at the other end of the field and I raced towards her to try and get her clear.

Gabriel sprinted past me as fast as a fucking aeroplane, cast an ice blade in his hand and slashed it through the air in front of me. I realised a thin vine had been stretched across my path ready to take me out and Gabriel tossed me a smirk before he threw the ice blade at a guy blocking Elise and it slammed into his foot. He shrieked like a baby, falling onto his ass and Elise dove over him and started running for the Pit.

Ethan barrelled into a girl beside her out of nowhere, taking her down before she could catch my girl. A ring of flames tore out of the ground around Elise and I flicked my fingers, opening a path in them so she could keep running, my adrenaline levels spiking. She sped past me and I collided with the girl on her heels, taking her to the ground and listening for the count of five before she was called out of the game.

The timer was down to ten seconds and I wheeled around to check if Elise was in the clear. She blasted one of the Pit Keepers out of her way, but the second one came at her with two vines in her grip, whipping them out and tripping Elise before she made it to the no magic zone ringing the Pit.

The ball slipped from her fingers and panic seized me as the Pit Keeper lunged for it. But suddenly Ryder was there, knocking him to the ground and shoving the ball back into Elise's hands. She clambered over the fallen Pit Keeper, took two bounding steps through the no magic zone and slammed the ball into the Pit, making my heart nearly leap from my chest.

"Aurora Academy are the winners!" the referee called the end of the game and the roar that left me was pure animal.

I tore off my shirt and my skin split apart into my huge Nemean Lion form as I ran across the pitch and pinned Elise beneath my paws, running my tongue over her whole face. We'd fucking done it. We were through to the finals!

Zodiac Academy, here we come!

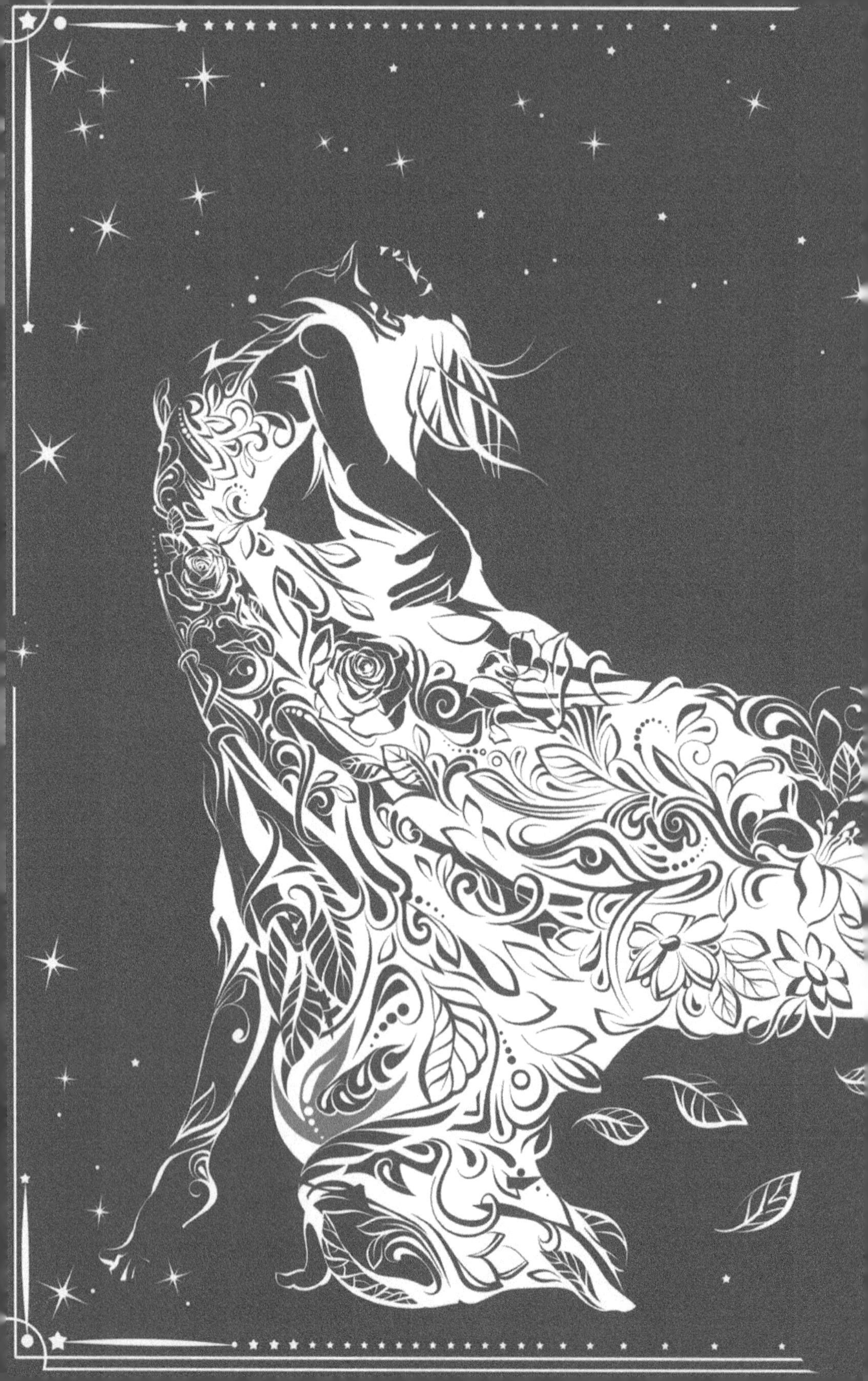

ELISE

CHAPTER THIRTY SEVEN

I sat on the roof of the Vega Dorms, watching Gabriel and Dante wheeling through the sky with Ryder at my side as the sun began to set and the end of another week at the academy drew to a close.

Leon was whooping and cheering as he rode on Dante's back and I smiled a little as I watched them, but it did nothing to settle the unease I was feeling.

"What is it?" Ryder asked me and I gave him a shrug as I released a sigh.

"King...Titan, whatever he likes to call himself. The agents the Altairs sent haven't found him and when I spoke to Caleb earlier, I kinda got the impression they were more interested in sweeping the whole thing under the carpet than they were in creating a manhunt."

"Fucking politicians," Ryder grunted, a sneer curling his upper lip.

"Yeah." I watched Gabriel loop around Dante then looked directly at Ryder. "Obviously they're pissed about what happened to Marlowe, and it's not like they're giving up. But they just seem so concerned with making sure no one figures out that some random Fae from Alestria managed to do that to an Altair that I know they're not going to up the investigation beyond the few agents they've assigned to it. And they won't even tell me much about them, so who knows if they're even close to tracking him down. Meanwhile, the full moon is approaching yet again and I'm worried, Ryder. I'm worried that he's going to up his game now that he knows we're on to him. How can he not? We need to act before it's too late, but it just feels like we're treading water all the damn time."

I picked up a small stone in my frustration, using the full strength of my gifts as I threw it away from me out across the grounds. A faint 'Ow!' broke the tension a second later followed by Professor Mars's booming voice.

"Who's up on the rooftops throwing stones?"

"Oh shit," I breathed, exchanging a glance with Ryder whose eyes shone with amusement.

"I'm coming up there and you can bet your asses you'll be in detention for a month!" Mars yelled.

Without giving it any more thought than just knowing we needed to run the hell away, I grabbed Ryder and shot towards the far side of the rooftop with him on my back.

I'd been practicing like crazy with my control over my air magic for weeks now and I was almost certain I could do this without killing us - but if not then I was going to rely on Ryder being able to soften the ground for us.

I leapt over the edge of the roof, stifling a scream as the twenty floors of the Vega Dorms started zooming by us as we fell.

Ryder chuckled in my ear like a freaking psychopath and before we could go splat, I wrangled the air around us and caught us in an updraft before using it to place us lightly on our feet right outside Ryder's window.

He leapt off my back and quickly disabled the spells he had protecting the place before tugging the window wide and hopping through it. I followed right behind him and he threw the window shut again, slapping a hand down over my mouth to stifle my laughter as he threw a silencing bubble up around us.

I bit my lip as the sound of Mars running up the fire escape reached us, and Ryder released me a moment later once we were sure he was gone.

"What am I going to do with you now?" he asked me, his hands moving to encircle the bare skin at my waist beneath my crop top.

"Actually, there was one thing I've been meaning to ask you to do," I said slowly, wondering if he'd make a fuss or if he'd accept my request.

"Anything," he replied instantly and I smiled.

"I want some new ink," I said, brushing my fingers over the tattoos on his wrist that he'd gotten for Gabriel and Leon. "One for each of you. On my back I think."

Ryder's eyes lit up and he ran his fingers up my spine in a feather soft touch. "Oh baby, you have no idea how many times I've dreamed about marking your pretty skin for me," he purred.

I licked my lips as I smiled up at him and his fingers curled around my waist as he started backing me up towards his bed.

Ryder caught the hem of my shirt and slowly peeled it off of me and I raised my arms to let him, my fangs extending as I caught the hem of his shirt and started to tug it off too.

"Why do I need to be naked for this?" he teased and I shrugged innocently.

"I'm just deciding where I want to bite you."

His smile darkened and he reached around behind my back, unhooking my bra for me and sliding it off too. His gaze ran down my body and I could see the battle in his eyes as he resisted the urge to touch my hardening nipples.

"When I'm done marking you, I want you to face the wall and sit that pretty little ass of yours on my lap so that I can fuck you while admiring my work."

"Deal," I purred, my thighs clenching at that suggestion.

I lunged at him, my fangs sinking into his neck as his hands grasped my ass and my nipples grazed against his bare chest.

The intoxicating taste of his blood washed over my tongue and I slid my arms around his neck, my fingers dragging over his closely cropped hair and nails biting into his scalp.

Ryder lifted me by my ass and I curled my legs around his waist, drinking mouthful after mouthful as he walked me to his bed, despite my venom weakening his muscles.

He dropped me onto my back, coming down on top of me and grinding his hips between my thighs while I continued to feed on him and moan in satisfaction.

When I finally pulled back, Ryder leaned down and licked a drop of his own blood from the corner of my lips before giving my tits a hungry look then flipping me over onto my front.

He slapped my ass hard and I gasped as he got off of the bed and left me there.

While Ryder gathered his tattoo equipment, I got myself comfortable on the bed but jolted in surprise as a little blue face suddenly appeared through the wall.

The ghost hound stared at me with unblinking eyes for several seconds like it hadn't expected me then looked over my head towards Ryder before happily trotting the rest of the way through the wall.

I stilled as it approached me, sniffing curiously before hopping over me and scurrying up to Ryder with its three tails wagging in greeting.

Ryder arched a brow as he spotted it, a little smile tugging at his lips before he banished it just as fast and sighed. "Back again then, are you?"

"She likes you," I said with a grin.

"No one likes me."

"I do."

"Yeah, well, you don't get points for that, baby. I'm pretty sure everyone else just thinks you're insane." Ryder leaned down to pet the creature who promptly started licking his fingers before leaping up onto his shoulders and snuggling into his face. He sighed then started towards the window as he tugged her into his arms.

"What are you doing?" I asked curiously.

"Putting it back out."

"Why?"

"Because..." Ryder frowned down at the ghost hound then looked back up at me and shrugged. "I dunno, it's a wild creature and it keeps following me about. So I just put it out whenever it appears."

"But why? She clearly wants to be here. In fact, I'm pretty sure she wants to be yours."

"Mine?" Ryder asked curiously, looking down at the little thing and tickling its ears. "Do you know that her venom is almost as lethal as mine?" he asked absentmindedly and it was so freaking cute that he was bonding with his little puppy over their deadly natures that I had to fight the urge to jump up and pinch his squishy cheeks.

"Sounds perfect for you then. Just let her stay. Make her a bed to snuggle in. Have you got something she can eat?"

Ryder frowned like he absolutely wouldn't be doing any of those things and the ghost hound leapt out of his arms before scurrying back over to me on the bed. She hopped up, bypassed me then started turning around and around in circles on Ryder's pillow before curling up in a little ball in the centre of it and covering her face with her tails.

Ryder looked somewhere between shocked and outraged and I rolled my eyes at him. "Come on. I want my new ink," I said to distract him before he could get any crazy ideas about putting the puppy out in the cold again and Ryder just shook his head as he carried his equipment over to me.

"Do you want me to do some sketches first or-"

"Nope. Just go with what comes naturally."

Ryder shrugged and I positioned myself on my front for him as he moved to straddle me and took a seat on my ass.

His fingers trailed down my spine softly before he cleaned the skin then the sound of the tattoo gun buzzing took up most of my attention.

I remained silent as the first prick of the needle hit my flesh between my shoulder blades and I focused on the feeling of the art being placed on my body.

Ryder concentrated on his work and I let my eyes fall closed, the prickle of pain distracting me from the hurt in my soul. I didn't know how much longer I could go on like this. The more time that passed without me discovering anymore clues as to Gareth's whereabouts, the more I felt certain that I wanted to try the dark magic Ryder had suggested.

I understood Gabriel's objections to it and Orion had made it clear that it would take time for me to build up the ability to have those kinds of visions, but if he was willing to guide me in doing it then I would gladly take the risk. I needed to find my brother. I was never going to be able to move on while these questions still hung over me.

When Ryder finally finished the fourth and final tattoo at the base of my spine, he switched the tattoo gun off and slowly ran his fingers over the new ink, healing my flesh and sealing the designs onto my skin permanently.

He leaned down and kissed the one between my shoulder blades before moving his mouth to the one below and the one beneath that. By the time his lips touched the final tattoo, I was practically panting for him and I pressed my ass up, wanting him to make good on that promise he'd made me before he'd started.

"Come and see what you think," he said, getting up and drawing me with him towards his closet. He pulled the door open to reveal a full-length mirror and I turned to look over my shoulder at the designs he'd inked onto my flesh.

A gasp escaped me as I drank in the sight of them, my gaze taking in the simple, black line drawn symbols for each of my men. At the top was a pair of open wings for Gabriel, beneath that a roaring lion's head represented Leon then a soaring Dragon for Dante and finally a coiled Basilisk for Ryder right where my spine began to curve towards my ass.

"Shit, Ryder," I breathed, drinking in the sight of them before returning my gaze to his and feasting on the hunger waiting for me there. "I love them."

The smile he gave me bit right into my skin and burrowed deep as he moved to stand against my back, his hands sliding around my waist as his fingers dragged along the length of my waistband.

A shiver tracked down my spine and I held my breath, waiting for him to make his next move. But before he could, the door burst open and I shrieked as Ryder yanked me behind his back to hide me from whoever the fuck had just let themselves in.

The fright dissipated as I spotted the other kings standing there, Gabriel stepping in first while Leon and Dante playfully shoved each other before Dante managed to get the upper hand and step inside before Leon.

"Bill just called me," Gabriel said, his eyes moving from Ryder to me as I stepped out from behind him. "Oh...sorry." His gaze fell to my tits and for several long seconds none of them spoke while they all got their fill of staring at me.

"What did he want?" I asked, folding my arms to hide my nipples, and cocking a brow.

"Oh err, yeah," Gabriel shook his head a little then went on. "He found a trail. A passport under the name of Frank Colder which has been in use throughout several cities spread across Solaria in the last year and a half." Gabriel took his Atlas from his pocket and held it out to me, showing me a copy of the passport, which stole my breath away.

"That's him, isn't it?" Leon asked excitedly, bouncing on the balls of his feet as I stared at the photograph of my brother. I gasped, my heart thundering so hard I was sure it was going to burst. His hair was longer than I'd last seen and he was wearing a pair of glasses but it was him. No doubt about it.

"Where?" I demanded, moving to grab my shirt and bra from the floor by the bed.

"Dalle stelle," Dante growled but Leon let out a squeal of excitement before rushing over and grabbing me so that I couldn't get dressed before he'd gotten a better look at my new tattoos.

"Oh my stars! Look at me! Look at all of us! Oh shit, now I've got a boner. Oh fuck, this is hot, too hot. I'm gonna need to look at this with my dick buried-"

"No fucking way," Ryder snarled, elbowing him aside. "Before you assholes showed up, that was the future I was about to achieve and I'll be the first one to claim her body now that it's marked for us."

"You can't seriously believe that we will all just agree to you monopolising her after-" Dante began but I growled at them to shut them all up.

"None of you will be putting your dicks anywhere near me any time soon," I snapped, fastening my bra as I gave them all a glare. "We are going to find Gareth. Right now. Where is he Gabriel?"

"Bill is working on finding the latest location where this passport has been used," Gabriel said. "He doesn't have anything from the last six months. So we actually have some time to kill..."

I yanked my shirt on, shaking my head. "No we don't. Let's just go to that hotel and ask about him then. They could have CCTV footage from his stay, something I can use to actually see him! No way am I just sitting around here waiting on Bill."

"I don't think any of us were planning to let you just sit around, little monster," Leon said as he reached out and pulled the hem of my shirt up to get another peek at my tattoos.

I slapped his hand away and narrowed my eyes. "Right now we need to-"

"Bill just found a record of that passport being used to check into a hotel in Terina yesterday," Gabriel interrupted suddenly, pulling his Atlas back out of my hand a second before the message from Bill arrived, containing a freaking address.

My heart stopped beating as I stared at the screen. My whole world stopped spinning and I just froze, realising this was it. This really was the moment I'd been aching for. I was going to find my brother and get the answer to all of the questions I'd been hunting for ever since I enrolled at this academy.

"Is she going to find him, falco?" Dante asked Gabriel in a low tone and my gaze snapped up to meet my Harpy's.

Gabriel frowned as he tried to get The Sight to give us more information and then a hesitant smile tugged at the corner of his lips.

"I *see* you, Elise. I *see* you in the hotel and...embracing Gareth," he breathed in astonishment and a huge exhale escaped my lungs as tears sprung to my eyes at his words.

Relief spilled through me in a torrent unlike anything I'd ever felt before and I fell down into a crouch, hugging my arms tight around myself as relieved sobs escaped me. He was alive. My brother was still with me and none of the pain or suffering I'd endured over losing him could hold a flame to the utter joy I felt at the idea of having him back at last.

Someone scooped me up into their arms and I didn't even have the presence of mind to realise it was Dante until I felt the electricity prickling against my skin while he walked, laughter surrounding me from him and Leon as they celebrated too.

I managed to recover from my shock enough to wrap my arms around Dante's neck and I placed excitable kisses against his cheek and jaw as my tears just kept coming and I fought to compose myself.

By the time Dante set me down on my feet again, we were standing outside the academy gates and the four of them were all huddled in close to me.

I glanced around at their faces. Dante and Leon looked full of joy while Gabriel seemed to be trying to *see* something else. But as I looked to Ryder, I found only trepidation in his eyes and that hardened mask he wore so well had slid right back down across his features.

"What is it?" I asked him as Dante took a pouch of stardust from his pocket, offering it up to Gabriel as he was the one who knew our destination.

Ryder glanced between the others and his brows lowered a little more before he shrugged. "Nothing, baby. I'm just being cautious. Seems to me like this could be the perfect kind of trap to lay for you and I don't want Titan getting his hands on you again. That's all."

"I don't *see* it being a trap," Gabriel replied as my eyes fell to him. "But I'm still getting bombarded with other visions which the stars seem more set on showing me right now so I'm not managing to *see* a whole hell of a lot about how this is going to play out. I did *see* Gareth's face though. So I say we just focus on finding him and I'll figure the rest of these visions out later." He shot a concerned look at Ryder and a shiver ran down my spine as I wondered what he could be *seeing* that would have The Sight so focused on it.

"Is everything okay?" I asked as Gabriel took a pinch of stardust from his pocket and he flashed me a smile instantly though it seemed a little forced.

"You know how the visions can be." He shrugged. "I'm sure I'll figure it out."

In the next breath, Gabriel tossed the stardust over us and we were whipped away within the clutches of the stars.

The world spun and starlight fanned over my skin before I was dumped back out again right in the middle of a busy street.

My eyes widened in fright as I spotted a bus heading straight for us and I threw my hands out, slamming a huge gust of air magic into my kings and knocking them all across the street to the sidewalk. I shot after them with my speed half a second before I could be flattened, and Dante leapt up from the pile of bodies with a cry of horror.

"What the fuck was that, stronzo?" he roared at Gabriel as soon as he was certain I was okay, throwing a punch which Gabriel blocked before it could land.

"Sorry!" he yelled back, shoving Leon's legs off of him as he scrambled upright too. "I can only direct us to places I don't know because I've *seen* them. That's not the same as actually being familiar with a place - obviously I wouldn't have chosen for us to land in the middle of the street and I was too distracted to *see* the fucking bus."

"Guys," Leon began, getting between them while Ryder cursed beneath his breath and dusted the ass of his jeans off. "I think we all need to take a moment for a hug circle."

"I'm not ever going to participate in a fucking hug circle," Ryder muttered and Leon huffed in frustration.

They all continued to bicker, but I just stepped past them, closing in on the glass front of the expensive hotel we'd arrived at as my gaze fell on a dark-haired Fae who was sitting at the bar inside.

"Gare Bear?" I breathed, moving right up to the glass door and pressing a hand to it, feeling the coldness of the pane against my flesh as I just stared at the back of his head and waited.

A bartender moved towards him, pouring out another drink and I sucked in a sharp breath as he turned to look at her, revealing the profile of his face and bringing every wish and prayer I'd had secretly or publicly over the last eighteen months to life right before me.

I shot inside, giving up on any kind of restraint as I raced towards my brother with my heart soaring and a laugh of pure joy tumbling from my lips.

"Gare Bear!" I yelled, drawing his attention over his shoulder half a second before I collided with him and sent us both crashing to the ground and onto the carpet, my arms wrapped tight around him as a strangled cry escaped me.

Gareth rolled us slightly so that he was on his back beneath me, and I pulled back enough to get a good look at him. His eyes were wild with concern for a moment before confusion filled his features as he took me in.

"Well, hey beautiful, what can I do for you?" he asked me with some weird, thick Fae Yorker accent and a voice that sounded nothing like his at all.

"I...Gareth, it's me," I bit out, rearing back a little more and blinking furiously to banish the tears from my eyes as my heart raced like humming bird wings in my chest. "It's Ella. What are you-"

"Sorry babe, I hit the blaze a little hard last night. Though I have to admit I'm surprised I don't remember you. Perhaps we could get a little more aquatinted now though, if you're down to party?" He slipped two fingers into his jacket pocket, tugging a test tube free so that I could see the electric blue Killblaze crystals inside it for a moment before his other hand landed on my thigh.

"What the fuck are you talking about?" I balked, my head spinning as I scoured the most familiar face in the world to me and started to notice more than one detail which just wasn't right. Why were his eyes that weird, pale blue colour? Where were the freckles which lined his nose? And why did his face seem somehow off in general, like he'd gained weight or lost some or... something.

Strong arms banded around my waist and I was suddenly hoisted off of Gareth as Leon dragged me into his grip and Ryder grabbed my brother by the front of his shirt and yanked him upright too.

I screamed as Ryder slammed him against the wall beside the bar and a bunch of the hotel customers leapt up and ran for it.

"Ryder, stop!" I yelled as Dante moved to stand at his side, slapping his palm over Gareth's face and snarling some curse at him in Faetalian.

"I'm so sorry, Elise," Gabriel breathed as he caught my jaw, forcing me to look at him and showing me nothing but heartbreak in his eyes. "I swear I couldn't *see* this. Not until you were already in here and it was too late to stop it from happening."

"*See* what?" I demanded, struggling against Leon's hold as a huge pit of dread opened up before me, beckoning me closer. But I refused to fall into it.

"Gareth?" I yelled, looking to my brother just as Dante used his power to rip apart the illusion clinging to his features.

I sucked in a sharp breath as some stranger was revealed to me. A guy I'd never laid eyes on before with a broad nose and those same, pale blue eyes which had looked so wrong on my brother's face.

"I don't understand," I breathed.

Leon released a pained sound as he nuzzled his face against mine, trying to comfort me while my heart was ripped from my chest and my brain tried to catch up to the reason why.

"I'm so sorry," Gabriel kept saying over and over, clutching onto my hand and trying to get me to look at him instead of the stranger Ryder and Dante were laying into. They weren't even using magic, just pummelling him with fists and fury while the guy yelled and begged for them to stop.

Ryder suddenly grabbed the man by his hair and whirled him around, shoving him to his knees before me and tearing a passport out of his back pocket before holding it out to me.

I stared at the picture of my brother, the false identity he'd had created to run with and I just shook my head in mute refusal of what I was seeing.

Dante threw a silencing bubble up around us, ignoring the panicking Fae who were all running the hell away from us. He raised a hand and electricity speared from his fingertips in multiple directions, frying every CCTV camera which could see us and no doubt destroying the recording system too.

"Tell her where you got that, stronzo. Or I'll happily string you up and start cutting pieces off until you're feeling more willing to share," Dante snarled and the guy before me looked like he was about to piss himself.

"You can speak willingly, or I can go inside your head and rip the answers out drop by drop," Ryder hissed.

"Okay, okay," the guy gasped. "I found that and two others like it in a car I boosted a while back."

"What car?" Dante demanded.

"Just some old rust bucket that I found on a little side alley in Alestria. It had been hidden with diversion spells and shit. But I really needed to walk down that alley to get to my dealer's place and after the third time I found myself diverted from it, I got suspicious and investigated. It took me like three days of trying, but eventually I managed to crack it then I just found this shitty old car. So I figured there was more to it than that, broke in and that's where I found the cash. I-I don't have it anymore though." He looked between my kings with terror written into his features like he'd just realised how badly he'd fucked up.

"We don't give a shit about the cash, just explain to us why you are walking around using stolen passports and wearing a stolen face?" Ryder snarled.

"I just...the passports were in there too and I knew that if anyone in Alestria figured out I had all of that cash they'd come looking for me. So I decided to use the dude's face and his fake identities to run. That's it, I swear. I haven't done anything other than that with it. I just wanted a fresh start, you know?"

I saw red, a scream bursting from me as I lurched out of Leon's grip and dove on the motherfucker before me without caring who saw or what came of it. I would kill him. I was going to rip his fucking head from his fucking shoulders and paint this entire room red with his blood.

My knuckles cracked into his cheek and I felt bone shatter beneath my blow before I started punching him again and again. The guy screamed for help, cowering beneath me and trying to fight me off with a meagre amount of fire magic, the burns only fuelling my fury as I hit him over and over and over again.

The wail of sirens drew closer somewhere in the distance, but I didn't care. And I didn't stop. I was going to destroy this piece of shit beneath me and damn the consequences. Because I knew that as soon as I let this fury fall away from me, all that awaited me in its place was a grief so dark and bleak I wasn't sure I'd ever find my way back out of it.

Hands grasped me and I jerked free of them more than once, but eventually one of them managed to wrench me upright.

I whirled around furiously, my fist crashing into Gabriel's face without him even trying to block it. The pain in his eyes only cut me deeper and I knew he thought he deserved that from me and worse.

"Run," Ryder snarled at the guy who was now trying to crawl away across the floor, covered in blood and looking well beyond terrified. "And if the cops catch up to you, I suggest you don't tell them a damn word about any of this or you'll find out first-hand how much pain a Fae can survive before death claims them."

Before any of us could say or do another thing, someone threw stardust over us and we were whipped away through the stars once again.

My feet hit hard ground and I shoved out of Leon's hold as I backed away from all of them, glancing around though my tears as I found us outside the Aurora Academy gates once again.

"Little monster," Leon breathed, reaching for me with pain and regret in his eyes but I just kept backing up, shaking my head.

"Leave me alone," I breathed. "I just want to be alone."

I shot away from all off them as fast as I could, racing into the depths of the Iron Wood until I couldn't hear a single sound and there was no chance at all of any of them catching up to me. Then I dropped down at the base of an oak tree, wrapped my arms over my head and fell apart.

I thought I'd lived through more pain in my life than any Fae should ever have to face, but as my heart broke from my lost brother all over again and I begged the uncaring stars to return him to me, I knew different. Fate had dealt me a hand filled with pain and loss.

This grief was built to destroy me. It had come sneaking up on me yet again when I'd finally started to believe I might be finding a way to survive it. It was a stab to the gut, a knife in the dark, an endless eternity of pain that would never truly leave me.

Had I been a fool to give in to the idea of hope? How could I keep doing this over and over, building myself up before crashing right back down even lower than I'd been to begin with.

"Are you out there Gare Bear?" I breathed to everything and no one. But of course I didn't get an answer.

And I knew the stars weren't done making me suffer yet.

Not even close.

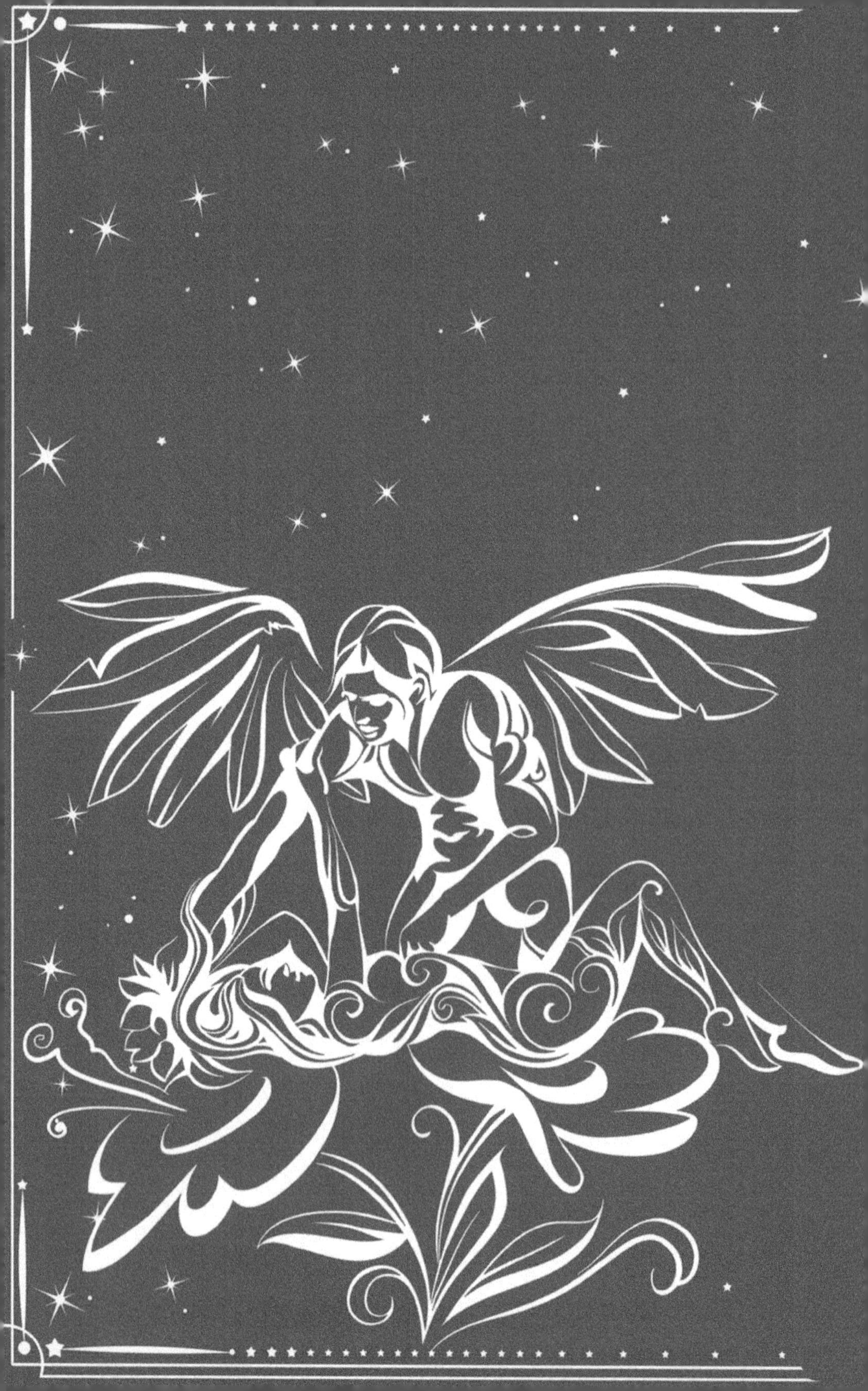

GABRIEL

CHAPTER THIRTY EIGHT

I circled the skies around campus, my heart crushing with the weight of Elise's grief. She'd gone off with Dante to talk at last and I kept a close eye on the boathouse where they were for a while before heading out to do a circuit of Aurora's perimeter. He'd been such a rock for her during this time, and honestly he'd been a rock for me too. That was why I'd gotten a tattoo just for him marking my flesh with the words *My Calm In The Storm* on my left bicep.

It was a perfectly calm day, the sun beating down on my wings as I let myself drift on the breeze and tried to *see* a way to King or Gareth or to a place where our girl could be happy again. But every time I tried to focus on those things, the stars were determined to pull my attention elsewhere and I finally gave in to their call.

Panic snared me as I was thrown into that same vision of Ryder being torn to pieces at the hands of the Lunars, but today the vision was keener than ever, more real than I'd ever experienced. I knew what that meant but couldn't bear to accept it. The path was set, fate solidifying and making me ache with the fear of it.

I'd been spending as many hours as possible every day hunting for a way out of this and making snap decisions to change Ryder's behaviour or actions in the hopes of causing a butterfly effect that sent him down a different path, but suddenly I felt I was out of time.

"Wait, not yet," I begged of the stars. "Give me more time, there must be a way to change this."

I sought out all of my options, from making Ryder hide or run, but I knew he wouldn't listen. He wasn't going to cower from this fate, but I needed to convince him otherwise. Because the Lunars wanted his blood. Today.

I dove from the sky, racing toward the gymnasium in a blur and landing outside it. I climbed in a window and ran across the gym floor, hunting for him. I knew he was here, but where?

The stars showed me a flash of his face and my head snapped around to where he was standing over Eugene, spotting him as his skinny arms lifted a surprising amount of weight.

"Ryder!" I called, running to him and he looked over at me with a frown. His chest was bare and soaked in perspiration, his shirt slung over his shoulder.

"What's wrong?" he asked immediately, racking Eugene's weight as a squeak of effort escaped him.

"We need to talk," I said darkly, grabbing his arm and dragging him into the locker room. A couple of juniors were in there, but I gave them a glare and pointed to the door. "Out," I barked and they ran from the room, clutching their clothes and bags to their bodies as they went. I shoved the door closed behind them before giving Ryder an intent look.

"The Lunars are out for your death today," I hissed, gripping his shoulder as anxiety warred in my chest.

He absorbed that knowledge with a slow nod, no hint of fear crossing his features. "So how do I avoid it?"

My throat thickened with emotion and I shook my head in despair. "I don't know. I can't *see* a way. The fate is becoming so set. Ryder, you need to run." I could already *see* his refusal, I could *see* the argument, could *see* him leaving and walking right into their arms if I pushed him, so I hung my head and cursed.

"I'm no coward," he said in a growl.

"It's not about being a coward," I tried, but The Sight showed me his refusal over and over again and I turned away from him, throwing my fist into the nearest locker. "They're going to come here and take you no matter what I say or do or…" My chest cracked open at the weight of *seeing* all of this, of *seeing* no way out and having to stare this terrible future right in the eye. The Sight was the cruellest kind of curse today and I hated the stars for giving me no other paths. No way to avoid it.

"Gabriel," Ryder said in a low voice. "I have to go to them and you're not to tell Elise." His hand pressed to my shoulder and I turned to face him once more with my upper lip peeling back.

"I'm not going to watch you die," I snarled.

"No," he agreed. "You're right. You're going to stay right by my side and you're going to *see* a way out." He said it with utter confidence in me and I hated that I was going to betray that trust, because I'd had these visions before and I'd steered him away from this fate as best I could, kept watch in the skies, made sure he was always nudged one way or another to avoid this path leading him to the Lunars' door. But I'd failed him. Because now here we were regardless and there were no more paths to take.

"Can you *see* your own fate today?" he asked. "Are you safe if you come with me?"

I frowned, then nodded. "It's not my fate to die today," I admitted.

"Good. And you might not trust yourself right now, but *I* trust you," he said, placing a hand on my shoulder and looking me in the eye. "And if I die, no blame lies on you. But I won't. You're going to do everything you can to save me and you're going to swear on it too, that way if you fail, you won't carry any guilt over it after I'm gone. You'll know without a doubt that there was nothing more you could have done."

"Ryder…" I dropped his gaze, my heart sinking like a lead weight. "It won't change anything."

"Then it'll do you no harm to shake my hand then, will it?" he growled and I sighed, shaking his hand and making the star vow with him so magic rang between our flesh. Then I pulled him in close and hugged him, cursing the stars for even daring to try and steal the Lunar King from this world.

I wanted to tell him to speak to Elise, to at least hold her in his arms one more time just in case, but that would lead to her coming with us into the fray, and that fate had too many chances for her death.

"I'm sorry, brother," I said in his ear.

"There's nothing to be sorry for. I'll return to our girl. We both will," Ryder said fiercely, slapping me on the back and drawing away.

I took a moment to clean the sweat from his body and clothes with my water magic, taking my time and knowing I was delaying the inevitable. When I was done, he pulled on his white shirt and we shared an intense look.

"You were always meant to be a part of my life, Ryder," I told him, pointing to the mark below my ribs which I'd recently gotten for him. Beneath the letter R were the words *My Darkest Saviour*. If it wasn't for Ryder, I was sure I'd still be alone, my heart unable to let any other companion into it. We were always meant to be friends, but I hadn't expected for him to become my family too.

Ryder showed me his left wrist, the Scorpio tattoo now embellished with intricate feathers surrounding it and the words *My Hope* curving underneath it. I followed the line of his forearm up to the Leo tattoo surrounded by flames with the words *My Joy* beneath it. Beyond that, he'd inked the Gemini symbol to his flesh with lightning daggering around it and the words *My Mercy* under it. Next was the Aquarius symbol with a rainbow arching over it like the stroke of a paintbrush and beneath it were the words *My Duty*, and finally Elise's symbol of Libra with small Xs all around it like the mark he had branded on his chest. The words *My Life* sat beneath it and I looked up at Ryder with a frown.

"The Aquarius?"

"Gareth," he answered immediately. "He did for Elise what I will try to do for her every day of my life. He's what I strive to be. My duty to him and to her. All of the words are what each of you gave back to me."

My heart squeezed like it was held in a fist and I gazed at this broken boy who'd grown into a man right before my eyes. I'd changed too. We all had. For Elise, for each other. And losing Ryder now after all we'd been through together was an unbearable thought.

I could feel the stars watching us as we walked from the room, the importance of this day seeming to cling to my very soul as energy hummed around us in the air. I'd march with my brother to the brink of death today and I prayed to all the stars who were watching, that they'd find a way to let me walk him back to the girl who'd saved him.

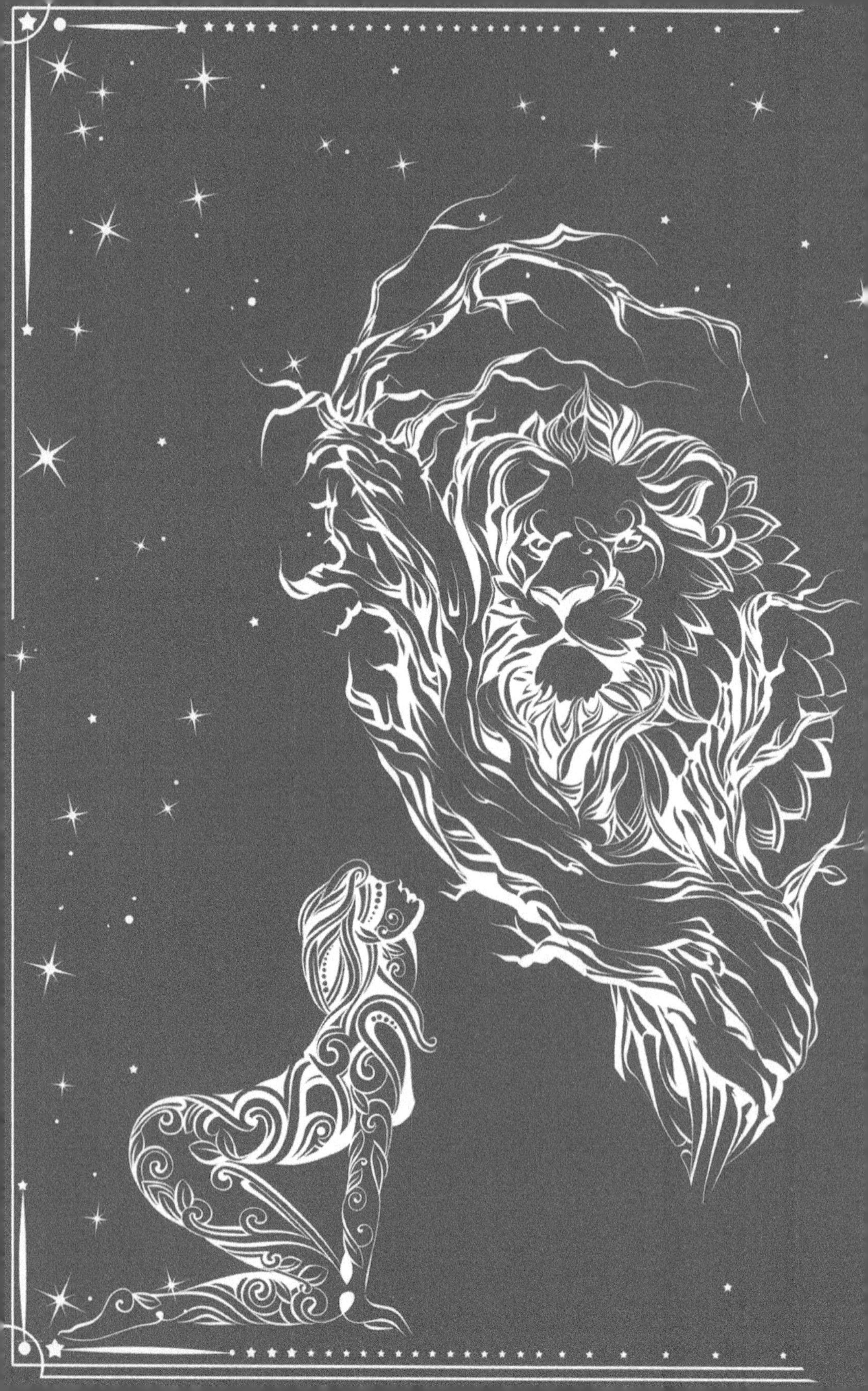

LEON

CHAPTER THIRTY NINE

I was scrunched up inside Ryder's locker in the gym changing room, my body paralysed by Medusa venom so I couldn't move or even make a sound. My fingers were twitching as I slowly gained back mobility and bit down on my tongue as I fought with everything I had to call out to Ryder and Gabriel. But they were gone and I was stuck here like a fucking idiot, desperate to shake off this power which froze my body in place.

I'd wanted to get Ryder back for the prank he'd pulled on me by falling out of his locker and pretending I was dead. I'd paid a Medusa guy fifty auras to let his snake hair bite the shit out of me then lock me in here with the antivenom in my pocket. Emotion was burning a hole in my chest and panic ripped down the centre of me from what I'd heard.

Ryder was walking himself to his death and I needed to get control of my limbs, chase after them and stop him. I'd tie him up in the trunk of my car and drive anywhere, making random decisions so fate couldn't catch us.

Hold on, Scar.

The venom was taking too long to wear off and I groaned in my throat as I tried to call out for someone to help me. The fake blood on my shirt was starting to dry and I cursed as I slowly got the movement back in my tongue and lips.

"Heeeelf," I groaned, trying to make my mouth work properly as I heard someone walk into the locker room. "Heeeelf meeeh."

"Hello?" Eugene Dipper squeaked in fear.

"Hugene," I said in what came out as a creepy ass voice which echoed around the locker.

"Who's there?" he gasped in fright.

"Leeenight," I forced out. "Open thadoor."

"I am brave, I am strong, I am a Daring Underdog," Eugene murmured under his breath. "Don't run, face your fears head on. Become a true Fae." The locker door yanked open and he screamed like a school girl as I tumbled out on top of him, crushing him to the floor, my face pressing to his.

"Helf meee," I begged as he struggled to push me off of him, but finally managed to roll me onto my front.

"Oh my stars! Did someone stab you?" he gasped.

"No," I slurred. "Medutha. Sheck my pocket."

He inched closer, bending down and rummaging around, pushing his fingers into my shirt pocket.

"Nothaone," I mumbled.

Eugene started patting me down, moving his fingers into my back jeans pocket.

"Nothaone," I repeated and he went for the left pocket next.

"Nothaone," I snarled and he shoved me over to check my front pockets. "Nothaone," I hissed as he went for the right pocket first. "Nothaone," I snarled as he tried that tiny nothing random jeans pocket within a pocket that no one ever used for anything. What the fuck was he thinking? Eugene finally shifted to check my left and final pocket. "Yethhhh."

Eugene snatched the syringe I had stashed in there with a triumphant flourish but turned pale at the sight of it.

"Sthab it in my ath," I said, my tongue lolling out and I couldn't make it go back in so I just licked the damn floor as my head fell sideways.

"Your ath?" Eugene squeaked in confusion.

"My athssss," I tried to pronounce the Ss better.

"Oh your *ass*," he said, blinking several times as he uncapped the syringe. "I don't like needles."

"Don't be a puthy," I growled and he rolled me again as he bent over, pulling my pants down to reveal some butt cheek. He stabbed me hard and I growled like a beast, making him squeak a little but he didn't run away.

The antivenom slowly ran through my veins and I gasped in relief as I got the strength back in my body and shoved to my feet. My right arm slammed into a locker and I cursed in pain. "Muvverthucker." My tongue still hung outside my mouth too and I couldn't seem to pull it back in.

"Thanks, Hugene," I slurred then raced from the room, my right arm flapping out beside me as I went and my jeans slipping down over my ass where Eugene had already half pulled them down.

It looked like Ryder and Gabriel were long gone, so I yanked my pants back up, took out my Atlas and called Elise in desperation. She didn't answer so I put out an academy wide alert on FaeBook for the Mindys to find her as panic gripped my heart.

I rang Dante, but he didn't answer either, the call going straight to voicemail. "Thante!" I cried down my Atlas. "Where da thuck are you? Call me athole, ith an emergenthy." I hung up, pushing my tongue back into my mouth with my finger but it immediately slid back out again. "Come on antivenom, do your thucking thing."

I made it to the Vega Dorms and ran up to our room, but no one was there. I sprinted to the window, searching the skies for Gabriel, but my gaze fell on Dante's huge Dragon form far, far away over the Iron Wood instead.

I darted back out into the corridor with my heart in my throat, racing downstairs as fast as I could, tripping over my feet which didn't want to work right then falling down the stairs, hitting every. Single. Fucking. One. On the way down and bursting outside into the sunshine.

"Thante!" I cried, waving my left arm, but he was way too far away.

The Kiplings were ahead of me on the grass, all of them stripping down and shifting into their Griffin forms. Middle Kipling's huge bronze body shone in the light as he lifted his large eagle head towards the sky and flexed his wings.

"Wait!" I cried, running at him and diving onto his back. "Chathe that Dragon!" I roared, kicking his sides and he released an indignant cry before I tossed my whole wallet at his brothers who gazed at me in mild curiosity. There was over a thousand auras of stolen cash in there plus a photo of some girl's grandma, so I was paying them well.

Middle Kipling took off towards the sky and I held on tight as he flew toward my best friend in the distance as fast as he could.

"Thante!" I bellowed as my right arm trailed behind me in the wind. "Thtooop!"

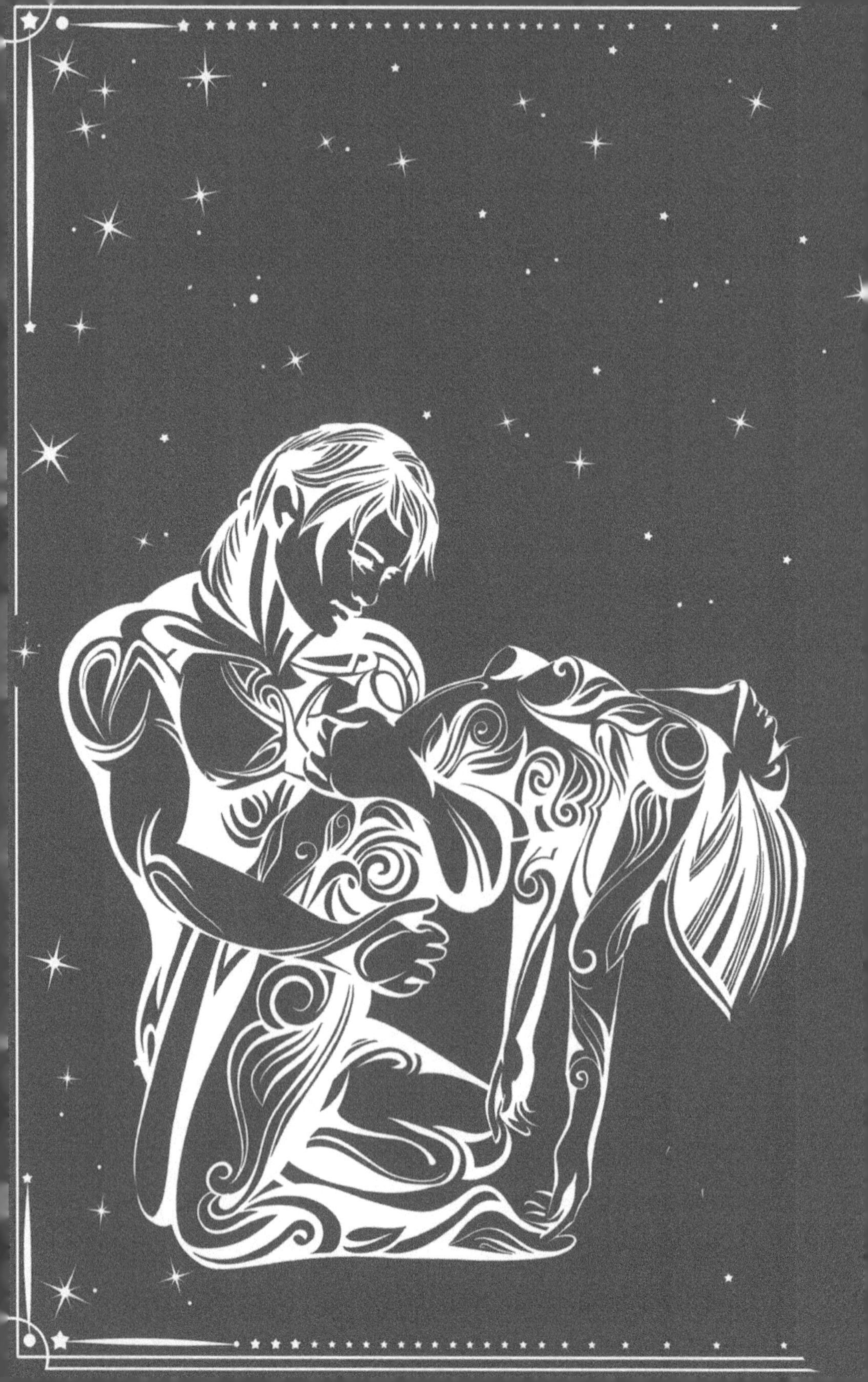

RYDER

CHAPTER FORTY

We arrived at the end of a street on the edge of Alestria where the traitorous members of the Lunar Brotherhood were gathered beside an old, abandoned hotel which towered over them.

The light filtered down the road in a golden glow that seemed almost unnatural for the time of day. I swear I could almost make out the stars in the azure sky too, all of them here to watch the Lunar King die. It was quite the audience for a nothing nobody like me, but I supposed the fate of Alestria would change one way or another today.

I didn't plan on my blood painting a new fate for our city, but I couldn't say I was entirely ruling it out. I trusted Gabriel though. He may not have *seen* a solution yet, but he was going to. He always did. I had faith in him, he just needed to find the faith in himself.

"You're not going to fight?" Gabriel hissed as we lingered in the shadows, clearly reading my mind.

"No," I admitted. "The tradition is to strip me of my bonds to the Brotherhood before my death. Scarlett will make a show of it." I looked to him. "Plenty of time for you to *see* a way out, Big Bird."

"How can you be so calm?" he growled, gripping my arm and not letting me walk beyond the shadows. "Aren't you even going to try and kill some of those assholes?"

"If there was a way to fight my way out of this fate, you would have *seen* it already," I said darkly then moved closer to him. "And you may be the one with The Sight, Gabriel, but if you think I can't read some of the future from your eyes too, you're wrong. Us being here alone means Elise and the others will stay out of harm. Otherwise we'd be standing here together as an army ready to fight and win together. As we are not, I assume that means you foresaw the possibility of Elise's death if she came with us."

He hung his head, nodding in admission.

"Good, so let's keep our girl safe," I growled then jerked my chin at the stars above us. "Look up, Gabriel. Your friends are here in the sky. Keep asking them for ways out and don't leave my side unless staying there equals your death." I strode out of the shadows and Gabriel cursed as he strode forward to keep right next to me.

"This is insane," he said under his breath as we marched up the street.

"I never claimed to be sane," I replied with a twisted smirk.

"Why aren't you panicking?" he growled.

"Because I trust you," I said through my teeth, taking in the riled up Lunars ahead of us as they all faced Scarlett who stood on a stage of ice she'd made for herself in front of the crumbling old hotel.

They hadn't noticed my approach yet, but I imagined it was only a matter of seconds before they did.

"You're asking me to save you when I can't," he growled, his terror over that clear, and it was strange to think of someone besides Elise caring for me so much.

"Have a little faith, Gabriel," I taunted.

"We will fight our away into Aurora Academy this very hour!" Scarlett cried out to a round of cheers. "We'll bring the traitor king to his knees and make him face the price of his crimes against our people!"

"No need to go on a witch hunt, Scarlett!" I bellowed and all eyes turned to me, making Gabriel straighten and step closer to me like he was my star-bound Guardian. I opened my arms wide. "You want my crown then fight me for it, Fae on Fae."

Mocking laughter rippled through the crowd and Scarlett sneered at me, placing her hands on her hips. She was wearing a skin tight leather catsuit, her dark hair blowing around her in the breeze. *What a fucking bitch.*

"Traitors don't get that courtesy," she said dismissively, trying to disguise her own cowardice, then waved her hand at her followers. "Seize him and the Seer!"

A tide of traitorous Lunars ran towards me and I stopped dead in my tracks as they surrounded me, not resisting as two of them grabbed my arms but I marked them, giving them a look which made it clear I had their deaths promised to them when I escaped this.

Gabriel blasted a couple of assholes with water as they got close to grabbing him, but the inevitability in his gaze made him snarl and give in. His eyes glazed as four Fae drew his arms behind his back and the crowd swarmed around me and dragged me toward Scarlett. The crowd started jeering us and lashing out at me and Gabriel even though we didn't have a single way to fight back. It was fucking repulsive.

I cast two subtle blades in my palms and clenched my jaw as I kept my gaze on the lying bitch of a woman who'd been a rat among my gang for years. She'd whispered lies in my ear when I'd escaped from Mariella, told me the Lunars had been there to watch as my father was killed by the Oscuras, then burned the letter that was meant to spark peace among the gangs rather than handing it to me like she should have. How many people had lost their lives because of her actions? She had so much to answer for and I didn't plan on letting her survive this day, even if the stars had other plans.

I was dragged to the front of the crowd to stand beneath Scarlett on her stage and she observed me with a scowl.

"Cast wards around us!" she commanded her followers. "No one leaves here until the Lunar King has fallen!"

A wild cheer went up and arms were stretched into the air as they all leant magic to a dome of wards which spread out to surround the whole area and ensured no one could get in or out.

And that was just fine by me.

I looked at the woman I'd once trusted more than any other and I was at peace with the knowledge that only one of us would be leaving here alive today. She'd blinded me with hatred for the Oscuras and fuelled my feud with Dante, but in the end my true enemy had been a rat in my own nest. If anyone should have been my Astral Adversary, it was her.

I was dragged up onto the stage, about to lunge at Scarlett with the blades in my grip when Gabriel shouted out to me, "Don't!"

I gritted my jaw, disintegrating the blades in my palms, seeing my death as clear as anything in his eyes. Then I let the motherfuckers bind my hands behind my back and they turned me to face the crowd. Gabriel was hauled up onto the other end of the stage and shoved to his knees while two assholes threw punches at him, roughing him up and splitting his lip. My gut clenched at that and I marked every single traitor here, promising them death for this.

Scarlett walked over to Gabriel, gripping his jaw and angling his face towards me.

"It's sweet you've come to watch your boyfriend die," she said to him and mocking laughter rang out around us, making my upper lip curl back.

"He's not my boyfriend," I scoffed and Scarlett looked over at me with a smirk. "He's my boyfriend-in-law."

They just laughed harder, but I lifted my chin higher, knowing I'd found something purer and more real than they ever would. I had a family, a life, and they could strip the skin from my bones, but nothing could take that from me.

Gabriel shook his head in desperation, and I shifted my gaze to Scarlett as she swaggered her way back to me and her cowardly henchman held onto my arms tighter. Not that I was fighting. And no matter what they did, I wasn't going to cry or beg for my life. I was the fucking Lunar King.

Scarlett cast a blade of ice in her hand and gripped my shirt in her fist, slicing through the middle of it and tearing it from my body.

"I'm a taken man, sweetheart," I said dryly. "And you're a little old and crotchety for my tastes."

"Shut up," she snapped then pressed the tip of the ice blade to the Lunar symbol just below my collar bone. She slashed her knife through it and I didn't even flinch as the blood poured down my chest. "Traitor," she hissed in my face.

"I already know your name," I said coolly. "You don't need to remind me."

She spat in my face to a round of cheers and I grimaced as the slick saliva slid down my cheek. I looked to Gabriel, my jaw grinding as I waited for the stars to give him an answer but he just stared at me at a loss and I tried not to think about the fact that I hadn't stolen a final moment with Elise. Maybe I really was fucked.

Don't think like that. Gabriel will find a way.

"Come here Clarence," Scarlett beckoned an asshole with no eyebrows closer and she took his hand, placing it on the mark she'd sliced open on my chest. "Burn it from his flesh."

Heat flared beneath his palm as a chorus of cheers carried to me from the Lunars and I glared impassively at Scarlett as the scalding pain gripped me, my skin melting beneath his hand and destroying the ink that lay there. I fed on the pain, my power reserves swelling and Scarlett's lips twitched in disappointment.

"Get him on his knees," she snarled and someone kicked out the backs of my legs as two sets of hands shoved their weight down on my shoulders. I hit the icy floor beneath me and awaited whatever torture she had in mind for me. Whatever it was wouldn't break me. There was no physical pain in this world I couldn't endure.

"Do your worst," I mocked her. "But you'll never hear me scream."

She leaned down so she was nose to nose with me, her eyes full of a power hungry madness and a twisted kind of hatred reserved just for me.

"You may not scream, Ryder Draconis. But you will feel more pain than you have ever faced in your life. And when our people have seen their traitor king pay, you will die in the bloodiest way I can think up."

The first sign of fear entered me at those words. Because as I looked to Gabriel for an answer he still didn't have, my doubts rose up and started to drown me.

I wasn't afraid for my own mortality. But I was afraid of missing out on the life I'd barely begun to live. Of missing out on Elise.

Forgive me, baby.

Scarlett struck the first blow against me, her knuckles cracking across my face and splitting open the inside of my cheek so blood washed over my tongue.

I felt the stars watching, seeming closer than ever before. And I wondered if they really had come here just to see me die.

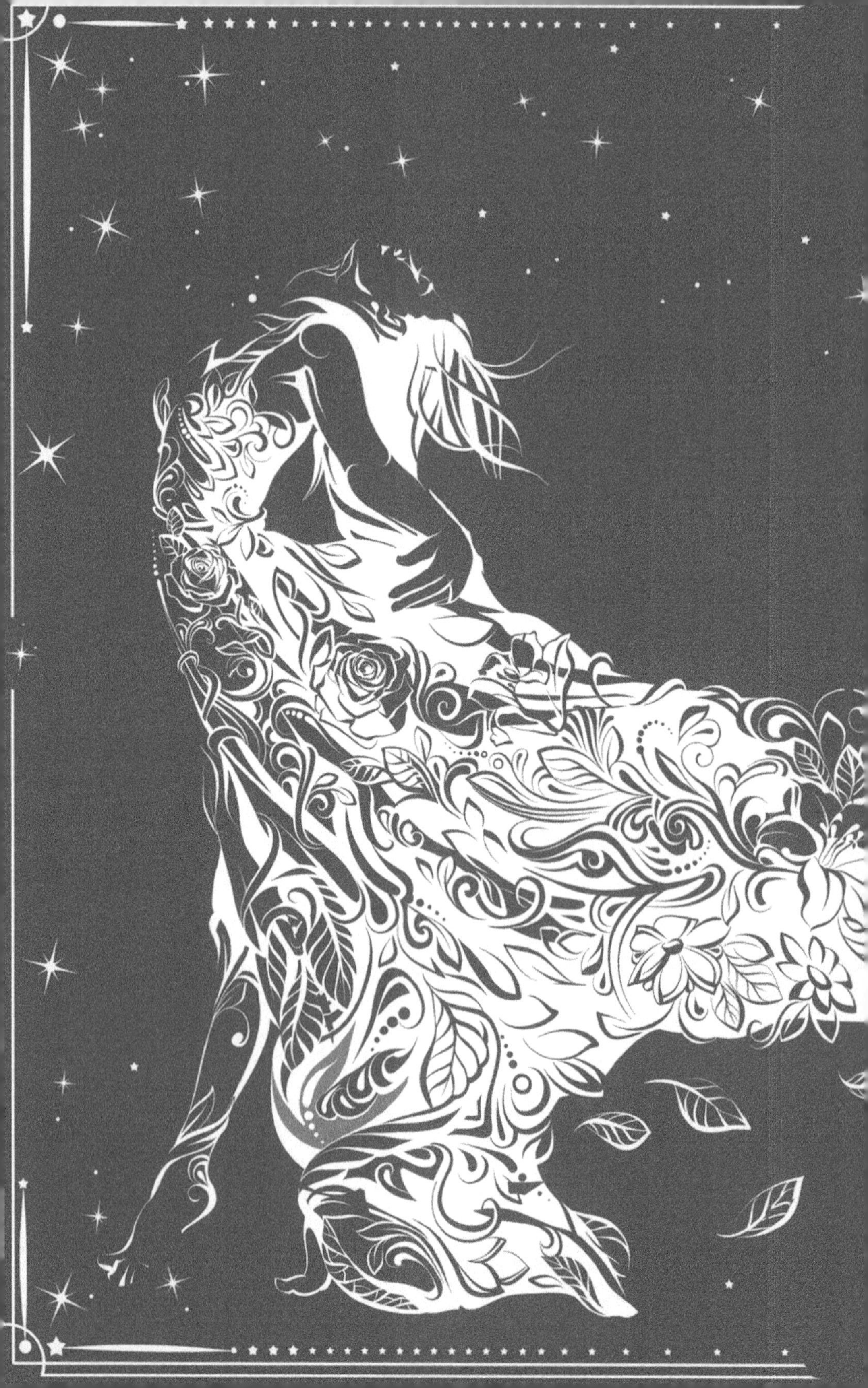

Elise

CHAPTER FORTY ONE

The wind whipped through my hair and electricity crackled along my skin as Dante flew hard and fast, speeding across the farmlands beyond the academy and stealing my pain and grief away from me as I lost myself in the moment.

It was an exhilarating ride, Dante pushing himself to his limits and making my heart race with adrenaline at every loop and swerve as he cut through the air with grace and powerful strokes of his wings.

The sky was blue and never ending above us and I could tell that Dante was working hard not to summon a storm today, allowing me to feel the heat of the sun on my skin as we sped through the sky.

I held on tightly to the huge spines which lined his back, using my air magic to keep me from falling when my grip failed me which was happening more and more often the harder he pushed me.

It was heaven. Freedom. Power. And I needed a taste of those things like a dying tree left bare in the desert. The last few days had been nothing but pain and grief for me. I'd hardly eaten. Hadn't wanted to talk. After Gabriel had found me in the forest and they brought me back to my dorm the night I'd lost all hope of finding my brother alive again, I'd wanted to do nothing but lay in bed and cry for everything I'd lost.

I hadn't been left alone once after they'd found me and the four of them hadn't so much as bickered as they'd worked together to look after me. They'd tempted me back to food then to speaking a little more and finally today, Dante had convinced me to come for this ride. And fuck had I needed it. Even more than I could have realised.

"Elise!" a faraway but determined cry caught my ear for the briefest of moments. But as I turned to try and look for the source of the call, Dante dropped into a barrel roll and I screamed as I fell from his back, tumbling down towards the ground at a furious pace.

Dante swept beneath me to catch me again a moment later and the call caught my ear for the second time, making me focus on my gifts as I twisted in my seat on Dante's back.

My eyes widened and a surprised breath of laughter fell from my lips as I spotted Leon waving furiously and yelling my name on the back of a seriously out of breath looking Griffin.

"Elise!" Leon yelled again and with my ears now trained on him, I detected the note of panic in his voice which stole my amusement and sent a dagger of fear into my gut.

"Turn around, Drago," I yelled to Dante. "Leon needs us."

Dante turned his scaly head to look up at me, his gaze moving to take in the Griffin who looked like it was seriously struggling to fly beneath Leon's weight and he whirled around suddenly.

Dante swept towards the Griffin, snapping his wings open and gliding beneath it at a slow enough pace for Leon to jump down to us.

He landed heavily, rolling across Dante's deep blue scales and I snatched his hand before he could roll all the way over his back and fall onto a wing.

"What the hell happened to you?" I asked in shock, my gut lurching with fear as I spotted the dry blood which coated his shirt and face.

"Nothing," Leon panted as he scrambled upright. "It's fake – prank – rat found me – stabbed ass - fell down stairs – hit every step - healed – not the point." I reached for him, frowning in confusion as I yanked him into place behind me.

The Griffin snared my attention as it raised its eagle head, screeched a goodbye then turned back away in the direction of the academy, its lion's ass end looking like it was running in mid-air.

"Ryder needs us," Leon gasped. "Gabriel *saw* him die. He said there's no way out of it and then Ryder said he was gonna go and face it himself. I was hiding in the locker room and I heard them, but they left so fast that I couldn't stop them because I was sort of paralysed at the time, but then I was fine because Eugene was there then I had to find you so we can help," he said in a tumble of words.

"Gabriel said there's no way out of that fate?" I breathed, my eyes widening as fear spilled through me.

"Ryder brought him with him, he said he trusted him to *see* something, some way for him to survive somehow. But I'm afraid, Elise. Gabe sounded so freaking cut up and I could tell he didn't believe that."

Dante roared loudly, the noise filled with anguish as he wheeled around and started flying hard and fast towards the city, using the connection we could all feel to one another to hunt down Ryder and Gabriel.

Leon wound his arms around my waist, gripping me tightly as his mouth fell against my ear. "We're going to change this fate, little monster," he growled. "There's no fucking way I'm letting my boyfriend-in-law die."

I nodded, unable to trust my voice in that moment as I dragged my focus away from that terrifying premonition and concentrated on what I needed to do.

"Can you refill your magic from the sun while we fly?" I asked Leon and he knew what I was asking before I even had to spell it out.

"I got you, little monster." He pressed his wrist to my mouth and I sank my fangs into him, drinking deeply from his burning hot power and filling my reserves to the brim as we sped towards our destination. I didn't know what we'd find when we got there, but I did know that I was going to be ready for a fight.

When my power was topped up, I healed the wound on Leon's wrist and took his shirt from him as he tore it off to allow the sun to find more of his flesh and recharge his power source too.

Within another few minutes, Dante dove downwards and my eyes widened as I spotted the gathered members of the Lunar Brotherhood, all of them screaming and baying for blood as they surrounded Ryder on a stage of ice.

My Basilisk was bloody and battered, his beautiful, scarred flesh cut open and bleeding while Scarlett Tide led the mob against him, letting them cut and beat him however they liked.

Gabriel was roaring threats at her from his position off to their left, his arms bound behind him and blood marking his face and chest from a beating too.

Some of the gathered members of the Brotherhood turned and spotted us coming, their yells of alarm reaching up to us as we sped closer and I threw an air shield around us before any of them could aim attacks our way.

"Ignore the Storm Dragon!" Scarlett yelled, my gifted senses picking out her words and my heart fractured as my gaze met Ryder's, his eyes full of regret and apology. He believed he was going to die here. But fuck that. "The wards won't falter," Scarlett continued. "They can't pass through them. By the time they get inside, the traitor will be long dead!"

As those words escaped her, I reached out with my power, feeling the dome of energy that surrounded them, realising she'd known we'd come and had been prepared for us. But I didn't believe for one second that they would be strong enough to keep my Dragon out.

"Tear them down, Drago!" I yelled and Dante roared as lightning exploded from his jaw, raining down on the dome of magic meant to keep us out and making the whole thing glow blue as a tremendous boom of thunder followed.

Members of the Lunar Brotherhood screamed in fright. They knew what would happen to them if that lightning penetrated their defences and it was only a matter of time before it did.

"Hold on, Scar! We're coming for you!" Leon bellowed from behind me, throwing his arms out and blasting the dome with an explosion of firepower which made it tremble and flicker as the Lunars below us fought to maintain their magic.

"Let's finish this," Scarlett yelled. "The reign of the Lunar King is over. Long live the queen!"

She advanced on Ryder with twin blades of ice in her hands and I screamed my defiance at her as Dante wheeled around, coming in hot for another attack and almost crashing into an abandoned hotel which stood beside the gathered crowd.

I slapped my hand into Leon's, the barriers around my power falling away just as he lowered his and I drove the full force of my magic into his flesh, gasping as our magic collided. Leon threw his free hand out and rained an inferno down on the wards once more, the combined might of our power making the flames burn blue with heat which licked against my skin even all the way up here.

In the same moment, Dante bellowed a roar which made the thunder crashing overhead seem tame and the lightning which burst from him was enough to rival the power of the stars themselves.

With a tremendous boom, the wards exploded beneath the might of our combined attack and the Lunars on the edge of the crowd were eviscerated before they even knew what had hit them.

Dante twisted his head, directing the immense bolt of power through their ranks before jerking it away from the spot where Ryder and Gabriel remained tied.

But before he could blast more members of the Brotherhood with his power, Scarlett raised her arms our way and a huge spear of ice shot towards us at a terrifying pace.

I snatched my hand out of Leon's, trying to throw a new air shield into place before it could hit, even though I knew I was too late.

Dante lurched aside to try and avoid the blow, but he was too big and he wasn't fast enough to escape it.

Dante roared in agony as the spear ripped through his right wing, knocking us off course and leaving me and Leon to cling onto his back for dear life.

The full power of the lightning which still poured from Dante's mouth struck the building to our left as he fought to regain control and there was an enormous boom as the entire thing shuddered ominously.

I managed to regain my balance, screaming as I lurched towards Dante's bleeding, broken wing and throwing my hands down on the edge of the wound as he fought to keep us airborne.

Healing magic poured from me in a torrent, seeking out and repairing the wound as fast as I could manage and a second before we could crash, Dante managed to right us. His claws brushed the ground before he beat his wings hard, launching himself skywards again with a roar. But I didn't have my grip in place and I rolled straight off of his back with a scream of fright.

I threw my hands out, catching myself on my air magic and landing on my feet just as Leon leapt down after me with a battle cry.

Dante continued skyward, roaring a challenge as the storm overhead built in fury and static energy crackled through the air.

I spun around, trying to gain my bearings as I lifted my hands and my fingers tingled with magic. But as my gaze fell on Ryder and Gabriel across the expanse of space that separated us, a scream of horror escaped me.

The building Dante had hit with his lightning was toppling, almost seeming to fall in slow motion toward my kings, Scarlett and the rest of the Lunar scumbags who had supported her in this.

I started to shoot towards them, but Leon caught my arm before I could move, jerking me to a halt before I could get myself killed.

The building collapsed with an ear-splitting boom in the next heartbeat, crushing everyone in its path beneath it.

"Ryder!" I roared. "Gabriel!"

I wrenched my arm out of Leon's hold, shooting up and over the rubble and coughing against the huge cloud of dust that had risen all around me in the destruction.

The bricks beneath my feet shifted suddenly and I was knocked onto my ass as one of the Lunar motherfuckers used his earth magic to rise up out of the debris.

I threw my hands out, knocking him away from me with a blast of wind and he shifted in mid-air, whinnying as he burst into a golden Pegasus and turning furious eyes on me.

But before he could come at me, a bolt of lightning blasted the rocks between us and Dante roared a challenge from the sky which the Pegasus met with a furious whinny before turning and flying after my Dragon.

I watched on in fear as more and more of the Lunars who'd avoided being crushed by the building shifted into flying Orders. They took to the sky after Dante, chasing him and using their Order gifts to attack him from behind. But as he roared again, blasting lightning strikes at them, I knew what he wanted me to do.

I shoved myself to my feet, stumbling on the uneven rubble as I used my connection to my kings to figure out where Gabriel and Ryder were. I could still feel them, so I had to believe they were alive. I just needed to get them out, heal them. It would all be okay. I had to have faith it would be or I really was going to break.

A hand gripped my elbow and Leon steadied me, his golden eyes alight with worry. "I'll go for Gabe, you find Ryder," he said. "But watch your back, little monster."

"You too," I breathed, my lips brushing his in a feather light touch before I shot away from him up the enormous mound of rubble, following the pull of the bond which would lead me to my Basilisk.

I dropped to my knees at the summit of the devastation, using my air magic to waft the cloud of dust away from me as I began to dig through the bricks, calling Ryder's name. My fingernails split and bled as I hurled more and more of the stones away from me using my gifts for strength and speed to make it go faster. But there was just so much of it. And as much as I wanted to deny the fear rising in my chest, I just couldn't see how they could have survived being pinned beneath all of this. Their hands had been tied, they couldn't use their magic to save themselves, so how could they possibly be alive amidst this devastation?

But I wouldn't give up on him. Not ever. So I gritted my teeth and moved even faster, digging and fighting and praying to all the stars in the sky for a miracle. Because he couldn't die today. I refused to let him. I'd already lost too much and Ryder hadn't even had a chance to really live. He'd suffered through so fucking much, fate couldn't be so cruel as to steal him away before he even got used to the taste of happiness on his tongue.

He wasn't going to die today.

He *wasn't*.

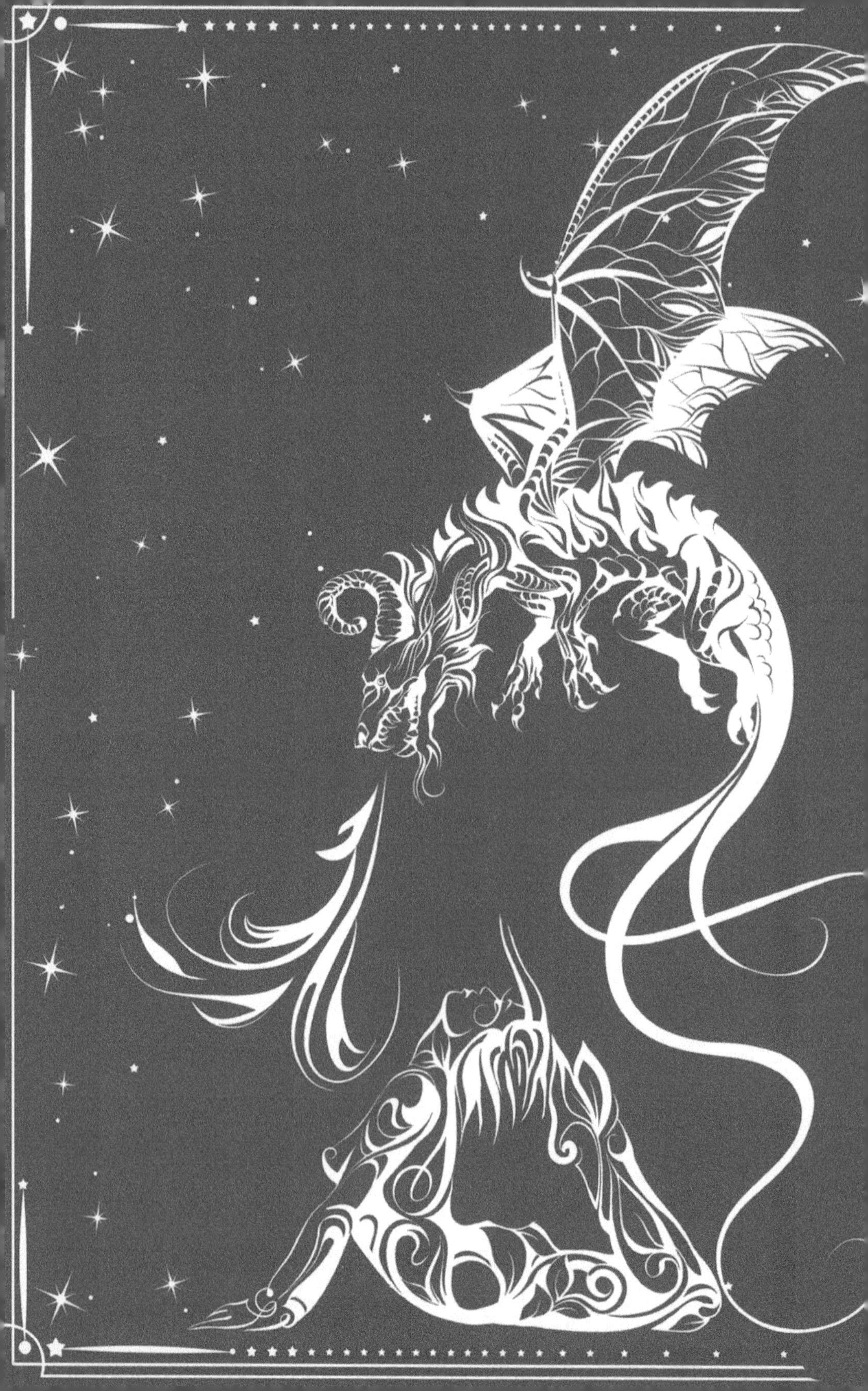

Dante

CHAPTER FORTY TWO

I led the gang of Pegasuses, Griffins, Harpies and any other flying stronzo who'd taken to the skies after me deeper into the city. I kept low, wheeling left and right down the streets and using the buildings as cover from the blasts of magic being fired at me.

A gold Pegasus was hot on my heels and it jammed its sharp horn into my flank. I roared in anger, putting on a burst of speed and whipping my tail hard to the side, smashing into the Pegasus and sending him crashing into a wall. He died on impact, glitter exploding from him as a shower of blood painted the wall red and he tumbled down toward the ground. My heart beat harder at the victory, but I wasn't out of the woods yet.

A Harpy girl flew after me with a scream, landing on my back and stabbing something sharp between my scales. I snarled furiously and sent a blast of electricity rolling down my spine that killed her instantly and she tumbled from my back, hitting the street below with a hard thwack.

The group behind me fell back as a line of lightning crackled off the end of my tail in warning and they realised touching me was a seriously bad idea.

I banked sharply down another street, my wings grazing the rooftops and my body shadowing the ground below, sending Fae screaming and running for cover as I sailed overhead. I needed to circle back to Elise, make sure she was safe. But I wasn't going to be bringing any of these stronzos with me.

I spotted a bridge up ahead that crossed the river and flew harder and faster towards it as an idea struck me.

A spear slammed into my back and I roared in anger just before another hit my leg. I flapped my wings, tearing along the road and sizing up the gap beneath the bridge. It would be a tight fit, but I could make it. And if they followed, they were going to fly right into my trap.

I weaved left and right to avoid the spears being thrown at me from a group of Harpies, my tail carving huge holes in the buildings as it smashed into them.

I snarled as a blue Pegasus flew beneath my belly and I swiped my claws at him as he tried to stab me with his horn. He flew faster, aiming for my throat with a furious whinny leaving him and the second he got near enough, I bent my head down and snapped him up between my jaws, swinging my head and sending him flying into a building beside me hard enough to finish him. I set my sights on the bridge ahead, counting down the seconds to reaching it.

Tre, due, uno-

I dipped down low at the last second, tucking my wings and sailing beneath the bridge just as a train went overhead, blaring its horn loudly, blocking my enemies' flight path and forcing them to follow me under the bridge.

I raced to the other side then pulled up hard, flapping my wings to gain height as quickly as possible before flipping back down to face the water. I drew on the storm within my soul, harnessing the wind and raising the water in a huge swell just as the flying Orders poured out from beneath the bridge.

The wave crashed over them as thunder boomed above me in the clouds and rain poured down. As they all went into the river's depths, I opened my jaws and released a bolt of lightning that shook me right down to my bones.

Electricity flashed out across the water, killing each and every one of them in an instant and their bodies floated up to the surface like driftwood.

I bellowed a roar at my victory as my chest swelled and a whole crowd of Fae watched from the streets in terror as I took off into the sky and raced back towards Elise and mio amicos.

I flew furiously back to the building I'd accidentally brought down in the street, fear weighing my heart down at the possibility that I'd killed my brothers. But they were strong, and both were earth Elementals. Maybe they'd acted quickly enough to save themselves. Maybe Leon and Elise had already found them.

As I made it back to destruction, I brought the rain down on the rising dust to clear my view of the rubble, hunting for any sign of mia famiglia. Panic clutched my heart and I prayed to the stars that they would keep them all safe.

I spotted Leon tearing through the rubble as he searched for my fratellos then Elise on the far side of the hill of debris, digging for them too.

My gaze suddenly hooked on some movement just beyond her where the surviving Lunars were regrouping and my blood turned to ice as Scarlett appeared from the wreckage, dragging a half-conscious Ryder out of the bricks and making my heart lurch with panic.

He was bloody, battered, weak and Scarlett had the smuggest kind of smile on her face as she hauled him along with a fierce determination. The Lunars clustered around them and I roared out to warn Elise, making her gaze flip up to me in the sky.

I swept forward with another roar, meaning to pluck Ryder right out of that bitch's grasp, but the Fae surrounding her turned on me as one, firing magic at me in ferocious blasts which forced me to wheel aside, beating my wings to gain more height.

I looked back over my shoulder as Elise tried to make a run for him too, but more of the Brotherhood rushed to fight her off.

Scarlett had two men tie ropes to Ryder's wrists and cranked him up to hang by his arms from a Centaur statue which somehow still stood tall amongst the rubble of the hotel I'd destroyed.

Terror beat a path through my body as Scarlett closed in on Ryder with a blade of ice in her hand and as I looked to Elise, I found more Lunars closing in around her.

I roared in anger as a bunch of them spotted me and more flying Orders shifted and took flight, readying to fight me and keep me away from the people I loved. I cursed in my mind as I flew down to intercept them, desperate to get to Ryder and help. But as they collided with me with powerful strikes of magic, I was lost to a battle of my own and I feared I would be too late.

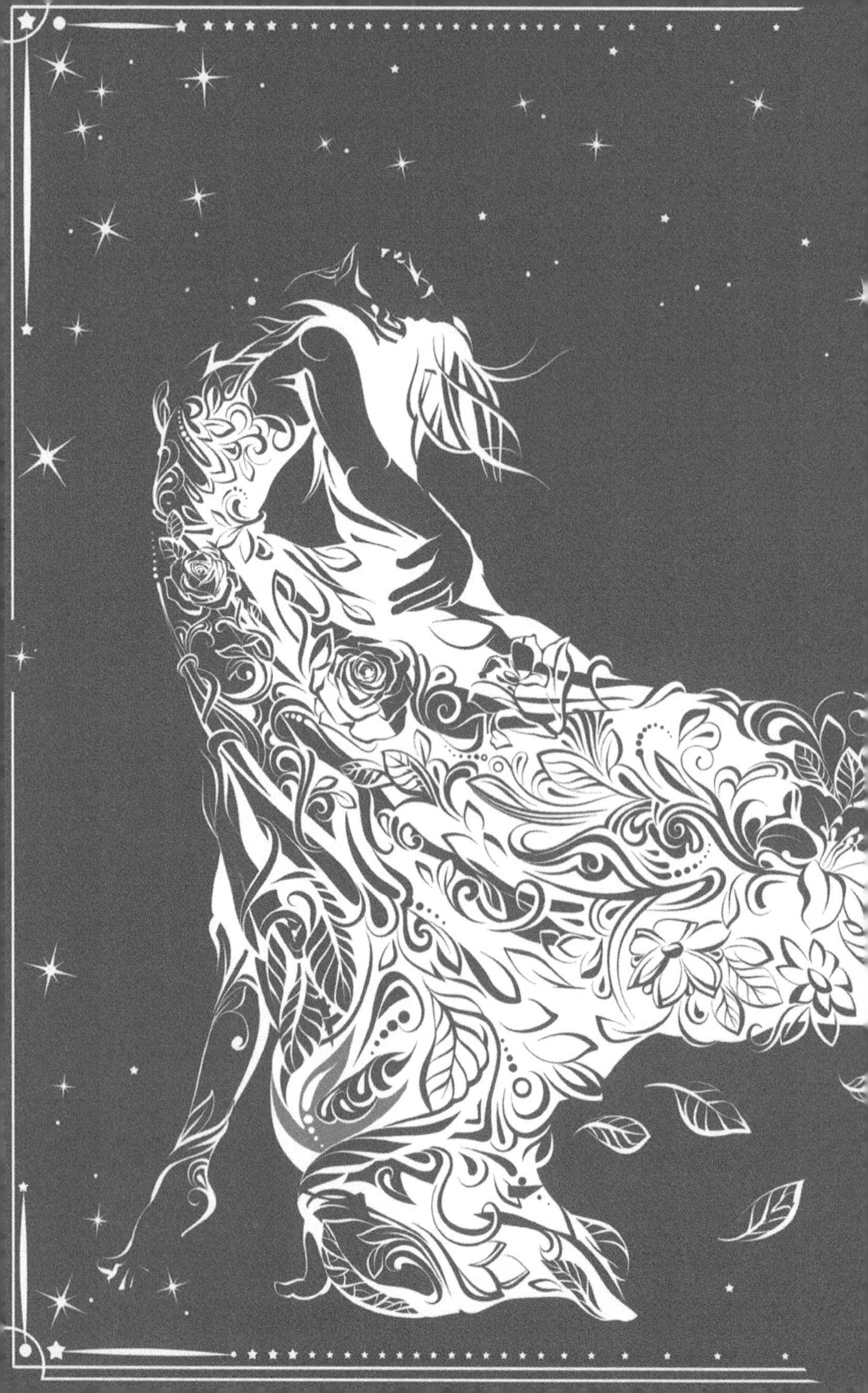

Elise

CHAPTER FORTY THREE

I shot across the heaped bricks, darting left and right as more and more of the Lunar Brotherhood emerged from the rubble of the destroyed building and started firing their magic at me while I fought to get close to Ryder.

He was tied to the statue of a Centaur which stood beside Scarlett, his arms pulled wide and feet just grazing the floor.

Scarlett was watching me, her eyes narrowed and a smirk tilting up the corner of her mouth as she got a bull of a man to force Ryder's jaws wide open.

"Ryder!" I screamed and his bright green eyes whirled to me, a thousand words filling his gaze as he watched me fighting for him.

But Scarlett wasn't going to give me the time to get there.

A wave of fire blasted into my air shield and I was forced to drop to one knee while I fought to maintain my magic. I snarled in fury as Scarlett lifted a blade into position, angling it towards Ryder's open mouth while he struggled against his bonds.

"Ryder!" I bellowed, my voice cracking as my thundering heart raced wildly with the desperate need to get to him and the rain from Dante's storm crashed down over us.

Scarlett reached into his mouth and with a savage swipe of her blade, she severed his tongue, laughing as she hurled the lump of flesh away from her, the silver flash of Ryder's piercing catching the light as it hit the ground.

I screamed so loud that it tore my throat and my concentration faltered enough for a bitch with water magic to shatter my shield.

A torrent of ice cold water sent me flying to the ground, my cheek smashing against a lump of broken brick and pain blinded me as blood spilled down my face.

Before I recovered from the agony of the wound, ice formed in thick and unbreakable lumps around my hands, a gasp escaping me as my magic was blocked off. The bitch who had beaten me cried out in triumph, fisting a hand in my hair, and casting a blade of ice into her hand which she pressed to my throat.

My gaze met with Ryder's as blood poured from his mouth, coating his jaw and painting him red as Dante was forced to fly further away from us and his storm went with him, the rain parting and leaving my view of the man I loved clear.

My heart seemed to still as I saw our deaths in Ryder's eyes, panic clawing at my insides as I realised this was it. Not just for him but for me as well.

I'd always known that the things I'd wanted to achieve when I enrolled at Aurora Academy might be the death of me. But as I knelt there with that blade pressing to my throat and my lungs expanding with their final breath, all I wanted in the world was more time. I'd found so much love while trying to fight back against my grief. In the darkest of places, the four men I'd once suspected of the worst of crimes had come to lead me to a position of peace and light. I'd barely even taken a taste of it yet and as I realised I'd already been gifted all that I would get to take from this world, I knew it wasn't nearly enough.

"I love you," I breathed, my eyes on Ryder, but my words for all of my kings. Because that was the one truest thing I owned. My love for them was too big and too powerful to die here with me. It was going to break free of my body and take flight on the wind. It would never be caged, never be tethered, never be controlled. I loved them and I needed them and I wanted so much more of them. But if this was all I got to have then at least for the briefest of times, I'd known what being loved by them felt like and that was the greatest gift the stars ever could have given me. I only wished I could have stolen a little more of it.

"Stop!" Scarlett bellowed just as the bitch pressed her knife in harder, my skin splitting and a bead of blood rolling down my neck. "She's mine. I want the whore who caused all of this to watch while I kill her mate and then I'm going to gut her myself."

Ryder yelled something but the stump that had once been his tongue made it impossible for anyone to understand his words before Scarlett backhanded him to shut him up.

"I've got Order Suppressant!" some asshole shouted as he ran forward, looking at Ryder's bleeding form with hunger in his eyes before turning that look on me. "Let's make sure his Vampire whore can't bite anyone."

Scarlett opened her mouth, almost looking like she was going to protest against anyone else interfering with her plans but then she just nodded, that cruel smirk back on her face. I narrowed my eyes at her, letting her know without words that I was going to rip her to fucking pieces for this if I got the slightest chance.

I hissed in anger as the needle was rammed into my neck and within seconds my gifts were stripped away from me, leaving me feeling weak and even more vulnerable before them. But that wouldn't stop me. If I got the opportunity, I was going to kill them all.

My gaze flicked up to the heavens where the roiling thunder clouds flashed with lightning repeatedly, but there was still no sign of Dante returning for us. Clearly his own battle was keeping him away, but I knew he'd come back for us as soon as he possibly could. Maybe all I had to do was stall for time.

Scarlett seemed to be thinking the same thing though and she turned to yell out to her followers, raising her bloody knife above her head like a trophy.

"Who wants to see the traitor king bleed?" she cried.

The crowd of Lunars screamed their approval to the sky and I tried to lurch to my feet, but the bitch holding me just cast more ice all around my legs and stomach to immobilise me completely.

Scarlett turned back to Ryder, her eyes alight with excitement as she held the blade pointed at his stomach and looked right at him.

"Any last words?" she taunted, knowing full well he couldn't reply.

Ryder glared at her, yelling something incomprehensible as he looked between the surrounding members of the Brotherhood like he was desperately looking for an ally among them, imploring them with his eyes to turn on this bitch and support their king.

As his gaze met mine, Scarlett drove the knife in hard and I screamed, lurching forward and fighting against the ice that contained me with everything I had, but it wouldn't budge an inch.

Scarlett laughed and stabbed him again. And again. Over and over until there was so much blood that the whole world seemed to run red with it, painting her and him and everyone standing close enough to them too.

Dante roared in the heavens above as my heart ripped into a million tiny pieces and I screamed Ryder's name in a desperate plea for him not to leave me.

Scarlett dropped her dagger and turned to one of the men beside her as the sky above lit with lightning and Dante burst from the clouds overhead.

The man handed her a heavy axe and she weighed it between her hands, laughing loudly as she lined it up with Ryder's neck before hefting it back.

"No!" I screamed and Ryder's green eyes lifted to mine, his gaze full of pain and regret which tore me apart.

"Long live the king!" Scarlett cried, swinging the axe with all her strength and the scream that escaped me was enough to tear the whole world apart and call the stars down from the sky as I watched Ryder's head tumble from his body.

It rolled and bounced across the heap of rubble and my whole universe imploded as it came to halt before me, his lifeless eyes reflecting the storm above as I fought against the ice containing me and screamed so hard, I was sure he could still hear me in the afterlife.

My beautiful, brave, strong mate was gone. His life cut too short and lived in so much pain. He was my soul, my heart, my torturous agony and one of the deepest loves I'd ever known. And as my screams of grief and pain continued to ring out into the heavens, I knew that this was a grief I would truly never recover from.

Ryder Draconis was dead. And my world would never again be filled with his light.

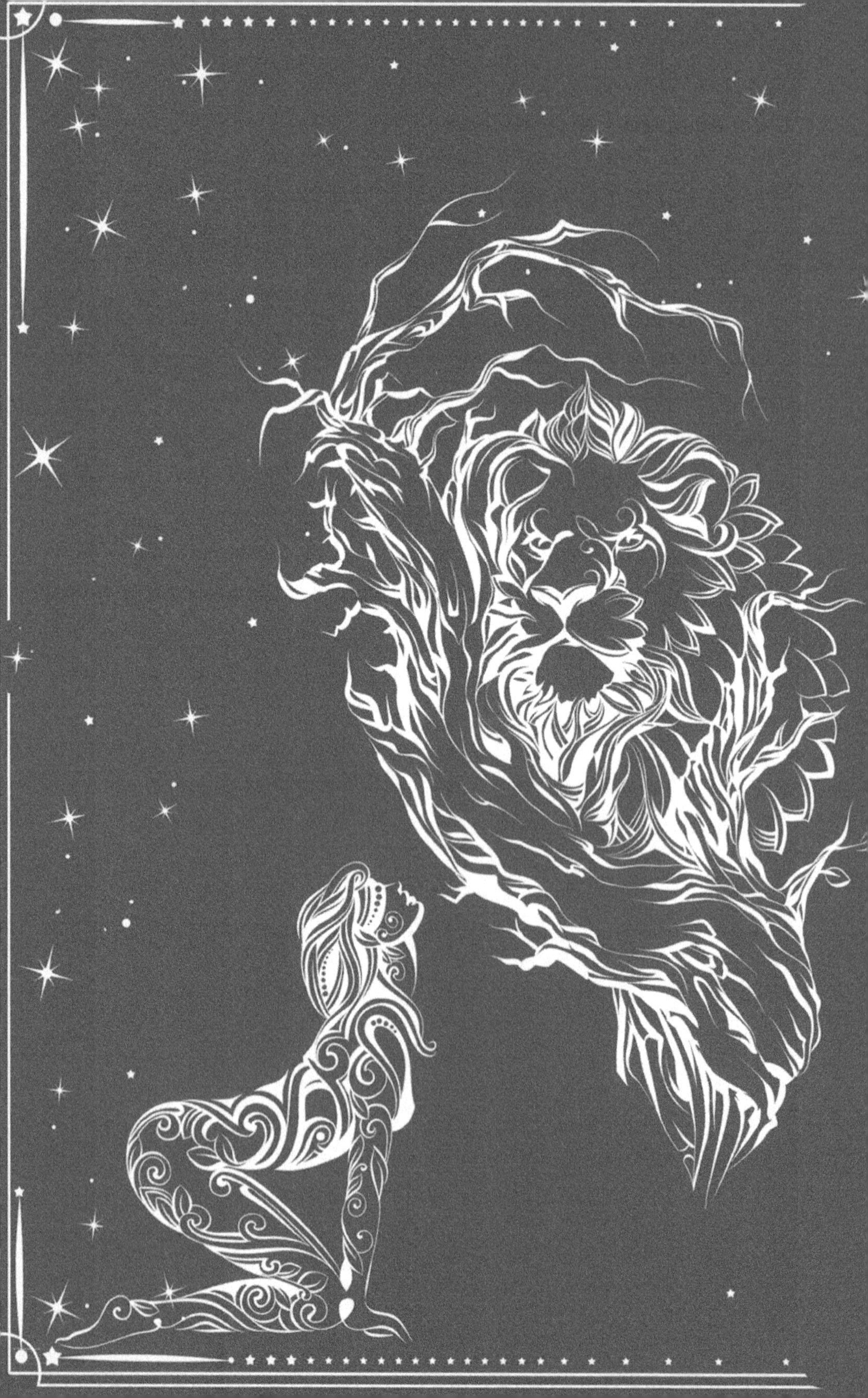

LEON

CHAPTER FORTY FOUR

I dug through the bricks in desperation, calling out for Gabriel. I couldn't see anything that was going on beyond the piled rubble to my right, but the Lunars were all shouting and were worked up into a frenzy somewhere close by. I just prayed that wasn't because they were winning this fight.

"Gabe!" I cried, sensing his connection to me growing closer and closer as I searched for him. "Gabe where are you?" I roared, throwing huge chunks of stone over my shoulder as I battled my way into the depths of the crumbling masonry.

I wasn't going to panic. I just needed to focus and find my Harpy. If he was conscious, he'd be able to *see* me digging for him. He'd know his Lion was coming.

"Hold on Gabe!" I called, digging furiously, my hands bloody and my teeth clenched as I battled to free him.

I glimpsed a black feather through the mass of bricks which made my heart race with a mixture of relief and terror as I dug more furiously, finding one twisted, broken wing before I glimpsed a bloody hand deeper in the rubble. Dante swept over me and rain beat down on my back, washing the sweat and grime from my body as I worked to free Gabe as fast as I could.

I unveiled his tattooed chest and the cuts all across his body before fighting the rubble away from his head. He groaned in agony, his limbs all twisted up and his face cut to shit.

"I'm here, Gabe, I'm here."

"Don't call me…Gabe," he rasped, then passed out, falling entirely still.

I pushed away the last of the bricks, hauling him out of the carnage into my arms and resting my hands on his torn flesh with a noise of anguish leaving me. I pressed my magic into his body, fear gripping me at how still he was as my power latched onto his and I began to heal him. He had so many injuries I didn't know where to begin, I just focused on spreading my magic into his chest and worked outwards from there. But when he didn't move, I started to freak out.

"Gabe!" I shook him, but he remained lifeless in my arms. "Gabriel Nox!" I shouted, slapping his cheek, but he still didn't wake up.

I kept healing him, laying him down on the rocks and rearing over him, pinching his nose with one hand and breathing straight into his mouth. I'd seen that shit on mortal TV and my mind was in a complete spiral so I couldn't think of anything else to try. I kept my hand on his chest, flooding his body with as much power as I had to give as I tried to heal him faster.

Wake up, dude, wake up.

His fingers suddenly pushed into my hair and I kept breathing into his mouth, figuring it was working.

"Elise," he murmured against my lips, then his tongue met mine and I laughed loudly, hugging him to me as he spluttered fully awake.

"*Leon*," he wheezed as I forced the breath out of his chest, crushing him in my arms.

"You're alive," I half sobbed, holding onto him and nuzzling his head. "I saved you."

"You kissed me," he growled.

"It was the kiss of life." I leaned back, inspecting his bloody face as the rain beat over it and washed it away.

"What?" he grunted, wincing from his wounds. I released him, gazing down at his broken wings and summoning the last of my power to finish what I'd started.

"Just stay still, I'll get you healed. I swear it." I pressed my hands to his wings, figuring he must have tried to fly out of harm's way when the building fell. The Sight sure hadn't helped him avoid this one, but I guessed as a bunch of Lunars were holding him down, he hadn't had much choice but to take the hit.

Dante flew overhead with a deafening roar, twisting through the air and blasting a Griffin to pieces with a shot of lightning that daggered through the sky.

"Ryder?" Gabriel rasped, a note of pain in his voice and I looked back down at him as a lump sharp rose in my throat.

"I don't know," I admitted, unable to see beyond the huge pile of bricks around us.

"I can't *see* anything. What if we're too late?" Gabriel tried to move, but he groaned, falling back down again and I pressed a hand to his shoulder, giving him a serious look.

"Stay still," I demanded. "You're not going anywhere like this. I'll get you healed then we'll find our family together."

Gabriel watched me as I worked as fast as I could to heal his twisted wings and he reached out to rest a hand on my shoulder.

"Thank you, Simba," he breathed.

I smiled tightly at him as a breath of relief left me. "You're welcome, Zazu."

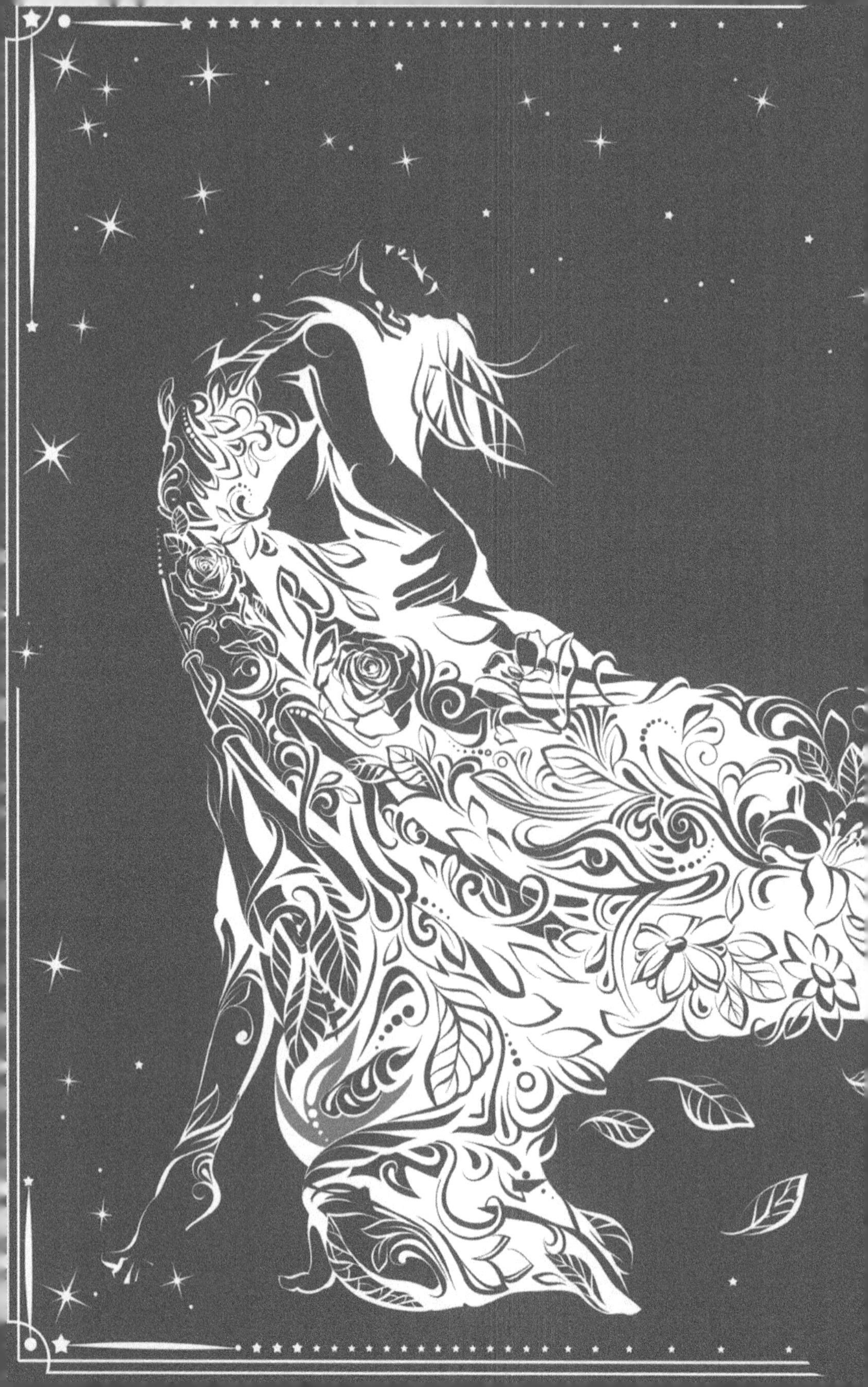

Elise

CHAPTER FORTY FIVE

The baying of a Wolf pack bit into my ears as the Lunar Brotherhood closed in around me while I trembled in the wake of Ryder's death.

My mind was a fog of grief and pain and I sucked in shuddering breaths as I tried to focus on anything other than the venomous pain that was destroying me from the inside out.

"Move aside," Scarlett snapped. "I told you, she's mine."

Booted feet came to a halt in front of me and I snarled as she reached out to grasp my chin, forcing my gaze up to meet hers so that she could drink in the pain in my eyes. Her fingers bit into my flesh, Ryder's blood making them slick and marking my skin as a cold, poisonous hatred seeped through my limbs.

There was room for one, single emotion in me besides this soul crushing grief. And that was rage. I was going to kill this bitch if it was the last thing I did. She would end her life bleeding out at my feet, and I would be sure to make it as painful as physically possible.

"Rip her apart!" someone yelled from behind me.

"Kill the whore!" another cried.

"Make her bleed!"

"Silence," Scarlett snapped, her gaze raking over me before darting around the crowd like she was considering how best to make me suffer. I only hoped she took her time so that I had an opportunity to destroy her.

The howling sounded again and Scarlett sucked in a sharp breath as she looked off to my right and her grip on my face angled my gaze that way too.

My eyes widened as I spotted the Wolf pack racing our way, many of them being ridden by other Fae who wielded magic and weapons in their hands like a force of warriors.

At first, I thought the Oscura Clan had arrived to take on the Lunars in a war which would break the peace deal and send Alestria into chaos and carnage once more. But as my gaze travelled over them and I spotted who led the charge, I realised it wasn't the Oscuras at all.

At the front of the pack, his muscular chest bare and blonde hair swept back from his face, Ethan Shadowbrook ran at full speed in his Fae form. His tattooed hands cupped around his mouth as he howled for the pack and they returned his call a hundred times over.

The rest of the Lunar Brotherhood had come to protect their king, their fury over this treason written into their features and their loyalty to Ryder branded onto their hearts. *If only they hadn't come too late.*

"For the true king!" Ethan roared, running even faster as the loyal members of the Lunar Brotherhood roared their approval and leapt into battle.

Ethan threw his hands out at us and a tsunami of water crashed over Scarlett and her followers, driving into me too and washing all of them away from me while the ice I was trapped in kept me in place.

I held my breath as the wave crashed over me before it finally fell away and I found Ethan standing before me, his eyes wild with fear as he melted the ice from my limbs.

"Tell me I'm not too late," he breathed as I scrambled to my feet, but I couldn't force myself to say the words.

I didn't need to anyway. Ryder's decapitated body was still strung up against the statue, his scars and tattoos making it clear exactly who he had been, and an agonised cry escaped Ethan's lips as he spotted him.

The grief hit me again too, the pain of it so raw that I could hardly breathe, but as my eyes burned with all the tears I knew I would cry for my Basilisk, my gaze fell on Scarlett Tide's retreating form as she turned tail and ran.

A furious, vengeful snarl escaped my lips and I broke into a run as I took chase, racing after her as she sped towards the buildings beyond the devastation, aiming for the shadows where she could escape her death.

But there was no fucking chance I was going to let that happen.

This was the one thing I had left to give to Ryder. The one thing I could do for him now after all he'd done for me.

Scarlett Tide would die today. And I was going to take pleasure in delivering her to her end.

I broke into a run, cursing as the rubble made me slip and stumble and the Order Suppressant kept my gifts locked away from me. But it didn't matter if I was without my speed or my strength. This was what I was designed for. The hunt was what my kind were built for. I had the scent of her blood now and fangs or not, I would be claiming her life this day.

Thumping footsteps raced along at my side and I glanced to my right, spotting Ethan beside me, keeping pace as he took to the hunt too.

"She's mine," I snarled, needing him to know that. This had to be me. Not him. Not anyone else. Her death was on *me*.

"I just need to see her pay," he growled back and the two of us leapt over the last of the rubble side by side before taking chase into the narrow streets.

Scarlett had a good head start on us, but none of the rage we held in our souls. Her need for life couldn't possibly match our thirst for her death.

My lungs laboured as I ran and my muscles burned, but I welcomed the pain, the lack of my gifts. I wanted it to be this way. Bloody and brutal and as painful as possible for everyone involved.

Scarlett darted down an alley and we tore after her, leaving the rest of the fight far behind as our footsteps pounded down the abandoned street. Any Fae who might have been close by when this started had clearly run as far from the carnage as possible and that suited me just fine. Because now there wouldn't be any witnesses to what I was about to do.

We rounded a corner and there she stood, her back to a brick wall, caught in a dead end like a rat in a trap.

"Wait," Scarlett breathed, but I had no interest in anything she had to say to me. I needed to feel her death on my hands, and I wasn't going to wait a moment longer.

Ethan tossed me something and I caught it on instinct, my gaze falling on a serrated blade carved from ice. It looked brutal and lethal and like the exact kind of weapon I needed to end this bitch.

I didn't want to do it with magic. I wanted to *feel* her die.

I bared my teeth as I ran at her and her eyes flared with something I couldn't quite place as she raised a hand between us.

But when I braced for her attack, none came, not a drop of magic accosted me and I grinned savagely as I realised she was tapped out. *Even better.*

I bellowed in fury as I swung the dagger back and her eyes widened.

"Wait, I'm-"

I stole the air from her lungs, not wanting to hear a single word from her vile mouth and in the next second my fist crashed into her jaw and I slammed into her hard enough to knock us both tumbling to the ground.

We rolled and she tried to pin me down, fighting to grasp my wrist and keep the blade away from her flesh.

I leaned down and sank my teeth into her hand, not giving a shit if I didn't have fangs and just ripping a chunk of flesh free, making her yank her hand away from me again as she gasped for air I wouldn't allow her.

That was her mistake.

I slammed the dagger into her stomach, the wet spill of her blood coated my fist as I ripped the jagged blade free and drove it in again and again, screaming my grief and fury at her as I tried to inflict as much fucking pain as I could.

Tears blurred my vision, but I blinked them away hard and as I looked back down at her hateful face, a horrified scream ripped from my throat.

Instead of looking down at Scarlett beneath me, I found Ryder there instead, his jaw gritted against the pain of the knife which was still buried in his gut and I instantly released the magic blocking the air from his lungs.

"Holy shit, baby," he wheezed, reaching for my face with bloodstained fingers which bumped against my cheek clumsily.

"Ryder?" I gasped, choking on my grief as confusion and relief warred together inside me and I just stared at him, trying to understand. My hand moved to cup his cheek, my thumb grazing over the stubble lining his jaw as I tried to figure out what I was seeing.

"By the stars, he needs healing," Ethan growled, recovering faster than me and hurrying forward. He dropped to his knees beside us while I just stared down at the man I loved and tried to figure out how I was possibly seeing him right now.

Ryder coughed, blood sliding from his lips and something clicked together in my brain, a gasp escaping me as I looked down at the ice blade I'd driven into his gut just as Ethan melted it out of existence.

A strangled cry escaped me as I realised what I'd just done and who I'd done it to, and I pressed my hand to one of the deepest stab wounds as Ethan worked to heal another. I threw every drop of my power into healing the injuries, tears slipping down my cheeks as apologies spilled from my lips over and over.

Ryder pushed his fingers into my hair, winding them tight as he forced me to raise my eyes to his.

"Don't you apologise to me for this, baby," he growled. "I almost got you killed out there. A few good hits to the gut are the least I deserve from you for that."

"Don't," I breathed, dropping my eyes from his to stare at the blood coating his chest again as I continued to heal him alongside Ethan. "Don't try and make me feel better for-"

"For what? For avenging me? For loving me so much that you chased that bitch out here and tried to inflict as much pain on her as you could manage in my name? I'm not mad at you, I'm fucking proud of you." He choked out a laugh but nothing about this was amusing.

I shook my head, my heart thumping painfully in my chest as I took in exactly what I'd done. I'd silenced him. What if I'd gone for his heart instead of his gut? I could have killed him without even knowing it was him. I'd come so close to destroying my own heart and my fingers were trembling with the shock of what I'd done.

Ryder growled at me, grasping my hair even tighter and making me look right at him. I fell into his gaze, sucking in a breath as he tugged me into his hypnosis and I was assaulted with so many images of the two of us that I could hardly take them all in.

I saw myself through his eyes and felt how he had felt around me in every moment we'd spent together since the very first time he'd seen me. I felt his lust, his jealousy, the pure, venomous rage he'd harboured over Dante and the others. And I felt the emptiness that had lived within him before me and exactly how I'd helped to fill that void with each touch, each caress, every word and moment spent together. Every time I failed to fear him or pushed him out of his comfort zone. I felt his damage and I felt my own, the way we'd come together and made something so new and pure out of so many fractured, broken pieces. He even showed me myself as I'd appeared at the end of this alleyway, my eyes alight with grief and fury, bloodlust spilling through every inch of my frame and he'd been so proud, felt so loved as he saw what his death had done to me. Even as I'd slammed a blade into his gut over and over, his love for me and his understanding of mine for him had been the biggest thing he felt. Pain was beautiful to him and he drank mine in like a dying man in desperate need of water.

"You're mine, baby," Ryder growled, appearing in front of me, whole and healed within the vision and cupping my face between his hands. "And I'm yours. There isn't anyone or any damn thing in this world which will ever tear us apart. You'd better believe that."

He kissed me, hard and brutal but totally unhurried, just drinking me in and letting me feel every one of those words as the vision slipped away and I found myself truly kissing him. Ethan had shifted back, the stab wounds healed and Ryder right there beneath me once more as I straddled him on the floor of the dirty alleyway.

And nothing in the world even mattered anymore. Because I had him and there was no way I was going to let him leave me ever again.

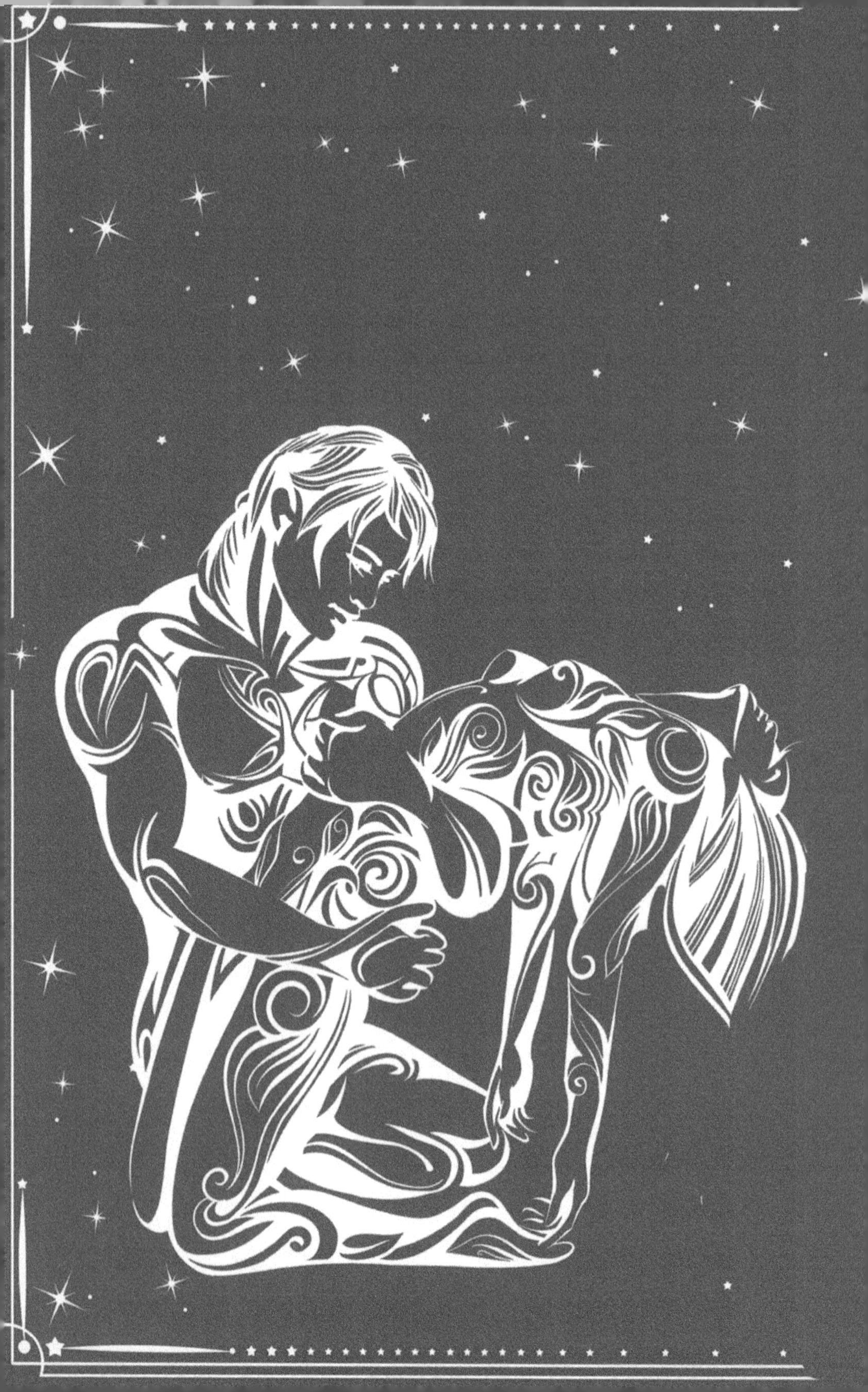

Ryder

CHAPTER FORTY SIX

Long before I wanted to, I broke the kiss with Elise, knowing we needed to get the fuck out of here and make ourselves scarce.

Elise stood up, tugging on my hand to help me to my feet too and Ethan dove at me, hugging me tight.

"My king," he growled in my ear, but those words didn't belong to me anymore.

I held him for a moment, thankful for the loyalty he'd shown me. He'd been at my side through every uprising over the peace deal, had put the bodies of our own people in the ground in the name of it. He'd been trying to prevent a rebellion for as long as I had in the name of a better future for this city, and I was endlessly grateful to him for it.

I released him and he looked down at the shredded leather catsuit I was wearing with a snort of laughter. My muscles had busted out of it and it was digging into my ass like a motherfucker, but I didn't exactly have time for a costume change right now.

"How'd you even pull this off, boss?" Ethan asked, carving his fingers through his blonde hair and looking at me in awe.

"I used my Order gifts to disguise her body as mine and mine as hers," I answered, my eyes snapping to Elise and her lips parted. "I didn't even know I could do it until I tried. Gabriel showed me how."

"So that means the Ryder I saw decapitated hanging from that statue was-"

"Scarlett," I confirmed with a smirk. "I'll explain everything fully, but first we need to get our family out of here and…" I looked to Ethan, sizing him up as he raised his chin and pride flared in his gaze. "There's no one in the Brotherhood more worthy of my crown than you, Shadowbrook."

His brows pulled together in confusion and a whine escaped his throat. "What's that supposed to mean?"

"It means I've got to disappear forever and you'll probably make a better king than I ever did anyway," I said.

"No," Ethan snarled furiously and I stepped forward, resting a hand on his shoulder as I gazed into his blue eyes.

"This isn't a request, it's a final order from your king. You're going to take my place and ensure the peace treaty is upheld. And you're not going to tell anyone I'm alive. As far as this city knows, that body back there is mine and it's going to stay that way."

"Ryder," Elise gasped. "You can't."

"I can," I growled. "It's the only way." I curled my hand around the back of Ethan's neck and yanked him forward so his forehead pressed to mine. "Consider this your coronation."

I released him and he howled mournfully, scraping a hand over his face. "You can't just cease to exist," he snarled. "What kind of fate is that? With everyone thinking you died at the hands of that traitor, unFae whore?"

"It's not up for debate," I snapped. "Ryder Draconis dies here today. This is the end of his story and you will tell it to our people. There is no other version. There will always be members of the Brotherhood who question my motives for peace while I rule. My bond to Dante makes it impossible for them not to and today will only end up repeating itself if I stay. They need a new leader now. One who they can back with the full knowledge that your motivations are purely for the good of the gang and their future. I was the leader they used to need. You're the one they deserve now."

Ethan shook his head, his face screwed up in horror at those words. "It's not what you deserve. No one is going to know how powerful you truly are, how you deceived us all and proved that you're the greatest Fae in this city."

I blew out a laugh, looking to Elise. "I don't need greatness, Ethan," I said seriously. "I have love and a family and a whole life waiting for me that the Brotherhood never could have offered me."

"You're really giving up everything you've worked for for *love*?" he scoffed like that made no sense to him at all and I hissed at him.

"If you're ever lucky enough to find what I have found, then you will realise you would give up everything to keep it," I spat and his eyes widened, clearly thinking I was mad, but I knew what real madness was now. Remaining in my past, alone with no one to care for but myself was the definition of it.

Elise took my hand, smiling sadly at Ethan. "The world is a small price to pay for your mate."

Ethan seemed confused, but didn't question either of us again, bowing his head in sadness as he accepted this fate. He would be a king, and a great one at that. But he would never understand why I so willingly handed him my crown until he didn't need it himself anymore. I hoped for his sake, that day would come for him.

Leon and Dante suddenly ran into the alley and I was accosted by them, dragged into the fiercest hug of my life.

"You fucking stronzo," Dante laughed.

"Gabe said you were here, but I didn't believe it. I saw your body back there. I saw your fucking decapitated head, dude!" Leon licked my face and I just let him as I held my brothers close then grabbed Elise to yank her into the fold as well.

Dante was very fucking naked and I didn't even give a shit as the love of my brothers and my girl surrounded me and I knew that with them I would always have a place where I belonged in this world.

"Yeah, yeah," I said gruffly, though I couldn't fight the smile off of my face. "We should get going. Where's Gabriel?"

"Here."

My family split apart and looked to him at the end of the alleyway, carrying a dead traitor bitch over his shoulder. Gabriel's chest was bare and splattered with blood. He looked like an angel of death, his hair matted with blood and the sharp angles of his handsome face thrown in shadow.

He tossed the dead woman at our feet then stepped over her and pulled me into a tight hug. "I could *see* how it was gonna play out, but finding your decapitated head still gave me a fucking heart attack." He released me then Elise dove at him and she kissed him hard as he stole a moment with her, his arms wrapping around her.

"I watched you get crushed by a building," she choked out and he gave her a sideways smile.

"Yeah, it hurt like a bitch too," he said then released her.

"What's the plan?" Leon asked urgently, taking hold of my hand and I shook him off. He might have been my boyfriend-in-law, but by the stars, we didn't need to start hand holding.

"Ryder, you need to use your chameleon gifts to disguise this dead girl as Scarlett," Gabriel said and I nodded, dropping down to do as he said.

"What about her clothes?" Ethan asked. "Won't someone notice they're gone?"

"Take them off, say she shifted," Gabriel supplied easily.

I finished up making the decoy body, it wasn't just an illusion, my power made this body Scarlett's completely, just as the decapitated body laying out in the rubble was mine. It was a fierce power that only I could control, so nothing could remove it but me. I stripped the clothes off of the dead Fae and Ethan picked up the fake Scarlett then nodded to me, emotion burning in his gaze.

"Take credit for her death," I told Ethan and he nodded though he still seemed unhappy with my decision. "Then make sure both the bodies are burned before the FIB arrive. I may be able to conceal them, but their DNA will show the truth."

"Okay. Will I ever see you again?" he asked tightly.

"I'll get in touch," I promised. "But whenever we speak from this day forward, call me Carson Alvion."

"Okay, Carson," Ethan said with his eyes glistening.

"Thank you," I said seriously then glanced at the others. "Everyone say goodbye to the new King of the Lunar Brotherhood."

"If you break the peace deal, I will become your worst nightmare," Dante warned Ethan and the new Lunar King raised his chin, his eyes narrowed.

"My word is iron."

"As is mine," Dante growled.

Leon started singing the Circle of Life by Elton John under his breath and I rolled my eyes. He was probably gonna try and hold Ethan above his head on the top of a building or some shit if I didn't get him out of here soon.

"Come on, Simba." I elbowed him. "Let's get the fuck out of here."

He took some stardust from his pocket and we all huddled close as he threw it into the air and the stars carried me away from the carnage of my old life towards a brand new future.

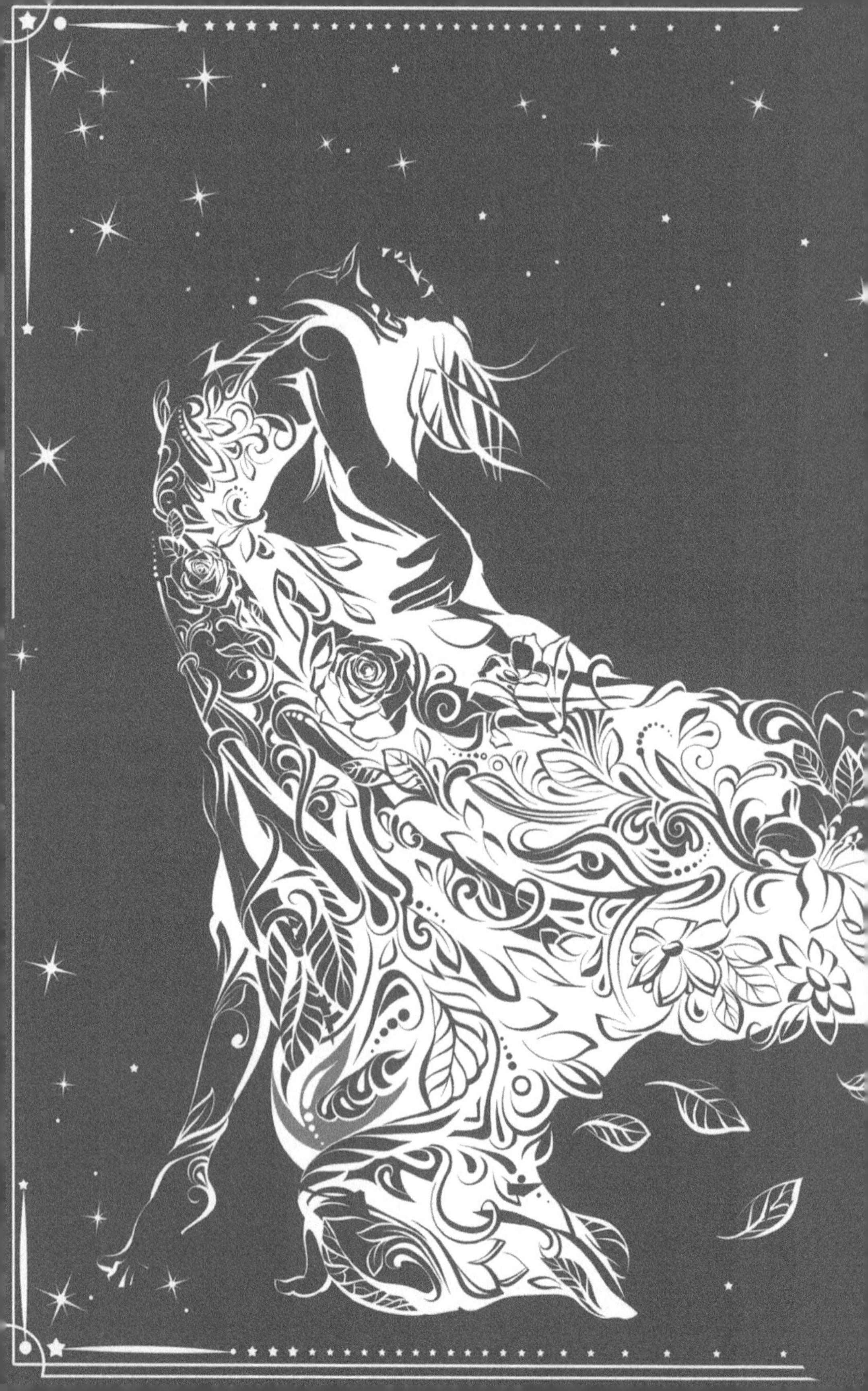

ELISE

CHAPTER FORTY SEVEN

We arrived in a snow filled landscape, the muted noise of the place so strange after the carnage of battle and I sighed as Leon wrapped his arms around me from behind, nuzzling against my neck. Then he released me and attempted to do the same to Ryder who huffed out a breath as he tried to push him back.

"Stop trying to make a habit out of this snuggly stuff, Simba," he growled, though the hint of a smile was playing around his lips again and I was beginning to think he didn't hate Leon fussing over him the way he always tried to insist he did.

Gabriel unlocked the door for us and we moved inside the cabin, but as I stepped over the threshold, Dante caught my hand and made me pause beside him.

He moved around me as he closed the wooden door and crowded me in against it with his body, leaning his forearm against the frame above my head as he cupped my cheek in his large hand and pressed his forehead to mine.

"Non potrei vivere in un mondo senza di te, amore mio," he breathed, tracing his fingers along my neck and making goosebumps rise across my flesh.

"I'm alright," I reassured him but he just shook his head, his eyes crinkling with pain as he thought back on what we'd just escaped.

"I could see them holding you in that ice, bella. I could see you in need of my help, but I couldn't fight my way to you. You have no idea how hard I was fighting to get to you."

I reached out to brush my fingers over his chest, frowning at the cuts which still marked his skin.

"Why haven't you healed these?"

"I deserve to feel the pain of them right now," he replied seriously.

I frowned, moving my hand so that I could heal them for him, but he caught my wrist, pinning it against the door above my head.

"Dante," I growled, reaching out with my other hand, but he just caught that too, moving it to join the first as he clasped both of my wrists in his one, big hand and pinned me in place.

"Just let me hurt for you, carina," he purred. "And let me remind myself that you're still right here, too."

My lips parted on a protest to that suggestion, but he leaned down and took a kiss from me before I could voice it, making electricity crackle across my skin as I gave in to him.

He kissed me slowly at first, tasting my lips and teasing my tongue with his and I sighed as some of the tension finally began to leak out of my limbs. He was here. He was safe. All of them were and we were together, exactly where we belonged.

Dante's free hand took hold of my waist as he pushed closer to me and I arched into him, our kiss deepening and my flesh tingling as the sparks of electricity washed over me, making my nipples harden and chafe against my bra.

"Non spaventarmi mai più così," he growled, a bite of warning to his tone as his mouth moved from mine and started tracking a path down my neck.

"Ti amo, Dante," I breathed, letting my head fall back against the door as he continued to kiss his way lower, the hand on my waist sliding around the front of my jeans and making my hips buck into him as he opened my fly.

"Ti ricorderò il posto a cui appartieni, bellissima," he growled into my collar bone. "E poi anche il resto dei tuoi uomini te lo ricorderà."

"What does that mean?" I begged as Dante pushed his fingers into the front of my jeans, seeking out the heat of my pussy and groaning as he found me wet and aching for him.

"It means that I'm going to make sure you don't forget who you belong to, bella," he replied. "And when I'm done with you and your legs are trembling, your body spent and your heart racing, the other men who own you are going to take their turns with you too."

"You want to punish me?" I asked in surprise, meeting his honey brown eyes as he lifted his head to stare me down.

"Today you took too many risks," Dante growled, sparks zapping against my flesh and making me gasp. "I love that you're brave and fearless and strong, amore mio. But I don't love when you're reckless. You have more than just yourself to consider now. You hold my heart in your keeping and you hold their hearts too. What do you think would become of us if we lost you?"

My lips parted as I felt the underlying fear in his words, the silver ring in his eyes glinting as it caught the light and reminding me of just how deep our bond ran. And I knew exactly what he was afraid of. I'd tasted that pain already today when I'd thought Ryder had been stolen from me. It had been oh so brief and yet had cut me so deep I knew I would have struggled to survive it beyond the length of my rage.

I lifted my gaze to look over Dante's shoulder, finding the rest of them watching us with hungry eyes and hardened expressions. They agreed with him on this. And I knew they were right. I *was* reckless. I'd made my mind up a long time ago that I would willingly trade my life to avenge Gareth and if I was being totally honest, since that moment I hadn't taken nearly enough care with my own mortality. But that had to stop. It had to because my life meant so much more now than just the continuation of my own, lonely existence. It meant the end of this bond between all of us, the end of this love which was so powerful it lit up the entire world around me.

I needed to stop seeing myself as a weapon primed to fire. I needed to accept the way they felt about me and the responsibility that placed upon my shoulders.

"I'm sorry," I breathed, looking between each of them in turn before my gaze met Dante's again. "I've been so caught up in the idea of revenge for so long that I stopped caring about my own life a long time ago. But it's not the same anymore. I have so much more now than I did when I made that choice. I should have stopped taking those kinds of risks as soon as I realised what I was to all of you and what you were to me. It was stupid and selfish of me."

"I'm glad you see that," Dante growled, gripping the back of my jeans and pushing them down over my ass. "But I'm still going to give you a reminder that won't easily slip your recollection."

I kicked my shoes off, followed by my socks and jeans and he just watched me, still pinning my arms above my head while keeping my gaze gripped in his, reading me.

"Are you ready for us to show you how selfish we can be, bella?" he asked me in a low, rough tone that had me swallowing thickly.

I bit down on my bottom lip, my gaze running down over the cut muscles of his bare torso and pausing as he roughly fisted his solid cock in his hand. His eyes were hard and full of lust and everything about the tension in his posture promised me that he was fully planning on destroying me as soon as I agreed to this.

"Yes," I breathed, my heart leaping as his lips crushed to mine the moment the word escaped me, his huge body pressing me back against the door so hard that I could feel every firm curve of his muscular frame through the thin fabric of my shirt.

Dante's free hand moved to clasp my ass and I hopped up as he lifted me, his fingers digging into my skin and delivering a bite of pain that had me moaning for him.

I locked my ankles together behind his back, flexing my hips and grinding against him, my clit riding over his cock as it swelled against the lace of my panties and my head spinning as he devoured me with his mouth.

My nipples were hard and aching within my bra and I wished he'd stop to rip my damn shirt off, but one look into his eyes told me I wasn't the one who would be calling the shots here. His grip on my wrists was bruising as he pinned them above my head and when I tried to tug a hand free he growled, squeezing harder and refusing me.

Heat skittered through my skin and he kissed me more fiercely, his free hand pushing between us where I was continuing to dry hump him so vigorously that I was pretty certain I'd be able to come from that friction alone.

The sound of him growling my name had me moaning again, my pussy throbbing with need as he shifted his hips and his hard cock drove against me, pressing into the soaked lace of my panties.

Dante found the edge of the material and dragged it out of his way.

I flexed my hips forward with a desperate need as his cock slid through my wetness, grazing over my clit before settling against my entrance, the head just pushing inside me the tiniest amount.

"Please," I breathed, pulling back to meet Dante's eyes and a dark smirk tilted his lips just as he thrust his hips forward and drove his cock into me all the way down to the base.

I cried out as electricity buzzed all over my flesh and Dante gripped my ass tightly as he began to fuck me hard and dirty, commanding complete control of my body and refusing to let me do more than just take it.

My head tipped back as I moaned and panted for him, his huge cock slamming deep inside me and making my pussy clamp tight around him, taking everything he had to give and more.

"Vieni per me," he demanded, his pace quickening as the pleasure in my body built and built like a dam ready to burst.

He thrust in again, somehow managing to drive in harder as his lips found mine and the second time he did it, I was lost.

My pussy clamped tight around his cock, a cry of pleasure bursting from me as I came all over his length and spots of darkness swirled across my vision while he slammed into me over and over, extending my orgasm and stealing my breath away.

With a Dragon's roar, Dante drove into me a final time, coming deep inside me and flattening me against the door for several heady seconds. Electricity crackled all over my body and made me cry out as aftershocks of pleasure cascaded through me, prolonging the ecstasy.

He kissed me once more, hard and rough, a reminder of who he was and what I was to him before he released my wrists suddenly and stepped back, pulling his cock out of me.

Dante set me on my feet, backing up as he looked me over and my legs trembled as I looked between my other three kings, feeling a lot like their next meal as their hungry gazes devoured me.

Gabriel stepped forward suddenly, answering the unspoken question between all of us and I licked my lips as I leaned back against the door, letting him come to me.

"Dirty little angel, aren't you?" he breathed, his gaze slipping down to my legs where Dante's cum was slowly rolling down my inner thigh. But if the heat in Gabriel's steely grey eyes was anything to judge by, he had absolutely no objections to that.

Gabriel stepped right up to me, grasping the hem of my shirt and tugging it over my head so that I was left in nothing but my underwear, and he tossed it aside as he drank in the sight of my body before him.

He still hadn't banished his wings and my gaze was drawn to them as he flexed them, the black feathers catching the light like a spill of oil and making me ache to run my fingers over them.

When he reached for me again, I tilted my chin, craving a taste of him. But his lips twitched with amusement like the idea of me calling the shots was a joke as he grasped my hips and spun me around so that my back was to him instead.

"Hands on the door," he commanded and I obeyed, bowing to my kings and giving in to their demands.

Gabriel took hold of the sides of my panties and rolled them down my legs, dropping to his knees as he waited for me to step out of them and I did so, my fingernails digging into the wooden door as anticipation ate me alive.

He stood again slowly, moving right up behind me and making me groan as he slid a hand around me and began to tease my clit.

The sound of his pants hitting the floor made a shiver race down my spine and the next thing I knew, he was pushing his cock between my thighs, coating it in the mixture of mine and Dante's arousal and making my pussy clench with need.

Gabriel kept stroking my clit, his movements firm and commanding and I moaned loudly for him, pushing my ass back in a clear demand for more.

But as he took hold of his cock to line it up for me, he didn't press the head against my pussy and I sucked in a breath as he pressed it to my ass instead.

"Yes," I moaned, arching back as he pushed in and the groan that escaped him as he drove into the tight confines of my flesh had my spine arching and me grinding back against him for more.

His fingers began moving faster against my clit and the moment he was fully seated inside me, I felt myself reaching the precipice and held my breath in anticipation of falling off of it.

Gabriel chuckled like an asshole, taking his fingers from my clit and spreading his wings wide behind us so that I was cast in shadow.

I wanted to complain, to beg him to come back and give my tingling clit exactly what I needed but he began to fuck my ass with deep, punishing thrusts the moment the words formed on my lips.

I cursed, bracing my arms against the wooden door as I fought to maintain my balance while Gabriel took hold of my hips and angled my body exactly the way he wanted it. He growled my name as he fucked me, his fingers biting into my flesh and my breaths heaving in and out of my body.

He grew impossibly harder inside me, my flesh feeling fit to burst as he chased down his own climax and used me for his pleasure.

His fingers moved back to my clit as suddenly as they'd abandoned me and I moaned in pleasure as he drove himself into my ass in time with the firm pressure he was delivering to that most sensitive spot.

He came with a savage thrust and a curse, groaning in a long and languid sound that was so fucking hot that it was enough to drive me over the edge too. My nails gouged scratch marks into the wooden door and I tipped my head back, something akin to a howl escaping me as I fell apart for him.

My heart was racing and my legs trembled violently as he tugged his cock back out of me again and I didn't even attempt to straighten myself, just leaning against the door and panting while another set of footsteps drew closer behind me.

Cold fingertips brushed along my spine, tracing the curves of my new tattoos from the one just above my ass right up to the one which rested between my shoulder blades.

"Ryder," I breathed, my gaze still on the floor beneath me as I stayed like that, waiting for him to take me the way he wanted.

His hand slid to the back of my neck and he tugged me upright, turning me to face him and looking at me like everything he was began and ended with me.

My hands landed on his bloodstained chest, my fingers tracing the X I'd painted there, branding him as my own, causing his muscles to flex beneath my touch.

"You broke for me today, baby," he growled as he started walking me backwards, his chest pressed to mine and his hand still clasped around the back of my neck.

I nodded, drinking in the lines of his face and bathing in the relief of knowing that he was still right here with me after watching his death play out in such a horrific way. Even knowing the truth wasn't enough to sear that memory from my flesh. I needed to see him like this, breathe him in and consume him, feel him possessing my body and dominating my soul in the way only he could.

I only realised he'd walked me into the shower when my back hit the tiles and he reached out to turn the tap on. Hot water suddenly cascaded over the two of us and Ryder slid his hand from the back of my neck down the centre of my spine to unclasp my bra.

He dragged it off of me, his eyes on mine the entire time as he tossed it aside and I fell into the depths of the emotions in his dark green eyes.

He was only wearing his boxers, but I found my fingers itching with the desire to peel them off of him as the water plastered them to his skin, outlining his thick cock and even the piercing that adorned it through the material.

My mouth dried out as I stared at him, my body still shaking a little from Dante and Gabriel's punishing treatment, but I wasn't done yet. Not even close.

I pressed my hands to the cold tiles at my back, watching him as he lathered up a sponge and slowly washed the blood from his body, covering every inch of his flesh in thick suds and drawing my eyes after the sponge as it carved its way across his muscles.

When he reached the V which dipped beneath the waistband of his boxers, he finally pushed them off of him, kicking them aside as his cock sprung free and I licked my lips hungrily at the sight of it.

He handed me the sponge, his gaze predatory as I took it and began to clean myself off next, watching him as he leaned back and let the water rinse away all evidence of what we'd survived today.

When I slid the sponge between my thighs, a deep rattle resounded through his chest and he gripped his swollen cock in his fist, slicking it up and down with languid motions that made my body tingle with need.

I tossed the sponge aside and dropped to my knees before him, needing to taste him, to fall for him, to show him he owned me in every way and worship him just for still being here with me.

Ryder's hands moved to grasp my hair as I slid my lips around his cock and I moaned as I took him into my mouth, looking up at him as he tipped his head back with a groan of pleasure.

I twisted my tongue around his tip, teasing the metal stud I loved so fucking much before sliding him in deep, loving the way he thrust in harder, his hands on the back of my head forcing me to take him all at once.

I pulled back then took him deep again, his hips driving forward as he began to fuck my mouth with a low rattle of pleasure tumbling from his chest. But then he jerked back, catching my wrist and tugging me to my feet so suddenly I missed my balance and fell against him.

His mouth collided with mine and I opened for him, loving the feeling of his tongue raking against mine, his stud dragging through my mouth as he owned me with that kiss.

His whole body pressed against me as he kissed me like he was trying to devour me, his rigid cock pushing into my stomach as I wound my arms around his neck to drag him closer.

Ryder ran the knuckles of his left fist down my chest, grazing my aching nipple with the word *free* as he continued to kiss me like we'd never get a chance to again.

His hand made it down to my thigh and he caught my leg, lifting it and hooking my knee over his arm, tugging until I pushed up onto my tiptoes with my other foot and his cock was aligned with my opening.

He broke our kiss, looking into my eyes as he held me in suspense there and my chest heaved between us.

"I love you, baby," he said. "And when I thought I was going to die today, the only thing in this world I cared about losing was you. I didn't want to be in an afterlife without you there. I didn't want to exist in darkness alone, pining for you. I spent too long in the dark before I found you. And I don't ever want to step back into it again."

"Ryder," I breathed but he pushed forward, sinking his cock into me deliciously slowly, letting me feel every single inch of him as his piercing rolled along my inner walls and my body drew him in all the way to the base of his shaft. "I love you," I whispered, forcing my eyes to remain locked on his as the incredible feeling of his body owning mine threatened to overwhelm me and we stayed locked in that position for several long seconds.

Then Ryder rolled his hips, keeping himself buried deep within me and grinding his pelvis against mine so that he rubbed against my clit.

I sucked in a sharp breath as he braced himself with one hand on the wall beside my head and I rocked my hips into his, finding a slow, deep rhythm which utterly annihilated me.

Ryder kissed my lips as he rocked his hips again then started carving a line down my jaw, the bite of his stubble making me moan as he drew his hips back just a little then drove his cock in deep again.

I kept one hand around the back of his neck to hold myself up but the other ran down his wet body, caressing his scars and tattoos and worshipping him as he continued to rock in and out of me.

When his mouth reached my neck, he bit down in time with a deep thrust, staying buried there as he ground against my clit even harder and I moaned his name, my fingernails biting into the back of his neck.

The angle he held me at let him hit me so deep that it was overwhelming, the feeling of his piercing scraping back and forth punctuated by him grinding against my clit. Every. Freaking. Time.

He kept his pace in check but upped the power of his thrusts, slamming in so fucking deep that I could hardly catch my breath between them.

I arched against him as my pussy pulsed and clenched him tight and as his mouth bit down on my nipple right in time with him grinding on my clit again, I fell apart for him.

My cries of pleasure echoed off of the tiles and Ryder groaned a deep, masculine sound that had my toes curling as my pussy gripped him so tight he had no choice but to come too. His cock pulsed inside me and his mouth found mine again, kissing me breathless as we rode out our pleasure in each other's arms.

When he finally pulled back, there was a wicked glint in his eyes and as he shut off the shower, I turned to find the others watching us.

Leon's gaze was scorching as he drank me in, all playfulness gone as he took my hand and tugged me towards him, clearly more than ready for it to be his turn.

He kept going, dragging me between Dante and Gabriel as he led me to the bedroom, the heat of his fire magic scorching my hand as I followed on mutely.

My legs were trembling, and my body felt utterly wrung out, but I still ached for the feeling of my Lion claiming me too. I needed him just like I needed all of them and I only hoped I'd be able to keep up with that burning desire in his gaze as he moved me to stand at the foot of the bed.

I reached out for him, clasping the hem of his shirt but he grasped my waist and tossed me onto the bed before I could remove it.

I breathed out a laugh as I bounced on the mattress, spread out beneath him while he looked down on me. But my amusement quickly died in the face of that look in his eyes. It was carnal and animal, hungry and full of wicked promises and I knew he wasn't going to go easy on me in any way.

Leon tugged his shirt over his head, tossing it away before slowly unbuckling his pants and I watched the show in eager anticipation as he dropped them to the floor.

I expected him to climb on top of me but as he dropped onto his knees and moved his face between my thighs, I couldn't help my moan.

"Are you tired, little monster?" he teased, slinging my legs over his shoulders as he held me in suspense. "Do you want me to do all of the work for you?"

"*Leo*," I groaned, bucking my hips as his mouth stayed too far from my pussy for my liking.

He growled at me then, meeting my gaze and holding it as he rolled his tongue over my clit. I moaned in relief, moving my hands to my tits as I squeezed them tight, releasing some of the pressure I felt building in my body as he began to work me over.

I couldn't hold his gaze for long, tipping my head back and bucking my hips as he fucked me with his mouth, and I loved every single second of it. I could feel the others watching us and I swear it just turned me on even more, knowing they could see this, that they were a part of it, it was just the perfect kind of sin.

Leon moved his hand up to join his mouth in destroying me and I bucked against his face as I came for him, pinching my nipples to extend the pleasure as he continued to lick and suck until he'd wrung every drop from my orgasm.

Leon growled in satisfaction as he drew back, moving on top of me and sinking his cock inside me before I could even finish riding it out.

His fingers laced with mine as he pinned me to the sheets and I wrapped my legs around his waist, driving my heels into his ass to encourage him deeper.

He kissed me hard and fucked me even harder, dominating my body and crushing me into the mattress beneath him as his dick hit me just the way I needed and my sounds of pleasure filled the room.

Then suddenly he was rolling us and I had to steady myself on his chest as I found myself on top of him, riding him instead, my thighs clamping tight around him as I got my balance.

Leon grasped my hips and took control of my movements as he slid me up and down the length of his cock, driving up into me and watching my tits bounce with a growl of appreciation.

Then his gaze cut beyond me and his eyes lit with excitement. "I think our girl needs a little more," he suggested in a low voice and the bed instantly dipped as three more bodies moved onto it with us.

Dante dropped his mouth to my right nipple, sucking it hard and making electricity crackle over all of us as Leon started fucking me harder, clearly enjoying the show.

Ryder took my other breast, kneading and pinching and dancing that delicious line between pleasure and pain as he started kissing my neck and biting my neck too.

Gabriel caught my chin as he moved into place behind me, tilting my head right back so that he could kiss me while his hand started to play with my ass.

It was so fucking much and my entire body began to quake with pleasure as hands and mouths moved across my flesh and Leon's hard cock dominated my pussy with every savage thrust.

Dante's electrically charged fingers found my clit as he continued to suck on my nipple and Leon thrust in even harder just as Gabriel pushed his fingers into my ass.

The cry that escaped me as I fell apart for them was pure, wanton animal and I came so hard I swear I almost blacked out from the pleasure that crashed through every single inch of my body.

It went on and on, wave after wave of utter bliss as Leon's cum filled me and my pussy gripped him in a vice. Their mouths all moved over my body as Leon sat up too and they worshipped me like I was a goddess they'd been born purely to serve.

I collapsed forward, falling onto Leon's chest as we all rearranged ourselves and shifted closer together.

Each of my kings found a way to touch me, not caring that they were just as entangled with each other as me. Because this was where we all belonged. Together. And now that I'd found the perfection these men could offer me, I was never going to be letting them go again. No matter what happened now or throughout the rest of our lives, I knew this was it for all of us. We were destined to be together.

We were a family.

And I'd finally found my home.

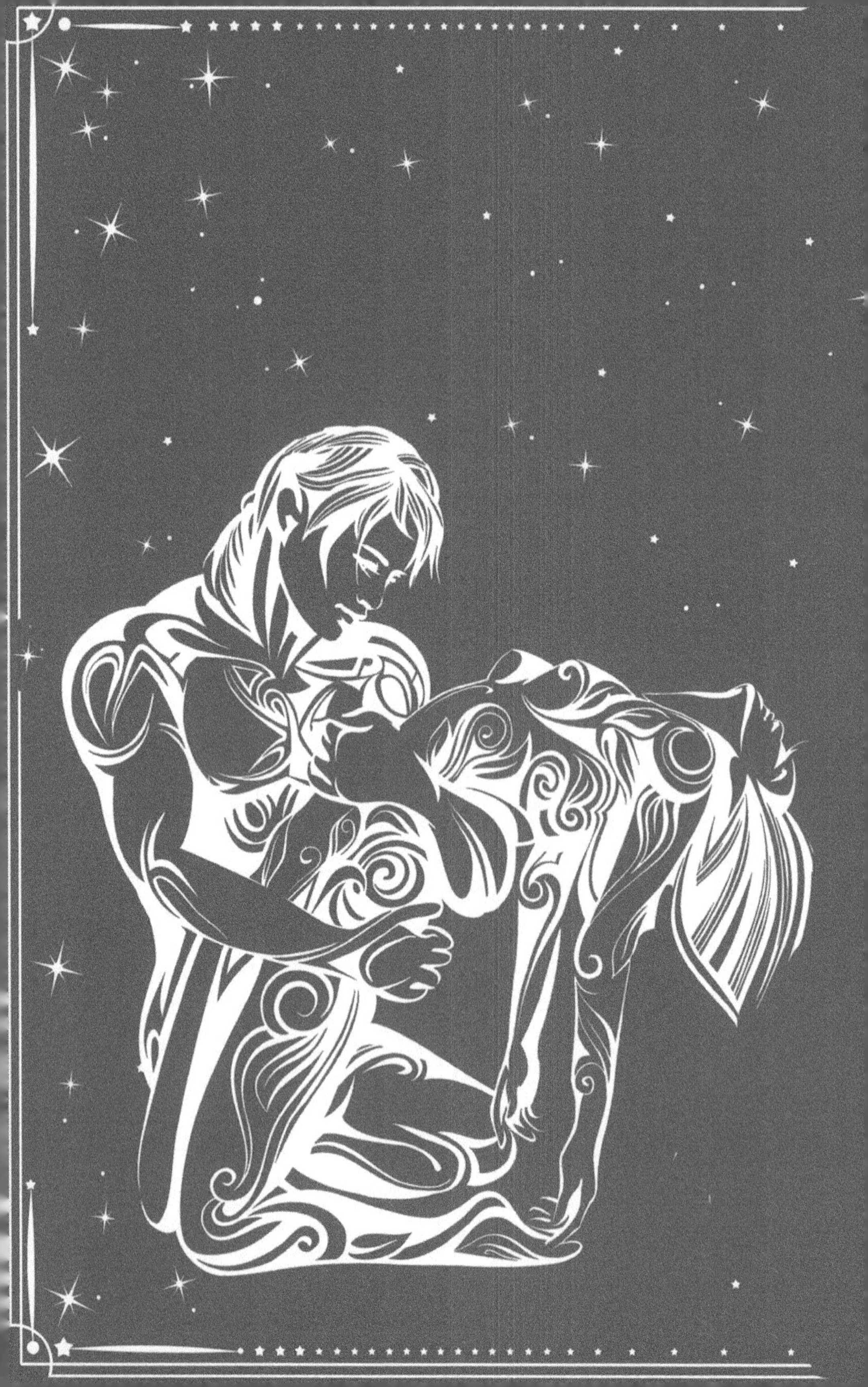

Ryder

CHAPTER FORTY EIGHT

"So how did you manage to fool the whole Lunar Brotherhood?" Elise asked in a husky tone as she snuggled against me, her finger tracing the cross over my heart, back and forth time and again.

"When the building fell, fate changed," Gabriel answered from her other side and Leon rested his head on his shoulder as he listened.

Dante was beside me draped in gold jewellery as he recharged his magic and the cold bite of the belt around his waist pressed to my hip. I didn't even give a shit about the dog pile we all inevitably ended up in these days. I would never admit it out loud, but I'd never gotten as good of a sleep as I did curled among my new family.

"So I don't have to feel like a royal stronzo for crushing you guys?" Dante groaned.

"The accident was unpredictable, so there was no way for me to *see* it coming. It changed everything, but I couldn't *see* any other paths until it happened," Gabriel said, reaching over me to clap Dante on the arm.

"Thank the stars you're a clumsy ass Dragon," Elise said, poking Dante in the ribs with a smirk and he chuckled.

"Why didn't you move out of the way, Gabe?" Leon asked.

"Because I had a vision the moment Dante's lightning struck the building," Gabriel said, his brow creasing. "And I only had a split second to act on it."

"He shouted *hypnosis* at me and I snared him in my power instantly," I said. "The thing about hypnosis is it gives you all the time in the world to have a conversation even if it's only a moment in reality."

"So what did you guys chat about?" Leon bounced on the bed a little, nuzzling into Gabriel.

"I told Ryder he needed to break his bonds, get hold of Scarlett then use his new chameleon powers to change both of their appearances. I *saw* a way he could use that gift to shift his appearance and Scarlett's and only he would be able to undo it. The magic isn't like an illusion, it won't break under pressure and can't even be detected by another Fae, so it was failproof," Gabriel explained.

"Holy shit," Elise laughed. "That's awesome." She grinned at me and I smirked.

"Gabriel said I had just enough time to create a stone chamber around me and Scarlett to protect us from the falling building and trap her in it with me," I said, looking to Gabriel with a frown.

"I needed to use my earth magic to strengthen that chamber though or else Ryder would be killed on impact," Gabriel said, his expression tightening. "So I just had to take the hit myself. I could *see* I wouldn't die, but it wasn't gonna be pretty either."

"Yeah, it was fucking badass," I said with a smirk. "Bet it hurt like a bitch, right?"

"Like a bitch with a sledgehammer smashing up every bone in my body," Gabriel agreed and Elise turned with a gasp, kissing his jaw. "I knew I wouldn't die," he added in a low tone to her. "But Ryder would if I didn't help him."

"You're a hero, dude," Leon whispered in his ear and Gabriel batted a hand at him.

"Nah, he's un guerriero," Dante said with a smirk. "A warrior."

Gabriel snorted a laugh, but none of us looked at him with anything except the highest of respect for the sacrifice he'd made for me. I'd never be able to repay him for it. My trust in him had been infallible and I hoped he had that same faith in himself in future.

"So you got hold of Scarlett?" Elise asked me, her eyes lighting up with the story.

"Yeah, once the chamber was in place, I just beat the shit out of her," I laughed. "The bitch was never strong enough to face me Fae on Fae, but I didn't give her a choice in the end."

"That's why you cut her tongue out," Elise said in realisation.

I grinned. "I had to shut her up fast, baby. Besides, I promised her I'd cut her lying tongue out when she first turned on me, so I had to make good on that."

Dante slapped my shoulder. "Genius, serpente."

Elise leaned up to kiss me and I hooked her leg up over my hip, grinning darkly against her mouth as I deepened it. I wasn't going to take a single second of my new life for granted. This was it. I was all in on this harem and I'd be damned if any asshole in this world was going to come between any of us ever again.

"Are you going to miss being a king, Rydikins?" Leon asked as he leaned over Gabriel to kiss Elise's neck.

"He's still a king," Elise said against my lips, her nails carving lines down my neck. "You're all *my* kings."

"I'd rather be a king to you than anyone else in Solaria," I said, rubbing my nose against hers.

"Is Ethan going to uphold the peace deal?" Dante asked with a note of concern in his voice.

"Yes," I swore, turning to look at him. "I trust him. He's proved his worth."

Dante nodded, satisfied by that and I felt the bond between us humming in the air for a moment.

"Why do you think Scarlett was such a whore?" Leon mused. "Do you think someone shoved a pointy stick up her ass at birth?"

Elise snorted a laugh.

"Her twin brother died at the hands of the Oscuras," I said and Elise's laughter fell away, making me unsure if I should continue this story.

"Her brother was psychotic," Dante chipped in darkly. "I was too young to really know everything that went on with him, but my papa told me about him once. Roland Tide used to capture pups from our family, take them away in vans and they'd turn up weeks later mutilated in a ditch or a river or a field." He shook his head, pain written into his features over those kids he hadn't known, yet felt the pain of their loss all the same.

I clenched my jaw at that dark knowledge, another fact that had been withheld from me.

"Papa went after him himself with the parents of those who'd lost children to him," Dante continued. "I don't know what they did exactly but-"

"They cut out his eyes and removed his hands before tying him to four stakes in the ground in the Imperian Desert, then left him for the Severis crows to finish," I supplied. "Scarlett liked to remind us all of that part, but I suppose the rest of it slipped her mind."

"She was never going to accept the peace deal," Dante said in a growl.

"She was probably planning my demise from the moment I reappeared from Mariella's and took back my place from her as the leader of the Brotherhood," I said in a hiss. "But she wouldn't have had the support back then to just take it so she waited, plotted, built her following and planned her move. If I hadn't trusted her word, maybe things could have been different..."

"You can't change the past, fratello," Dante said, resting a hand on my shoulder. "Il passato non ha altro da dire, ma il futuro è una canzone senza fine."

"What does that mean?" I asked, already liking the sound of it.

"The past has nothing else to say, but the future is an endless song," he replied and we sat in the silence following those words as hope caressed my heart.

I could see a life unfolding before me that I'd never dreamed of before, and all the choices within it were yet to be written. For the first time ever, I couldn't wait to read the next chapter of my story.

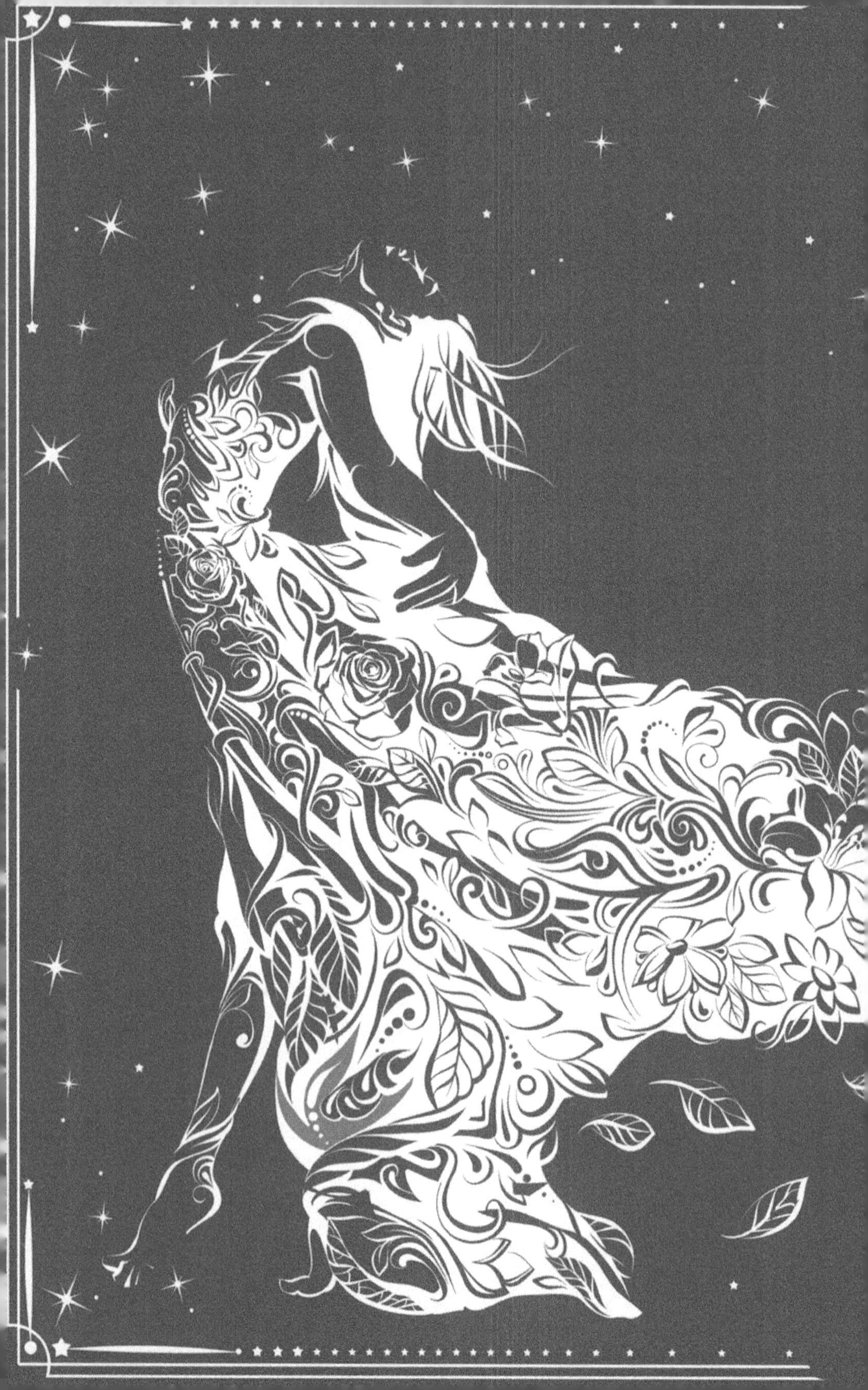

ELISE

CHAPTER FORTY NINE

I woke the next morning to the smell of burning toast and a whole lot of cursing coming from Leon somewhere beyond the bedroom.

I groaned, feeling the delicious stiffness in my limbs from our session last night as well as a rather more intriguing stiffness grinding into my ass from Dante.

"Good morning, amore mio," he purred, tugging my back against his chest more firmly as he ran electrified fingertips down the side of my naked body.

"Good morning, Drago," I murmured through a yawn. My fangs were tingling and I sighed in relief as I felt my Order gifts back within reach, the Suppressant was clearly gone from my system and I guessed I had Ryder to thank for that.

Dante kissed my neck and I sighed, peeking through my lashes and finding the rest of the bed empty and the bedroom door cracked open.

"Just stick a knife in there and force it out," Ryder snapped from somewhere beyond the room, sounding more than a little irritated.

"I thought you weren't supposed to stick metal things in toasters?"

Leon asked curiously. "Or is that lawn mowers?"

"Give it a try and I guess we'll find out," Ryder suggested.

Dante didn't seem to be the least bit interested in their conversation as he casually parted my thighs, lifting my knee so that his cock could line up perfectly with my pussy and I half laughed, half moaned as he continued to kiss my neck.

I felt more than a little tender after yesterday, but I could easily heal that and the harder he worked to tempt me into another round, the more consideration I was giving it.

There was a sudden bang and the lights all went out at once followed by the sound of Ryder bursting out laughing.

"Very funny, Simba, but you can get up now," Ryder said and I stilled as concern warred in my gut. "Come on, *get up*," Ryder said a little more firmly, followed by a curse. "Shit, are you alright? Hang on, I'll fix you, I didn't mean to-"

I shot out of bed and raced towards the door in a blur, finding Ryder bent over Leon who had collapsed on the floor. Green healing light spilled from Ryder's palms as he muttered something about not wanting him to die and his brow furrowed in clear concern.

Leon suddenly lurched upright, planting a kiss right on Ryder's mouth and grinning from ear to ear. "I knew you loved me, Rydikins!"

Ryder hissed threateningly, making a move to lunge at him for that prank, but then the two of them noticed me standing there butt naked and they got distracted.

"Do I smell a terrible breakfast?" I asked with another yawn, reaching out to snag a shirt from the back of the couch which I was pretty sure belonged to Gabriel.

I dropped the black material over my head and it fell almost all the way down to my knees, covering the important bits so that I could eat and heal. Dante may have come close to tempting me, but I was freaking starving and

I was almost certain that if I let him lead me down that path, one cock would soon become four and the only thing I'd be getting in my mouth before dinner would be dicks. And as much as I loved a good cock sandwich, there was really no nutritional value to that meal. Who would have thought maintaining my own harem would come with such hazards to my stomach? A girl needed to eat.

"Thanks for cock blocking me, stronzos," Dante grumbled as he stepped into the room behind me and I glanced around to find him standing there shirtless in a pair of low slung grey sweatpants.

I narrowed my eyes at his outfit and he shrugged innocently, but he knew exactly what he was doing. I never should have shown him those grey sweatpants thirst traps on FaeBook. He was practically wearing lingerie and begging me to lick him, and dammit if I wasn't tempted.

My stomach rumbled loudly and I tore my eyes away from my too freaking hot Dragon as I headed to the kitchen to see what damage control I could do with the breakfast.

"Where's Gabriel?" I asked, eyeing the charred remains of what I guessed had once been a slice of bread in the toaster. I unplugged the thing before upending it over the sink and slapping it on the ass to make it spit out the inedible food.

"Gone to his vision room to try and *see* some stuff and things," Leon replied, prowling over to me and looking all Lion with his golden mane hanging around his shoulders.

Shit, I really needed to eat because he was definitely giving me the orgy eyes again.

The charred lump of toast finally dislodged itself from the toaster and I set it down before turning to find something for my growling stomach.

Ryder moved away to find the fuse box while I started hunting in the fridge and Leon wrapped his arms around me from behind, watching as I tried to decide on what I wanted.

"What are we eating?" he purred.

"I'm thinking scrambled eggs and toast," I said, reaching for the eggs. "Assuming you didn't cremate all of the bread?"

"Just that one slice," he assured me before leaning in close to my ear to whisper the rest. "And it was a Ryder trap."

"You knew he'd get you to stick a knife in the toaster?" I asked as I grabbed some butter and milk too before moving to the counter to start making our food. Leon stayed right behind me, still holding me close like a limpet and making it about ten times harder to prepare the food, but I was enjoying it too much to complain.

"No. I was planning on giving it to him to eat and seeing if he'd say anything or if he'd just crunch his way through the layer of charcoal like the psycho he is. Clearly me getting electrocuted was a much better play in the end though. I swear, he was crying over me. Actual freaking tears."

Dante barked a laugh clearly listening in and Ryder hissed from the far side of the room just as he finished with the fuse box and the power came back on again.

"The only thing I would have been crying about was the fact that the toaster had managed to kill you before I got the chance," he said, moving to sit at the breakfast bar with Dante, their arms brushing against each other's.

I started mixing up the eggs while Leon asked me what I was doing with every single step and I explained in painstaking detail every little thing, knowing he was going to be attempting this himself whenever he next got the chance. It was pretty simple, but I still didn't rate his chances of success.

Leon brushed my hair away from my neck, healing magic sweeping along my skin as he removed the bruises one of them had left there last night and I smiled at him as he started rubbing my shoulders to work some of the kinks out too.

I put the eggs on to cook and started off the first round of toast then spun in his arms and ran my own fingers though his hair.

"You know what you could do if you really wanna help me out, Leo?" I asked, eyeing the thumping pulse in his neck with my fangs tingling and he sighed dramatically.

"Sorry, little monster, I'm almost tapped out. I haven't had a chance to get some rays since the fight yesterday and it's so freaking cold and cloudy outside that I can't do it here. I say we all go and spend a few days in that vacation house I bought for you. Then we can spend every day lazing in the sun while you suck on any piece of me that you want to."

I pouted at him in disappointment, turning to bat my lashes at the others only to find Dante in the process of decorating himself in as much jewellery as he could possibly fit onto his body.

"Sorry, bella. I should have slept in gold last night, but you distracted me and I took it all off again," he said with a shrug.

"Come here, baby," Ryder said, patting his knee and looking smug as fuck. "Having a whole gang try to murder you hurts like a bitch, so I'm good to go."

"Don't joke about that," I growled, giving the eggs a mix and tossing some more bread into the toaster before shooting around the breakfast bar and hopping into his lap.

"Well, the lot of them are dead now," he replied with a shrug, taking his Atlas from his pocket and showing me an article in The Celestial Times detailing the scene of the fight yesterday with the title *Ryder Draconis and Scarlett Tide killed in Lunar Brotherhood in-fighting*.

I swallowed thickly, frowning at the public declaration to the world that he was dead

"Are you sure about this, Ryder?" I asked hesitantly.

"This is what matters to me now, baby," he said, taking the Atlas from me and setting it down on the breakfast bar as he held his arm out to show me the inside of his forearm. With everything that had happened yesterday, I hadn't even noticed the new ink on his arm - or maybe he'd been hiding it like he had with Leon's star sign, but I couldn't help but suck in a sharp breath as I reached out to brush my fingers along his new tattoos.

"You got one for Dante?" I asked, tears pricking the backs of my eyes as my finger followed the lines of the Gemini symbol he'd marked onto his skin and Dante looked around suddenly, clearly knowing nothing about this either.

"What?" he asked with a deep laugh, grabbing Ryder's arm and tugging it closer for inspection. "Have you gone and fallen in love with me now, stronzo? Because I'm sorry to say, your tits aren't big enough for my liking."

"Well at least if you were sucking my dick, I wouldn't have to listen to you speaking," Ryder shot back, failing to hold a smirk in as he tugged his arm away again.

"Wow," Leon said with a sigh as he started plating up the toast and eggs, though for some unknown reason he was putting the eggs on the plates first with the toast sitting like hats on top with no butter and he also kept dropping big lumps of egg as he went. "Ryder got tattoos for all of us. Elise got tattoos for all of us. Gabriel bought me that huge gift basket of mane grooming products and wrote me that massive letter detailing how much I mean to him… and you just didn't get me anything, did you *Dante?*" He shot a pointed look at the medallion hanging around Dante's neck and I snorted a laugh. I very much doubted Gabriel had done any such thing, but I was staying out of this.

"Seriously, stronzo?" Dante asked irritably. "You're still harping on about this? Why are you so damn set on taking it from me? It belongs in my family. It has been passed down for generations."

"Oh so I'm not your family then?" Leon shot back, passing a plate across to Ryder and accidentally knocking the toast off onto the floor.

"I didn't say that," Dante groaned. "But you're not an Oscura."

"Well what about the ring you gave to Elise?" Leon asked, pointing at it.

"That's different," Dante growled.

"Because you love her?" Leon asked, passing a plate towards me which he'd forgotten to put any eggs on at all meaning it was just dry toast.

"You know I do."

"But you don't love me?"

"For the love of the stars," Dante growled. "Fine. Have it." he tugged the medallion over his head and tossed it to Leon who dropped the plate he'd been holding in favour of catching it.

I threw my hand out, somehow managing to catch the plate and food with my air magic before it could hit the ground and I quickly wrangled it back into place before setting it down in front of Dante.

Leon had started up some kind of crazy celebration dance while singing Treasure by Bruno Mars and making a big show of placing the medallion around his neck and I couldn't help but laugh at his antics as Dante rolled his eyes and started on his food.

Ryder shifted me on his lap and I caught hold of his arm again so that I could finish my inspection of his tattoo and I could feel his eyes on me as he fell still.

"Your Duty?" I murmured, running my fingers over the Aquarius symbol and the rainbow that adorned it. "Who-"

"Gareth," he replied in a low voice meant just for me. "These tattoos represent the things each of you has given back to me." He slid my fingers further up his arm until they rested over my own star sign by the crook of his elbow and leaned in to press his forehead to mine. "After Mariella, I wasn't even half a person anymore. I was just this cold, empty vessel so full of hurt and hate. But you saw what little was left of me, baby. You brought me back from that. And through you..." He dragged my hand down his forearm over each and every other tattoo until he laced his fingers with mine, the word *free* broken apart by our hold on one another. "I found all of them too."

Tears prickled in the backs of my eyes but Ryder kissed me before they could fall, stealing that emotion for himself before pulling back and baring his throat for me.

I slid my hand up the back of his neck to hold him in place as I bit him, a sigh escaping me as the wash of his dark power flooded my senses and swept over my tongue.

Ryder drew me closer and I held him tight, trying to fight off the memories of what I'd almost lost yesterday. He was here in my arms now and that was all that counted.

The door banged open behind us and I drew away from Ryder to look at Gabriel as he stepped into the room, shaking snow from his hair and giving us a grave look.

"The stars have shown me the future," he said in a low tone, his brow pinching as he took a step towards us. "And I'm afraid it doesn't look good."

"What is it?" I asked, pulling away from Ryder so that I could see him better.

"I've *seen* so many different paths, but there is one certain thing which I know - tonight is the full moon and Titan is planning to do his biggest ritual yet. He's taken over Alestria, preparing to make his stand against the Celestial Counsellors. If he succeeds, then the fate of the kingdom will be thrown into so much turmoil that the only guaranteed things are death and carnage."

"So let's make sure that doesn't happen," Leon said firmly and Gabriel nodded.

"We have a shot. Just this one. I've *seen* it working out but..." His eyes cut to me and he frowned. "I've *seen* death too. For all of us. This could be the end for any of us or even for our entire family. But if we don't try tonight, then I don't think we'll get another shot."

"What do we need to do?" I asked as my pulse thundered in my ears.

"I think I've got some ideas," he said, looking between each of us in turn. "But the one thing I know for certain is that this is it. All or nothing. Our fates hang in the balance tonight and whatever way the dice falls, nothing will ever be the same for us again. Are you ready for that?"

Silence fell as we all looked between each other and I got to my feet, moving across the room until I was cupping Gabriel's cheek in my palm.

"I trust you," I breathed.

"We all do," Dante agreed firmly, and I turned, finding the three of them right behind me.

"Then let's finish this," Ryder growled. "It's time that motherfucker met his end."

Leon leaned in, throwing one arm around Ryder's neck and another around Gabriel's. "I think it's time for a group hug," he said, fighting off a grin.

Dante breathed a laugh as he threw an arm around Ryder and Gabriel too, the four of them forming a circle around me as we all pulled in close to each other.

"I love all of you," I said, not wanting it to sound like a goodbye but needing it to be as clear as possible in that moment. "And when this is done, we are all gonna live long, peaceful, boring lives with no more evil assholes or people out to murder us."

"That seems unlikely," Ryder muttered and Gabriel winced, confirming it.

"Unlikely or not, that's the future I want," I insisted.

"Then we'll give it to you, little monster," Leon promised.

"Just so long as we survive the night," Gabriel added darkly and we all crowded closer together, just holding onto each other for a moment, knowing that when we broke apart again that would be it. We'd plan our strike and make our move.

The rest was up to fate.

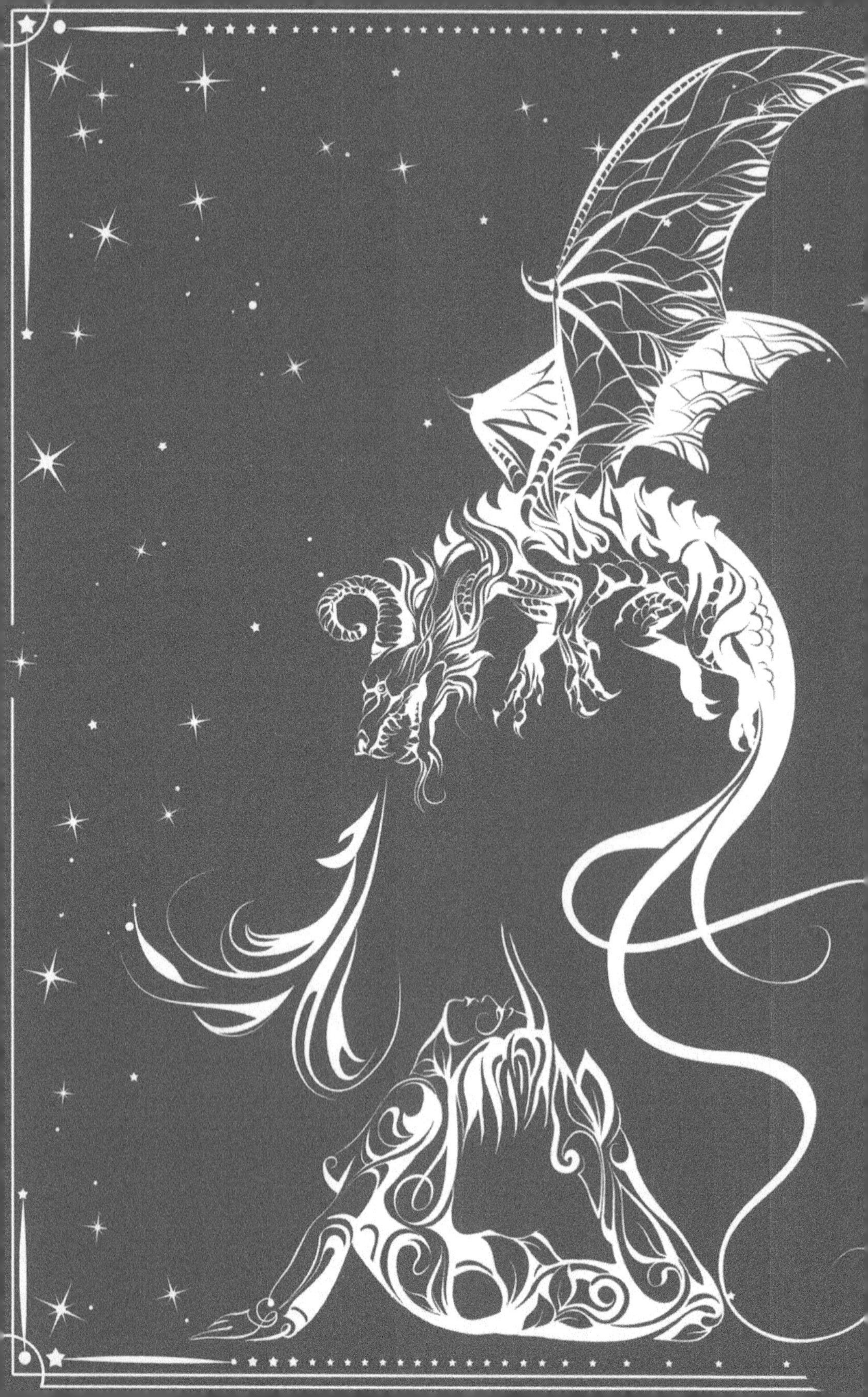

Dante

CHAPTER FIFTY

King had the city on lockdown and every one of his stronzo Black Card members were out patrolling the streets. Gabriel said they were hunting for us and I'd already sent a warning to every member of mia famiglia to remain at home and keep the pups safe.

King wouldn't be able to find it let alone be able to get in there, but it still soothed my heart knowing they were safe.

The FIB had already questioned my mamma and Leon's famiglia about our whereabouts after the Lunar attack in the city. We'd all been seen and our faces were plastered throughout the newspapers in Alestria in connection to the deaths and destruction that had occurred. Lucky for me, I was still a hot commodity to the Dragon Lord bastardo though and I'd had a message from him informing me I owed him several more jars of lightning in payment for him calling the FIB off and keeping me out of Darkmore. Not that I was grateful to him in the least, but at least I'd been able to force him to include the others under that layer of protection. He couldn't even outwardly show Elise disdain anymore now that it turned out she was an Altair. I guessed political bullshit did come in handy sometimes.

Elise and I had stardusted into the alley that backed on to The Sparkling Uranus and we made our way out of the shadows onto the road, casting concealment spells around us to keep us hidden. Gabriel couldn't *see* Titan directly, but he knew the Black Card were gathering at the town hall in central Alestria so that was where we were heading.

I narrowed my gaze on a hooded bastardo at the end of the street, talking on his Atlas. "-all quiet down here, Barry. Just caught a couple of kids breaking curfew and taught them a lesson." He chuckled. "Yeah, the little assholes will learn who's the real power in town soon enough."

A growl built in my throat which was echoed by Elise and I looked to her, finding her fangs bared and her gaze locked on our prey.

"He's all yours, bella," I said and she smiled darkly before shooting forward and diving onto his back. She snapped his neck and he slumped to the ground at her feet before she tossed him into the dark alcove of a doorway.

"One down," she purred as I jogged up to her.

"I bet I get more kills than you tonight," I challenged and her eyes lit up.

"That's a bet you're gonna lose, Drago." She smirked, leading the way down the street and I hurried to her side, keeping the shadows close around us.

"You're as bloodthirsty as Ryder," I teased and her savage smile said she agreed with that.

"He's gonna be pissed he's missing out on all the fun," I said.

"I don't wanna let him go anywhere in this city until the dust's settled after his fake death," Elise whispered and I nodded my agreement. After some time, Ryder was going to create a new identity and use his chameleon powers to change his appearance then he would just slide back into our lives and we would be able to live in peace at last.

We rounded the next corner and Elise pressed her finger to her lips, clearly hearing something I couldn't as we hugged a wall and crept up behind two large dumpsters. I threw a look around the side of one, spotting two Black

Card members patrolling the street like wraiths moving along in their long cloaks.

"Mine," I hissed, then flicked my fingers, sending a bolt of lightning that split apart and struck the two of them dead in the backs of the heads. They fell to the ground with smoke coiling up from their fried hair and I shot a grin at Elise. "Two to me."

"Oh shit, Nigel!" a woman wailed from beyond the bodies and Elise tore out from our hiding place in the direction of her voice.

I stepped out after her, watching as she collided with the new arrival, the two of them hitting the ground. Elise silenced her scream with one vicious bite of her throat then fed deeply from the Black Card member as she died beneath her. I walked up behind amore mio, releasing a low whistle of approval as Elise got to her feet and wiped the blood from her mouth with the back of her hand.

"Now it's a draw." She beamed then danced away from me like a little psychotic pixie and I followed, entranced by my ragazza matta.

We took the backstreets to the heart of the city, Elise knowing them as well as I did as we moved through the dark. Alestria was quieter than I'd ever experienced, the bars closed up and no one out on the sidewalks. Titan had worked fast to get the city under his control and I prayed there hadn't been too much bloodshed during his rise to power. But his reign was going to be cut short before it had even really begun. We weren't going to allow this self-righteous bastard to get away with everything he'd done. He was asking for a fight and we were certain to give him one this very night.

We reached the town hall, the tall white stone building with cracking walls and large pillars along the front of it standing out starkly under the full moon. A low, collective chanting sounded from within its walls and I eyed the many guards at the front door with a frown. I could take them out with my lightning, but that wasn't what Gabriel had told us to do. And despite how tempting it was to destroy those stronzos who were like sitting ducks in front of me, there was no chance of me deviating from our Seer's instructions.

I nodded to Elise and she picked me up, throwing me over her shoulder and shooting around the back of the town hall in a furious blur. She placed me down before a maintenance ladder that ran up the wall towards the roof and I gestured for her to go first with a sideways smile.

"Ever the gentlefae," she said, kissing my cheek before stepping onto the ladder and starting to climb.

"Don't be so sure of yourself, bella. I'm only going second so I can enjoy the view." I gazed up at the roundness of her ass in her tight jeans and she threw a grin down at me as I followed.

We made it to the roof and crept across the flat concrete space, heading to the door that would gain us access to the building. Gabriel had warned us about what lay beyond it so I pressed my hand to the door, charging electricity beneath it and releasing it in a blast that tore through the metal to the other side. Half a yelp was cut off abruptly and I forced the door open, finding a couple of dead Black Card members inside.

"Four to me," I murmured to Elise and she cursed as she followed me inside, stepping over their bodies.

We jogged down a narrow stairway and the chanting grew louder as we made it to a balcony and dropped to our knees. We crawled forward, peeking over the edge of it between the railings and my gaze fell on Titan at the heart of the enormous hall with splashes of blood marking the ground at his feet.

My gut clenched in disgust as he walked along a line of Blazers, offering a blade to them one at a time and whenever they chose death, they ran it across their own throats while he absorbed the magic from them as he cast his dark spell. The Black Card were ringed around them all with Titan in the middle, forming a protective wall, but the stronzo hadn't thought to protect himself from above.

The ominous chanting grew to a din in my ears and I looked to Elise beside me with a flare of determination in my soul. We were going to make

Titan hurt, make him scream, make him pay. And when it was done, we'd cast his body into hell and finish what Elise had started on her quest to destroy King.

I stripped out of my clothes and Elise readied the stardust in her grip while she flexed her other hand, preparing to cast magic.

I leaned in close, stealing a hard kiss from her mouth and whispering against her lips. "You just lost the game, amore mio." Then I stood up and dove off of the balcony, shifting as I fell in mid-air and my enormous Dragon form exploded from my flesh.

I roared loudly as Titan looked up in alarm and the Black Card screamed in fright.

Lightning blasted from my throat as I circled the room, incinerating each and every Black Card bastardo surrounding Titan while Elise shielded the Blazers with a strong air shield.

"No!" Titan cried, though his face was hidden beneath that dark concealment spell which hid his true identity from the world. But we knew the truth now and we were coming for him.

Elise leapt off the balcony with a battle cry and I swept around towards her, anticipating her moves. Titan raised his hands, water blasting from his fingertips in a huge torrent aimed at Elise and I sailed beneath her, taking the hit to my chest as she landed on my back, ran up my neck and swan dived off of my head. I flew up as she tossed the stardust over Titan, catching her feet between my talons at the last second as her hand latched around Titan's arm.

"Wait – Elise!' he cried but the stardust twisted around us and the three of us were yanked away by its power, tearing into the ether between worlds as we were transported to where the others were waiting for us.

Elise dropped Titan as I flew us up and away from the sweeping farm field we'd just arrived in, banking hard as he tumbled into the middle of the huge zodiac circle which had been burned into the ground. It wasn't just any circle either, that was dark magic at its finest, a trap to hold a Fae within its grip, but its power had to charge before it could work. Titan needed to remain there for several minutes before it could bind him to its power.

Gabriel, Leon, Ryder and Orion all stood around him and worked together, casting a fierce ward over Titan to keep him in place.

"Land, Drago!" Elise cried and I swept towards the field, laying Elise lightly down before shifting in the air and hitting the ground on my feet. She shot away to the circle, throwing out her palms to aid the wards around Titan as the bastardo fought furiously to get free. Magic swirled around him, crashing against the barrier and I ran to help mio amicos, scooping up a pair of sweatpants which had been waiting for me behind Leon and tugging them on before diving onto the Gemini symbol of the zodiac circle and adding my own power to the wards.

Each of my famiglia stood on their own zodiac symbols, Orion and Elise standing together on the Libra mark as they fought to keep the wards strong. Powerful artefacts stood on the rest of the zodiac star signs that Gabriel had spent the evening gathering; he'd been shown where to find each of them by the stars. There were all kinds of stunning treasures from chalices to beautiful ornaments and jewellery, and I had to tear my gaze from it all as the Dragon in me urged me to hoard it all.

A huge blast of air magic tore out from Titan, slamming into the wards so hard, I felt them start to crack.

"Fuck!" Gabriel cried as part of the wards gave out and his gaze whipped onto Orion. He tugged something from his pocket, throwing it hard as Titan cast a glinting metal spear in his hand and threw it furiously out of the circle towards Orion. The stardust pouch hit Orion in the chest, glitter flying everywhere as he was transported away into the stars to safety and the spear went sailing through that very spot half a millisecond later.

"Holy shit," Elise gasped as we closed the wards once more and Titan attacked that spot again with a blast of air magic, battling her power with his own and making her brow pinch in concentration.

"Start the chant!" Gabriel bellowed and we all shouted out the spell which could strip the stolen Elements from King. We'd taken the potion before we left to capture him and now we were ready to finish this.

Titan dropped the concealments around him with a curse, a snarl on his lips as he conserved his energy. "I don't want to hurt you, Elise. You don't know what you're doing!"

"I know exactly what I'm doing!" she cried back and his lips pressed together before he threw his hands to the sides and water poured out from him in a raging whirlpool. The wards all came down and I braced for impact, casting air against my back and planting my feet.

"Stay on the circle!" Gabriel cried, him and Ryder focusing on anchoring all of the artefacts in place as water flooded over us. Leon was cast away in the tide and Ryder threw out a vine to pluck him from the waves and place him straight back on the Leo mark.

Titan rose up on a pillar of earth so high it cast us all in its shadow and terror squeezed my heart as his gaze latched onto Gabriel.

"Enough of this!" Titan roared and the whole sky seemed to fall as a tornado swirled around him and dragged Gabriel away into its grip.

I raised my hands with a bellow of rage and clouds answered my call with a deafening boom of thunder. The full moon was lost to the storm and lightning blasted down from the sky, all of it daggering towards Titan with the full fury of my power.

He cried out as it hit, using an air shield to keep himself safe but my lightning struck over and over and over, making his concentration wane. His tornado died and suddenly Gabriel was falling through the sky, his wings snapping out and tearing through his shirt as he swept down to the ground and landed back on his mark with a snarl on his lips.

Ryder blasted the tower of earth away beneath Titan and he fell down to the middle of the circle once more. I let my storm subside as we all picked up the chant again and Titan cried out as we weakened his power, holding him within the zodiac trap. He shot air at Ryder and Leon countered it with a blaze of fire which devoured the oxygen, tearing back towards Titan like a flame thrower. Titan cast a wall of ice to protect himself and the flames went out against it before he shouted loudly and sent the ice wall shattering into a million tiny daggers, all tearing out towards every one of us but Elise.

I threw out my hands, casting away as many blades as I could on a breeze, but several slammed into me and I growled in pain as Elise screamed in fear for the rest of us.

"Don't move!" I barked at her as she took a step toward me and I stole a moment to heal myself as the others drew Titan's attention toward them.

"Stop!" Titan snarled. "You don't know what you're doing. I'm the saviour of this world!"

"You're a monster," Elise spat and his brows pinched at her words before she sent a barrage of air towards our enemy and our chant grew louder and louder.

Titan groaned as he fought the power of the dark magic that surrounded him, all of us playing him at his own game. If he hadn't realised that we were his death yet, then he was about to get a rude awakening. Because we all stood here as kings beside their queen, our home threatened by this beast. And he was about to find out what happened to the people who crossed us.

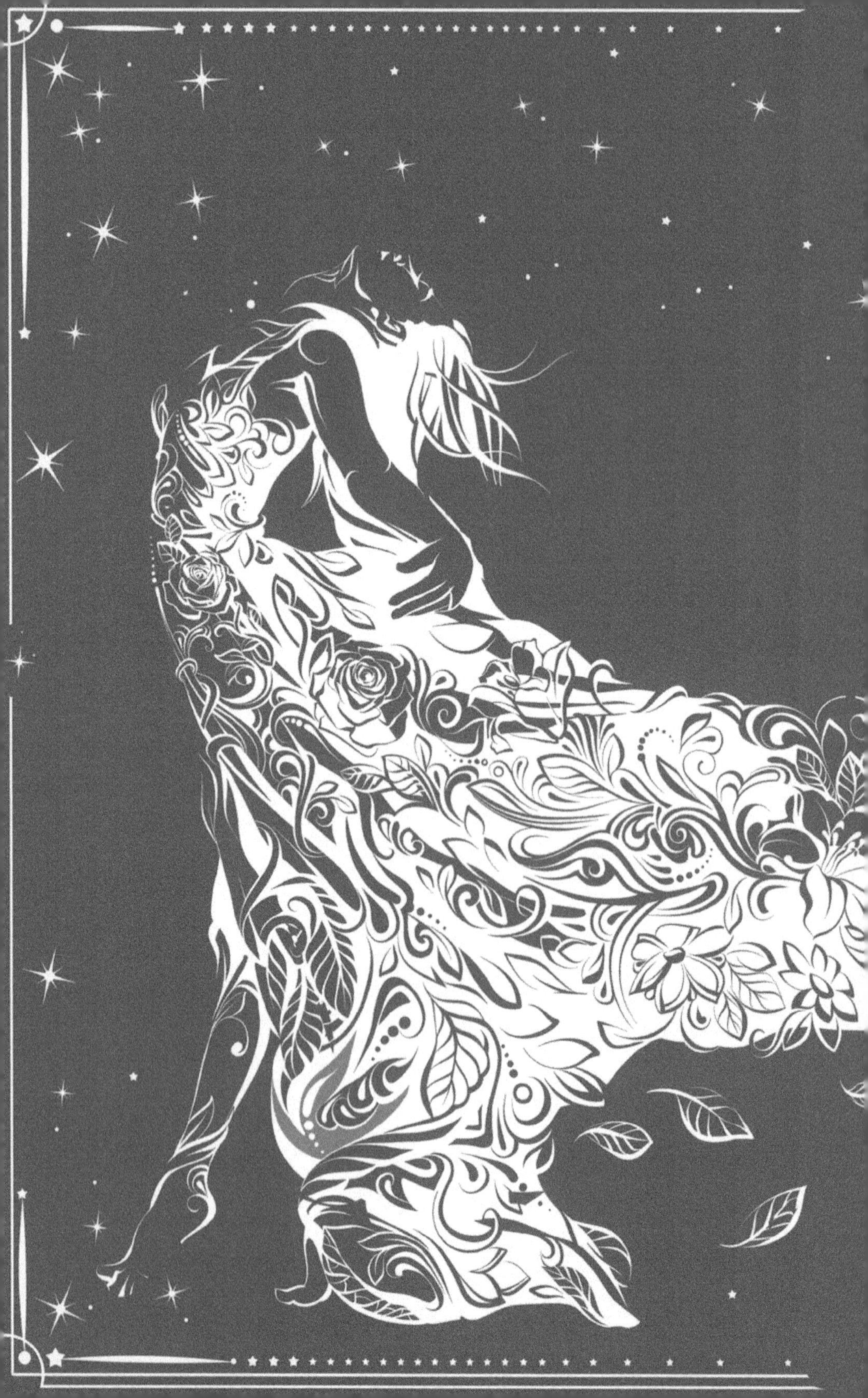

ELISE

CHAPTER FIFTY ONE

The wind whipped between us as a maelstrom of magic tore around us in a whirlwind, tugging strands of lilac hair across my eyes. I shouted above the thunderous sound of the magic colliding, chanting in time with the others and locking Titan in the centre of the circle.

"You don't want to do this, Elise!" Titan yelled suddenly, fighting to remain upright while he tried to battle against the power of the dark magic we were using against him. "I know you understand me. We're kindred spirits you and I!"

Pain burrowed into my chest and twisted into my heart at his words. He'd known how much he meant to me. Hell, he'd probably just been grooming me to try and get me to be a willing participant in his bullshit. I'd been vulnerable and he'd been right there, ready to step in and use me for his own agenda.

"Was any of it real?" I demanded, leaving the chanting to the others because I needed to know. I needed to hear him tell me to my face that he'd just been using me, fooling me.

"Of course it was," Titan replied, his eyes swimming with the emotions of the man I'd thought I'd known. "I'm not the monster your mates have painted me out to be."

I glanced away from him to my kings, but they were all focused on the magic they were wielding, the power of it flowing between them in a rush of energy so potent that I could see the golden glow of it hanging in the air.

The artefacts Gabriel had gathered to represent the other zodiac signs were all vibrating as they remained locked in their positions around the circle, channelling the immense power that we were building to complete this task.

"How can you really believe that?" I spat at Titan, my heart cracking open as I looked upon the true face of this man who I'd let slip into my heart. "Your own daughter was murdered. And now you've been killing vulnerable Fae to suit your own desires, stealing their power from them and taking them from their own families who have to suffer through the grief you know all too well. And then you're spouting all this shit about wanting to save Alestria. What kind of saviour preys on their weakest people?"

"I didn't prey on them," Titan snarled and my eyes widened as leaves began to peel away from his fingertips, each of them bright green but withering and turning brown as they fell from his body to litter the ground. The earth Element was being stripped away from him and my kings chanted ever louder as they threw all of their power into this. My magic was warring right along with theirs, but I needed these answers, had to hear them if I was ever going to be able to claim any peace after this. "I only took what was offered."

"You dosed those poor Fae with Killblaze," I spat. "It was designed to push them over the edge, to fund your greed for power. You're no better than any other power-hungry Fae in Solaria - you just found a way to take claiming your power more literally than most."

"Killblaze only sped up the inevitable. Those souls were already lost to despair. The drug was a kindness, it allowed them to go without pain, to fall into death with a smile on their faces and to gift their magic to a cause which would save many more from a much worse fate. Any who came to me and chose not to take their lives were sent on their way, their memories wiped, and new hope injected into their souls. Think about it, Elise. I sent Eugene Dipper your way when he was teetering on the edge. If all I cared about was power then I could have just encouraged you to find more powerful friends, to leave him isolated and alone and spiralling towards suicide as he had been."

"Well why the fuck didn't you?" I demanded, my heart wrenching for the poor, bullied boy who had become one of my dearest friends.

"Because he embodies what I'm trying to achieve - a better world. I saw his potential just as I saw yours and I knew the two of you would be able to become so much greater if you united in friendship."

I shook my head, not wanting to hear that because it made hating this beast before me so much harder. How could he have been helping Eugene when he was clearly more than capable of hurting so many others? His logic was a twisted, convoluted thing which had a whisper of sense to it that I didn't want to hear.

Titan cried out in pain as the last of the leaves were ripped from his body, his head throwing back to look up at the stars which were bright in the sky overhead like they were watching the show with interest.

"Keep going!" Gabriel cried, his voice hoarse from the force of the chanting as he and the others chanted the ancient words even louder, the air vibrating with the power of what we were doing.

I opened my mouth to join them once again, needing this over, needing it done, but I had more questions to ask, and I had to hear the answers.

Titan beat me to it though, his head falling forward again as he locked eyes with me again.

"Your father wanted this, you know? He believed in it just as fiercely as I do. He knew we needed to do something about Alestria and the corruption which was tearing this city apart."

"You stole my father from me!" I yelled, my throat thick with unshed tears which I battled away, refusing to allow him to see me cry. My life could have been so different. Me and Gareth could have been loved and cared for.

Our mom could have been happy. We could have had food in the fridge and clothes without holes in them and more importantly than any of that, we could have had the security his love would have provided us with. Everything might have been so different, but Titan had stolen the opportunity for me to ever know whether or not it would have been. "He clearly saw what you were about to become and changed his mind about supporting a monster in his rise to power. But you wouldn't allow that would you?"

"I couldn't," Titan said, shaking his head sadly like the knowledge of what he'd done to Marlowe Altair actually hurt him. But that wasn't fucking good enough. "I needed his blood. We were already on this path and I couldn't allow him to go to his sister about our work - the very woman who should have come to help deal with the gangs and violence in this city in the first place. The very one who is responsible for how bad things have gotten here. She and the other Celestial Councillors don't deserve their position above the rest of us if they refuse to take their responsibilities to us seriously."

I shook my head, hating how his words twisted things and made them sound so fucking reasonable. Yes, the Councillors could have done a lot more for our city and yes, I'd cursed them for leaving us to toil under gang rule more than once in my lifetime, but it was a big fucking kingdom and I knew they had a lot to deal with outside of our shitty corner of it. Besides, whatever they'd done or hadn't done couldn't excuse everything Titan was responsible for. Could it?

"Stop this, Elise. Join me. I'll allow you to have just as much say in the way we go forwards as I have now. Look at all you've done already - you created peace between the gangs, you made a family out of men destined to let their hatred cause so much death and violence that countless lives would have been destroyed by them. You feel the call of this work just the way your father once did, just the way I do. It's why we formed the connection we did. You know it in your heart, what I'm doing, what I want to achieve is the right thing."

I shook my head again, over and over because I didn't want his words to make sense to me. I didn't want to agree with any of them. Water was running from Titan's hands now, the power of that Element being ripped away too and I knew that soon the only Element left in his grasp would be the air magic he'd been born with. Then we had to finish this. But my heart was racing and doubts were creeping in as the feelings I had for him and the reasons he was giving started to pull at my resolve.

Leon caught my eye across the circle, his muscles taut beneath the onslaught of raw power which was billowing between all of us and though he never stopped chanting, there was a question in his eyes. One more thing I needed to know the answer to before I could make any kind of insane decisions right now.

"What about Gareth Tempa?" I demanded, my voice rough but strong and my gaze snapped back to Titan. "If you want me to consider your point of view then tell me what happened to him. What did you do to my brother?"

Titan's lips parted, his eyes wide with a sudden understanding as the last of the missing pieces slotted together for him and he realised exactly who I was and what I'd lost before he met me. I waited for him to say something, to give me this last piece of the puzzle. The question which had brought me here, had delivered me to my kings and embroiled me in this fucking mess in the first place. *Who killed my brother?* And as I looked into the eyes of the man who had become something so much more than a teacher to me, who had held me when I cried and had understood my grief in such a beautiful, tangible way, I saw the truth there.

He was the one I had been hunting for all this time.

He was the one who had taken Gareth from me and destroyed the only good thing I'd ever truly owned before I came here.

And as he closed his mouth again, keeping his secrets and hoarding the truth I so desperately needed to hear, I knew.

There was no way I could ever join forces with him. There was no way

I could ever understand his play for power or accept the methods he'd used to achieve all he had up until this moment.

There was no excusing the things he'd done. He was a tyrant, hell bent on reshaping the world into the mould he thought fit best. And like all tyrants, he'd chosen to crush anyone who tried to question him or stand in his way.

Like my brother.

Titan may have begun this journey from a place of grief and injustice, but he'd more than become the monster he was so desperate to rid the world of.

And it was time his story came to an end.

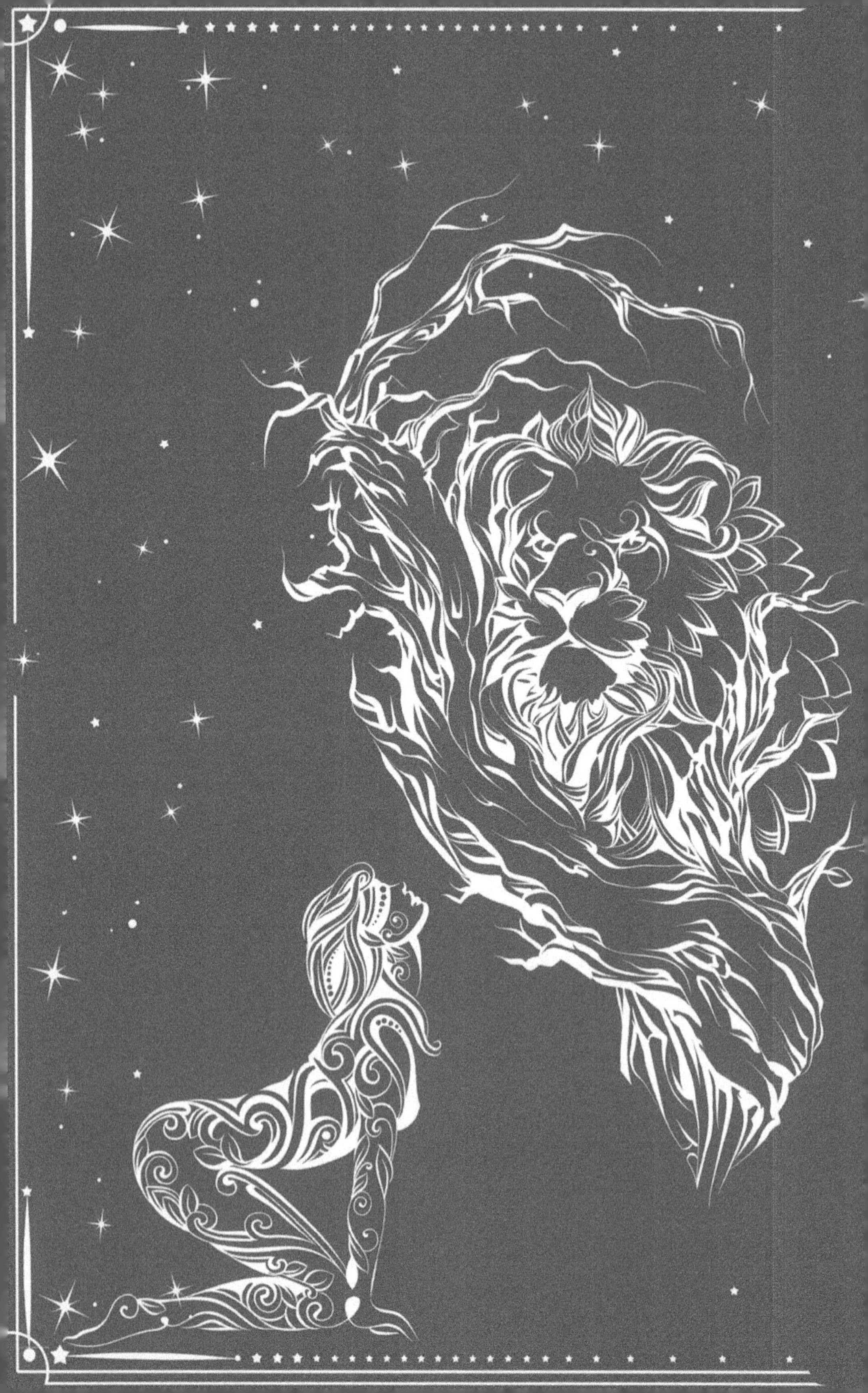

LEON

CHAPTER FIFTY TWO

The water Element started to swirl away from Titan's body, water droplets spinning out around him as we stole from him what he'd stolen from countless others. A sweet satisfaction filled me to see him hurt as he cried out, trying to fight our combined power. But it was too late. The dude was done for. And our girl wasn't going to be swayed by the bullshit spewing from his lips, she saw him for what he was. Which was a dark Fae hellbent on stealing power in the name of a cause he'd long since lost his morals to.

"That's it," Gabriel said through his teeth as we chanted louder at Titan and he wailed, stumbling to his knees as the last of the water Element was torn from his body then spiralled up towards the stars in a glittering swirl of blue light.

Titan panted, sweat beading on his brow as his hands pressed to the earth, his back hunched as his features twisted in pain.

Silence fell and my jaw tightened as our chant fell quiet and we stared at the pathetic Fae between us.

"How could you?" Titan growled, raising his head and glowering at

Elise. "I welcomed you into my arms, I wanted more for us, I loved you when you had no one else. And *this* is how you repay me?"

"I'm not your daughter, Titan," Elise hissed. "Our relationship was built on a lie. I know what you are. And I know what you did to my brother."

"Gareth Tempa didn't have to face the fate he did," he spat. "He couldn't keep his nose out of things that didn't concern him."

"So you silenced him because he interfered with your fucking plans?" Elise roared, still desperate for that one truth which seemed so determined to elude her.

"You'll never understand. Sacrifices had to be made for the greater good," Titan snarled, then leapt to his feet and threw out his palms. A huge blast of air exploded from him and we were all thrown backwards off the circle, slamming to the ground. "You may have taken my access to the other Elements, but you cannot strip my own Element from my bones, I am still all powerful with air magic alone!" he cried.

We needed to get back to the circle, had to start the final part of the incantation to strip the last of his stolen power from him before he managed to escape.

But as Elise shot to her feet, I knew she wasn't going to risk that. A Vampire could drain the stolen magic faster than we could do it as one with the spell and the look of furious determination in her eyes said her mind was already made up on that. She wanted to end this. And now that he was weakened and his stolen Elements were gone, she could do it.

Gabriel leapt upright, crying out, "Wait!" as he ran to catch her. But his arms closed around air as she shot forward with the speed of her Order, tearing into the circle and colliding with Titan. "No!" he yelled and my heart lurched with concern. Why was he trying to stop this? Didn't he trust our girl with that power? Had he *seen* something bad?

My heart pounded unevenly as Elise's fist cracked across Titan's face before she drove her fangs into his neck. He shouted out in horror as she immobilised his magic and started drinking and Gabriel stared on in fear as his eyes glazed with a vision.

"Gabriel, what do we do?!" I shouted, looking to the others.

"She's strong enough to do this. This is the fastest way to take the magic from Titan so that it can be released back to the stars where it belongs with the souls of the Fae who owned it," Dante called and my heart lifted, but Gabriel's face only twisted with more terror as he was lost to some dark vision.

Shit, this isn't good. Or is it? I don't know, I don't know.

"Go on, baby!" Ryder roared as he got to his feet.

Elise drained Titan dry as he screamed in pain, tearing at her arms in vain as he tried to fight her off. She drank and drank from him and Titan turned pale, his eyes widening as he realised she wasn't going to stop. He thrashed and fought, but my little monster was in full savage mode as she fed from him, stealing away his life. It was brutal, wild, poetic. And I was so here for it.

Titan crumpled to his knees, holding onto her waist almost like an embrace as he gazed up at her. "I'm not a bad m-man," he stammered in fear then she gripped his head, leaning down to talk directly to him.

"That's the thing about bad people, Titan, they always think they're in the right. But you've destroyed countless lives, you've killed those who needed help. And if you think that doing it in the name of some grand cause redeems you, then why don't you ask the stars for mercy when you meet them in the sky?" she hissed then whipped his head sideways with a loud snap, breaking his neck and letting him fall dead on the ground.

She hung her head, her shoulders heaving and I pushed to my feet, running to her.

"Elise!" I cried, whooping to the sky as I leapt forward to pull her into my arms. We'd done it. Titan was dead, the world was saved, we were all heroes and it was time to have a celebration orgy on top of Titan's dead body. Too much? Nah.

I reached for Elise, but she suddenly whipped around and a storm of air exploded out from her so powerfully that I was thrown to the ground again, tumbling away across the field.

I slammed into Gabriel and he gasped as he was jolted out of his vision.

"Elise?" Dante called, a note of panic in his voice and I looked over to her, finding her eyes wide and sparking with an almighty kind of power. A crazed, frantic look fell over her face before she turned and shot away with her Vampire speed, tearing off into the night.

"Elise!" I bellowed in fear, turning to Gabriel as he shoved me off his lap and my ass hit the ground. "Where did she go?" I begged of him as Ryder and Dante came running over in alarm.

"She took his power," Gabriel rasped. "Not just his magic, every scrap of dark power in his veins. She took it all. She was supposed to release it to the stars, but her heart was so full of pain over Titan and Gareth that when that moment came and the power offered to take the pain from her, she let it instead of banishing it from her body." His face paled as he looked to the stars in terror, his eyes glazing before he spoke in a strange whisper that wasn't his voice at all, the strength of it sending a tremor through the earth beneath us. *"Death is coming."*

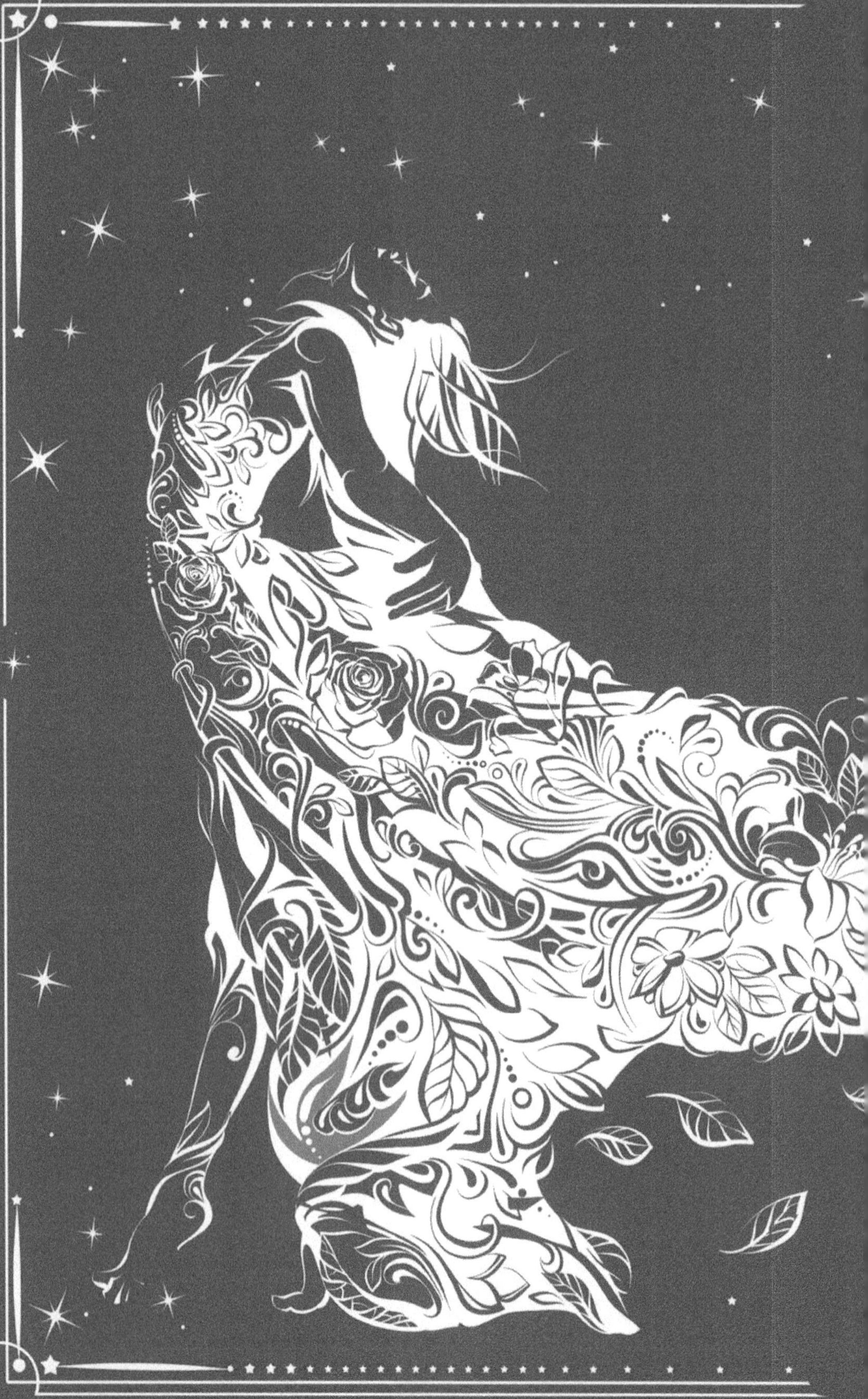

ELISE

CHAPTER FIFTY THREE

I ran and ran, shooting south towards Alestria as the sheer weight of the power now crashing through my body was almost enough to crush me. It was all I could think about, all I could feel, this unending torrent of raw power which was begging for me to use it as much as my body was begging for blood.

I needed an outlet for it. I needed to release it into the world and bring about every wish and desire I'd ever owned. This was my time. Mine alone. They said absolute power could corrupt absolutely and my soul had clearly been corrupted by the vengeful need of mine.

But I didn't care, because nothing in the world could ever compare to the feeling of this energy coursing through my limbs. I was unstoppable, unbeatable, a fucking all powerful being given flesh. A motherfucking star walking the earth and bleeding power for all to see.

My mind was clamouring with whispers I couldn't quite hear, urging me on, begging for vengeance, showing me faces of Fae who deserved death and I realised that these were the voices of the Fae whose magic I now owned.

This magic was so powerful that I was peeling back the veil and speaking with the dead.

Titan may have been the one they gifted their Elements to but when I stole that power from him, their magic had passed to me along with their wants, needs desires and hatred.

The world really was a dark and twisted place. There was so much evil here. So many villainous Fae who deserved death for the things they'd done and the lives they'd ruined. Titan had stolen this power from Fae who had suffered worse than most. Who had ended their lives rather than go on living with the hand they'd been dealt by fate. But in gifting their magic, they'd gifted so much more than that. They'd left their need for vengeance and thirst for retribution behind too.

And I was their tool now.

I ran at the fullest speed available to me with my gifts, but the bloodlust was raging through my veins and I wasn't moving nearly fast enough to sate the need in me for violence.

With a roar of fury at the injustices the original owners of this power had faced, I leapt into the air, throwing my hands out and propelling myself skyward with the full force of my power, the air magic so much more potent than what I was used to as it catapulted me into the sky.

I moaned as the power rushed through me, filling me up and pouring from me in waves of ecstasy as I took a moment to adjust to my new position in the sky and set the glowing lights of Alestria on the horizon in my sight.

The voices inside me cried out, begging me to avenge them, showing me the faces of the Fae who had ruined them and filling my entire being with a thirst for blood that was so powerful I couldn't even begin to resist it.

I shot forward, flying without need for wings and moving so fast that the world beneath me was nothing but a blur, the city growing closer and closer by the second.

I groaned in ecstasy as I went, this power so much more than I ever could have imagined. This raw energy so much greater than anything else I'd ever desired in all my life.

I didn't need anything aside from this. I was a slave to this potent magic, and I was more than willing to be its vessel. There was no pain here, no grief or heartache or anything soft. If I gave myself to this power, let it corrupt me, I'd be unstoppable. And that was one of the most tempting offers I'd ever known.

A memory that wasn't mine flashed in my head of a house with a blue door and a man who lived there. His daughter was one of the Fae whose power I now held, and she screamed at me to take his life the way he had destroyed hers by creeping into her room in the dark, night after night. Her thirst for vengeance coated my tongue and the vile taste of loathing swept through my body.

He was going to die by my hand. And if the screaming pleas of the others I owed my power to was anything to go by, he would be the first of many.

I dropped out of the sky like a missile, my fangs snapping free a moment before I collided with the roof of the house, crashing through tiles and bricks with an explosion of power. I slammed to halt in the middle of a shabby front room with wallpaper peeling off the faded blue walls.

A man sat in an armchair right in front of me, a beer clutched loosely in one hand and stains on his shirt as he gaped at me in shock and fear. He was a vile creature, one who had caused so much pain and suffering to his own daughter, who had made this house a hell to the child he should have loved and protected above all else.

"Hello, Ed," I purred, my lips peeling back to reveal my fangs as his daughter screamed encouragement at me from beyond the veil.

I shot forward as Ed screamed, my fangs ripping his throat out as my power slammed into him and tore his limbs from his body, hurling them in every direction before eviscerating him entirely.

A cry of pure bliss tore from my lungs as my power swelled at the kill and the taste of blood on my lips spurred me on. But it wasn't enough. The names on this list were endless. The vengeance I sought unstoppable.

The power in me was humming with pleasure and my entire being was coming alive with it. Tonight, I was a predator on the hunt. The most powerful being in the entire kingdom, and Solaria would run red with the blood of the guilty before dawn.

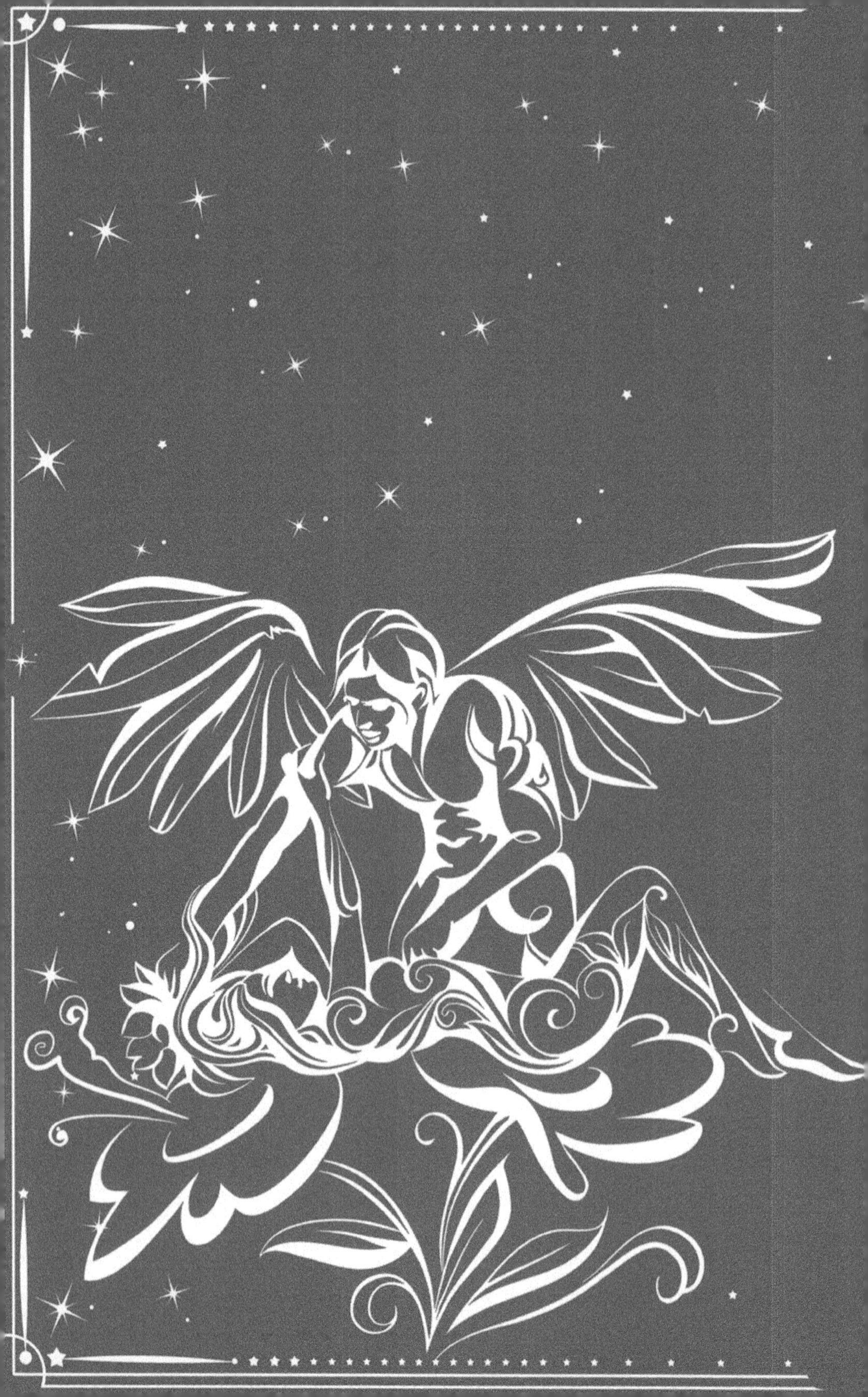

GABRIEL

CHAPTER FIFTY FOUR

I *saw* Elise cleansing the whole kingdom of the cruellest Fae she could find, the dead whispering in her ears and urging her towards their destruction. But the power would corrupt her if she stayed within it too long and we were already wasting too much time.

"I have to go," I called to the others as they rode on Dante's back and I flew along beside them. "I can get to her before you can. Just keep following the tracking spell."

"Bring her back to us," Leon called in desperation and I nodded, a promise in my gaze before I put on a burst of speed and tore away from them.

Elise had the only fucking stardust we had with her because I'd thrown my supply at Orion to save his damn life. His death had been inevitable tonight if I hadn't gotten rid of him so completely and The Sight had shown me that he wouldn't be able to get to another supply of stardust in time to come back to the fight.

The stars were playing with us and the thrill of our victory was cast into despair instead as I saw the dangers Elise faced. If she couldn't find a way to anchor herself and release this power, her soul was going to be corrupted.

She'd stop hunting down the blood of the guilty and start killing blindly as the power consumed her. I had to reach her, had to find a way to save her before it was too late.

I flew across Alestria, the world a blur as I focused on nothing but the tracking spell binding me to her.

I raced towards the outskirts of the city, my gaze locking on a flash of movement below me on the dark street. Elise was tearing along it at a furious pace and I clenched my jaw in determination as I dove from the sky, my gaze fixed on my girl.

"Elise!" I cried to her, but the wind stole my voice away as I flew harder and faster to catch her.

Flashes of The Sight sped across my vision and I lost all view of the world as I was shown the future. Elise's fangs were in my throat, she needed to feed on me, she needed my taste to remember who she was, to ground her before the power became too much and stole her from us forever. Gareth's plea to me in a vision suddenly rang loudly in my head once more, his meaning suddenly clear. *"The power will destroy her and all that she loves, let her bite you, it's the only way!"*

The visions showed me what would happen if that fate came to pass, the light fading from my body, death stealing me away beyond the veil. It was a real possibility that I would die in this endeavour. But I needed to save her soul from being forever blackened by this power living in her. She had to release it. And if my death was the answer, then so be it.

The Sight released me and I found myself two feet from Elise, unable to stop as I collided with her. We hit the ground, tumbling furiously along the tarmac and I wrapped my wings around her to protect her from the worst of the blows, softening the earth with my magic a little too late. We finally came to a halt with me pinning her down as we remained within the feathery cocoon of my wings.

"Angel, I'm here," I said breathlessly, but her eyes were wild and gleaming with darkness and it didn't look like she recognised me at all.

She was painted red with blood and the need for more of it burned within her gaze. She lunged up and I didn't fight as her fangs drove into my neck while I held her against me in an embrace.

"I love you," I told her as she drank from me savagely, clawing at my back as she fed like she was starved. "You don't need this power, angel. Come back to me."

She thrashed, rolling us over and slamming me against the ground as she continued to feed, hungry groans leaving her.

"I've loved you every day. The more I fought it, the more I wanted you." I clutched her arm, feeling blood dripping down it and I healed the wound with a curse as it rushed over her wrist, coating the bracelet there in red. "If I could meet you for the first time again, I'd do it all differently. I'd love you as you deserved to be loved from day one," I gritted out as she swallowed mouthful after mouthful of my blood and I prayed my words would reach her as I started to weaken. "I'd make sure you never felt alone, and we would have worked to find King together from the very beginning. I fucked up, angel. I'm not your equal, I'm not your mate. But I do love you with the entirety of my heart and there isn't a force in this world which could change that. I just figured it out all too late and I'm sorry for how I treated you. I'm sorry I caused you pain. But I'm here now and I'm not going anywhere. If I'm destined for someone else, let them wait forever, because I'm never going to leave your side, Elise."

Her feeding started to slow and I dragged in a breath which didn't seem to give me any air at all. I felt fate shifting, a life opening up for Elise once more with a million beautiful paths for her to follow. But just as many without me in them. My heartbeat slowed and I *saw* my death coming for me as clear as day, like a blanket of darkness tucking me into an eternal sleep. I feared it stealing me away from my love. My heart surely would be ripped out, left here with her. It couldn't exist anywhere without her now.

I dragged my fingers along her cheek as darkness descended on me, the stars shining blindingly bright in my periphery. But I didn't want to look at them, the only goddess in this world I wanted to gaze at was right in front of me. And I'd look at her until I could look no more.

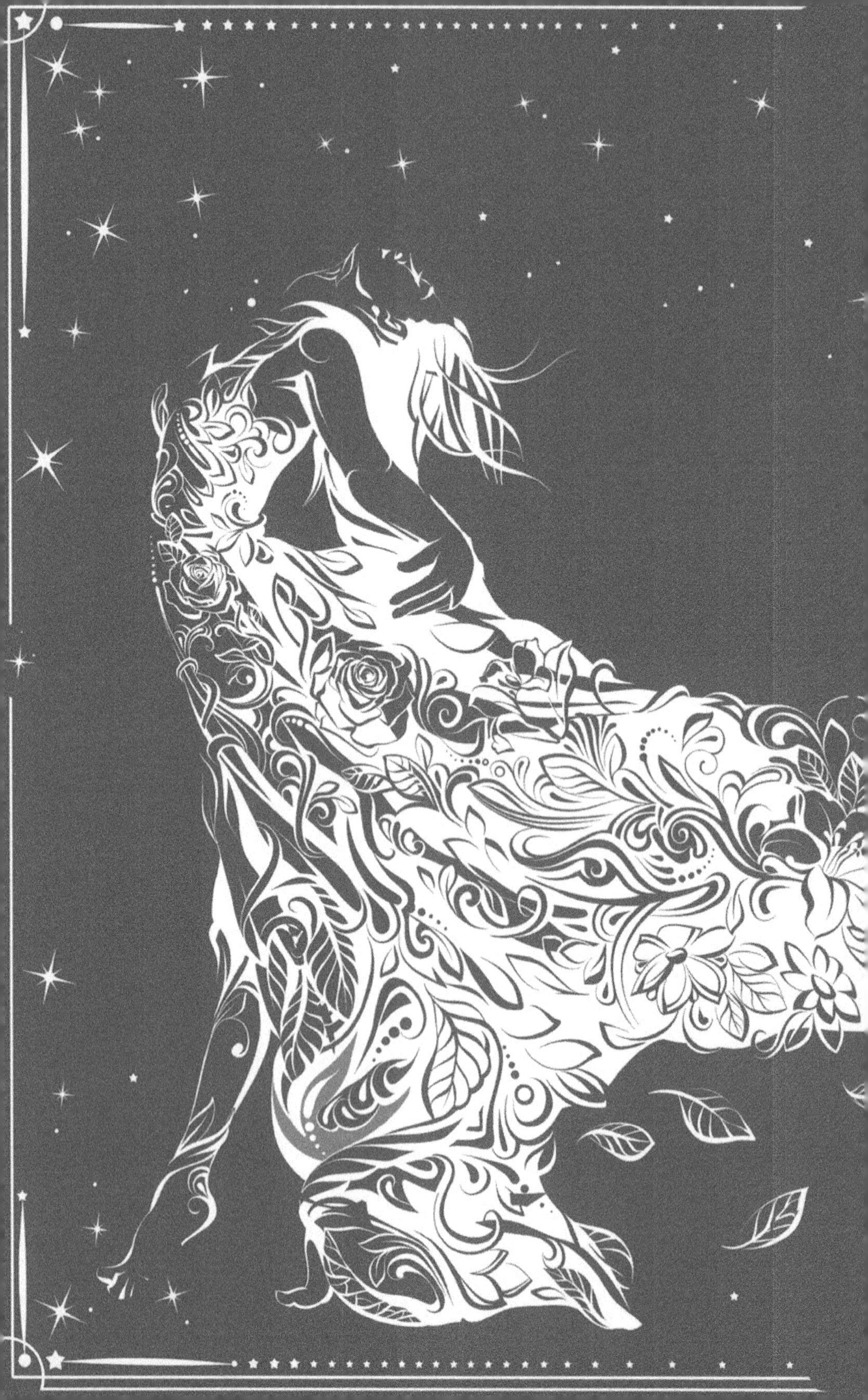

Elise

CHAPTER FIFTY FIVE

My teeth sank deep into flesh, the rich, unbridled taste of the power I was consuming lighting me up in the dark, calling to my soul and making me groan as a memory tried to force its way beneath my skin. Like I was forgetting something. Something important. But as the blood rolled over my tongue and I swallowed greedily, it was hard to focus on anything other than my desire for more and more of it.

But as I began to fall into that dark place where my unending power and insatiable bloodlust met and all else was forgotten, something else began to force its way into my thoughts and I gasped as my attention was snared by it, ripping my fangs free of the flesh I'd been draining.

The white jasper crystal on my wrist hummed and burned with power and memories began to press in on me from all around. I gasped as I was torn out of the present and into the past, recognising the dreams I'd been having lately alongside many other happy times me and Gareth had spent together. I felt the way he'd felt when he looked at me. I felt the weight of his love as it wrapped itself all around me. And I felt the pain of his absence more sharply than I had in a long, long time. It was like he was right here with me, like I could reach out and hold his hand, feel him at my side where he always should have been...

A sharp slice of grief cut through me as I thought about the time I'd spent missing him, aching to know where he was and what had happened to him. My head snapped around with this strange place that had taken me hostage and I found myself looking at a memory which was much darker than the rest, a forbidding sense of unease filling me as I looked upon it and I knew in my heart that not only did I not want to know what was contained within it, but that this was where I would finally get the answer I'd been seeking.

"What happened to you?" I breathed to the dark, needing to know, no matter what it cost me.

Suddenly I was falling, tumbling backwards through time and space and landing in a body which wasn't mine and spoke with my brother's voice.

"Out with it then, Gareth, why are you lurking here instead of waiting for us with the others?" King asked again and I licked my lips, standing before him in the corridor of Altair halls.

"I'll go and see that the final preparations are being made to your satisfaction, Card Master," Nightshade said in a clipped tone, giving me a sweeping look before brushing past us. She headed towards the entrance to the secret corridor which would bring her out to the woods where the ceremony was being held and left me there alone with the monster I was trying to escape.

"I should get going too," I said, hastily, hoping he'd believe I was just on my way out to the woods as well.

"Why are you running so late, Gareth?" King enquired, stepping towards me as their ever-shifting face and voice changed once more, this time revealing an old woman within the hood of their cloak.

"I got caught up with a bunch of stuff with some of the kids in my class," I said, trying to shrug it off and follow after Nightshade with my heart racing and my palms slick.

I pushed my fingers into my pockets to hide the nervous tremor which tumbled through me and found the white jasper crystal in my left pocket. I hooked it into my grip, holding it tight as it burned hot in my hand and taking a little comfort from the thing.

King watched me as I stepped around him and I gave a little bow of my head in a show of respect as I headed towards the same secret passage Nightshade had gone for.

For a few, blissful seconds, I thought that was it. I'd gotten away with it, had made it past his notice and could still try and figure out a way to run tonight before it was too late. But then a strong hand wrapped around my bicep and I was tugged to a halt.

"Look at me, Gareth," King said in the honey sweet tone of a woman.

I swallowed thickly, taking half a second to compose myself as I turned to meet their gaze, my throat bobbing.

"Can I help you with something else, Card Master?" I asked diligently, the crystal burning hotter in my hand as I gripped it even tighter.

"You should be gathering the others, not engaging in anything with other students at this vital time."

"I'm sorry," I said quickly, dropping my eyes and inspecting the floor between us as my pulse thundered and I tried to think of the right thing to say. "I...was actually ambushed by Gabriel Nox."

"Nox?" King asked curiously.

"Yeah...he's erm, a total asshole and he hates me. And I guess he just saw me walking alone and he jumped me. Beat the shit out of me if I'm being totally honest. It, ah, just took me a little while to come around after. And then I had to heal and stuff. I'm really sorry, truly. I promise I'll work even harder to make it up to you." I forced myself to raise my eyes to theirs, to let them see the truth my words held and hope they accepted that was all there was to know.

King sighed as they inspected me with the eyes of a young man who could have been my age. They nodded, releasing my arm. "Fae on Fae fights cannot be helped, but I hope to build a mantra of respect and dignity among my new world where such vicious, random attacks are no longer a concern for the innocents. It is one thing to fight with someone who deserves it, but quite another to prey on those weaker than you for nothing more than sport."

They sneered that last word and I nodded profusely. Obviously I wasn't about to tell them that Gabriel had a perfectly valid reason to attack me.

"Run along then. The moon is rising, and we don't have time to delay."

"Yes, Card Master." I bowed my head again and took off, relief spilling through me as I managed to escape at last.

I took four long strides down the corridor, fighting against the urge to run as I tried to figure out exactly how I was still going to pull this off.

"Oh, Gareth?" King called, their voice changed once again.

I fell still, taking a breath before looking back at them. "Yes?"

"I have to ask you, as tonight I will be interrogating all members of the Deck anyway. But I need to know if you hold any knowledge about a book which was stolen from me?"

"A book?" I squeaked, the pitch of my voice spiking alongside my pulse and I cleared my throat quickly as I hurried on. "What kind of book?"

"The Magicae Mortuorum. It is filled with spells and magic too powerful for most Fae to understand. I need it for my work, but in the wrong hands it could be very dangerous indeed. I have of course had to punish the man who was responsible for its safe keeping. But unfortunately, he was unable to shed any light on its whereabouts before he died and I have good reason to suspect he wasn't the one responsible for the theft. That being said, the only other logical conclusion is that there is a traitor in our midst. So I have to ask you just like everyone else. Did you steal from me?"

I shook my head too fast, or maybe not fast enough. My heart was thrashing so hard that my pulse was thundering in my eardrums and it took me a moment to summon the words I needed.

"No," I breathed. "I would never do anything to hurt the Deck. I know *how important your work is to the future of Alestria."*

"How disappointing," King sighed, their voice shifting again to a dark and menacing growl. "I do believe you're lying to me."

I stood frozen in place, my limbs locking up as I stared at them and a thousand lies tumbled through my mind, but as I tried to force myself to voice any of them, a louder more desperate voice screamed in the back of my head that it was too late. They knew. They fucking knew. They were so powerful that I was certain they had all kinds of detection spells surrounding us to seek out lies and falsehoods. And even if they didn't, I could feel the last remaining bonds which bound my soul to theirs thrumming with energy, digging deep beneath my skin and seeking out my deception. They knew. And I was out of time.

Shit on it.

In what was either one of the bravest or stupidest things I'd ever done in my life, I raised my hand and threw a blast of air magic at King with the full power of my strength, knocking them flying back down the corridor as it took them by surprise.

Then I was running, sprinting, racing as far and as fast as I could go. The white jasper burned hot in my left hand, the thing seeming to radiate energy which I drew on for strength as I sprinted down the corridor and ripped open the door. I sped out into Acrux Courtyard, a terrified whinny escaping my throat as I ran for my fucking life.

I needed to shift then I had to fly far, far away from here. The second I hit the clouds, I'd turn my nose north and just keep going until even the rising sun couldn't catch up to me. I'd have to figure the rest out after that. I couldn't risk trying to get to the car and cash I'd hidden downtown with my fake documents inside it. I couldn't risk going home to grab Ella or Mom no matter how much I ached to do exactly that. I'd left the clues for Ella to find, she'd catch up to me eventually, I had to have faith in her. And right now, I just had to run the fuck away and hope King didn't catch me.

My body shivered as the shift started to take hold, but before I could sprout a single feather, let alone a wing, I slammed into a wall of solid air so hard that I felt my nose shatter on impact.

I fell back to the hard stone of the courtyard, blinking through the agony as my eyes took in the sight of the meteors streaming across the sky one after another, not paying me any attention as they went on their way at a colossal speed.

Footsteps approached me and I rolled over, panic tumbling through me as I scrambled up onto my knees, my eyes widening in fear as the cloaked figure stalked closer.

"You betrayed me," King said in a low voice filled with disappointment like he was scolding a naughty child. "You stole from me. Tried to run from me. I thought you were one of us, Gareth? I thought our vision for the future was aligned?"

"All I ever wanted was a future of freedom," I breathed, my hands shaking a little as I thought of Ella, wondering what would become of her if I wasn't around to set her free like I'd always promised.

"But I was giving that to you. To all Fae in Alestria," King said, coming to a halt right in front of me.

I tried to get up, but vines coiled around my arms, pinning me in place and making sure I remained there, kneeling at King's feet like some pious believer. He reached out to place a hand on my shoulder and healing magic washed through me, fixing my nose before he used water magic to remove the blood from my face and clothes too.

"I would have given you the world," King breathed sadly, looking down at me like doing this really did upset him, but I could see the decision in their cold, grey eyes and it didn't shift away when their face changed either.

"I don't want the world," I replied, my voice stronger than it had any right to be because I knew in that moment that I was looking my death in the eyes. "All I wanted was to make my own freedom." I didn't mention

Ella, I couldn't risk that, but my heart was breaking for her, my gut twisting and writhing at the thought of what would happen to her now. I was the one who was supposed to get us out of here. I was the one who had come to this academy to steal us a better life and opportunities the likes of us were never meant to be privy to.

What would she do now? How would she find her way free without me there to hold her hand? I wasn't even grieving the life I knew I was about to lose; I was grieving the one I knew I couldn't give her anymore. The one I'd promised her time and again. The only thing I'd ever wanted. I'd dreamed of taking her somewhere that she could thrive and become the woman I knew she was capable of being, but now I was going to leave her all alone in this dark and hateful world and I couldn't bear the thought of that.

I'm so sorry, Ella. I'm so fucking sorry I failed you.

"Tell me where the Magicae Mortuorum is and I'll make this quick," King said, their face hardening with a decision which was the end of me.

I straightened my spine, lifting my chin as I clung onto the one thing in this world that truly mattered to me. My sister wasn't going to be subjected to a world ruled over by this monster. The girl I loved more than life itself would never be forced to kneel before King the way I was now. And if that meant days, weeks, months of torture as they tried to rip the location of that book from me then so be it. I wouldn't give it up. I'd cast a blow against them which they couldn't easily recover from. There was dark magic in that thing which they needed to complete their plans and there was no way I'd ever give it back to them.

"Gone," I growled. "Sold on the black market, never to be seen again."

King's spine straightened and rage flashed through their eyes, the vines restraining me squeezing tighter as they crushed me with their power. But I stayed silent. Even if they shattered all of my bones, that answer was never going to change.

"You sold it?" King hissed.

"Money is freedom," I replied with a sneer. "Only those who have never lived at the bottom of the barrel fail to understand that. And all I ever wanted was to be free."

King's face changed again and again, their concealment spell seeming to writhe with their anger as they reached into the pocket of their cloak and pulled out five vials filled with electric blue crystals.

"Perhaps your tongue will loosen under the influence of these," he said slowly.

I stiffened, eyeing that drug fearfully and knowing full well what it was capable of. I'd seen too many Fae sacrifice their own lives with it, had watched Lorenzo's life get torn apart by it. It was a plague amongst our city which was being spread by this monster and his greed and the mere sight of it was enough to turn my stomach. I didn't want to take that. I didn't want a single breath of it entering my lungs.

But as King began to shake the vials, activating the crystals and turning them to vapour, I knew that wasn't going to be up to me. They were taking my own choice in it away, just like they would take my life away too.

I didn't beg, didn't cry, or plead or try to make King pity me. I knew that wouldn't work. I knew in my heart that it was already too late for any of that.

Instead, I closed my eyes and fell into all the best memories I had of my sister and me. Of every smile and laugh. Every moment we'd spent together planning the life we ached to live. I remembered all the moments in which I'd held her and comforted her and how much she'd made my life better. She'd been it for me. My guiding star, my little angel and the one person in this miserable world who had made everything worth surviving, every day worth living. She'd been my light and my dark and the most honest, unending love I'd ever known or ever would.

The crystal in my palm burned hot as it drank in the memories and I hoped that one day she might find it and see them. See and feel just how much I'd loved her and know that I wouldn't have changed a single thing. Every risk

I had taken had been for her. Every mistake I'd made and every pain I'd felt had all been worth it if it only meant she got to smile a little more often and live a little better. I willed the white jasper to keep the memories safe for her, to lock them away from prying eyes and make sure no one could unlock the secrets I was leaving here.

King cast the air around my head into a bubble as he opened the vials of Killblaze, containing the smoke within it. I held my breath as I tried to fight off the inevitable with the memory of my sister's hand in mine so vivid in my mind that I swear I could almost feel it.

My lungs burned and ached as the Killblaze pressed to my lips and nose, contained there by King's magic and I held out for as long as I possibly could.

But eventually my body betrayed me, my mouth opening as I sucked in a deep breath laced with the poison this monster had created to serve their twisted purpose.

The drug rushed into my system and King removed the vines that had been restraining me as I crashed backwards, landing hard on the solid ground with a laugh tearing from my lungs.

I was smiling, smiling so big that it was a surprise my face hadn't torn in two.

I watched the pretty lights zipping through the sky overhead. Zip. Zip. Zip. Where were they going? Somewhere better than here? Somewhere far, far away where people were happy, and dreams were fulfilled? There were so many things I'd wanted to do with my life. So, so many things. But now they were gone, zipping away just like those meteors, and leaving me behind down here in the dirt.

A face floated before me, eyes like fire and full of malice.

"Where is the book?" King asked me and I laughed again.

"Gone," I whispered because I knew that was the right thing to say. They were a demon and they couldn't have it. It was gone. "Gone, gone, gone,

far away forever and a day." I screamed like a banshee just because I could, and a thick hand slapped down across my mouth.

"Tell me-" The face stopped talking abruptly, a curse escaping them which made me twitch. In fact, my entire body was twitching and writhing and something in my chest was beating so fast it sounded like a drum, bang, bang, bang. It was too fast, too fast for me and it hurt almost as much as it made me laugh.

I watched as the man with all the faces tugged his fancy cloak off and suddenly there was a flash of fire which made me gasp as it went up in flames that warmed me up and then burned me through until I felt like I was burning with it and I began to kick and flail even more while I screamed against his palm over my mouth.

The man holding me down growled something at me and suddenly I recognised him. His face wasn't changing anymore, and he was someone I knew. Professor Titan frowned down at me as another voice called out from far, far away.

I thought he was nice. He seemed so nice in class. But now I was looking on his true face and I could see that wasn't right at all. He wasn't a nice man, he was a harbinger of hatred and a thief of power. He was a liar and a manipulator and now he was going to be my death too.

"Offer up your power to me," Titan hissed, taking my free hand in his. "I will use it to create the kind of world where everyone is free as you wish."

Magic tingled along my arm and I looked at his kind smile, wondering why not? Why not let him have it and use it like he said? I wouldn't need it anymore anyway. I was slipping away. My body was crashing and burning and soon I would be gone for good. Far away and I was never coming back.

The white jasper in my other hand seemed to flare with heat suddenly and I was shaking my head at Titan, words tumbling from my lips which I wasn't sure were even words at all as I pulled my power back into me and kept it close to my heart with my love for the only girl I'd ever really needed. It was mine. He couldn't have it just like he couldn't have her.

"Never," I hissed against his palm, my voice stronger for a moment as I found some resilience in my love for her.

I wouldn't give it to him. Not even while I could feel my body spasming and my organs constricting, and my heart still thundered like a war drum in my chest, racing towards the end while battling for it not to be over. Not ever.

That voice called to me from far away again and a funny little piece of me wondered if they might be able to help me.

"Help!" I cried, my voice cracking and punctuated with laughter as my spine arched against the hard stone beneath me and my body fought against this agony consuming it.

Titan cursed, looking over his shoulder before calling out too. "Help, me! I've found a student in trouble - I think he's overdosing!"

Thundering footsteps raced closer, and Titan leaned in once more. "I wish you could have just stuck by me like you promised."

I turned my eyes on him and laughed louder. I laughed and laughed as I felt my body giving up.

Professor Mars appeared then, cursing and pressing his hands to my chest as he tried to heal me. But Killblaze didn't work like that. No, no, no. Once it was inside you there was no getting it back out until it ran its course. And this dose was going to consume me before my body could consume it.

I turned my eyes from the man who was trying to rescue me and gripped the crystal in my hand even tighter as I looked up at the sky. I didn't want to look at someone battling against my fate when I knew it couldn't be changed, and I didn't want Titan to be the last thing I saw on this cruel earth. So I watched the meteors speeding by in the sky overhead. They were so beautiful, so peaceful and free. I hoped Ella could see them too.

I love you, my little angel. And I'm so, so sorry. I wish I could have set you free like I promised. I wish I hadn't failed you.

The lights in the heavens above began to dim and the pain in my body *fell away too. Or maybe it was me who was falling. Maybe I was the one who was saying goodbye. I just wished I didn't have to. Because all I'd ever wanted was to live a real life with real choices and to spend days in the sun with my sister by my side without anymore worries hanging over us.*

But that was gone now. It was gone and so was I and I just hoped that somehow, she'd find a way to claim it for herself without me. Because the worst thing about dying, was knowing that I was leaving her alone…

I crashed back out of that memory with agony tearing through my limbs and grief clutching my heart in a vice as I finally got the answers I'd been hunting for and they ripped me apart more truly than anything I'd ever known.

The power raging through my body was nothing to this pain. The loss I felt so visceral that it cut me to the bone.

I looked down at my blood which was coating the crystal. The crystal which had needed Gareth's blood to unlock it – but he and I shared blood just like we had always shared everything else. He really had left me these answers and I'd had them with me all along.

The pain of what I'd just learned was ripping into me soul deep but as I dropped my head, my eyes fell from the crystal to the man beneath me, horror spilling into me as I found my Harpy there, bleeding and falling away from me too, threatening to rip the last fractured pieces of my heart to shreds if I didn't do something to save him.

I cradled him against me as I poured healing magic from my body into his and my tears cascaded down onto his cheeks in a torrent.

"Come back to me," I demanded as my magic took root and began to heal him with all the desperation of everything I was. And as the stars sparkled overhead, for once, I wondered if they might be listening.

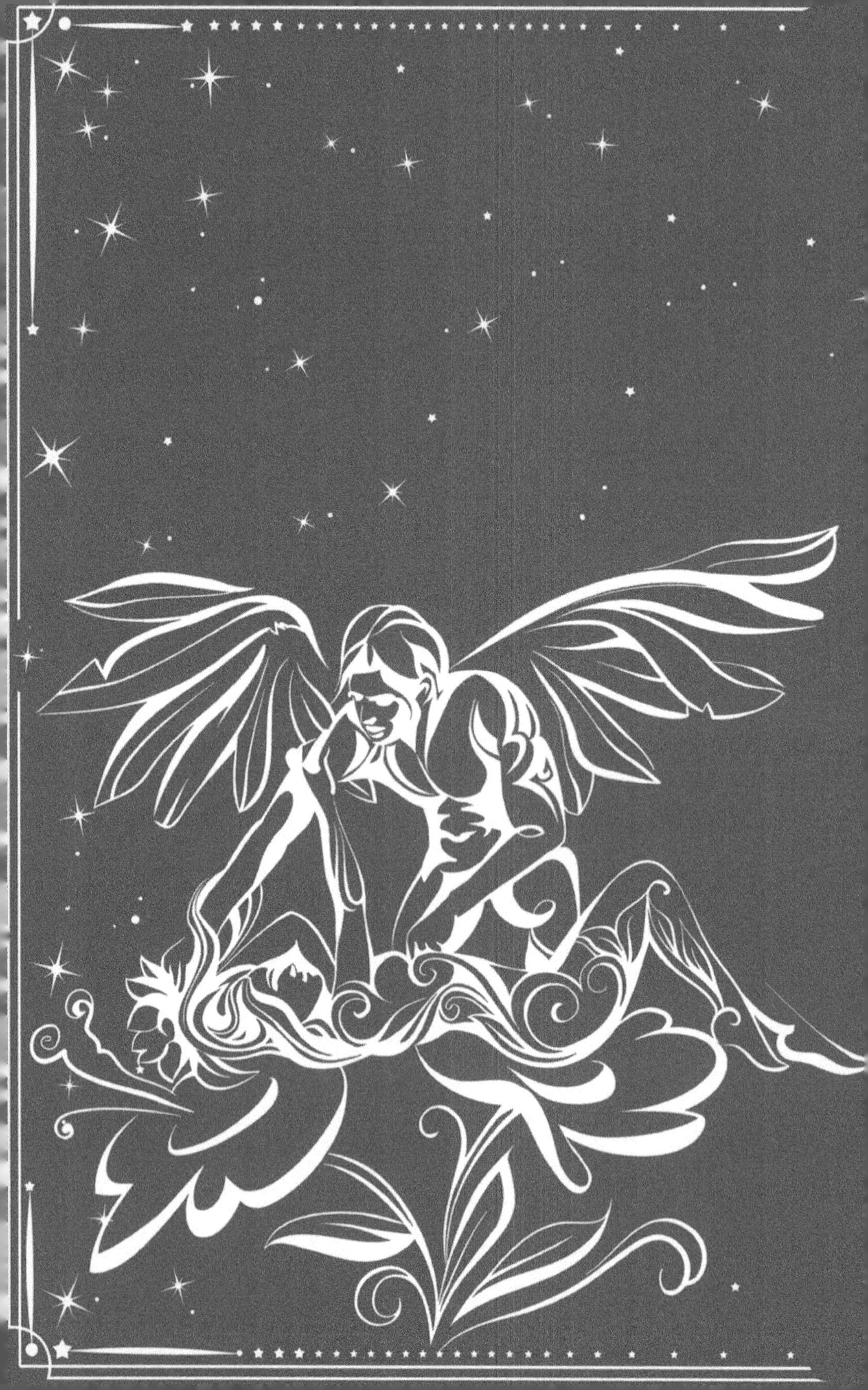

GABRIEL

CHAPTER FIFTY SIX

"*Wake up, son of fate,*" the ethereal voice whispered in my mind and my eyes flickered open, but only darkness greeted me. *"Your fate hangs in the balance."*

I tried to reach for the place Elise's fangs had sliced into my throat, but I couldn't feel my body at all. I was hanging suspended in an expanse of eternity and slowly, the darkness began to flutter before me like a veil.

"Gabriel?" a woman called to me from beyond it and I desperately tried to see her as the darkness continued to ripple in a breeze I couldn't feel. There was light beyond there, the sound of water running and laughter carrying from its depths.

"Hello?" I called, an ache in my soul drawing me to that voice.

"The world will fall without you, those in your future need you," the stars spoke to me, their power ringing through the depths of my soul.

"Then send me back," I demanded, panic flaring in my chest. "I want to be with Elise."

"The daughter of blood has many mates."

"And I'm her fourth," I snarled fiercely.

The stars started whispering in a language I couldn't understand, and my heart pounded furiously.

"Gabriel!" the woman called again from beyond the veil and something deep inside me dragged me towards her. I fought it hard, not wanting to move an inch towards that eternal place where Elise didn't exist. "You must go back!" she cried and a lump shifted in my throat.

"Who are you?" I called, but before she could reply, the stars' voices filled my head again.

"A great burden awaits you on your path. Four years from now, the dice of fate will be rolled once more. Are you strong enough to face the tests placed in your path? Are you strong enough to save your family?"

My heart beat furiously. "I'd do anything for my family."

"Then beware the lord of shadow, and seek the twin flames."

"What does that mean?" I begged of the stars, but I was suddenly dragged away from the dark and pain burst through my neck. My eyes flew open and I found Elise healing me, holding me close as tears coated her cheeks and she begged me to return to her.

"I'm here," I rasped, my throat dry and my mind whirling from all I'd heard. She shifted back to look at my face, her gaze frantic as she took me in and confirmed I was really here with her.

"You're okay," she choked out then leaned down and crushed her lips to mine. I tasted her tears, her pain, her love. It was all tangled into this furious kiss that made my soul rise to the edges of my flesh in a desperate bid to join with hers.

When she leaned back, unimaginable power flared in her eyes and I could see her fighting against the call of it to stay here with me. I needed to make her let go.

"Release it, angel," I begged of her, but she shook her head.

"Not yet," she said, her eyes flicking up to gaze down the road we were on.

I slid her off of me, moving to sit up and follow her line of sight to where two headlights punctured the dark in the distance. I could only make them out with the use of my Harpy vision but I got the feeling they were headed here for us. "What is it?" I asked, holding her hand, afraid she might run away at any moment. If I lost her again, I feared I'd never get her back.

A vision flashed through my mind which answered the question I'd asked, the Celestial Councillors were in that car, Melinda Altair, Tiberius Rigel, Antonia Capella and Lionel Acrux. They'd come to deal with King at long last, but it was all too fucking late, wasn't it?

I saw them chatting back and forth, casual as anything like our whole kingdom wasn't at risk.

"Did we really need to take the car for this stretch of the journey, Lionel?" Melinda clipped.

"I like to take in the scenery." He shrugged. "We stardusted most of the way. I don't know why you're in such a rush."

"The upholstery is rather nice in here," Tiberius commented, bouncing in his seat a little. "Isn't it, Antonia?"

Antonia smiled brightly with a nod, nuzzling into Tiberius. "I haven't taken a car journey for years, it is rather novel, isn't it?"

"If this Fae has taken over a whole city, maybe they are of more concern than we expect," Melinda said with a frown.

"I highly doubt it. You're talking about Alestria, Mel, it's more of a cesspit than a city," Lionel said and they all laughed just before I jolted out of the vision. *Fucking politicians.*

"I can finish the Dragon lord," she bit out, rising to her feet and pulling me after her.

My heart beat furiously at those words, fear snaring my heart. "It's too dangerous."

She turned to me with the decision already made in her eyes. "I'm strong enough, Gabriel. I could take them all on tonight and not break a sweat."

"Elise," I started to protest but then a vision flashed across my eyes of that fate. Lionel Acrux would die if Elise struck at him now and countless atrocities would be avoided. A thousand terrible paths closed before my eyes and a vision of peace stretched out ahead of me instead.

Excitement built inside me as the stars released me from that image and I urged Elise forward. She could do this before she needed to release that power, she could change the darkest of fates if she could just hold out a little longer then I would draw her back to me and she could set the tempest inside her free at last.

"Go, angel. You'll save the whole kingdom with that one death," I said heavily.

I couldn't grasp the details of exactly what Lionel would do if he survived this night, but the future was like a great wall of blackness whenever I tried to focus on it. I could hear screams, sense the terrible fear across the land. And I knew it was all because of him.

Elise shot away from me up the road, powering toward the car and a smile split across my cheeks as she built an enormous storm of magic around her. A tornado tore across the road, stretching out so we were at the heart of it with the approaching car. Her power was immense, a roaring flame that could never go out. But as soon as she finished Lionel, I needed to be ready to capture her, help her release this power. And before that, I needed to ensure the Councillors never saw who struck the blow so she couldn't be punished for this. We would make them believe it had been Titan and all of our troubles could die tonight as one.

I spread my wings and took off into the swirling air, chasing after her and throwing out a palm to cast her in shadow whilst working to conceal my own body. She closed in on the vehicle as it came to a stop and Lionel Acrux stepped out of the car with flames in his palms, his eyes narrowed in confusion at the shadowy blur moving towards him.

My heart beat like a war drum in my chest as I feared for my girl, but I had faith in her too and the stars showed me her power, how easily she could destroy him right now.

A tingle along my spine made me snap my head up and look to the sky far above the tunnel of the raging tornado and my gaze fell on the stars. My heart seemed to slow and I blinked as I lost all train of thought, all passage of time.

I dragged my gaze back down to Elise and the tornado fell away in a whoosh of air that sent a storm out across the land in every direction. She leapt into the sky on a gust of air beneath her and time shifted once again, making my mind drift and lose track of everything.

Elise suddenly stood before me on the air and I couldn't draw my gaze from her beautiful face. The wind fell still at our backs, a perfect bubble of absolute calm surrounding us as I slowly beat my wings to remain airborne.

The stars rearranged themselves just for us and shock jarred through my core as I stared up at the Libra constellation sitting beside the Scorpio constellation in the sky.

I'd longed for this moment for so long, it almost didn't seem real for it to be truly happening now. Elise was everything I wanted, but I had accepted I'd never be her Elysian Mate and now it turned out…I was.

Elise smiled at me, moving closer until we were almost touching and I saw my whole future in her eyes. But the vortex of power in her gaze burned brighter for a moment and I could see her slipping away from me, moving toward the edge of this circle as the power tried to corrupt her.

"Elise!" I cried. "If you leave, you'll Starcross us!" Panic ripped through me as I caught hold of her hand and her face contorted in pain as she struggled with the dark power in her body.

"Look at me," I commanded and her eyes raised to mine, her breaths seeming to even out as she remained in my gaze. "Stay with me, angel," I said in a low tone and slowly, she nodded.

A smile graced her lips as she looked around and control returned to her expression as she focused back on me. "It's our Divine Moment, Gabriel."

I flew closer to her as I accepted that impossibility, unbelievably blessed to be here before her under the stars.

"I want you to know… I didn't need the silver rings in my eyes to love you with everything that I am or ever could be, angel," I said, baring my truth to her. "And honestly, after everything I've done, I don't feel worthy to be here, chosen for you."

"Gabriel." She shook her head at me, reaching out to cup my cheek and I could feel the raging tempest of that stolen power humming beneath her skin, but for now she was in control of it. "We chose each other long before the stars decided it. I'm glad they finally agree, but it doesn't change anything really. I already wanted you as deeply as the others, I want you in every way a woman can want a man. And I wouldn't change the path we've walked to get here, because it's been our story. And I love every word from the raw and hurtful to the pure and beautiful. You're my Harpy, my guardian, my protector. I'll love you always in every way I can, in every moment we're offered from here on out."

I cupped her hand against my cheek then drew her fingers to my lips to kiss them, my heartbeat slowing to a thrumming tune that felt more right than anything I'd known before. This was true peace. Absolute contentment.

"Maybe the love in your eyes is more than I deserve," I said softly. "But I do know that there isn't a Fae in this world who'd fight harder to be worthy of it than me. I have loved you from the first moment I saw you. I love how you shattered my walls, how you gave me the family I so desperately craved. I love that you have made me a man I am proud of, Elise. But more than all that…" I took hold of her waist, pulling her flush against me and dipping my head to speak my final words against her lips. "I love *you*."

Power flared in her eyes and crackled along her skin, but there was something even more powerful than that swirling storm of magic which she held trapped inside her flesh and I could feel the depths of that love just as fiercely as she clearly could. She tiptoed to mould our lips together and I felt the bond take hold of us as we embraced this gift from the stars, our lives irremovably linked from this time forward. Our Divine Moment was perfection, the sum of all we were tangling together never to be unbound. And I knew in the depths of my soul that I would love this girl until there was nothing left of us but stardust and memories. I'd follow her through life, through the good, the bad, and eventually, I'd follow her into the sky.

The world seemed to start spinning around us in a blur of stars and suddenly the sky returned to normal and we were left suspended in the clouds as I held my Elysian Mate in my arms.

The memories of what we'd been doing before this came rushing back and I looked down to the road, finding us nowhere near the road where the Councillors' car had been and Leon, Dante and Ryder all standing beneath us instead, looking up towards the stars.

"Our family's waiting, angel," I said, her hand sliding into mine like it was made to fit there.

Elise stilled and amidst the endless silver of her eyes, I could see that eternal power calling to her once again, corrupting her and tempting her away from me. She blinked hard and I could feel her forcing her own will over it, but it was still there, burning with the desire to break free. Her time to release it was running short.

We dropped from the sky, landing on the road in front of them and Leon gasped, staring from me to Elise before his gaze locked on my eyes.

"Oh my stars, it's happened!" He ran at me, colliding with me so hard he knocked me onto my ass. He started licking my face and purring so loud his whole chest rattled.

"By the stars, Leon," I growled, trying to push him off but he was a determined asshole.

Elise was yanked into the pile and Ryder and Dante promptly joined us. Ryder knocked his knuckles against my cheek and Dante scruffed my hair and I just started laughing as I gave in to the love of my people and hugged them all back.

"Family forged and family bound," the stars whispered and the way everyone stilled and looked up made me know they'd heard it too. *"A gift for a fractured soul, for cruel fates and crueller paths. When the world grows dark, look to each other to find the light."*

"Look!" Leon cried as the weight of that voice lifted and I raised my head to find him pointing at the half figure of eight mark between the crook of his forefinger and thumb. "You have one too!" He grabbed my hand, yanking it up to lock with mine and as our marks connected to make an infinity symbol, I felt my bond with him flare and burn.

"Ohhh fuck that feels like coming," Leon sighed and I yanked my hand back, smacking him with it.

"Don't ruin it, dipshit," I said and he smirked.

"Holy shit, I've got two," Elise said, gazing down at her hands which were both marked with the symbol but as I reached out to touch one of them, I felt the burning power within her skin and knew she was struggling to contain it. Her cheeks were still marked with tear tracks and though she looked at me with a desperate and unending love in her gaze, I knew that pain and grief were warring inside her too.

"We can make an infinity circle," Leon said, his eyes bugging out of his head.

Before he could make us do that, I caught the back of Elise's neck, dragging her into a fierce kiss, the need to solidify this new bond between us raging inside me. She melted against me, moaning softly and it took everything I had not to rip her clothes off right here in the middle of the road. But as the air around us seemed to hum and buzz with the power she was battling to contain, I knew there were more important things for us to do right now. She needed to end this. That stolen magic had to be returned to the stars or our happily ever after wasn't going to last beyond this moment.

I held her tight, lending her some of my strength, and Elise sucked in a sharp breath, power rippling across her body as she rolled over to lay beside me and I knew the moment had come for her to banish that power.

I wondered if the stars had always planned for the five of us to end up here, or if every fate was always just a spinning coin waiting to fall. As the stars winked and glinted at us, a vision descended on me of the future now opening up before us, the perfect sweetness awaiting us in our lives. But in the periphery of my Sight, I could *see* Lionel walking the whole kingdom towards some impenetrable darkness that made my heart twist uncomfortably. And I knew a time would eventually come when I had to step into a war I knew nothing of yet. But as I looked to my girl and the power brimming in her eyes, I knew we had our own war to face now. She needed to let go of that unending magic, or we'd lose her forever.

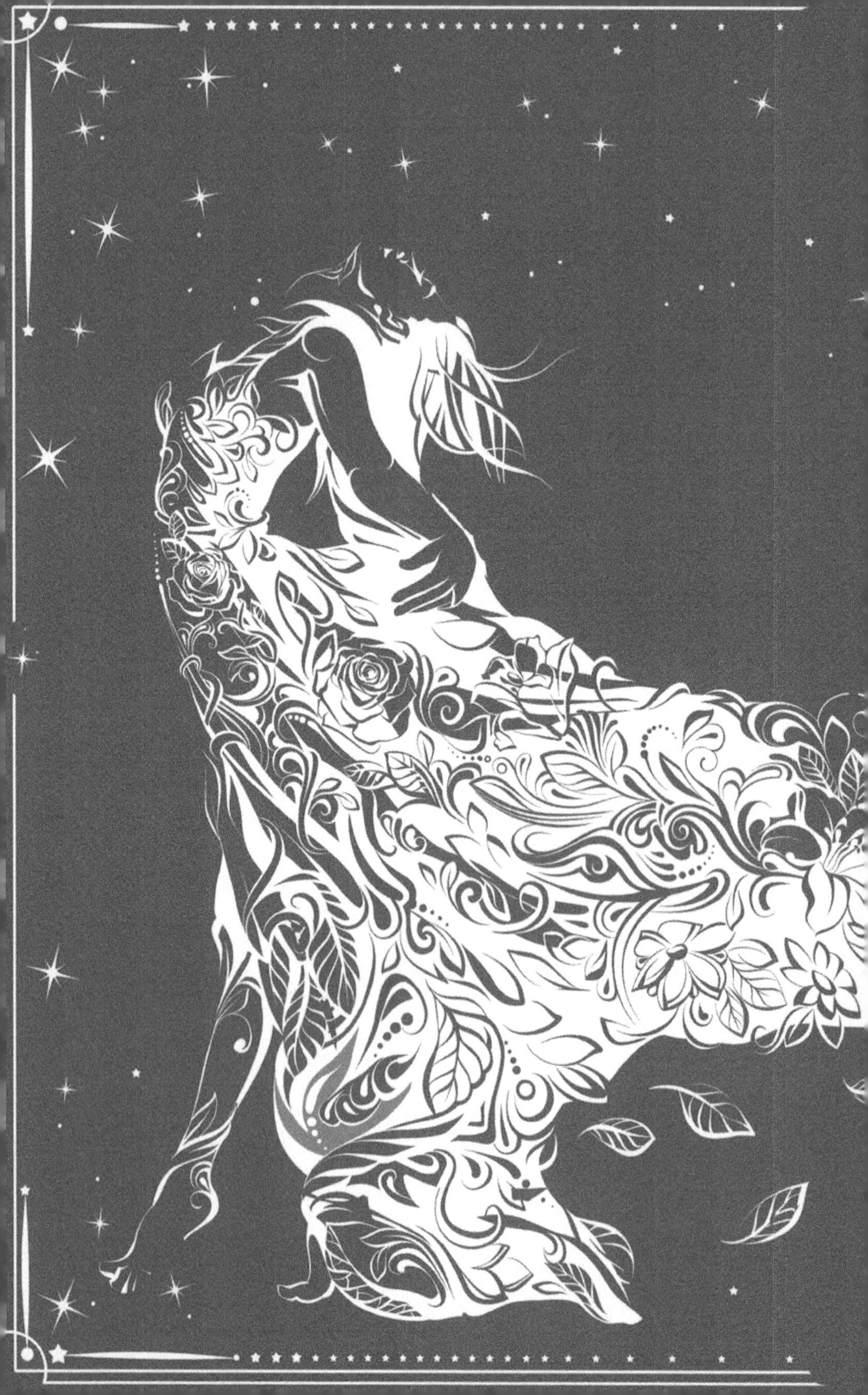

ELISE

CHAPTER FIFTY SEVEN

I was a wash of conflicting emotions, as grief and pain collided with love and happiness inside my chest and the immense power within me burned with the desire to do something about all of it.

But it wasn't the way it had been before. The voices urging me to action had been quieted by the blood I'd spilled on their behalf and I was able to push their wants aside and concentrate on my own. This power needed an outlet and there were things I wanted to do with it.

I stood from the group of my mates, tempted away from them by this blinding power as it swirled in my veins and drowned away everything in me but the need to use it.

"Elise," Gabriel called to me and my eyes snapped to his as power crackled along my limbs and lit me up with pleasure. All of them were on their feet, gazing at me like I held their hearts in my hands and was about to steal them away forever. "You need to release it to the stars. You can't control it like this for long. It wasn't meant for you."

I frowned at him, the power in me flaring like it didn't like the sound of that. It wanted to stay locked inside me. It wanted me to use it and do all of the things I hungered to do. It was endless, limitless and with it, nothing could ever hurt me again.

"Baby," Ryder growled. "Listen to him. You have everything you need right here without it."

"Torna da noi, amore mio," Dante added.

"We're right here, little monster," Leon said, reaching towards me. But Gabriel placed a hand on his shoulder in warning and I took a step back, wondering what he'd *seen* to make him do that. But I wouldn't hurt them. Never. I would do anything to avoid causing them pain. Pain like the agony I felt over Gareth.

As my mind landed on my brother, that sharp slice of grief cut into me even deeper and I hissed at the agony of it, my power rising up like a tornado around me as I tipped my head back to the stars.

"Why?!" I screamed at them, knowing they could hear me, that they were the masters of fate and that they'd allowed Gareth to fall prey to his. But they didn't answer, just twinkling serenely like nothing a mere mortal could do or say could ever affect them.

But fuck that. I was no mere mortal anymore after all and if they refused to give me what I needed then I'd damn well take it for myself.

I turned away from my kings, glaring out at the fields beyond us as I drew the full might of my stolen power closer, and I released a scream so loud that the heavens themselves must have trembled beneath the rage in it.

I twisted my hands into claws as I reached out in front of me on instinct and drove my fingernails into the very fabric of the world surrounding me, ripping it from the grip of the stars and forcing the veil back as I tore down the barrier between life and death.

Power crashed through my body like an oncoming storm, my entire being vibrating with the weight of it and my bones screamed in agony as it tore through my flesh and burned me alive. But I refused to stop. I refused to let this power control me – I was the vessel, and I was taking back control. I didn't care what the stars had to say on it, this divide was going to open for me or so help me I'd tear every motherfucking star right out of the sky.

Finally, a dark doorway seemed to burn itself into existence before me as I clawed it open and I gasped as the weight of all the dead beyond it pressed forward eagerly, looking for a way through.

I threw my hands up in front of me and snarled as I forced them back, not knowing what havoc they might wreak upon the world if I were to set them free. That wasn't why I was here. There was only one soul I ached to see and I wasn't going to allow any but him to pass through.

"Gareth!" I yelled, my heart racing as I fought to hold back the tide of dead before me and I could feel my kings moving to stand at my back, staying close, refusing to flee even though it was clear they should. I wasn't sure how long I could hold this rift in check now that I'd torn it open. "Gareth Tempa!" I screamed because I needed him. I needed him so much that I didn't care what this cost me, I just had to see his face. I refused to accept his fate and I was going to fucking change it.

The shadows beyond the rift began to move aside as a figure drew closer and a sob caught in my throat as my brother appeared before me at last.

He looked just as I remembered and yet utterly different at the same time, his body seeming to only hold form because I wished it so. Or maybe he did. I wasn't certain, but there was something fluid to his flesh which felt like he might just scatter into a billion tiny pieces at any given moment and abandon me here.

"Gare Bear?" I choked out, a tear burning a hot trail down my cheek as I looked into his familiar eyes and he gave me a sad smile.

"My little angel," he breathed, tilting his head to survey me. "Look at you."

"Step through," I begged, my body trembling as I fought to hold this power in check, knowing my time was short and that it wouldn't last. "Come back to me."

Gareth's eyes filled with sadness as he reached out to place a palm against the space which divided our worlds. "It doesn't work like that, Ella. I can't just step through. Not without opening the way for others."

"So let them come too," I begged, not caring about that. I needed him and he was right there, I *needed* this.

He shook his head, his gaze moving from me to the men at my back and a smile touched his lips. "All I ever wanted was for you to be free and loved," he said softly. "And you have that now. Even if I wouldn't have exactly chosen this particular brand of happiness for you while I was alive." He arched a brow at me and the teasing expression was so familiar that it ripped right into my chest.

I choked out a laugh as more tears fell. "You'll learn to love them too," I promised him.

Gareth smiled softly. "I already do, Ella. I've been watching over you. I've seen how fiercely they love you. No matter how unexpected the men who provide you that love may have been for me, I can feel it. All of it. They can give you the life I couldn't."

"But you did give me this," I choked out. "I wouldn't have met them if it wasn't for losing you." The weight of that truth hurt me so deeply that I didn't think I'd ever be able to accept it. Losing Gareth had equalled me finding my Elysian Mates. But why couldn't I have them all? Why did my brother have to be that price?

His face brightened as he grinned wide and boyishly. "I guess you're right," he said, his eyes full of so much love it pained me that I couldn't just drag him into my arms and hold onto him forever. "I can't wait to see you live the life we always dreamed of, Ella."

"So step through. Come and live it with us," I pleaded, my limbs trembling from the use of so much power and the figures beyond Gareth stepping closer again like they could tell the rift was about to come crashing down. I thought I recognised a few of the faces, Dante and Ryder's fathers, and a man and woman who peered in Gabriel's direction with pride in their eyes and regrets weighing them down. But I couldn't concentrate on any of that. My focus was on Gareth as I felt our time slipping away from us.

"Please, Gare Bear," I begged. "Don't leave me again. Step through. I need you."

"You don't, little angel. Not anymore. My time on your plane is over and there's nothing either of us can do to change that. Just know I love you. I love you so fucking much, and you made my life complete. And know that I wouldn't have changed a single thing. I hate that I had to leave you before we were ready, and I hate that I can't give you what you want now. But you have love, Ella. You have men who would tear the world apart for you and a future just waiting for you to claim it. You don't need me anymore."

"I'll always need you," I sobbed, refusing to accept what he was saying.

"You're almost out of time," Gabriel said in a low voice behind me. "You have to close the rift, Elise. If you don't, everyone in Solaria will be in peril."

I sobbed even louder, stepping forward, intending to grasp my brother and rip him through to me because I couldn't just accept this. He was so close. So fucking close. How could I just close this door between us and know I'd never see his face again?

"Go," Gareth urged. "My time is over but yours is only just beginning."

"I don't want to say goodbye," I choked out.

"You're free to claim the happiness I always wanted for you. That's all I ask - be happy for me, Ella. Live life to the fullest and love with all your heart. And know that I'm always with you, no matter where you go. I'll never truly leave."

Tears raced down my cheeks as I shook my head in denial, but I could feel the power I was holding rattling through me now. My body was trembling and my flesh was burning. I couldn't contain it much longer. We were running out of time all over again. And I would never be able to claim enough of it.

"I love you, Gare Bear," I sobbed as magic flared within me and my grip on the rift tightened against the flood of dead who wanted to break through. But the divide was rattling against my hold now, the weight of so many dead aching to steal this freedom bearing down on my shoulders.

"I love you too," he swore. "Always."

Gabriel's hand landed on my arm and I knew that this was it. Our time was up, and it never could have been enough.

I pressed forward and leaned my forehead to the barrier between me and my brother and he mimicked the gesture as I began to pull the veil across once more, my heart carving open as I was forced to close this door for the final time.

I cried out as the dead tried to fight me, their combined might battling with the explosive force of the power caged within my flesh as I fought to slam the doorway shut again.

Magic burned through me but I managed to maintain my hold on it as Gareth lent me his power and helped me make the final push then with a grunt of effort, the veil was forced closed once more.

Just as the last of the magic closed over and my body felt ready to explode from the weight of so much power, Gareth spoke one, final time.

"Be free, little angel. *Live.*"

I forced the veil shut with a cry of effort and fell to my knees in the mud as the magic in me boiled and burned, writhing within my body and calling on my bloodlust once more. I was losing myself to it again, but as I turned and looked at the four men who stood at my back, I knew I couldn't let that happen.

As much as this pain made me ache to give myself up to the power and become its plaything rather than feel it, my love for the four of them burned so much hotter. I wouldn't give them up. Not for anything.

With a cry of relief, I tipped my head back to the stars and threw my hands up towards them, letting the magic burn a path right out of me as I cut the bonds which anchored it to my flesh and set it loose, restoring the balance just as should have happened with the death of every Fae who had owned it when they died.

My body shook and trembled as the power ripped its way free of me and darkness closed in around me as I forced myself to release every last drop.

But as the final pieces of that energy fell from my body, an empty abyss closed in and I fell back with a hard smack, colliding with the grass as the air was driven from my lungs.

I stared up at the stars for a long, peaceful moment before four concerned faces appeared in my line of sight and my heart swelled with the love I felt for these men.

It was over. Titan was dead and I had the answers I'd so desperately needed even if it had broken me to find out the truth. So as the darkness rolled in to claim me, I knew that despite the ache in my soul and the grief I would forever carry over losing my brother, I could find peace now too. And I held onto that knowledge as I drifted away into the dark.

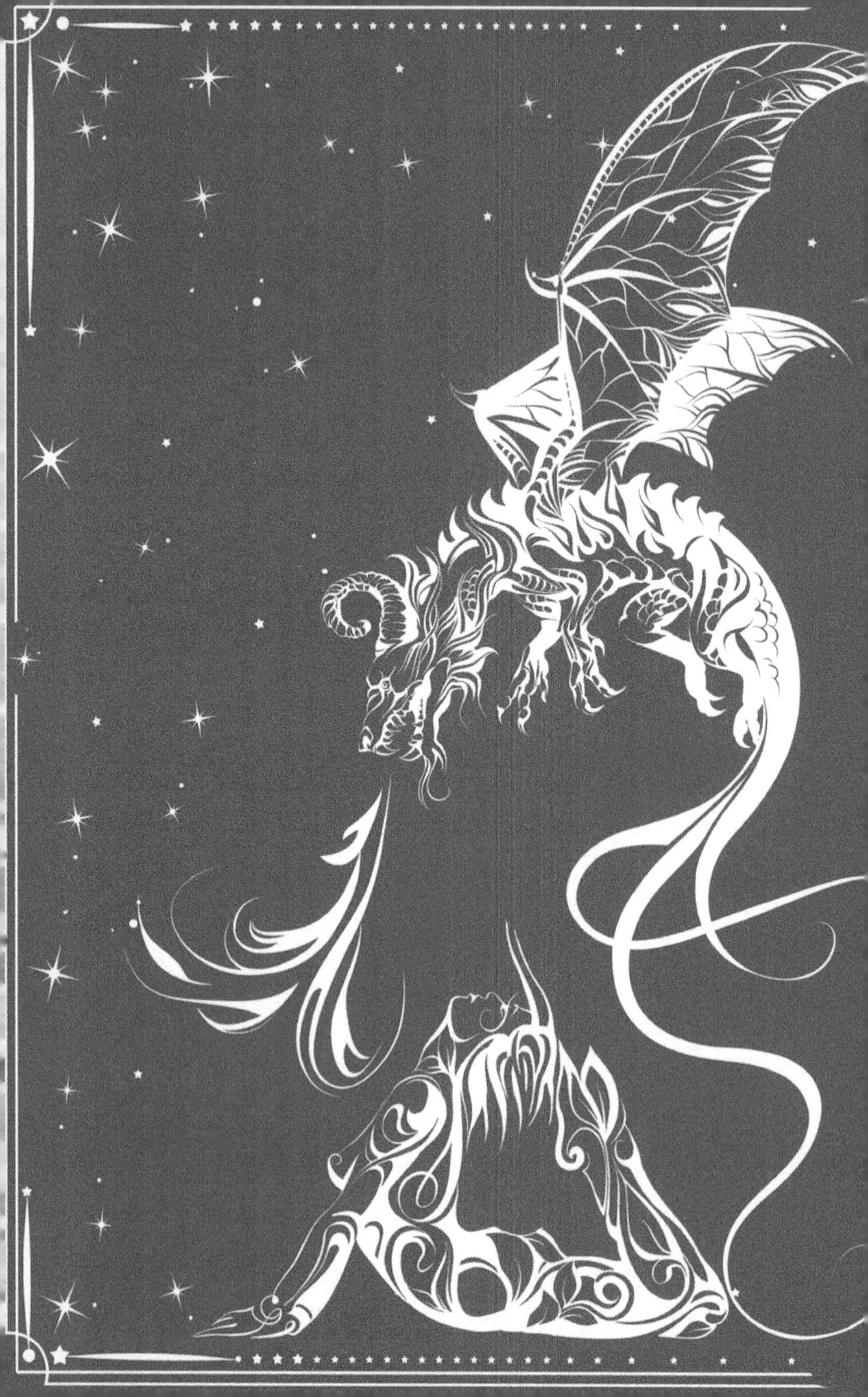

DANTE

CHAPTER FIFTY EIGHT

"Torna da noi, amore nostro," I begged of Elise as we crowded around her, sending healing magic into her body together. Her eyelashes fluttered and my shoulders pressed to the other guys', leaning in close as she finally woke up.

A heavy breath of relief left me as I gazed at her purely silver eyes, our beautiful mate safe and alive. "Are you okay, bella?" I asked her.

Seeing Gareth must have been impossibly hard for her, but it had settled a weight in my own heart to find that he was alright beyond the veil. He wasn't tormented by the life he'd lost. He was at peace. And I was relieved over that for my cavallo.

"Yeah," she said, a sad smile pulling at her lips. "At least, I will be."

Leon nuzzled against her cheek and she pushed her fingers into his hair. "We love you, little monster. And we love Gareth too. Don't we, Scar?" He elbowed Ryder beside him and for once he didn't put on his emotionless front, he nodded and took Elise's hand and the flare of magic in his eyes told me he was feeling every ounce of her pain.

"We're his brothers in this life and the next," he said firmly.

"One day, when we join him beyond the veil, we will have time to know him properly," Gabriel said, taking her other hand and kissing her palm.

She shuddered beneath us, drawing in a long breath. "I'm so tired."

"Then let's go home. Tomorrow is the beginning of a new world, amore mio," I promised, pulling her to her feet between us and she took a moment surrounded by our arms, our love. I felt tethered to each and every one of these Fae and now that Gabriel had bonded to Elise, it was like we were all united in an unbreakable circle, each of us as vital as the other in keeping it whole.

I was only in my sweatpants since I'd shifted to carry Leon and Ryder here, but as I went to drop my pants to carry us back to my famiglia's home, Gabriel held out a hand to stop me.

"Wait," he growled, his eyes glazing with a vision.

"What now?" Ryder gritted out.

"Please tell me this night is over already," Elise groaned.

"Gabe?" Leon questioned, shaking his arm.

"Don't disturb him." I knocked Leon's hand away from him and Gabriel jolted out of his stupor.

"There's a rally in the city," he said.

"Right now?" Elise asked in confusion. It must have been almost midnight.

"Fly us there, Drago," Gabriel asked and my brows arched at the use of my nickname for a moment before I nodded and dropped my pants, shifting into my Dragon form.

They all climbed onto my back and I took off into the sky, following Gabriel's directions as he called them out to me. We made it to the town hall at the centre of the city and the others cast thick concealment spells and a silencing bubble around us I swooped down, landing on top of it in the shadows.

My harem slid from my back and I shifted into my Fae form, pulling my sweatpants back on as Leon passed them to me and we moved to the very edge of the building, gazing down at the massive crowd gathered in front of the town hall, filling the streets and cheering at something. Ryder had shifted his appearance using his chameleon Order gifts so he looked like a pretty nondescript man with blonde hair, so even if anyone did happen to notice us, they wouldn't recognise him.

My breath snagged as I spotted the four Celestial Councillors standing up on the steps before the hall and my blood ran cold as my gaze fell on Lionel Acrux at the heart of them.

"Your city is safe!" he boomed, his voice amplified ten times by a spell so it rang out across the streets. "The Fae who called himself King is dead and their followers have been eradicated. We have discovered that it was none other than Colin Titan, a professor at Aurora Academy and we have brought his body here to dispose of to be sure you rest well at night, knowing he is gone." He whipped out a hand and a concealment spell lifted, showing Titan lying dead at their feet in his robes.

A wild cheer went up as the people of Alestria clapped and celebrated over his death. Lionel was such a stronzo.

"How did they even find his body?" Elise hissed.

"My friend used her Seer gifts to show us where to find Titan this very night and we must all give a round of applause to Destiny Moonshine for her great service to our kingdom." Antonia pointed to the woman at the front of the crowd wearing flowing yellow robes and she blushed as the crowd applauded her.

"Dalle stelle. They used that bitch to find his body and steal our glory," I growled.

Lionel threw out his palms, using his fire magic to turn Titan's body to ash and the crowd cheered even louder.

"Know that Alestria will always be protected by us," Melinda Altair called out and I looked to Elise beside me as she pouted.

"You have nothing more to fear," Tiberius Rigel cried, smiling like a superhero in a cape.

"Merda santa, they're taking credit for what we did," I muttered.

"We will now take questions from the press," Antonia Capella said, straightening out her fancy blue dress and Leon pouted.

"We did all the work," he growled. "I'm gonna go down there and tell them."

Gabriel slammed a hand to his chest, shaking his head. "No," he sighed. "We can't. We won't be believed."

"Fuck them," Elise growled.

"High Lords and Ladies," a peppy reporter called out. "Would you have any objections to a statue being erected in each of your honours here at the town hall?"

"For the love of the moon," Leon cursed.

"No, not at all," Lionel said, pushing a hand through his hair like a suave bastardo and the crowd went mad again.

"I've seen enough," Elise said tiredly, sliding her hand into mine and leaning her head against my shoulder. "At least it's over now, that's all I really care about. Let's go home, Drago."

I kissed her temple, turning away from the skeevy Councillors who'd stolen our glory and fighting my Alpha instincts which told me to fly down there and put the story straight. But before we could leave, another reporter shouted out a question which piqued my interest.

"Lord Acrux, do you have any comment on Dante Oscura's connection to the Lunar-Oscura gang fight? Sources say he has been seen spending time at your manor in Tucana."

I turned back the same moment Elise did and we looked down at Lionel as he casually straightened his tie. "Mr Oscura has in fact been of great help to us in locating the Fae who called himself King this very night. He was not involved in any gang fights and as far as I understand it, the offending parties in that little disagreement are now dead. Dante, his mate, Elise Altair, and the rest of her harem are of course cleared of any suspicion considering the tip-offs they provided this evening which led to us saving Alestria."

My brows arched at that and though the stronzo had spun this whole thing so that him and his friends looked like the city's saviours, at least that was one good thing that had come out of this. My family were now free from any FIB investigations, but I had the feeling Lionel would be calling in favours in response to his so-called kindness soon enough.

I shifted into my Dragon form and my famiglia climbed onto my back as I took to the skies once more without a single concealment spell around me so the crowd gasped and pointed as they spotted us. I didn't look back, offering the Councillors a passive aggressive fuck you as we sailed away into the night.

Following Titan's death, Alestria entered the first stretch of peace it had seen in two hundred years. The end of the year came and went and we enjoyed a long summer which turned into a pretty extensive mating-moon as we headed to the vacation house Leon had bought for Elise. We spent plenty of time at my family home too as well as with Bill and Leon's family once we got home. The days in the sun slid by all too quickly as the first day of school in our final year at Aurora arrived.

And at last, we decided it was time for Ryder to re-join the academy under a new identity. Gabriel had tutored him through anything he'd missed in the last weeks of term before summer to keep him up to speed and I was pretty sure he enjoyed their little bestie bro time.

Our group was more bonded than ever, rarely a flicker of a fight breaking out between us – except during the two week mood Leon threw after our team was disqualified from playing Zodiac Academy in the final of the inter-academy Pitball tournament thanks to one of our Pit Keepers testing positive for fucking Faeroids just before the match. The only way we'd gotten him to cheer up was when we all made a star vow that promised we'd work doubly hard in Pitball training our final year to make sure we got one last shot at the cup. That, and Elise had given him titty rights for a week. It had been a long damn week, that's for sure.

After so many lazy mornings, lazy days and lazy nights, I was actually quite excited to be returning to Aurora Academy. Especially as there were no more wars to fight or megalomaniacs to hunt down and destroy.

"Drum roll!" Elise cried as she leapt out of my en-suite bathroom, looking seriously excited.

Leon bounced on the bed beside me, drumming out a tune on his knees as Periwinkle jumped up beside him with a bark. My famiglia's dog Lupo was obsessed with the little blue ghost hound and she loved leading him all around the property, running him ragged by letting him chase her while she evaded him by slipping through walls and fences and driving him crazy. She kind of reminded me of Elise in that way, maybe that was why Ryder and Periwinkle got along so well.

"I'm so ready for this," Leon said. "Is he brunette, or blonde? Is he still a man? Oh my stars, is he a girl? With big tits? Dibs on titty rights!"

I roared a laugh and Elise smirked. I looked to Gabriel who was leaning against the wall with his arms folded and a knowing look in his eyes. The stronzo already knew exactly what Ryder's new identity looked like but he clearly wasn't going to say a word until we saw him for ourselves.

"Come on, serpente," I called.

Elise dove onto the bed between me and Leon, folding her legs up beneath her. She was wearing a cute ass blue yoga pants and crop top combo that kept drawing my attention to her pushed up tits. She caught me staring and pushed my face around to look back at the bathroom door as I got snared by them again then took my hand and Leon's in hers.

"I think the dramatics are pretty overkill, don't you?" Ryder called then kicked the bathroom door open, stepping out into the room.

My jaw dropped and Leon gasped. He had long, silky black hair that fell down to his chest in soft waves and his face was chiselled, his jaw strong, his eyes still the same shade of green that belonged to him, though missing the silver ring in them. His skin was kissed gold and was covered in colourful tattoos, his muscular arms folded across his chest.

"Meet Carson Alvion," Elise announced excitedly.

"Oh my stars!" Leon dove off the bed, shoving Ryder's arms apart to examine him, tugging at the white wifebeater he was wearing and tearing it off of him to expose more tattoos over his body. "They're Disney tattoos!" he practically squealed and I pushed off of the bed, walking over to see for myself.

I barked a laugh at his tattoos which were twisted, gritty versions of Disney characters. His left bicep was covered with a roaring Beast who was being ridden by Belle who held a sword in her hand and looked like a warrior. Beneath that was Cinderella getting tatted up by her Prince Charming while she bent over a chair in a tiny blue lingerie set with a crown in her hair, beneath her was Thumper on the back of a very beefy Bambi with large antlers covered in blood. On his other bicep was Ariel bursting from the waves as a shark dove over her head and a knife was raised in her hand as she battled with it. Below that one was Anna and Elsa from Frozen, building a snowman that looked like a monster version of Olaf with snarling teeth and a blade for a nose. Across his chest was the entire pride from The Lion King, all of them roaring while Zazu soared above them looking more like a vicious eagle than a little bird. It was fucking perfect and as I looked between each of the tatted up, sexy ass princesses on his body, I realised they all very much resembled Elise and the princes all had a hint of each of us. There was even a Lady and the Tramp mark near his hip and Lady definitely resembled Periwinkle and the Tramp looked like Lupo.

"I'm a Lion Shifter," Ryder announced with a smirk and Leon gaped at him as his gaze roamed all over his silky hair and the V cutting away beneath his pants. "Oh, just one final touch." He tracked his fingers over his left eye and marked a faint scar running through it.

"Scar!" Leon cried, throwing himself at Ryder and crushing him in a fierce hug. "Best. Day. Ever."

"You won't be saying that when I steal your Mindys and show you who's the better Lion," Ryder taunted and Leon growled in a challenge.

"Wait, look, you haven't seen the best part yet." Elise ran over and grabbed his left arm, turning it over to show us the line of tattoos running up his forearm. He'd kept the star signs for all of us, but had concealed them under the guise of Disney characters, hiding the symbols within them. Leon's was Simba, mine was Mushu the dragon from Mulan, Gabriel's was Blu the parrot from Rio, Gareth's was the Pegasus from Hercules, and Elise's was Tinkerbell in a lilac dress with shimmering wings.

"Are you okay with me looking different in public, baby?" Ryder asked Elise and she lifted her hand to Ryder's face, gazing into his eyes.

"Whenever it feels weird, I can look right here and see you," she said.

"So what's your backstory?" Leon demanded, bouncing around Ryder and inspecting every inch of him. "Are you my long lost brother from a faraway land who was imprisoned by a Nymph and used as a sex slave for years and they cut your eye with a magical stone which they found in an enchanted well that your father-"

"No," Ryder cut him off. "But we are going to pose as family. Your father hooked me up with some papers that say I'm your distant cousin."

Leon squealed his delight, nuzzling into his head. "Do you want me to teach you to purr, Rydikins?" He whispered in his ear from behind as he started purring loudly. "Listen to my purr rumbling through you, pushing deep into you, can you feel it vibrating?"

"Stop that. I'm never going to purr." Ryder batted a hand at him and Leon danced away.

"All Lions purr, Carson," Leon taunted. "Or should I call you *Scar*son?"

A smirk pulled at the corners of Ryder's mouth and I had to wonder why he'd chosen this identity if he hadn't wanted Leon to react like this.

A low growl came from behind us and I turned, spotting Periwinkle on the bed, her ears flat and her teeth bared at Ryder.

"It's okay, girl," he said, walking toward her and she backed up a few steps as he reached out for her. "It's me, Periwinkle."

She stilled, tiptoeing forward and sniffing his hand as he offered it. Then as she caught his scent, she yipped and jumped up, licking his face as she rested her paws on his chest.

"We're gonna be late for school," Gabriel said, making me jump as he appeared right beside me.

"You wanna come with me, girl?" Ryder asked the ghost hound and she barked in agreement. "I think you're gonna need a new look too though, hmm..."

"Make her into a Lion cub," Leon suggested.

"No," Ryder growled. "Greyshine's not gonna let me bring a damn Lion cub around campus."

"Is he going to let you bring *any* animal around campus?" I snorted.

"He will if you tell him to allow it, Drago," Gabriel said with a smirk and I chuckled as I nodded my agreement.

Ryder pressed his hand to Periwinkle's head and changed her fur to a deep rust colour before making her three tails into one so she looked like a pretty normal little dog.

"Come on. Get dressed, Ryder." Elise shoved him back into the bathroom, grinning brightly as she moved to stroke Periwinkle and admire her new look.

I grabbed my blazer from the bed and pulled it on as Elise shot in front of me, doing up my shirt buttons for me which I'd left hanging open. Her fingers grazed my flesh as she worked and a hungry growl rolled through my chest.

"Nope. No time for that." Gabriel smacked me around the head and I sighed. "We can't be late, Ryder needs to register for classes."

We were soon all ready to go and we made our way through the house, being hugged by every single member of my famiglia while they all fussed and cooed over Ryder's new look and Periwinkle got a bunch of fuss too. Lupo licked Periwinkle all over and she lifted her chin, not seeming to mind that so much and I wondered if she knew the dangerous game she was playing by flirting with a dog five times her size. If he tried to mate her, I'd castrate him.

I'd made my whole famiglia swear a star vow to me to keep Ryder's identity secret. I wouldn't lie to them and I knew they'd never tell anyway, but since Felix, I couldn't take any risks.

"Oh look at you, nuovo figlio," Mamma cooed as we made it to her at the front door. "My Rosa will be blushing all over you, she always did love a dark haired Leone." She winked and Rosalie turned red beside her.

"Aunt Bianca," she hissed.

"Oh hush, we all know of your fondness for Roary, piccolo lupa," she said, waving a hand like it was nothing and I felt bad for Rosalie as she struggled to keep her composure. At the mention of Leon's brother, a weight fell over us and I put an arm around Leon, pulling him close.

"Don't worry, Leo, when I'm old enough and trained well enough, I'm gonna break Roary out of Darkmore," Rosa said and Bianca laughed.

"You will do no such thing, cucciolo pazzo," she scoffed and Rosa scowled at her. I swear she actually believed she'd do it and I smiled at her tenacity.

Leon reached out and scruffed her hair, his mood brightening at her words. "Thanks, pup."

We said our goodbyes and headed outside, walking off of the property and enjoying the feeling of the sunshine on our skin as the lingering summer air fluttered around us. It was the perfect day, the flowers blooming and the golden sunlight making the horizon seem to shimmer.

As we stepped out of the gates, I took a pouch of stardust from my pocket and threw it over us, carrying us to Aurora Academy for our first day of term. Peace gilded my soul as we arrived in front of the academy gates and I felt that at last, we were going to be able to enjoy our time here without the weight of the stars on our shoulders.

We walked inside together and I took Elise's hand, wanting to show the world that she was my girl and mia famiglia were all around me in an unbreakable unit. Periwinkle trotted happily along beside us, her coat rippling in the breeze as she sniffed the air.

A large group of girls were gathered near the gate and they all burst into excited screams as they spotted Leon arriving, jumping up and down while waving signs with his face on with phrases like "we missed you, Leon!", "the king has returned', and 'this Mindy is at your service'.

Ryder took a hipflask from inside his blazer pocket as Leon waved to them, drinking out of it and I narrowed my gaze on him. A beat after he'd swallowed, the Mindys' eyes flicked to Ryder and some of them dropped the signs in their hands.

"Who is *that*?" one of them gasped, fanning herself.

"Oh my stars, he's so *big*."

"So handsome."

"Look how shiny his hair is," another added.

A flock of half the Mindys came bounding up the path towards Ryder and Leon twisted around in confusion as he glared at him.

"What the fuck?" Leon demanded of Ryder and the Mindys and some of them glanced back at him guiltily before moving to try and stroke Ryder's chest and arms.

Elise shot in front of them, baring her fangs and they fell back with yelps of alarm, bowing their heads in submission before darting away again.

But many of them looked back over their shoulders at Ryder with parted lips, exchanging excited whispers as they went.

"What did you do?" Leon demanded, grabbing the hipflask from Ryder's fingers and sniffing the contents.

Ryder flicked up a silencing bubble as we walked past the Mindys and a bunch of them swooned, looking between Ryder and Leon like they couldn't decide who they were more affected by.

"It's a Charisma potion, brewed from the essence of the strongest Lion I know," Ryder said with a smirk playing around his mouth as he gave Leon a pointed look.

Leon held a hand to his heart in horror. "You stole my *essence*? My Lion juice?"

"Don't say it like that." Ryder's nose wrinkled. "I have to commit to the role."

"You can't steal my Mindys," Leon growled ferociously.

"I'm not stealing anything," Ryder said tauntingly. "They came to me." He shrugged and snatched the hipflask back from Leon, tucking it into his inside pocket.

"I'll cut a Mindy if they try and touch either of you," Elise muttered, her fangs still exposed as she circled around our group like a huntress guarding its prey. I loved when she got like this and I caught her hand, tugging her against my hip as Gabriel chuckled.

"I'll take you to see Greyshine," Gabriel said to Ryder. "I can *see* how to make your admission go smoothly."

"Are you sure you don't want me to scare his shiny ass into overlooking any discrepancies?" I offered and Gabriel shook his head.

"I can handle it for now. I'll tell him you'll be on his case if he doesn't let Periwinkle hang out on campus too. But if anything comes up in the future, I know you'll be able to keep him in line." He walked off with Ryder and Periwinkle as we stepped into Altair Halls, marching up the stairs while me,

Leon and Elise walked to our Potions lesson.

"Bing-bong," Principal Greyshine's voice sang through the tannoy. "Welcome back to Aurora Academy all you boss boys and gals. I hope you had a tremenderific summer and you're looking forward to getting stuck in to class. Just a little announceroo that the old storage shed – lovingly nicknamed the Dead Shed – has now been converted into a hangout for all you cool cucumbers during your down time. Have a wicked day!"

"Pretty sure I'll be hanging out there never," Elise said with a shudder.

After work had started on converting the Dead Shed at the end of last term, the Elemental workforce had uncovered a pristine fake body hidden there in the exact image of Gareth along with a whole portfolio of designs for what he termed 'Tempa Pego bags'. He'd hand drawn designs for all kinds of Orders, the bags made to put Fae's clothes in while they shifted, magically stretching out to accommodate the Order form of the Fae using it. It was kind of a miracle no one had thought of the idea sooner.

After they were discovered, Principal Greyshine had been an absolute stronzo by sending Elise pictures of the fake body and upsetting her all over again – I'd scared him shitless in payment for that. The one good thing that had come out of it was that the portfolio had been recovered and we'd all been so impressed with the bags that I'd suggested Elise send them to my cousin Lilliana who was starting up her own fashion label in Tucana. They'd been a hit straight away with all Orders. And after Leon had done a video on FaeTok while wearing a sparkly rainbow one on his back, shifting into his Lion form and doing a ridiculous ass shakey dance, it had gone viral and made Elise a ton of money. We couldn't walk down the street these days without seeing one, and it made her smile every time, that little piece of her brother scattered throughout the entire kingdom.

Elise slowed her pace as we headed down into the basement where Titan had taught us so many classes, pausing outside the door with a frown creasing her brow. Greyshine had finally employed a new professor for the job and we hadn't been in here since before Titan had been killed. We'd only had a few weeks left of term when we'd returned to school last year so I guessed Greyshine hadn't seen the need to hire anyone else until now.

"Elise?" I said gently and she looked to me, the pain in her eyes hardening.

"I'm fine, it's just…" She shook her head. "He was like two different people, you know? The man he was at the academy wasn't the same as King."

"He had to hide that part of him," Leon said softly and Elise nodded.

"I know, I just sometimes think about that good part of him," she said, sucking her lower lip for a moment. "And I feel guilty that I…"

"You can tell us anything, amore mio." I took her hand, guiding her closer to me and Leon as he nodded his agreement.

She released a breath. "I only wonder how things might have been different if he hadn't gotten the Magicae Mortuorum. If he'd never been corrupted by dark magic. I know what it's like to feel the temptation of all that power, I know how easily I could have given in to it myself."

"But you didn't," I growled fiercely and she clenched her jaw, nodding.

"I'm not excusing what he did," she added, a bite to her tone over everything King had done to her, to Gareth, to our city. "It just seems like fate can twist one way or another so easily."

"It comes down to our choices, little monster," Leon said gently, running his fingers along her jaw as he tilted her head up to look at him. "The stars might lay out fates for us, place obstacles or temptations in our way, but ultimately it's us who decides which path to follow. Titan chose poorly."

"Did Gareth choose poorly too?" she rasped out, her eyes filling with tears.

"No, amore mio," I said with absolute certainty to my words. "Gareth faced a thousand challenges to save you. And he did. He was willing to give his life for that, and sadly he had to in the end."

She sighed, her spine straightening as she took comfort in those words and nodded. "You're right." She leaned in to kiss me before kissing Leon too and we headed into our Potions class where a tall, smiling woman awaited us at her desk.

The whole room had been redecorated with pictures of all kinds of magical herbs and flowers on the walls, and she'd even replaced the desks with tables and benches which all now faced the opposite wall. It was like a whole new space and the tension ran out of Elise's body as we moved to take the back row bench together. There were no more reminders in this room of Titan, and I had the feeling, Elise had finally closed the door on him for good.

ONE MONTH LATER…

"By the stars, Elise," Gabriel groaned as he leaned his hand on the wall above her and she took his cock to the back of her throat. We were in an empty classroom after hours and Leon had specific instructions for me and Elise to keep Gabriel distracted from The Sight. She'd been more than happy to go this route and I was trying my best not to get hard as our deadline approached.

I checked my Atlas behind Gabriel's back as he groaned and fisted his hands in Elise's hair.

Leon:
Bring him to the Cafaeteria in two minutes xxxxx

I didn't think the kisses were really necessary, but Leon was in a particularly peppy mood today.

"Hang on…" Gabriel said breathlessly and I stepped around him, finding his eyes starting to glaze with a vision. I slapped him hard around the face and he snarled at me.

"Focus on your mate, falco," I commanded and his gaze fell to her as he sucked in air between his teeth.

She looked so good on her knees in her school uniform, her skirt riding up over her hips to reveal her little pink panties beneath. *Dalle stelle, I mustn't get hard.*

"Wait," Gabriel hissed, his eyes glazing again and I spanked his ass through his pants, making him grunt in anger. "What's your problem?" he demanded.

"I want her," I growled. "So hurry up."

He went to curse me out, but then Elise upped her pace and he swore, pressing his hands to the wall again and driving his cock deep into her mouth as he came.

She swallowed everything he gave her then got to her feet, tugging up his pants and grabbing his hand as she looked to me and I nodded.

"Time to go." She tossed him over her shoulder and shot away with her Vampire speed and I barked a laugh, running out the door after them.

I hurried through the corridors and tore through the exit into the sunshine before making my way to the Cafaeteria where Elise was planting Gabriel down.

"What the hell?" Gabriel balked, still in a post orgasm daze as I jogged up behind them.

Elise didn't waste any more time for him to figure it out, shoving the doors to the Cafaeteria open and pushing him inside.

"Surprise!" a mass of people shouted with Leon at the front of them, shooting a glittering party popper in his face.

Gabriel's lips parted and his eyes fell to the lilac t-shirt Leon was wearing with the words Elise-ian Mate written on it in black letters. He had another in his hand which he dragged over Gabriel's head, locking his arms to his sides before he kissed him right on the mouth. "It's our Elysian Mate party extraordinaire!" Leon cried, grabbing another t-shirt from a Mindy and throwing it at me. I chuckled as Gabriel started laughing and Elise towed him inside by the hand. "And it's dedicated to you, Gabe, because you thought it would never happen. But I told you it would happen, didn't I Gabe?" Leon said excitedly.

"Don't call me Gabe," Gabriel said but a grin was pulling at his mouth. The whole place was decorated the same lilac colour as Elise's hair and the hall was thronging with our friends, the Mindys, the Oscuras and Lunars alike. Ethan Shadowbrook was wearing a little party hat with the words *Fated, Mated, Elated* on it while he ate chocolates and spoke to Ryder. The two of them had slowly started spending more time together as they faked creating a new friendship through Pitball. Ryder had had to try out for the team again and Mars had been overjoyed to find an earth Elemental as good as Ryder at the game. He'd had to change up some of his signature moves so as not to draw attention, but after Mars had given him some pointers based on 'an old member of the team', he was back to playing the game exactly how he used to and no one was any the wiser. It was fucking fantastico. And his new identity was fool proof on account of the fact that nobody even knew Ryder had chameleon powers and if they had, no one would have believed he'd disguise himself as a Lion Shifter covered in Disney tattoos.

Leon handed Elise a lilac dress with the words Elise-ian Queen on it and she started stripping out of her clothes to change into it with a smile on her lips. I casually cast a storm cloud around her body to keep her concealed and she smirked at me as I zapped her pert ass with a little lightning. When she emerged from the cloud, she looked hot as fuck in the fitted dress that clung to her curves perfectly.

"Look what Winkle's wearing!" Leon yelled, calling her over.

Periwinkle ran to greet us in her dog form, wearing a small lilac shirt with the words Elise-ian Mutt on the back of it. I snorted, dropping down to stroke her ears and she licked my palm before diving at Elise with a bark of happiness.

Gabriel changed properly into the shirt Leon had given him, embracing the party and smiling as Mindys came over to congratulate him.

"You really didn't know about this?" Leon asked, batting his lashes at him.

"No idea," Gabriel said, patting him on the shoulder and Leon grinned from ear to ear.

"I'm gonna get the cake, you have to see it. It's got tiny moulds of all five of us on top of it, plus Periwinkle too! *And* it's covered in our constellations." He ran away, practically skipping through the crowd as the Mindys ran after him, asking if he needed anything. I hooked a couple of beers out of a block of ice on one of the tables and headed over to Gabriel, passing him one and clinking my bottle to his before I took out my chalice and poured the beer into it.

"You knew about the party, didn't you?" I murmured to him.

"Yup," he said. "I've known since he started planning it."

I smirked, taking a swig of my beer. "You gonna tell him?"

"Nah," he said. "Look how happy he is."

My gaze fell on Leon as music started up and he began grinding on Ryder and Ethan, shouting about the cake and freaking twerking.

Elise nestled her way between us and we wrapped our arms around her as the lights were dimmed and the party got into full swing. My pack started howling and I knew it wouldn't be long before they started tearing their clothes off. It was inevitable really when Oscuras were involved. I loved the wildness of my famiglia though, and after feeling like an outsider as the only Dragon among them for so long, I realised I no longer felt that way. I'd found four Alphas who matched me in every way and showed me that it didn't matter what your Order was, whose blood ran in your veins, or even your gang affiliation. In the end, family was anyone you loved. And the five of us were anime gemelle. Soul mates. But better than that, we were mated souls.

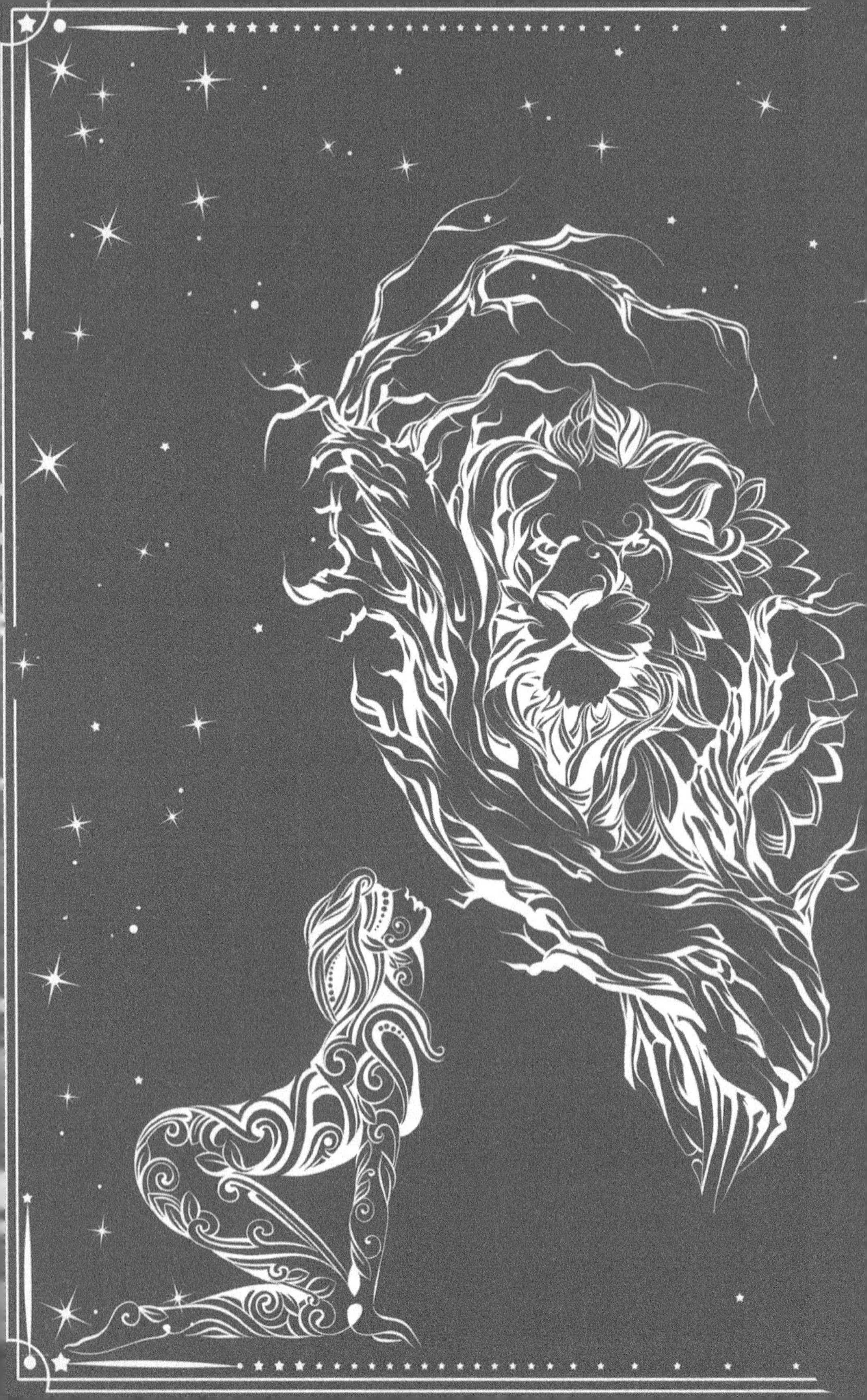

LEON

CHAPTER FIFTY NINE

NINE MONTHS LATER THAN THAT…

"Today is the day you become a king or queen among Fae!" I bellowed, pounding my fist against my chest. "You will fight like a warrior and when you feel no strength left in your bones, you'll dig deeper and deeper until you scrape out the very essence of your soul and dish it out to your enemies in fists and fury!" A cry of ascent went up and I lifted my chin high. "This is a war and you will stand at my back and paint our opposition's field red with their blood. We won't be leaving here without their heads torn from their bodies and-"

"Alright, Mr Night," Coach Mars clipped. "Round it up."

"This. Is. Alestriaaaaa!" I roared and my team hollered it back at me, jumping up and down with excitement.

We'd made it to the Pitball finals once more up against Zodiac Academy and I wasn't going to have my win stolen from me again. Last year, some helpful little grapefruit of a Pit Keeper on our team got us disqualified after testing positive for Faeroids just before the big game, so Omega Academy had played Zodiac Academy in the final. I'd. Been. Livid.

So this was it. My last shot. My only chance of winning the tournament and thrashing Zodiac, making them my Mindy. It was my dream, my dreeeeam. And I had to fulfil it or I'd end up like Lance Orion, because, welp, the guy had fallen from grace like the shiniest apple on the tree, to a fallen pile of mush on the ground. Poor dude. Gabriel knew more about it than me, but he was all sworn to secrecy by the stars or some shit. Sounded like old Asscrux was involved though, and when that Dragon prick stuck his nose in anywhere, no one ended up happy. Orion had shadows in his eyes these days and a heaviness about him since he'd started drinking on the reg. Bro was in training to be a professor now at this very school and was currently working as the youngest coach ever of the Zodiac Academy team in the meantime.

I felt sorry for the guy, I really did. His dream to join The Solarian Pitball League had dissolved before his shiny little eyes like a fart in the wind. I couldn't imagine how that must have felt, but I reckoned it was close to gouging your own eyes out with a teaspoon. I was kinda sad we hadn't gotten to thrash Zodiac Academy while he'd been on their team, but since he'd graduated half the seniors had left and were replaced with newbs. They were strong ass Elementals too, but they didn't have the experience we did. I mean yeah, they'd made it to the final and Orion had done a bang up job of getting them into shape so fast, but we were the fucking pros in the tournament dammit and I intended to thrash their little rich Fae asses today so good that they'd never forget my name. *Leonidas Night. King of the pitch. Lord of balls.*

I jumped down off of the bench and grabbed Elise and Scar, tugging them in close as everyone else got the message and crowded around for a group huddle. Gabe was opposite me with Ethan beside him and Dante on his other side. The weak link in our team was the freshman who'd replaced our dodgy ass Pit Keeper at the start of this year. She was sparky though and this win would bolster her confidence if we could pull it off, I just needed her to focus instead of getting distracted by Ethan Shadowbrook every time he ran past her. She'd legit let in three Pits during training the other day because Ethan's shirt had gotten ripped and he'd played the final rounds without it on.

"Get in here, Coach," I called, waving Mars over and pride filled his eyes as he joined our huddle under my arm and I kissed his bald head. This was my last game and he'd been a damn good teacher over the years. It made me kinda emosh to be graduating soon and leaving him behind. "Sir, of all the professors at Aurora, you've been the most killer," I told him and everyone nodded their agreement. "You always gave a shit about us, you know? And that's all most of us ever needed."

"Oh Leon." Mars waved me off, but his eyes glimmered a little and I felt myself tearing up too.

It was over. The lazy days on Devil's Hill, the morning breakfasts with my little monster and my Lionesses in the Cafaeteria, the Mindys at my constant beck and call, the long evenings of Pitball training and the endless runs in the Iron Wood. I'd loved Aurora Academy with my whole heart, it had been my second home and the place I'd found my mate. Through all the bad we'd faced together, there had been so much good to outweigh it in the end and I wanted to win this tournament not just for me, but for that school. Because it deserved the funding, it deserved to be taken notice of and the kids within it deserved to be seen. So I'd win this thing for Aurora and give her a parting gift that would hopefully give the kids of Alestria a chance to be someone in this ruthless kingdom.

"Thank you, Mars," Elise said and a chorus of thank yous sounded around the ring as Mars lost it completely and started sobbing. I patted his back and started up a chant to bring everyone's focus back to the game and boost their spirits. "Aurora, Aurora, Aurora, Aurora."

Everyone chanted it louder and louder and we started spinning around in a circle as fast as we could until we were all laughing and breathless.

I led the way out of the changing room and Ryder walked behind me, pulling his long black mane up into a top knot like mine was.

"We're matching," I whispered back at him and he rolled his eyes. "If we win this thing, I wanna hear you purr out there, Scar."

He smirked. "Fine, I'll purr if we win. Is that incentive enough, Simba?"

"Now we've definitely got this in the bag." I grinned.

Sometimes I was sure his new identity had helped him to be himself in front of everyone outside of our pride. He didn't give a shit if people saw him eating cereal or munching on doughnuts in the Cafaeteria. He laughed openly and loudly and smiled without trying to suppress it when we were in public. It was freeing for him and when he got to shed the mask and be in his true image with the rest of us, that weightlessness about him remained. Though I was sure that had more to do with Elise than anything else. Our girl had healed his soul and he'd come to be a man with a heart bigger than mine. Well alright, the same size. I mean sure, he still loved to take part in underground cage fights and got off on pain and torture and freaking loved blood and maiming and all that jazz, but he did those things with a smile on his face like an utter cutie pie these days.

I led my team onto the pitch to a roar of cheers that filled my whole head. Our entire school had come to watch us play, half the stands filled with them in our purple colours and the other half in Zodiac's navy and silver colours. Zodiac's boos were lost to the enthusiasm of our school and I waved to everyone, trying to seek out my parents among them. It wasn't too hard, the Oscuras had taken up a whole section of the stands and an inflatable Storm Dragon bounced over their heads as they jumped up and down like animals, howling and barking for us. In front of them, freaking Pitside, was Dante's Mamma, my moms and Dad, Bill, Marlowe and – holy shit, Melinda Altair was right beside him with her son Caleb. She was pumping her fist like an anime character, and the two of them were wearing Aurora Pitball jerseys with Elise's number on it.

"Look, little monster!" I cried, pointing them out and Elise jumped up and down, waving at them all with the brightest smile on her face.

"Go on Alpha!" one of Dante's uncles roared, suddenly losing his grip on a plastic cup in his hand and it went sailing down, sending wine splashing all over Melinda.

The Oscuras seemed to hold their breath as they awaited her reaction, then Melinda started laughing as camera flashes from the press went off and she smiled through it all like a good sport. *Awesome.*

Rosalie climbed up onto a railing with a few of the younger pups, wearing a crop top and open Pitball jacket, waving to all of us and I grinned at her, my heart swelling with how many people had come to watch us. Ethan's eyes moved to her and a hungry look entered them which made me step forward and slap him good.

"Get horny after the match, not during," I growled but he just shook his head. "Besides, she's fifteen, dude, way too fucking young for you."

"Dunno what you're talking about. As if I'd ever be interested in an Oscura. I'm ready to crush this," he replied fiercely, turning away to focus on the game again. *Good.*

Now we really did have to win this shit.

Mars jogged off ahead of us to stand beside Orion who wore the black uniform of the Zodiac coach on the side lines of the field. His arms were folded and he briefly shook Mars's hand before his gaze returned to us and I suddenly saw a whole world of pain in his eyes. This wasn't where he was supposed to be. He was meant to be off winning tournaments all around the kingdom as part of the Skylarks team. It had been all over the news when he'd announced that he wouldn't be taking any of the spots offered to him from The League, instead choosing to follow his dream to be a Cardinal Magic professor at Zodiac Academy. But if that was the face of someone following their dream then sign me up for a one-way ticket to failure. Because he looked broken beyond repair.

I offered him a wave and he nodded to me, a slight smile pulling at his lips for a moment before it fell away again just as quickly.

"Poor dude," I murmured.

"I hate seeing him like that," Gabriel said quietly from a little further down the line as we moved to stand in front of the Zodiac team.

The referee jogged forward and I frowned at the man with ultra tanned skin and shorts on which were way too high up his thighs for a normal ref kit. "Morning guys, I'm Professor Washer!" he said brightly. "I'm not the usual Zodiac referee, but I'm doing a teeny weenie favour for a colleague of mine. Are we all ready to get down and dirty today?" he asked and my nose wrinkled as he started doing lunges, making his shorts ride right up into his groin. "Don't mind me, my hiney is a little tight today. I was up late last night doing naked moon yoga, has anyone given that a try?"

The Zodiac team captain, Nila Krovan, took a pointed step away from Washer and I couldn't blame her. She had short blonde hair, muscular arms and a determined glint in her gaze. But she was going down, down to loser town.

"Okay, Team Captains, scooch a little closer to me, that's it." Washer beckoned us nearer and he gave me an appraising look. "Well aren't you a strapping young lad? I hope you stretched out those big thighs of yours this morning. If you want to give me your email address after the game, I'd be happy to forward you my naked moon yoga routine. I made a video."

"I'm good, thanks," I said, unable to hide my grimace. *No I do not wanna see a video of your naked ass doing yoga, creepo. I'll figure out my own naked moon yoga routine thank you very much.*

"Well just let me know." He patted my arm then squeezed my bicep and I fought a shudder as he tried to skim a little of my magic with his Siren gifts, but I had that shit locked down tighter than a duck's ass so he quickly gave up with a pout. "Let's get this game in gear then, shall we?" Washer turned and Orion tossed him a Pitball so hard it nearly hit him in the face. He fumbled the catch, but kept it in his arms and chuckled, wafting a hand at Orion like they were playing some game, but Orion's face said they weren't. Washer stepped between us, doing a couple of squats and I pressed my lips together impatiently.

"Okay now, no foul play on the pitch, I'll be watching your backsides very closely." He gave us each a pointed look.

"Go on, Leon!" Rosalie's voice carried from the crowd and I smirked as I concentrated and Washer readied to toss the ball.

A buzzer sounded the start of the game and the crowd went crazy as Washer threw the ball into the air. Kroven dove at me with a scream, going for an attack first over trying to catch the ball and I braced myself as she collided with my chest, caught her by the hips and threw her backwards over my shoulder to crash to the dirt. With a surge of energy, I dove forward, picked up the ball and started running, knocking two of the opposition to the ground as I tore down the pitch, glancing back over my shoulder to check on my team as they moved into their positions.

Ethan got himself clear first so I threw the ball to him and he leapt into the air to catch it while Elise ran to meet him. They sprinted along the pitch together while Dante and Gabriel took down as many Zodiac members as they could and Ryder hung back, waiting to wield the earth beneath the opposition if needs be.

I started circling around towards the Pit, coming up behind one of their Pit Keepers and pouncing on them, knocking them flat to the ground as Elise and Ethan charged towards us. A huge meathead of an Earthbacker took Ethan down in a furious collision but he manged to toss the ball as he fell. Elise caught it with a whoop and leapt over my head, narrowly avoiding a blast of flames from the other Zodiac Pit Keeper before throwing the ball into the Pit.

"Aurora takes the first point!" Washer called out as the magical leader board above the pitch showed our lead.

I roared my excitement, grabbing my little monster and kissing her hard before slapping her ass and directing her to the Air Quarter of the field.

Everyone readied for the next round and my heart thrashed as I awaited the buzzer.

"Nonith!" Orion barked at a guy on his team who'd been as useful as a wet fish in that round. "Get your head in the game or I'll fucking sub you."

Woah, temper much? A bunch of the female students in the stands behind Orion started muttering and pointing to him as they blushed. Then suddenly the buzzer was sounding again and the game was in play.

I charged at Captain Kroven with my teeth clenched as she took down one of our Pit Keepers and made a run for the next. I caught her by the hair, spun her around and knocked her onto the dirt, throwing my body on hers to hold her down as Washer counted for five and she was out, losing their team a point. *Sucker.*

I shoved myself up, finding their Earthraider with the ball, racing forward to score with Dante right on her tail. I cast a wall of flames to stop her, but she rose up on a hill of dirt, diving over the flames before hitting a solid wall of air and crumpling to the ground with a wail. Dante picked up the ball with a wicked laugh, tossed it to me and I threw it over my shoulder into the Pit.

The crowd went wild and Dante ran over to me, high fiving me hard, his skin zapping me with electricity as our hands connected.

"You're killing it, Leone," he said.

"You too, bro." I grinned.

We lost the next two rounds and enough of our team members were put on their asses to make both teams even Stevens. I called my team in for a huddle before the next round started up, needing to regroup.

"Do you *see* anything we should watch out for in the next round, Gabe?" I asked him and he frowned.

"Their Fireshield is gonna set Carson's ass on fire to start the next round so watch out for that." He nodded to Ryder and my Rydikins' eyes darkened with the challenge. I loved when he went all Lunar King psycho on the pitch. "Keep an eye on their Waterguard and Airsentry, Ethan, they're gonna shadow you the next couple of rounds and you're not gonna get anything in the Pit but you can distract them and keep them away from the rest of the team. That's all that's fixed, every other fate is too fluid."

I nodded. "Okay, I think we should change up tactics then. Ethan, run laps and keep those two assholes busy. Dante and Carson, I want you guys to take out their Earthbacker and Fireshield. I'm gonna go for their best shooter."

"She's fast," Elise commented with a frown. "Are you sure you can catch her?"

"I can catch her, little monster," I said with a cocky grin. "And Gabe, I want you knocking out the Pit Keepers." I finished up giving the rest of them directions then we spread out into our positions across the field as the Zodiac team broke apart from their own huddle.

When the buzzer rang out, I raced down the field like a charging bull, my gaze locked on the Zodiac Earthraider. She caught an earthball as it shot out of the earth hole and I powered along like the Terminator to cut her off. She threw huge mounds of dirt into my path to try and stop me, but I leapt over each one, then cast a flash fire in front of her, making her scream and stumble back. Those few seconds cost her everything as I collided with her and the ball rolled from her hands. Elise appeared, picking it up and ducking as someone shot a massive blast of water at her, missing it narrowly before she started racing up the pitch.

"Go on, Elise!" I roared as the Aurora crowd began shouting out encouragements, going mad as she made a beeline for the Pit.

The Zodiac Fireshield shot into her path, throwing a fistful of flames into her gut and knocking her backwards. Ryder collided with him in a bone-crushing tackle, taking him to the ground so Elise could leap over them and keep sprinting towards the Pit.

Gabriel knocked one Zodiac Pit Keeper into the Pit, but the other one made it past him, tearing towards Elise and turning the ground to ice beneath her feet. Elise nearly fell over and I ran after her, throwing out my palms and melting the ice before she could slip. She knocked the Pit Keeper aside with a blast of air, sending them flying across the field with a wail and Elise dove forward, slamming the ball into the Pit with a scream of victory.

Gabriel tossed her over his shoulder, running around the perimeter of the Pit while I roared to the sky in excitement and the whistle sounded for half time.

We all trailed into the locker rooms, muddy, bruised and battered and started healing ourselves as we went. We were one Pit up on Zodiac, but this was a seriously close game. They were fighting for their lives out there and so were we.

"Did you hear?" Ethan bounded up to me, clapping me on the shoulder.

"What?" I asked.

"There are officials from The League are here looking for new talent," he said, his eyes bright. "Can you imagine if they picked some of you lot? I could say I went to school with a bunch of famous Pitball stars."

My heart thundered furiously in my chest at that. Was I good enough to be picked? I'd never really thought about playing beyond my school team, but now the idea was presented to me, it was fucking all I could think about.

"Awesome, dude. Maybe they'll pick *us*." I grinned and Ethan laughed.

"That'd be cool but nah, I'm the Lunar King, remember?" He smirked. "My main job outside of leading my people is not getting killed or arrested and sent to Darkmore Penitentiary.

I snorted a laugh. "You're too pretty to go to Darkmore, dude," I told him. "You'd have to fight every day to stop Big Burt trying to trick you into picking up his fallen soap in the shower so he can dick you."

He barked a laugh. "Nah, I'd kill him. No one's going near my ass without consent."

We had to fight for our lives in the next half of the match, every Pit we scored countered by Zodiac scoring straight after. We were in a furious game of push and pull, desperate to just get another point ahead to try and stretch our lead a little further. But every time we got close, the Zodiac team managed to steal it from us and gain back a point. No one dropped a single ball either, forcing us to keep up this maddening fight until we were down to the second to last round and an asshole got Dante on his back, meaning we lost one point and evened up the scores to a dead even draw.

"Fuck," I growled as everyone crowded in for the final huddle. This next round was it. We *had* to get that Pit or knock out at least one more teammate than they did ours.

"Take a breath, Leo," Elise urged and I did, trying to keep my head clear as the pressure mounted up on me.

"Gabe?" I asked. "Got anything for us?"

Gabriel shook his head with a frown. "I can't *see* anything."

"Gah," I spat in frustration, kicking the grassy ground at my feet.

"The last two rounds have had airballs shot into the game," Dante said. "Chances are it won't be that again."

"They're gonna think the same thing," I growled. "So everyone's gonna be flanking the other holes."

"So what if it is an airball?" Elise said. "It's random, technically there's no greater chance that it won't be that."

"But the law of averages says it'll be one of the other Elemental balls," I said with a frown.

"I'm just saying, we shouldn't rule it out," Elise said and I nodded, deep in thought as I tried to work out our best play here.

"How are we doing for magic?" I asked.

"I'm almost out," Dante said.

"Same," Gabriel agreed along with one of our Pit Keepers and Ethan nodded too.

"I'm good," Ryder said and I turned to him with a twisted smile, knowing that all of the pain he inflicted in this game kept him topped up even if everyone else had to believe he was running on sunlight like me.

"Then I say we use everything you've got. Blast the pitch to shit and take out as many Zodiac players as we can," I said.

"Their Fireshield has been reserving power," Ethan said.

"Alright, I'll focus on them," I said. "Elise, how's your power?"

"I've got enough for one strong shield," she said. "I don't think I can blast anyone too far out of my way though."

"Okay, focus on getting the ball then use that shield to slow down anyone behind you. I want everyone else on defence. Block all members of their team and get Elise to the Pit at all costs."

"Are you sure?" my Fireside gasped, her eyes wide.

"Yes, I'm sure," I growled. "We give Elise the best shot possible. Go Aurora!"

"Go Aurora!" they all shouted back and we broke apart, spreading out across the pitch and Elise moved to the air hole quarter.

"Come on, little monster, you got this," I said under my breath then laid my attention on the Zodiac Fireshield with his fuzzy hair and bulky shoulders. *Dead. Meat.*

The buzzer sounded and adrenaline fuelled my veins, every hope I'd ever had about winning the tournament pinning on these final five minutes of the game. I waited by the fire hole, but with a fwoomph an airball shot out of the air hole. *No fucking way!*

Elise leapt up to catch it then hit the ground running, casting a wall of air behind her which the other Zodiac player immediately ran into and crashed to the ground on her back with a yelp.

Elise's gaze was fixed in determination as every single Zodiac player on the pitch turned and ran at her.

A tremendous boom sounded as the ground split apart and Ryder dropped half the Zodiac team into it in one fell swoop. I cheered as I ran forward, but as I made it to the edge of the ravine, I was forced to stop, cut off from the rest of the game.

"Go on, Simba!" Ryder called, casting a bridge of earth in front of me and I raced across it with a grin, charging toward the Zodiac Fireshield once more.

Dante and Gabriel took down Zodiac members as fast as they could but the opposition's Earthbacker made it to Elise, taking her down with a furious collision that sent them rolling over the ground.

I smashed into the Fireshield just before he took out Gabriel and something crunched beneath me in his body as I held him down for the count. I barely even heard it as my gaze hooked on Elise again, trapped beneath the Earthbacker. She had to get up. Right fucking now, before the count was up and she was out of the round.

"Get to Elise!" I bellowed to anyone close enough to hear me.

Ethan was suddenly there, his shirt torn open at the back and blood running down his skin as he fell onto the Earthbacker and ripped him off of Elise. Half a second later, one of their Pit Keepers set Ethan alight and he cried out, dropping to the ground and rolling to put out the flames, clearly tapped out on water magic. Elise had already raced way, running for the Pit as I got up and the guy beneath me crawled off the field. Dante and Gabriel were out too and as I did a mental count of how many of each team members were out, I realised we were still in a fucking draw. We needed this damn Pit.

"Go on Elise!" I shouted and the chant was taken up by our entire school as she pelted down the field.

I had barely any magic left, but what little I had, I cast at the Pit Keepers and fire flashed around them. One of them stumbled to the ground to avoid the fire, but the other doused the flames and ran to intercept Elise, throwing out his hands, but no magic came out. *Ha!*

Elise punched him right in face, flooring him before she ran to the edge of the Pit and slammed the ball into its depths.

"Aurora Academy are the winners!" Washer's voice filled the entire stadium and I was stunned for two full seconds before I tore my shirt off and ran to grab my girl.

I dipped her into a crazy, passionate kiss before the rest of my team collided with us and we all fell into a dog pile, laughing and cheering and celebrating. My heart was pounding like mad and I had the biggest victory boner ever.

Ryder slapped his hand to my back and I managed to roll over as I hugged him.

"Purr for me, Scar," I begged and he rolled his eyes, using his snake rattle to create a low purr in his throat and I squeezed him even harder for that. It was so good, he must have been practising in secret.

Dante was so excited that we all started getting electrocuted and quickly had to get up and stand away from him as he sprinted off to meet the Oscuras who were all pouring onto the pitch, half of them tearing their clothes off as the Zodiac professors tried to restore order.

"We did it, Leo!" Elise threw herself at me again and I hugged her tight, nuzzling into her head and soaking in every perfect second of this moment.

"Mr Night, Miss Callisto?" someone called and we looked over, finding an official looking man there in a suit, smiling at us.

My heart dropped out of my chest into my gut then swirled around in there in a whirlpool. This was Guy Vellios. The fucking chairman for the whole motherfucking League. He held out his hand to us and I lunged forward, gripping it in mine and pulling him in close to lick his face.

"Leo!" Elise gasped, but Guy just laughed as he drew back and offered his hand to her instead.

"It's quite alright," he said as he shook her hand. "I'm incredibly impressed with both of you, we've been watching you for quite some time."

I supressed a squeal, placing a hand to my mouth as I stared at him unblinkingly.

"If you'd like, we'd love to chat with you both more about the possibility of you joining The League. There are a few spots opening across some of the major teams and we'd love for you both to try out." He handed us each a shiny silver business card and I gaped at him, speechless for once.

"We'd love to." Elise elbowed me and I started nodding, not able to get a single word out as he smiled again and headed away across the field.

My gaze fell on Orion as he watched the interaction, looking like we'd just stoned his mother to death and my heart tugged with guilt for a moment.

Elise caught my hand, turning me to her and a grin split across my face once more as I got captured in her eyes.

"You did it, Leo. You got us here," she said with emotion in her gaze.

"I couldn't have done it without you, little monster." I ran my thumb over her muddy cheek as a party broke out on the field and the Oscuras started singing some old song in Faetalian.

It was the most incredible moment, not a single piece of darkness in our world right then.

Pure happiness spilled from Elise and my muscular, muddy Lionesses and it was the most blissful feeling of my existence. Somehow, my lazy ass had grown into someone capable of creating a whole pride, of winning the academy Pitball tournament and of impossibly capturing the heart of this perfect creature in front of me. And I realised I may have longed for this Pitball dream to come true for years, but my truest dream was standing right in front of me. And I'd never let her go.

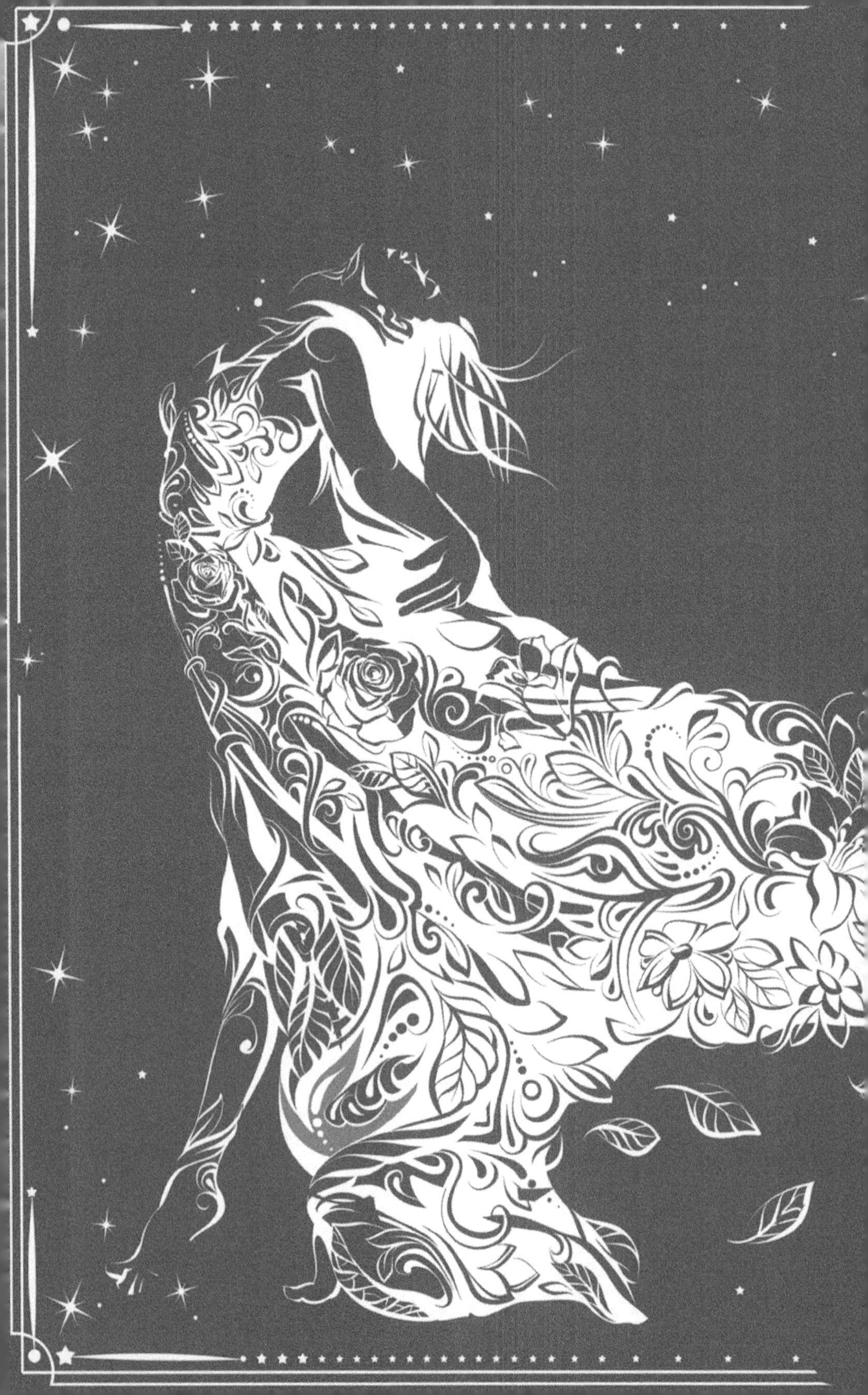

ELISE

CHAPTER SIXTY

ANOTHER THREE YEARS LATER...

The sound of a crowd big enough to fill a freaking rock concert accosted my ears from the sweeping lawn beyond the window as the heady scent of summer flowers swept in on the breeze and tugged my long, lilac wedding dress around my legs.

"For the love of the moon!" Bianca cursed between the pins jammed between her lips as she caught the fabric and continued with her final adjustments.

"It already looks perfect, Auntie," Rosa groaned as she flopped back down on the bed, ruffling her pale pink bridesmaid's dress and causing Bianca to curse even louder. "Besides, you know Dante and the others won't let her stay in it five minutes longer than the ceremony anyway."

"Hush your mouth you naughty pup!" Bianca gasped, wafting a hand at Rosalie and sending a vine snaking towards her so that she could heave her back up onto her feet.

"You'd better watch out, Auntie - when I'm Awakened I'm gonna use my earth magic to lift you off of your feet whenever I want in retaliation for all of this abuse!" Rosalie complained while I laughed.

"Did anybody order eighty-five flower girls and page boys?" Leon called from the other side of the door and Bianca shrieked in alarm, diving on top of me and constructing a wall of earth between us and the door.

"Calm down, Auntie!" Rosalie said with a laugh as she leapt over us and hurried to the door. "He hasn't even opened it."

"I won't have this union cursed by the stars before it's even begun!" Bianca snapped before descending into Faetalian as she heaved me upright again and began fluffing the intricate lace detailing of my dress as she fixed it for me.

"Umm, I don't wanna interrupt or anything," I said hesitantly.

"What is it, cara mia? We don't have long to finish up here," she muttered, adjusting the hem of my skirt so that it pooled just to her liking behind me.

"I know," I agreed. "It's just that you kinda stabbed me with that pin when you took me out and I'm pretty sure I'm bleeding on the dress-"

Bianca shrieked in alarm as Rosalie burst out laughing from beyond the wall of earth and the sound of the door opening followed. There was a stampede of tiny feet and laughter as all of Dante's youngest siblings, cousins and even second cousins poured into the room, racing around the space and howling excitedly. I spotted my little cousins Jenna and Iris running amongst them too, giggling wildly as the Oscura Wolf pups got over excited and jumped all over the place. Each of the girls wore a baby pink dress with a huge tulle skirt while the boys wore grey suits with little pink bowties. I had officially lost count of the number of page boys and flower girls I had when it passed thirty and I decided I would no longer give any fucks about how big this freaking wedding turned out to be.

"I was just wondering if you could get a bunch of photos for Roary," Leon's voice came from beyond my hiding place. "I don't want him to miss a moment of this so-"

"Someone get a water Elemental in here!" Bianca howled, interrupting Leon and Rosalie as she tugged the pin out of my leg and slapped a hand down over the tiny wound to heal it for me.

"Yeah. I'll do it," Rosa replied to Leon, the amusement falling out of her voice at the request.

"Stop beating yourself up, little pup," Leon said firmly. "Roary is a big boy. He made his choices and he would hate to think of you out here feeling responsible for them. I know it sucks that he's stuck in there, but if you don't even enjoy the life you're living out here then it makes his sacrifice less meaningful."

"I'm still going to get him out one day," she swore.

"I know you will," Leon agreed. "Anyway, I have to get back, my moms are going way overboard in their work at getting the four of us ready and they'll lose their shit if I'm not back for my head massage soon. Plus they keep trying to convince Ryder to grow a moustache and he is being awkward about it. I'll see you out there, little monster!" he called excitedly and the sound of his footsteps receding reached me. I snorted a laugh, wondering what the Lionesses were putting my guys through in preparation for today and wishing I could be a fly on the wall for them fussing over all of them.

Rosa started taking more photos than could possibly have been called for, but I knew she just wanted to make sure Roary didn't miss out like Leon had said so I kept quiet about it.

Four of Dante's aunts all raced into the room a moment later, squabbling over which of them was the most powerful water Elemental and before I knew it, the tiny bloodstain on my dress was gone and I was being shoved in front of a huge mirror to inspect myself.

"Wow," I breathed, my eyes glistening as I stared at the hand-stitched dress which Bianca had spent the last year working on without any magic at all.

The lace detailing was the finest I'd ever seen and she'd worked countless zodiac signs and constellations into it. It fit me like a glove and the tiny white flowers she'd grown into place amongst the lilac strands of my hair were stunning. I didn't even feel like me in this. I looked like a freaking princess in the most amazing way.

"It's almost time!" Rosalie called. "You look shit hot, Elise. Don't forget to make those stronzos work for it tonight. I'll get the pups in position downstairs."

I grinned at her as she cupped her hands around her mouth and howled before jogging out of the room, still taking photos and causing all of the pups and my cousins to charge after her in a stampede.

I released a long breath as silence fell at last.

"How are you feeling, cara mia?" Bianca asked me kindly, reaching out to take my hands and giving me a teary-eyed look.

"Well, I already knew the five of us were forever," I reasoned. "I'm mostly doing this for the ring."

Bianca burst out laughing and then started crying, wafting me away as I tried to reach out to comfort her. "It's nothing," she insisted, patting at her eyes. "I just wish Micah could be here to see his oldest boy marry the girl of his dreams. But I know he's close by watching us with your sweet fratello, amore mio."

I swallowed thickly at her words, nodding as my own tears blossomed and I fought to keep them at bay. Gareth wouldn't have wanted me crying over him on my wedding day, but these were the kinds of occasions when I missed him the most sharply. He should have been here as my best man, teasing me for matching my dress to my hair and squeezing me tight as he told me how happy he was for me. But I knew he was close by even if I couldn't see him and I wasn't going to let my grief paint sadness onto the days I wished he didn't have to miss.

A soft knock came at the door and we both looked around as we fought off our tears and I breathed in sharply as I spotted my mom standing there awkwardly, clasping a white box in her hands as she looked between me and Dante's mom.

"Hi," she said, her gaze roaming over me and way too many words hanging in the air between us. I'd invited her of course, but I really hadn't had any idea whether or not she'd show up until that moment. She'd accepted the invite, but reliable really wasn't her bag these days and my heart swelled a little in relief as I saw her.

Things had been a bit better between us in the last few years. She'd finally moved out of the wellness centre where she'd been staying and had even managed to start up her own business teaching strippers to dance and choreographing routines for them. It didn't exactly pay all of her bills and between The Black Hole and The Sparkling Uranus – which was now called the Cosmic Strip and run by the Oscuras too - we provided her with most of her clients. And I covered the bills she couldn't afford on top of that, but she seemed to like it and she hadn't felt the need to go back to stripping or whoring so far as I knew.

We spoke more than we used to, but there was just something broken between us now, the hole where Gareth should have been too wide to breach and too deep to venture into. But that didn't hurt the way it once had. She'd had her chances to fix things with me and though they were improved, I'd accepted the fact that we were never going to be close like I'd once wished we could be.

The news of Marlowe's discovery had hit her hard - mostly because once he'd learned a lot about my upbringing and the things I'd been subjected to in and around The Sparkling Uranus, he hadn't been interested in reconnecting with her romantically. I still wasn't totally sure who had informed him of all of that shit, but Ryder was mysteriously vague about the conversations he'd had with my newfound father and I was almost certain it had been him. Not because he'd wanted to hurt me by giving up the truth of my upbringing, but because he'd wanted Marlowe to understand me better and appreciate my trust issues.

And I had to admit, that once Marlowe had a full understanding of my life and he'd spent months in various recovery therapies arranged by his sister, he'd actually proved himself to be a man worth the love I had to give. He was loyal and protective and noble in a way that not many Fae I knew were. He'd even restarted his charity work following his recovery and was still determined to improve the lives of as many Fae as he could - even if that meant he was a little unpredictable and didn't always follow the family line, much to Melinda's clear distress. But even she didn't try too hard to rein him in. I was guessing after knowing he'd been kept under the control of another Fae for years, she didn't want to subject him to that again so she just gave press releases covering for his more unpredictable moves and for the most part, he just did whatever the fuck he liked despite his link to the Celestial Councillors.

"I hope it's okay I came," Mom said, stepping forward cautiously. "I just thought, maybe it would be nice for you to have something borrowed from me? Though I'm not sure they'll really match this whole classy thing you've got going." Her eyes swept over the priceless dress and I could feel her discomfort.

"What is it?" I asked softly, moving closer to her as Bianca backed away to give us a little space.

"They're my lucky stripping shoes," she said with a breath of laughter, flipping the lid open and revealing the pair of diamanté covered platforms with a killer heel. "I always made my best tips when I wore them." She shrugged looking embarrassed and I grinned, reaching out to grab them.

"I might be dressed up like a princess right now," I said as I slid my feet into the shoes one at a time. "But I'm never going to forget where I came from, Mom."

Her smile widened as I held my foot out towards her for inspection before dropping the dress down to cover them.

"Okay. Great. I'll go find my seat," she said, turning back towards the door then stopping herself and turning back to me. She hesitated a moment and then lurched forward, wrapping her arms around me and squeezing me tighter than I could ever remember her holding me. "I do love you, baby girl," she whispered. "And I'm so very proud of you. I'm just sorry I wasn't...better."

"Mom," I began but she released me and waved me off as she stepped back.

"Enjoy your big day," she said firmly. "Gareth would want that."

My throat thickened and something in my heart seemed to swell as she turned to hurry out of the room again before jolting to a halt.

I sidestepped to see what had stopped her and bit my lip as I found Marlowe standing there in his grey suit, the two of them staring at each other as the lives they might have lived hung in the space between them.

The moment seemed to drag on for eternity before they murmured a greeting to one another then Mom hurried away.

"Where's my beautiful girl?" Marlowe asked excitedly, shooting forward with no warning and skidding to a halt right in front of me. He grinned widely, flashing his dimples and reaching out to cup my face between his hands as he inspected me. "Are you ready?"

"Yeah, Dad, I think I am," I agreed.

Marlowe's lips parted and his eyes began to water as he opened and closed his mouth like a fish and I nudged him to make him stop it.

"Don't cry or I'll cry," I said.

"Did you just call me Da-"

"Per amore della luna! We're late! Scoot, scoot!" Bianca cried suddenly, wafting her hands at us and making me laugh as she chased us out into the hallway.

"It's one thing to keep the grooms waiting, cara mia, but quite another to make them serve the Wedding Breakfast late for the rest of us!"

Bianca raced away down the hall and I grinned at my dad as we followed on behind her more slowly.

When we reached the wide staircase in the centre of the Oscura house, a string quartet started playing from somewhere beyond the wide open doors where the bright sunlight was streaming in and the scent of flowers filled the air.

The noise of three hundred Werewolves plus every other Fae we knew and could trust in the whole of Solaria - thanks to the input from the Oscuras and the Nights - suddenly died down and my heart began to race as we descended the stairs.

"Are you ready for this, my girl?" Marlowe whispered and I grinned at him as I nodded.

"Damn straight I am. It's about time those assholes put a ring on it."

Marlowe started laughing and I fought a snigger too as we made it to the foot of the stairs just in time to see the last of the flower girls and page boys moving out of the aisle on the lawn ahead of me.

I took a deep breath as the bridesmaids and groomsmen strode down the aisle next - pretty much entirely made up of Dante's family with my cousins Caleb and Hadley thrown in for a little variety.

Then it was our turn. Marlowe squeezed my hand where I held onto his arm and as the music changed to an instrumental arrangement of Can You Feel The Love Tonight - *thanks Leo* - I stepped out into the sunshine.

The sweeping lawn to the south of the Oscura stronghold had been transformed with a sea of chairs tied with white tulle and pale pink ribbons, an enormous archway smothered in white roses covered the entire congregation and at the far end of the seemingly endless aisle, four men stood waiting for me in a circle beneath the sun, ready for me to take my place at the heart of them.

The smile that bit into my cheeks grew and grew with each step I took and my pulse thundered until I finally made it past every member of the congregation and Marlowe released my arm.

I stepped forward to take my place between my four kings and before so much as a word of the ceremony was spoken between us, I knew that I had made it to my perfect place in the world. Because so long as I was surrounded by them, I knew I'd be surrounded by happiness. And really, what more could a girl from the worst part of Alestria ask for?

The full moon hung low in the sky and the dancing and celebrations had been taking place for hours before I found a moment to catch my breath.

I stumbled away from the dance floor, healing my sore feet for what must have been the hundredth time and dropping down into a chair as Dante and Leon competed to do the limbo under Lasita's dingy stick.

"Who's turn is it on cake duty?" Bianca called as she raced by me and I laughed as I glanced across the room to the towering white wedding cake which we still hadn't gotten around to cutting yet. She'd made it herself of course and had hand-frosted every inch of it including the five figurines which sat on top of it. She'd been warning hungry pups away from it all night and I made up my mind to get the guys to come cut it with me just as soon as I'd had a breather so that she didn't have to keep worrying about them ruining it.

"Of course, it would make your disguise so much easier to maintain if you grew a true mane," Safira's voice caught my ear and I couldn't help but get to my feet to investigate as Ryder replied.

"I prefer my normal look," he said firmly as I caught sight of him lingering by the buffet while Leon's moms all pouted at him.

"But a long mane is so appealing," Latisha sighed, stroking his short cropped hair sadly.

Everyone in attendance here was in on the ruse about Ryder's 'death' and they knew his Carson alter-ego well by now, but it was so much better when he didn't have to wear it. Which since we'd graduated, he hadn't had to most of the time as we didn't spend much time in Alestria aside from visiting the families and obviously then he was safe inside their homes.

"Or a moustache," Marie added, stroking his upper lip. "Your pride is lacking moustaches."

"Seems like a shame," Safira agreed.

"Such a shame," Latisha said with a nod.

"I don't want to grow a-"

"Oooh or a goatee?" Marie suggested excitedly.

"Yes! Like a *real* gangster," Safira cooed.

"People might even be afraid of you then," Latisha added. "Wouldn't you like to be dark and terrifying?"

"I am terrifying," Ryder growled indignantly. "Everyone knows that I can-"

"Perhaps a full beard?" Safira said thoughtfully. "You might even seem intimidating if you had a beard."

"I *am* intimidating," Ryder snarled and I took pity on him as I darted between Leon's moms and stole him away.

"Can I just grab this cuddly bear?" I asked them, linking my fingers through his as he growled at me.

Leon's moms all started giggling about newlyweds and commenting on how cute we were and I grinned at Ryder as he scowled my way.

Gabriel yelled a challenge to Dante and started limboing too, while Orion was forced to join in by Bill but instantly fell on his ass, drawing plenty of attention to the dance floor and I yanked on Ryder's hand while everyone was distracted, tugging him behind a huge floral display and stealing a kiss where no one could see us.

"I should spank your ass for that cuddly comment," he growled, eyeing me hungrily as I smirked up at him.

"Wait for our wedding night, Cuddles," I teased, making the rattle go off in his chest.

"Or maybe I should just pin you to this weird trellis thing and remind you of exactly who you-"

"Group photo out by the vineyard!" Bianca yelled suddenly, her voice magnified by some spell. "I'm missing the bride and one groom!"

Ryder groaned and I laughed as I tugged him back out of our hiding place, slipping between the huge crowd as we re-joined the others and moved outside like requested.

"You look beautiful, Elise," Laini gushed, taking my hand and squeezing it as I found myself beside her for a few moments. The day had been an absolute whirlwind and I'd barely managed to scrape a couple of sentences with most of the guests so I had to grab every moment I could with everyone.

"So do you. Did I spy you and one of Dante's cousins getting cosy by the buffet earlier?" I asked her conspiratorially.

Laini blushed, looking over at the girl who I was pretty sure was called Greta and catching her attention. Greta waved, biting her lip and Laini gave me an excited grin. "She seems really nice."

"Go get her then," I hissed in encouragement before I was swept through the crowd and positioned at the front of everyone with my kings either side of me.

The photographer lifted himself up into the air using his magic as he positioned himself for the perfect shot and Bianca barked instructions at all the Oscuras to make sure everyone got in.

"Are we missing anyone?" Bianca yelled once she was satisfied.

"Our brother isn't here," Kipling Senior commented.

"The middle one," Junior added and a collective sigh went up.

"Well where could he have gotten to?" Bianca cried just as Leon gasped in horror.

"Who was looking after the cake?" he demanded.

"Oh no," I breathed, catching Dante's eye as a horrified look passed between us.

"I'm coming, my beauty!" Leon roared, talking off and racing back against the lawn.

I took a step to follow him but Gabriel caught my arm, a look of disgust written across his features. "It's too late," he breathed. "Far too fucking late."

"You *saw* that?" Ryder snorted and Gabriel grimaced.

"Sometimes The Sight is a curse."

Leon's screams of horror filled the air a moment later and Bianca started swearing in Faetalian.

Dante wrapped his arms around me and I couldn't help but laugh as the truth began to spread and the Wolves all howled their grief over losing the cake to the cock of a Griffin with a weird as fuck fetish.

"I'm so sorry, carina," Dante breathed against my neck.

"He saved you from having to give that Dragon Lord asshole your sperm, Drago," I said, shaking my head. "The least we can allow him is a wedding cake to remember."

Gabriel began dry heaving and Ryder scrunched his nose up while I looked up at the camera and grinned just as the flash went off.

It sure as fuck wasn't a perfect picture, especially as a Griffin with his pants around his ankles and frosting smeared all over his junk ran past being chased by a raging Nemean Lion just as it was taken, but I had to admit, it was definitely a moment to remember.

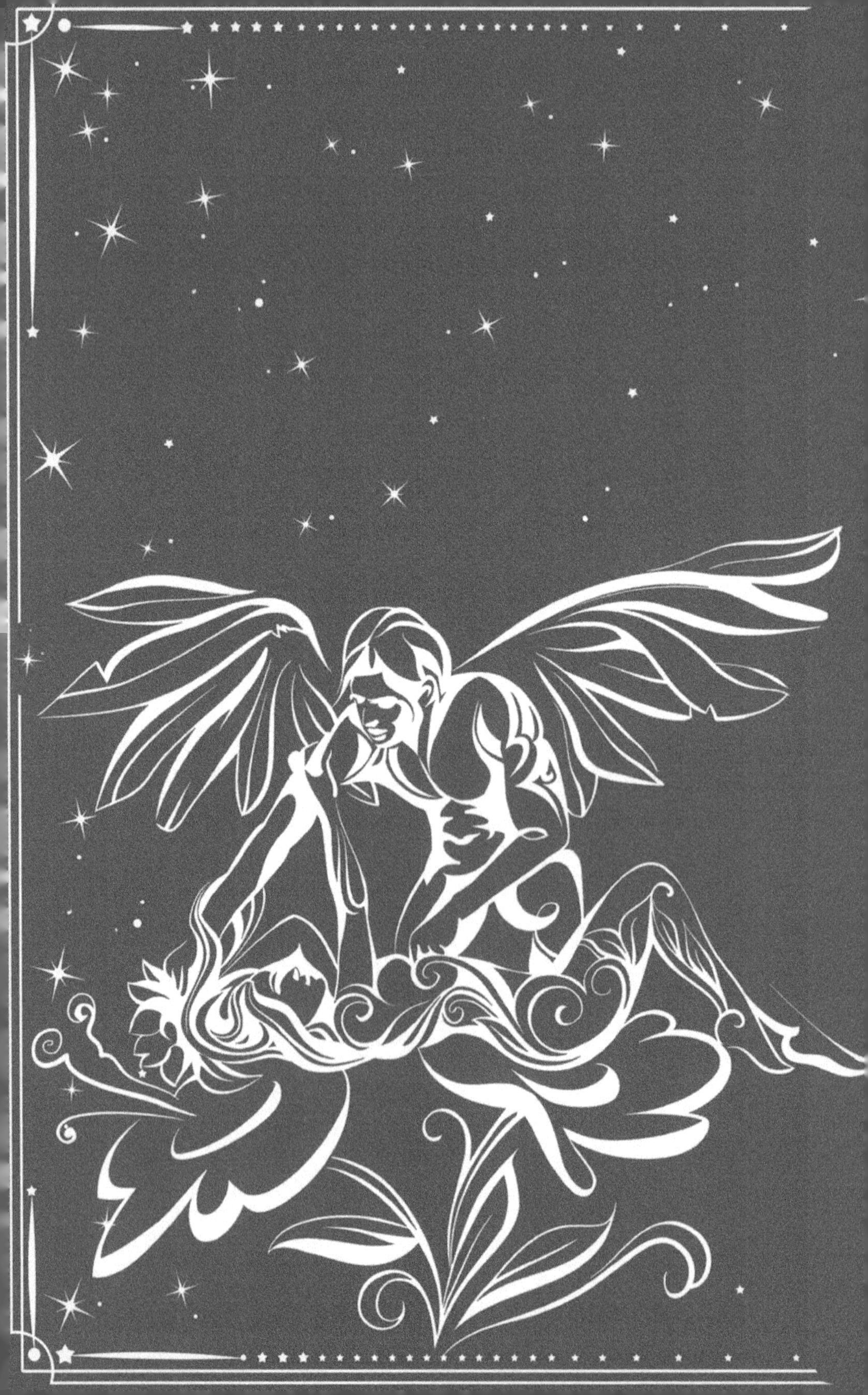

Gabriel

CHAPTER SIXTY ONE

TWO MONTHS AFTER THE WEDDING…

I stepped up to the front door of the house I'd been building for months in between teaching part time at Aurora Academy. Elise and Leon would be home from Pitball training with the Skylarks team soon. I'd gotten Rosalie to distract Dante and Ryder from looking for me with the tracking bond between us by taking them on a hunt in the woods at the edge of the Oscura vineyards for a bear which had been spotted on the grounds and needed to be chased off.

I fixed the special branch Elise and the guys had made for me into the middle of the door, using my earth magic to wield the wood around it and hold it there and satisfaction ran through me.

I'd been getting the urge to build this place for a long time, but it needed to be absolutely perfect. It was going to be our home, our nest. And I'd painstakingly worked to make sure every detail of it was just right.

I jogged off of the wide stone porch onto the path out front and admired my work. The house was large with three floors, a white balcony on each level. The grey tiles were sleek and sloped over the roofs of each bedroom on the second level. And on the top level, the roof rose into a point, but to the east side of it was a sculpted wooden lookout tower with carved wings on the side of it. I could see all across the land from up there and the roof was able to open to let the morning light in if I ever didn't want to sleep there without waking for the sunrise. I'd bought this land which backed onto the Oscuras' northern vineyard in secret; it lay at the boundary to a tall mountain which rose up to my left, the dying sun glinting off of its peak as it sank away behind it.

I took my Atlas from my pocket, sending a message in our group chat with a smirk pulling at my lips.

Gabriel:

Need help. Come find me.

I had placed protective boundaries all around this place to keep it safe, but their magical signatures would all be recognised to let them through. I'd left the stardust wards down for now so they could travel directly to me and get the surprise of their lives.

My family all appeared in front of me on the path, rushing forward with fear in their eyes as I smirked, pushing my hands into my pockets.

"What's going on?" Elise asked, her hair still wet and her dress on backwards as if she'd pulled it on mid shower. In fact, it was turning kind of transparent now as I looked at it. And I was definitely looking. Mmm… I got a vision of all of us in the massive bed I'd had installed upstairs and started grinning.

"Gabriel?" she snapped, shaking me out of it and I pulled her into my arms, smelling her sweet cherry scent and kissing her forehead.

"Sorry, angel, but you look hot as shit right now." I glanced at Leon who hadn't faired much better than Elise in the getting dressed department, his hair soaked and only a pair of blue sweatpants on him.

Dante and Ryder folded their arms, mimicking each other as they cocked their heads towards one another. Ryder was currently concealing himself as Carson, but he let the identity fall away as he realised we were alone. Periwinkle was at his heels, her own dog guise dropping away to reveal her vibrant blue colour and three tails which started wagging.

"You gave me a heart attack, what's going on?" Elise demanded and a flash of guilt ran through me at worrying her.

"Turn around, angel," I told her.

"No, I'm not gonna turn around. I wanna know why-"

I grabbed her, whipping her around and the guys looked too as she fell still in my arms.

"Welcome home," I told them, suddenly feeling nervous that I'd gotten this wrong, or that it wasn't what they'd imagined, or that I'd been too presumptuous building this place without asking for their input. But it was my Harpy nature to make my mate a home and I'd wanted to provide that for all of her men too.

"What?" Elise breathed and I started walking her toward it.

"This is ours," I said. "I built it."

"Are you serious?" Leon gasped, his wet hair flying around him as he turned and ran at me. I braced myself for impact as he knocked Elise into my chest and wrapped his arms around both of us, jumping up and down. "Let me see inside, Gabe. Show me inside. I wanna get in there deep and explore every dark corner and thrust myself into its beautiful-"

"Stop talking about it like that," I growled and he shut up sharpish, nuzzling my face instead.

"You really did this for us, falco?" Dante asked as Ryder continued to stare up at the place, apparently having no comment.

"Yeah." I ran a hand down the back of my neck as Elise and Leon released me, heading up to the front door in anticipation. "What do you think?"

"I think it's fantastico," Dante grinned, lightning sparkling in his eyes.

"It backs right onto Oscura land so you'll always be close for pack business," I said and he looked even more excited, running over to hug me. "Grazie, mio amico." He stepped back, jogging over to join Elise and Leon by the door as they inspected the porch and cooed over all the intricate details in the woodwork.

"Look, there's carvings here of all of us!" Leon cried as I moved to Ryder's side and my shoulder brushed his.

"Do you...like it?" I asked uncertainly, glancing at his expression which gave nothing away.

"I never thought I'd have a home again," he said in a rough voice and my chest tightened. I slid an arm around his shoulders and he looked to me with a crooked smile. "Is it really ours?"

"Yes," I swore. "All ours."

He turned to embrace me, clapping my back hard and I felt our bond burning hotter for a moment before we broke apart and headed up the porch steps to join the others.

"Can we go inside?" Elise shot over to me, taking my hand in hers.

"Of course." I beamed. "Just touch the door to get in, the magic will recognise you."

I guided her forward and she gasped as she spotted the special branch she'd gifted me embedded in the centre of the door. "I love it."

"Go on in," I urged.

She reached out a hesitant hand, glancing up at me as her fingers paused before the wood.

"Angel?" I questioned and I looked to her as emotion pinched her features. "Are you okay?"

"Yeah, I just..." She took a breath. "I always thought Gareth would walk through the door of my first home with me, right here at my side."

My gut knotted and I squeezed her fingers just as a wind picked up around us and twisted her hair in its embrace. She gasped and a low laugh escaped me as I felt her brother's presence as fiercely as if he was right beside us. A whinny seemed to carry on that wind and Elise closed her eyes as she took a moment to feel the embrace of her brother, a tear slipping from her eye. Ryder moved beside her, wiping it away with this thumb before resting a hand on her lower back.

"Looks like he showed up for the occasion, baby," he said in a low tone and she nodded, sniffing a little before reaching for the door again.

"Love you, Gare Bear," she whispered as the wind continued to flutter around us and as she pressed her hand to the door, it clicked as it unlocked

"Wind me, Gareth!" Leon cried and we all laughed as he broke the sad mood, turning to him and finding his hair spinning out in the breeze before it whipped Dante in the face and he roared a laugh, running his fingers through the breeze and adding a gust of his own to play with our lost brother.

Elise pushed the door wide and we stepped into the hall, the sunset light pouring across the floorboards in sweeping strokes of pink. The white walls were cast in it too and Elise rushed forward to look at the huge Pegasus silhouette painted on the wall beside the stairs, rearing up as his horn seemed to pierce the stars above it.

"Gabriel, it's beautiful," she breathed in awe, placing her hand to it then trailing her fingers along as she wound further down the hall to where countless photographs hung on the walls. I'd used The Sight to get hold of Leon's scrapbook for a night and copied all of the best ones, having them framed, plus I'd managed to get my hands on some of Elise's childhood photos from her Atlas. Pictures of her and Gareth were sprinkled between all of our family, binding him to us as clear as anything.

Leon and Dante tore off upstairs, racing along as their shoulders butted against each other's and their laughter carried back to us as they explored the upper levels together. Ryder and I followed Elise to the huge open plan kitchen built of honey wood with a lounge beyond it decorated in cream colours. It had three huge couches angled towards a stone fireplace beyond the breakfast bar. Floor length windows led out to the back porch where there was a hot tub and outdoor bar too, but Elise didn't head that way, she circled into the next room which had a long dining table in it and bookshelves all around it. We soon made it back to the entrance hall and headed upstairs, checking out all of the guest bedrooms before I showed them the master bedroom with its enormous bed at the heart of it taking up most of the space.

Leon and Dante were already there, bouncing up and down on it and I laughed as they grabbed hold of Ryder and dragged him onto it on his back, bouncing either side of him as he fought to get up.

I took Elise's hand, guiding her to the next room down the hall and pushing it open to show her the nursery I'd made there in pale blue tones. A bunch of teddy bears were in the cot, including a snake and a Lion that kinda resembled Roary.

"Gabriel…" Elise started, but I just pulled her against me and smirked.

"Well, we might need it sooner than you think," I murmured and she laughed, slapping my arm but it didn't look like that idea scared her so much. It didn't scare me at all. In fact, I was ready to start a family just as soon as the stars saw fit.

I led her to the next level up and guided her to a secret door which was hidden behind a roaring Lion mural. We slipped through it and I pressed it shut behind us with a mischievous grin, leading her up the wooden stairway to the lookout on top of the house.

The place was lit by fairylights and fur blankets were laid everywhere, plus a cosy armchair in the corner was angled to gaze out across our land.

"Wow," Elise breathed as she stood gazing out through the glassless windows ringing around the lookout.

I stepped up behind her, kissing her neck and working my way up to her ear. "Do you like it, angel?"

"I love it," she said, a smile in her voice as I wound my hands around her waist and held her against me.

"It's all yours," I said. "Every piece. Including the man who made it."

She twisted her head to capture my lips and I held my wife in my arms, kissing her sweetly as the last of the sunlight fell from the world. And the night that came held only peace.

SEVERAL MONTHS LATER…

I woke with a tremendous weight crushing me to the mattress and I growled as I tried to move but couldn't. My Atlas was buzzing on the nightstand and I shoved the beast crushing me to the bed. At some point in the night, Leon had apparently shifted into his Lion form and was now spread out over all of us.

"Fucking, Mufasa," Ryder growled beyond Elise as she grunted, trying to push him off with her Vampire strength, but he wouldn't budge.

"All together," Dante commanded and we fought to get purchase on him as we shoved hard, but he just rolled over, his legs sticking in the air.

Periwinkle yelped as one of her tails got crushed and Ryder grabbed her and put her on his pillow out of harm's way where she snuggled into his head and went back to sleep.

"Leo!" Elise jabbed him in the ribs and he farted.

"Nooo!" Dante cried, stuck at the ass end of Leon as he fought to get away.

"By the stars," I growled, trying to a *see* a way to wake him up.

"Merda santa, it smells like some gross animal crawled up his ass and died," Dante growled, using his air magic to waft the fart away.

My Atlas kept buzzing and I tried to reach it, but I couldn't. The Sight gave me an answer at last and I sighed. "Ryder help me lift him with vines." I cast two thick ones around Leon's front end and Ryder did the back end before we hoisted him with our magic toward the ceiling and left him hanging there as he continued to sleep, his tongue lolling out of his mouth. Elise stretched out, rubbing her hand over her round belly and I leaned down, kissing the bump. A big fat cat lying on our baby wasn't going to do them any harm, they were too Fae to be bothered by that.

I swiped up my Atlas and found Orion calling, pushing out of bed and answering as I exited onto the balcony, leaving the others to curl back up together and go to sleep again.

"Hey Orio," I said through a yawn. "Everything alright?" He'd been dealing with all kinds of shit lately after there'd been some incidents of Nymph attacks at Zodiac Academy and I swear every time I spoke to him, his aura was even heavier.

I helped him as best I could, but I still worried about him. I knew there was more going on with him than he was letting on too, I'd *seen* it, and honestly the shit he was getting himself wrapped up in with a certain student made me fear what was going to happen to him. I didn't want to call him out though, if he didn't want to discuss the details of everything going on with him then I could understand that, all things considered. I just wished The Sight would give me more answers on how to help him.

"I've got some good news for once," he said and my heart lifted.

The morning sunlight ran over me and I soaked it in, letting it fill up my magic reserves as I dropped into a swinging chair and kicked off of the railing to make it rock.

"Oh yeah?"

"Yeah, we've got an opening for a Tarot and Arcane Arts professor at Zodiac Academy. Elaine Nova asked me if I knew anyone suitable and obviously, I thought of you."

My lips parted in surprise and I paused as I waited for The Sight to give me any sense of whether I should take it or not. I didn't *see* anything immediately and I looked back over my shoulder through the window, gazing at my family with a frown. "I dunno, man, that's a long way from home."

"You'd get a stipend of stardust so you can go home anytime you like," he said, the hope in his tone clear that I'd agree to this.

"Well…alright, I'll think about it," I agreed.

"Don't take too long," he said.

"I won't. Is all else good with you?" I asked and he fell quiet for a moment.

"Yeah," he said though it didn't sound like that was entirely true. "But maybe you could come visit soon and we can talk? Or better yet, take the job and I'll see you next week."

I chuckled at his enthusiasm. "Alright, I'll let you know as soon as I've spoken to Elise and the guys about it."

"Okay, Noxy," he said and I felt him lingering on the line a moment longer like he wanted to say more before he eventually said goodbye and I was left with a leaden weight in my chest.

He was in one hell of a lot of trouble right now, maybe it would be good to be near him so that I could keep an eye on the stars for him.

As I had that thought, my gaze snagged on something shining far out in the lawn ahead of me and I frowned, pushing to my feet and resting my hands on the railing. It kept twinkling and I felt the most desperate need to go and find out what it was.

I climbed up onto the railing, freeing my wings from my flesh and taking off into the air.

I swept towards it then circled it a few times, trying to figure out what it could be before I landed and reached down, plucking a shimmering Tarot card from the stalks of grass.

It was The Fool which usually signified new beginnings.

"What the…" My brows knitted as I turned it over, finding curling silver script written across it.

The twin flames await.
You must answer the call of your ally and go to their aid.
The world needs you, Gabriel Nox.
-Falling Star

Visions flashed through my mind in a blur and I *saw* a terrible fate befalling the twins from my dreams, Lance Orion and Darius Acrux. My heart beat out of rhythm as I *saw* so many dark fates playing out before my eyes and I knew in the depths of my soul, that I needed to take the job Orion had offered me.

The stars seemed to draw closer and I felt them urging me down this path like they were desperate for me to go that way. Like I needed to do it or else the fate of Solaria could take a turn for the worse.

"It is time, son of fate," they whispered to me. *"The questions of your origin will be answered. Follow the footprints of the past and you shall find all that you have lost."*

My mind rattled with the weight of that voice and I took in two deep breaths of the cool morning air as I made my decision, knowing in my soul it was the only one I could really make.

Looks like I'm going to work at [Zodiac Academy](.)*.*

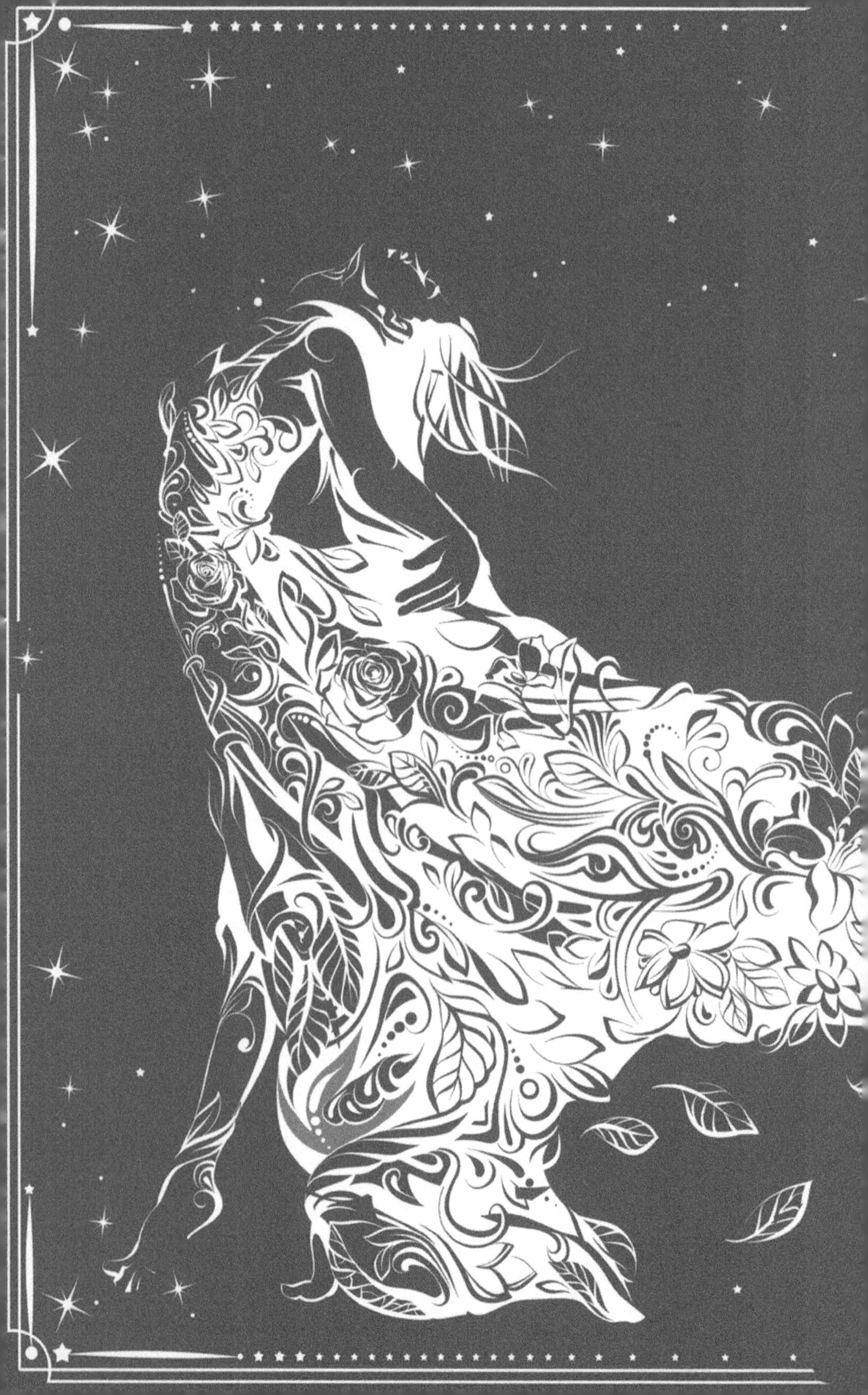

Elise

CHAPTER SIXTY TWO

THREE YEARS AFTER THAT...

Screams of agony coloured the air intermingled with the midwife yelling, "Push! That's it!" and I threw my head back against my pillows as sweat made lilac strands of hair cling to my face.

"Oh-my-stars there's so much blood," Leon gasped, clutching his face and looking seriously pale.

"Let me see," Ryder snarled, shoving him aside so that he could get a look too. His face dropped and an eyebrow arched as he got a good look right at the money shot where the baby was crowning. "Holy fuck. I've gutted a whole lot of people and skinned them and burned them alive and cut them into pieces and done things with a corkscrew that would give your granny nightmares from beyond the grave - but this shit is fucked up."

"Don't be such a stronzo," Dante growled as the sound of panting and screams mingled in the air and the midwife's voice drowned them all out again.

"It's okay! You're doing great! I just need to perform an episiotomy."

I caught sight of a scalpel and the pain in my huge belly sharpened as the thought of her putting that thing down there made me shake my head furiously. Surely not? That couldn't be the way they had to do that shit? Why the hell were babies too freaking big to fit out of the exit hole comfortably? Someone had to be at fault for that design flaw, I mean, what the actual fuck?

I lost sight of the scalpel as the midwife ducked down and my kings all shoved into each other to get a closer look.

Gabriel flinched back and a collective "Ooooh," sounded from all of them as Leon bit down on his knuckles and glanced between the show and me with horror written into his features.

"I'm sorry, little monster, but this shit is so fucking terrifying," he said, wincing again as more screams filled the air.

"I can't look at that anymore," Gabriel announced, moving around the bed and hurrying over to grasp my hand. "I've seen a lot of things," he breathed, looking into my eyes. "But some images just scar you for life, you know?"

"Why is it so fucking hot in here?" I panted, swiping a hand across my forehead as another wave of pain moved across my belly and I gritted my teeth against it.

"Because babies like it hot," Leon said firmly. "It's all warm inside you and if it was freezing cold out here then when he came out it would be a right shock to the teeny weiner!"

"I can't look away," Ryder murmured, almost to himself as the midwife barked orders to make sure the attention was on her again. "Why can't I look away?"

"It's like staring at the sun, fratello," Dante breathed in horror. "Once you lay eyes on it, she catches you in her grasp and even though it burns to watch, you just can't stop."

"Can the three of you please-" Gabriel snapped, but he was cut off by their collective gasps of horror.

"This is like watching a massacre," Ryder growled.

"RIP her poor vagina," Leon breathed, wincing as he continued staring.

"I think I'm going to be sick," Dante whispered as the screams got so loud that they bit through my skull and made it ring just as my body was overwhelmed with another contraction.

I tightened my grip on Gabriel's hand and had to force myself not to use my gifts just so that I didn't break his fingers.

"Switch that shit off," Gabriel barked. "Elise has had seven contractions now and that's four more than I planned on letting her suffer through."

"I can't look away," Leon whispered, his eyes still glued on the bloody scene before him. "I keep trying and trying but I just...can't."

"Well then I'm just going to cut this baby out myself," I growled, pushing up onto my elbows as I tried to reach around Gabriel for the surgical blade which lay ready on the nightstand.

That got their attention at last and the three of them whirled around towards me, protesting loudly and quickly surrounding the bed.

I grabbed the remote instead of the knife, giving them all death glares as I flicked the TV off and the sound of all that screaming finally left us. Why the hell they'd thought it would be a good idea to watch a show about mortals giving birth on the day our baby was going to be born was beyond me. Fuck being a mortal though - like seriously, they had to force a big ass baby out of their vaginas?? And it clearly hurt like a bitch and it didn't even seem to fit right. By the stars, mortals had it rough.

"I'm just glad you don't have to suffer through childbirth like that, angel," Gabriel murmured, placing a kiss on my forehead as he tucked my sweaty hair behind my ear.

"Fuck that," I agreed. "That latest contraction actually twinged a bit though, so I think we should crack on with this." I held my hand out for the blade but of course that just started them off.

"I won the race last night, so that means I get to cut the baby out," Dante said firmly, trying to reach for it but Ryder pushed him back a step, shaking his head firmly.

"No. Because I won that bet this morning, asshole," he growled.

"That didn't have anything to do with this," Dante replied, narrowing his eyes and squaring off against Ryder as electricity crackled through the air.

Gabriel sighed, rolling his eyes at them as they continued to bicker and shove each other. "It's not going to be either of you," he said in a tired tone.

"You know, falco," Dante began, rounding on him and making Gabriel turn away from me. "You may have The Sight, but that doesn't mean you can just get your way all the time by pretending that you've already *seen* it happening."

"Yeah," Ryder agreed firmly. "Like how you made out that you'd already *seen* you were the one who was going to drink the last beer the other night. I was thinking about it afterwards, and I think that was bullshit."

Gabriel broke a laugh and Dante and Ryder got all outraged as they turned their bickering on him instead.

While the three of them were distracted with that, Leon crept up to me, grinning excitedly as he rolled my shirt up and leaned down to kiss my super pregnant belly. He started singing something to the baby in a low voice, but with the others still arguing I couldn't catch what it was.

Leon grabbed the numbing potion Ryder had brewed for me and began rubbing it into my belly for me while I sucked in a breath at the next contraction. Fuck, those things really twinged when they started to get going. No way would I want to know what the bad ones felt like. That mortal's screams had been a clear enough reason for me not to find out.

"You strut around here telling everyone you already know what the future holds when really you could just be using that to turn every situation to your own advantage," Dante said loudly.

"Yeah, like this," Ryder agreed. "You think if you just say that you're going to be the one to cut the baby out of her because you've already *seen* it happen then that makes it so."

"I just said it wouldn't be you two, I didn't say it was going to be me," Gabriel protested but I knew full well he did pull that shit with The Sight whenever it suited him. I just so happened to think it was funny, so I wasn't gonna point it out.

Leon casually grabbed the surgical blade and leaned forward to place a rough kiss against my lips. "I can't wait for you to be a momma again, little monster," he said with a purr and I grinned at him as he moved back down to look at my belly, singing his song once more.

I could barely even feel the blade sliding across my skin as he carefully sliced me open and in the next breath, all arguments were cut short as Leon belted out the chorus to Circle of Life by Elton John and raised a little blood covered baby up into the air above his head like Simba on Pride fucking Rock.

"Holy shit," Ryder breathed, moving closer to help remove my placenta and heal me up.

"It's a girl," Dante murmured excitedly, taking my hand as tears of joy filled his eyes.

"Oh, no way," Gabriel said, feigning surprise as he hurried over to grasp my shoulder. I wanted to chew him out for that shit because I had banned him from using The Sight to figure out the baby's sex but just like last time, he'd clearly cheated.

I held my hands out for her and Leon grinned big as he obliged me, still singing the end of his song in a low tone as he passed her over. The moment he finished singing, she began to cry and I did too, relief and excitement overwhelming me as I looked at her beautiful face.

I nestled the perfect little thing in close to my chest, murmuring greetings to her as Gabriel carefully used his water magic to clean her off and her cries faded away again as she snuggled in tight.

The door burst open with a bang and our eldest, Luca, barrelled into the room, stumbling on his toddler feet and yelling, "Baby!" excitedly. His dark hair was a mess of curls which were sticking up on one side from his nap and I was guessing he'd given poor Bianca the slip for about the fiftieth time today.

He tripped over nothing and went flying, but Gabriel was already there, catching him by the back of his shirt and setting him on his feet again.

"Stop doing that," Ryder hissed as he finished healing me up and I shifted to cross my legs between me, sighing as my lungs expanded fully for the first time in months and I adjusted to the difference of having my flat stomach back again at last. "If you never let him fall he won't learn his limits."

"And I've told you that I'm not going to just let him crack his head open because you have it in your mind that he might be a Basilisk and enjoy hurting himself," Gabriel replied with a shrug.

Luca scrambled away from the two of them as they continued to grumble at each other over their preferred parenting methods and I grinned as our little rascal tried to clamber up onto the bed to meet his new sister.

"I thought it was meant to be your nap time?" I teased him as he crawled up the sheets.

"Baby!" he replied like that was answer enough and I couldn't help but grin as he leaned in really close to get a look at his baby sister.

I adjusted my hold on her for him to see and the smile that lit his face up made my heart ache with that old need for my own brother.

"*My* baby," Luca cooed, leaning down to kiss her forehead and a tear ran down my cheek as I watched them falling in love with each other at first sight.

"So we're going with Ruby, yeah?" Leon asked excitedly.

"We decided on Jane, stronzo," Dante replied.

"Pretty sure we didn't," Leon disagreed, leaning down to rub his nose against our little girl's. "She says that's not fancy enough. And I think we can all agree, this kid is fancy as fuck."

"Daddy fuck," Luca said brightly and I tossed Leon a scowl.

"Nooo, little Lion cub, Daddy said duck," Leon replied quickly.

"Quack?" Luca asked suspiciously. He was only two, but I could tell he was already catching onto his Daddy's bullshit.

"Yep," Leon agreed firmly.

"Papa fly?" Luca asked suddenly, his attention shifting to Dante as he scrambled back upright and dove off of the bed.

Gabriel made a move to catch him while Ryder hissed at him, but Dante had been ready and he quickly shot the little rascal around the room on a gust of air magic while I leaned back against my pillows and just stared at the little miracle in my arms.

Leon wriggled up to lay beside me, his chin on my shoulder as he looked down at her lovingly.

"Hey Ruby," he whispered.

"It's *Jane*," Dante growled, most of his concentration still fixed on our giggling two-year-old as he zoomed around the room.

"Why not just call her Ruby Jane then if you two won't stop arguing about it?" Ryder asked as he moved to my other side and reached out to give the tiny bundle in my arms a finger to hold on to.

"We could call her RJ for short," Gabriel added, brushing his fingers over her soft golden hair and cuddling in with us too.

Dante set Luca down on the foot of the bed again and he promptly scrambled up into my lap to take another look at his sister. "RJ," he said in the cutest freaking baby voice and I knew right then that we wouldn't be changing it.

"RJ," I agreed with a sigh, looking around at my four kings as they huddled closer and we all just stared at these two little miracles we'd created. "I get the feeling you're going to be trouble."

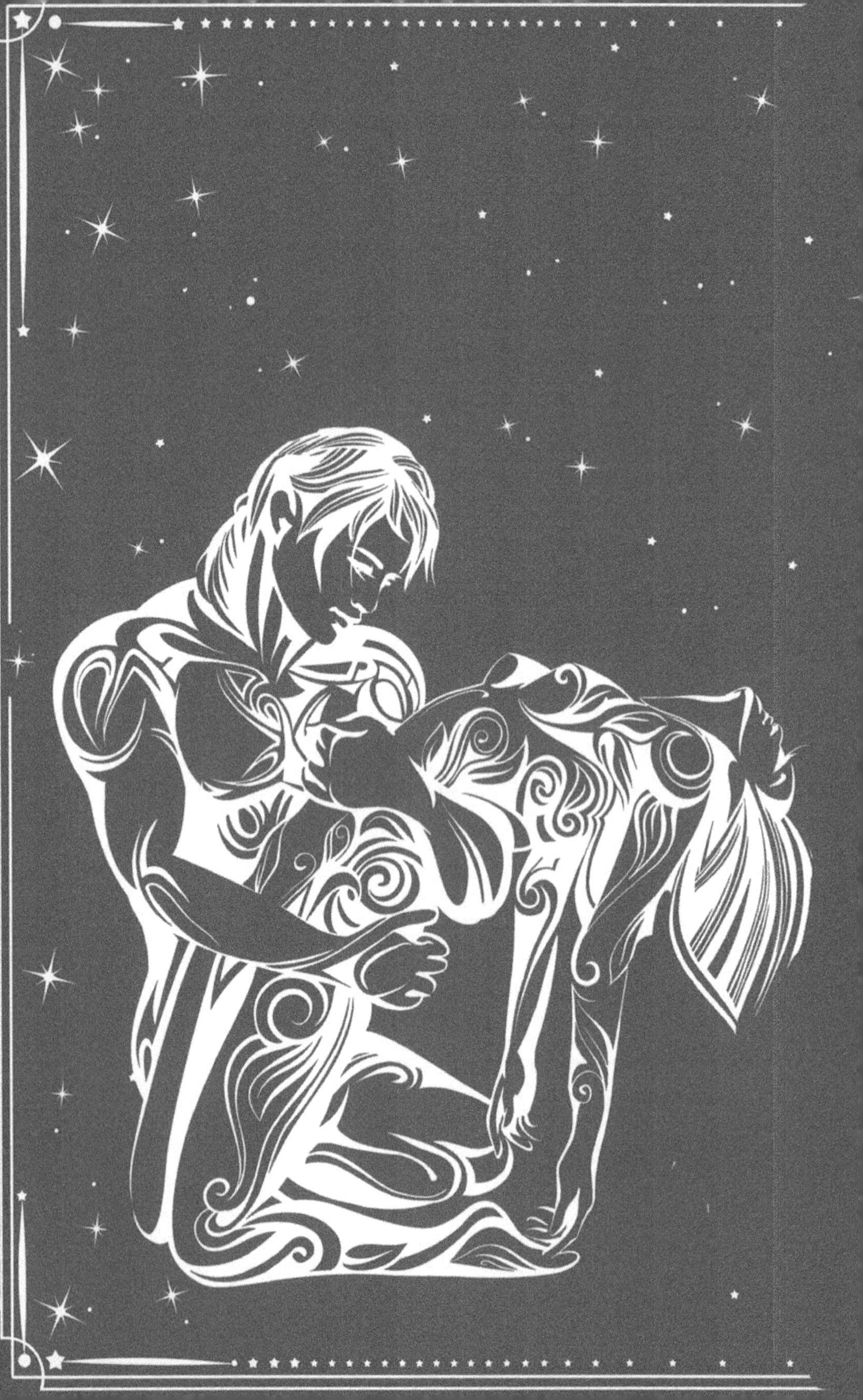

Ryder

CHAPTER SIXTY THREE

SIXTEEN YEARS LATER THAN THAT…

"Luca is going to Emerge today," Gabriel announced as he leaned down to place a plate of pancakes in front of Elise on the breakfast bar and her eyes widened in surprise.

"What's he gonna be?" she whispered excitedly.

Leon lunged across the surface, grabbing Gabriel's arm. "He's a Lion, isn't he? I told him to grow his hair long, but would he listen? No, and now-"

"I'm not telling," Gabriel cut him off with a sparkle in his gaze.

"He's obviously a Basilisk," I said, eyeing up my own plate of pancakes as Gabriel brought it over and placed it down. "And maybe we'd know how he reacted to pain if you let him fall more often when he was a kid, Gabriel." I gave him a pointed look.

"Why would I let my child hurt himself if I could *see* a way to avoid it?" Gabriel scoffed. We'd had this argument a thousand times, but Luca had learned all about pain in the end anyway when I took him to the underground fights at Serpens. They let unAwakened teens have fist fights on Thursday evenings and the first kid Luca had faced, he'd beaten senseless. If that wasn't Basilisk energy, I didn't know what was.

"If he's anything with scales on it, it's a Dragon," Dante said from beside me with a smug smile. "Plus there are only so many Orders that Emerge this late. He's eighteen years old."

"Which is three years older than you were when you Emerged, wasn't it?" I taunted.

"Yes, not much younger than you were when you Emerged as a Basilisk," he shot back.

"Pfft, that was different," I said. "I was in danger, my Order Emerged to save my ass."

"Well my great, great Uncle Clawd didn't Emerge as a Lion until he was nearly nineteen," Leon added which he constantly reminded us of lately.

"Lions nearly always Emerge when they're kids, Leo," Elise laughed. "But Vampires Emerge when they're Awakened. Are we going to get a special early Awakening for him like the Celestial Heirs got?" She looked to Gabriel, but pouted when he didn't agree to that.

"Wait...look how smug Gabe is today," Leon said suspiciously, narrowing his eyes on him.

"Don't call me Gabe," he sighed.

"Is our boy gonna be a Harpy, Gabe?" Leon demanded, completely ignoring Gabriel's exasperation with his nickname for him. "When do they Emerge?"

"I Emerged when I was seventeen," he said, but gave no further clue of what Luca was gonna be.

I looked over at the clock, but my gaze snagged on Periwinkle's fluffy bed on the floor and my heart tugged as I missed her. I looked quickly away again and checked the time. "Are the kids getting up for school today, or what?"

"I'll get them!" Leon bounced out of his seat. "They love when I'm peppy in the morning."

I snorted a laugh. "Didn't RJ throat punch you the last time you woke her up singing Hakuna Matata at seven am?" I'd been damn certain she was going to be a Basilisk too, but then she'd gone and Emerged as a Pegasus last year and by the stars was it a fucking drama. She'd Emerged in the shower, exploded through the glass, cut herself to shit and whinnied like the house was falling down. I loved her no matter what her Order, but by the stars, don't get me started on the glitter. It got everywhere. And while Leon and Elise were off winning Pitball tournaments, Gabriel was working as a professor and Dante was off overseeing Oscura gang duties, guess who was left here to clean it up all the time? Me.

Of all our family, was I really the most suited to being a star damned house husband?

Since RJ had Emerged, she also seemed to have turned into a full-blown teenager. She screamed at me three times a day and burst into tears over shit I didn't even understand. Apparently she wanted to dye her fur red instead of its natural duck egg blue. But hell if I'd be letting her put any of those cheap chemical Pegasus dyes near her skin. I said I'd brew her a wash out dye and she'd slammed her bedroom door in my face saying she didn't want my 'homebrew bullshit'. My potions were the best in the fucking kingdom dammit.

I'd sent her to toil in the Oscura vineyards for a week for that and she'd gotten a lot less mouthy with me since. No one ever told me that raising a teenager was akin to raising a demon sent from the depths of hell and moulding them into a functioning Fae. In hindsight, it was probably a blessing my parents hadn't been around during my teens, I would have been a fucking nightmare.

"Ahh get out, Dad – get out!" Luca's voice boomed from upstairs.

"Oh shit, it's alright, cub, let's just talk about it. It's totally normal-" Leon tried but the distinctive slam of a door in a face came and cut him off. He ran back downstairs and pointed an accusing finger at Gabriel. "Why didn't you warn me?"

"About what?" Gabriel looked up from where his face had been buried against Elise's neck, making her laugh breathily. "Oh…"

"Yeah, *oh*," Leon growled, rubbing his face. "I'm scarred for life."

"You're not the one who has to wash his sheets," I said with pursed lips and Leon snorted.

"Yeah, fuck cleaning up his room, please tell me he hasn't got a stash of porn in there somewhere, Rydikins?" Leon took his seat, tucking into his pancakes, quickly moving on from the drama in favour of his breakfast.

"No one has porn magazines these days, Leone, it's all online," Dante chuckled.

Elise chewed her lip. "Do you think I should go and talk to him?"

"No," all four of us guys said immediately.

"Trust me, amore mio, the last thing a guy at his age needs is his mom trying to talk to him about his sexuality," Dante said.

"Your mamma must have caught you so many times, dude," Leon said with a pitying frown.

"What about your moms?" Dante tossed back. "They have zero boundaries."

"Yeah, the worst time was when they cheered me on through the door and wouldn't leave," he said.

"Shit, what did you do?" Gabriel asked with a snort.

"I climbed out the window and finished on the roof in peace." He shrugged and I barked a laugh. "Oh shit, should I go check the roof?"

Before anyone could answer, Luca stepped into the room, his dark hair sticking up in every direction and his jaw tight. A faint red blush lined his cheeks as he moved to join us, grabbing some pancakes from the side and tucking into them.

We all shared a look as an awkward silence descended over us.

"Ready for school today?" Elise asked casually.

"I wasn't jerking off," he blurted at the same time and a laugh hitched in my throat.

"It's perfectly normal, figlio," Dante said gently.

"If you want to read page sixty six in my Lion book, it explains how male cubs like to-" Leon started.

"I don't wanna read your book, Dad, I know what I'm doing," Luca said firmly then cursed as he realised what he'd said.

I released a low laugh and Dante fell apart next until we were all losing it and Luca finally cracked a grin.

"Morning," RJ said brightly, appearing dressed in her dark blue Elderhills Highschool uniform, her skirt rolled up to way above her mid-thigh.

"No." I flicked a finger so a vine grabbed hold of the hem and forced it to unroll.

"Ergh, Dad, you're such a prude," she hissed then grabbed a plate of pancakes, dropping down beside Gabriel who kissed her on the head.

"Hello, sweetheart, you're in a good mood this morning," Gabriel said, his eyes narrowing with suspicion as he clearly tried to get a vision on why that was the case.

"Well I swear I got a touch of The Sight again when I woke up." She tucked into her breakfast, telling us about the flicker of a vision she'd *seen* of her teacher giving her detention today for backchatting him.

"You're gonna be a better Seer than I am, I didn't get clear visions until I was eighteen," Gabriel said proudly.

When it was time for school and Luca was dressed at last, Dante tossed Luca the keys to his car and we all walked them off the property to the main gate.

"Do you really have to do this every day?" RJ groaned as Leon yanked her in for a hug and a nuzzle while Gabriel pulled Luca into his arms.

"You love our hugs," Leon insisted, purring loudly as he passed RJ to

Gabriel's arms and I hugged Luca.

Elise fussed over them both, kissing their cheeks and whizzing around us with her speed until everyone had been hugged and our kids stepped off the property to head to school. They got into the super safe, super slow car Leon had stolen for them despite their requests for a flashy death trap and we all waved goodbye like the cheesiest motherfucking parents ever as Luca rolled his eyes and they pulled away. I loved embarrassing those two. It was too fucking easy.

I sighed, missing Periwinkle again and Leon moved to rest a hand on my arm. "They'll be back before you know it."

"Yeah, I know. I was just thinking about Peri," I muttered.

"I miss Winkle too," he sighed and I punched him in the ribs.

"You two are obsessed with her," Elise laughed. "She'll be back from the groomers in an hour." Peri loved getting pampered, so she went to the groomers once a week to have her coat brushed. I'd been pretty surprised when I found out ghost hounds could live up to two hundred years and the pup had barely aged a day since I'd first found her.

I caught Elise's hand, tugging her against me as I kissed her. "Sounds like we have an hour to kill then, baby."

Dante kissed our wife's neck from behind and I slipped my fingers under the long shirt of Gabriel's which she'd slept in.

"I think you're right," Elise purred.

"Are you gonna ride her, Ryder?" Leon whispered in my ear and I smacked him in the head as he laughed and tickled my sides.

"I'm gonna punch you in the face first," I said as I swung around and he shot away, tearing off his clothes as he prepared to shift.

I sprinted after him while Gabriel called, "You won't catch him!" and I took that as a challenge as I threw out vines, two of them tearing toward him and trying to snare his legs. Leon jumped out the way of them, shifting into his Lion form and roaring a laugh as he sprinted off into the vineyard beside the house.

I slowed to a halt and turned to Gabriel with an idea coming to mind.

"Oh, that'll work," Gabriel called and I noticed Dante had stolen Elise's attention, kissing her fiercely on the ground like a damn savage.

I had to teach the damn Lion a lesson though now and stick to my word about punching him, but I was gonna hurry up about it and return to our girl just as soon as I'd done that.

Gabriel ran up to me, patting his pocket and I rolled my eyes before I shifted into my tiniest snake form, waiting for him. His wings split out from his back as he scooped me up and took off into the sky, pushing me into his pocket so I could see out across our beautiful homeland.

Gabriel gained on Leon easily and we chased him into the woods at the edge of our property as he tried to lose us, but Gabriel laughed knowingly and I knew we'd win this fight.

I gazed down at him, my tongue flicking in the wind and my gaze set on the golden beast powering along through the trees. *Nothing can ssssstop me now, Sssimba.*

"Did Luca Emerge yet?" Leon asked Gabriel.

"No," he growled.

"Now?" Leon pushed.

"No, Leon," Gabriel snapped. "And if you ask me again, I'll shove this wine bottle up your ass." He plucked the Arucso bottle up off the coffee table and brandished it at him.

Elise nestled closer to me where she sat in my lap in the armchair, sighing contentedly after our dinner.

"Oh you'd love that wouldn't you, Gabe?" Leon taunted. "You're always up for experimenting after a few drinks."

I barked a laugh and Gabriel rolled his eyes, kicking his feet up on the coffee table as he leaned back on the couch beside Dante.

Elise ran her hand down my chest, slipping her fingers inside my shirt and caressing the X inked there. Periwinkle was up on the arm of my chair, watching us curiously with her head cocked to one side. I swear she was waiting her turn to sit in my lap.

"Oh my stars!" Gabriel suddenly roared, leaping to his feet.

"Is it happening?" Leon jumped out of his chair onto the coffee table, his eyes gleaming with excitement.

"No, but we need to go right now. Elise stay here," he barked, striding to the door.

"What the hell's going on?" Elise gasped as I got up, placing her in my seat as Peri yapped in concern.

"It's a man thing, trust us, angel." He shot over, kissing her hard on the lips and she reluctantly stayed in her seat as Gabriel led the four of us to the door.

We kicked on our shoes, heading out into the twilight and hurrying after him as he practically ran down the drive to the gate.

"What the fuck is going on, Big Bird?" I demanded, struggling to keep pace with him. He was like a fucking seagull on an updraft.

As we stepped beyond the boundary of our property, he turned sharply around to face us all, his eyes swirling with darkness.

"Is it the pups?" Dante asked in concern. "Are they okay, falco?"

"They're fine," Gabriel bit out. "But RJ won't be if we don't hurry."

"What's happened?" Leon rocked from one foot to the other, knotting his fingers in his mane.

"It's that Corbin boy," Gabriel spat.

"No," Leon gasped.

"Yes," Gabriel hissed and the rattle went off in my chest. "He's going to take our girl's virginity."

"He's dead," I snarled. "Bring me to him and I'll break his fucking neck."

"A morte e ritorno," Dante hissed.

Gabriel nodded, taking a pouch of stardust from his pocket and throwing it over all of us, dragging us away into the stars.

We arrived in a woodland at the top of a hill, glimpsing a viewpoint ahead of us where a car was parked looking over the glittering lights of Alestria.

A moan caught my ear from inside it and I hissed furiously, tearing off my clothes and shifting into a snake the size of a python.

"We need to surround the car," Gabriel said in a low voice. "Or the little prick will make a run for it."

Leon pulled his clothes off, a growl rumbling through his chest before he shifted into a Lion and waited for Gabriel's commands as his upper lip peeled back in a snarl. Storm clouds drew in over the gleaming stars above and a ripple of static electricity ran down my spine.

"You take the front," Gabriel whispered to me and I didn't wait to hear the rest of his instructions to the others as I slithered across the ground, making my way under the car towards the hood.

"I'm so in love with you, Ruby-Jane," Jett Corbin growled and I hissed furiously. What kind of a name was Jett anyway? It was a fucking asshole of a name.

I made my way to the front of the car just as thunder boomed above us in the sky and RJ gasped.

"Wait a second," she said frantically then Leon leapt on top of the car with a loud bang. Gabriel swooped over him, landing gracefully on the driver's side of the car and as the door flew open, he swung it sharply shut in Jett's face, knocking him back into his seat.

"Is that your Dads!?" he yelled in alarm and I was glad the little shit sounded afraid.

I shifted back into my Fae form, leaping onto the bonnet in a squat to glare in at them.

RJ screamed as she struggled to do her shirt up which was wide open and exposing her glittery black bra. "Put your dick away, Dad!" she begged in a wail.

Leon dropped down onto the other side of the car, shifting back into his Fae form and staring in at Jett in the driver's seat, his dick pressed firmly to the window.

"Dad!" she screamed at him, mortified and that was least she fucking deserved for this. Dante circled above us in the sky, a beast of terror as lighting crackled off his wings and he roared his rage into the clouds. Rain spilled down on us and I slid off of the bonnet, joining Leon as he opened the driver's door and yanked Jett out by the scruff of his neck.

"Leave him alone!" RJ snapped, wriggling back into her school skirt and I slammed the door in her face, binding all of the doors shut with vines.

Gabriel snarled, the three of us surrounding Jett in a circle as rain pounded down on us from above.

"I wasn't gonna-" Jett started in terror, but Gabriel cut over him.

"Don't lie to me, I can *see* every dirty thought in your head, kid," he snapped and the guy paled. I wasn't sure that was entirely true, but Jett certainly believed it.

"Dads!" RJ wailed. "Let me out this second!"

"You don't touch our girl," Leon snarled. "Ever. She's gonna be a virgin until her wedding night, you hear me?"

"What?" RJ shrieked. "You're all crazy!"

"Did you hear me, cub?" Leon shoved Jett's shoulders so he knocked into me and he looked around at me with fear in his eyes.

I wasn't gonna hide who I was to this boy. I'd either slip him a memory potion and make him forget, or better yet, I'd bind him in a star vow to keep my secret and make him swear not to lay a finger on my girl unless he married her while I was at it.

I snared him in my hypnosis as his gaze locked with mine, showing him a torture chamber where he lay tied to a wooden bench while I tore his limbs off. He roared in pain and spat curses at me, and I might have admired his tenacity if he'd been interested in any other girl than my little princess.

"You're gonna stay away from her, aren't you, Corbin?" I snarled and his mouth opened and closed.

"But I love her," he said fiercely and the fire in his eyes made me hiss. I released him from the vision, throwing him over my shoulder while RJ screamed and I strode right to the edge of the sheer drop at the crest of the hill.

"Wait, Mr Altair - stop!" he cried.

"I'm not an Altair, I'm far, far blood thirstier than every Vampire in that family. And you had your chance, now you're gonna pay for bringing our princess out here like a cheap hooker."

"Wait!" he begged, but I threw him over the edge of the sheer hill and RJ screamed louder, banging her fists on the windscreen.

Dante swooped out of the sky as Corbin's yells carried down towards the city below, falling and falling like a rock as Inferno raced to catch up.

Almost too late, Dante sailed beneath him and Jett slammed into his scaley back with a thump, his screams carrying off into the city as our Storm Dragon sailed into the distance.

"You're all psychos and I hate you!" RJ started kicking the door and I released the vines keeping her inside, so she spilled out in a tumble.

She snorted indignantly as she regained her feet, stamping her foot on the ground like it was a hoof.

"We're here to protect you," Leon said, opening his arms for a hug and RJ punched him in the gut, making him wheeze.

"Hey, don't hit your Dad," Gabriel growled, catching her hand and drawing her closer to him. "We only want to look out for you."

Her features softened a little at that and I walked over to them, placing a hand on her shoulder.

"Please put some clothes on," she begged of us and Leon sighed, jogging off to fetch our pants and tossing mine to me when he returned.

I tugged them on then pulled RJ around into my arms. "Did he hurt you?" I demanded.

"No, Dad, I asked him to bring me here," she said, raising her chin. "He's cool and I want him to be my first."

I cringed and Leon slammed his hands over his ears and started singing loudly.

"You're sixteen," Gabriel snarled.

"Yeah, and?" she threw at him. "I'm old enough to know what I want."

I scoffed. "You're not even Awakened, you don't know anything yet. Especially not about sex."

"Oh that's rich," she snarled. "Coming from the guy who tattooed *lust* on his knuckles when you were around my age." She folded her arms, cocking an eyebrow and I growled.

"Who told you that?"

"Mom." She shrugged and Leon lowered his hands from his ears, sensing he could listen again. "She also told me *you* were a complete player who beguiled every Lioness at Aurora Academy with your Charisma." She prodded Leon in the chest. "And *you* spent the night with Mom way before you got together while you were being a total dickwad." She arched a brow at Gabriel and his lips popped open.

"What the hell else has she told you?" Leon gasped.

"Everything," RJ said simply. "She doesn't keep secrets from me because she's cool, unlike my overbearing Dads." She stomped her foot again and I sighed. *Dammit Elise.*

"Be that as it may, the way we behaved has no bearing on how *you* can behave," Gabriel said sternly and Leon and I nodded our agreement.

Screams sailed by in the distance again as Dante did a loop the loop and Jett held on for dear life.

"That's so unfair," RJ growled.

"Fair doesn't come into it," I hissed. "You're grounded. And you can only see that boy again with an escort present."

"What?" she gasped. "That's ridiculous! Literally every girl in my class has lost their V card, how come I have to be V-pressed?"

Leon sniggered at that word, then fought away his smile and rearranged his serious face.

I stepped closer to her to draw her attention again. "The difference is, you don't own your V card - we do. So suck it up, buttercup." I folded my arms and RJ whinnied furiously.

"Don't be mad, little cub, we've got pizza and ice cream at home," Leon said. "That's waaaay better than sex anyway."

"Ha," Gabriel laughed then cleared his throat, looking away and RJ glared at him.

"Don't be mad, princess." I caught her hand, tugging her into my chest and forcing a hug on her as she wriggled and clawed at me. But she finally gave in, sighing heavily against me and I squeezed her tight.

"It's just because we love you." Leon joined the hug and Gabriel wrapped his arms around us too, crushing her in the middle of us.

Dante came to land beside us, shifting back into his Fae form and tugging on his sweatpants as he strode over.

"Where's Jett?" RJ gasped in horror as we broke apart.

"I gave him a ride home and put him in his mamma's lemon tree." Dante smirked before tossing a bunch of keys into Jett's car. "He can come pick this up tomorrow."

"You guys are such assholes," RJ muttered, but she was already getting over our behaviour because this was pretty normal when it came to us protecting her.

"By the stars," Gabriel gasped. "We need to get home, come on!" He threw stardust over us before we could say another word and my heart beat harder at what the hell else the stars had in store for us today. But as we landed outside the gates to our house, I spotted the reason, my lips parting in complete shock.

Elise was sitting on the back of an enormous shaggy black Monolrian Bear Shifter while Periwinkle ran circles around it.

"Look!" Elise cried, grinning as the bear bounded towards us and a smile split across my face.

"Holy shit, is that Luca?!" Leon cried, running towards him and our son nuzzled his hand as Elise confirmed it. "My great, great, great, great, great aunt was a Monolrian Bear!"

"Pretty sure I had a distant cousin who was one too," Dante said, running forward to hug him.

"You look awesome, Luca." RJ ran over to him, climbing up to ride on his back behind Elise. Gabriel took off into the sky, flying around them and laughing as Luca playfully tried to buck his mom and sister off his back and they held on tight, laughing wildly.

My heart burned so warm in my chest at seeing my whole family together, happy, safe, home.

There was no place in the kingdom I'd rather be than here. And nothing that made my life more complete than them.

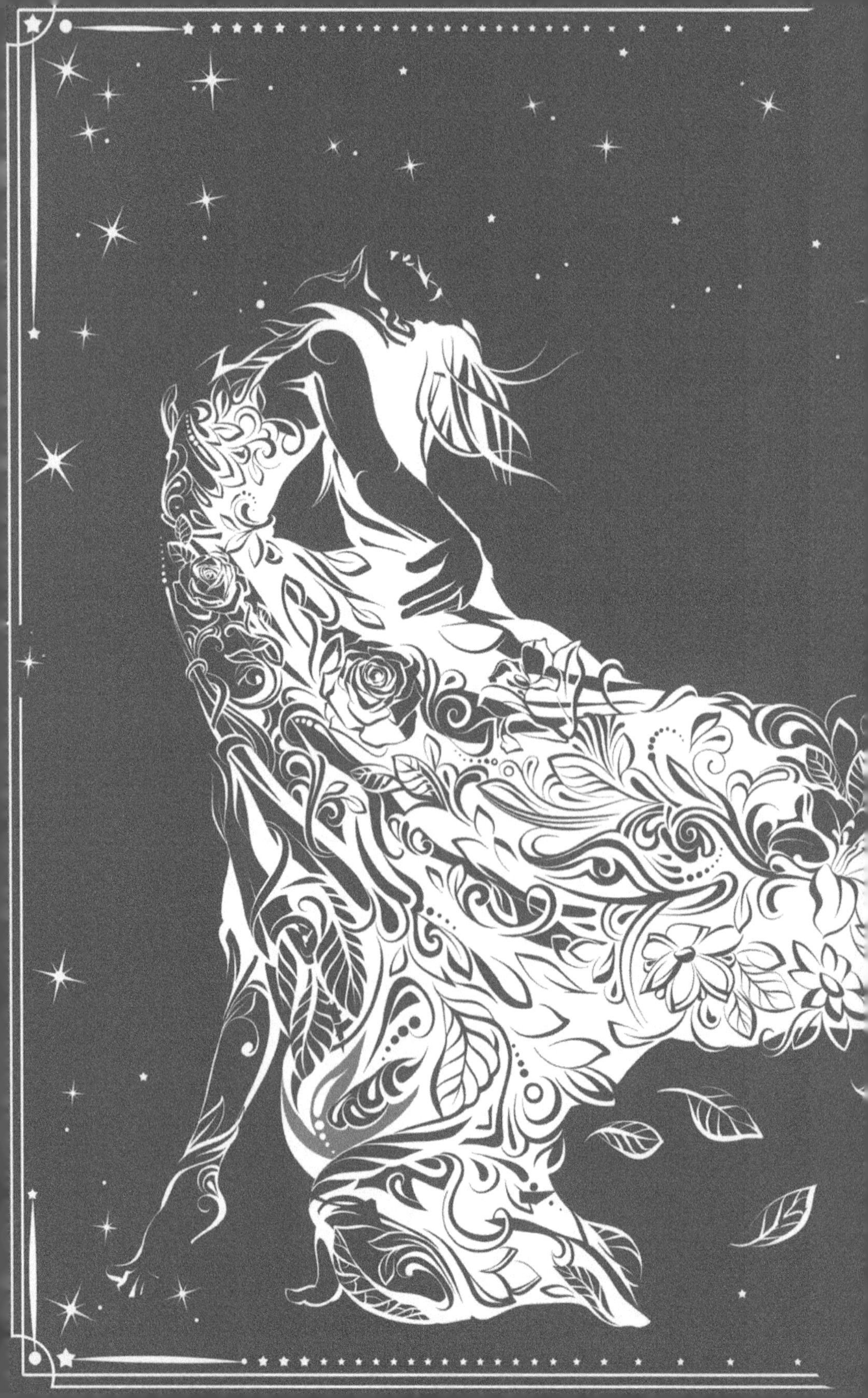

ELISE

CHAPTER SIXTY FOUR

AAAAND ANOTHER SIX YEARS LATER FOR THE LAST TIME...

The moon was rising in the distance and the five of us leaned back against the mound of earth magic that Ryder had cast for us as we sat on the rooftop and felt the vibrations of the music from the building beneath us rattling through our bones.

"You do realise that this is insane, don't you?" I asked as Gabriel leaned back and laid his arm around me, lending me some body heat.

"I don't know what you mean, amore mio," Dante purred, laying back and folding his hands behind his head as he looked up at the stars which twinkled in the dark sky overhead. "We're Fae. It's perfectly normal for us to spend our free time star gazing."

"Uh huh." I rolled my eyes at the four of them, leaning forward to snag a bag of chips from the huge snack bag Leon had brought for this little adventure. Chances were, this would be a long night.

Leon snarled at me half-heartedly, but most of his attention was on the space below us, where Fae in fancy suits and dresses moved in and out of the building we'd selected for this little night out.

"So what are the heavens telling you, Gabriel?" I asked him, snuggling in closer to him as I ate a salty chip. "Is fate inclined to be any kinder to Solaria in the future than it has been up until now?"

Gabriel winced slightly but tried to cover it and Ryder chuckled darkly as he leaned forward, resting his forearms on his knees.

"The stars love predicting carnage, baby," he said, glancing up at the heavens. "I think they enjoy making us all hurt."

"Why would they enjoy that?" I asked curiously.

"Because happily ever after always tastes sweetest when it's been earned through agony," he replied simply. "The best things in life hurt us the most."

"Always so negative, stronzo," Dante teased. "I for one am happy with the life the stars have gifted us. I have the woman of my dreams, children I would kill and die for, a pack of ferocious Fae who love and respect me...and you four bastardos to keep me on my toes. What else could a man want?"

"I'm happy too," I agreed, my gaze moving to the Pegasus constellation sparkling in the sky overhead as I thought of Gareth for a moment. I let a smile touch my lips as I imagined what he'd say about what we were doing here right now, knowing he'd be just as bad as the rest of them. "For the longest time I never could have believed I would be. I have the four of you to thank for that."

"The stars knew we needed each other," Leon said, smiling around at us and stealing my half eaten bag of chips. "They could see we'd make the purrrfect Pride. Isn't that right, Gabe?" He slapped Gabriel on the arm and my Harpy sighed.

"Don't call me..." Gabriel paused, looking between Leon and me for a moment and then rolling his eyes before finally going on. "In fact, you know what? I've been telling you not to call me that for more than twenty years and

I'm done. So go ahead, call me Gabe. I'm cool with it."

Leon sucked in a breath and started bouncing up and down like an excited cub while Ryder shook his head and tried to hide his smile.

"If Leo gets to call you Gabe-" I began but RJ's laughter interrupted us and all four of my kings sat bolt upright, suddenly alert and scowling at everything and nothing.

"Jett," Leon growled, spitting his name like it was a curse and I sighed, wondering if they'd ever stop with this shit.

"Don't you think you're taking this too far?" I asked them, trying for the hundredth time to rein them in.

"I think you're underestimating the sex drive of a teenage boy, little monster. This isn't too far, in fact it's an under reaction. We should have castrated the little fucker like I wanted to last week," Leon growled as he moved to the edge of the roof and looked down at his prey, wriggling his ass from side to side like he was preparing to pounce right over the edge and take RJ's boyfriend out here and now.

"She'll hate you for ruining her party," I warned them as the others moved to look over the edge too. The concealment spells which hid us up here on top of the Cafaeteria meant no one had seen us yet, but it was only a matter of time.

"No she won't," Gabriel said in his I-know-everything voice and I huffed out a breath. "Besides, I've *seen* her perfect mate and it is *not* Jett."

"I'm going down there," Ryder growled as Jett took RJ's hand and started to tug her toward the Iron Wood.

"Wait for it," Gabriel warned before any of the others could make a move and I shook my head at their bullshit. When we'd been their age, we'd been getting up to a lot more than hand holding and they knew it.

"Wait for what?" Dante asked, electricity crackling off of him as he narrowed his eyes on our daughter's boyfriend.

"That." Gabriel pointed in the direction of Altair Halls just as a group of around ten FIB officers rounded the building and started running towards the party.

"This is an official investigation!" the lead officer called. "We have been informed that there is Killblaze being consumed at this party!"

That was bullshit because the secret of how to create Killblaze had died with Titan and it hadn't been heard of for years, but one look at Gabriel told me he'd been the one to tip them off on that.

The teenagers all started yelling and running away from the cops even though I doubted any of them were doing anything illegal and Gabriel chuckled as he pointed our daughter out as she tried to make a run for it into the trees.

"Light them up, Leon," he commanded and my Lion grinned as he shot fire magic their way, illuminating RJ and Jett for an officer who hadn't made it inside yet.

I watched with interest as the young officer took off at full speed, his dark hair blowing away from his attractive face as he called out for RJ and Jett to stop.

"What's your plan?" I asked Gabriel, noticing him grinning like he already knew exactly what was about to happen.

"Wait for it," he said so we did and I chewed on my lip as I watched the agent gaining on RJ, wondering how she was going to escape him.

But I got my answer a second later when the agent pounced on her, tackling her and making her scream as the two of them slammed down into the mud.

Jett shot RJ a desperate look then ran for it, saving his own ass and proving that my kings had been right in thinking he wasn't good enough for our girl after all.

"What the fuck, falco?" Dante demanded, making a move to lunge forward and go to her aid, but Gabriel grabbed his arm to stop him.

"Look," Gabriel said as my heart pounded and we all stared on, watching as the agent pinned our girl to the ground and she threw her head forward, cracking his nose with her forehead and making blood spill everywhere.

"Merda," Dante cursed while Ryder hissed and Leon snarled. I was about three seconds away from shooting down there to help her myself when Gabriel spoke again.

"That's her perfect mate," he said, choking up a little as he looked at our daughter hurling insults at the huge officer who still had her pinned beneath him while he bled all over both of them and called her a crazy whore loud enough for all of us to hear him. "Isn't it beautiful?"

"You have to be shitting me," Ryder snarled. "No way our girl is destined to end up with a cop."

"The stars really do hate us," Dante breathed in horror.

"What about my stolen riches?" Leon gasped. "What will he say of my riches?"

"Are you sure about this Gabriel?" I asked tentatively, watching as the agent hauled RJ to her feet, the dress she'd spent weeks picking out now torn and filthy, the night she'd been so looking forward to utterly ruined.

"Yes, my angel," Gabriel said firmly. "He's the one for her."

"That love story isn't going to be a pretty one," Ryder muttered, his narrowed gaze trailing the agent as he hauled our daughter away. "Shouldn't we be helping her?"

"No," Gabriel said firmly. "RJ is about to have one of the worst nights of her life while stuck in a holding cell thanks to him. She's going to hate that Fae more than any other she's ever met."

"And that's a good thing?" I asked dubiously.

"Yeah," Gabriel sighed dreamily, while we all watched as RJ was cuffed and forced to walk towards the gates, curses and threats spilling from her lips with every step she took. "Everything will work out in the end. We just need to trust in destiny."

I forced myself to stay where I was, standing between my four kings as our daughter was arrested and thought back on all the things it had taken for us to get here.

Destiny was a bitch.

But in the end, it had led me here.

So maybe he was right, and all I needed was a little faith.

―――――――――

AUTHOR'S NOTE

Phew, that was a big one! Warrior Fae was one hell of a ride and officially our biggest book to date - we poured blood, sweat and tears into this one and it really was one hell of a ride.

These characters are something else. This series was our first ever dip into the reverse harem pool and I'd like to think these boys and our badass, broken girl taught us how to swim. There have been highs and lows, deaths and almost deaths - don't go getting cocky though, guys - I feel the need for a nice, messy blood bath coming up and believe me when I say no one will survive that!!! Dun, dun duuuuuun....

Ahem.

Anyway, megalomaniac and psychotic tendencies aside, we just wanted to say thank you to you for reading the story of Elise and her kings all the way through to the end and for living and breathing every agony filled moment of grief, every heart pounding second of lust and for falling in love right alongside them.

Goodbyes are always bittersweet, but we hope you agree that their story is finished and that you got to hear it in full. But of course, if you do want a few more glimpses of them and some of the other characters who have featured in this story, then you can chase down Gabriel's final mysteries about his past in Zodiac Academy which also features Orion and has a few cameos from Dante, Rosalie, Caleb, Eugene and maybe a Dragon obsessed stalker twat too. And if you've been a bad, bad Fae and want to find out what happens in the depths of Darkmore Penitentiary then you can follow Rosalie on her mission to bust Roary out and return his life to him - you may even spot Ethan Shadowbrook and a few other characters banged up with them too.

It's been fun living inside the minds of this fucked-up fivesome, but all good things must come to an end.

If you want to be on the frontline for more of our ramblings and to find out first about new releases as well as getting access to exclusive teasers and more, then come join the best group of people we know in our [Facebook reader group](#).

Thank you for being you, we love and appreciate you just like Leon loves his Mindys, Dante loves his family, Elise loves blood, Ryder loves violence and Gabriel loves being a smug all seeing, all knowing bastard.

See you in the next adventure - but be warned, we don't plan on going easy on you mwahahahhahahahaha!

Love, Susanne & Caroline xxx

ALSO BY CAROLINE PECKHAM & SUSANNE VALENTI

Brutal Boys of Everlake Prep

(Complete Reverse Harem Bully Romance Contemporary Series)

Kings of Quarantine

Kings of Lockdown

Kings of Anarchy

Queen of Quarentine

Dead Men Walking

(Reverse Harem Dark Romance Contemporary Series)

The Death Club

Society of Psychos

**

The Harlequin Crew

(Reverse Harem Mafia Romance Contemporary Series)

Sinners Playground

Dead Man's Isle

Carnival Hill

Paradise Lagoon

Harlequinn Crew Novellas

Devil's Pass

**

Dark Empire

(Dark Mafia Contemporary Standalones)

Beautiful Carnage

Beautiful Savage

**

The Ruthless Boys of the Zodiac

(Reverse Harem Paranormal Romance Series - Set in the world of Solaria)

Dark Fae

Savage Fae

Vicious Fae

Broken Fae

Warrior Fae

Zodiac Academy

(M/F Bully Romance Series- Set in the world of Solaria, five years after Dark Fae)

The Awakening

Ruthless Fae

The Reckoning

Shadow Princess

Cursed Fates

Fated Thrones

Heartless Sky

The Awakening - As told by the Boys

Zodiac Academy Novellas

Origins of an Academy Bully

The Big A.S.S. Party

Darkmore Penitentiary

(Reverse Harem Paranormal Romance Series - Set in the world of Solaria, ten years after Dark Fae)

Caged Wolf

Alpha Wolf

Feral Wolf

**

The Age of Vampires

(Complete M/F Paranormal Romance/Dystopian Series)

Eternal Reign

Eternal Shade

Eternal Curse

Eternal Vow

Eternal Night

Eternal Love

**

Cage of Lies

(M/F Dystopian Series)

Rebel Rising

**

Tainted Earth

(M/F Dystopian Series)

Afflicted

Altered

Adapted

Advanced

**

The Vampire Games

(Complete M/F Paranormal Romance Trilogy)

V Games

V Games: Fresh From The Grave

V Games: Dead Before Dawn

*

The Vampire Games: Season Two

(Complete M/F Paranormal Romance Trilogy)

Wolf Games

Wolf Games: Island of Shade

Wolf Games: Severed Fates

*

The Vampire Games: Season Three

Hunter Trials

*

The Vampire Games Novellas

A Game of Vampires

**

The Rise of Issac

(Complete YA Fantasy Series)

Creeping Shadow

Bleeding Snow

Turning Tide

Weeping Sky

Failing Light

Milton Keynes UK
Ingram Content Group UK Ltd.
UKHW030834021124
450589UK00002B/401